The Swans Are Swimming

By

Mansfield Campbell

07:15. The tranquillity was disturbed by the piercing sound. Before the second beat was sounding, a hand reached out and stopped the alarm. On automatic, he rose immediately and exited the bedroom. It was only several steps to reach the bathroom where he lazily disturbed the door handle to no avail.

He knocked gently three times and quietly said, 'Charlie, are you in there?' and after several seconds he turned away and descended the stairs.

Not one third of the way down the stairs, a small dog made his pass and headed into the kitchen with purpose. Once in the kitchen, the man was drawn to the small dog whose eyes were demanding that the back door was opened as a matter of urgency. The two dead bolts were undone and the key in the lock placed in the middle of the door was unlocked. The dog was already on its hind legs frantically pawing at the door. Before the door was one quarter open, the dog had forced its way through, tail wagging and into the back garden.

The kettle that had been half filled the previous evening was set to boil and then two pieces of bread placed in the toaster. A PG Tips teabag was placed in a mug and then the margarine and marmalade and milk retrieved from the fridge. Once the kettle had boiled, the mug was swiftly filled with the tea bag, hot water and a dash of milk. The bread was put into the toaster and then he headed back upstairs and dressed. Returning back to the kitchen, the tea and toast were promptly dispatched. A final return upstairs and he tried the bathroom door handle. It opened immediately and he entered. A quick brush of his teeth followed by emptying his bladder and a cursory face wash. This was all that he had time for.

His pace quickened now that the fug was clearing as he descended the stairs. He went back into the kitchen and opened the back door. The dog was sitting alert and patiently waiting to be let back into the house.

The back door was locked securely and he walked to the front door where he momentarily stopped and shouted out, 'Bye everyone, have a nice day.' There was no reply other than the dog retreating up the stairs as he shut the front door.

The walk to Finchley Road station was a brisk twelve minutes downhill all the way. This was a well-trodden walk that he had taken for several years on a regular basis. The platform was crowded as usual and when the train pulled in and stopped, as was customary the crowd on the platform parted to let off fellow commuters before everyone squeezed onboard. On this journey, he never got a seat but was always contained in the central part of the carriage, standing and partially crushed. He had become accustomed to this journey and its foibles, and anyway, it was only for twelve minutes. Surrounding him were mainly bankers using the Jubilee line to ferry them to Canary Wharf. This was the 'new City' housing the 'new bankers'. He regularly spent the journey ruminating about his brood, and this always put a smile on his face. His beautiful, slim wife with a long sensuous neck. His fifteen-year-old daughter who was beginning to resemble his wife with high cheek bones, slim with a generous but not over long neck. And lastly, his five-year-old daughter who loved everyone, everything and the world. She was brimming to almost bursting point with love. She had a look of ET but in a cute and beautiful way, with a permanent smile perched delicately on a long neck. Yes, they were Swans but they were his Swans and they were beautiful and with very individualistic personalities. He wistfully thought that there wasn't anything that he'd alter about his Swans. Distracted by these pleasant thoughts, he was still smiling absently from the crush of humanity that was engulfing him. He involuntarily clenched his buttocks and his smile was replaced immediately by a grimace. He needed a shit and he needed it very, very soon. Actually, there was one aspect about his bevy of Swans that he would change.

The carriage doors opened at Westminster and commuter etiquette kicked in. The worker bees buzzing on the platform hummed and parted. They parted enough to allow off the small number of fellow worker bees who belonged to other hives located above in the Heart of Democracy. The larger number of banker bees then swarmed onto the train, filing every nook and cranny as they headed off to their banker hives in Canary Wharf. He ascended the escalators from the deepest station in London up to ground level and then marched briskly to work. Upon entering his place of work, he was immediately met with the stern-looking security guards. They were scanning every individual entering the building, probing for any abnormal behaviour. Working there for seventeen years cut no ice with these individuals – everyone was a potential threat and no pleasantries were proffered. The secure lock needed a pass input followed by keying in a unique code, and finally a retina scan. The lifts in the lobby accessed most floors but access to some floors required further security requirements. He chose the floor number directly below the floor that he worked on. Exiting the lift, he headed into the men's toilet and quickly entered a spare cubicle. This was a tactic that he adopted in the last several months as he didn't want his colleagues judging him and sharing crude jokes based on either the noise or the smell emanating from his morning ablutions. Now it was a dash up the stairs and through the office to his cubicle with a few pleasantries passed en route.

As he eased into his seat, he was aware that Sandra Carruthers was prowling about. It was 08:32 and she was staring at him, long enough to get his attention and then deliberately diverted her gaze to the wall clock before letting out an audible tut. She swung around and haughtily returned to her raised glass office that dominated the entire floor. Once inside and seated, Carruthers activated her terminal and fired off a curt email to HR. The email had an attachment that she drafted originally and it was a typical petty note reminding all staff that they needed to be at their workstations and logged on by 08:30 when working in the office. This was then sent out by HR as an edict which drew universally condemnation from all employees. His transgression was the main thrust of her email.

Meanwhile, he was looking out of the window whilst all of his systems booted up and came online. John Pope was sitting at his desk in Thames House, the home of MI5, and he was a spy.

2

John Pope's team converged on the meeting room furthest away from the glass office known as Sandra's Solarium. It was a daily occurrence at a minimum in order that any critical information was disseminated quickly and efficiently amongst the members that were working onsite and then was reconstructed electronically and shared with all field agents. Emails, despite attempting to make them crystal clear, were prone to interpretation and unfortunately mis-interpretation. Pope accepted that team members working in the field had to rely on this type of communication, but a quick chat always trumped an email. Emails worked very well as an audit trail, but the culture of sending emails was becoming the norm. It was also a key tool for the arse-lickers and they were a growing band in The Service. All emails were encrypted using PGP (Pretty Good Privacy encryption) and meant that there was a high degree of security, unless there was a security breach and an agent allowed a third party to access their phone. Pope was a renowned technophobe and distrusted the way that technology had become the vogue over the last decade.

In the room with Pope were Clare Hawkins and Chris Gould. Clare was thirty years old, tall, slim, with dark-brown hair cut in a bob style. She had been with MI5 seven years having been recruited through the old network via Oxford University. She'd had a typical middle-class upbringing, was a very good driver, calm under pressure and possessed an analytical mind. Chris was twenty-eight years old, medium height, a squat build, had thinning sandy hair and suffered from a lack of dress sense. Like Clare, he was recruited direct from Oxford as was the natural order, or was that obsession? He was constantly about to start a diet and restart a mythical training regime. When chasing suspects, he tailed off due to lack of breath but once on the scene always subdued them, relying on his natural strength, and then handcuffed them.

The agenda revolved around several covert surveillances that were being conducted on potential homegrown ISIS terrorists. The Intel had been expanding in the last couple of months and all noises suggested that young Muslim Brits are going to be involved in a bomb attack in the UK. Once again, it was impressionable young men who were purported to be radicalised. Aligned with MI5 Intel, there was intel from GCHQ that was damming and supported the proposition that an attack was being planned. The "Golden Balls" had picked up chatter from a number of burner phones, emails and websites that plans were in motion. GCHQ used ECHELON which was a computer package with the capability to suck in huge amounts of phone, email, faxes and computer details. It then used key phrases/words in many languages to interrogate the data and flag all that are suspect for further human analysis. In addition to UK intelligence, there was now a steady stream coming from the National Security Agency (NSA) in the USA. NSA were picking up similar chatter via ECHELON. However, NSA had a global view of data which also included data coming out of GCHQ's version of ECHELON (NSA had created a backdoor entrance into UK's system).

The three team members poured over the latest data, sharing views and ideas. By the end of the meeting, several action points had been both agreed and assigned. The list was written up by Clare and distributed to both themselves and all of the agents currently working in the field. Once back at their desks, they would contact each agent via secure text and request a verbal contact within six hours.

John Pope sat at his desk knowing that they desperately needed a breakthrough soon. A frown appeared on his face, and whilst he was deep in thought, an email appeared in his inbox. He looked at the sender and saw it was from HR.

3

11:00. The sun was creeping towards its zenith and it was already a hot, humid and sticky day in Luton. The Volkswagen people carrier slowed to a stop adjacent to the building's rear door. It was a T-Porter SE130 five-door model painted black with tinted windows apart from the driver's and front seat passenger's windows. A tall young man in his early twenties exited from the front passenger seat and walked slowly towards the building. He removed a set of keys from his trouser pocket and unlocked the door. He then opened the door and peaked inside. Without turning around, he raised his right arm up with a thumbs up hand signal. The rear passenger door opened automatically as commanded by the driver. Out stepped another young man who was small both in height and build, and he gesticulated to the other occupants to exit. Out next came a tall slim man wearing a thobe, which is a long robe, a black turban and a scarf that covered his neck and partially covered his face. He stretched languidly, and out popped the final passenger who was a medium-built youth. The people carrier then reversed back and headed towards a free parking space on the opposite side of the car park. The three-man column walked in single file into the building. Once inside, the door was re-locked by the man on sentry duty and then all four set off. The three young men who were all wearing Western clothes surrounded the senior man who was dressed in traditional Arabic garments in an escort pattern. So far, no words had been exchanged between anyone in this group since exiting the people carrier. One took the lead, the second person walked adjacent to him, placing him on the inside, nearest to the wall, whilst the last man walked directly behind him. As they walked purposefully along a couple of corridors, a stare from the lead person was enough for whoever was blocking them to move aside and clear the pathway forward.

Mr Butt thrust aside both of his arms in his typical greeting manner. 'Hamiza, greetings. How are you?'

Mr Butt was a rotund man, gregarious, wearing a dark suit with a Kufi adorning his head. He was a pillar of the community and made it his business to know as many people within it as possible. Hamiza was taken aback momentarily and stopped – this was not part of the plan. His brain froze as he hadn't been brought up to ignore, or be rude to, elders of the community.

'Good morning, Mr Butt, I'm well, thank you.'

And with that, Hamiza attempted to restart walking, but Mr Butt stood his ground, still with both arms spread wide and said, 'Hamiza, please introduce me to the gentleman in your company.'

Hamiza could feel his internal temperature rapidly climbing, beads of perspiration beginning to form on his forehead. He said, quietly averting Mr Butt's gaze, 'My apologies. He is a visiting Imam who is here for a period and doesn't speak any English. Please excuse us as we are late for a meeting.'

Mr Butt nodded his head in deference and moved aside. The Imam in return gave the smallest of acknowledgements. And with that, the group moved off down the corridor and turned right towards a door that led down into the basement. Mr Butt turned around and looked with puzzlement at the group.

The group descended the stairs and entered the fourth and last room on the right-hand side. Once inside and the lights switched on, the door was locked by Usman. The Imam's eyes scanned all corners of the room and everything in between. It was a small room with shelves on three of the walls containing a collection of items that were found in all basements e.g. paint tins, brushes, cloths, brackets, boxes of nails and screws etc. There was a musty smell that was overbearing due to the fact that there were neither windows nor ventilation. There were several plastic chairs around a battered wooden table that clearly had seen better days. In one corner was one plastic chair and an antiquated desk. There simply wasn't room to accommodate anything else here.

Usam, the taller of the group, looked towards the Imam and spoke. 'This was a storeroom which we cleared out. I hope that it meets all of your needs.'

The Imam brushed his hand away in a dismissive fashion, his black pupils staring hard back at Usam, 'Who is that man Butt and why did we stop when the orders were clear that there was to be no contact?'

All three collaborators shot pensive glances between each other before Usam spoke. 'Imam, we are sorry. Mr Butt is an elder and was being friendly. I'm sure that nothing will come from that.' He added quickly, 'Hamiza did well to say that you didn't speak English and also to not offend him.'

The Imam spat back, 'Enough. No more mistakes. Now go and fetch the Martyrs.'

Rahan, who was the smallest and youngest of the three, turned and waited for Usman to unlock the door before scurrying out.

Upstairs in the main community hall, Mr Butt was staring at the main noticeboard where all sorts of communications were posted. Despite it being the age of electronic communication, all community-related communiques were printed off and posted on noticeboards spread out throughout the building along with many handwritten notes. The community had many individuals who either had little to no education or who were of an age that they were computer illiterate. He was clearly searching for something in particular without being able to locate it.

Ahmed Hussain sidled up to Mr Butt and said, 'Good morning, how are you?'

Mr Butt involuntarily shook before replying, 'Sorry, you surprised me as I was looking for something.' He continued. 'Good morning, Ahmed. I'm well, and how are you?'

Ahmed smiled affably and said, 'I'm well, thanks. So, what are you looking for? Perhaps I can help.'

Mr Butt shook his head in a way to display that he was unable to understand what was giving him concern and went on. 'When we have visiting Imams, the details of their names and the duration of their visit are approved by the council and then posted on the board. I met earlier today a visiting Imam and not only was I not aware of his visit but I also can't find any details of it posted anywhere.'

Ahmed smiled broadly and replied instantly, 'Mr Butt, you know how things can be a little muddled here and occasionally chaotic. I'm sure that it's the same old story of information lost in the system. Give it a couple of days and it will appear.'

Mr Butt sounded reassured and said, 'Ahmed, I'm sure that you are right. Oh, by the way, are you losing weight?'

Ahmed bridled at the weight loss comment but kept his composure and said, 'Just training for a half marathon. Bye now.'

And with that, Ahmed headed off towards the cafe. Mr Butt remained at the noticeboard staring at it and imploring it to supply an answer.

In the basement, Rahan knocked three times on the door, paused then added a further two knocks and a further pause before delivering one final knock. The door was unlocked from the inside and Rahan entered with seven young men. The Imam was standing and pointed with one hand to the seats surrounding the old desk. All of the seven young men shuffled around the desk and sat obediently.

The Imam, without addressing anyone in particular, said, 'You can leave now.'

The three men who had escorted him into the building left without speaking and locked the door from the outside. They would then perform their next task which was to guard the entrance to the basement and also to the actual room itself. No one inside the room spoke and there was a palpable silence for a couple of minutes. During this period, some of them fidgeted awkwardly and there were a couple of nervous coughs.

The Imam broke the quiet, saying firmly, 'Sons of Mohammad, you all have been chosen. Your rewards will be immortality.'

There was an immediate change in the collective body language of the group and electricity shot through the group. Thus the final programming stage of this group had begun.

They would be dedicated to the cause and weaponised. Seven more young British-born men radicalised.

Ahmed was in the cafe nursing an espresso, in a small mosque in the north east of Luton.

Ahmed withdrew his phone and saw that he had one message in his inbox. He downed the espresso and left the cafe. Acknowledging several people on his route, he nonchalantly walked out of the mosque and down the road. He turned off into a quiet cul-de-sac and scanned his surroundings. Satisfied that he was on his own, he withdrew his phone, accessed his inbox and read the message. He typed in a short reply and sent it. The phone shutdown and returned back into his trouser pocket, he then headed back into the mosque. Ahmed Hussain was an undercover agent working for MI5.

4

19:43. Pope entered his detached house in leafy Finchley and shouted out, 'Hi, everyone, I'm home.'

There were a couple of muffled replies from the kitchen and a yelp followed by urgent scratching emanating from the lounge door. Putting down his briefcase, he stretched out and pushed open the angry lounge door. The small dog sprang out, tail wagging furiously, and leaped up, bouncing off his thigh. The dog then lengthened and rested its two front paws on his legs. Pope leant forward and patted the dog on his head.

The dog adjusted its head and urgently licked his fingers. 'Hi there, Doodle,' he said to this customary greeting.

Pope turned around and flicked off his dark-brown brogues that were beginning to show signs of ageing despite regular care and headed off up the stairs. The dog had already returned into the lounge using its nose to push on through the tiny gap between the door and the door frame. Pope hung up his lightweight linen suit and tie and then threw his shirt and socks into the washing basket. He put on a t-shirt and loose-fitting jogging bottoms before going into the bathroom where he quickly washed his face and combed his hair. He retrieved his phone from his suit jacket pocket and headed off. Picking up his shoes en route, he walked into the kitchen.

'Hi, darling,' he said to his wife before looking at Charlie, smiling and saying, 'Charlie, fancy cleaning old Pop's shoes?'

His fifteen-year-old daughter Charlie wrinkled her nose and screwed up her eyes simultaneously before replying, 'Dad, no way, they smell gross.'

Every day Pope asked his daughter to clean his shoes and every day she refused. This was their own private banter. Charlie was prone to mood swings in the last two years and could be very surly but always played along. She was also heavy-handed with her younger sister and bossy, which often triggered rows between her and both of her parents. The rows followed a particular pattern where Charlie became hysterical, screaming and crying, before storming off to her room. Academically she was in the top quartile and was very studious.

Pope sat at the kitchen table which was propped up against the wall. A small extension had been built by the previous owners and this allowed for a decent-sized table and chairs to be housed there. This was where the family mainly ate all of their meals. The evening meal was set for 18:00 on weekdays and it was unusual for John to eat with the rest of his family due to his work commitments. His meal was reheated. The dining room was reserved for formal family gatherings or important dinners such as Christmas or Easter. Charlie was also using it to do her ever-burgeoning amount of homework and to sneakily play PC games and enter online chat rooms.

Jane placed his meal in front of him, returned to the kitchen sink and continued to wash and clean vegetables. Jane was thirty-nine years old with shoulder-length blond hair. She had the remnants of a Yorkshire accent having spent all of her life up to the age of eighteen in Leeds. She studied chemistry at The Imperial College London and was seduced by the life that London offered, vowing never to settle back in Leeds. It was whilst studying she met John Pope. She was on another boozy, crazy and carefree night out with ten fellow female students. The objective of these nights out was to drink copious amounts of alcohol, smoke a bit of dope, take the piss out of men who regularly hit on them but not before cadging drinks off of them, occasionally slink off with someone or go back to the halls of residence with whoever from the semi-wild group that was left single. Jane took a fancy to the tall slim young man who was talking to another man of similar height also sporting a military-styled haircut in a south Kensington basement wine bar. Fuelled by booze, she broke away from the group and walked up to the two men and introduced herself. John could see that she was clearly under the influence but was physically attracted to her and found her funny. She clinched the deal when she insisted on standing her round. This was an act that John had never encountered before from uni students, and quite frankly was an act that Jane had never performed before either. Her group implored her to drink up as they were heading off to another wine bar, but she waved them away. Eventually John's friend made his excuses and left as he was beginning to realise that three was a crowd. John asked to walk Jane back to her room and she agreed. They chatted all of the way with Jane setting out all of her life's goals and ambitions, with John nodding or grunting at the appropriate pause in the drunken monologue. Outside the main gate, Jane turned to John and, without pausing, asked for his phone number. The number was handed over and Jane promptly threw up all over John's jeans and trainers. This was the beginning of their joint journey.

Pope had just finished his dinner when Daisy, his five-year-old daughter, entered the kitchen.

'Daddy's home,' enthused Daisy as she raced over to him and launched herself at him.

He caught her and in one movement picked her up and sat her on his lap. Her little face was beaming and she planted kisses on his face, threw her arms around him, hugging him. For the next few minutes Daisy used her hands to contort Pope's face. Smiles were replaced by frowns which were replaced by pursed lips and changes to his hair style were also performed. All of the time a compliant Pope listened to his daughter's squeals of laughter filling the room whilst both his wife and Charlie looked on, entranced, caught up in this family happening.

Jane broke the performance. 'Daisy, go and wash your hands thoroughly and get ready for bed. I'll be up shortly and we'll brush your teeth.'

John Pope put Daisy down and she rushed out of the kitchen. Daisy was very tactile and was going to go through life with that as a dominant trait. He frowned. Daisy was, as his wife put it, 'going through a phase'. This involved spending hours with Doodle sitting on her lap whilst she inspected his bum. Daisy was convinced that Doodle had an issue and was happy to prod, probe and explore his anus. Doodle, however, wasn't that happy with this turn of events but nevertheless complied.

John decamped to the lounge, Jane veered off upstairs to get Daisy settled and Charlie went into the dining room. His phone was put on the charger. Doodle gingerly sat on Jane's lap when she returned following an earlier thorough examination from Daisy as soon as she sat down. With the TV on low, Jane talked through her day. John was always attentive as his family was the perfect antidote to a job that was highly challenging, heaping huge pressure on him that was relentless. Jane talked about dropping off and picking up the kids as well as the staff and customers' dramas that unfolded daily at the antiques shop in Hampstead Heath where she worked part time.

'I bumped into Nadia today and she asked whether you would take Zayhan for a drink. Apparently Zayhan wants to go to the pub but doesn't know anyone there.'

Pope had batted away four previous requests from his wife, but this wasn't going to go away.

'Ok.'

'Thanks.'

They had an unwritten agreement never to discuss anything connected to his work. As his partner, she understood that when John walked through the front door he wanted to switch off. His family kept him sane, gave him pleasure and reaffirmed why he was doing this job. All of the Pope family dramas and incidents were treated phlegmatically because his family was his highest priority. Well, certainly on par with the rising number of terrorist acts and potential acts of UK terrorism that filled up his work time.

John joined the British Army at the age of eighteen following his A levels. He was born and raised in Slough, a large town on the fringes of London. He didn't want an office job like his father and didn't want to do an apprenticeship either like many of his school friends. Without consulting his parents, knowing that they would put up objections, he walked into an Army recruiting office and two months later joined The Royal Green Jackets. The RGJ is an Infantry regiment specialising in rifleman duties. He was a natural with either a gun or a rile and he honed his skills on the range. He was selected and qualified as a sniper. It wasn't surprising when he came to the notice of the SAS and was seconded. Regular tours of Northern Ireland were punctuated with secondments to other UK-based organisations, notably Special Branch and MI5. He was recruited by MI5 and joined them in 1992 at the age of twenty-four. He was now forty-two years old and had been in The Service eighteen years. This period of time had seen a huge change in the role of MI5, the adversaries, the MI5 personnel and the UK as a country.

He put his mobile phone in his pocket, slipped out and polished his brogues, giving them a deep-brown shine. It was 22:00 and he picked up Doodle's lead from the dog basket. Doodle flew out of the lounge and circled whilst Pope put on his lead. Doodle was a West Highland terrier with a snow-white coat offset by two black pupils and an even blacker snout. He was two years old with bundles of energy and always alert and ready for any outdoor activity.

He popped his head into the lounge and said, 'We'll do the twenty minutes circle as it's too humid.'

And with that, man and dog headed off up the street incline towards Hampstead Heath. They had passed several houses when there was shouting coming out of the front bedroom windows from the next house.

A male voice with a London accent unleashed '…and who pays for everything? Who is working whilst everyone here waits for handouts?'

Dogs have intuition. Put them in a car and head to the seaside; they will try and stick their noses out of the window or leap about the car in anticipation. Put them in a car and head to the vet; they will howl, whimper and shake involuntarily all of the way. Pope momentarily glanced up at the curtained window and Doodle growled and bared his teeth. Doodle knew what Pope was feeling. They picked up the pace and went on their way.

Back at the house, Doodle scooted into the kitchen and lapped up water from his bowl before bounding upstairs. Pope checked that all of the doors were locked and that Charlie was not in the dining room and then went upstairs. He put his phone on charger by his bed (it always needed topping up), picked up his shorts and went into the bathroom where he took a shower. From his Army days, showers were always had first thing in the morning and this activity continued when he joined MI5. In recent months however he'd had to adjust as the bathroom in the morning had become the exclusive property of Charlie.

Jane had explained this matter-of-factually to him. 'Just going through a phase.'

It seemed to him that his brood were going through mutually exclusive phases but that was ok(ish). Finishing up, he went into his bedroom and reset his alarm clock to 07:05.

Jane said, 'Early start tomorrow?'

'No, just need to be in by 08:30.'

02:45. The black Volkswagen people carrier eased to a stop outside a terraced house in the south west of Luton. There was an imperceptible movement of the curtain in the lounge. Less than thirty seconds passed before the old wooden front door creaked open and a cloaked figure walked out and slinked into the already opened rear passenger door. Rahan was positioned by the door and nodded politely as the person passed by him, but there was no acknowledgement. The people carrier moved off slowly down the darkened street that was bereft of traffic.

The terraced house was occupied by an elderly Afghanistan couple who had lived there since 1989. In that time they had learnt very little English, had no friends, did not work, living off of welfare handouts, and did not attend any Mosque. Neither had particularly good health and had come to rely on the cocktail of medicines proved by their caring Pakistani doctor. He spoke Pashto and was able to gain their confidence whilst he medicated them against the plethora of illnesses that ravaged the elderly. They regularly communicated via letters to their large family who mainly lived in the rugged mountainous region of Hindu Kush. The return letters which often included photos of family members and friends were read, reread and treasured. Their love for the UK diminished when a unmanned Predator drone targeted a family wedding in a mountain village in 2005. This was their family. The celebrations were curtailed when a Hellfire missile struck the group and atomised everything within a 120-metre radius. Over a hundred people were either killed or injured in the attack by The Predator that acted as judge, jury and executioner. The intended target was not attending the wedding and the information supplied erroneously to the CIA only managed to turn more people against the West. The Taliban were winning. This village was where these two Afghani immigrants originated from. They had recently received a letter from a family member saying that an important person was going to go to the UK and they needed to extend their hospitality for the duration of his stay. It was their physical and social isolation that made them attractive to a cell in Kabul dedicated to finding safe houses anywhere in the world for Jihadists.

The occupants of the people carrier had arrived at the mosque at 03:15 and quickly made their way to the room in the basement. The driver had driven a circuitous route, checking regularly for any car that could be following them. The driver had been given strict instructions that the journey both to and from the mosque must be by a different route, with regular stops to flush out any tails. A further ten minutes had passed before the seven young men had taken their seats and the room was secured.

Outside the room, Rahan spoke softly. 'He's not very sociable.'

Hamiza replied, 'No, and he's fucking paranoid.'

Usam spoke next. 'Listen. He knows what he's doing. We need to make sure everything goes ok and we all follow his orders.'

Rahan said, 'Paranoid 100%. He wraps himself up like a mummy. You can't see his face other than those evil eyes and that big hooked nose. We now are here at fuck o'clock because he doesn't want to bump into old man Butt.'

Hamiza said, 'Yeah, pain in the Butt.'

Both Hamiza and Rahan sniggered.

Usam said, 'Mr Butt generally gets here around 11:00 and stays until midday prayer is over and he's met with other elders. So he's out of here by 15:30. He's back at 20:00 for sunset prayer and then stays for night prayer before leaving around 23:00. We need to keep an eye on him if he changes his routine.'

Rahan said, 'So we're up in the middle of the night and away by 09:30.'

Hamiza said, 'This is going to be a bitch.'

Usam said, 'Ok, let's take up our posts.'

07:05. Pope's alarm burst the peace again. It was another day. The only change to his morning routine was that he planned to take his morning shit in the toilets on the floor above where he worked as part of his rotational dump policy. That and he'd be at his desk by 08:25. At 09:00, Pope, Clare Hawkins and Chris Gould sat around the table in the meeting room. They all brought into the room plastic cups filled with coffee from the vending machine that lingered in the corner of the office. The coffee was crap but at least it was free. No doubt at some stage, the free vending machines would disappear courtesy of further cuts. Some may even support that, but it would be bad for morale despite the frequent complaints about the quality of the drinks dispensed.

Clare started the meeting. 'We aren't giving any time to a number of the designated objectives.'

Chris blurted out, 'It's about prioritisation.'

Clare's body language betrayed her views and she shook her head. 'We can't just ignore them.'

This was a conversation that they had had several times and it was time to find a solution that would be acceptable.

Pope looked at the list and said, 'Boris is running around London and the Home Counties unfettered with his two gorillas in tow. He'll be running standard dry cleaning even though we aren't tailing him. At least he'll be wasting most of his day losing imaginary tails. Look, I'll meet up with him and have a chat. The industrial espionage angle does need to be looked at. We can't have the Frogs nicking our ideas. Chris, grab everything that you can on it and let's catch up early next week. Oh, and get anything that Golden Balls (GCHQ) has also. As for the assortment of right-wing and left-wing activists, Clare go and speak to SO15 (Met Police Counter Terrorism Command) and see what they've got. Bring it back to the meeting that Chris is setting up next week re the Frogs. Now, let's get out and meet the team. I want HUMINT (Human Intelligence) asap. There must be something out there. I'll run south London, Clare north London and Chris take Luton.'

The meeting was over and there was Intel to gather. Pope had analysts sifting through data gathered from London and Luton. Clare and Chris assisted with running both undercover agents and informers in these locations. It was a large area accompanied with a large population to cover. Other areas of the UK were similarly split up within MI5, and John had the added responsibility for ensuring that info was shared with his counterparts.

SO15 Counter Terrorism Command was an amalgamation of the Anti-Terrorist Branch and Special Branch within The Metropolitan Police. Golden Balls was the nickname given to GCHQ by other departments and organisations who were also involved in Defence of the Realm. They were the darlings of the press and were credited with being on the frontline of all things security, not only for the UK but all of EEC, and they were also a senior partner to the NSA (National Security Agency – equivalent to GCHQ in USA but several times larger with a global reach).

Successive UK governments were seduced by the power of electronic eavesdropping and poured in untold funds into the hardware and software that was run by GCHQ and the geeks that lived and breathed the widgets and digits that spewed out SIGINT. SIGINT is a combination of communication between people and electronic signals that aren't verbal or handwritten communications and are often encrypted. HUMINT is the gathering of intel from human sources, and this isn't sexy or magical, and departments and organisations that rely on HUMINT had their budgets regularly reduced.

MI5 was one organisation that suffered budget reductions, and they relied heavily on HUMINT, as did MI6. The seeds were sowed when the Berlin Wall came down in 1989 and when in 1991 the Soviet Union's Communism collapsed and was usurped by Boris Yeltsin's democratic force, and then the powers that be questioned the need for such a large joint force. Defence budgets were similarly slashed. The Cold War was over and with that no nuclear and conventional weapon enemy was out there. It was time to scale back.

With the rise of the Taliban, Muslim terrorist cells and now ISIS, it was clear that SIGINT alone would not be enough to defeat them. They were countering this form of intelligence gathering by limiting use of technology and dividing and sub-dividing multiple times into cells that effectively did not have contact with other cells. MI5 had been saved from extinction but had to restructure, regroup and recruit following on from patterns and behaviours developed for combating the Cold War that kicked off in 1945. 9/11 was the global wake-up call for all intelligence agencies. The most powerful nation on Earth had been caught with its trousers down. There were serious failings within key security agencies, and it highlighted that they didn't share critical information with each other. Bloodletting followed, there was a rise in Homeland Securities profiles, patriotic laws were passed and the USA would never again be caught out.

London suffered a catastrophic episode, '7/7 in 2005', and escaped a bungled attempt within two years. The threat to the UK did not come from foreign extremists but from homegrown radicalised young men. This was what MI5 was arming itself to not only defend against but attack.

As the meeting at MI5 was breaking up, another meeting at the Luton mosque had just concluded. Once again, the seven young men left one at a time and headed out into the streets of Luton where they went their separate ways. They had all been taught the basics of dry cleaning and went on meandering journeys back to their safe houses. It was already a hot, humid day, and a couple of them decided to take the most direct route back to their safe house following such an early start. The Imam would have meted out physical punishment if he was aware of such indiscipline. Meanwhile, he headed back to his own safe house and the company of two serfs. He would spend his time alone in his room researching online and would only vacate the room to either eat or use the bathroom. He also was able to pray four times a day in there. The first prayer of the day was with the group in the small room in the basement.

Chris Gould took the 10:01 train from St Pancras International Station and arrived at Luton station at 10:22. Getting out of the office was something he relished, and he took every opportunity to be involved in field work. Chris wanted to prove his worth and migrate to a job that wasn't so paper orientated and had more excitement. He had set up two meetings each for two hours in which he would update both undercover agents with the latest intel, get feedback and impress on them the need to exhaust all avenues looking for the latest and possibly imminent threat.

There were over twenty mosques and associated community buildings within Luton, and they were all concentrated in the north-west of the Town. MI5 had inserted two undercover agents and they had split up their surveillance into two equal groups of twelve buildings. Deepak Chopra was recruited from Nottingham University in 2007 and was fast-tracked into working undercover due to the shortage of ethnic agents who had the capability to operate within Muslim communities. Chopra was from an Indian Hindu background and spoke English, Hindi and French. In the absence of anyone better equipped, MI5 thrust him into the field. Having brown skin was enough apparently. He was softly spoken and mild-mannered, and Chris had arranged that meeting for 13:15. The first meeting was with Ahmed Hussain at 10:45 in a greasy spoon cafe ten minutes' walk from Luton station. Chris planned to have two full breakfasts today as a treat to himself for being out of the office. He would put this on his expenses and they were small enough to be sanctioned without any scrutiny. This evening he would have the homemade lasagne and chips lovingly cooked by his live-in girlfriend Melanie followed by a doze in front of the TV.

Chris sat at a table in the corner of the cafe and ordered a full English breakfast. A mug of milky tea was placed before him with a small tea bag swimming inside. He prodded away at the tea bag and then switched on the recorder that was in his jacket. He pulled out of his sports bag a notebook and pen. His large breakfast arrived and the plate was filled to the brim with eggs, bacon, sausage, mushrooms, tomatoes and hash browns, all swimming in grease. Baked beans were also on the plate, and a round of toast on a small separate plate finished off the calorific, high-cholesterol, heart-attack feast. Chris powdered the contents with both salt and pepper and was in the tricky process of firing copious amounts of tomato sauce from a reluctant bottle over the food when Ahmed Hussain sat down opposite him.

'Fucking hell, bruv, you got enough on that plate?' Ahmed said in his now undisguised Cockney accent.

'Growing lad, growing lad,' came back the reply before the first heaped forkful entered his gob.

'Too much pig on the plate, bro. I'll order something less likely to fucking kill me,' Ahmed said before looking at the man behind the counter and shouting out, 'Cheese omelette and one coffee.'

Breakfast was demolished in relative silence before they went through the agenda that Chris wanted to cover. Ahmed explained that he was rotating between each mosque and covering prayers and meetings, as well as hanging around the communal areas. He was close to a group of young guys in one mosque, but they were into criminal activities to earn money. Stealing cars for a chop shop and transporting drugs seemed to be their focus. There was a whisper that a group of men were targeting vulnerable young white girls and forcing them to have sex with them. He would file reports when he had more information and that could then be forwarded to the police. He said that he was speaking to as many people as possible, but having to cover the amount of buildings as he was being asked to was a tough assignment. He said that to cover everything, in his opinion, they needed at least six undercover agents.

'Deepak doesn't have the same concerns.'

'Course not. He's a fucking Paki.'

'As you well know, Deepak is an Indian.' Chris wanted to press his buttons.

He knew that Ahmed was 100% from Pakistani stock on both sides of his family, and he was equally amused and puzzled by the racist comment made in the current politically correct society.

'Same difference. Listen, I go to prayers every day, my knees are fucked from all that kneeling and after last prayer and bullshit chat it's gone midnight before I get home. I'm living on coffee and energy drinks just to stay awake. I have no time to go to the gym, watch a film or even have a McDonalds.'

'McDonalds is bad for you,' quipped Chris.

'Says the man who just ate 10,000 greasy calories.'

They both laughed.

Chris said, 'What about the new Imam you mentioned a couple of days ago?'

'Nothing, bruv. He hasn't been back but I'll keep an eye out for him.'

Chris nodded, followed by a deep burp, and said, 'Ok. Keep at it. And by the way, are you losing weight?'

Ahmed frowned, got up and made to leave.

'Hey, don't forget to pay for your omelette,' said Chris.

'Bruv, put it on expenses.' And with that, Ahmed left.

Ahmed had omitted one critical point in the two-hour conversation. He no longer went to first prayer of the day at any mosque He simply did not have the energy to be full on 24/7. He knew that if he told Chris this then there would be a bollocking and he would be forced to get back at it. Chris wasn't working undercover and Ahmed knew that no one turned up for first prayer, or those few who did were just religious nuts. Ahmed was wrong.

Chris rested at the table for a further ten minutes before strolling off for his second meeting, and more importantly his second all-day breakfast. Luton had a variety of top-notch greasy spoons. Deepak was punctual and serious and studious throughout the meeting whilst he watched Chris devour a humongous plate of grease-infused food.

'Chris, you must be very hungry, mate. The way that you wolfed that lot down. Missus gone on strike?'

'Can't beat a traditional breakfast.'

Chris knew that Ahmed and Deepak worked in silos. They never had contact with each other and that was how MI5 wanted their undercover agents to behave. If there ever was a 'life and death'-type incident, then any agent in the vicinity would be despatched to assist until the troops could get there, even if that meant breaking cover. Deepak would never know that Chris had just eaten a similar-sized plate of food. The meeting went according to Chris's agenda. Deepak raised no concerns about his workload. His upbringing meant that it was impolite to question anything, so he wasn't about to buck the trend here and now. Chris was impressed with Deepak's methodical feedback but missed that unlike Ahmed, who knew the nuances, customs and languages spoken, Deepak wasn't able to really integrate himself into the heart of the community and would always be marginalised. Plus, he didn't even look right.

Deepak only drank a bottle of water throughout the meeting and Chris decided that he wouldn't ask for the money but if questioned then he'd say that he had the water and Deepak had the full English breakfast. MI5 was suffocating from petty bureaucracy and too many were focusing on non-essential crap. Overall this had been a successful couple of meetings and Chris waddled back to the station in time to catch the 15:45 into London. Once on the train, he unbuckled his belt as his trousers were now straining and snoozed all of the way back. He decided that it was pointless to return back to the office but went home instead. He would avoid the worst part of rush hour on another hot day and he'd actually have more time to devote to work rather than spend time rammed in the underground. Once home he could reread his notes, listen to the tapes, type up the two field reports and complete his expenses claims form. The plan disintegrated as soon as he stepped through his front door as he lay on the settee and promptly fell asleep, only awakening when Melanie said that dinner would be ready in fifteen minutes. He spent the interim time thinking about what new exercise regime he would start tomorrow.

Pope entered the small Syrian restaurant off of the Edgware Road at 20:00 and headed to the table at the rear. There were three large men folded uncomfortably around a table that, because of their size, resembled a child's table. It was apparent that the senior man had chosen the table purposefully. He sat with his back to the wall and was able to surveil the whole room, which is standard tradecraft. He was a middle-aged man with short peppered hair that sat on top of a very large square head that sat on top of a very large square body. He was a bear of a man and was a representative for a bear of a nation.

He stood up, extended his bear-sized hand, smiled and said, 'John, good to see you.'

'Victor, likewise,' came the reply as the handshake was completed. 'Perhaps we could have some privacy.'

Victor flicked his eyes at his two companions and they both got up and moved to a table further down the small restaurant. Victor Sokolov was a senior officer in the SVR which was responsible for gathering intelligence in foreign countries on behalf of Russia. Victor was a decorated soldier who fought with distinction in the Soviet–Afghan War. It was a bloody war that lasted nearly ten years, beginning in 1979 and finished when the USSR withdrew, defeated. Victor was fearless, faithful to his men, a master of weapons and battlefield tactics and an ideal recruit for SVR who were recruiting in the early 1990s with a purpose. The two men accompanying him were not SVR and did not have the nous to be credible agents. They were men who in a different life were soldiers who'd served under Victor. Their reward for unswerving loyalty was that they were his batmen, chauffeur and bodyguards.

'John, the guys don't speak any English. No need to push them away.'

'Why are they here then?'

'Friends. Everyone needs friends. Right?'

Victor picked up the bottle of Russian vodka and poured a healthy measure into a glass and gently pushed it across the table towards John Pope. It was no coincidence that they met here. It was one of only a few places in London that served Rodnik vodka. This was a brand with over 100 years' heritage and not like the dozens of poor imitation brands that had popped up in the last ten years and flooded the market. Victor liked his vodka old school as he liked friends and foes alike. There were no mixers and no ice, just a bottle to be shared between two friends.

The glasses were raised, clinked and 'Nostrovia' shared.

'Victor, everything is quiet on the streets of London and we want it to stay that way.'

'John, what do you mean? It's UK kids that you need to worry about. Do you want our help?'

'Victor. London is teaming with Russians. There's more oligarchs than I could shake a stick at. There's Russian mafia running and muscling in on drugs and human trafficking. Football clubs are being run with Russian money. There are dissidents plotted up here trying to sell their stories. All in all, roubles are flowing here like fucking water and, like water, are handy when it comes to washing and laundering. Do not resolve any more feuds or vendettas here.'

'John, we don't do that.'

'No? Litvinenko got a lethal dose of Polonium 123 for embracing democracy.'

'That was 2006 and no one has proof as to what happened.'

'Take it as a friendly warning then. But we have other things to focus on, so zero tolerance to any fucking about.'

'John, this is exquisite vodka, let's enjoy. I don't think that you have anything to worry about.'

Pope took one further large shot, stood up and bade Victor a good evening. The message had been passed over and accepted. Both men respected each other because they shared a similar background of outstanding military service which led them to being head-hunted for a spy career. They had shared a bottle or two of vodka or drank several pints of real ale in the past whilst bonding and grappling with mutual problems and would do so in the future, but this was neither the time nor the place for pleasantries. Before he had left the restaurant, the two gorillas had sat back down at the table and were helping their boss finish off the bottle of vodka. The small Syrian owner looked on nonchalantly, but he would be making a phone call to the Syrian embassy once they had cleared off.

02:35. The Volkswagen people carrier was nearing its destination and there had been deathly silence since all four people had entered it.

'I see that the Ayatollah of Doom has given the red card to four of the team,' said Zeehan, the driver of the people carrier, to no one in particular.

'Yeah, I heard that they have been sent to Coventry, literally,' replied Rahan. 'Apparently he doesn't want everyone together just in case.'

'Just in case of what? Corr, he's a miserable bastard anyway. More like the Ayatollah of Doom and Gloom,' said Zeehan.

'Stop now,' interrupted Usam. 'You all know that we aren't to speak of any operational matters.'

'He'll have Hamiza flogged and stoned,' said Rahan, grinning widely.

'Nah, he comes from a model Muslim family. More likely to give him a medal,' piped up Usam, trying to keep the mood light.

'He's already had his Sunday bacon sandwich. Ain't that right, bruv?' said Rahan.

'Shut up, man,' retorted Hamiza.

'What's this about?' fired out Zeehan, who was always ferreting around for gossip. He always enhanced any gossip salaciously before spreading it to the four winds.

'Oh, I thought you all knew,' said Rahan, feigning innocence. 'The Ali family sit down every Sunday morning and devour bacon sarnies.'

Hamiza hung his head, feeling shame now as his face burned because his family secret was being exposed by his so-called mate.

'Yeah, Mrs Ali drives down to the south of Luton into a nice white area and buys her pig rashers every week,' continued Rahan.

'Well, Mr Ali can stop banging on at me about attending prayers and reading the Quran. That's major hypocrisy, man. Eating swine ain't on, no way, bro,' laughed Zeehan.

'Does Grandpa eat the pig?' asked Rahan.

The game was up, so there was no point denying anything.

Hamiza said, 'Nah, he lies in on a Sunday and doesn't get up until 11:00. Mum tells him that he's entitled to a lie in. We have our bacon sarnies at 09:30, so he doesn't know.'

'Wait till I tell Mum, she'll love this, bruv,' said Zeehan.

'Bruv, don't, please. You might as well put a two pager in *The Luton Herald & News*. That would be too much for Mum and Dad.'

'What about Ramadan?' questioned Zeehan.

'Bruv, we love the sarnies too much.'

The people carrier exploded with laughter as the four men whooped and hollered. Snorts of derision were quickly replaced with snorts followed by grunts and squeals. That was the extent of the group's imitation of pig noises. The group would start their early daily rises from this day forward by journeying together, making pig noises and giggling. The car was still visibly shaking from the merriment as it slowed to a stop and everyone put on their game faces. Time to pick up the Ayatollah of Doom and Gloom and confirmed pig hater.

09:00. Pope rolled out of bed, stretched lazily and headed into the bathroom. He scratched his head before commencing his ablutions. Strange that the bathroom was always vacant at weekends but barricaded during the week when he really needed it. He went back into his bedroom and put on his running gear. Every weekend, work and family permitting, he went for an hour's run up and over Hampstead Heath. He was joined on these jaunts by his ever-present running companion – Doodle. He went downstairs and was greeted in the kitchen by Jane, Daisy and Doodle. Kisses all round including Doodle, who never wanted to be excluded from anything, followed by a strong cup of black coffee and then it was time for the off. Doodle was yapping and hovering around his dog basket where his lead lay. Daisy always put his lead on, even though it was a laborious process between an uncoordinated child and hyperactive dog spinning in opposite orbits. Any interference would only provoke tears, screams and tantrums. Common sense prevailed and it was best to let the protagonists duke it out. Besides, both Jane and John enjoyed watching the animal version of Twisters. Having harnessed Doodle, Daisy went through the cuddle-and-kiss ritual, but Doodle wanted to get out now and didn't engage enthusiastically with the young girl.

Pope held Doodle on a short leash as they gently jogged up the road. He glanced at his watch and made a mental note of the time. It would be a further twelve minutes on mostly incline pavements before they entered Hampstead Heath. This part of the run was always taken at a modest pace and served as a warmup. Once into the woods, John released Doodle, who took off at a sprint. There were several paths that John ran along and they were all a series of inclines, flats and declines. He alternated his runs because he felt that it alleviated boredom. The truth was different; once he started to run at a decent pace, his body focused on both the mechanical effort required and the breathing technique required to support the physical effort expended. Doodle swept ahead of him in an arc but always circled back. He would stop, sniff and move swiftly on. The heath offered up a lot of different smells and scents to a dog. Other dogs were acknowledged but were no more than a mere distraction as he focused on his primary roll of forward scout. Occasionally Doodle would take a different route at an intersection, but a sharp whistle from John and Doodle would reappear and overtake him on the correct path without even a look. Having completed a circuit, John was covered in sweat and after putting Doodle back on the lead, he headed home at a brisk pace. At the front door, John glanced at his watch and calculated that the run had taken one hour and four minutes, which was acceptable as he aimed to run for one hour at least per session.

Released from his lead, Doddle headed into the kitchen and set about lapping up noisily the fresh water in his bowel. He then turned his attention to the food that had also been deposited into the food part of the bowl and despatched that manically. John walked into the kitchen and was met with a long cold glass of water sitting on the table. He imitated Doodle and gulped it down loudly.

'Thanks, Jane. That hit the spot. It was hot out there.'

'Good,' came the reply as Jane scooped a tired Doodle up in a checkered blanket and headed out of the back door quietly.

John went upstairs and into the bathroom for a long, cool shower. When he reappeared in the kitchen casually dressed in an open-neck shirt, chinos and deck shoes, he was greeted by a surly Charlie and breakfast cooked by Jane.

'Anything interesting in the Sunday papers?' he enquired.

'No. It's all scandal and gossip. I don't know why we buy them.'

Jane's reply was something that he heard regularly since they had started dating. Jane also chose the Sunday papers that they bought and not only read them religiously but repeated verbatim many of the stories to him over the coming days. John read the front page and scanned the sports pages and that was more than enough for him.

Charlie, like her mother, enjoyed reading all of the gossip and spent time every Sunday memorising the most sensational stories. At school on Monday, all of the girls would be swapping stories and correcting each other if there were any inaccuracies, and it was super, super important to be up to date with 'the goss'.

As John was drinking a cuppa post breakfast, Daisy walked in still dressed in her pyjamas. Her face was a combination of frustration and annoyance.

'Mummy, I can't find Doodle.'

'Darling, Doodle is resting. He's been out for a long run with Daddy and will see you when he's ready.'

'Why does he have to go out running anyway?'

'Darling, all dogs like to run. You know that it makes them happy.'

'Happy and tired,' chipped in a now-smiling Charlie.

'That's enough,' said Jane, staring at Charlie.

She nipped it in the bud before a full-scale screaming session erupted.

'Go and watch TV and Doodle will be with you soon,' soothed Jane.

Daisy left the kitchen unhappy with the explanation. She knew Doodle was in the house but despite relentless searches over many months, she was unable to find him. Even the garden searches were unable to track him down. And for a long while she was convinced that he was in the loft. Her mum had explained to her that Doodle couldn't open the loft and climb in it, and even when Daddy picked her up and showed her the inside of the dusty, musty loft, she still wasn't fully convinced. She would do one more search of all of the rooms before watching TV.

Meanwhile, Doodle was wrapped up in his blanket on the front passenger seat of the car in the garage. All of the windows were open as was the side door into the garage. Anyone looking into the car would only see a crumpled blanket on the seat. Doodle slept deeply and blissfully, dreaming doggie dreams. He and, more importantly, his anus was safe in here for a couple of hours.

12:05. John got up and headed for the front door.
'I'm off for a pint.'
'OK. Dinner's at 15:00. Oh, and don't forget if you see Zayhan to ask him along.'

Pope frowned and exited the house. He could hear the high-pitched buzzing sounds of several lawn mowers as neighbours cut their gardens. Positioned in the middle of his front lawn, making a poor attempt to mow it, was Zayhan Khan. He had already seen Pope leave his house and was watching him walk up the road towards him. A 1,000-watt smile lit Khan's face as John closed in.
'Good morning, John. How are you today? It's going to be a real cracker,' beamed Khan as he stepped aside from the idle lawnmower.
'Yes,' came the reluctant reply.
There was an embarrassing pause when neither man spoke. Khan's face was frozen with a pleading smile plastered all over it.
Pope thought of Jane's conversation with Nadia, who was Khan's wife, and reluctantly said, 'I'm going to have a swift pint. Do you fancy one?'

'Give me two secs and I'll grab my keys.'

The front door was ajar and Pope could hear Khan shout in a threatening tone, 'Boys, get out and cut the grass and put it in the green bin. I'll be back soon and will expect it done.'

Khan reappeared, smile in place, hair coiffured, with a jacket folded over his arm. Pope thought to himself, *How many men mow their lawn dressed in black trousers, black shirt, medallion shining on a pigeon chest and polished black shoes? This man was deliberately hanging around, waiting for me.*

Once up on the Heath, they passed two pubs before Pope said, 'Here we are.'

They entered the Red Lion with its low ceiling and dark interior and went to the bar where Pope nodded at a couple of elderly gentleman sitting on their own before walking to the bar and immediately getting the attention of the young buxom barmaid.

'Yes, luv, what will it be?' she said, looking Pope in the eye and smiling.

'A pint of your guest beer for me, and Zayhan, what you having?'

'Whiskey and lemonade for me. Whatever is house is OK.'

With the drinks poured and ice added by Khan from the bucket on the bar, Pope directed them both to a small table in the corner. Pope sat with his back to the wall and was facing out towards the whole of the pub. Subconsciously tradecraft kicked in.

'Nice place,' said the always beaming Khan.

'Yes. Cheers.'

The conversation followed a standard format. Pope explained that he was a civil servant in a job that focused on pensions for civil servants both in the UK and abroad, and he had to travel a bit because there were offices everywhere. Pretty dull stuff really. And before that he was in the army but was a desk jockey who again looked after soldiers' current and past pensions. Khan larged it up that he was a city highflyer in a job with great money and great opportunities for promotions. In fact, he worked in the back office of a small European bank and was a lowly clerk inputting FX deal tickets into their back office system. He was the only male inputter surrounded by eight young women, and that was the only positive thing that could really be said about his job. Surprisingly, they both enjoyed similar tastes in music and that was an area where Pope warmed to Khan. The ice had been broken, four drinks bought and consumed, and they hadn't even spoken about families or, more importantly, sports.

Pope looked at his watch which read 13:20 and said, 'Is that the time? I'm off to see an old colleague who's not well.'

Khan was taken aback as Pope stood up and reacted immediately.

'John, that was great. We must do it again soon.'

'Sure,' came the non-committal reply.

Outside they shook hands and Khan headed back home. Pope strolled up the street, turned right then second left and entered the old pub.

He made several nods and hellos to people he knew before he stopped on the edge of a group of men whose ages ranged from mid-thirties to mid-sixties.

'Here he is. Pint of special, John?'

'Sounds good.'

'Bit late for you, John,' said another member of the group.

'Yeah, but I'm here now.'

09:00. Pope, Clare Hawkins and Chris Gould were back in the same corner meeting room, each with a plastic cup of something described as coffee but which would fail miserably under the trades description act. There was a five- minute entree when everyone described what they did at the weekend, which amounted to very little. This was a custom-honoured tradition up and down the country in every business and all walks of life every Monday morning. In most cases, people went through the motions showing little interest, as there was little to actually be interested in. Pope then dove into the detail.

'I spoke with Boris and that's closed. I met with five agents, three informers and four Walker teams. There's nothing out there that suggests anything is going down soon.' Boris was the cover name for Victor Sokolov. All contacts were given a cover name.

Clare spoke next. 'I spoke to seven agents, eight informers and six Walker teams and it's the same. I met with SO15 and they say that the tabs are tight on all left and right-wing activists and they aren't up to anything that we should be concerned about.'

Chris chirped in. 'Nothing from the two guys in Luton and GCHQ hasn't come back yet re the Frogs.'

Pope tapped his pen on his pad thoughtfully.

'The Walker teams have been on their targets 24/7 for four months solid and they think that we need to wrap it up. They aren't even remotely right. The intel we are getting isn't picking up real targets. We are assigning teams based on weak intel and tittle-tattle. Worst of all, the teams are worn out and look demoralised. Same for the undercover guys who look burnt out,' said Pope. The Walker teams were surveillance teams who follow, photo, eavesdrop electronically and report back on targets.

Clare looked at Chris and they both nodded.

'OK, I've got a division meeting at 11:00 and will bring it up,' continued Pope.

'That won't go down well,' said Chris.

'Bad news never does,' said Pope with a deadpan expression.

11:00. The divisional meeting was held in The Cage. It was a room in a level below ground that had no external electronic communications installed. The walls, ceiling and floor were all built with mesh designing to obstruct any form of eavesdropping. Anyone entering the room had to deposit all phones, laptops and any other electronic equipment at the desk of the secretary whose job was to manage the meetings in The Cage. Everyone walking into The Cage walked through a detector and this alerted when someone accidentally attempted to access it with any electronic device. Sandra Carruthers was seated at the head of the table. To her left was her assistant-cum-secretary-cum-general dogsbody. There were six regional heads of England and one head each for Scotland, Wales and Northern Ireland. John Pope was regional head for London but for a very odd, historical reason, Luton, which was in the Midlands region, was included within his remit.

Carruthers set the scene, stating that information from both GCHQ and US-based intelligence suggested that there was a high probability that an attack in the UK was being planned. The information had been passed up the chain and the threat level had been upgraded from Substantial to Severe by JTAC (Joint Terrorism Analysis Centre) today. This breaking news brought a shift in the body language of the collective group. Sharing this news had the desired effect that Carruthers wanted; she now had their undivided attention. She went on to berate the group for the lack of results despite the fact that only scraps of information had been shared with them. Now in full flow, she asked each regional head individually what information they had regarding the imminent attack. It was obvious that she was using this meeting to brow-beat everyone and pass onto them accountability for bringing to book the terrorists. More importantly, she was letting them know that failure to arrest any impending attackers would be their responsibility and not hers.

Carruthers delivered her coup de grace when she announced that all holidays and leave would be cancelled with immediate effect. She finished her sermon and, looking at the group, asked them if there were any questions. In fact, she dared them to ask any questions.

This was met with stunned silence and Carruthers was just about to get up when Pope spoke. 'There are people in this room as well as many others who have booked family holidays and—'

'Are you saying that holidays are more important than stopping a terrorist attack?' interrupted Carruthers.

'Of course not. But we can't take kids out of school during term time.'

'Families should go alone then without MI5 agents. Everyone mans their stations,' snapped Carruthers.

'Spoken like someone who doesn't have a family,' said Pope, coolly staring at Carruthers.

'My decision is final,' said a red-faced Carruthers as she stood, indicating that the meeting was closed.

'We have undercover agents and Walkers who are close to burn out because they have been full on for a few months. It's counterproductive to getting results if we keep driving them this hard. We need to manage smarter...' went on Pope.

'You have your orders. Get on with them,' shouted Carruthers. And with that, she stormed out of The Cage.

Her assistant picked up the papers that Carruthers left in her slipstream and scuttled out after her. A couple of divisional heads picked up their own papers and left. Seven people were left in the room and no one spoke for a minute, stunned by how badly Carruthers had managed the fiasco.

'Well, that went well,' said Tony Crook in his thick Scottish brogue accent.

Laughter reverberated around the table.

'Let's all agree not to be seen with John Pope for the next several months. No need for all of us to blot our copy books,' added Steve McLeish.

'She hasn't got a fucking clue,' piped up James Davidson.

'Anyway, I'd like to go on record and say thanks to everyone for showing tremendous solidarity in the meeting,' said Pope.

'Any time, old chap. Please send out the invite for your leaving do,' roared Tony Crook.

And with that, the meeting truly finished and the remaining participants disbursed.

At 14:45, Pope's desk phone rang. It was an internal call and the name of the person and their extension was displayed.

'Hi, John. Everything OK?' said the caller.

'Good thanks. And you?'

'Fine. Are you available for a catch up?'

'Sure. Do you want me to pop up?'

'How about 17:30 at the usual?'

'Sure.'

John Pope walked into the small pub in Pimlico at 17:28 and saw the familiar tall, lean figure of Sebastian Drake taking a decent slake from a pint of real ale.

'Ah, John. Just poured. I took the liberty of choosing a CAMERA best ale. It's got good flavour,' said Sebastian as he picked up the full pint with a frothy head from the bar and handed it to John.

'Cheers,' they both said in unison as the pint glasses clinked.

A pregnant pause ensued whilst both men swallowed and absorbed the flavours on their taste buds.

'So I hear that you've had a busy day,' said Sebastian.

'Ah. News travels fast, Seb.'

'Well, bad news certainly does.'

'Is that how it is?'

'It's kicked up a hornet's nest and a few people are ruffled.'

'Really? It shouldn't have needed me to state the bleeding obvious.'

'Quite so, quite so. But as you know, nothing is ever black and white.'

'She's trampling over everyone. We've got shit intel and she's raising the threat level as a stick to beat us with. Everyone out in the field is knackered; we want more from them and now fucking holidays are cancelled. We aren't machines, and morale is at an all-time low.'

'John, we get it. But she does have a point. We need to get on top of this asap.'

'Seb. It's not bringing in this load of middle managers that have no experience in the field or anywhere that I'm railing against. It's the way we gather data, the fact that we get little support from the Muslim communities and that we surveil people for months when it's clear from the get go that they are either petty criminals or just illegals working in the black economy. We're spinning wheels.'

'It's a long game. We need the support from the Muslim communities but they want to be isolated and that's a political decision to force integration. We do need to surveil better, but we are focusing on people who travel to areas that are terrorist training camps and known for radicalisation, but again people are allowed to travel freely. And the amount of calls we get are increasing, but sifting through the hoaxes, malicious people and time wasters is time consuming. Anyway, with all that, we are making progress and we have thwarted several genuine threats. The papers keep on with headlines about immigrants who want to get in and cause chaos and that doesn't help at all. We know from 7/7 and other attempts that it's homegrown where the threat really is. And we know that some of the new middle managers as you call them aren't suitable, but we need to change as an organisation to meet the ever-changing threats, and they do bring in new ideas,' retorted Seb.

'Throw out the baby with the bath water springs to mind with the sweeping changes that are blowing through.'

'And that's where we on the top floor need better feedback,' said Seb with empathy.

'Is that what this meeting is about? You want me to be a snitch?'

'No. We want to avoid meetings that turn into slanging matches and it would be helpful if decisions that are counterproductive are flagged up. We'll deal with it.'

'What, like cancelling everyone's holidays? What she should have said was make sure that you have adequate cover and if not then flag it up.'

'As I said, we'll deal with it,' said Seb. 'Don't push too hard. Sandra upward manages. She has made a point of getting to know some very influential people not only in the Service, but politicians, civil servants, Police, 6 (MI6) and elsewhere.

She has friends and they have opened up doors for her and helped her get a lot of attention in a relatively short period of time.'

'Good for her. But she doesn't ask for feedback from the troops and doesn't want anyone questioning her poor decisions.'

'Then time will tell whether she's right. If not, then all of her friends will disappear and she'll sink without trace.'

'Time for one more?' asked Pope.

'Why not. It's a decent pint.'

They enjoyed the second pint in relative silence.

'Just one more thing, John. I've received some information from a friend in Military Intelligence and it seems that 6 have been sitting on intel. I'll share it with you once I've got it squared off, but it's going to buy brownie points with your mate Boris.'

'OK. Always good to be in the black with him.'

Just as they were leaving the pub at 18:00, HR had sent out a communication to all staff. It reiterated that all staff holidays would be honoured despite the fact that the threat level had been raised today. It said that holidays would be honoured even if the threat level was raised further. The mail went on to say that everyone had a responsibility to check that in their absence their workload was fully covered and if they had any concerns then they must be raised to their direct line manager. Only in the event of an actual event would there be a need to potentially cancel leave and then everyone would pull together for the duration. The email finished off by wishing everyone a happy holiday and a reminder to use up their holiday by the end of February, as carrying holidays forward was at the discretion of management. Of the people who attended the 11:00 meeting, a couple laughed out loud after opening the email, a couple smiled and the other three didn't react as they didn't want to take sides. Other staff who opened the email were puzzled as they weren't aware that their holidays were under threat. Sandra Carruthers read it and looked up toward John Pope's desk, raging inside with fury. Several minutes later, she heard a ping alerting her to another email arriving into her inbox. She looked at the sender. It was from the top floor.

09:30. Usam exited the people carrier at the end of the High Street. He yawned lazily and stretched himself out before lolloping forward into the early morning shoppers. His mind wasn't focusing on anything but he was feeling tired and looking forward to getting home and going straight to bed after he had a fag and looked at the sports pages. He knew that his mum would wake him up promptly at 14:00 with a lunch awaiting.

Mr Butt was making his way along the High Street on his daily morning walk. He was a small rotund man who gathered weight easily around his middle. His weight had been gathering steadily since he was a teenager, and without either a healthy diet or an exercise programme, he had entered middle age with high blood pressure. He was a ticking time bomb; it was only a matter of time before he suffered the first of many strokes. Being a natural worrier only exasperated his condition. His doctor sympathised with him but warned him that he needed to radically change his lifestyle and worry less about things that he had no control over. Pills were prescribed to lower his blood pressure and a commitment to eat healthier and exercise regularly promised. Regular checkups were diarised and all of this added to the ever-increasing sack of worries that Mr Butt lugged around with him. He used the morning walk as an opportunity to stop and chat to as many people as possible, which he found relaxing. The same could not be said for the counterparts, who were generally strapped for time and needed to complete their shopping expeditions as quickly as possible before heading on to their next task. Many found the experience tortuous and changed their routine in order to avoid being trapped with him. In a couple of extreme cases, they sought medical assistance and were medicated because of their overwhelming feelings of nervous exhaustion. Mr Butt meticulously recorded his daily walks, and his morning stroll could take up to two hours despite 70% of that time being taken up by jawing. What he never diarised were the treats that he earned whenever he 'walked' for more than one hour, which were two generous cream doughnuts supplemented with two mugs of sweet tea.

Mr Butt was chatting with young Mrs Mia and her two young fidgety children when he was momentarily distracted. Mrs Mia spotted her opportunity, said goodbye and left in a similar fashion as a Formula One car exiting the starting grid of a Grand Prix. Before he had time to reply, she was wheel-spinning and burning rubber as she swerved through the idling pedestrians, dragging two bemused children with her. Mr Butt didn't have time to walk ten metres to the pelican crossing, so he hopped out into the road and negotiated the traffic, earning a loud blast from one driver's horn who had to stop to avoid hitting him. His stubby little legs picked up the pace as he hunted down his unsuspecting quarry.

'Good morning, Usam,' said a breathless Mr Butt.

Caught completely off guard, Usam froze in his tracks. Plans to buy a packet of cigarettes and a daily newspaper then have a smoke and a quick read in the local park were in tatters. This man could talk for England…and possibly several other countries also. Shit!

'Oh. Hi, Mr Butt,' he replied, trying not to break stride.

A master of cornering people, Mr Butt shot out his right hand to proffer a handshake whilst simultaneously placing his left hand out towards Usam's right shoulder. Any chance of Usam escaping had been blocked. Reluctantly, he stopped and shook Mr Butt's hand.

'Another fine day,' said a smiling although somewhat out of breath Mr Butt. 'Where are you off to in such a hurry then?'

'Just getting a paper for Mum.'

'And how is your mum and dad?'

'They are both well thanks. I'll say that you asked after them,' Usam replied, trying to extricate himself and move off.

'I'm puzzled, and perhaps you can help me,' implored Mr Butt.

'Of course.'

'I checked all of the noticeboards and spoke to a few council members as well as a couple of respectable elders, and no one is aware of a visit from an Imam.'

Usam looked at Mr Butt, sporting a vacant expression with his mouth hanging partially open. He made no sound at all and was the perfect example of someone catching flies.

'As he was with you and your friends, I thought that you could shed some light on this holy man and his visit.'

Still no sound came from Usam, but his impression of a man catching flies elongated, and to a neutral observer it would have been mightily impressive.

'Is he still here?'

'Er. We just met him outside,' bluffed Usam.

'OK.'

'He wanted to go to the side prayer room,' said Usam, getting into his stride.

'Who was he meeting then?'

'No idea.'

'But he doesn't speak English. How did he ask you directions to the side prayer room?'

Usam was aware that he was tripping himself up and beads of sweat were forming on his forehead.

'One of the elderly women was outside and she translated.'

'Who was that then?'

'I'm sorry, I don't know her name, or any of their names.'

'Well, what did she look like then?'

'I don't know. You know they all look the same.'

Mr Butt was about to carry on his inquisition when Usam started to walk on.

'Mum reads the paper with a cuppa and I need to go.'

'Of course. Have a good day.'

Mr Butt turned around and watched Usam as he scurried off down the road. The sketchy answers to his questions meant that Mr Butt had another set of worries to add to the sack of worries that he carried around with him.

Usam had already decided that he wasn't going to mention this conversation to anyone and definitely not to the Ayatollah of Doom and Gloom. In fact, he was going to go straight home and go to bed. His day was already fucking ruined.

11:00. All heads were seated around the table in The Cage. Carruthers and her assistant entered and took their seats at the head of the table.

'Senior management has decided that a review of all targets currently under surveillance must be done. Within one working week, I require written reports on all candidates for the withdrawal of surveillance. The report must include reasons for withdrawing surveillance. Most important is the views must either come from Walker teams or be endorsed by Walker teams. We are focusing on reducing the surveillance on targets that aren't credible and want to free up resources. The cost of running operations needs to managed better.'

Carruthers paused and looked around the room.

'Any questions?'

There was a pregnant pause and it looked like the answer was no.

'Yes, Sandra,' said Pope.

He awaited any form of reply but was met with silence.

'I was thinking that rather than focus on watching people brought to our attention by public feedback only that we try a slightly different tact.'

Another pause and still no verbal feedback from Carruthers other than a blank stare.

'If we look at young men who have travelled in the last several years to known terrorist training areas and cross reference that with feedback from the public, we then have a group more likely to harvest real targets. We should eliminate public feedback only that has been raised for any number of spurious reasons.'

Carruthers' hands tightened around her pen and her knuckles were turning white from where the blood was draining from them, and she was about to say something when another voice piped up.

'That's a cracking idea,' boomed Tony Crook in his Scottish brogue.

'It certainly will help,' endorsed James Davidson.

Carruthers smiled thinly. 'I'll push that up the chain and see what they think. In the meantime, get out to the Walker teams and have the reports back by this time next week. OK, anything else?'

Another pregnant pause. With that, Carruthers got up and marched out of The Cage followed by her assistant. Nothing was said in The Cage until four heads got up and left.

Frank Selly, who was the regional head for south-west England, said in a burred accent, 'Good idea, John. We need to get a better handle on choosing targets. It's far too scatter gun.'

'What the fuck about managing the cost better? More corporate bullshit speak from the latest offsite managed by some overpaid consultant twat,' roared Tony Crook.

'We do need to manage costs though,' said John Pope.

'Don't defend her. I'd like to interrogate all of the consultant twats,' went on Tony Crook.

'Now, now we don't do rendition anymore,' said Pope. 'Not that we ever did...'

'I thought when she asked for questions, John was going to ask if it will affect our holidays,' said a smiling Callum Drake, head for Northern Ireland.

Laughter broke out amongst the group.

'How about that though. HR yanked her chain yesterday. John must have friends in high places,' screeched Tony Crook.

More laughter and then all eyes fell on John Pope.

'Not guilty. But I'm off to Welsh Wales on Thursday for a ten dayer with the family and the dog.'

'That's quick. When did you book that? Last night after HR's love note?' quipped Tony Crook.

'Nope. All tied up several months ago. We were going to go to Crete but when Daisy found out that the pooch would be kennelled that caused a major meltdown. So Welsh Wales it is.'

'Same difference,' said Frank Selly, 'apart from the shite weather and the Taffies.'

'Talking of meltdown. Don't forget Sandy wants her reports tout suite. Best do your handover asap,' laughed Tony Crook.

'Yeah. Thanks. I don't want to come back and spend time on the naughty step,' fired back Pope.

With that, the meeting concluded and the group dispersed.

14:00. Pope, Clare Hawkins and Chris Gould were sitting in the corner meeting room. All had finished their cups of awful coffee without commenting on the abysmal taste. Pope had just finished going through his handover ahead of his ten-day holiday. It was standard fare: keep up weekly meeting with agenda and action points. Contact with his undercover agents and Walker teams would be shared equally between both of them. He'd remotely dial into any heads' meetings. Any crisis, they were to contact him immediately. At this point, the meeting would generally be winding down but Pope had a surprise item to throw out there.

'There has been an order from on high,' he started. 'A full review of all targets under surveillance must be conducted, a report written and a proposal included on whether surveillance should cease. If so, then this needs to be substantiated. The Walker teams must either recommend or endorse all proposals to shut down the operation. Reports into Carruthers by close of business this time next week.'

'Wow, that's a seismic shift,' said Chris. 'Good news though, everyone thinks we have too many non-relevants under the microscope.'

'Yeah, and as we are constantly being reminded about budgets, costs and the need to be more frugal, then it's got to be a good thing. What with the cost of a 24/7 surveillance, that alone burns a hole in the annual budget,' chirped Clare.

'So what happens next then?' questioned Chris.

'A review of how a person or group gets onto The List is going to be done. Rather than target people who have been supplied from Joe Public, we are going to cross reference that group with young men who have travelled to known hot spots in the last several years. This should weed out a lot of false positives that are gumming up the works,' replied Pope.

'So no plans to reduce the size of Walker teams?' asked Chris.

'None whatsoever. We are trying to tune up and refine the initial process. In fact, we need to add more criteria to further improve the process, but this is the start,' came back Pope.

He handed out a list of all Walker teams, their targets, length of time the operation had been ongoing, source and reason for surveil. Each one was assigned to either Chris or Clare.

'OK, if you are comfortable with adding this to both of your own workloads and covering my holiday then I propose that when you have completed a draft report, reviewed by the Walker team, then you send it to me for final review. I'll review and comment. Once agreed, then send the report to Sandra.'

'What if we aren't comfortable with this workload and deadlines?' said Chris mischievously.

'Well, I'll cancel my holiday and draw up a new workload list,' said Pope without any sign of emotion.

'No, that won't be necessary,' laughed Chris, having drawn the response that he expected from his fully committed boss.

Clare nodded her head in agreement, not really understanding that Chris was only pulling Pope's leg.

'OK, that's everything unless there's any further business,' said Pope.

Clare cleared her throat and her hands slightly trembled.

'There is one thing,' she said, looking at the table. 'I did hear that you made a very personal comment to Sandra in the recent heads' meeting.'

'Go on,' said Pope.

Chris shifted uncomfortably in his seat, caught out by the turn of events. He couldn't think of a reason to get up and leave. But then again, he wanted to stay, hear the gossip and see how it played out. It may be a good story to discuss with the boys over a pint. Especially as they shared information with each other once the beers flowed. Offices are the same the world over, even if your job is dealing in secrets. No, *especially* if your job is dealing in secrets.

'Sandra is of a certain age now and I doubt that she is... how can I put it... fertile,' went on Clare.

'Sorry, I haven't a clue what you are talking about,' said a puzzled Pope.

'Women have careers and that means that they sacrifice having families when they are at their most fertile. It isn't an easy decision to put aside having children, but that is a choice modern women have to make,' whispered Clare.

Pope was even more confused now. Chris didn't have any idea what Clare was on about but noted that she was now behaving and talking like his live-in girlfriend Melanie.

'What exactly was it you were told?' said Pope, trying to cut to the chase.

'Well, I was told confidentially that there was a conversation about potentially cancelling everyone's holidays, and you said that it was alright for her as she didn't have children. You were referring to the fact that she's potentially barren. That's very hurtful to any woman,' said a now near-distraught Clare.

Chris thought that at last there may be a story here to be recounted over a few beers.

'Clare, that's wholly incorrect. I'll tell you what was said and then you can go back to whoever told this tale and correct them,' said a calm Pope. 'First, it is true that Sandra tried to impose a unilateral ban on all holidays for the foreseeable future for everyone. I mentioned that for those of us with children this meant we wouldn't be able to have a family holiday as we can't take kids out of school during term time. I did say that cancelling holidays if you aren't a parent is easy because there's no impact as there aren't any kids to consider. There was no inference direct or otherwise to Sandra's ability to have children. What was said in that meeting has been grotesquely misrepresented.'

'Thanks, John. I had to bring it up, you do understand.'

'Of course. And I have put the record straight.'

Clare smiled meekly, trying to recompose herself. She slowly gathered her papers up and left the meeting room. The years were ticking by and she was soon going to have to make a decision about starting a family. First though, it would be nice to have a steady boyfriend and not a lazy dope like most of her poor choices. Someone like John Pope would do nicely, but that was a thought buried deep in her subconscious.

'Fucking gossips,' quipped Chris. 'This place is a whore house for gossip.'

'Never heard that expression before.'

'Nah, but it's good all the same,' said Chris. 'Wasn't sure if Clare was talking about Sandra or herself at one point there.'

Pope wasn't about to be drawn into another conversation that could be misrepresented and shared amongst the avaricious gossip mongers.

'OK. Catch you later,' said Pope as he got up to leave.

Chris would have a nice story for the boys. Obviously it would be suitably embellished before rolling out.

16:30. Pope opened an email shortly after it pinged in his inbox.

JP,

Peace and harmony broken out again.

Look forward to seeing new approach to selecting targets rolled out.

We'll catch up after your hols.

Seb

PS I'll have info ready for Boris.

04:35. The door to the basement room opened abruptly and caught the three people outside off guard. The Imam turned around without looking at them, reached into his Bisht, a flowing over-cloak made of wool, and produced a key. He locked the door, checked that it was secure, placed the key in his pocket and turned to face the startled triumvirate who were gathered in a tight group. They stared at him, wondering what he wanted. It was rare that anyone left the room during the session and never him. It was as if he never needed water or food or had the need to use the toilet.

'Is there an emergency?' the Imam said in almost a whisper.

The three of them hesitated, looking mostly at the floor but not offering a response.

'In the room where these holy warriors are preparing for glory in Paradise, all I can hear is the sound of a pack of hyenas. Laughing and chattering for at least twenty minutes,' he said as he slowly approached them.

'Imam, we are sorry,' said Usam. 'The walls in the basement amplify noise and makes it sound a lot louder.' He hoped that this explanation would placate the Imam.

Ignoring the reply, the Imam continued to close the gap between himself and the group.

'Were my instructions unclear?'

'Imam?' said Usam.

'Specifically, one was to stand at the top of the stairs and bar entrance to the basement to anyone. One was to stand outside of the room. And finally, one was to stand at the bottom of the stairs and support the other two,' said the Imam. 'And yet here you all are, laughing and joking. Doing anything but your job.'

Rahan was now the closest of the group to the Imam and he smiled weakly at him. In an instant, a Janbiya, a short, curved dagger, was pressing against Rahan's neck. Rahan could smell cardamom on the Imam's breath. Cardamom is added to make a popular Arabic tea, and he was reeking from it. No one spoke for several seconds and all three were frozen still in a state of both terror and shock. The blade pressed a fraction harder against Rahan's neck and he involuntarily stretched his head back and away from the blade fractionally.

'If any of you are unable to perform the simplest tasks then perhaps I need to find a replacement,' warned the Imam, his jet-black pupils darting with venom from one to each of the other two.

'Imam, it won't happen again,' said Usam in a high-pitched voice betraying panic.

'No, it won't,' instructed the Imam.

As swiftly as the dagger appeared and was pressed against Rahan's throat, it was removed and secreted back into the Bisht.

'Get back to your stations,' was the final command.

And with that, the Imam turned around and headed back into the room. The three sentries scurried back to their posts suitably chastised and frankly glad that they weren't relieved from their positions permanently. The drive back to the safe house was sullen as usual. Once the people carrier had exited the road, Zeehan, the driver, broke out into pig impersonations. After a couple of minutes of doing his solo impressions, he realised that no one else was participating. The rest of the journey was completed in silence, as if the presence of the Imam was still in the car. It was.

10:00. The car was fully loaded. The cases had been placed in the boot late yesterday evening after the car had been filled to the brim with petrol, oil added and all tyres inflated. The car had been through the car wash at the weekend followed by a hoovering and a general internal clean up. Air freshener was sprayed everywhere inside and that meant no one could go inside it until it wasn't so toxic. Even the spare tyre was inspected. Very rarely was so much time afforded to the car. After all, it was just a mode of transport for the family. It was used mostly by Jane Pope for ferrying the kids from A to B and pottering to and from work. Even John had complimented on how well it looked after a little TLC.

John was going to drive for all of the journey and the plan was that they would stop for refreshments around 12:30 and take the opportunity to stretch their legs and grab some fresh air. A sound plan that everyone understood and bought into. Jane sat in the front passenger seat and put the destination into the GPS. It sprang into life and produced a map, highlighting their home address. John had read the route in his A-Z roadmap atlas of GB the previous evening and was comfortable that he would get there without the need for GPS assistance. He wasn't a fan of the ever-burgeoning list of apps and technology that was invading everyday life. Well, a technophobe would say that anyway. Most of the route he had done many times and as it was motorway for the lion's share of the journey, there was little opportunity to get lost. In the back seat behind him sat Charlie, who was typing into her phone and pushing Doodle away from her at the same time. Daisy was sitting behind her mother, trying to drag Doodle into a headlock. Jane opened a packet of peppermint sweets and popped one into John's mouth before leaning over the seat and offering both girls the packet. Charlie took out one and Daisy took out two. Daisy opened out her hand and Doodle wasted no time accepting the offer of the sweet and semi-settling down next to her. Daisy popped the other sweet into her own mouth and started to chew frantically.

John eased the car out into the road and turned right.

The GPS hollered, 'Turn left.'

The car was travelling slowly along the street whilst the GPS repeated several times, 'Turn around. Turn left.'

Pope lamented internally that this was going to be a long journey. Jane inserted a CD into the car CD player and adjusted the volume. She had chosen a U2 album that both her and John enjoyed. They shared similar tastes in music even before they met, and this pastime helped cement their union. U2 was up there with soul music. They enjoyed dancing in the discos in the 80s and there was a wealth of artists that they bopped along to. Chic, Change, Micheal Jackson and Prince were the main staples of their listening and dancing. Spandau Ballet was another that held a high position in their list of favourites, and there were several albums of theirs in their collection. John had never told Jane that they weren't really his style, but a little white lie can sometimes go a long way. The first dispute came as they turned right at the end of the road and headed downhill towards Finchley.

'God. Do we have to listen to that? It's sooo old and out of date,' ranted Charlie. 'And they are old too.'

Jane caught a sly grin from John and said, 'OK, what do you want?'

'Justin Bieber, obviously.'

A new CD was inserted and the car filled with the sounds of his first album, *My World*.

'That's better. Doodle likes this album,' said Daisy, always trying to win favour from her older sister.

Less than three minutes into a five-hour journey and harmony was restored. The car headed towards the North Circular Road which skirts around the busy centre of London. Charlie started singing along to the songs that she'd heard many, many times. Daisy tried valiantly to join in but had to settle for humming. It wasn't long before the atmosphere in the car was a combination of relaxation and enjoyment. Charlie's head bobbed to the music on her longish neck. Daisy, not quite co-ordinated, bobbed her head on a developing long neck and Jane was swaying gently supported by her long, elegant neck. Straddled between the two girls in the rear seat, Doodle leapt about, planting licks on both of them. John Pope was smiling and thinking to himself that life was good.

The Swan family were paddling in unison albeit in their family car.

Further peppermint sweets were shared out after twenty-five minutes and everyone including Doodle partook. The Justin Bieber album ran its course after fifty minutes.

'Can we play that again? That was good fun,' asked Daisy, looking at Charlie.

'OK, but then we'll play Taylor Swift,' replied Charlie.

'Goody, Doodle really likes her,' said Daisy before continuing. 'Come on, Mummy, get Justin on.'

A further five minutes passed before Daisy asked, 'Mummy, can I have a packet of crisps?'

'OK, but lunch is only one hour away.'

'Me too,' said Charlie.

Two packets of crisps were passed back and the singing became disjointed whilst mouthfuls of crisps were chewed and swallowed. Daisy's opened packet was a signal for Doodle to assist her with the task. Twenty minutes later, Daisy's next request was made.

'Can I have a drink, Mummy? I'm thirsty.'

Jane handed back two small cartons of orange, anticipating Charlie's request. Jane and John shared a bottle of water. John could hear regular pings from his phone in his jacket pocket as emails arrived in his inbox. Even singing could become monotonous, and Charlie broke off.

'Daddy, we are going on holiday and you are still wearing your smelly work shoes.'

'Comfortable for driving.'

'No way. They are heavier than deep sea divers' boots.'

This observation drew laughter from everyone, although Daisy had no idea who or what a deep sea diver was, never mind his (smelly) boots.

'Well Daddy, did you know that Doodle sleeps with his head on your shoes?' said Daisy.

'How do you know that he's asleep?' asked Pope.

'He snores and he sleeps with his tongue out. And sometimes his eyes twitch.'

'Darling, he's dreaming when his eyes twitch,' interjected Jane.

This set of Doodle comments drew more laughter and he danced around the back seat, becoming even more excited about this wondrous adventure with his personal pack of dogs. After two hours and forty-five minutes of driving, mostly on the motorway, the car pulled into a service centre. Jane took the girls off to find the ladies' toilet whilst John walked Doodle around the car park. Jane returned with coffee, sandwiches and some sweets. Everything was devoured whilst sitting in and out of the car. Doodle once again ate 50% of everything given to Daisy. A further visit to the toilets and then everyone packed away and was ready for the final part of the journey. The thirty-five-minute stop meant that they had one hour fifty minutes' travelling before they reached Port Eynon on the Gower Peninsular. Their family run hotel catered for pets and was minutes away from the beach. The journey continued uneventfully with peppermint sweets doled out regularly and a further couple of cartons of orange slaked by the kids. Daisy managed to persuade her mum that Doodle wanted to sniff out of the window, and Jane reluctantly lowered the rear window enough for him to stand up on Daisy and stick his snout out. Daisy was delighted. After a while, even Doodle had had enough and curled up in the middle of the backseat. Taylor Swift had finished and now the car was quiet. Jane was napping, Daisy was deep asleep, Charlie was dozing fitfully in and out of sleep and Doodle was gently snoring.

Like any major battle, once both protagonists have set up their heavy artillery and deployed their battalions in placements to offer offensive advantages whilst also having further deployments to offer equally defensive cover, what follows is carnage. Who fires the first cannon is irrelevant as the outcome is all that matters. Charlie swore and stuck with her version for the rest of her life that it was the truth and that her version was the actual sequence of events. Charlie protested her innocence at the merest mention of this story and immediately took over, changing and challenging all comers with her 'truthful' version. It all began when Doodle threw up on the seat between Daisy and her. Daisy looked over and saw what Doodle was doing and then she started throwing up, apparently mostly through her nose. A fair-sized portion of the projectile vomit enveloped Doodle's back. It was both Daisy and Doodle throwing up combined with the gross smell that forced an unwilling Charlie to empty the contents of her stomach on the floor. And no, she didn't know how puke ended up on the back of her dad's jacket. Daisy, who was in a state of shock, never spoke about the awful event. As the years went by, she suspected that there might be an alternative version to that expounded by Charlie, but she never challenged her older sister. John remembered the sequence of events unfolding in a different order than that regaled by Charlie, but he kept it firmly to himself. He remembered Charlie's hands gripped tightly around his headrest for several minutes before it all kicked off. Charlie was making repeat noises during this period, trying not to throw up.

Eventually she couldn't hold back the tide. Once she started to throw up, some onto his jacket, he began manoeuvring the car towards the hard shoulder. Doodle started yapping and Charlie turned her head towards him, which led to only one outcome. Daisy started crying because Doodle was covered in puke and then joined in. Finally, Doodle threw up. Despite varying versions of this tale, everyone agreed that Jane did not cover herself with glory. Waking up confused, she became hysterical and was swearing uncontrollably. Under pressure and disorientated, she caved in and, worst of all, had a Tourette's moment. That was always how the story ended. Mum was the butt of the joke – especially as she rarely swore and, if so, never ever the 'F' word.

The quiet was broken by two kids vomiting, assisted by a little dog. Pope reacted immediately; checking his rear mirror, he indicated and moved from the middle lane into the slow lane and then again checking his mirror, he moved onto the hard shoulder where the car slowed to a stop. He had already auto-wound down the rear windows.

Jane had woken up with a start and, on seeing the ensuing spew fest, screamed, 'Out the window. Out the window. Out the fucking window.'

Neither children nor dog took any notice, but once the car had stopped, Charlie did put her head out of the window and promptly chundered down the door. Pope flew out of his door and opened the rear door before dragging out the still-puking Charlie and holding her up whist she retched on the embankment. Jane had performed a similar act with Daisy, who was vomiting and crying as her mum held her horizontally. A couple of minutes passed and both children had no more to vomit or cry. They were both covered in puke. John reluctantly poked his head through the back door. He was hit by a brick wall of stench. It took all of his years of battlefield experience not to involuntarily join the puke gang. He focused on Doodle, whose snow-white coat was matted with puke. Doodle had already begun the tasks of eating up the puke that he had not three minutes ago delivered onto the previously clean back seat. Doodle looked up and a soggy tail started wagging back at

Pope. Pope leant in, deliberately avoiding touching anything, and snatched the dog out. Jane was stripping the soiled clothes off of both of the girls, who were compliant. She looked at John and Doodle and was unable to say anything. John looked at his phone and searched. There was a motorway service station three miles away. With no more water onboard, there was only one option available. Mum and the two girls stripped to their underwear would sit in the front passenger seat. Doodle would sit in the footwell. All windows would be open, no arguing, and once at the service station, everyone and the car would be cleaned up. Indicator on, silence, and the car drifted back into the slow lane, leaving a vile smell in its wake.

When the car stopped, Jane said, 'John, you need to sort out your jacket, there's stuff on your back.'

Jane then took the girls into the toilets and began the cleaning up process and bagging the soiled clothes after washing them thoroughly in the sinks. John had a tired Doodle under his arm as he walked into the gents'. Doodle wasn't happy when he was made to stand in a sink whilst water was poured all over him. Worst still, liquid soap was applied to his coat vigorously. Once Pope was happy, he used the fixed towel to dry off the little dog. A couple of odd stares from other patrons were ignored. Finally, his jacket was scrubbed in the sink.

An elderly gentleman entered the toilets and spoke to Pope with an educated accent. 'I hope that you don't mind. I saw your good lady and lovely children head into the rest room. I couldn't but help notice that they were not looking well. I am a doctor and there is an uncommon strain of Norovirus going around. I would suggest that you and your family contact a doctor just in case.'

'It's worse than that. They've had a nasty dose of Justin Bieber,' replied Pope as he exited with Doodle, who now looked more like a large wet rodent, tucked under him arm.

Doodle never missed an opportunity to show affection; he stuck out his hot tongue and licked the man on the back of his hand. The elderly gentleman quickly went to the sink and began forcefully washing his hands. Pope bought two eight-litre bottles of water and sluiced the back seat, floor and the outside rear door. The smell was atrocious but at least the food parts and sludge had mostly been removed. Jane returned with both partially clothed girls and sprayed most of her bottle of 'Seductive' perfume into the rear of the car. The after-effect wasn't that pleasant. Everyone again crammed into the front of the car with all of the windows open. As they drove through the Port Eynon village streets, they attracted strange looks from both pedestrians and fellow car travellers alike. John was driving at a careful pace with his head protruding out of the driver's door window. There were three heads protruding out of the passenger door window sucking in fresh air. Doodle was still imprisoned in the footwell for his part in this dastardly affair. Some five hours ten minutes after leaving Finchley, the Pope family had reached their holiday destination. Jane, girls, dog and cases were rapidly plonked into the hotel. Pope returned to the car from smell hell and drove with purpose to a local garage that also offered a car valet service. Pope parked and found the manager. He explained the situation and the manager walked slowly over to the car, careful not to get too close.

'OK. We can do it. But it's not a normal job. It will be triple steaming and the guys don't like doing this,' said the manager, thinking pound notes.

'Fine. What's the damage?'

'It's going to be £80.00.'

'Done,' he said, and he whipped out four £20 notes.

The manager was crestfallen. He should have charged £120, rich fucking Londoners. He'd know better next time. 'Ready in two hours.'

Pope was already marching off when he saw two Romanians stroll over to the car and gingerly open the doors.

Best eighty quid I've ever spent, thought a now-smiling Pope.

20:00. Usam looked at his phone for the third time in twenty minutes. It irritated his father that his family spent so much time monitoring their phones. And the pinging when a message was received sent the recipient into a frenzy. Conversation was dead, he often said to anyone and everyone in his family, but they just rolled their eyes. The text Usam received was short. He fired back a reply immediately and then walked out of the room dialling the sender.

21:00. Pope walked into the local pub and spotted Terry Gibbons standing at the bar.

'Hi, mate. What are you having?' said Terry as he extended his right hand.

'Pint of Best.'

'So, how's life?'

'Great. Family all well and growing. Daisy is five, Charlie is fifteen and we've now got a dog.'

'Bloody hell. They'll be married next and then you'll be a granddad.'

'Yeah, time is racing by. And what's happening with you? Still a lumberjack?'

'Same old. Still a tree surgeon to give it its correct title. And working the doors every Friday and Saturday in Cardiff centre.'

'Now that sounds like busy work.'

'Can be occasionally but they are a good crew of lads.'

'Like the Green Jackets, eh.'

'How would you know? You made new mates and pissed off.'

'Technically I was seconded.'

'Yeah right. Still working for that toff spook with a plumb in his mouth? What's his name, Seb the fucking duck.'

'Well remembered. Seb Drake is around still. You know, we are always looking for a good man.'

'Christ. At least wait until I'm pissed before you try and recruit me.'

'Well?'

'No chance. I'm not cut out for Spook Street.'

'OK. Well, cheers and let's enjoy the next few days.'

'Jane OK with me gatecrashing your family holiday?'

'If she wasn't then you wouldn't be here.'

'No change then. Still under the thumb.'

'Bollocks. Anyway, anyone on the arm?'

'Nope. Just the groupies who hang around bouncers.'

'Really?'

'Trust me, mate. You can't fail. Well, unless you are Frank Poole.'

'Now there's a blast from the past. Whatever happened to him?'

'Some of the boys at Green Jacket reunions reckon he got banged up in Sweden for counterfeiting. Probably tried to pass Monopoly money, the soppy bastard.'

Gibbons pointed to a table and they walked to it. He caught a feint whiff of sick smell and was annoyed that the manager didn't clean the place. They reminisced about the times and people they encountered in the Green Jackets as they both started at the same time. Gibbons was an excellent soldier but Pope was a natural with a rifle, and that was why he was spirited away. After several pints, that dam whiff was still there and still annoying Gibbons.

Pope smiled and recounted the story of earlier today when the rear of the car became Barf City.

'I swear the only thing missing was Mike Oldfield playing Tubular Bells. It was *The Exorcist* on wheels.'

'Yeah. Whatever happened to Mike Oldfield?'

'No idea. But I'm calling in a priest to exorcise the motor before we go back.'

'Mate, you need to do the same to your clobber.'

'Oops. Sorry, mate, it's been a very odd day.'

Gibbons got up and went to the bar to buy the next round. There were two large, hairy bikers at the bar. They were baiting the small barman and making homophobic comments towards him. The barman was intimidated both by their behaviour and their menacing appearance. Gibbons waited patiently for several minutes to be served whilst the two bikers continued haranguing the barman. Gibbons was never one to shy away from conflict and disliked their bullying behaviour.

'Lads. Turn it in. He's just trying to do his job,' said Gibbons, staring at the two tormentors.

'Move on, mate,' said the larger one, now facing Gibbons.

'That won't happen, you fucking dipshit.'

A swinging right hand missed Gibbons's head as he ducked inside. Gibbons's forehead connected hard and true on the bridge of his opposition's nose. A crimson shower cascaded from the now broken nose, and tears rolled down his fat cheeks. All of his fighting spirit had been quelled. His mate broke a bottle on the bar and all eyes in the bar were now focused on a situation that was quickly escalating out of control. Pope, who had witnessed the scene, had moved behind the bottle-wielding thug and delivered a heavy left-footed kick into the biker's left hamstring. The thug winced and hopped as a result of the blow. Pope then delivered a right-footed kick into the thug's right calf and he flopped onto the floor, writhing in agony from both blows. The broken bottle was voluntarily released from his grasp, as his hands immediately wrapped around his intensely painful injuries.

The barman looked at Gibbons without any gratitude. 'Thanks a lot. I have to live here and these are regulars.'

Gibbons looked at the thug nursing a broken nose. 'Fuck off and don't come back. I'll be in here every day for the next few days. I live in Cardiff and if I hear that either of you are sniffing around here then I'll be back.'

Both thugs sheepishly left the pub and several locals were silently pleased to see them finally get their comeuppance.

The barman poured them both another beer.

'John. Still wearing those steel toe caps I see,' said Gibbons.

'Don't forget the heels also.'

'No, I won't, and don't forget to fumigate them. Bloody soon, mate.'

Both men laughed.

'Don't tell me that you still have that old pop gun also. The only thing that's good for is the *Antiques Roadshow*.'

Pope tapped the side of his nose twice. 'No comment. Covered by the Official Secrets Act,' said a grinning Pope.

'Last time that hunk of scrap iron was fired in anger was in the Crimean War. And by the bloody other side. Hidden steel toecaps, old Ruskie guns. Those Reds in Afghanistan sure made an indelible impression on you.'

'Some good guys. No doubt now reaping the rewards of state capitalism.'

'Is that was it is? Seems like a few oligarchs making out like bandits whilst the rest struggle on.'

'And here endeth the party political broadcast.'

'Well, if you were with your chums now, they'd have sold you the gun and the steel toecaps. No free handouts and toasting shite with their rocket fuel vodka. That's your state capitalism.'

'Maybe. Anyway, up for a run tomorrow? Seven o'clock sharp outside the hotel for a one-hour, you on point with me and Doodle?'

'Who's Doodle?'

'You know. I mentioned that we have a dog now.'

Gibbons shrugged his shoulders and headed off into the village. That was the best he could manage, but it was a confirmation. Pope turned the opposite way and walked back to the hotel. He entered the room quietly and the bedside lights were on. Jane was sitting upright in the old double bed watching the news on a small colour TV.

'So, how's Terry?'

'Good. He's got two jobs now. He's a tree surgeon and also works a couple of nights as door security.'

'Typical Terry. A lumberjack and a bouncer.'

'He's happy and that's what counts.'

'I hope he didn't lead you astray. He can sniff out trouble at two miles, that one.'

'No. Just a chat reminiscing over old times,' lied Pope, deliberately not making eye contact with Jane. 'Anyway, how are the girls? No more dramas, I hope.'

'No. Everyone went to bed and were asleep within ten minutes,' said Jane. 'Daisy did say though that both her and Doodle would stay at home next year. Apparently they don't like holidays.'

Pope laughed aloud. His family always made him laugh.

'Well, we've got a busy day tomorrow and no one will remember today. Down to the beach in the morning, then flying kites in the afternoon.'

'That's relaxing, and no car journeys, which is best,' smirked Jane.

'About that. For the journey home, it will be a light breakfast for everyone. No food or drinks allowed in the car apart from water.'

'What about Doodle?' bantered Jane.

'Especially Doodle. I'm up early for a run with Terry and I need to quickly check a few reports from work that I'm expecting. Hopefully I won't be too long. Do you want anything from the mini bar?'

Jane shook her head and continued watching TV. John took out his laptop and went through the security logon sequence.

02:45. The Imam enters the people carrier. The door was automatically shut and they drive away. As per usual, there was complete silence.

Usam turned around and broke the quiet. 'Imam, Rahan isn't with us today.'

The Imam's black pupils fixed on Usam, 'Yes, he is carrying out a task.'

Usam seized the opportunity to continue. 'Will he be gone long?'

'As long as it takes.'

'I see. Do we need to recruit cover then?'

'No. The driver will now be a sentry.'

'The driver?'

'The driver,' said the Imam, pointing at Zeehan.

Zeehan was quiet up to this point, driving slowly as he listened intently to the conversation.

'What, me?' Zeehan stammered.

'Yes, you. Park the car and we all go in together. They will tell you what to do.'

With that, the conversation was finished. No one knew where Rahan was or what he was doing, and Zeehan had been promoted to fill the vacancy.

The Imam thought back to the previous evening. He had used a burner phone to text Rahan. A simple message said to meet at the park, which was several streets away from his house. He had to pack a small bag and on leaving tell his parents that he was taking a break and going to stay with friends in Bradford. His mum and dad, who were settled in front of the TV, didn't have time to challenge him or elicit any information out of him. Rahan poked his head into the lounge, uttered two sentences and fled out of the front door. Filled with importance, he pounded the pavement to the park. The events earlier in the day when his life was physically threatened had all but evaporated. He saw the Imam sitting in the back seat of a battered Vauxhall Nova and strolled over to it. The driver was unknown to Rahan but leant over and opened the passenger door. Rahan and his small case sat in the passenger seat.

'Welcome,' said a smiling Imam.

Rahan wasn't accustomed to this level of friendliness, and when the driver also smiled he relaxed.

'We are going to meet someone of importance to the success of this mission. He is waiting for us in a secluded place and will pass on vital information. You are here to act as lookout,' said the Imam.

Rahan smiled, as this was promotion in his eyes. He was being given a role of importance and he was moving up the organisation and ahead of his friends. The car stopped in a lay-by and Rahan got out along with the Imam. There were no other cars or lorries parked there this particular evening. The driver remained in the car but smiled at Rahan as he exited. The Imam and Rahan walked in silence along the footpath deep into the ancient wood. They had driven further up Bedfordshire to Malden Woods.

After ten minutes they reached a point where the Imam said, 'We are here. Now we wait.'

The Imam checked his watch and a further ten minutes passed when they heard footsteps coming from the same path that they had recently trodden.

'Is that him?' said Rahan, looking back towards the direction that they had come from.

The Imam had stealthily removed his Janbiya from his Bisht and with a weighty slash severed the carotid artery in Rahan's neck. The blow was fatal as blood began spewing out of the wound. Rahan couldn't comprehend what was happening and did not make a sound. That was partially due to the fact that his body had quickly gone into a state of shock. His life ebbed away as he fell to the ground, eyes still open whilst a pool of blood formed around his head. Unconsciousness followed rapidly and within a few minutes Rahan was dead. The small docile rabbit was no match for the cunning fox. The fox didn't have to use its hunting skills honed over decades to pursue its quarry. It merely nudged it gently and willingly to the kill zone and despatched it without mercy or feeling. The rabbit's eyes, full of innocence and expectation, gazed into the eyes of its foe with disbelief, and its fragile limbs shook involuntarily, hoping against all hope that this was a mistake and that the fox would change its mind and come to the timid creature's aid. There was no change of mind; there never was going to be a change of mind. The cunning fox was hard-wired without some basic human emotions that included sadness, shame and guilt. The emotions that swelled inside him abnormally were aggression, contempt and disapproval, and they drove him on with his own personal obsession. The driver had already walked up carrying a shovel and Rahan's case. He walked over to a hole that had recently been dug beside the path and threw Rahan's case into it. The Imam had removed Rahan's phone from his pocket and was in the process of pocketing it when the driver came back and dragged Rahan by his feet towards the hole. The driver was careful not to get any blood on his clothes. Rahan was rolled into the pit and the driver filled it up with the recently excavated earth. Leaves and twigs were then placed on top and it now looked as if there never was a hole there, and certainly not a grave. The driver continued shovelling earth and twigs back towards and onto the path. He completely covered all traces of blood. The Imam gave the area one final inspection and then they left. From the point of the murder until the final inspection, fifteen minutes had elapsed. The Imam and his accomplice went back to the car in silence and then drove back to Luton. Mission accomplished.

19:30. Sandra Carruthers had dressed in an Alexander McQueen dress and jacket. She dressed to impress at least three times a week, and McQueen was her favourite designer. She had acquired a very expensive wardrobe of designer labels that were only rolled out when she went out. Carruthers wasn't someone who socialised or enjoyed socialising. She had a purpose and that purpose was self-promotion, social networking and upward managing. Tonight was no exception. Carruthers was going to another gathering in another club in Pall Mall where she would be introduced to more people who hopefully would at some stage of her career assist her in her obsession with promotion. At the age of forty-eight years old and single, it was obvious to one and all that she was a single-minded lady who was career driven. She was tall at five feet nine inches, slim with a dyed-blonde short-layered bob haircut and, despite makeup and her hair cut, looked her age. The car arrived and she was whisked off to Brooks's club in St James Street. This was a gentlemen's club that had stood there for over two hundred years. It was a favourite for European royalty, writers and the Diplomatic Corps. She would be admitted as a guest but confined to a certain number of rooms only. No women members and no access to areas restricted to men, and then only men of rare breeding or global power. Carruthers put up with this boorish behaviour that was endemic in Pall Mall because the potential rewards outweighed everything else. She would be charming, engaging and attentive as always.

'Ah, Sandra, glad you could make it,' said Lord Wickham.

Sandra crossed the room lit by several candelabras and joined the table where Lord Wickham was sitting with four other elderly men. They all stood and waited for the formal introductions.

'General Quinton Foulkes, Judge Creasy, Doctor Irwin and Mr Smith, who is a quantum physics scientist,' said Lord Wickham. 'And this delightful lady is Sandra Carruthers, who is tasked with the very important role of keeping our streets safe.'

'Bravo,' said Judge Creasy.

With that, the ice was broken and they all sat back down. Confidential stories were swapped. No gentleman would ever repeat anything uttered in this prestigious inner sanctum outside no matter how salacious. For tonight, Carruthers was an honorary gentleman. She eased through her standard set of tales practiced and delivered many times in the various Pall Mall clubs. They were an attentive audience, hanging off her every word. As usual, the conversation veered towards her background and how she entered the Service. She had this off pat and was convincing, although not as convincing as she thought. She was approached whilst at Oxford but declined as she wanted to work for one of the many advisory bodies that work for the Civil Service. This was rewarding work as it helped shape and reform the Civil Service without being caught up in any internal politics. Then an opportunity came to work in the HR department of MI5. She excelled here as her main role was cost cutting. The fall of the Soviet Union late 1991 meant that MI6 in particular, but also MI5, needed to restructure. Having rolled out a programme of cost cutting, she was moved sideways into an analyst role. Here again, she analysed data and made recommendations. Some were critical in the defence of the realm, and she rose steadily through the roles and ranks of analysts. Eventually she was promoted to a role where she oversaw and managed field agents and ongoing operations until now, where she had oversight and management of UK regions.

MI5 was as guilty as other agencies of overlooking women and indeed ethnic minorities, and had been publicly scolded by successive governments. Haste had driven through a number of appointments that filled agreed quotas, but not all were made on merit. Carruthers was one of those. She was a desk jockey with no field experience and this evening was rubbing shoulders with people who at some stage in their own careers had had to get their hands dirty.

The evening finished off with the usual exchange of cards and words along the lines that 'we'll keep in touch and if there's anything you need then don't hesitate to contact us.' Carruthers was systematically working her way through all of the clubs of Pall Mall. A veritable who's who of the rich and powerful. A tactic that she hoped would bear fruit. She was working through a similar list for members of parliament, civil servants, police, GCHQ, MI6, CIA, NSA, and other security agencies belonging to European countries. Carruthers was thorough if nothing else. However, her self-centred efforts were being scrutinised by senior people not only within her own agency but also other agencies.

11:15. Mr Butt was talking with a small group of elderly men in the community hall. As usual they were sharing the gossip gleaned from the local community. They spoke in a hushed reverence, heads nodding in unison at the appropriate times. Their body language was in symmetry and displayed seriousness. Whoever had been to the doctor, their ailment and diagnosis and prescription was shared. It seemed that there was a pill available to cure every ailment, and no one left the doctor's surgery without a meaningful prescription and a follow up appointment. Next on their agenda was sharing tales about who was going to go on holiday and who was currently on holiday. Anyone buying a car was next because that act signified both wealth and status. Then there was the list of relatives visiting Luton from all corners of the globe, and any personal details about them were aired. They skirted discussing any members of the community involved in criminality. Those who were burglars, dealt drugs, took drugs, stole cars and menaced people. These items were taboo partly because some of these men were fathers, grandfathers and uncles to the perpetrators. Mr Butt broke away from the group once the conversation had run its course and surveyed everyone else in the room. He spied his targets and headed off towards them.

'Hi, Mr Butt,' said Ahmed, crossing his path.

'Good morning, Ahmed. How are you this fine day?'

'Very good thanks, and you?'

'Busy but well, thanks.'

Busy my arse, thought Ahmed. 'Any news?' he said.

'Well actually, now that you ask, there's one thing. Do you know the Iqbal family? The mum and dad are hardworking and pillars of the community. Two wonderful daughters who are excellent students and will eventually go to university.'

Not pausing for either a breath or a chance of a reply, Mr Butt ploughed on. Ahmed was used to Mr Butt's behaviour and hoped that this wasn't going to be a long, rambling pointless monologue.

'Well, their son Rahan upped and left Thursday evening without any warning.'

'Did he say anything?'

'Apparently he has friends in Bradford and is going to stay with them.'

'I don't understand. What's wrong then?'

'First, his parents say he doesn't have any friends in Bradford. Second, he's never done anything like this before, just left.'

'With the internet chat rooms, Facebook etc., kids are making friends all over the world. Anyway, they can call him and talk to him.'

'They've called him, as have his sisters, and his phone is off. But he has sent a couple of texts saying he's OK. Apparently, the texts aren't how he writes. Normally it's all short words with pictures but these text are polite and no pictures.'

'No emojis doesn't mean anything. He's a young guy just growing up, that's all.'

'Maybe. Anyway, I need to be going.'

'Yeah, but before you go. Did you ever find out about the visiting Imam?'

'Another mystery. No elders or holy men were aware of any visit. And when I spoke with Usam, he says that he met him outside and was only showing him to a side room. It's as if he doesn't exist.'

'Strange.'

'Yes, very strange. Anyway, why are you asking?' questioned Mr Butt.

'No reason. Have a good day and if I hear anything about Rahan from the younger guys then I'll let you know.'

'That would be useful, we all need to stick together. And you have a pleasant day,' smiled Mr Butt. 'And Ahmed, try and eat more. You look far too thin for a young man.'

Ahmed was thoroughly pissed off with the last comment. This particular undercover gig was the fucking pits. He wasn't concerned with the disappearance of Rahan but the case of the visiting 'now you see him, now you don't' Imam needed a bit of investigating. No gym and no muscle-building food was dulling not only his investigative skills but his self-image. The comments from everyone were only hammering home the image problem. He was deep in a generation who were obsessed with their bodies courtesy of the constant barrage from film stars, influencers and music stars, whose images along with their training routines and diets were everywhere. Ahmed suffered from body dysmorphia.

He resolved to spend more time in and around this particular mosque and to get to the bottom of the vanishing Imam, and stuff the rotation strategy. Then he'd start up training again. Best though to update HQ and keep them in the loop. With that, he headed out of the mosque to send an update.

19:00. Terry Gibbons was propping up the bar and gently easing himself through his second pint of local ale. It had a fruity aftertaste which took a little getting used to, but he was determined to try it anyway. Nevertheless, it had a decent head and that was always a plus point. He had gleaned from the nervous barman that neither of the two thugs had revisited the pub since the incident. The barman had also mentioned that the landlord was unhappy because they were regulars and he was going to lose trade. *Typical*, thought Gibbons. *The twat was only worried about losing pound notes and was not interested in the welfare of his staff.* He'd resolve that if the landlord brought it up, then he'd confront him. He had handed over his telephone number to the barman and said that if they ever returned, he should call him and he'd come back and sort them out. The barman looked even more nervous and blanched. Gibbons had to then reassure him that he didn't expect that would happen and it was better to have a backup option just in case.

Pope, family and dog entered the pub. Gibbons bought everyone a drink along with a couple of bags of crisps and they all decamped to a table away from the bar. Gibbons was relaxed and told a few family friendly stories about his current life in Cardiff. The conversation meandered and everyone contributed.
Charlie attempted to introduce a small measure of mischievousness and began by saying, 'So these early morning runs. Who is the fastest then?'

Pope was used to her antics and wasn't going to rise to the bait so just sat there enjoying his pint. Gibbons, who had a competitive nature, replied, 'Well, we are fairly evenly matched but I think that if it was a real race then there would only be one outcome.'

Daisy butted in. 'Doodle is the fastest runner, obviously. Even if he has a sore bum.'

Gibbons was reminded that he was in the company of a young family and corrected himself. 'Yes, Daisy, you are correct, Doodle is the best runner.' Although he wasn't sure what to make of the comment about Doodle's rectum.

Upon hearing his name, Doodle, who was sitting next to Daisy, stood up and jumped up on Gibbons's legs. His front paws bounced off the seated thighs of Gibbons. Doodle went back to sitting beside Daisy and continued to help her eat the opened packet of crisps. It was a gesture by Doodle; Gibbons was part of his pack now. Admittedly Gibbons was low in the pecking order and that was why a short bounce off was all that was required.

'But you were there when Mum and Dad met,' said Charlie, changing tack.

'That was a long time ago,' replied Gibbons.

Jane was silent, but ancient memories were instantly flooding her mind. Pope remained indifferent to this new line of conversation.

'So tell us then,' pressed Charlie.

Daisy was disinterested with this conversation and continued to feed a grateful Doodle with crisps.

'Well, me and your dad were having a drink in a fancy Kensington wine bar and your mum was in there with her friends, and that's where they met.'

'But who spoke first?'

'As I remember it, your mum came over and spoke to us.'

'Did she come over on her own or did any of her friends come with her?'

Gibbons realised that he was being interrogated and wasn't sure now how to respond.

'Can't remember.'

'OK, how many friends were with Mum?'

'Can't remember.'

'Who left with who?'

'Can't remember.'

'How many altogether with you and Dad. Can you remember that then?'

'I told you that already.'

'OK girls, time for the loo. Daisy, leave Doodle here with Daddy,' interceded Jane as she stood up.

Both girls accepted their orders and all three females headed off towards the ladies' toilet.

'Fucking hell, mate, is it always like that?' asked Gibbons.

'Pretty much. Anyway, you handled it OK.'

'Cheers, mate.'

'Well, if you hadn't then Jane would have had your balls.'

'I knew those army interrogation sessions would come in handy one day.'

Both men laughed and Doodle was rewarded with some more crisps. The females returned and the conversation just rolled on. During the course of the evening, a couple of elderly men smiled at Gibbons and Pope, and an elderly lady stopped at their table on the way to the ladies' and made a point of saying that everyone who was a regular was grateful for their help the other evening.

After she doddered off, Jane said, 'What was all that about?'

'No idea,' replied Pope.

'Case of mistaken identity,' added Gibbons.

'Really?' said Jane.

'Yeah. You know what old people are like,' went on Gibbons. 'Confused.'

Charlie watched on, hoping that the situation might escalate. Jane decided that this was getting nowhere and let it go. Well, at least until she got back to their room with Pope. This reminded her why she used to be irritated when Gibbons was around back in the day.

09:10. Ahmed Hussain was standing in the main hallway studying the noticeboards and looking for any information that may give him even the slightest lead. Having read and reread all of the assorted bag of items pinned on the boards, Ahmed was about to head off and interrogate all of the other noticeboards dotted throughout the mosque. In his peripheral vision, he noticed someone moving in an unnatural way. His years of undercover work and specialised training kicked in and he slightly turned his body and headed towards the main door entrance. It was an imperceptible movement that wouldn't draw attention towards him from anyone, and especially anyone trained in counter-surveillance techniques.

Moving from the main hall towards the front door was a young, slim early twenties man dressed in Western clothes. He had a baseball cap slung low on his head, the peak unnaturally positioned low, covering most of his face. He walked quickly with his head deliberately facing towards the floor in front of him. Hands in his jeans pockets, shoulders hunched and avoiding eye contact, he was the epitome of someone exhibiting furtive behaviour. He was deliberately avoiding any contact with anyone and in fairness was achieving that goal.

No one in the main hall was paying any attention to the young man and he was moving through it stealthily. In fact, no one had ever noticed him move through the hall several times before and would never be able to provide a description of his physical appearance. He walked out into the street, turning left and heading towards the town centre without glancing back. This was part of the technique of drawing no attention towards him from anyone who attended the mosque. Ahmed had followed him outside and watched him slopping off. Ahmed decided not to follow him but would log the contact with his superiors.

Back inside, Ahmed continued standing facing the noticeboards, replaying the details of the event over in his mind. Was he imagining something that wasn't worth further investigation? It was important to be sure that there was something worth expending effort on as too often flags were raised and then operations mounted on flimsy feedback and quite frankly poor judgement. As he was grappling with these thoughts, another young man almost identical in both appearance and behaviour appeared from the main hall and headed towards the front door. Ahmed literally froze; this was not a coincidence. He followed this young man outside, keeping a respectable distance, and saw that he was also heading towards the town centre. Ahmed's head was spinning; there was something going on here and he was in the epicentre of it. He decided once again that he wouldn't follow this individual and instead returned to his haunt in front of the noticeboards. After a couple of minutes, an elder sidled up besides Ahmed.

'Good morning.'

'Good morning,' replied Ahmed. He wanted to carry on observing and tried to move away.

'Did you go to sunrise prayer?'

'No,' replied Ahmed, trying to move away.

Just then a third young man appeared in the main hall and everything about him was very similar to the two previous guys who had left separately. Ahmed now wanted to escape from the clutches of this busybody and focus entirely on what was happening around him here in this seemingly harmless mosque.

'Do you ever attend sunrise prayer?' banged on the elder. 'It's important for spiritual expansion to partake and as often as you can.'

Ahmed casually asked, 'Do you know that young guy who just walked past us?'

'No,' came the reply.

The elder did not actually notice the young guy walking past, nor did he look towards the main door to see him leaving. In fact, the elder did not know anyone apart from the group that he belonged to and the clerics. His short-term memory was poor and he talked to random people to stave off the loneliness that was encroaching his daily life.

'I think he's my cousin. I must dash as I need to speak to him. Bye.' And with that, Ahmed hurried towards the main door.

The elder stood there, annoyed by the abrupt behaviour. He thought to himself that young people were not respectful and did not share their time easily with the older generation. In his day, if he walked off he would have been beaten with a broom by his mum for such disrespect. He would remember this young man and report his tardy behaviour. But he wouldn't, because he had dementia and this event was already being erased from his memory.

Ahmed stood outside and saw the guy tracing the same steps as his confederates. He started to process all of the information from this morning and was looking to draw some conclusions:

A) What exact location were they in at the mosque

B) Who were they meeting with

C) Were they all together all of the time

D) What were they doing there

E) How often do they meet and at what time

F) When will they meet again.

With these thoughts flowing through his mind, Ahmed turned around and saw four guys leave the rear of the mosque and walk across the car park towards where several cars were already parked. He knew two of them and decided to make contact. He hurried towards them as they headed towards the black Volkswagen people carrier. Ahmed had to think hard to remember the name of one of the guys.

'Hamiza, how are you?' he shouted out as he quickened his pace.

The group didn't break their pace but subtly reorganised their formation. The older one in the group dressed in traditional Arabic Imam clothes was now shielded from Ahmed's view. Usam and Hamiza peeled off and walked towards Ahmed, intentionally blocking off his view of the

Imam. Ahmed caught sight of the Imam, who shot a glance at him as he entered the rear passenger door of the people carrier. Ahmed took a mental photograph of the Imam. This was imprinted in his memory; it was a profile. A man with a hooked nose, chinless, dark Arabic-type complexion, black soulless eyes and no excess flesh on his face. This profile reminded Ahmed of a hawk.

'What do you want?' flashed Hamiza.

Taken aback by Hamiza's curtness, Ahmed replied, 'Just came to say hello. That's all.'

'Sorry but we are in a hurry.'

Ahmed went on, 'Apologies for interrupting you. Anyway, who is the other man? Is he a Holy Man?'

Usam blurted out, 'No, he's Rahan Iqbal's uncle.'

'Oh, I heard that Rahan has run off to Bradford,' Ahmed said, trying to lighten the mood.

'Rahan hasn't run off anywhere,' snapped Usam.

'So you have heard from him then?'

'No, er, yes,' fired back Usam. 'We're late. Goodbye.'

And with that, they spun on their heels and walked smartly back to the people carrier. The engine was already started and was idling. As the people carrier passed Ahmed, he casually made a mental note of the number plate whilst nodding absently at the driver. Despite his best efforts, he was unable to get a further look at the mystery man who was obscured by the tinted windows.

Once the journey was under way, the Imam asked, 'What was that all about?'

Hamiza replied, 'Nothing. Just a busybody being nosey. That place is full of them.'

The Imam said, 'Don't tell him anything if he comes back again. Say you don't know anything and walk away. Understood?'

'Yes,' came the reply in unison.

When the people carrier stopped outside of the Afghani house, the Imam produced a piece of paper and handed it to Usam.

'I want you to buy all of the items on this list. The goods must be delivered to the Afghanis in the next seven days. They are expecting the items and know what to do with them. Deliver everything early morning and be quiet. I don't want the neighbours waking up and watching deliveries being made here.' The Imam went on, 'There won't be any more early morning sessions at the mosque. The martyrs won't be going there. I will be away for a while and will make contact when I get back. Until I get back, none of you must go to that mosque. Is all of that understood?'

'Yes,' came the reply again.

The Imam handed over a bundle of notes to Usam.

'This will cover the purchase of the goods.'

'Do you need a lift anywhere?' asked Zeehan.

'No. Just stick to the plan,' came the reply. 'It's important everything is carried out exactly as I have told you.'

They all nodded gravely and again said yes. The Imam got out of the people carrier and walked into the terraced house.

The people carrier drove off with the occupants sitting in silence. Usam opened up the note and read out aloud the list of items:

1. Fifty small boxes of assorted nails and washers
2. Three small travel alarm clocks and batteries for each of them
3. Three men's sports rucksacks
4. Seven large bottles of cleaning fluid
5. Several electrical items and batteries for them.

They all joined in slagging off the Imam. He was a thoroughly unlikeable character and treated them like something unpleasant that he found stuck to the bottom of his shoe. The discussion then turned to their young friend Rahan. None of them could understand why he wasn't returning any of their calls. Rahan monitored his phone religiously and was someone who sent a reply or returned a call literally within a couple of minutes of receiving a message, day or night. He was known for being someone with little sense of humour, but boy did he try hard to be funny. Not returning calls or messages wasn't something that he had ever done, and they were worried about his welfare. They talked about the implications of what would happen once all of the items on the list were purchased. There were no pig imitations for the rest of the journey. Things were getting serious, very, very serious, and they were completely out of their depth.

The Imam explained to the two old Afghanis once again what they needed to do over the coming weeks. The goods were going to be delivered early in the morning and they needed to make sure that both the delivery team and themselves were quiet and not to disturb any of the neighbours. They must unpack all of the goods, dispose of the packaging in their bins and then place the goods around their house in a way that will look to anyone that they belong there. The alarm clocks must be put in every bedroom, batteries fitted and the correct times set. The cleaning agents must be placed under the sink. The boxes of nails and washers must be put in the garden shed. The other electrical components and batteries were also to be stored in the garden shed. The sports rucksacks were to be wrapped up as if they were gifts ready to be sent back home. He gave them a copy of the list and told them to check off all of the items upon receipt. If any items were missing, they must tell the tall one who will be delivering the items to go and fetch it. If they had any problems once the items were delivered, they should speak to the tall one and he will help. They nodded that they understood their orders but didn't say anything. They despised this man who didn't treat them with respect but was happy to live in their home and take their food and hospitality. He was a dog. He went upstairs and picked up his already packed bag. A car arrived outside as he walked back down the stairs. He told them again that he was going away for a while but would return. In the meantime, they weren't to talk to anyone and definitely were not to share any information of his visit with their family back in Afghanistan. He left. They looked at each other but said nothing. They had no one to speak to; well, apart from their caring doctor.

12:00. Ahmed saw Mr Butt ambling through the cafe and casually walked over.

'Good day, Mr Butt.'

'Good day, Ahmed. How are you?'

'Well, thanks. I remember that you were concerned about Rahan. I was wondering whether you were aware that his uncle was visiting. In fact I saw him here early with Hamiza when they were leaving.'

'Well, that is news to me. Who exactly was with him?'

Ahmed replied, 'Hamiza and two others. I know the driver by face but can't remember his name. He drives a tinted-windowed black Volkswagen people carrier and the other guy was tall. Er, now what's his name. Ah, that's it. It's Usam.'

'Ahmed, this is all very puzzling. I'll check with my friends and see if any of them can shed any light on this.' And with that, Mr Butt scurried off.

In all of the years he had been coming to this small mosque, he had never known there to be three unexplained incidents, and he was determined to dig deep. He was a man on a mission. Who was that visiting Imam? Why had Rahan disappeared off to Bradford? And who was this mystery uncle who was being ferried around Luton? Ten minutes later, after consulting with his cronies, Mr Butt returned back to where Ahmed was now seated.

'The plot thickens. No one is aware of any visits scheduled for either now or in the near future for any Iqbal family relatives. And a couple of them are close to Mr Iqbal and they would definitely be aware of any visit. I did however find out the name of the driver of the black Volkswagen people carrier. He's Zeehan Begum and comes from a very good family. He does a lot of private jobs driving his people carrier, mainly to and from Luton airport and also weddings,' said Mr Butt.

'Thanks for that,' replied Ahmed. 'I'm going to go outside for a bit of fresh air before midday prayer. See you later.'

Ahmed walked outside, cautiously surveilling everyone en route for any more young men similar in both appearance and behaviour to the three guys he saw early this morning. Once outside, Ahmed turned into the car park in order that he could check whether there was any suspicious activity worth investigating. He saw Hamiza standing next to a silver Ford

Fiesta talking to an older man, and without hesitation he walked over to them.

'Hi, Hamiza, I was just talking with Mr Butt and mentioned that you were driving Rahan Iqbal's uncle around. He said that no one was aware that his uncle was over here from Pakistan.'

'Oh, well, that was what I was told.'

'Really? Who told you that then?'

'I can't remember,' said Hamiza.

'OK then, where did you take this uncle?'

'We dropped him off at Luton station.'

'Did he have any luggage with him?'

'What's this, twenty questions? Anyway, why are you so interested?' fired back Hamiza.

'No reason. Mr Butt was asking, that's all.'

'Yeah. He's always poking his nose in. Nothing better to do with his time.'

'Hamiza, please,' said the older man gently.

'Sorry, Dad, but you know how he is.'

'Come, Hamiza, we'll be late for midday prayer,' said Mr Ali.

Hamiza shrugged his shoulders. That was the sign that the conversation was over. Ahmed smiled and then turned around and headed back towards the front of the mosque. Mr Ali looked at his son and squirmed thinking about what he had just heard his son say. It was obvious that Hamiza was lying but Mr Ali didn't want to press. Pressing would start a ferocious row again between father and son and he would end up being none the wiser. Worse still, if he did get a truthful answer, he may not like what it meant. Mr Ali did not want to know what his son was involved in.

Ahmed walked past the mosque and headed into the cul de sac. He retrieved his phone from his jeans pocket and dialled Chris Gould. Ahmed went through all of events for today and then requested that Chris gathered CCTV between 09:30 and 11:00 in and around Luton station. He gave Chris the Volkswagen people carrier description along with its number plate. They needed to identify this mysterious uncle. Ahmed then as an afterthought requested CCTV for in and around Luton airport, as he suspected that he had been given misleading information. Chris said that he'd create the paperwork and get the tapes set up to run through, and Ahmed needed to make his way back to Thames House immediately. Ahmed signed off and went back to his flat to pick up his car and dash back down the M1.

15:00. Chris and Ahmed, along with a couple of analysts, started trawling through all of the CCTV tapes for both Luton station and Luton airport, and the people carrier did not appear anywhere. They also looked at CCTV from both station platforms and within Luton airport and, despite there being a couple of possible candidates, there was no positive sighting of 'Uncle'. Chris and Ahmed then went into the corner meeting room for a full debrief of all of the happenings from earlier today. Chris agreed that a report needed to be written up and flagged as high priority. Ahmed then produced a draft of the encounter with the three young guys, followed by the brush with 'Uncle', then the chat with Mr Butt and finally the conversation with Hamiza.

The checking of all of the CCTV footage was also included, along with Rahan Iqbal's disappearance. Chris called up the draft report on his screen and reviewed it, making online changes which he agreed with Ahmed, who was looking at the report over his shoulder. The report was completed and sent off to John Pope, cc Chris, Ahmed and Clare Hawkins at 20:00.

Pope opened up the report at 21:30 in his hotel bedroom. Having absorbed all of the information, Pope recommended that Ahmed and Deepak Chopra go onto 24/7 surveillance of the mosque, with Walker teams on key targets and extra surveillance on the mosque, all supported by a backup team and an analyst team working out of Thames House. Someone from London East would be reassigned to backfill Deepak. Deepak would need to provide the replacement person with a comprehensive handover. London East would provide ongoing cover within their own resource group for the absence of their colleague. Everything would take effect first thing tomorrow morning. Chris Gould would go up to Luton, meet with Ahmed and Deepak, set up surveillance and all support necessary, and the operation would be effective by midday when this report would be updated accordingly.

Pope authorised the report and sent it back to the regional recipients. In addition, the report was sent to Sandra Carruthers and Group Support. Pope then sent a text to Chris Gould saying that if he needed anything then Pope would cancel his family holiday and head back. Chris replied within one minute saying that he would be able to cope. Chris actually relished the opportunity to manage something of this magnitude and hopefully raise his own profile within the organisation.

05:45. There was a light rap on the front door. A couple of minutes later after a further rap, although stronger this time, the front door was opened slightly and a small dishevelled face peered out through the gap. Zeehan smiled at the craggy face and whispered that he had come to deliver the goods. The face of the small lady looked back at him quizzically. He picked up the black holdall and showed it to her, still smiling. She glanced behind and looked at her husband who was also dishevelled, and he mumbled something to her. This was enough for her to open the door further and stand aside. Zeehan walked in smartly, followed by Hamiza who was also carrying a similar-sized black holdall. The old man dressed in fading pyjamas and torn slippers pointed to the kitchen, which lay straight ahead. Both of the unwanted guests walked into the room and stood. Behind them shuffled in the Afghani couple, and the small dilapidated kitchen was now crowded. Zeehan unzipped his holdall and started putting all of the items on the Formica table. Once he completed the task, Hamiza followed suit and cleared out his holdall. Hamiza turned and was about to walk out when the elderly man put his wrinkled arthritic hand on Zeehan's forearm and squeezed gently. Zeehan looked at the old man and understood.

'Hamiza, wait. They want to check that everything has been delivered.'

'OK,' said Hamiza gruffly.

The old man spat out several words towards the ailing female and she left the kitchen. They could hear her footfalls as she ascended the creaking staircase. The creaks continued as she walked into her main bedroom, and then after retrieving something from the small bedside table, she slowly and arthritically returned back into the kitchen. A folded piece of paper along with a pair of battered and unclean glasses was handed over to the old man. He slowly put on his glasses and stared at the items written on the folded piece of paper. He continued to stare at the piece of paper for a minute as his eyes adjusted to both reading via spectacles and the added annoyance of being woken up so early. Once everything was in focus, he mumbled something else to his wife. She went out of the kitchen into the front room and retuned with a blue biro pen. Hamiza craftily gazed at Zeehan and raised both of his eyebrows. Zeehan shook his head slightly as if to say 'let them get on with it.' Hamiza was impatient at the best of times, and watching this scene unfold in agonisingly slow motion was winding him up.

The old man picked up each item, studied it, looked at his list and either ticked an item or made a note next to it. He then handed the item to the old lady who took it and placed it in the front room. Whilst she was out of the kitchen, the old man stood still and only when she had returned did he restart the process. This activity went on for some fifteen minutes until all of the items had disappeared from the kitchen. The old man then stood there for a further two minutes, frowning and staring at the list. Finally he mumbled something, and the old women gave him a curt reply.

'OK,' said the old man, looking at Zeehan.

'Good,' came back the reply.

Zeehan and Hamiza gathered up their empty holdalls and walked out of the terraced house. Zeehan turned around to say goodbye, but the distressed front door had already been shut.

'That was bloody painful,' said Hamiza, putting on his seatbelt.

'Well it's done now,' replied Zeehan, putting the people carrier into gear and driving off.

The Afghani couple walked into the front room and looked at all of the items spread out everywhere.

'Let's get some sleep and then we can unpack everything and put it away,' said the tired old man.

'Yes. I'll make breakfast at eleven and after that we can sort all of this out.'

The couple wearily ascended the stairs, knowing that they had several hours of work ahead of them before everything would be completed as tasked by the Imam. They were a couple in every sense, as their advanced age meant that individually they lacked the physical capacity to perform even the most mundane of tasks. But by working together as a team, they were able to get by, although the man was the ganger and the female was the labourer.

08:30. Chris Gould was sitting in his favoured Luton cafe, large all-day breakfast in front of him smothered in ketchup and brown sauce, salted to death, with a hot steaming mug of sweet tea next to the plate of buttered toast. He was again with his back to the wall in the corner table and was digging into the food, ravenous as if he hadn't eaten for a week. Well, apart from the baguette he had eaten not one hour earlier at St Pancras station, along with an espresso. Deepak sauntered into the cafe, nodded towards Chris and sat opposite him. Just as they were about to exchange greetings, Ahmed walked into the cafe and planted himself next to Deepak.

'Everyone good?' Ahmed said.

'Yeah,' replied Chris.

Deepak, who was shy, politely nodded with a small boyish smile.

'Guys, order some grub and then we'll get started,' said Chris through a mouthful of food, managing not to cover them in food particles.

The owner walked over and took their orders. Nothing like the mountain of food that Chris was wading through, and two sandwiches with two coffees were delivered to the table within three minutes. With the food, drinks and accoutrements, the table was already busy. They each took out their laptops and then stacked plates and accoutrements in the corner, making just enough room to work and eat at the same time. Remote log on took a few minutes as the various security protocols were activated. Finally they were all logged onto MI5's mainframe computer and looking at the report written by Ahmed, reviewed by Chris and authorised by Pope.

'OK, guys. We'll go through each item one at a time and agree it,' said Chris.

'First. The operation is called Alastor.'

'Where did that name come from?' asked Ahmed.

'Alastor was the Greek God for family feuds.'

'Of course he was. Who thinks up these bloody names?' said Ahmed.

Chris glared at him. 'Let's focus.'

Chris was taking the lead on this operation until Pope returned from his holiday, and he had chosen that name. He was in angst for nearly one hour yesterday evening thinking and rethinking over a suitable name that hopefully would impress the great and the good. The report had been titled Operation Alastor by Chris before he went to bed, exhausted by that exercise.

'So, you are both on 24/7 onsite surveillance. How do you want to play it?'

'I think we should do ten-hour shifts,' replied Ahmed.

He knew this was coming and had thought through the various options. This for him was the best of a bad bunch. He had experienced various long shifts over an extended period and none of them were easy. At least with this shift pattern, you could get time to have a decent kip; assuming that you could actually switch off.

'Deepak, you OK with that?' asked Chris.

'Sure, seems OK,' replied Deepak. Actually, Deepak would agree with anything. He was by nature a follower and not a leader.

'OK, agreed then,' said Chris. He updated the Operation Alastor report online and both Ahmed and Deepak watched the changes appear on their screens real time.

'Right. Next, what is your cover? Both of you need a reason to be at the mosque for such long periods.'

'Well, it's coming up to the start of the next academic year. Why don't we say that we are doing online university courses for mature students? We find it difficult to study where we live. That way we can have our laptops out and sit around doing not a lot. Just like real students,' laughed Ahmed.

'Deepak, any thoughts?' asked Chris.

'No. I like Ahmed's idea. It's good cover.'

'Let's keep it simple. I studied Computer Science at Nottingham so I'll be doing the course online. I can get the material and reread it just in case someone checks up,' said Ahmed.

'I did History and Economics at Bristol,' added Deepak.

'Good. The backup team will enrol both of you. That will be on your legends asap. Anyone digging around will see that,' said Chris as he updated Operation Alastor.

'OK, next. You must attend every prayer. We want photos of everyone attending with their names, and names of the clerics and Imams. Times of start and finish of every prayer. There are various groups running in and out of the mosque and we want all of their details. We want names and photos of people working in the cafe and their hours, and the same for the cleaners, and in fact everyone. It's a tall order but we need to build up a picture fast of what is going on in there. We want you to access every room in that building, take photos and draw maps. We want every telephone, PC, and fax documented down to their model number. Even the cars in the car park; photograph and document everything. Join every group and go along, you know the drill,' said Chris.

'Wow, that's a fucking tall order, bro,' said Ahmed.

"We know that. You send everything back to Analysis Team Four. They are as of now working full-time on Operation Alastor. Yes, there will be gaps such as a photo without a name, but they will also try and fill in any gaps. They will be looking into the background of everyone who steps foot into that mosque. All phones, faxes and PCs will be tapped but we need to make sure that we have all of them. That's why we need you to confirm that information.'

'What about the three guys Ahmed identified and the 'uncle', anything special for them?' asked Deepak.

'Yes. If they show up, then you need to alert Team Four immediately. But if support isn't available, then you must follow them. We need to know where the high-value targets are staying.'

Both Deepak and Ahmed nodded.

'We are going full court press on this. A camera is being installed at the end of the street. It will see all cars going into and out of the car park, and if necessary we'll be able to watch the main entrance. It will be disguised as a traffic camera. The two main suspects, Usam Mia and Hamiza Ali, will now be under 24/7 surveillance by Walker teams. Golden Balls will start monitoring their mobile phones, home phones and their internet traffic, along with data held on their PCs. Team Four will intercept their Royal Mail home ingoing and outgoing post. They will look into their bank accounts. Also Mia's people carrier will have a tracker fitted to it today. We will have them in a vice and will start to squeeze. Team Four will be doing deep background on both of them,' stated Chris as he continued to update online everything that was being discussed.

Ahmed said earnestly, 'There is a problem with a lot of the women. They are covered from head to foot and getting any ID will be impossible.'

'True, but they aren't generally involved in terrorist activities, so we don't want you to waste time and effort on any women whose face is covered,' said Chris. 'But you both remember Mustaf Jama who escaped via Heathrow Airport in 2006 wearing a Niqab? He was over six foot and built like a brick shit house. If there's any veiled women who look like that then take a photo of them and try and ID them.'

Again they both nodded.

'It's best that you both avoid contact at the mosque. It may arouse suspicion. Use the laptop cameras to film everything as they are hidden and no one will see them. Phone cameras are a bit more conspicuous so use them with caution,' said Chris. 'One other thing. Here's a few body trackers. If you have a target and can plant a tracker on them then do it,' he said as he passed over a small plastic bag to each of them.

'Any questions?' Chris asked.

'No,' came the reply.

'Anything at all, contact me.'

Chris shut down his laptop and put it back in its case. He then put on a baseball cap and Ray-Ban sunglasses, stood up, shook both of their hands and went to the till to pay the bill. He cut a very odd sight as he waddled out of the cafe dressed in a suit that was looking both threadbare and far too tight and wearing sunglasses and a baseball cap. Especially as it wasn't even sunny.

'Deepak, let's swap mobile numbers.'

The numbers were swapped and they both sat there absorbing what had just transpired.

'Guess I'll take first shift,' volunteered Ahmed, looking at his watch. 'I'll be in the mosque at twelve. When you arrive at ten, send me a text. I'll be in the cafe, so if you stay in the main hall we won't meet. I'll text you as soon as I'm outside. That will be our in and out routine.'

'Sure.'

'Anyway, where are you staying?' inquired Ahmed, trying to break the ice.

'I've got a tiny bedsit above a furniture shop, but you can't swing a cat in it, southeast of the town centre. You?'

'I'm in a two-bed shithole above a chicken shop in the town centre. Piss heads shouting most of the night when they aren't fighting and throwing the food up and down the road.'

'MI5 have salubrious places for us, eh,' said Deepak.

'Listen, if you want to move in there's a spare room. Fucking noisy, stinks, but at least there's space and it's not too far from the mosque.'

'Thanks. I'll think on it. Might sublet my gaff to a family of four midgets and make a few quid on my place.'

Both of them laughed.

'What the fuck is going on with Chris? Suit, baseball cap and shades. Serious wardrobe malfunction. If he thinks that's being inconspicuous then he's fucking mad.'

'As my dad used to say, "What a plonker,"' said Deepak.

'Wasn't that Del Boy?'

'No, it was definitely my dad.'

Ahmed opened his mouth to say something but for once decided to let it go.

'He's banging on and there's baked beans in sauce dripping down his shirt.'

'Yeah, I noticed that.'

'Well, last time he came up, he had a similar mountain of food when we met. He's heading for a jam tart attack.'

'No way. I met him after you, so only about an hour later and he had the same as he had today.'

'What a fucking fat bastard,' said Ahmed.

Both of them roared with laughter and several other patrons turned around to see what the commotion was all about.

'But he's a good bloke and knows what he's doing,' said Deepak, trying to put some perspective and respect back into the conversation.

Ahmed looked at him seriously and went on. 'Yeah, he's one who always has your back.' Then he paused before adding, 'If he ain't at breakfast.'

More laughter before they logged off, packed away their laptops and left the cafe.

11:15. Sebastian Drake knocked politely and entered the anteroom. Sheila Beavers was sitting at her antique oak desk studying her PC. The carpet was deep shag pile and, like everything else in the room, expensive.

'Good morning, Seb, I don't believe that we were expecting you,' she said, raising her head from the screen and smiling at the visitor.

Sheila Beavers was the personal secretary to the director general for all of his tenure. If fact, she had been his personal secretary when his was deputy director general, and even before that lofty appointment. Some rumours suggested that she serviced him outside of work hours also for the same period. For a lady in her mid-fifties, admittedly without a husband or children, she was well preserved. Whatever, Sheila was extremely competent, managed his diary skilfully and was at his side night and day throughout a myriad of crises over the last twenty-three years. Prime ministers come and go, but MI5 remains a rock, and Sheila was one amongst many who galvanised and supported the rock.

'Just popping in for a quick update, if possible,' replied Seb Drake.

'Now, let me have a quick look,' said Sheila, knowing exactly what the director general would be doing hour by hour for the next several days, even down to when he would be brushing his teeth. She studied her PC screen, 'Well, you may be in luck. I'll just check because he's reviewing stuff at the moment.'

Seb smiled. He knew exactly what she meant when she said 'the DG was reviewing stuff'.

'Sir Dickie, I have Sebastian Drake here,' she said into the phone. Sheila listened to the reply. 'Right, Sir Dickie, I'll send him through.'

Sheila pressed the button secreted under her side of the desk and said, 'Please go through, Seb.'

'Thanks, Sheila.'

Seb Drake pulled back the steel door that Sheila had remotely unlocked and opened the huge oak door that opened back into the DG's office. The DG was a tall man standing six feet five inches with silver hair and bushy eyebrows on a face that was craggy and displayed every year of his sixty-six years. His black with grey charcoal pinstripes suit was tailor-made and fitted him well. He did not look up but was stooped over, intense and in the middle of a serious enterprise. Seb closed the oak door and waited patiently until the DG had finished. Once finished, the DG frowned, shot a glance at Seb as if to say that the interruption had affected him and then stood up to his full height.

'Seb, what's on your mind?' said Sir Dickie Crampton through a gravelly voice caused by years of chain smoking.

'Just checking that you have seen the latest operation starting up in Luton.'

'Yes. I saw the report authorised by John Pope. You spoke with him about our French friends plucking some of our better ideas. Causing a bit of a stir and "we" need to put a lid on this. Captains of industry are bending the PM's ear and that won't do.'

'I know that the PM is aware there's possibly something in the offing. If there's anything that you need by way of background or latest intel then I'm happy to provide it. John is running with the French problem.'

'Thanks. COBRA is meeting later but I don't plan to share anything yet,' said Sir Dickie, once again stooping. 'Trouble is, the foreign minister and home secretary jump on every crumb, blow it out of proportion and then want to micro-manage the damn show. No, I'll wait and see what pops up first.'

'Understood.'

'Operation Alastor. Who came up with that bloody name?'

'A Greek god, I believe.'

'Pope wouldn't have assigned anything as pretentious as that, so I'm guessing it's a Carruthers attempt at being smart.'

'I think she is in the clear.'

'Well, whoever it was is a tit.'

Seb smiled.

Sir Dickie finished addressing the ball and then putted a twenty-footer right into the middle of a brass bowl that spun around and then spat out the golf ball.

'Good putt,' said Seb.

'Having a damn time of it. Just can't get into the groove,' said Sir Dickie. 'Have been using this belly putter now for three years. I often think about shooting the golf club coach. He put me onto this foul contraption and now I can't use a normal putter. Worst still, you look a real wanker with this anyway, and when you miss, well, every Tom, Dick and Harry wants to take a poke.'

'Yes. I see how that could be a problem,' sympathised Seb.

'Not a golfer Seb?' asked the DG, addressing the next golf ball.

'Afraid not. Family takes up any spare time.'

'Of course. Mind you, that's why I took up golf in the first place. Get away from the bloody rabble.'

'I hear it can be addictive,' added Seb.

'No more than heroin,' said the DG as he stroked the ball. 'I expect HR and budget to be up here today. No doubt this operation will cost a pretty penny and they will be jumping up and down.'

The golf ball hit the lip of the brass cup and flew away. The DG stood up again and was clearly becoming agitated. Consistent putting was critical. Budgets, spreadsheets and their unholy owners were not.

'Anyway Seb, I won't keep you,' said Sir Dickie, addressing another golf ball.

Seb left, closing the oak door behind him. Sheila looked up from her screen and mouthed goodbye, and with that, Seb went back to his own office, comfortable that the DG was supporting the operation and any associated costs and was ready to keep COBRA in tow. All good apart from his putting.

The carpet in Sir Dickie's office was not shag pile. His carpet had a fast run to it. It was very expensive, but it ran true, very similar to that of any top-class green. The furniture was all antique and priceless, as were the paintings that adorned the walls of this spacious office. Paintings of British victories in battles fought centuries ago. All painted by famous painters, and priceless works of art owned by the British people but hanging here for the pleasure of the DG in his private practice putting green. There was an odd collection of hickory golf clubs, polo sticks, real tennis racquets and even rowing oars, all donated by previous DGs displayed in a wall-mounted case. A book perched on a small antique table below the case explained each particular piece of sports equipment and had a synopsis written by its owner. An eclectic group of sports equipment with memories written down and shared.

Sir Dickie hadn't added his custom-made, hugely expensive belly putter into the book. There were days when he seriously thought about burning the whole sodding collection along with the book. Golf had that effect on him. However, he was a competitive player and generally won the vast majority of his matches. PMs and cabinet ministers were fodder for this serious player. He was happy to crush captains of industry, senior CIA bods, the latest US ambassador in particular and any other ambassador, as well as heads of European security agencies and senior dignitaries from the Commonwealth. To offset his putting inconsistencies, Sir Dickie manipulated his golf handicap, and it worked a treat. No opponent would openly challenge the DG's handicap. Behind his back, he had grown a worldwide reputation for being a golf bandit. He had opponents queuing up to play him and it was a huge headache for Sheila Beaver to fit in some work around all of his matches. The amount of information shared, gleaned and in some cases stolen whilst on a golf round was enormous. There was also misinformation that needed to be put out there and Sir Dickie was the master.

The only group that Sir Dickie had disdain for were the African dictators who were cruel men to anyone who dared cross their paths. The despots were a goldmine for information and were always accommodated whenever they were in town and fancied a round. Sir Dickie masked his disdain well because what he hated most of all was that to a man, they were hackers. They would churn up tees, fairways, roughs and greens without favour or flavour. Probably the same way that they treated their own population, he often thought. Such was his obsession with golf, he'd have the PM and anyone down from him on the speaker phone whilst he practiced his putting. In his mind, he thought it was good simulation to putt whilst there was a hostile crowd baying for his blood.

23:25. At 40,000 feet travelling east at a cruising speed of 550 kilometres per hour, a Boeing 777-200 heads along its flight path. In business class, a gentleman of Arabic determination settles back into the comfortable extended chair and closes his weary eyes. It had been a long journey in the last two days and still there was one more stop before he could head back home.

At 09:40 on Sunday morning, he had left his accommodation in Luton and was driven to Harwich. The journey was uneventful and went along the M25 and A12. There wasn't much traffic around on this particular Sunday morning and thankfully there were no breakdowns or motorway accidents on the M25 stretch, which can delay the journey for up to several hours. The car arrived in Harwich some two hours thirty-five minutes after setting off. The car parked outside a mid-terrace house in the heart of a council estate. No words were spoken and both the driver and passenger got out of the vehicle and walked smartly to the front door. The door was already opened and they both walked inside. The Imam carrying his bag went upstairs where he changed into Western clothes. They remained in the small house for the remainder of Sunday.

At 07:45 on Monday, the two men left the terraced house and, using the car, drove direct to the Harwich ferry. The Imam was now travelling under a false passport. His name and all other details all bore details of a Belgium citizen. His driver was also travelling under similar false documentation and was a nephew, should they be stopped and questioned. But they never were; travelling within Europe had been made very easy. Borders had been removed as part of the policy of freedom of movement introduced by Germany. The EEC set the policies that governed changes within the EEC, and Germany dictated that policy. A federal Europe was the ultimate goal and it was being achieved over decades, dragging along all of the other countries who were members of the EEC. Freedom of movement was key to achieving a federal Europe. This also was key for criminal elements working within the EEC who exposed and exploited this weakness.

Human trafficking, smuggling all forms of contraband and firearms along with moving stolen cars formed their staple business. It was expanding exponentially due to the lack of border control, and the criminal fraternities were making huge amounts of money on the back of exploitation. In their large shadow were the terrorists who used the same networks as the criminals. They needed stolen vehicles with clean or stolen number plates, firearms, and most importantly, forged European passports. Belgium passports were the favourite choice and these forgers were pumping out as many as they could produce. French, German and Dutch false passport documentation were also popular along with the related country ID cards. An unlikely alliance had formed, with the forgers providing the link between both nefarious groups. There was a heavy price to pay for creating a federal Europe, but Germany was prepared to pay that price. As for all of the other countries, it was dawning on some of them that the price would be high and paid with the blood of innocent civilians.

The car drove onto the P&O ferry which set sail promptly at 09:00. The journey across the North Sea was choppy and took thirteen hours and fifteen minutes to complete. The Belgium nephew did not enjoy the sea journey and took several visits to the small toilets, where he emptied out the contents of his stomach. He left the toilets every time with eyes still streaming, a fierce headache, hair unkempt, shirt hanging of out his trousers and foul breath. Once sea sickness took hold, there was really nothing anyone could do. The motion of the boat continued to deeply affect the person until they were back on land.

When the ferry docked at 17:15 local time, the cars and lorries disembarked in an orderly fashion. Some fifteen minutes later, the car had left the port, passing through minimal security checks. This route had been selected after careful thought and was a regular route to shuttle terrorists to and from mainland Europe. The car windows were left open at the behest of the Imam. His driver needed to urgently attend to his personal hygiene, and in particular he needed to brush his teeth several times. The driver was ordered not to speak for the whole of the car journey, and that would also help minimise the stench.

The car journey from the Hook of Holland to Schiphol airport in Amsterdam took only forty-eight minutes driving through Rotterdam. The Imam departed the car outside the departures terminal, taking his bag with him. His Belgium passport had already been left with his nephew. The nephew had instructions to destroy both the Imam's and his own Belgium passports and ID cards as soon as possible. Throwaway IDs were used once and then burned. They were easy to come by and left no footprint. The nephew would also change the car number plates for another set of European stolen plates, use his own passport and return to his own home in the centre of Brussels.

The Imam glowered as he entered the departures terminal, thinking that the driver would need to be replaced. Yes, he had performed skilfully and professionally both as a driver and aiding with the burial of that idiot kid Iqbal, but he drew attention to himself. He was a spectacle, constantly being sick on the ferry, and boy did he smell. He walked over to the counter of the airline carrier and joined the small queue who were business class passengers. At the front of the queue, he presented his diplomatic passport. This always impressed the attendant, and he passed over his case to be transported in the plane's hold whilst keeping a shoulder bag containing his laptop, toiletries and a book which would go with him as hand luggage. The attendant barely glanced at his passport details, handed him back his passports with a luggage ticket stuck on to it and bade him a safe and pleasant journey. His flight would depart at 21:25 and after one stop would land at 09:20 local time next morning. The journey would take nine hours fifty-five minutes and he would land at Dubai International Airport.

11:50. There was a long queue of gleaming taxis waiting outside the departure terminals of Dubai International Airport. The Imam, now dressed as a businessman, joined the queue and was bustled into the clean vehicle within three minutes. Taxis here were very inexpensive and it was almost impossible to travel anywhere on foot. Pavements had not been part of the infrastructure development, as oil is in abundance and driving encouraged.

Fifteen minutes later, the taxi pulled up in front of one of the opulent skyscraper hotels that dominated Downtown. He exited the taxi, carrying his case and shoulder bag and crossed the huge foyer towards the bank of glass-fronted lifts that were the centrepiece. He kept his head down thus avoiding detection from the plethora of CCTV cameras that monitored the foyer area. He waved away a couple of bellboys who were dashing over to him, hoping to assist with carrying his bags to wherever he was going.

Once in the lift, he pressed the button for floor twelve and the lift gently rose up. The door opened and he was confronted by three burly men, all with wrestler builds who were bursting out of their suits. He drew out of his inside jacket pocket his passport, and the smallest of the gorillas scanned it. The gorilla nodded at him, passed back his passport and pointed to the room in the middle of the floor. Outside this room there were a further two security guards posted, and once again he had to produce his passport for inspection. This time he was subjected to a physical body frisk followed by a body check from an electronic handheld wand. The guards motioned that his cases would not be allowed into the room and that they would be returned to him after the meeting had completed and he had left the room.

The door was opened by one of the security guards and he entered the large suite which was set up as a conference room. Sitting around a large conference table were six middle-aged men, some dressed like him in Western garb and the others dressed in traditional Arabic clothes.

He walked up to each of the men and when they rose, he shook their hands and embraced them.

'Come sit,' said the man dressed in Arabic clothes. 'Please have a coffee,' he continued as he poured a small cup of thick coffee and handed it over to him.

Another of the group said, 'You have timed this well. You have had the longest journey of anyone and here you are on time. Impressive.'

All of the others nodded and smiled at him.

He took a sip of his favourite coffee, composed himself and said with conviction, 'Gentlemen, the plan is underway. I have been to Germany and there are many refugees pouring in. Hamburg has no control over the immigrants. They are throwing money at the immigrants, along with housing, food, clothes, medical treatment and anything else that they want. No one has paperwork; well, very few anyway, and they are just required to fill in questionnaires. It was easy to infiltrate fifteen agent provocateurs into that chaotic place. The Hamburg mosques are equally overrun, and it was also easy to work there for several weeks without any interference.'

He paused before continuing. 'It is a similar situation in Paris, and there are nine agents inserted there. Some will head off now to Marseilles where they will be able to go about their business undetected and invisible. In Brussels, the management of immigrants is virtually non-existent. Twelve agents have been inserted there. In all cases, local recruitment has begun both in the mosques and at the workplaces. Local cells will be created and once their training has been completed then a concerted battery of high-profile attacks will take place. They will for all intent and purposes look like either lone wolf or radicalised individuals who had planned and carried out the attacks. The agents will not be involved in any of the attacks. They will identify, recruit and train the individuals. I will select the targets along with the date and time of the attack and pass this critical information on to the agents. The agents will move around from city to city implementing our agenda having exhausted all local recruits first in that particular city.'

Impromptu applause broke out from the group. The Imam paused and then raised both of his hands, which was the cue for the applause to stop.

'The last stop in England was more difficult,' the Imam went on cautiously. 'The mosques are full of busybodies. The locals are Westernised and lack discipline. It will be troublesome as we can't introduce agents; they will stand out. Their security services are more vigilant and will be worthy adversaries. But I'm confident that we will achieve our goal and strike a blow there that will reverberate around the world.'

More applause.

The main man called Mr Manzur who spoke at the beginning again spoke to all of the group.

'Everyone is committed. We have infinite funding and anything that the Imam needs will be purchased. The funds that you have requested for the next phase is available. Two million in cash in each euros, US dollars and GB sterling, totalling six million in cash. In addition, your fee for this phase has been deposited into the various accounts as you requested. The infidels are looking in the wrong direction. Allahu Akbar.' *God is Greater.*

More applause, this time louder and accompanied by fists being beaten on the large table.

'Let us all acknowledge and applaud the fantastic work that both Mr Salhi and Mr Tariq have done in recruiting all of the agents requested by the Imam. They also organised their training and infiltration into Europe hidden amongst the ever-growing band of refugees. This is no mean feat and has taken several years. Let us not underestimate the enormity of the operation, and we'll need another batch identified, trained and sent to Europe. The operation will take many years to complete, but with the dedication of our group, it will succeed,' went on Mr Manzur.

The group stood as one and too-loud shouts and hoots applauded vigorously.

'Gentlemen. We have turned off the security cameras that would normally track everyone's movements in this hotel. The security team is under our control and they will check that no film identifying anyone here is available. This floor has been booked out to a shell company and there are no records leading back to anyone. Please leave the building after the meeting and return to wherever you are staying. A meeting will be arranged when the next phase has been completed in another venue, and once again security at the venue will be assured,' said the man sitting next to the Imam known as Mr Salhi.

All of the men stood up, shook hands and hugged each other. They then filed out of the room, remembering to pick up their belongings that were being stored by the security guards.

Of the six men that had met the Imam, a couple were representatives of radical factions within benign Arab governments who openly supported the West. Another couple represented factions within two Middle Eastern banks who were based in benign Arab countries, and one was a senior executive in a multinational corporation based in a benign country, whilst the final one was a senior army figure in one of the benign Arab countries. The West and in particular USA and Great Britain focused their military might on the mountains, foothills, cities and towns of Afghanistan. In addition, there was mistrust of Pakistan's alleged involvement in supporting terrorist groups. Especially as Osama bin Laden was still out there. Evidence pointed towards him being supported and even shielded by a country. Iraq was getting US support in an effort to introduce democracy and Iran remained defiant. No intelligence agency was putting the oil-rich states that were pro-Western in the spotlight. These countries were, after all, friends. This mistake was allowing radical factions within them to plan and orchestrate a prolonged terrorist attack against Western Europe with impunity.

The Imam was handed his cases as he left the room. In the short time that he had been in the meeting, six million in cash had been expertly secreted into the purpose-built areas within them. These places would not easily be detected, and certainly not by the naked eye. The extra layer of security was that his baggage travelled under the global protectorate and immunity of diplomatic luggage. His persona of religious zealot was played out to the full when planning, recruiting and implementing 'the

Plan in Europe'. He was a pious man, ferociously dedicated to the cause, with a ruthless streak creating fear rather than respect in all subordinates and followers. He needed the latest personal payment of two million US dollars that had been wired into his several bank accounts located in countries that were not under any US federal jurisdictions. He was never questioned on whether all of the cash funds had been spent when he returned from his forays into Europe, and he overfunded each trip. Not because he thought that he would encounter an unexpected overspend, but because he secreted away at least one million into one of his own accounts.

There were many countries who take a lax view to banking oversight and compliance. This allowed illegal funds to flow freely into their banks, making both the banks concerned and the concerned country wealthier. The Imam was a man with an expensive and lavish lifestyle. He practiced polygyny and had three wives. From his three wives he sired twelve children. The families had homes near to each other, more for his convenience, and were comfortable with this arrangement. They all got along well together and accepted the fact that their husband, father and provider had to spend large periods of time away from home working on behalf of their government. The children were educated in the finest academic establishments in the world. That alone cost a fortune. For example, one son was studying law at Harvard University, another son was studying economics at Oxford University and three daughters were at finishing school in Switzerland. All of his children were destined from a young age to be pushed towards a profession that would assist the development of promoting a global Muslim society. Doctors, bankers, politicians, lawyers and judges, and military generals would be his legacy. He had his own agenda and where it crossed with that of more fanatical elements then he was prepared to accept their patronage and funds.

He realised that he could command huge fees for doing the bidding of extremist elements and this would provide him with the means to live a life in the way that he wanted. It did mean that he had to work under extremely dangerous conditions and severe pressure, but with his lifestyle and outgoings, it was a price that he was prepared to pay. His own values and that of his large family were not aligned to that of his paymasters. In fact, his family would have been shocked to find out that their husband and father was an international terrorist who indiscriminately planned attacks that murdered many, many innocent civilians. There was total hypocrisy in that he educated his children in the finest Western educational establishments, and these same establishments Westernised them with their culture, values and sense of tolerance. He saw them growing physically, growing intellectually along with developing rounded personalities and drew pleasure from the efforts and sacrifices that he made.

Sitting around chatting with his family as they shared their own trials and experiences was the ultimate pleasure for him, and living a lie to his own family was just another lie in the web of lies that he lived within.

He left the hotel and headed back to Dubai International Airport. The flight time is under one hour back to his home country. And then it was another hour back to his family dwellings. He would be home early evening and then will be in the bosom of his family, eager to hear all of their tales. Skype would allow him to catch up with all of his children who were currently studying abroad and be brought up to date with everything going on in their lives. He would swap gossip gleaned from other family members with those who were currently living abroad. He would immerse himself fully within his family for a few days. This would allow him to recharge his own batteries before he began the planning stage of the next phase. The cases containing the money would be left in his main wardrobe. He had no need for it and knew that the cash would be distributed once he returned to Europe.

Four men entered the lift on the twelfth floor heading towards the ground floor. General Faisal pressed his hands against his jacket pocket and said, 'I must have left my glasses in the meeting room.'

One of the other men immediately pressed the 'Open door' button and the doors to the elevator that were slowly closing sprung open. General Faisal smiled and said thanks before exiting. The security guards in the hallway looked at him curiously. He fumbled with his jacket pockets and then produced a glasses case.

'I thought that I had left my glasses in the room but they're here,' he announced as he showed the glasses case to them as proof.

He swivelled around and pressed the elevator button. An elevator appeared and he pressed the button for the ground floor. The lift started to descend before stopping at the fourth floor where four people were waiting to enter it. He exited the lift and then called for a lift to go up to the twenty-fourth floor. Once the lift arrived with several people in it, he entered. His eyes darted towards the panel that displayed all of the floors that the lift would be stopping at. He slyly smiled as the nineteenth floor had already been chosen.

When the lift stopped at the nineteenth floor, he exited along with two other gentlemen. Without speaking, they all made their way into the cocktail lounge. General Faisal headed towards the bar and ordered a Jameson eighteen-year-old Reserve. The barman poured a generous measure, placing the cut glass tumbler along with a small pitcher of water in front of the general. The general's eyes flickered and the barman retreated.

After several minutes, the drink had been despatched and the general nodded towards the barman. Another generous measure was poured and delivered along with a fresh pitcher of water. Again, the barman was dismissed without any payment or gratitude. The general turned around and surveyed the length and breadth of the cocktail bar. There were small groups of young Eastern European women. Some were engaging in conversation and drinks with Arabic men; others were standing round chatting to each other, and others were dancing energetically to the disco music that was being pumped out via an expensive sound system. He had particular tastes and scanned the young women until he saw his prey. Once he had selected her, he stared at her intently. Her companion noticed him first and whispered in her ear.

The diminutive blonde Russian girl who looked no more than a thirteen-year old prepubescent schoolgirl sipped seductively on her non-alcoholic drink and stared back at him across the room. Once again, he motioned with his eyes and the girl sauntered over. She was expecting that he would buy her a drink and engage in small talk. She spoke a few languages but not Arabic. This was OK here because almost all of the men who frequented this place spoke English.

The general's expression did not change as he looked into the girl's eyes as she smiled at him. From his jacket pocket he withdrew a room key and handed it to the girl. She looked at the key, nodded towards him and then left the cocktail lounge. All of the while, her friend had continued to watch the events unfold and knew by his actions that this was a callous man who treated the girls as pieces of meat.

He leisurely finished his drink and put the glass back on the counter. The barman took this as his cue to obtain payment and walked over. The general fixed him with a menacing glare and the barman returned to the most important job of making sure that the bottles of expensive spirits were lined up correctly on the shelves behind him.

The general made his way via the lift to the twenty-second floor where he exited and walked along the brightly lit corridor to the fifth door on the right and stopped. He knocked and the door was opened by the young girl who was now scantily clad. The predator devoured his prey, but not before administering a physical beating. He went into the bathroom and briskly showered. The young girl was still crying and bleeding from her nose, both eyes were blackened, her lips were swollen and she had bruising to her arms, abdomen and back and bite marks that were bleeding on both of her thighs when he returned into the bedroom. He looked at her with disdain as he threw several 100 US dollar bills onto the bed. Instinctively, she curled up into the foetal position, anticipating further punishment, but he calmly walked out of the room. From the moment he left the twelfth floor, he had not uttered one word to anyone but had managed to have two drinks without paying for them, violent sex with a young girl followed by administering a beating to her, and now he was leaving the hotel. A nondescript van was parked outside of the hotel with all of its windows opaque.

As soon as the general exited, a zoom camera started taking photos of him. The person next to the photographer was adding a running commentary into a throat mike. The general got into a taxi and a Mercedes parked further down the entrance slipped out after his taxi had passed it. The film and commentary was encrypted and uploaded via a laptop to a secure website that was hosted in Tel Aviv within thirty seconds. The van then pulled out and headed in the opposite direction to General Faisal's taxi and his tail.

The mobile phone rang several times. Mr Manzur retrieved it from where it was lying on the table and looked at the name of the caller.

'Yes, Mr Salhi, what can I do for you?' he boomed into the phone.

'Sir. We may have a problem.'

'Yes. Please go on.'

'Your instructions for everyone to leave the hotel immediately were not carried out,' said Mr Salhi, who was the person in charge of security at the meeting held three hours ago. 'I checked with our security people and one person was not accounted for. It's the general. They tracked him via the CCTV to the cocktail lounge on the nineteenth floor. He picked up a prostitute and went to a room on the twenty-second floor. The girl was beaten and I've arranged for her to have medical attention. He walked out of the bar without paying for his drinks and, worst of all, he booked the room in his own name. This is a mess and he is sloppy. I've had to arrange for all of the relevant tapes to be wiped but that will now take a few hours. The room booked in his name will be changed to a false name. The girl won't be able to work for several days and I've paid her not only for loss of earnings but extra for her to forget about the whole incident.'

Mr Manzur, who had organised the meeting, calmly said, 'You have done well. I will deal with it from here. Thanks.'

The call ended. Mr Manzur knew that this was a delicate situation and needed handling with kid gloves. General Faisal was critical to the whole plan. He controlled the army of the largest country involved in the operation. His support may be called upon and the army's allegiance to him would outweigh that of their country's political leaders. How ironic that the man charged with providing military security was their highest security risk. His predilection for young girls and beating them to a pulp was putting everything at risk. He was an arrogant, brutal man.

Mr Manzur knew that there was only one solution to this problem. Trying to reason with someone who flouted basic security and even booked a room in his own name in a hotel where great lengths had been gone to to erase any trace of them ever being there would be a waste of time. In fact, the general may withdraw his support or even damage the operation if challenged, as he was that unbalanced. No, the solution was that all future meetings would be in remote but secure locations. If Faisal wanted to fuck then he could stick it up a goat, beat the shit out of it and then eat it. That deranged bastard wasn't going to fuck up this holy operation.

09:00. Mr Ebeid was sitting in his office and he nonchalantly logged into his bank's mainframe computer. He was director for Internal Audit and a high-profile officer within his bank. He represented his bank at user groups within the Middle East. He also represented his bank at global banking events and regularly visited branches of his bank in Europe and North America. His secretary entered his office.

'Good morning, Mr Ebeid. How was your trip to Europe?'

'So, so.'

'I'll bring in your coffee.'

'Thanks.'

Mr Ebeid was also logging onto his personal accounts which were numbered accounts in three Swiss Cantonal banks via the internet. He was checking that the one million in euros that he'd personally deposited in cash last week was showing up. On his recent trip to Europe whilst visiting a couple of branches and attending a banking conference in Paris, he withdrew from several banks based in Luxembourg the princely sum of seven million in cash. Six million was for the Imam as requested for the next part of his mission and that was handed over to him yesterday in the meeting in Dubai that he attended. The other one million euros was syphoned off for his own personal use and that lot he had deposited into the three Swiss Cantonal banks. He had no compunction about embezzling the funds as it was a drop in the ocean. The people, institutions and countries behind this scheme were pouring multimillions of US dollars or equivalent into it. His role was to manage the funds paid into a number of shell companies through a number of banks in tax havens until the funds arrived in various accounts held in banks domiciled in Luxembourg. Once the funds were washed through multiple companies and multiple banks, then they were untraceable. As director of Internal Audit, he was an expert on money laundering and, using those skills, he was the perfect man to launder the money. He would then go and pick up all cash that the Imam requested plus his own skim.

His skimming was adding up and he planned to retire and live in Switzerland where everything was expensive. That being said, he would be able to live a very comfortable lifestyle there and indulge in his favourite passions of gambling on horses and the casino card game Baccarat chemin de fer. Both were costing him a fortune already and as director of Internal Audit, his wages were insufficient to cover his ever-increasing debts. Moving to Switzerland would also get him away from the infernal heat that blasted away day after day out here in the desert. He had a grownup family and a nagging wife. A few more drawdowns by the Imam and he would have enough to retire from this dreary job. He'd leave the wife here in the desert and hopefully she'd fry but he'd keep paying the bills; anything that kept her away from him was money well spent.

His planning and scheming was all that kept him going. Within the Internal Audit department, he had identified and recruited a lowly female employee. She was easily manipulated and sworn to secrecy regarding the setting up of a number of fictitious accounts. He would create the paperwork and leave it in her in tray in an envelope marked private and confidential. She would then input the details and open the account, returning all of the paperwork back to him. She had authority to open an account in any branch of the bank around the world. He would authorise the opening of the account by using a super user account. A super user account had a generic name and authority to action all activities.

In reality he should not have a super user account, but he'd demanded it from the security officer who'd reported to him and was his junior by several levels. He waited several months and then arranged via HR for the security officer's contract to be terminated. His replacement would not be aware of the super user account. It was a breach of standard protocol to have security report to Internal Audit.

Opening these accounts was critical in the processing of money laundering. Others within the group of six would transfer funds from their own institutions from accounts that had been set up there and funds deposited there to these accounts. He would then arrange onward transfers until the funds eventually ended up in the banks in Luxembourg. By midday, he was satisfied that everything was in order.

Mr Manzur was sitting in his plush city office when he received a call on his private line. Very few people were given this number, and he immediately answered the call.

'Hello.'

'Good morning. We need to meet.'

'When?'

'Now.'

He put the phone down, grabbed his jacket and headed towards the lift. Ten minutes later, he entered the coffee house and saw the gentleman sitting in the corner with the familiar sight of three large security men seated at the table in front of him. It was clear they were expecting him; none of them paid much attention to him as he passed by them and sat opposite the elderly gentleman.

'How did the meeting go yesterday?'

'Very well. The Imam has put in place all of the operatives as previously discussed. Germany, France and Belgium were easy to infiltrate. England remains an issue but he is using local recruits and that too is going to plan. He moves around Europe as if he is wearing an invisible cloak. No one is aware of him, nor are they aware of the agents.'

'Good. But we need to be vigilant for any complacency.'

'He is a gift from Allah. A true soldier of the faith.'

'And the funds?'

'Everything is working like clockwork. The Internal Auditor gets the funds washed and then brings back all of the cash that the Imam requires.'

'So are there any issues at all?'

Without hesitating, Mr Manzur said, 'No.'

'Very well. Keep me posted.'

'Of course, Your Highness,' said Mr Manzur as he bowed before leaving.

The elderly man sat in his seat for several minutes. He was thinking through what was briefly discussed and what he had gleaned separately from Mr Salhi, who also attended the meeting. Mr Manzur was the overall man in charge of the group of six and the Imam, but he had not mentioned just now that General Faisal had behaved inappropriately after the meeting had finished. He concluded that Mr Manzur was dealing with it and he would not interfere and micromanage. He would wait and see how the next meeting was managed and how the general behaved before he interceded. General Faisal was a key cog in this operation and would not easily be replaced, so patience was what was required for the moment. Unknown to Mr Manzur, Mr Salhi also reported everything that happened direct to His Highness. He was originally uncomfortable with what appeared to be spying but was assured by a senior aide to His Highness that it was necessary to get independent validation as any misunderstanding can then be smoothed out. After a period of time Mr Salhi became comfortable with this arrangement and endorsed it even though Mr Manzur was one of the most thorough and professional men he'd ever met. It did also help that as part of the arrangement, Mr Salhi was receiving regular payments into an account set up for him in the Bahamas.

General Faisal's car pulled up outside of the heavily camouflaged aircraft hangar that was located on the edge of the military base. This area was heavily guarded and off limits to general military personnel. He exited from the chauffeur-driven limousine and walked into the hangar. Immediately, two senior officers approached him and saluted stiffly. One was a colonel and the other was a brigadier.

'Sir, the birds are assembled and ready for inspection,' said the more senior brigadier.

The general returned their salute and marched forward towards where the birds were parked.

'Since they arrived last week, we have been assembling them. The pilots and co-pilots are undergoing their final training at Fort Rucker, Alabama, where they are now using live ammo in exercises and learning night combat tactics.'

'When will they return?' asked the general.

'It will be another nine weeks and then we will give them two weeks' furlough as they have been away over nine months,' went on the brigadier. 'The ground crew will be working on the birds all of that time, familiarising themselves with every inch of them. Spares will be delivered in the next two weeks and the first batch of ordnance will be delivered here in sixteen weeks.'

'And the Americans?'

'The technicians arrive next week and will check that the assembly has been done correctly. They will also fly them and even without ordnance will check that the firing mechanisms are working.'

'Good. The first batch of ordnance will include both live and blank rounds?'

'As ordered. The Americans have even doubled the blanks that will be delivered. They expect us to begin a rigorous testing phase and put the pilots through their paces, and that will require a lot of ammo.'

'When do the Americans pack up and leave?'

'They will be here for four weeks.'

The general had reached the first of the four birds and there was a lot of activity around all of them from the ground support crews. The ground support crews assembled and stood to attention. The general saluted the group after they had saluted him.

'Men, your work here is of the utmost importance. We live in dangerous times and our small country needs the latest military equipment to defend our borders and our people. I know that all of you are patriotic and will never let our country down. Together we will repel any attack from any foe.'

The men cheered the general. He was one of them and a man that they would follow into battle.

The general put his hand on the body of the Apache AH-64D Longbow helicopter. Beneath the cockpit that housed both the pilot and co-pilot sat a gaping hole. Here the 30mm Chain Gun M230E1 would soon be installed. The Stub wing pylons looked naked without any armaments affixed. A combination of AGM-114 Hellfire anti-tank missiles and Hydra 70 general-purpose missiles would be arranged when in combat mode. He slowly walked around the lethal warbird, admiring its physical appearance. He mounted the steps and peered into the cockpit. It was like looking at something out of *Star Trek*. The pilot sat in the rear seat behind and elevated from the front seat where the co-pilot/gunner sat. Should either one be incapacitated then the other one had the functionality to fly and/or shoot. What made this military platform even more like something out of *Star Trek* was the flight helmet, which provided all of the information directly in front of the pilot's eyes. They had no distraction by having to refer to the instruments on the cockpit panels as it was displayed on their Heads Up Display (HUD) helmets.

The general dismounted the steps as his large frame would not fit into the cockpit, and as much as he wanted to sit inside it, he knew that getting out would be a problem. Walking back to his car, he listened to more details bellowed out by the brigadier, but he had a small attention span and he was no longer listening to anything said to him.

A final set of salutes and he got into the car. Sitting in the rear, he contemplated what destruction he could wreak once he got the Apache numbers up to full strength. Countries within the region had superior armies in terms of numbers of soldiers and numbers of military equipment, but most of their equipment was 1980s technology and earlier. He would be commanding an army with twenty-first-century technology, and that was far more advanced than anything they would encounter. He relished the opportunity to cross swords with those countries driven by opposing ideology. He also wanted to face off to Israel, but that would never happen. They followed the same path that his country had chosen and were armed with the latest military hardware that the US would sell them. His imagination was now running riot as he would relish the opportunity to use his firepower against the US, but that would never happen. Their firepower was unimaginable and was always being upgraded.

Mr Karim had been sitting at his desk all morning clearing up the backlog of emails and work that accumulated from taking yesterday off. His secretary knocked and walked in.

'Can I get you anything for lunch, Mr Karim?'

'Yes. Just a couple of sandwiches with any filling.'

'OK. Oh, and did you have a good day off yesterday?'

'Yes. I spent it relaxing with the family.'

She smiled and walked out of his office. *Interesting*, she thought. *His wife called and asked where he was. She obviously thought he was at work. I can't believe that he has a mistress; he's far too dull. Anyway, some gossip to share with the girls.*

Mr Karim was chief operating officer at one of the premier banks in his country. He was a well-respected figure not only within his bank but within the banks in his country, the central bank of that country and within the banking community of the whole region. He ensured that funds meant for the terrorist operation and channelled via accounts through his bank were processed and did not come under scrutiny of compliance or any regulatory checks. Flags weren't raised because the accounts, although fictitious, were not in names or countries that would raise alerts, as were the sums that flowed through them. He supported the ideology that was not only backing this operation but was steering its agenda and resourcing it both with people at all levels and funds. His life outside of work revolved around his family and he had little other interests. Within the organisation, he played a supporting role to Mr Ebeid in terms of money laundering. Mr Ebeid was the kingpin who set up all of the offshore accounts and managed the funds through to their final destination in Luxembourg.

There was something that had been troubling him for a while and he didn't have a chance to speak privately with Mr Ebeid yesterday at the meeting. Only Mr Ebeid had the whole picture, but when some figures were mentioned at a previous meeting, it looked to him that not all of the funds were reaching the end point. It was just a hunch but a hunch born out of twenty years' banking experience. He respected Mr Ebeid and trusted him implicitly, and there was only one thing to do.

'Good afternoon, Mr Ebeid speaking, how can I help you?'

'Good afternoon, Mr Ebeid. It's Mr Karim here. Can you talk?'

'Of course. What can I do for you?'

Mr Karim stuttered through his concerns with deference and then asked Mr Ebeid if he had any concerns about funds being misappropriated. There was a long pause before Mr Ebeid spoke.

'Do you think that I am in any way involved?'

'No, sir, not at all. My gut tells me that if anything the funds are being skimmed in the Cayman Islands. The place is run by crooks for crooks. Mafia and drug cartel money swills around there openly and it breeds corruption. Stealing a million here and there, who's to know, and more importantly, who's going to tell?'

'I see your point. Let me backtrack over everything and see if I can find any discrepancies.'

'Thank you. Is there anything that I can do to help?'

'No, please leave it with me. It's a delicate situation and I think under the circumstances it's best not to raise this with Mr Manzur and the group until we have the full picture.'

'Of course. Thanks for your time. Good bye.'

'No, thank you. We'll speak again. Good bye.'

Mr Ebeid sat there staring at his phone.

His gut, he thought. *His fucking gut. Well, I'll give his gut something to think about.*

He pressed his intercom to his secretary and said, 'No calls, and cancel my afternoon meetings. Something urgent has come up that I need to attend to urgently.'

And with that, Mr Ebeid started planning the demise of Mr Karim.

Mr Tariq left his office and headed downtown. He was a senior civil servant in the finance ministry and had been there for over ten years. The running of the country was based on oil and everyone had a decent lifestyle. It was important to the ruling elite that the general population were kept in line as there wasn't any democracy. Throwing money at the proletariat was an easy way to control them and he was part of the inner circle that controlled the public purse. He entered an empty office located on the seventh floor of a nondescript office block. This unused office was the regular meeting place selected by his contact. En route he performed a couple of cursory checks, but there wasn't anyone tailing him. In the office, his contact was leaning against the wall, smoking as he looked out at the traffic passing by on the highway below.

'Well then, spill the beans,' said his nondescript contact in the nondescript office.

Mr Tariq eagerly went through everything that had happened at the meeting, before the meeting and after the meeting. He was going into such detail that he was positively anal. His contact nodded appreciatively, still smoking. Smoking was the only thing that kept him awake whilst Mr Tariq performed his soliloquy. Once he had finished, the contact thanked him for providing all of that information and added that it was invaluable. Mr Tariq knew that his contact used a recorder to record the information and even though he looked half asleep whilst he chain-smoked, that was all part of the act.

It was several years earlier, after he had agreed to be involved in this operation, that he was approached. He met two men who said that they were working for the government's internal Secret Service. They claimed that they knew he was getting involved with activities that were against that of the government and that he was committing treason. If he were to assist then the government would not act lethally against both him and his family. He agreed that he was involved in something although he wasn't sure what it really was and that it was a mistake on his behalf. From that day forward he met with his contact in this very room and talked about everything that he and his confederates were involved in.

His contact went into the car park and drove directly back to his headquarters.

'How was it?' asked his boss.

'Usual. He left nothing out.'

'Good. Any need then to listen to it?'

'No,' said the agent as he tossed the recorder over to his boss.

His boss caught the recorder and pressed the delete button. He then sent an encrypted email saying that Mr T had been debriefed and everything was OK.

At the same time as Mr Tariq was approached by the Secret Service, so was all of the other five members of the group. Obviously they were approached by the Secret Service agency of their respective countries. Unlike Mr Tariq, they didn't buckle and demanded proof of any alleged wrongdoing. Despite being pressed on a few occasions, they didn't acquiesce. It was a test set up by the Overseers as they wanted to probe for any security leaks. Mr Tariq proved to be the only security leak and, after much discussion, the decision was made to keep him in the group as he had skills that were critical to the operation. He would feed all of his information to someone who was designated to be his controller without ever knowing that he was being duped.

From the outset, a huge amount of thought had gone into the type of people who would be needed to manage this operation over a long period of time. Their skill sets, their commitment to the cause and their ability to manage under extreme pressure were probed and tested before they were selected. This group of six knew that they had a huge responsibility sitting heavily on their shoulders. They had accepted that responsibility along with the dangers and picked up the mantle.

Somewhere, somehow, their commitments and personal values had changed. Either that or they had been extremely well hidden up till now. What was originally a tight-knit group working seamlessly towards delivering the same goal had over time turned into a dysfunctional group with their own hidden agendas. They still were determined to deliver the same end results but now with personal goals intertwined. Time would tell if these would derail the operation.

On top of the group of six who were no longer dedicated solely to delivering their agreed ultimate goal, the Imam was also delivering his own personal goal in parallel to that of the operation.

14:00. Ahmed was four hours into his fourth ten-hour shift and was sitting in the large community room nestling a large espresso between both hands. He had just attended midday prayer and had managed to surreptitiously photo all of the attendees. He arrived early and knelt at the back. He waited until the prayer had finished and he then set off the miniature camera secreted in his jacket pocket to film every three seconds. It recorded the face of every person attending as they exited from the prayer room. Once everyone had left, he arose and left. The Imam was photographed at the start of the prayer. Ahmed busily put names to the faces in his laptop computer where the film had been uploaded from his miniature camera. Once he had added all of the names that he knew, he timed and dated the file prefixing it with 'Midday Prayer'. He then sent the encrypted file to Team 4 and they started the laborious process of filling in background details on everyone identified and to see whether they could put names to the number of people who were not identified. The set of photos were all passed through the facial recognition system that checked the faces against a database of photos. The database had been created taking photos of everyone who had for whatever reason been photographed by all security agencies, Interpol or the police forces' combined database. The check took several minutes to complete and returned a null result.

Ahmed sipped his espresso and decided that he'd while away some time going through the beginning of the Computer Science online degree course. He'd spent the start of his shift walking around every room, familiarising himself with the activities going on in there. He wasn't popular as he knocked and entered into rooms that were holding private group meetings and prayers. These assemblies were all innocent affairs and where there were women-only meetings, his intrusion was met with some hostility. His camera was firing away and he was able to glean information that helped formulate the bigger picture. He had also been out into the car park on several occasions and photographed all of the cars there. It was whilst he was outside that he noticed that the surveillance camera disguised as a traffic camera had been installed and was currently pointed at the entrance to the car park. He made a mental note to raise with Chris Gould in a couple of days whether the requirement for both him and Deepak to photograph all of the cars was now necessary. He opened up the introduction to the Computer Science course and began reading it. He instantly became engrossed in the material. At heart he was a computer geek, and he noticed that he had become rusty; there were gaps in his knowledge caused by not using the information on a regular basis. Frustration was setting in when he looked at his watch and was taken aback. One and a half hours had flown by. He needed to focus on what was happening in and around the mosque, and he saved the data and closed the online course.

Ahmed got up and stretched, yawned and was about to purchase another espresso when Mr Butt waddled over to him.

'Ahmed, how are you?' said the smiling Mr Butt.

'Well thanks, and you?'

'The knees are playing up but that's old age for you.'

'Out of curiosity, did you find out any more about Rahan Iqbal's uncle?'

'No. It seems that the boys had helped a stranger who had come in to pray. They are good boys and even dropped him off after prayer.'

Ahmed smiled. He knew that was a blatant lie that had easily duped Mr Butt. He would need to try another avenue without exposing himself if he was going to uncover who that person was and, more importantly, what was he up to.

'Of course. On a separate subject, I noticed three new faces here Sunday. They were all young men around early twenties and they left about 09:30.'

'I wasn't here until before midday prayer. Why do you ask?'

'No reason. They just looked a little suspicious. Maybe I'm being over cautious but three young guys, you never know. Things go missing.'

'No, Ahmed, you are being very sensible. Stuff does go missing but no one wants to point the finger. What I have noticed is one young man acting very suspicious though.'

Ahmed's attention rose immediately. 'Go on.'

'This young chap comes into the general community room and sits there studying on his PC. Every now and then he gets up with his PC and walks around the hallways and rooms. He never talks to anyone and his behaviour is suspicious. This has been going on since Tuesday.'

'Now that does sound strange. Can you describe him?'

'Yes. He's about five feet six inches tall, slim with jet-black hair cut short. He has boyish features with a permanent grin on his face. I don't think he's Muslim. His head bobbles all of the time and if you ask me he's an Indian, probably a Hindu.'

Ahmed could barely disguise his annoyance. Mr Butt had just described Deepak Chopra to a tee.

'Let me follow this up, Mr Butt. I'll come back to you in a couple of days.'

'Are you sure? I can speak with the elders.'

'No. He's a young guy and I can easily find out who he is.'

'OK. I'm off now as there's a young lady over there that I need to speak with.'

And with that, Mr Butt toddled off.

I knew that Indian would stick out like a sore thumb. Undercover? Undercover my arse, thought Ahmed. *I need to speak with him before he blows the whole damn show. And I need to get some Lemsip as I feel like shit.*

Ahmed composed an email detailing everything raised by Mr Butt, adding what Deepak needed to do, and sent it to Deepak. He considered copying in Chris Gould and John Pope but decided against that. He didn't want to escalate or inflame the situation, rather Deepak needed to start integrating himself within the mosque community, talk to people, use his legend, stop ferreting about and stop his bloody head from bobbling. What a giveaway. Ahmed's next activity was to access MI5's identikit software package from his laptop and create a photo fit of the Imam that he had seen on Sunday morning. It was only a glimpse and mostly a profile with the top of his head and body covered. The profile did however exaggerate his hooked nose, weak chin and thin face. Ahmed took his time refining the image until he was content that it was as perfect at it could be. Yet again, he was reminded that the image he had created using the software was remarkably similar to that of a hawk. He then added text explaining everything that had happened on Sunday regarding this individual and the people who'd assisted him and that there was no evidence that he was deposited at either Luton train station or Luton airport. A final paragraph was added recounting Mr Butt's comment earlier claiming that this individual was a visitor who was then helped with his onward journey after attending prayer. He submitted the image to Team 4, copying in Deepak and Chris Gould. Looking at his watch, it was now 18:30 and there was only one and a half hours to go before he finished his shift. Ahmed's energy levels were plummeting fast. He had the beginnings of a thumping headache. He knew that he needed to get into bed and sleep as he was definitely coming down with something.

19:00. Chris Gould was standing by the desk of Team 4's leader. The conversation had been brief and the team leader had assured Chris that all of the tasks had been completed and everything requested had been implemented. Data was flowing into the analyst team and they were categorising everything and beginning to sift though it methodically. GCHQ was sending over all of the electronic and voice data that they had been requested to capture. The Walker teams were in place, the car tracker fixed and the CCTV feed from outside the mosque was rolling in live. All of the noticeboards had been photo'd and every item on each board was going to be processed. In fact, the noticeboard data had been forwarded to Team 5 and sharing the workload would speed up the process. Team 5 would also look into the financials of all of the key targets, again bringing everything up to speed as soon as possible. Chris nodded his head in acknowledgement and walked back to his desk. He ran through everything again as he walked. He didn't want anything to drop between the cracks or get missed. In the absence of John Pope, this was his opportunity to shine. Operation Alastor was his baby, and he even christened it.

A car pulled up outside the back entrance that led up the flight of stairs to the small flat over the chicken shop. The driver, who was in his late fifties, got out. He was a small man, no more than five feet three inches, with salt and pepper hair. He popped open the boot and retrieved a holdall. Slowly, he walked up the metal stairs, straining under the weight of the bag. He knocked loudly on the grungy door where the red paint was peeling off liberally. The door was opened in seconds and he was greeted by a smiling face.

'Hello, Dad, come in.'

'Thanks, son. Where shall I put this?'

'Through here, in the kitchen,' said Deepak, walking ahead.

'I see that the tax office has put you up in another rat hole.'

'Oh, it's not that bad. I've started cleaning it and it will be fine in a few days.'

'Your mum worries, you know. Anyway, here's enough food to feed an army for several days,' said Mr Chopra, unpacking a multitude of dishes all covered up in aluminium foil. 'Did you bring your microwave oven?'

'Yes, don't tell me Mum sent one up.'

'You know your mother. Anyway, at least I don't have to lug that up here from the car.'

Mr Chopra walked throughout the flat without asking permission.

Once he had inspected every room, he said, 'Not a bad size. I see that you are sharing this flat.'

'Oh yes. Just a temp guy up here from the tax office.'

Mr Chopra eyed his son. He knew that he worked for the government in some capacity but it sure wasn't the tax office. It was a balancing act; Deepak wanted to follow his own career and the family didn't want to be excluded. This was a compromise; wherever Deepak went, food parcels would be delivered and there would be occasional family gatherings once the dwelling had been scrubbed. His mum didn't approve of living in a dirty place.

'OK, well I'll be off then. Phone your mum.'

'Absolutely, Dad. And thanks.'

Mr Chopra left the flat, got into his car and drove back to London. MI5 forbade contact with anyone at undercover agents' residences as this breached security protocols. Deepak's cultural background meant that he couldn't just switch off and ignore his family. Up until now he was able to circumvent MI5 rules easily because he had always been housed on his own. He rationalised that there was little harm in the odd family visit, but now he was sharing with someone else and that someone may be a stickler for rules and procedures. A few white lies may throw his flat mate off the track. Anyway, it was time to get ready and go to work. It had already been a fairly long day as he had moved all of his gear from his tiny flat here and had started the process of cleaning this place up.

08:00. Deepak had been back in the flat for over one and a half hours. He had spent that time cleaning the small bathroom and the elbow grease that he poured into the cleaning was beginning to show. He knew that he'd need to spend several more hours at it before it was transformed from a health hazard into something half decent. Years of neglect could not be turned around quickly, especially if the inhabitants continued to use the facilities but refused to ever clean them. How Ahmed lived like this was a mystery to him.

The kettle had boiled and he shouted out, 'Hey, Ahmed, fancy a cuppa?'

'Yeah, I'll be right out.'

Ahmed was lazing on the two-seater sofa wrapped in a blanket, hair in a mess and eyes full of sleep when Deepak walked in with two mugs of tea, milked, sugared and tea bags still swimming in them. He put both mugs on the rickety table and sat in the unsprung chair, which had the stuffing poking out of it from several small holes.

'I got your email yesterday evening before I left for work. We need to talk about everything that you brought up. But first, how are you?' said Deepak flatly.

'I feel like shit. This has been building up for some time. I'm run down. Nothing that a few days' rest won't cure,' replied Ahmed before he took his first slurp of tea.

'Are you going to call it in then?'

'Nope. A couple of shifts will be all that I miss. They can't get anyone else in and you are already pulling a long shift.'

'But what about the daily postings back to Team 4?'

'I thought about that. I'll doctor them and use data that I've already sent with just a few minor adjustments.'

'Man, that's not good.'

'It will do. I need to rest. They've had me running around now for several months.'

'Let's go through all of your points then in your email.'

Ahmed was fully awake now and he rubbed the remains of the sleep out of his eyes. He sat up, keeping the blanket wrapped around him, and took another slurp of tea.

'I could murder a couple of biscuits,' Ahmed said, looking forlornly at Deepak.

Deepak jumped out of his seat and returned with a plate full of Rich Tea biscuits. They both sat there dunking their biscuits in their mugs of tea and eating the soggy outcomes.

'First, you can't mention that I've gone AWOL.'

Deepak was uncomfortable with being made an accomplice but solemnly nodded in agreement.

'Ta. You need to speak to people there. They have noticed you sitting in the main community room, then dashing off periodically and coming back. It all looks suspicious and your behaviour is making you stand out.'

'I guess there's something there that I need to improve upon.'

'You don't look like or act like a Muslim and that adds to them being suspicious.'

'What do you mean?'

'Well, you have a boy's haircut and that ain't cool. Get a number two on the back and sides and gel the top.'

'I thought it was a smart haircut.'

'No, bro. It's Indian through and through. And when you sit there, your head bobbles and that's a 100% giveaway.'

Deepak's head was now gently moving from side to side as if it was a branch of a small tree caught in a breeze.

'Really. I never knew that was an Indian trait and I certainly didn't know that I was doing it.'

'Bruv, you are doing it now,' said Ahmed before going on. 'Don't creep around with your head down all subservient and polite. Have some edge and a bit of swagger, that's how to roll. Yeah, be polite to the elders but don't grovel.'

The information was coming thick and fast at Deepak and it all sounded like something that he heard in a film about gangs in east LA. However, he conceded that he did need to take this information on board as he didn't want this operation to unravel because of him.

'What you need to do is change your legend and spread that around as your cover story. It's the only way to move forward now that you are being watched.'

'OK, what do you suggest?'

'Well, you need to say that you were brought up as an Indian Hindu and that you decided to convert to the Muslim faith when you became an adult. You need to say that this caused a rift in your family and you moved out to follow your faith and you also decided to take further education and get a career. Say that your family held you back and you now plan to follow your true path.'

'Why can't I be an Indian Muslim?'

'Because you don't look or behave like one. We just went through all of that.'

'OK. You know better I suppose, so what next?'

'Pull up your legend and we'll update it online with everything that we've discussed.'

'Right, you shout it out and I'll type.'

Ten minutes later, Deepak's legend had been updated in MI5's database. The rule of thumb was to create a legend that resembled their own real life as closely as possible. That way it was less likely that an undercover agent would accidentally let slip anything that might expose their cover. They even kept their real names but changed where they grew up and were schooled. Legends were the bedrock on which an undercover agent plied his trade, and his life depended on it. Facebook and other social media networks meant that it was easy to snoop on anyone under a certain age. MI5 did create, maintain and update legends on social networks, adding fictitious friends, family and acquaintances, and the 'real' person was strongly advised to not keep any information about them in the public domain. This was the tricky bit as family and friends wanted to post both information and photos and didn't always either agree or understand why someone was being so vehemently obstructive. This in some cases led to major fallouts, some of which were permanent.

'There's a middle-aged man called Mr Butt who is a busybody but is really useful. He's there most days around midday prayer. Do you know him?'

'No.'

'OK. Best avoid him if you can for now. When I go back there, I'll have a chat with him and explain everything that we've covered regarding updating your legend. Once I've had that chat, he'll be more relaxed and then you can start working him. He's just the type of person that we need to cultivate, not only here but in every mosque. The only way we'll ever make any progress is if we have people on the inside who keep their ear to the ground and share all of their information with us.'

'Right. Anything else?'

'Just one thing. Where has all of that food come from?'

'I cooked it at the other place and brought it here,' lied Deepak. 'There's plenty there. Have as much as you want.'

'I thought you lot are vegetarians.'

'No, we eat meat but not cow. There's some that are strict vegetarians but not us.'

'Well I'll take you up on that as eating good food will help me recover quicker.'

'OK. I'm going to clean a bit more then grab some sleep.'

Despite feeling unwell, Ahmed couldn't resist getting on his soap box, especially as he had a captured audience.

'Bruv, the flats that we are given are shitholes. You will go down with something, I'm telling you. Dysentery, TB or maybe bubonic plague. The white Oxbridge rowers working undercover will never be given them places. They stay in penthouses, it's us that get stuck in these crap houses.'

'I'm not sure about that,' replied a smiling Deepak, whose head was bobbling again.

'Fucking white institutional racists, bro. We are being royally fucked, trust me on this.'

'Cleaning up the place is easy. It only takes a bit of time and good old honest sweat.'

'Do you think Farquhar fucking Twitcher has to clean his crib when he's undercover at Henley regatta? No fucking way. His cleaner does that shit whilst his butler irons his spats.'

Deepak laughed and his head started bobbling even more. 'Is Farquhar-Twitcher a real name?'

'They are conning you, bro.'

'Listen, I've been in a few places that the Walker teams end up in and they are rough. They stakeout anywhere opposite the target, and the lofts that they commandeer are dusty, smelly and even have mice running around.'

'Bruv, think about it. That whole crew are weird. They enjoy sitting anywhere just listening and spying on people. They all graduated from watching all that reality TV and fly-on-the-wall documentary shit and get paid to do something that they'd pay you to do.'

'I'm not sure about that. As well as MI5 guys there are SAS and SO15 in the Walker teams.'

'Exactly. White institutionalised racists, every one of them.'

'I'm going now. Get some rest.'

'OK, but first we need to update your legend.'

'Fine. What now?'

'Input that you have a hereditary neck disease that causes your head to bobble. It hasn't stopped whilst we've been talking.'

'Piss off.'

'There's no need for that. I didn't think that you swore.'

'You'd make a saint swear,' said Deepak, picking up the two empty mugs and the plate cleared of biscuits.

'And get your hair cut,' smiled a sickly Ahmed.

11:00. The young man pushed open the glass door and walked in. He went up to the counter and the tall, willowy Somalian said in broken English, 'Yeah man, you want?'

'One hour and a flat white.'

The Somalian typed a few keys into a screen behind the counter and waited for the screen to supply the answer.

'Two pounds, and you table nine,' he said, pointing to the back of the cafe by the window.

The young man searched his front jeans pocket and withdrew a handful of change. He sifted through the collection and put several coins on the counter. The Somalian looked at the coins, mentally counting their collective value, swept them up and deposited them in the open till. The young man hadn't waited for any confirmation but had walked over to the PC station, sat down and was already logging in. He looked around and checked whether anyone could oversee his screen and was content that he had enough privacy. He took out of his pocket a piece of paper which contained three email names and their associated passwords. He chose number two on the list and logged on.

His daily routine was to rotate the use of each email name and use a different internet cafe for accessing the internet. He logged onto specific websites that were also provided and written on the piece of paper. He sat there, cap perched low over his eyes, and watched the first set of content appear. A cup of coffee was placed on the table supplied by the Somalian, who didn't bother to look at the PC screen. The preacher was speaking in English and he was giving his interpretation of quotes taken directly from the Quran. There were at least 109 verses that speak of war with non-believers. Some of them were very graphic, with commands to chop off heads and kill infidels. Muslims who did not join the fight were called 'hypocrites' and were warned that Allah would send them to hell.

The preacher had a powerful personality, repeating over and over his interpretation of Allah's will. He had a substantial amount of material to choose from and didn't draw breath for twenty minutes whilst he increased his rage to near-boiling point. All of the while, the young man absorbed the invective sermon, further cementing his already twisted ideological view. He logged onto two further websites, one showing acts of violence. There were scenes of villages after a drone strike and the slaughter of innocent civilians, as well as the injured and mutilated survivors. There were video messages from suicide bombers and there were beheadings.

The other website was similar to the first website that he visited. Same message only different quotes from the Quran by an equally irate preacher. At the end of his hour, his head and heart had been filled with equal measures of hatred and promoted the thought that he was an avenging angel. He cleared out the links that he had created when accessing the three websites from the PC, logged off, got up and walked out of the internet cafe without speaking to anyone.

13:00. Another young man entered another internet cafe and went through a similar process as per the previous young man. Once logged on though, he accessed an internet chat room. A couple of minutes later, another person logged on. The other person explained that the family were missing him and that his mum was upset. The other person asked where he was, but he didn't get a reply. The conversation moved onto football and their favourite football team. Would United win the league title this season? They both agreed that they would. But they said this at the start of every season, and by and large United did. The other person said that their dad didn't mean anything by the way that he behaved. He was strict and wanted everyone to make the best for themselves, and why not come home. No was the answer, and the young man abruptly left the chat room. He was both frustrated and angry and then logged onto the prescribed websites for the remainder of his hour's time.

15:00. The third young man entered a busy internet cafe full of noise and laughter. Several young kids were playing games against each other. He sat at his PC and looked around with annoyance. There were girls who were displaying too much flesh. They should cover themselves up as they dressed and behaved immodestly. This irritated him more than the young boys who swore loudly and pushed and shoved each other. He logged onto the websites but after forty minutes logged off and left the cafe. His annoyance at the girls' behaviour had distracted him and he was barely in control of his anger. He decided that he would go for a long run and that would quell the demons that permeated his brain.

Before the Imam had departed, he had given all three of the young men a number of items. Each of them was given cash; there was enough for them to live on for the next several months. They had each been given a piece of paper with three email names and passwords and a number of websites. They had to log on daily and spend one hour accessing the websites, and they had to change daily which internet cafe they went to. There were quite a few of them in and around Luton and they should in the course of time use all of them. They were not to make contact with each other, and one was told to use internet cafes in the north of Luton, one in the south of Luton and one in west of Luton. Once they had used every internet cafe in that region, they would move clockwise onto the next region. They could not use the mosque where their training had been conducted, but should pray at least three times a day in a different mosque and regularly change mosques. They should read the Quran daily and become well versed in the contents, and they must exercise daily for at least one hour. Constant reaffirmation is a key tool controlling people use over people who are impressionable. This tool was well known to the Imam, and he planned to use it and maximise its effect whilst the operation moved on to the next phase.

09:30. The Pope family were leaving the hotel and going home after their ten-day holiday in Port Eynon. The sky was a pale blue with smatterings of clouds moving lazily across it. It was going to be a sunny, warm day with a strong breeze here on the Gower Peninsular. Ideal for sailing, outdoor activities and just ambling about. All of the bags had been packed by Pope before breakfast in the car. He had thoroughly searched both his ensuite room and the ensuite room that Charlie, Daisy and Doodle shared. He had learnt through painful experience that items were routinely left behind, some valuable and some inconsequential, but all caused a major drama leading to having to return and hunt for the unaccounted for item. Leaning against their car was a smiling Terry Gibson. Doodle wagged his tail, strained on the lead and dragged Daisy towards Gibson.

'Hi, boy,' said a smiling Gibson as he petted Doodle, who was excitedly greeting him. 'Just popped back to see you all off.'

'Thanks, mate,' said Pope. 'Well, girls, say goodbye to Terry.'

'Goodbye,' said Charlie.

'We had good fun building sandcastles and will probably come back,' shouted the ever-smiling Daisy. 'And Doodle's bum is better.'

Gibson smiled and patted Daisy on the head, saying, 'Yeah, I enjoyed building the sandcastles.'

'Take care, Terry. You must come up and visit us some time,' said Jane as she gave him a peck on the cheek and a gentle hug.

'I'll take you up on that.'

'Yes, we can take Doodle over Hampstead Heath, he loves that,' interjected Daisy.

'And we'll build sandcastles,' replied Gibson.

'Don't be silly, there's no sand or sea there,' said Daisy.

Everyone laughed. Pope proffered his hand and Gibson shook it.

'What's the journey time to Cardiff?' asked Pope.

'One hour twenty pushing it on the bike. I just noticed; how long have you been wearing glasses?'

'Not long. Well, ride safely.'

The Pope family loaded up in the car and, waving frantically to Gibson, they drove off. He mounted his bike and rode back into the town where he was going to spend the morning riding one of the barmaids that he had met when he was down here the previous weekend. In the Pope car there was an air of disappointment. The holiday was over and it was time to get back to work for the adults and back to school for the girls. Pope, who generally let Jane make all of the family related decisions, had given her a strict agenda the night before whilst they were lying in bed.

'Everyone will have a light breakfast. Don't pack any sweets, chocolates or crisps for the journey, just a couple of bottles of water. We'll stop after two hours or so for a break, but no food, only drinks, and that includes Doodle.'

'John, don't be too hard on them.'

'I'm not. I just don't want a repeat performance of what happened coming down here.'

Jane's silence was her reply.

'Listen, it's five hours with a stop to get back home and then everyone can eat and drink as much as they want.'

Pope stopped now as he knew anything else would only trigger a row and end what had been a fun holiday that he had both enjoyed and needed.

In the car, the girls sat in silence. No one asked to listen to the car radio. Doodle, who was curled up in the middle of the back seat, suddenly scooted through the gap between the passenger's seat and the driver's seat, jumping awkwardly over the gear knob. He pushed himself into the passenger footwell, curled up, and Jane adjusted her feet to accommodate him. He had also remembered the journey down and was taking his own preventative measures.

'Mummy, where is Doodle?' cried a worried Daisy.

'Don't worry. He's tired and is going to go to sleep.'

'He's never done that before. He always sits with me.'

'Yes, but he's never been tired before. Why don't you close your eyes and rest.'

The journey home was uneventful and the family arrived at 14:15. Pope unloaded the cases whilst Jane prepared sandwiches and drinks for everyone. Whilst the family were eating in the kitchen, Pope heard the familiar sound alerting him that a new email had just arrived on his phone. He checked the email and finished his snack.

'That was nice. Listen, I need to pop into work and catch up. I'll see you all later.'

'Dinner will be at 06:30,' said Jane phlegmatically.

Pope was sitting in the nondescript pub that he met Seb Drake in whenever there was a need to catch up. He was nursing a pint of the latest guest bitter and it was a woody hoppy flavour that he enjoyed.

'Hi JP, how was your holiday?' said Seb, bounding over to the table where John was sitting.

'Very good, Seb. Probably went too quick. What can I get you?'

'Sit. I'll get them. Best or guest?'

'Guest please.'

'Right you are.'

Drake returned with two pints of guest bitter, and Pope, in his short absence, had taken a keen slug out of the pint that he was holding. The table that Pope had chosen was in the corner and away from prying eyes and ears.

'Operation Alastor is in full swing and the DG is in the picture. He's happy to let it unfold and hasn't mentioned anything to COBRA. He feels that it's just a standard operation and raising it will only bring unwelcome intrusion. He wants to wait until there's something definitive and only then will he brief them.'

'Sounds reasonable.'

'The French problem that we discussed.'

'Ah, that.' Pope now knew why he had been summoned on the afternoon that he had returned from his holiday.

'Yes. Where are we with that?'

'No progress. A brief review by my team so far but nothing has popped out. Everything has been focused on Luton and what with my holiday...'

'Well, you need to take personal charge. Holidays are over and we don't work 09:00 to 17:00,' interrupted Drake.

Pope had rarely seen Drake take such a strong stance.

'Seb, understood. I'll get onto it right away. Just for my own benefit, what is pushing this up the priority pole?'

'JP, keep this under your hat. The squeeze is coming from a group who have the ear of the PM. We need to demonstrate that we are on top of this. It's the usual...politics.'

'Sure. Not a bad pint.'

'No, it's very good.'

Drake went on then to recount in full the account given to him by a current serving SAS signals officer from D squadron of a covert counter surveillance operation carried out in Afghanistan in late 2008. Pope listened intently for nearly one hour until Drake finished.

'So this is the information that you want me to pass onto Boris.'

'Yes. MI6 have sat on this and maybe they have their reasons. But we feel that we need to share it with our Russian friends. We need to get some credit in the bank. Their current prime minister is building himself a very strong power base and in all likeliness will be the next president. He is modernising their army and updating all of their Cold War military hardware. They are not going to stagnate and they are in parallel rejuvenating their global commercial model. Their natural resources are unlimited and their oligarchs are fronting their latest revolution.'

'I see. We're back to politics again.'

'Yes. But you sell it to Boris that Her Majesty's government does not condone nor support drug trafficking and will assist any country that is being threatened by this scourge.'

'And what about the fact that we've known about this for two years?'

'Easy. Just say that, like Russia, events happen and aren't always shared with the correct body who will deal with it. Right hand not knowing what the left hand is doing and all that.'

'Right. I'll set up the meet and let you know the outcome.'

'Good. I need to crack on,' said Drake as he drained the dregs from his third pint of guest bitter.

Pope watched him leave, drained the remainder of his fourth pint and sent a brief text to his wife saying that he'd be in the office until late and not to wait up. He then sent a text to Victor Sokolov and received a reply within two minutes confirming the meeting later that evening at their usual haunt – the Syrian restaurant off the Edward Road.

Pope walked back to Thames House where he had previously parked his car. He needed to dig out everything now regarding the French problem and start from scratch. He'd catch up with Chris Gould tomorrow and go through what he had gleaned from studying everything so far. A few hours in the office would allow those four pints to work their way through his system before he drove to the restaurant located off of Edgware Road for his 22:00 meeting. Pope accessed the latest updates created by Chris Gould which were sketchy and then the two files that had been originally created which were raised specifically as items of concern and potential industrial espionage by French nationals.

The first file related to a British pharmaceutical company that had invested millions on creating a vaccine for one of the most deadly of viruses known to mankind, that being Ebola. There had been many vaccines created over the previous decade but none had been approved and none had a good track record of curing anyone infected. The pharmaceutical company had focused on cutting-edge science and genetic engineering at DNA level. They were years ahead of anyone else trying to create a foolproof vaccine. Their vaccine, whilst still at a theoretical stage of development, was being developed to counter not only strains of Ebola that were predicted but also a mutated and more virulent version of it. They anticipated that a vaccine would be developed and ready for trialling in 2014.

The second file related to a Water Research and Development company who had invested millions on developing a solution for purifying water and making it clean enough to drink. They were developing a solution that was cheap to build per unit, resilient and portable. Africa was their target because of their high mortality and illness rates, caused by people and livestock drinking unclean water. Fifty per cent of all of the world's illness was caused by drinking unclean water. There were other companies developing solutions but this company had focused their effort on creating a membrane filtration that would pass unclean water through and release clean water after processing. They were using advanced Nanofiltration within three layers of filtration and were creating a robust Nanofiltration layer that, as to date, had eluded the industry. They were targeting testing to begin in 2013 and rollout standalone portable filters in 2015.

Both companies had been in research and development since 2005 and as part of their due diligence had been audited for sound security by MI5 in 2008. MI5 acted as paid consultants for companies involved in classified technologies and rigorously examined all facets of their security. They ran security background checks on all employees, from CEO to the cleaners and anyone in between. They scrutinised the physical security of their premises. They probed electronically all of their computer firewalls and made sure that terminals did not allow outside access or unauthorised software to be loaded. They reviewed the user permissions that were granted to all employees and made sure that employees did not leave their screens on when they left their workstations. They ran a similar suite of checks on all of the subcontractors who were involved in delivering the end solution.

In both cases, in 2009 French commercial companies announced publicly that they were developing solutions similar if not exactly the same to the ones being developed in England. But without having put in the same level of research, they were at a similar level of development and were aiming to bring their product to market at least one year earlier than that of their English competitors. It was not possible to do no research on products using advanced and as yet theoretical technologies and have a product ready in a few years to rollout. Somehow, some way, they had acquired the intellectual property of the British companies.

Pope realised that he was going to have to go back to the very start and read through everything. This was going to be a long process and he knew that engaging the assistance of any of the analyst teams was out of the question. Seb Drake had been very specific in that he and he alone was responsible for getting to the bottom of this espionage. Seb had more than hinted that his weekends and evenings now would be filled with this and the rest of his time should be devoted to hunting the terrorists.

For Pope's next task he went through the information that Drake had shared with him regarding the SAS covert mission in late 2008 and wrote everything up into a report, marking it highly classified. He then added restricted access, making it only available to Seb Drake and himself. He reread the report and formulated what information he'd share with Boris and the reason for sharing the information as proffered by Drake. He looked at his watch and it was already 21:40, so he briskly tidied up, logged off and shut down his PC before heading off to the car park.

22:00. Pope walked up to the table where Victor Sokolov, aka Boris, was already seated and smiled. He ignored the two large men sitting on the table adjacent to Victor's and they did likewise. Their roles were described as diplomatic cultural attachés on their embassy visa forms, but they were more agricultural than cultural.

'Good evening, Victor, thanks for dropping whatever you were doing and turning up.'

'No problem, John, *Match of the Day* wasn't going to be that good anyway. What can I do for you?'

'Actually, Victor, there's something that I can do for you.'

'Really? Well in that case let's first share a drink,' said Victor, pouring a large Rodnik vodka into a glass.

The glasses clinked. 'Nostrovia.'

Pope embarked on his historical story, omitting details that involved things to do with American involvement and MI6. The version recounted was that of an SAS covert mission to track down a high-value target based on local intel. It was thirty minutes before Pope had finished, and during that time Boris sat there, saying nothing, not even blinking. He listened intently, not a muscle moving on his big square head. There was an uncomfortable pause only broken when Boris picked up the bottle of vodka and poured two more generous measures. Pope looked at the quadruple measure of fire water, thinking that he would be over the limit to drive home, but he needed Boris to share his thoughts, so he picked up the glass and again both men toasted. 'Nostrovia.'

'John, why do you share this information with me now?'

'Victor, the information has only recently reached MI5. Overseas military operations and especially covert ones generally aren't shared. In this case, the intel wasn't relevant to the original mission and the military simply filed it. You know how they are. Anyway, someone on that mission was swapping yarns with one of our blokes and he flagged it up. We did some digging around and it checked out. The decision was made that we should share this with you. When it comes to smuggling heroin, Her Majesty's government has a zero tolerance policy and we hope that you would do the same for us.'

'So this has full authorisation?'

'Straight from the Top Floor.'

'I see. And what do you want in return?'

'Absolutely nothing.'

'Well, in that case, on behalf of Mother Russia, please pass on our deepest gratitude to those who decided to share this information with us.'

Pope finished off his drink, shook hands with the large bear and left. Boris passed over the bottle of vodka to his two cronies who gratefully accepted the gift and shared out the remainder into two equal measures. He sat there in reverie for several minutes.

There were a number of points that didn't make sense. Why were the SAS operating unilaterally in a US-controlled area? The US had their own covert teams supported by drones and air cover controlling that area, and dropping in an unannounced team could be potentially lethal. Friendly fire was far too common since the first Iraq war, and the protocols put in place to restrict this happening were strict. Were either the CIA or MI6 involved in this mission? It had the hallmark of something that one or both would attempt with full plausible deniability. Why were MI5 sharing this information? They had a history of never sharing anything with anyone.

He decided that the best course of action was to send everything back to the Federal Secret Service known as the FSB. They would deal with this and he would act as a liaison officer should they want anything else from MI5. When the KGB was dismantled in the mid 1990s, the FSB was set up to maintain security in Russia. Victor Sokolov worked for the Foreign Intelligence Service known as SVR who were also part of the dismantled KGB, and the SVR worked exclusively abroad, focusing on espionage.

Sokolov got up, which prompted both of his companions to also get up. He passed over three twenty-pound notes to the manager and walked out. Before he had got into his car, the manager was on the phone to his contact at the Syrian embassy.

07:00. Ahmed was loafing on the two-seater sofa with the blanket around his shoulders. The blanket had moulded around his body and was in need of a wash nearly as much as Ahmed. Being ill was the perfect excuse for him to become a slob. He hadn't washed, brushed his teeth or combed his hair for three days and was becoming a health hazard. He had however managed to eat a significant portion of Deepak's rations. Deepak knew that the pots of food were rapidly diminishing but acknowledged that Ahmed was benefiting from eating a healthy diet and was looking a lot better than he'd looked a couple of days ago. It would be great, he thought, if Ahmed could manage to use the shower and toothpaste though rather than go around with dog's breath.

'So how are you feeling?' enquired Deepak.

'Getting there. I reckon that I'll go back for my next shift?'

'Really? You feel that much better?'

'Yeah. As I said, a bit of rest was all that was needed.'

'Good, I don't like covering for you. Saying you are there when you aren't isn't right. What if—'

'What if, what if. You nag like an old lady. I'm back in this evening at 20:00, so let it go.'

'Just saying.'

'Anyway, what happened with your haircut?'

'I did what you asked, why?'

'I said number two on the back and sides, not all over. The idea was to make you look like the other young guys there.'

Deepak ran his hand over the fuzz on the top of his head.

'Don't you like this?'

'Are you sure, bruv? You looked like a schoolboy with that other haircut. Now you look like a schoolboy from borstal with a number two all over.'

'Well, I'm going to get ready and head off to work. Oh, and by the way, now that you are feeling better, the shower is in the first room on the left.'

'Very funny.'

09:00. Chris Gould and Clare Hawkins were seated in their corner meeting room when Pope entered.

'Morning, everyone.'

'Morning, John, how was your holiday?' said a rotund Chris Gould.

'Good. The family had a great time and the weather was good.'

'I guess you want an update then,' went on Chris.

Chris apprised Pope with all of the details and that mainly focused on the activities of both Team 4 and Team 5 who were pulling together the information. Walker teams, GCHQ and the two undercover agents made up the remainder of the information. Pope nodded at various points. The information provided by Chris wasn't throwing up anything that suggested there were nefarious activities being performed at the mosque. Pope wasn't in the least concerned. It was important to get everything in place and then watch, listen, wait and see.

'OK, Chris, that's all fine. Listen, I just want to quickly go back over the GCHQ information regarding the industrial espionage stuff that you looked into before I went on holiday.'

'Right. They ran historical data through ECHELON and it came back zero. They used phones, computers, emails and social media from 2006 to 2009. Both main companies and their subcontractors were included. It was a big job and took five days to run. Why? Is there anything else that you want me to do?'

'No. I will share this with both of you but please do not share any of it with anyone else.'

Both Chris and Clare shifted in their chairs; clearly there was something afoot.

'I'm going to review everything relating to both cases. Call it a personal project. I'm going to do a root-and-branch review. I've had a quick scout around and now I'm going to look under every rock. I think that it'll probably take many months.'

'Why not bring in an Analysis team? Surely that's quicker,' said Clare.

'I thought about that but I think that I'll see what I can figure out.'

'So what does this mean to Operation Alastor?' asked Chris, hoping secretly that he'd be allowed to carry on managing it.

'Nothing. As I said, I'm going to look at this stuff separately. Operation Alastor remains our main focus.'

Clare smiled. She knew that Chris wanted the opportunity to head up a high-profile operation and grab the kudos that went with it.

'At some stage, I may need one or both of you to help out, but that's going to be further down the track.'

Both heads nodded back to Pope at that comment.

Back at his workstation, Pope created a memo detailing the activities that he was going to undertake as part of the root-and-branch review. He would first go through all of the documents created originally. If that threw up nothing, then he would authorise background checks on all employees of both companies and their subcontractors for the period from 2006 up until today. He would be looking at whether their finances had drastically improved and whether they had taken up a position in either the French counterparts or a subcontractor of them. He would then look at the French companies and subcontractors and gather background details on both the companies and their employees, looking for any connection with the British companies and whether they had been involved in any way with industrial espionage. He would then look at French companies that were employed in industrial espionage. Finally he would investigate whether the French government had been involved using either of their security agencies i.e. General Directorate for External Security DGSE (the equivalent to MI6) or Central Directorate of Interior Intelligence DCRI (the equivalent to MI5). This was his plan of action and he estimated that if needed to complete everything, it would take in excess of one and a half years. He added in estimates of costs and forwarded the memo to Seb Drake.

At 13:45 Pope received back a separate email from Drake approving the approach, the timeframe and the estimated costs. Pope filed that email away but was slightly uncomfortable. Drake had told him that the DG wanted this investigated and resolved as there was group of people who had the ear of the

PM and this was urgent. And yet he had put a completion date of at least one year and six months, which wasn't challenged. Something wasn't quite right about the whole thing. It was very, very fishy.

20:30. Ahmed was sitting in the community room with his laptop open. He was logged onto his Open University course and was planning to crack on for an hour before getting ready for night prayer which was scheduled for 21:50. A body plunged itself into the seat opposite.

'Good evening, Ahmed. How are you?' huffed Mr Butt.

'Good, Mr Butt, and you?' said Ahmed as he logged onto MI5's photofit software application.

'A bit tired but plodding on.'

'Can I show you something?' enquired Ahmed as he swiftly pressed several keystrokes.

'Of course.'

The laptop was swivelled around so that the screen was now facing Mr Butt, and Ahmed got up from his seat and walked around the wooden table and stood behind him.

'I constructed a facial likeness of Hamiza's uncle. You remember the gentleman that was visiting here last Sunday? Anyway, take a look and let me know if you recognise him.'

Mr Butt stared at the image on the screen for several seconds and shook his head.

'Here, what about his profile?' said Ahmed as he pressed a key, and another image filled the screen instantly.

Mr Butt gazed at the profile photofit and again shook his head.

'Ahmed, where did you get this from?'

'It's part of my Computer Science degree. I'm playing around with Open Source Code and developing my own program,' replied Ahmed, knowing that Mr Butt wouldn't have a clue what he was talking about.

'Very good. The technology available to your generation is a marvel. You have opportunities that we could only dream about. Well, in my day it was an artist who drew the likeness and it never looked like anyone. Then they moved onto selecting facial bits and sticking them together and that wasn't any better.'

'Yes, we are lucky. Anyway, it was worth a try.'

'Ahmed, you are a very determined young man. I don't know why you are putting so much effort into this.'

'Just curiosity, and it was a useful exercise for my degree.'

'Anyway, that Indian boy is still here. He spends a lot of time on his PC but I noticed him speaking to a couple of young men who have a reputation.'

'A reputation for what?'

'They get into trouble and shame their family who are good, hard-working people.'

'About him. I dug around and he's converted to Islam. He was a Hindu but converted and fell out with his family. That's why he moved here. He wanted a fresh start.'

'That makes sense then. Do you know his name?'

'Yes, Deepak Chopra. He's studying for an online degree in English history. I expect that he'll end up being a teacher,' said Ahmed, trying to inflate Deepak's personal profile.

Mr Butt softened some. He respected anyone who had a professional career.

'Well, that is good but you are judged by the company that you keep.'

'I bet he doesn't know anything about them. He's lonely and talking to people of his own age, that's all. Why don't you chat to him?'

'Maybe I will. But what puts me off is his haircut. Honestly, he looks like a football thug,' said Mr Butt as he got up. 'Bye.'

Mr Butt shuffled off but stopped and returned.

'I knew I knew that face,' he said, pointing at the laptop screen that was now blank.

'Really, where from?'

'It looks like the face of the visiting Imam from the beginning of August. You remember the Imam that no one knew anything about?'

'Are you sure?'

'I can't be positive because it was a while ago and I only got a glimpse of him, but it sure looks like him.'

'Thanks.'

'Probably coincidence.'

Ahmed fired off an update to Team 4 of a potential ID from the photofit of the Hawk and potentially two sightings, one by him and another by Mr Butt. He added that they were allegedly two different people. Ahmed then sent Deepak a separate email saying that Mr Butt would probably contact him, and that Ahmed mentioned that Deepak was going to be an English history teacher and to update his legend. He added that Mr Butt thought he was mixing with the wrong crowd and added a PS: his haircut made him look a football hooligan. The PS made Ahmed smile; he was going to extract the maximum mileage out of Deepak's hair raid.

09:00. Pope, Chris Gould and Clare Hawkins were sitting in the corner meeting room, each holding a cup of in-house imitation coffee.

'I'm sure that the rumour mill is in full swing regarding the Luton mosque operation,' said Pope.

'There's some chat that the op may be about to fold,' said Clare matter-of-factly.

'Why? We need to be patient,' said Chris defensively.

'I think we need to be prepared for anything,' said Pope.

'What's the driver for closing down the op?' queried Chris.

'It's only natural that after a while, and it has been several weeks, that questions are asked if nothing has come up,' replied Pope, trying to be even-handed.

'It's all down to cost. Bloody budget, that's all that matters,' said a bitter Chris.

'Budgets do matter but we need to see a reason or something that warrants this level of surveillance, and frankly we aren't,' Pope said.

Internally he was incandescent but he didn't want to show his true feelings to his subordinates. He needed them to buy into whatever decision was coming, be professional and not take it personally. When people took work decisions personally it affected their work and morale, and in this game any dip in performance could have massive ramifications.

'Anyway, the op name was dodgy,' said Clare.

'What's wrong with Alastor,' said Chris defensively.

'A few people were questioning it,' replied Clare.

'What!' squawked Chris.

'Listen, there's nothing wrong with the name. Let's focus. Right, if the op folds, then plan to reassign the full undercover team and prepare to debrief the two guys working undercover at the primary site. Team 4 will need to square off everything that they are currently following up. I don't want them to just shut down. If they are following any leads then they must be completed. No loose ends. The Walker teams will need standing down, the tracker removed from the target's people carrier and the CCTV removed from the street outside the mosque as well as GCHQ advised and their ECHELON surveillance closed down,' said Pope calmly.

Chris and Clare nodded.

'Chris, create a full close down plan and a partial close down plan. I'll review it tomorrow and then we can roll it out if necessary,' said Pope.

'Will do.'

'I don't need to say this but please don't share this. We just need to be ready to react to any decision, that's all,' said Pope, swallowing the last mouthful of dodgy coffee.

11:00. Everyone was seated in the Cage. Carruthers looked up from the mound of papers on the table in front of her.

'Thanks, everyone, for coming here today. Can we go around the room and provide an update?'

One after the other, each regional head gave an update on the many operations that were currently underway. Pope sensed that this was window dressing and that Carruthers was about to drop the hammer on the Luton operation. Whilst the updates were being made, Carruthers' interest was barely registering. And finally it came to Pope's turn. He gave a brief on the multiple operations currently ongoing in London, deliberately leaving Luton until the end.

'The Luton mosque operation has two targets under 24/7 surveillance. We have CCTV surveillance outside the mosque and we have two undercover agents onsite full time. We have a strong picture of what is going on inside the mosque when it goes on and who attends the activities. Team 4 have been sifting through all of the information as it becomes available and we have ongoing support from GCHQ.'

'Thanks, John,' said Carruthers, coiled like a snake ready to strike. 'The two targets under 24/7 surveillance, have we seen any evidence that they are in any way behaving suspiciously?'

'Not really.'

'The driver of the people carrier, what has he been doing?' asked Carruthers, not looking up from her mound of papers.

'He's been driving people to and from Luton airport and running groups of people mainly up to Bradford for weddings.'

'And the other target?'

'Pretty much working full-time in his father's electrical goods shop.'

'I see. And the sightings of the Imam and or the uncle. Have there been any more than the two before we set up this operation?'

'No.'

'What about the three young men that agent Hussain identified on the Sunday before we set up the operation? Have they been seen since then?'

'No.'

'Finally, has either of the two undercover agents flagged anything since the start of the operation that we should be concerned about?'

'No.'

'So, in summary, Team 4 haven't found out anything, neither has GCHQ and all of our surveillance hasn't unearthed a jot,' said Carruthers, leaving it hanging in the air.

Pope chose not to verbally respond to her summation. Everyone else around the table sat still, waiting for the snake to strike.

'I think that in the circumstances, I need to recommend to the powers that be that the operation is downscaled and all resources reassigned. The costs associated with an operation of this magnitude cannot be justified,' said Carruthers, raising her head and looking directly at Pope.

'Well, that is certainly one conclusion that you could draw,' said Pope, stonily holding her gaze.

'Why? Are there others?'

'Yes. I do wonder whether we came across the end of a phase of a long-term operation and that we set up shop after that particular phase had finished,' continued Pope.

All of the other participants around the table now resembled a crowd of spectators at the final of a tennis tournament. All were absorbed and their heads followed from each tennis player to the other as they smashed the ball across the net hoping to find a winning shot.

'Let's say that there was a visiting Imam and he was conducting hate preaching and indoctrination of three young men, and that target one and target two were part of his support team. Once he had completed his work, everyone disbursed.'

'Go on,' said Carruthers, not showing her hand yet.

The crowd were on the edge of their seats. This match could still go either way.

'Both targets were regular attendees of that mosque and since that Sunday they have never been back. The three young guys go to ground and the Imam/uncle vanishes. That can't all be brushed off as coincidences,' persisted Pope.

'It's circumstantial and just a hypothesis. We can only deal with the facts and there isn't anything that merits the operation to continue. I'll make my recommendation and see whether the Top Floor wants to continue with it,' bit the venomous snake. 'Thanks, everyone.'

And with that, Carruthers and her assistant slithered off.

The match was over; the crowd relaxed back in their seats. No clapping as that would be inappropriate, but there was acknowledgement of the winning shot. Several of them got up and left, leaving the usual gang to pick over the bones.

'John, tough luck,' said Tony Crook, beefing up his Scottish accent.

'Difficult one really,' sympathised Frank Selly.

'Part of the problem is that she has no field experience,' added Steve McLeish.

'All part of the new broom. Spreadsheets, budgets and reports. Do more with less,' said James Davidson.

'Sometimes you need to go with your gut. Instinct can drive when you have the experience to trust it,' lamented Pope.

'John, we're all becoming dinosaurs. The bottom line now is the pound note and how much does it cost,' said Tony Crook.

'The cost is simple. Innocent people will be murdered on our streets if we continue down this road,' said Pope, getting up and walking out of the Cage.

16:00. Seb Drake was seated at a corner table in the pub when Pope walked in and waved at him. Pope walked over and took a seat immediately after noticing that there were two frothing pints already sitting on the table.

'Another guest beer. Tastes good. This battle cruiser has been a lifesaver by promoting so many non-commercial beers,' said Drake in his posh accent with Cockney rhyming slang thrown in for good measure.

'Cheers,' responded Pope as he took a decent slug of it. 'Yeah, that's a fine old ale.'

Neither man spoke for a couple of minutes as they allowed their taste buds to savour the malty ale.

'So, Operation Alastor is going to close,' said Drake.

'It looks that way,' replied Pope.

'And your view?' enquired Drake.

'First we had a lot of noise from GCHQ and NSA. Heavy traffic over the airways that something was cooking. Everyone from the PM down was dancing on hot coals. Then we see something really out of the ordinary up in Luton and we go into overdrive to put a blanket over the top of it. But then pretty much nothing. So now it's classified as a wild goose chase and now it's time to close it down.'

'Pray continue,' said Drake, taking another swig from his pint.

'Everything points to the preparation phase of a big operation being completed just before we arrived. This isn't over; it's just begun.'

'So what would you have us do then?'

'Run with it.'

'Well that can't happen. Carruthers is paid to make decisions and recommendations and we can't ignore her.'

'The consequence though are unimaginable.'

'Perhaps there's a compromise.'

'Really?'

'Let's say that the two undercover agents remain onsite and we leave the CCTV surveillance camera outside there. London gets their undercover agent back. Team 4 process the camera footage, which isn't a biggy. Best of all from Carruthers' point of view, this change is cost neutral. We keep the same number of undercover agents at Luton as before, London gets back their agent and Team 4 only has a minimal amount of checking from the street CCTV camera as the software programme script is written and will flag up only exceptions. Not ideal, but under the circumstances,' said Drake in appeasement, hands spread out wide.

'Well, that means we lose cover on all of the other mosques in Luton,' said Pope.

'Yes it does, but if you really think this is the place to focus on then so be it.'

'I do,' said Pope.

'So what do you think of our start to the Euros then?' quizzed Drake, deciding it was time to change the subject.

'Two wins is a great start and we have Montenegro at home in several days, so it's looking good. We should be OK to qualify for the finals in 2012.'

'Yes, but the World Cup was a disappointment. We looked flat and despite Lampard's shot being three feet over the line and not being given, Germany were the better team.'

'Can't argue with the 4-1 result. They are building a fine young team. Who knows, a decent bet for the next World Cup in Brazil.'

'Yes, they look good. We're struggling though, but don't want to admit it. Can't understand employing a manager who can't speak English. That's strange, especially as the job is all about communication.'

'And winning,' added Drake.

18:30. Pope was sitting at the kitchen table with Charlie sitting opposite him in her usual seat. Charlie was midway through the courses for several GCSEs, with the exams at the end of the educational year in June 2011. It was going to be a stressful year for her and she would be sixteen years old in January. She was relaxing ahead of a few hours' studying in the dining room. Daisy burst into the kitchen and then proceeded to cross the floor 'jumping across flowers'. This was a technique that she'd been learning since she started her Saturday morning ballet classes at the beginning of September. She half stumbled at the end and fell into Pope's arms. He swept her up, sat her on his lap and she planted several kisses on his cheeks.

'Daddy, did you like my ballet steps?' squealed Daisy.

'Yes. You are very good.'

'Well, I practise every day. I want to be a ballerina when I get older.'

'I will come and watch you in your shows.'

'Yes, and Mummy and Charlie and Doodle.'

'Doodle won't be there,' sniped Charlie.

'Please,' said Jane.

'Nor will I,' added Charlie.

Daisy's face crumpled. 'Doodle will be there.'

Pope said, 'Show me some more,' and gently put Daisy down.

Daisy galloped around the kitchen for a couple of minutes whilst everyone watched her. She was happy to be the centre of attention. But her own attention span was limited and she abruptly stopped.

'I need to check Doodle's bum,' she declared to no one in particular.

And with that, Daisy continued galloping somewhat uncoordinatedly out of the kitchen.

Pope was momentarily absorbed in his own thoughts. Jane had decided to enrol Daisy in ballet classes for a few reasons. First, it was exercise, and children weren't encouraged with the modern lifestyle to get enough exercise. Second, she would make new friends. Third, Daisy was slightly uncoordinated, almost clumsy, and ballet would sharpen her up.

Pope understood and endorsed her reasoning. However, there were unforeseen consequences. Since starting the ballet classes, Daisy moved around in a series of dance movements all of the time. At home, walking down the street and even when they went to buy the family shopping, Daisy would be jumping, leaping and spinning around like a demented dervish. Also, she had taken to wearing her ballet outfit of leotard, skirt, tights and ballet shoes all in luminous pink all of the time. The only concession that Daisy made was that she wouldn't wear her ballet shoes in the house. Jane had persuaded her that if she wore them then they would wear out. The other accessory that Daisy insisted on wearing were her fairy wings in a garish pink. After a couple of weeks, Pope casually mentioned to Jane that wearing the same clothes all of the time was a tad unhygienic.

Jane answered that the clothes were regularly washed and ironed whilst Daisy was at school and that ended any further discussion.

'Besides,' said Jane, 'it's only a phase Daisy is going through.'

Several weeks on now, Pope wasn't sure whether this was a new phase or if it was an addendum to the phase that included regular inspections of Doodle's arse. Whatever was going on here, he was definitely no more than a bit player, a mere observer, and he knew better than to try and fathom any of it out. Perhaps he was going through a phase, he mused.

'John, fancy a cuppa?' asked Jane.

'Yes please.'

That shook him out of his trance and back into the real world.

07:35. Despite several taps on the bathroom door, there was no acknowledgement from its occupant and it remained locked. Pope continued to complete dressing and gathered his mobile phone from the bedroom before heading back downstairs. He combed his hair over the kitchen sink, applying a liberal amount of water to the comb in order that his dishevelled hair would take on a groomed appearance. He then slipped on his trusty brown brogues but wasn't ready yet to leave for work. He ran his tongue around the inside of his mouth and across his teeth. There was a sensation of furriness on his tongue. He wasn't comfortable with this response and a light bulb went on inside his head.

When serving in the armed forces, whisky was a potent tool and adaptable in the battlefield. It was used to clean wounds, to fortify someone ahead of an extreme mission, as an anaesthetic and in many more situations. He went into the front room and took out his malt whisky bottle from the drinks cabinet. He unscrewed the top and took a slug from the bottle before re-screwing it and replacing it back in its customary place. He walked into the kitchen, head tilted back and slooshing as he went. He spat some of the liquid out into the sink and then began rubbing his teeth and his tongue vigorously with the index finger of his right hand. He completed this exercise within a minute and, once satisfied that the furriness was gone, he sluiced his mouth under the cold tap. Doodle had been a constant if somewhat bemused companion throughout this exercise. Finally, he quickly washed the inside of the basin with water and dried both his hands and mouth on the kitchen tablecloth. He smiled to himself. The tricks learned in his army career were always useful. He exited the front door shouting out goodbye and was only greeted with Doodle's sprint up the stairs.

08:23. Seated at his desk, Pope watched as Carruthers forcefully approached.

'Good morning,' Pope said without any emotion.

'Good morning,' came the reply. 'I see that there's an ongoing debate on downscaling the Luton operation.'

'I wouldn't know, I'm not privy to those conversations.'

Carruthers leaned in closely to Pope. 'Really?'

'Yes, really,' he said, leaning back slightly as she had invaded his personal space.

Carruthers held her stance, momentarily sucking in air, and then swivelled around and, without saying a word, strode back to her glass castle. Pope was slightly bemused by her body language throughout this minor encounter. She had leant so close to his face, he thought that she was planning to kiss him.

Carruthers logged onto her PC and created an email which she fired off to HR, marking it as high priority. Several minutes later, Pope had all of his applications loaded onto his PC and he was checking the daily headlines from all of the newspapers. He always went through this routine in order that anything globally that may be of interest was captured, and partly because he liked to keep abreast of news events anyway. Even the tittle tattle tabloids were useful for amusement if not much else.

The audible ping alerted him that he had an email just deposited in his inbox. He opened his Office application and in his inbox saw a high priority email from HR sitting at the top of the queue. He opened it and reread it twice. It was a summons to immediately go to the medical centre where he would be required to undertake a random drugs and alcohol blood test. He thought about just getting up and exiting the building. With everything going on at the moment, what was this bullshit about? He did know that his whereabouts were logged and security knew that he was currently sitting on the 7th floor and was logged onto his workstation PC. If he tried to leave the building, his pass would not be accepted and his exact whereabouts would instantly be flagged to security. This was because he had been flagged for a drugs test and all egress points would deny him departure. He replied to the HR email stating that he was logging off his workstation and then going directly to the medical centre.

Pope exited the lift at level -3. He had never been to this floor before and from that point of view it was a novelty. He was required to perform a yearly medical and fitness test but that was conducted at MI5's training centre. Fort Monckton in Portsmouth was the base shared by several agencies as budgets had been tightened by successive governments. The artificial light lit the long corridor and further down it he could see two armed guards posted in front of secure doors that blocked the corridor. Whatever else was going on down here, clearly some of it was highly sensitive and classified.

Above the first door on the left was a sign that read 'Medical Centre'. Pope opened it without knocking and was confronted by a typical doctor's waiting room. There were plastic seats in rows and at the far end was a nurses' station where a young Filipino nurse was engrossed by the screen in front of her. The front row of seats was occupied by five men, all of whom Pope didn't know.

He walked up to the desk and the Filipino, without looking up, said in broken English as she extended her hand, 'Card.'

Pope thought for a second and then handed over his security pass. The nurse put his card into a slot in the hard drive and looked at her screen.

'Go, room three pleeeze,' she said again in broken English and handed Pope's security pass back to him.

He looked around the room and saw that there were no doors here other than the door that he had entered. Without glancing at the front row incumbents, he walked back out of the waiting room and saw that there were several more doors on either side of the corridor that were numbered. He walked up to door number three and opened the door. Inside was a couch, a screen, a number of medical gizmos and a desk with two seats on this side of it and a seat on the other side that was occupied by an overweight middle-aged man dressed in a long white coat. The man stood up and over the top of his half-moon spectacles gazed at Pope with a welcoming smile.

'Please come in and sit down,' said the ruddy-faced man in a pleasant manner, with his hands pointing to one of the seats opposite him. 'Thanks for coming. You know why you are here?' continued the man.

'Yes.'

'Good. Let me introduce myself. I'm Doctor Stephen Hempel-Smith. May I call you John?'

'Sure.'

'This won't take too long. I know that you are busy and can do without interruptions. Please slip your jacket off, roll up your sleeve and we'll do the blood pressure test first.'

Pope complied and Dr Hempel-Smith applied the cuff and then read the reading.

'Just relax, John. We'll take another reading.'

The good doctor took a further two readings and then typed into his screen the best reading.

'OK, now we'll take the blood. Please make a fist and squeeze,' he said, passing over a small plastic cylindrical contraption.

Pope squeezed hard and the veins in the crook of his elbow became prominent. A sharp hypodermic needle was shallowly inserted into one of the veins and a phial of blood withdrawn.

'Good. Now hold the cotton wool,' said Dr Hempel-Smith as he applied a small plaster over the top of it.

Dr Hempel-Smith put the full phial in a container by the sink and then sat back down behind his desk where he stared at the information on his screen. He scrolled down several times and then looked at Pope, smiling.

'Are you sleeping well?'

'Why do you ask?'

'I see here that you have been late into work occasionally.'

'Two minutes late twice isn't late. Besides, I don't work a nine to five job like some people.'

'Anything at home or at work worrying you?' said the doctor, ignoring Pope's waspish reply.

'Nope.'

'Not drinking excessively then?'

Pope looked at the doctor and thought that *he* was exhibiting the outward signs of excessive drinking. If anyone in the room was 'on the sauce' then it was the doctor. His profession had one of the highest rates of alcoholism.

'Listen, what's this all about?' said Pope, becoming irritated.

'You know it's a random check. I'm just following protocol.'

'No is the answer then.'

'OK, John. The blood test results will be back in a few days and I'll give you a call. See you then,' said Dr Hempel-Smith, once again smiling.

'Sure, doc,' replied Pope, rolling down his sleeve and putting his jacket back on.

Dr Hemel-Smith continued to read the information on his screen after Pope had left the room. Sandra Carruthers' email to HR earlier this morning demanded that Pope was subjected to a random blood test. According to her, Pope was reeking of whisky when he arrived at work, slurring his speech, and he was unkempt in appearance. She alleged that he must have been drinking heavily before he came into the office. Hempel-Smith had not observed any of those traits during Pope's appointment, although there was a mild smell of whisky on his breath. Hempel-Smith then read through Pope's record and it was very impressive. This man had served his country with distinction both in the armed forces and in MI5. If he had succumbed to alcohol then Hempel-Smith would do everything in his power to help him. After all, he also had served Queen and Country and knew that it wasn't easy adjusting to civvy street albeit in MI5.

He drifted back to his army days serving in both Iraq and Afghanistan where he was a psychiatrist dealing with soldiers suffering from Combat Stress Reaction and sitting in on interrogations that were not always carried out under the rules of the Geneva Conventions. The Americans wanted answers at any costs and the British PM gave the green light for unethical behaviours to be performed by interrogators. As he'd raised then, it would be a waste of time because the detainee would give the answers that the interrogators wanted just to stop the torture. He was repulsed by this gratuitous behaviour, and indeed it contributed significantly to his self-diagnosis that he was burnt out.

Working here was an opportunity to help others who may also be burnt out, but was also a way of rebuilding his own shattered mind. His final act before closing Pope's record was to update it with the medical activities carried out and then send an update back to HR. The HR update was succinct and stated that in his medical opinion Pope didn't exhibit any signs that he was under the influence of alcohol, that he was lucid and fit for work duties. This endorsement would ensure that the current access denial was removed from Pope's security pass and, more importantly, that he wasn't suspended from duties with immediate effect.

Pope didn't realise that Carruthers' allegations meant that he was a hair's breadth away from being suspended from work and subject to formal disciplinary procedures. Hempel-Smith wondered what was motivating Carruthers to attack Pope in such a vicious and public way. A fraternity and brotherhood was extended by all to all who'd served on the battlefield. Only they knew the horrors and sacrifices made during those extreme times when it's kill or be killed. Pope was his brother and he would help him in any way that he could.

11:15. Seb Drake knocked on the door and entered the room. Sheila Beavers, who was the PA to Sir Dickie Crampton, looked up from her PC screen and smiled.

'Good morning, Seb, how are you?'

'Well thanks, and how are you?'

'Good thanks. Are you looking for an appointment?'

'I was hoping to catch Sir Dickie for a quick chat.'

'Important?'

'Not super urgent.'

'I see. Well, he's in the middle of reviewing and it's been a difficult morning so far.'

'Right-oh. Maybe I'll pop back later,' replied Seb Drake, taking the hint from Sheila.

Sheila Beavers was staring hard at her PC screen and then looked up. 'How about I ring you about 14:30 ish. I expect that after lunch everything will be fine and Sir Dickie will be interruptible.'

'Sounds good. Thanks, Sheila.'

'My pleasure.'

Drake exited and headed back to his own office. Sir Dickie had a legendary temper if disturbed when in the midst of a troublesome reviewing session. More than one person had barged in and found themselves on the wrong end of a tongue lashing. Drake always welcomed Sheila's guiding hand when attempting to broach the director general for an impromptu meeting. Reviewing/putting could be a frustrating exercise at times.

11:30. Sandra Carruthers knocked on the door and entered the room. Sheila Beavers looked up from her PC screen and smiled.

'Good morning, Sandra,' Sheila said without any warmth.

'Good morning. Can I speak with the DG?' said Carruthers, all businesslike.

'Do you want an appointment then?'

'No, I'd like to crash in now.'

'Well, he's currently reviewing and it's been a difficult morning.'

'If he's reviewing, then perhaps I can grab several minutes of his time.'

Sheila picked up her telephone and pressed one key.

'Sir Dickie, I have Sandra Carruthers here, she would like to speak with you.'

There was a garbled reply that Carruthers couldn't quite make out.

'No, Sir Dickie, she doesn't want to make an appointment.'

There was more garbled noise emitted from the earpiece of Sheila's phone but louder this time, causing her to move the phone away from her ear.

'He'll be right with you. Please take a seat.'

Sheila returned to looking at her PC screen. After two minutes there was an audible buzz on Sheila's phone.

'Sir Dickie is ready now,' Sheila said, activating the door release mechanism.

Carruthers strode purposefully into the DG's splendidly furnished office.

'Ah, Sandra, take a seat. Now, what can I do for you?' said Sir Dickie, barley able to conceal his anger.

Without any preamble, Carruthers launched into her monologue.

'Sir Dickie, I assume you have seen the update to Operation Alastor.'

His dewy eyes pierced her gaze, but he didn't respond.

'There's been changes to my recommendation and I feel that I should have been consulted first.'

Again, Sir Dickie held her gaze without one muscle on his face moving. He took on the appearance of a waxworks dummy.

'Pope no doubt has had a hand in this,' blurted out Carruthers.

'Young lady, the time-honoured process was followed here, the exact same as with every other recommendation sent up the pole. It went to three senior heads who reviewed it. You know who they are because all of them have signed it off. They then sent the final recommendation to me. Based on their seniority and experience, I endorsed their recommendation.'

'My position has been undermined.'

'Young lady, the field experience that the three heads have runs into in excess of seventy-five years. They use that experience along with their intuition to adapt and modify any recommendation as they see fit. I see no reason in this instance to challenge their recommendation. Furthermore, once you send something up the chain, it does not loop back through to subordinates. Pope has had no say in their decision, nor has he had access to the report update prior to my approval.'

'But he...'

'I have told you what happened, now don't challenge me.'

Carruthers didn't believe him but had pushed it as far as she could.

'The changes made aren't exactly off the chart. What exactly are your objections?' said Sir Dickie, trying to be conciliatory.

'There's work still for Team 4 and we don't have cover across all of the other mosques in the Luton area,' blurted out Carruthers.

'My understanding is that the software program for facial recognition and vehicle ID has been written. Only exceptions will be flagged and that isn't an onerous job for Team 4. Probably not even one hour per week. As for full coverage of all mosques, the collective view is that we focus on this one mosque as it is the only one where we have seen anything out of the ordinary.'

'We should be covering all of the mosques,' insisted Carruthers.

'First, the operation has been scaled back at your request. I have my doubts but I'm prepared to go along with it. Second, senior people with immense field experience say that we should keep a presence at this particular mosque.'

'The cost of this operation is burning a hole in my budget...'

'Young lady, my concern is the safety of all of our agents in the field, right after the safety of all of the people living in the UK and all of our visitors. The budget will not compromise those values. I see that you don't have any field experience. Perhaps that's what is clouding your judgement.'

'Sir Dickie, my contribution isn't defined by field work. I have made significant contributions in both the finance department and the HR department and am doing likewise in my current role.'

'Your comments have been noted,' said Sir Dickie in a dismissive fashion.

Carruthers got up from her seat and left the office briskly. Without casting an eye towards Sheila Beavers, she marched out of her office and headed to the lift.

Once the lift arrived, Carruthers entered and muttered, 'Young lady. Young lady. Condescending old codger. That fucking dinosaur's days are numbered. He's heading for extinction, where he belongs.'

14:35. Seb Drake was seated opposite Sir Dickie's seat. Sir Dickie was pacing about the office, agitated with his belly putter swinging from one hand.

'Everything good?' enquired Drake.

'Bloody putting is not in the groove. I have a four-ball at the club tomorrow and don't want to lose to hedge fund managers. More money than sense, that lot. They make Premiership footballers look like tramps and throw their money about willy-nilly. Quite vulgar, really. I'd black ball the lot of them but for the fact that they have donated millions to pay for a new state-of-the-art irrigation system. Tees, Greens and Fairways all have automated sprinklers. The course will soon be Championship standard, so I can't complain.'

'Good luck with the match. I just wanted to catch up regarding Operation Alastor.'

'Go on.'

'It's a difficult one. Yes, the cost of the whole operation is big, but shutting it down does seem extreme. Granted, we haven't seen anything of interest since we went operational but that's all part of the game. We need to be patient. We know that they are learning our tactics and will adapt their own tactics as a result, but dipping in and out changes everything. It becomes more random and therefore less likely that we'll catch the big operations. Everyone with experience feels that this is the right place to put in a chokehold, but we're downscaling because of budget.'

'Right. Carruthers didn't consult anyone on the top floor first. She made a unilateral decision and expects 100% support. She's gone out on a limb and if this backfires then she'll be held fully accountable,' replied Sir Dickie.

'We don't want to create a blame culture though. God, I'm beginning to sound like a fucking consultant.'

'No, we don't. But neither do we want someone without any field experience making decisions that quite frankly they aren't qualified to make,' said Sir Dickie.

'Well, she was given that role and she's entitled to a lot of latitude, which she's using here.'

'Carol Jenkins had an impeccable field record, even the Yanks thought highly of her and yet she was passed over.'

'I remember. It shouldn't have even been a tight call and yet Carruthers managed to get the post. Politics again. HR pushed for a pencil pusher and one of their own. It sent out a message that if you excelled behind a desk *and* you were a woman, then there were career opportunities here. She's their poster girl,' said Sir Dickie through gritted teeth. 'Carruthers had external support also. She's been wining and dining the great and the good for years and lobbied her supporters when the decision was going to be made. She represents the future if we're not careful.'

'What are you suggesting?'

'Well, I've got a little surprise for our Ms Carruthers, but I also need you and the others to have an informal chat with her.

Get her onboard with sharing her thoughts about any future recommendations with the Top Floor. Information is a two-way flow and she needs to also leverage off of all of your experiences. We can't have a disjointed approach, it simply doesn't work.'

'Yes, sir. I'll get right on to it.'

'Good. And one final thing.'

'Sir?'

'Yes, you are beginning to sound like a consultant.'

Both men laughed as Drake sauntered out of the office.

Sir Dickie picked up his phone and pressed one key. The phone was answered immediately. 'Sheila, can you pop in here?'

'Of course.'

Sir Dickie continued to pace around his office, belly putter still swinging gently in one hand. Sheila took up the chair that Drake had just vacated and had a pen and pad in her hand ready to write down everything in short-hand.

'Right, Sheila, take a note to HR. I'm looking for Sandra Carruthers to go on a two-week course. It needs to be a combo. A few days on the Brecon Beacons with a couple of hairy arsed SAS types for a bit of survival training should start this jolly off. Then down to Fort Monckton for tradecraft training and some weapons skills. Make sure she uses live ammo when shooting down range. Blanks are only good for honing accuracy. She needs to feel, smell and hear real guns being fired. Then out with a Walker team for 24/7 surveillance for a couple of days. Pad it out and send it off.'

'Sir Dickie, what is the reason for this training? I need to complete a Purpose of Training box.'

'Oh. Management development or similar bollocks. Looking to hone the skills and add another few strings to the bow etc, etc. You know better than me how to fill in the paperwork.'

'OK. And when will this course start?'

'No point hanging around, Saturday will be fine.'

'One final question. Will the SAS be required to perform extreme interrogation techniques on her?'

Sir Dickie smiled at the images conjured up of Carruthers wearing her haute couture clobber, blindfolded, wearing ear defenders with screaming white noise drowning her ears, covered in her own piss and shit, sitting in a shed up in the Beacons.

'No. I think that she'll have enough to contend with.'

Five minutes later a high priority message entered the inbox of HR.

15:15. Carruthers opened up the email sent from HR. Her instant reaction was to storm up to the Top Floor. She gathered her thoughts and then contacted someone she knew well in HR to see if there was any way that she could wheedle out of this course. She mentioned that they were in the middle of a delicate operation and that she really needed to be around, but it didn't wash. The course had been approved, dates set and training instructors' time approved. She was told that this was an opportunity to prove herself and she should seize it with both hands. She muttered something that the other person couldn't hear, but the only thing that she wanted to seize with both hands was the windpipe of that decrepit dinosaur, and maybe the neck of the bitch who worked for him also.

It hadn't been a great day so far. Carruthers had seen the update given by the medical officer and he had given Pope a clean bill of health. Her hopes now rested on the blood test results. She was adamant that he was reeking of whisky this morning. OK, maybe she had embellished it somewhat when she added that his speech was slurred and that he was dishevelled, but that was just garnish. She went into her private online diary and looked at her evening appointments for the rest of the week. She then went about cancelling all of them by sending out bland emails. She was going to go to the gym every evening now as preparation for this two-week bullshit course. In addition, she booked two sessions on the gun range. Guns and exercise, two things that she really hated. This was going to be a tedious week. Her final act was to cancel all of her meetings in her calendar for the next two weeks and block it out. That way no one could book any meetings with her until she returned to work.

09:15. Pope and Chris Gould were walking into The Mall shopping centre in Luton.

'It's a good idea to have this face to face,' said Chris.

'Yes, it's important that the guys hear the message, say their piece and then we all move on,' replied Pope.

The Mall was fairly empty but there were some shoppers milling about. Already inside The Mall and scanning around was Mr Butt. For a change of routine, today he'd decided to walk a different route that included a circuit of all of the floors of The Mall. He wasn't a fan of these concrete towers that lacked the friendliness of locally owned shops. For him, popping into a shop and having a natter with the shop owner was always useful as he gleaned much information, but in these homogenised shops manned by young people, that wasn't possible.

Chris studied the floor plan and then said to Pope, 'Follow me.'

They entered Costa Coffee and queued up for two flat whites before settling into a corner table. Not five minutes had passed before Ahmed had joined them, holding a croissant and double espresso.

'Morning,' said Ahmed, sitting next to Pope, placing both the food and drink on the table in front of himself.

'Morning, Ahmed,' came back the reply in unison.

Idle chitchat commenced for a couple of minutes before Deepak plonked himself down next to Chris Gould. He was also carrying a double espresso. Field agents naturally gravitated towards caffeine, and the stronger the better. Staying awake was their top priority and caffeine was their preferred prop.

Chris couldn't stop himself, 'Hey, Deepak, what's with the haircut? A change of image, I see.'

Deepak ran his hand through the fuzz on his head, 'Yeah, do you like it?'

'Brutal,' came back Chris's jolly reply.

Like Chris and Ahmed, Deepak took out his laptop and opened it up on the table and went through the remote logon access sequence. Pope didn't bother to logon to his laptop but had his phone logged on to to work applications and it was also sitting on the table. Anyone looking over to their table would assume that a group of travelling salesmen were having a catchup whilst on the road.

'Guys, thanks for coming,' started off Pope. 'It's important that you hear for yourselves what the next steps for Operation Alastor are and why.'

Both Ahmed and Deepak were looking at Operation Alastor on their screens and everything looked normal. There were updates flowing into the designated components by the relevant operators.

'A decision has been made to downgrade the operation.'

Both Ahmed and Deepak looked up from their screens and exchanged glances. Neither of them had had any idea that this was coming. Neither said anything but were clearly shocked from hearing Pope's opening salvo.

'As and from today, the operation will be dismantled. Team 4 will be stood down, GCHQ will cease electronic surveillance of the two targets and the Walker teams will be pulled. What will remain is the surveillance of the Luton mosque. Both of you will continue with that facet of the operation as will the CCTV surveillance of the street and car park. But the knock-on effect is that there won't be any other units surveilling other Luton mosques as everyone else is being reassigned back to their own teams. Whilst the op officially closes today, anything that is unresolved will continue. This relates to Team 4 in particular; they will run with anything on their books and in all likelihood they will be out in ten days roughly.'

Pope deliberately paused for several seconds in order that this information could be absorbed by both Ahmed and Deepak. 'Guys, we really appreciate all of the effort that both of you have put in so far. Your dedication has been noted, I can assure you. But we need both of you to carry on as this is still our primary target.'

'If that's true, then why is the op being run down?' spat out Ahmed.

'The decision was made to release resources for deployment elsewhere. These are always tough decisions but that's part of the bigger picture,' said Pope diplomatically.

'Sounds like budget rules,' replied Ahmed.

'Listen, we haven't shut it down but without anything at all since we've resourced up, it was always going to be a question of how long we can keep manned up here.'

'So what about us then? What do you want us to do?' said Deepak timidly.

'Well, the ten-hour back-to-back shifts can't continue. I guess you guys are cream crackered. Let's go with covering all of the prayers excluding sunrise. So, first shift gets in at 07:00 until 15:00 then second shift 15:00 until 11:00. You decide between yourselves how you want to play it. Personally, I'd go with one week early then one week late but that's your choice. Also, you both need to take off one day a week and that's again your choice,' continued Pope.

'Who will be monitoring the updates if Team 4 are pulled off?' asked Deepak.

'Chris will be on that end of things. But if it blows up, then call Chris, Clare and me. Don't rely on Chris monitoring the operation real time because that won't be happening. Chris will be multitasking and will probably check for updates two to three times a day.'

Chris, who had sat there motionless, nodded stoically.

'Just a couple of more points and we're finished. First, Deepak, you are lodging further away. Do you want us to find you a place nearer now that this is going to be a long-term gig?'

'How about I doss in with Ahmed?' quizzed Deepak.

'That's not normal protocol. But under the circumstances I'm happy to authorise that, if Ahmed agrees of course,' said Pope, hoping that this compromise would boost morale.

'OK with me,' said Ahmed nonchalantly.

'Done. But this isn't official and don't ask again in the future. Are we clear?'

Both Ahmed and Deepak nodded somewhat sheepishly.

'In the circumstances, do you need any assistance moving?'

'Nah, we can handle that. We'll sort it out in the next day or so,' piped up Ahmed.

'Right-oh then. Deepak, keep the keys and don't sublet the gaff,' said Pope in a jocular fashion.

'I wouldn't have ever thought of doing that,' said a wide-eyed Deepak, sounding like butter wouldn't melt in his mouth.

'Last point. As both of you have been at it now for several weeks, take a three-day furlough starting from tomorrow. You have both earned it, and thanks for your efforts so far. I can tell you that a good number of senior people think that the Luton mosque will herald something and we are backing you guys to bring it.'

Both Ahmed and Deepak smiled. The rah-rah speech had the desired effect and they were both reenergised, refocused and ready to continue with their mission.

At that moment, Mr Butt was waddling past Costa Coffee shop and gazed into the window, mildly admiring his reflection. He slowed down to a stop and stared intensively at the group of men seated at the far corner table. His eyes focused, and he recognised both Ahmed and the skinhead Deepak. With them he also noticed two white middle-class men, and one of them was podgy. He deliberated for a short while and decided not to intervene. He'd catch up with the very respectful Ahmed later as he was easy to chat with. The other one came across as modest and friendly, but being a convert with a skinhead haircut meant that he couldn't really be trusted in the eyes of Mr Butt. In other words, 'Always judge a book by its cover.'

Pope waited until Chris had packed away his laptop, then stood up.

'Right then, we're off. We're going to speak to both of the Walker teams and explain the situation, then it's back to London and we'll inform Team 4. If you check Operation Alastor early evening, then everything will be up to date.'

Pope shook both Deepak and Ahmed's hands, as did Chris before they headed off for their next rendezvous.

'Bro, quick fucking thinking there regarding our housing arrangements,' whispered Ahmed.

'Thanks.'

'Carruthers and her singing and dancing spreadsheets are behind this, I'm telling you, bro. This op has been sunk by the bean counters, I'm telling you,' ranted Ahmed.

'Not quite, we're still in play.'

'On our fucking own, bruv.'

'Don't forget Chris is still with us,' said Deepak innocently.

'Yeah, that fucking helps. I bet he gives John Pope the slip now and has two fuck off builder breakfasts. I swear he's getting fatter. I watched you sitting next to him and it was like watching Gulliver sitting next to a Lilliputian.'

'Come on now. Anyway, we have three days off, what do you plan to do?'

'Nothing. Go to a gym and carry on with my online course.'

'Really? I'm going home.'

'Fuck it. Let's just call it a day right now. Why don't you piss off and I can reclaim my pad. I could do with some peace and quiet.'

'You are a bad influence but I'll take your advice this time.'

They both packed away their laptops and headed out of The Mall. A few minutes ahead of them, Chris and Pope had walked past a young man with a baseball cap perched low over his head. They didn't recognise him and he didn't recognise them. He was heading towards an internet cafe in the middle of Luton to continue with his daily dose of indoctrination. The young man passed by The Mall as both Ahmed and Deepak were exiting and literally brushed shoulders with them. Again, neither party took notice of the other one. They were all lawfully going about their business on the streets of an English town. The young man busied himself down the street and overtook an overweight man who was ambling along, just out for a morning stroll. Mr Butt looked at the young man's profile but it wasn't a face that he recognised from either his mosque or his immediate circle of acquaintances, and he didn't attempt to converse with him.

Literally in the space of several minutes, several parties who were inextricably intertwined had passed by each other and most had not recognised each other, nor their conflicting agendas.

19:15. Pope was seated at his place in the kitchen and had just finished his evening meal. It had been a long and taxing day. Standing down an operation was draining emotionally. Agents who worked both in the field and in the office worked extraordinarily long hours and it was tedious sitting there waiting for something to happen or sifting through mountains of data looking for clues or trying to link data to other data or to targets' movements and behaviours. He had spent the day selling something that he knew many didn't agree with, but for the sake of morale and harmony, he towed the party line. As aggrieved as many were, inside he was incandescent.

The females had been upstairs for nearly an hour. This evening was a big event in the Pope social calendar. It was the first school disco that Charlie was going to attend. The school had a policy that school discos weren't something to entertain but at the insistence of the Parent Governors Committee, they put on an annual disco for pupils studying A levels and also for those sitting GCSEs. There were multiple feet heading down the staircase and then the kitchen door opened and in walked Charlie followed by Jane. Pope looked up and immediately noticed the transformation in Charlie. She was wearing a short, and in his opinion, provocative, dress, and her straight shiny hair had now been curled and set. But what struck him most was the difference made by Charlie wearing makeup. She had rouge gloss lipstick, light eye shadow and eye liner with a thick layer of eye mascara. His little girl was growing up fast and he hadn't even noticed it.

'Who hit you then?' said Pope jokingly.

Charlie's face changed from a smile to a scowl and then she stormed out of the room. Jane threw him a stern stare and retreated after Charlie, who was heading upstairs rapidly. Pope sat there glumly. What a bastard day this had been so far. He knew better than to get involved. Jane would have to fix this, and all because his joke was taken out of context. He wondered what it would have been like if he had had two boys rather than two girls. Playing football, sharing a pint, ogling young women when out driving. In all probability they would have caused problems. Granted, there would be different problems, but problems nonetheless. Nah, he'd stick with the Swans, although he expected to be in the doghouse over this faux pas.

A further ten minutes passed and he could hear raised voices and a burst of screaming from upstairs. There was a brief silence and then he heard sets of feet hurriedly descending the stairs followed by the front door being opened. Pope crept out of the kitchen and was confronted by Daisy who was scuttling after the other two. Daisy was dressed in her dressing gown, pyjamas, bobble hat and gloves offset by short blue wellington boots. She stopped, put her arms on her hips and stared at him before haughtily walking out of the front door. She hadn't mastered the act of closing the front door yet and he walked towards it. Sitting on the mat staring out of the front door was Doddle.

From the distance, Daisy squealed, 'Doooodle.'

Doodle reacted immediately and after a small glance towards Pope, he took off like a sprinter coming out of blocks in the Olympic final of the 100-metre sprint.

'Fucking traitor,' shouted Pope.

Pope made a brave decision and walked out of the house and was standing in the porch.

'Bye,' he said, waving at the car.

In the car, the three female heads remained facing forward, not acknowledging his gesture. He could see in the gloom the silhouettes of all of them, heads facing forwards gently swaying on their slender necks. He sensed that it was a frosty atmosphere in the car as it pulled off. There was one exception who had his nose desperately sniffing out of the small gap at the top of the window. Front paws resting on the inside of the car window to assist his balance with his tail wagging wildly was Judas Iscariot. Pope went back inside and closed the front door.

Pope was sitting in the front room watching the TV when Jane returned. Jane poured herself and Pope a drink and sat down next to him. A few minutes passed before the silence was broken.

'Do you want me to go and pick up Charlie?'

'No. Charlotte's mum is picking up a few of them and she is going to drop Charlie off.'

'Is she upset?'

'John, what do you think? And don't say that it was just a joke.'

'Christ, is everyone sensitive. Come on, there was nothing in what I said.'

'Why not just say, "You look nice." She's growing up, you know.'

'Yes, I know. But her skirt is very short.'

'John, we agreed that we wanted our girls to grow up normal. All of the girls are wearing short skirts, it's part of the fashion. She needs to be part of the group, not dressed up like your mum.'

'Well any shorter and she'll catch a cold.'

'Still cracking the jokes.'

Pope finished his drink in silence and then decided to take Doodle out for a longer walk. Doodle didn't do family politics or take sides and so off they went.

09:30. Ahmed was strolling along the High Street just getting some much-needed exercise when he stopped abruptly.

'Ahmed, good morning, and how are you?' said an out-of-breath Mr Butt having jogged inelegantly across the road and stopping the traffic in the process.

'Good. And how are you?'

'Still here,' came back the reply. 'Still nothing from young Rahan Iqbal.'

'Really? I'm sure that he'll turn up when he's ready.'

'His family are worried. They get replies to text messages but his messages are curt.'

'Well, at least he's replying. Some kids don't even do that.'

'I suppose you are right.'

'Well, I must be off...'

'Ah, just one thing,' said Mr Butt, holding out both of his arms.

'Sure.'

'I was passing Costa Coffee in The Mall yesterday and I saw you in there.'

'Yes.'

'Well, I thought that I knew the two men you were with but I couldn't remember their names.'

Crafty old bastard. He could be a spook the way he noses about, thought Ahmed.

'Oh yes, those two, right,' said Ahmed, trying to buy some time in order that he could concoct a decent cover story.

'Myself and Deepak met with our university lecturers for a face to face.'

Mr Butt smiled and was interested in worming out the details from Ahmed. Ahmed on the other hand was getting into full flow and continued.

'Occasionally lecturers meet up with online students and it's an opportunity to not only ask them questions but also for them to see how we are progressing. I think that it works really well and they really know their stuff.'

'Very good. Studying is so important nowadays as getting a job without qualifications is difficult. I know that I shouldn't say this but with all of those bloody foreigners coming over from Europe soon there won't jobs for anyone.'

'Yeah, like we aren't foreigners.'

'No, we come from the Commonwealth and respect the Queen.'

Ahmed was about to explode into a series of profanities, but that would both alienate his best source at the mosque and blow his cover.

'Well, I hope that I'll get a job in IT once I get my degree.'

'Yes, a polite young man like yourself deserves that opportunity. As for your friend being a teacher, I don't know if he's cut out for it. What with being a skinhead and a convert,' mused Mr Butt aloud.

'Thanks. I think Deepak cut his hair because he has some form of scalp disease.'

'Oh, is it communicable?'

'No, but it's very itchy. That's why he's always rubbing his head,' said Ahmed, trying not to laugh.

'Right, well I must be off,' blurted out Mr Butt as he had extracted as much information as he wanted. Well, enough to share with his cronies anyway.

'Good bye,' smiled Ahmed whilst thinking to himself, *What a Pakistani fucking racist.*

Ahmed pulled out his phone and sent Deepak a quick email detailing everything discussed with Mr Butt and emphasising that he looked like a skinhead. He also thought that he was lucky that Mr Butt knew nothing about online uni courses because if he did then he'd have queried Ahmed's load of twaddle.

Ahmed walked into his favourite cafe and ordered tea and toast and seated himself by the window. He spent a relaxing twenty minutes going through a couple of tabloid papers that had been left on the various tables that morning. On the way back to his flat he decided to call his mum.

'Hi Mum, it's Ahmed.'

'Ahmed, how are you, my son?'

'Very well, and how are you?'

'Tired,' came the reply.

'And the family?'

'Your brothers and sisters are all well.'

'And Dad?'

'He's already gone to work.'

Ahmed knew that his dad would have already left and that was why he chose to call at this particular time.

'When are you coming to visit then?' enquired his mum.

'It's difficult, Mum. I'm very busy at the moment working on a project with a tight deadline and there's no chance of getting home.'

'Well, Ahmed, you need to make time. Family is important and life's not all about work.'

'Sure.'

'Your brothers and sisters miss you.'

'I know. Mum, I'll call you soon. Bye.' said Ahmed, wanting to close this circular conversation that he always had with his mum.

'Bye, Ahmed.'

Ahmed carried on walking. The call calmed Ahmed and frustrated him in equal measures. He was pleased that his brothers and sisters were all well, although he did know that, as he texted all of them on a regular basis and had banter with them. His mum had been suffering from health problems in recent years and was taking a number of prescription tablets on a daily basis. She wasn't someone who shared her personal health problems with anyone and refused to discuss the details of her health issues with anyone in the family. She would only say that she was feeling tired. She also didn't want other members in her extended family or in the local community to know her personal problems. She thought and often said that there were too many gossips around and she wasn't going to feed their insatiable quest for family information.

Ahmed had a difficult relationship with his dad. His dad was born in Pakistan and came over to England as a young child. He had lived all of his life in East London and had been brought up as a Muslim. He married a girl with a similar background and tried to embrace the English culture at work, which was offset by being strict at home with many rules that he forced on both his wife and all of his children. After a number of jobs, he finally settled for a clerical role in his local council and had served there for twenty-odd years. He was planning to see out the rest of his working life there. A relatively easy job followed by the council pension was the combined sum of routine and ambition that he aspired to.

Ahmed clashed with him from a young age, always questioning his rules and dictatorial style. His father used the belt on him several times but it only served to make Ahmed more angry. Once Ahmed was a teenager, their conversations were carried out via his mum as their relationship had deteriorated. In a way, it paved the way for his younger siblings to have a slightly less strict upbringing, but there were still far too many rules. Ahmed wanted to enjoy the opportunities of living in a multicultural society and had friends at school and uni from every ethnic background, and he mixed with equals who, like him, were interested in technology and football. He was an Arsenal supporter and went along to as many games as he could, and after the game he always stayed and had a few beers, discussing either a great victory where they played the opposition off of the park or a defeat where the cheating bastard ref had robbed them. His dad neither approved of football nor drinking and that fuelled even more rows. Going to uni was a win win situation. Ahmed was calmer but his personality had been moulded through his confrontational relationship with his dad. The family also benefited from the reduction in rows and confrontations whilst Ahmed was away. He had decided that he wouldn't be going home after uni and that he'd find a job in IT somewhere.

Post 9/11, the recruitment drive to recruit ethnic minorities began slowly within MI5 and MI6. Agencies didn't see that the landscape for several generations had already changed and that they were going to have to recruit ethnic groups, and in particular Muslims, in large numbers if they were going to combat both the threat at home and abroad. Infiltrating middle-class white Oxbridge graduates into UK Muslim communities and abroad wasn't going to work. George Smiley and hunting

Reds under the bed was all but dead. The thing was that the UK had many ethnic communities and was a very fertile hunting ground for procuring the next generation of spies. It just required a change of policy backed by belief in the ability and allegiance of this next generation.

Ahmed Hussain was ripe for recruiting and when he was approached at Nottingham University, he literally jumped at the opportunity. At last he would be integrated into the society and would be fulfilling a role of both purpose and responsibility. He would dedicate his ability, skills and life to serving the greater good. He didn't know it but when he joined and became a field agent, his performance was scrutinised even more than a normal recruit. He was a pioneer and his performance gave confidence to the Service that the new recruitment policy would reap rewards. It was just a case of getting the selection process correct and weeding out the ineffective, subversive or incompatible candidates. In the brainstorming sessions, the policy makers even thought that the first batch of ethnic recruits post-9/11 would eventually become the future selectors and interviewers of future recruits. They would make up the frontline in the selection process and would also become the trainers of the newbies passing on their experiences and rewriting the training manuals. Heavy expectations hung on the shoulders of Ahmed and his class, but for now it was time to go for a run, watch a few DVDs and then eat some more of Deepak's great grub.

11:00. Pope descended to level -5 and walked the short distance to a set of doors that were locked and blocked further access along the corridor. He placed his security pass against the card reader and waited for a beep and a green light to confirm that stage one had been completed. He then placed his right-hand index finger into the biometric reader. The scanner checked his fingerprint against the internal record, and stage two was completed successfully. The several door locks disengaged and Pope walked into the room. The door swiftly reengaged all of the locking mechanisms and the door was secure again. Pope walked up to the desk where a man was seated.

'Good morning, Jenkins,' said Pope with warmth.

'Good morning, sir,' came the cockney reply.

'Just want some time on the range,' went on Pope.

'Of course, sir. What weapon are you wanting to fire today?' asked Jenkins.

'Any small arms and live ammo,' said Pope flatly.

Jenkins looked at his screen and typed in a number of keys. Once the information was displayed, he repeated the action three more times and on each occasion further information was presented back to him.

'Sir, you have already used up your monthly allocation of both time on the range and live ammo quota, but I see that you haven't used up your allocation of dummy ammo. Under the circumstances, I think that I can supply you with a box of dummy rounds for a Browning High-Power handgun.'

'Perfect.'

Jenkins typed into the screen and printed off a form which he handed over to Pope. He turned around on his chair and wheeled it along the cabinets until he reached the right one and punched in the code to unlock it. He retrieved the Browning High-Power which was the favoured handgun of the SAS and then relocked the cabinet. He wheeled himself further along the wall full of cabinets and unlocked another cabinet, withdrawing a box of ammo. After locking the cabinet he scuttled back to his place without ever leaving the chair and handed both the gun and the ammo over to Pope. Whilst Jenkins was away from his station, Pope had signed and dated the form which was now facing Jenkins.

'Lane six,' said Jenkins, putting the form into a folder and buzzing the door behind him open.

Pope walked through and was now in the shooting range. He went to the cabinet and took from it a pair of ear defenders, a pair of safety glasses and four targets before heading off to lane six. In the shooting stall, he fixed his target and sent it down range. He then put on the safety glasses over his own glasses and put on the ear defenders. Finally he loaded the gun with thirteen bullets. Fully loaded, the semi-automatic weapon could kill a man up to fifty metres away, had a small recoil and weighed 1kg fully loaded. Pope put the gun into the inside pocket of his jacket and composed himself. He drew the gun from his pocket, aimed and unloaded the complement of bullets in the magazine. After he had fired thirteen times, he checked his magazine and weapon to ensure that it was fully empty and set the safety. He used the target retrieval mechanism to retrieve the target and studied the grouping of the bullets. This was necessary in order that he made any needed adjustments to his firing technique before he fired off his next full magazine. Pope went through the same routine another three times. The only change to the routine was that he placed the gun in a different pocket and chose a slightly different firing stance.

He practised for being ready to combat any eventuality. He wasn't a gun enthusiast who took a standard firing stance and breathed rhythmically between each shot. His life, lives of comrades and lives of Joe Public may well rest on Pope's ability to fire under adverse circumstances and this was what he practised for.

He collected all four targets and would study them at great length later. He would go over in meticulous detail every shot and what firing position he took, along with which pocket the gun was actually retrieved from. He would write up in detail everything and study the results against previous results. That data along with what he wanted to practise next time would actually assist him in how he would structure his next shooting exercise at the gun range.

There was one issue with his approach. Due to cuts, operators were only allowed a certain amount of time and ammo per month on the gun range and this was significantly less than marksmen needed to hone and craft their skills. Pope was lucky because Jenkins managed to assist with allocating both extra time and extra ammo. Today, Pope had been booked in under the name of an employee who rarely used the gun range. In fact, the head of catering wasn't known to ever fire any weapons, but he did make a mean pavlova. Jenkins was very creative with how he managed the gun range and several regulars benefitted from his management style. Pope signed the form earlier with an illegible signature as part of this charade. Many operatives also belonged to private gun clubs in the

Metropolis and there they were able to fire a variety of guns and rifles along with ammo up to and including armoured piercing bullets. This was at their own cost which some begrudged. Pope was happy to use the company range as this allowed him to keep familiar with the weapons and ammo that he would use in the field. He promised himself that if his marksmanship ever dipped, he would join a club and put in extra practice. But at the moment and with Jenkins' assistance, he was maintaining the standard that he had set himself.

Jenkins was also the custodian of Pope's pride and joy. It was a Russian-owned gun that had been heavily modified and had been 'liberated' from a quarry in Afghanistan many years before, and it had phenomenal accuracy over a great distance. Long-range shooting was the property of rifles and this gun had quite unique traits.

Pope exited the range and returned the gun to Jenkins, who checked the weapon for any bullets in the chamber or magazine and also checked that the safety was on.

'Everything OK with the gun, sir?'

'Trigger is a bit sticky.'

'Right. I'll see to that immediately.'

'Thanks, Jenkins.'

'Have a good day and see you soon.'

Jenkins was a sergeant in the Paras, serving fifteen years before he joined civvy street. He was a chatty, affable man who believed in discipline and the values of good, hard, honest work. All of the weapons in his armoury were stripped down, cleaned and oiled regularly. If the weapons were reported to be firing incorrectly or inaccurately, he'd check them himself and if necessary retool them. Very rarely was a weapon sent back to the manufacturer as Jenkins managed to fix most faults reported in-house. He was a craftsman who had learnt his trade whilst being in the field and out there, there wasn't DHL around to post off for spare parts. People who used the gun range or booked out weapons for field activities respected Jenkins, and in return he served one and all with equipment maintained to the highest of standards.

11:00. Pope, Chris Gould and Clare Hawkins were seated in their customary seats in the corner office. Humans are by nature creatures of habit and without either thinking or being told will tend to sit in the same seat if they for whatever reason regularly end up in the same room.

'What's happening then, Chris?' asked Pope.

'Well, Team 4 are still following up on a few leads. I've spoken with them just now and they reckon that everything will be completed by the middle of next week. The tracker has been removed from Target One's car and the Walkers teams have dismantled everything and are back in the fold. GCHQ have confirmed that the specific eavesdropping of the two targets is now shut down. The CCTV street camera is still on, our guys are on R & R and their house moving is complete.'

'What house moving?' piped up Clare.

Chris shoots Pope a glance.

'I asked Deepak to move in with Ahmed,' said Pope impassively.

'Oh, isn't that against protocol?' rebuffed Clare.

'I weighed up several factors and thought that the move made sense. They are both working in the mosque and can figure things out on the hoof if they are able to chat away from the site.'

Hhhmm,' breathed Clare.

'I trust the guys, and it's delegated responsibility. They need to be empowered. And besides, Chris will pop up there regularly and keep an eye on them.'

'Is that something that I can consider for my ops then?' enquired Clare.

'Clare, this particular op has demanded some thinking outside of our normal operating parameters. Everything else both now and in future will continue to operate under standard parameters,' replied Pope.

'Sure.'

'Anything else?' asked Pope, hoping to bring this meeting to a close.

'Yes,' said Chris. 'What's Sandra up to?'

'No idea. What specifically are you referring to?' said Pope.

Silently he was hoping that he wasn't about to go through again why she insisted on shutting the op down, or at least downscaling it to a minimum.

'Well, she's out of the office for a couple of weeks and no one knows what's going on. Her PA creeps around and won't even answer other than to say just check her calendar for when she's in the office and book all future meetings for when she's back.'

'I'm not aware of why she's not going to be in. An email was sent out to all section heads this morning from HR saying that she will be out from close of business today for two weeks and that she's not contactable. In her absence we go straight to the Top Floor,' replied Pope.

'Isn't that unusual?' went on Chris, digging gently.

'Look, you now know as much as I do,' said Pope, looking straight at Chris.

'OK.'

16:00. Carruthers left her office and marched towards the lift. Standing patiently waiting for a lift was Pope. He looked at her as she positioned herself next to him and he smiled insincerely. She returned the smile with a curt nod and just at that moment the lift arrived and the doors opened. They both walked into the empty lift and Pope positioned himself in front of the control panel.

'Which floor, Sandra?' he asked.

'Ground, please.'

Pope hit the ground floor button and the level -three button.

Carruthers had her coat on and was carrying three bags, and one of those included her laptop. She had evidently packed up for the day and wouldn't be coming back. No words were spoken in the lift and they both stared at the control button panel as it displayed what floor the lift was currently on. The lift halted at the ground floor and Carruthers swept past Pope.

'Have a nice weekend,' said Pope.

'And you.'

The doors closed and the lift continued on its journey. Pope speculated on where Carruthers was going to be over the next two weeks and came to the conclusion that she was probably going to be off having a medical procedure and that was why she hadn't divulged any information. If he was a betting man, he'd go for a plumbing job.

No further people entered the lift and Pope exited at the level -three floor. He went straight into the reception room and, without looking at the glum people occupying the front row seats, headed to the nurse's desk and presented his security pass before the Filipino nurse even asked for it. He remembered her brusque manner from his recent visit. With his card checked and returned, he headed off to Dr Hemel-Smith's room. Knocking on the door, he then entered.

Hempel-Smith stood, smiled and offered his hand. Pope accepted the clammy handshake and smiled back at the pleasantly mannered man.

'John, please take a seat. I'll just call up your records,' went on the good doctor as he scrolled down through several screens of information. 'The blood test results for drugs or alcohol are negative.'

'No surprise.'

'Good. But your cholesterol is slightly higher than it should be and you have elevated blood pressure.'

'I see.'

'It's common, especially with your work and the modern lifestyle. I would recommend perhaps a bit more exercise, moderate your alcohol intake and eat more fibre and fruit.'

'I thought that you'd ask how much I drink per week.'

'No point. No one ever tells the truth.'

Pope laughed. He was a good judge of people and Hempel-Smith was a decent bloke.

'I see that you wear glasses. When was your last eye test?'

Pope thought for several seconds and then answered, 'Probably a couple of years ago.'

'I'll arrange for an eye test and we'll meet again.'

'Is that it?'

'Yes. I'll put in the diary an appointment for six months and we'll check your blood pressure and do another blood test just to check how your cholesterol level is.'

'No drugs and alcohol then.'

'No. That was at the behest of HR and as I said, you have passed that. I'll see you after your eye test next week. Have a very pleasant weekend.'

'Thanks, and you also enjoy your weekend, Doc.'

After Pope left, Dr Hempel-Smith updated his medical records and sent back a bland reply to HR stating that Pope's blood testing had returned a negative result. The information regarding Pope's blood pressure, cholesterol and pending eye test were all omitted as it was subject to patient confidentiality and not for their preying eyes.

Fifteen minutes later, Carruthers heard the familiar ping of an incoming email. She quickly accessed her inbox and read the email from HR and cursed under her breath – Pope had passed his bloods.

She was seated in her favoured hairdresser in an exclusive salon in Mayfair and explained that she wanted a cut, wash and some more colouring. The colouring was now an integral feature to her regular visits to this particular salon as, despite the colouring, grey hairs were becoming an ever-increasing invasion. The whole process took just over an hour and two cups of coffee. Once completed, Carruthers inspected the results in the mirror and the hand mirror held by the stylist and smiled at her. Including tip, the job cost £95.00 and she actually looked exactly the same as when she had entered the salon, mostly because she had gone through this procedure not three weeks ago.

Carruthers went downstairs into the area reserved for other services offered by this salon. Here she had her hands, feet and nails all polished, painted and cared for. This activity took a further forty-five minutes and another cup of coffee. And all for the price including a tip of £55.00. Carruthers went back home feeling relaxed. The pampering exercise was worth every penny and she felt a lot better not only about herself but also about this management training exercise that she was going to be going on tomorrow.

The evening was spent packing and repacking for the next two weeks. She knew from the agenda what was going to happen and it was important that she presented an image of a powerful, well-groomed modern female executive. She laid out open on her bed three cases of various sizes from her Louis Vuitton set and hoped that she would be able to squeeze into these behemoths all of the designer clothes, lingerie, high-heeled shoes, makeup products, hair dryer and bath lotions for a two-week sojourn. Once everything had been finally packed after two hours of serious effort, she then added her lurid pink Lycra gym kit, fire engine red cross trainers and bright yellow running trainers for the exercise sessions.

By now, Carruthers was feeling much more positive about the whole thing. A couple of weeks out of the office would give her a chance to recharge her batteries and get in a bit of exercise. Not too much though as, in her opinion, exercise accelerated the ageing process and that was something that she was constantly battling against. She was always first in the queue to buy the latest anti-ageing product on the market endorsed by someone with genetics that meant they looked amazing without this snake oil. She was still very wide awake and alert as she applied the various lotions and potions prior to retiring and knew that she wouldn't drop off for some time and sat up in bed looking as if she was wearing a death mask. A regular stream of coffees during the day followed by a further three cups during her pampering session meant that both her body and mind were on full alert, and she started reading her latest pulp novel.

Carruthers arrived at Victoria Barracks at 08:50 via a black taxi and was dropped off outside with her designer luggage. This barracks was the home of the Coldstream Guards and they performed the ceremonial duties at both Buckingham Palace and Windsor Castle. They also had an operational role as a light infantry division and had a long-standing connection with the Parachute Regiment. Leaving her luggage on the pavement, she walked up to the guard room and presented her MI5 ID card to the soldier who was standing outside the guard box.

'Good morning. I'm expecting to be met here,' said Carruthers confidently.

'Good morning, ma'am. Please wait here and I'll check for you,' said the tall young soldier dressed in camouflaged fatigues with his L85A2 rifle slung across his chest.

He went back into his box and checked through a list on a clipboard. He then picked up the telephone and had a short conversation before replacing the receiver. He then chatted to his colleague who was seated at the desk in the box and then made notes against one of the items on his list. A couple of minutes later a slightly battered blue Ford Transit twelve-seater minibus arrived from inside the barracks and stopped at the barrier. The driver wound down his window and passed over a chit to the soldier who had now exited the box. After inspecting the chit, the soldier nodded to his mate who then activated the lift sequence to lift up the barrier. The van drove out and stopped next to Carruthers.

'Miss Brown. I'm your lift,' said the man getting out.

He was wearing jeans, trainers and sweatshirt and had medium-length dark brown hair. He slid back the passenger door behind him and waited whilst Carruthers picked up her luggage.

'Sling that in there,' he said, not offering to carry any of her luggage.

She placed her bags on the seats and patted them back into them to make sure that they were secure on them. He then slammed the door shut, causing the luggage to shift in their seats.

'Right. You can sit upfront with me,' he said, looking at the well-dressed lady whose hair and makeup was all firmly cemented in place.

She tottered around in her high heels to the passenger door and bordered as elegantly as she could. It was a high step up into the cabin and probably best not attempted in a tight-fitting designer two-piece suit and heels. Once seated, she adjusted her clothes and gently touched her hair in several different places, just checking that everything was still in place.

'OK. Belt up and we're off,' came the instruction from the driver as he put the minibus into gear and nosed out into the Saturday morning traffic.

Carruthers obeyed the instruction and secured her seat belt. There was an uncomfortable silence for a few minutes before Carruthers broke it.

'How long is the journey?' asked Carruthers.

She was hoping to extract some information from the driver as, whilst she had received an agenda, it was very sketchy. She only knew that she would be doing a field exercise for three days that focused on teamwork. This was going to be the start of the two-week course.

'Not too long,' came back the reply as his left hand reached down and put on the radio.

Bloody great, she thought. *Radio Two now for however long this takes with a monosyllabic moron for company. I bet he won't change over to classical music. Probably never heard of it.*

The journey took three hours twenty-five minutes without stopping for a break. The minibus pulled up in a gravel car park where there were three men chatting. At their feet were two large rucksacks and two of the men were dressed in battle fatigues with army boots and beanie hats on. The other man was scruffily dressed; in fact, he looked very similar to the driver and all three of them were smoking. They barely looked up as the minibus swung around and pointed out towards the way that it had just entered the car park. It finally came to a stop next to the men. There were no other cars in the car park. The only other item was a brick-built small toilet. The driver of the minibus didn't attempt to get out, and he nodded towards the three men. Carruthers undid her seat belt and stepped ungainly out into the cold wind.

The man dressed in civilian clothing looked directly into her eyes and said, 'Major Smith. Can I see your ID please?'

Carruthers fumbled in her inside pocket and withdrew a laminated card which she passed over to him. Major Smith gave the card a cursory glance before returning the card,

'Good. Everything is in order, Miss Brown. Everything that you need for the next three days will be provided. Your clothes are put out in the cubicle,' went on Major Smith, pointing at the brick toilet. 'Please change in there. You can keep on your underwear.'

Carruthers looked at him and was about to say something when she decided to hold her tongue. She went into the foul-smelling room and noticed straight away that the lock had been vandalised, so there was no way to lock the external door. There was one dirty stall, and the door was missing with a half-used toilet roll sitting on the cistern. A small hand basin squashed in the corner with half a wall mirror above it was the only other bathroom accessory in this bleak room. Hanging over the door frame was a hessian sack, a green T-shirt, a long piece of string, a pair of thick woolly socks, a pair of green gloves without fingers and a plastic shopping bag. On the floor was a pair of well-worn but clean military issue boots size 5 and a half. Carruthers stood there for a minute before marching outside.

'Is this some kind of joke?' she said, relatively composed, looking at Major Smith.

'Miss Brown, all of your equipment and clothing is provided courtesy of Her Majesty's Armed Forces along with your instructors. You are at liberty to withdraw at any stage but that will mean that you cannot continue with the rest of your course as you will be marked as failed. Furthermore, if you disobey any instruction then you will also fail and be sent back immediately. Is that clear?' replied Major Smith.

There was no reply.

'Good, then please get changed and report back here in five minutes.'

Carruthers went back inside and stripped off to her underwear, carefully folding all of her neatly pressed designer clothes and hanging them over the grimy door frame. She put on the green T-shirt which was a bit too baggy and noticed the goose pimples forming on her arms and legs. It was colder in the shit house than outside. That gave her added incentive to get dressed and get out of there. Next she put on the socks and pulled them up above her knees. She then put on the hessian sack which had a hole cut out for her head and two others where she could put her arms through. She treble-folded the string around her waist and tied a knot in her front at waist height. Then she put on the boots which fitted her perfectly and thought that HR must having given these bastards her shoe size. In anger, she threw the plastic bag against the wall behind the dirty, dank sink. Finally, she put on the fingerless gloves. Now dressed, she carefully picked up her clothes and shoes and walked outside.

'Pack your gear away and it will be returned in three days' time,' instructed Major Smith.

Carruthers walked over to the passenger door behind the driver and opened it. She opened the nearest case and it sprung out the clothes trying to escape. She put her clothes and shoes on top of the rest of her pristine clothes and had to use some exertion to close the case. She closed the minibus door without exchanging any words with the disinterested driver and walked back to the three men.

'Where is your hat? Outdoors you lose most of your body heat through your head,' said Major Smith.

'What hat? I didn't see a hat,' replied a confused Carruthers.

'It's the plastic bag. You'll be glad of it when it's cold and pissing down.'

Carruthers spun around and went back into the toilet and picked up the wet Lidl plastic shopping bag, stuffed it down her sock and walked back outside. When she stopped in front of the three men, she pulled down her sock to reveal the scrunched-up plastic bag.

'Well, I'll leave you to it then,' said Major Smith at no one in particular as he turned around and walked towards the minibus. The newly formed group watched as the minibus drove out of car park and disappeared from view as it descended the hilly road.

'Right. Introductions first and then we're off. Two hours of walking and we'll stop for a brew.'

Carruthers looked at the small stocky man standing next to Spud and smiled.

'Hello, Twiggy,' she said.

'No, he's called Puke Up,' said Spud. 'Twiggy is over there,' he continued whilst pointing at a five-foot long branch on the curb.

'Twiggy will be carried everywhere and both you and Puke Up will be carrying it. If you break it, damage it or lose Twiggy then there will be penalties and forfeits to pay. You decide how you carry it but carry it you will. Any questions, Miss Brown?' said Spud.

Carruthers shook her head and thought, *OK if this is how they want to play it then I'll go with it.*

She walked over to the branch and said, 'I'll be in front, Puke Up, and we'll carry it resting it on our right shoulder.'

Puke Up picked up his heavy Bergen rucksack and hoisted it onto his back. At the same time, Spud did likewise with his equally heavy Bergen rucksack. Puke Up walked over and picked up one end of Twiggy. Carruthers hoisted the other end clumsily onto her shoulder then the odd couple fell in behind Spud.

'It's 12:45 now, brew up at 14:45,' said Spud, looking at his watch as he headed off out of the car park onto a footpath.

Puke Up checked his watch and said, 'Roger that.'

Carruthers didn't have a watch on and didn't speak at all. The footpath started off with a steep ascent and was surrounded by wild, open moorland. The views were spectacular and Carruthers took in the unspoilt beauty. The wind became more biting now that they were out and in the exposed landscape and it was a crisp nine degrees Celsius. Walking offset the cold day and Carruthers was surprised how warm she actually felt. Twiggy felt light but that was partially due to the fact that Puke Up was a good few inches smaller than her and was only five foot four inches tall. Therefore the larger part of its weight was being carried by him. She thought that he must be strong as an ox because he was fully laden with the rucksack and he was carrying Twiggy as well. The two hours sped past without much conversation when Spud's watch began chiming.

'Time for a brew up,' said Spud as he headed off the footpath some twenty-five metres and put down his Bergen.

He promptly opened it up and produced a ground sheet which he spread out. He then pulled out of the Bergen a flask, three plastic cups and a packet of digestive biscuits. Carruthers and Puke Up walked over and put Twiggy down next to the ground sheet and Puke Up took off his own Bergen. Carruthers accepted the hot, sweet, milky tea along with three digestives. This was one of the best cuppas that she'd ever tasted. She was very fussy when it came to drinking tea normally. It had to be Earl Grey tea and the milk was always added to a warmed cup before the steeped tea (approximately five minutes) was finally added.

'So where exactly are we then?' she said, dunking her digestives, copying what both of her instructors were doing.

'We're in the Brecon Beacons. Today we are going to do an easy route up to Pen y Fan which is the highest peak at 886 metres.'

'Fantastic views, I believe. And how long will the walk take?'

'It's five miles up and back down. We're taking a route parallel to the most popular path known as "The Motorway". At this pace, I reckon we'll be finished about 17:15. We tend to stay away from the tourists and walkers as much as possible. We'll camp out for the night and we'll be off on another harder route tomorrow. Whenever we stop, it's best to check your feet for chaffing or cuts and then dry them. So, off with your boots and socks and check them now,' said Spud.

Carruthers removed her boots and socks and exposed her painted toenails and recently pedicured feet. Everything looked in order and she put everything back on, remembering to put her 'hat' back in her sock. Puke Up got up and went a further twenty metres away and out of Carruthers' direct line of sight and relieved himself.

Spud looked at her and said, 'If you need to go then go over there. Unfortunately there aren't any toilets until we get back.'

'I'm fine,' she replied.

'From now on we stop every hour to take on water and we'll have a cuppa at the peak. Hydration is vitally important when out. If you need a pee then shout and we'll stop.'

Carruthers nodded. She was determined to make it up and back without suffering that indignation on her first day. Spud packed everything away and both he and Puke Up put back on their Bergens. Puke Up stood by Twiggy and waited for Carruthers to make her decision.

'Same again. I'll take the front and we'll carry it on our right shoulder,' she said.

Puke Up nodded and picked up one end of Twiggy. Spud took the lead and then headed off upwards. Pen y Fan is one of the most dangerous areas in all of Great Britain because the weather can change in an instant, and this has caused both civilian and military injuries and even deaths. Spud and Puke Up had trained here many times and also served as instructors and members of rescue parties, and they respected this challenging environment. They had read the weather forecasts and would receive any updates from their regiment but were continually scanning the sky for any imminent change.

After a further thirty minutes of uphill walking, they finally reached the summit of Pen y Fan. Once there, Twiggy and the rucksacks were put down. Spud passed round a chocolate bar to everyone, not only as a reward for reaching the top but as a good source of fast absorbing energy. They all had a drink of cold water from one of Puke Up's military water canteens and Carruthers didn't object to sharing the same canteen. A further cuppa was had by all three. The stop was only ten minutes as it was beginning to get very cold on the exposed top, but the views were excellent. Once again, the rucksacks were put back on and Carruthers took the front of Twiggy, which meant that she would be carrying the heavier portion of it now, and she also placed it on the same shoulder. Puke Up followed suit.

Almost at the same spot that they had their original brew up, Spud shouted out for a water break and stepped off the path. Although this path wasn't used by walkers, Spud observed the Countryside Code. Once again, Puke Up's canteen was passed around and they all took on board water whilst Twiggy rested quietly on the moorland. In less than three minutes they were back on the path and off again.

Very little conversation passed between the group until they stopped for their next water stop where once again they stepped off the path and shared from the same canteen. Carruthers' thigh muscles were beginning to feel a bit tight from all of the walking. She wasn't used to walking uphill, and walking downhill was even harder. Stopping didn't make it any easier as her muscles tightened up further, and the first set of steps after the stop weren't pleasant until the blood started flowing back through her legs and loosened them up. She noticed that her breathing had become easier and she was getting her second wind. She also didn't feel that cold despite wearing a sack!

They set off again and she realised then that despite Spud taking the lead, he was actually walking at her pace. They walked for another hour and the car park from where they started was insight, but again it was time for a water break and that was exactly what they did. Then they walked back down to a spot close to the car park where Spud ordered them to stop.

Looking at his watch, Spud said, 'OK, 17:10, we'll set up camp here.'

Then, looking at Carruthers, he went on. 'Why don't you pop down and use the loo.'

Carruthers nodded and walked back down to the toilet and relieved herself. She stood in front of the hand basin and turned on both taps. They responded by trickling cold water into the basin. She took off her hessian sack, boots and socks and performed a fast strip wash. Once done and feeling mildly invigorated, she redressed and looked at her reflection in the broken mirror that had a haze over it. All things considered, not too bad, she thought. She retraced her steps back to where she had left her instructors and was surprised by what she saw. There were already two tents up and a large ground sheet spread out and secured by small rocks. Everything surrounded a small stove with a pot on top bubbling away. When she reached the freshly erected campsite, Spud passed her a plastic mug with hot sweet tea and some more digestive biscuits.

'Take the weight off,' gestured Spud, pointing to the ground sheet.

Carruthers complied and sat down, enjoying her brew up. The other two joined her and everyone had a brew and biscuits.

'Dinner is on and grub will be served in fifteen minutes. Best to inspect your feet and check for any sign of blisters or cuts,' went on Spud.

Carruthers did as ordered and everything was in order and still buffed from the pedicure.

'The small tent is yours, by the way,' said Puke Up. 'Well, you and Twiggy actually.'

'Come on,' she replied.

'No, Twiggy is your responsibility for the whole of the exercise,' said Spud. 'Part of the team-building exercise is looking after Twiggy.'

'OK, so tell me. What exactly is the point of our dear friend Twiggy?'

'Twiggy represents someone in your group that needs help or assistance all of the time. Let's say for example in a battlefield, Twiggy would represent a wounded colleague. You need to care for Twiggy and work with everyone else to ensure that Twiggy gets the right assistance 24/7,' replied Spud.

'I guess that Twiggy won't be part of the fire then,' joked Carruthers, trying to lighten the mood.

'No. We never cremate our colleagues. At least not whilst they are alive,' quipped Spud.

'So anyway, how did you get the nickname then?' asked a relaxed Carruthers.

'Short story. Earlier in my army career, I didn't follow orders and ended up on jankers far too often. I was forever peeling potatoes and that's how I got the nickname.'

'I won't ask how you got your nickname,' Carruthers said, looking at Puke Up.

'No, and I won't ask how you got your nickname of Miss Brown. We get a few spooks to look after either here or out in the field and it's always Brown, Black or White. Very original. Did someone over there fall in love with Reservoir Dogs?' remarked a semi-smiling Puke Up.

'Very good,' said Carruthers, laughing out aloud.

'OK, let's eat now,' said Spud.

The army field rations were dished out on plastic plates with plastic cutlery. They all ate in silence and then had another mug of tea with a chocolate bar. Once the dinner was over, Spud picked up the plates, cutlery, mugs and the plastic and paper that they were originally wrapped in and walked off to the toilet. He disposed of all the plastic and paper in the bin and returned some ten minutes later with everything washed. When he got back, Puke Up then headed off to the toilet. He returned some fifteen minutes later armed with assorted branches and twigs from the near woodland and set it all down away from the fire which had been started by Spud who had also by now packed the stove away in his rucksack.

The fire was periodically perked up by feeding it with the branches and twigs during the evening. Spud explained that their camp was 500 metres away from the car park as this was a Countryside Code requirement. He explained that the Army used the Brecon Beacons for a lot of their training and were mindful of respecting the environment.

Carruthers listened to everything spoken and was genuinely interested in learning more about both the Army and their practices. She suspected that her instructors were from the SAS regiment but didn't ask them that question. The fact that she was on the Brecon Beacons, which was a favourite training ground for the Regiment and that the soldiers didn't have regular haircuts along with both her driver and Major Smith were, in her opinion, dead giveaways. She was actually pleased; at least she was being trained by the best of the best. Pleased; well, apart from wearing a sack, that was.

Spud then spent time teaching her how to map read using a compass for the rest of the evening. No GPS or phones or Google Earth on this exercise. They would ascend Pen y Fan tomorrow by a more difficult route than today and she would navigate them both up and back down. She went over the route one final time and then it was time to hit the sack. They would be up at 07:00 and then off on the route by 08:00. Carruthers retired to her tent with Twiggy and found that there was a sleeping bag in there. She secured the front flap of her tent, put Twiggy adjacent to her, stripped off to her underwear and climbed into the sleeping bag. Within ten minutes she fell into a deep sleep. The two instructors remained seated around the fire for another hour before they put the fire out, packed away the ground sheet and also retired to their tent.

07:00. Carruthers was awoken from her sleep.

'Miss Brown, time to get up.'

'OK, I'll be out in a minute.'

She quickly dressed and went outside. Both Spud and Puke Up were already in their army fatigues and the stove was boiling a pan of water. Nearby, another smaller fire was already burning steadily in the early morning mist. It was a cold, crisp morning and she could see her breath as she exhaled.

'If you want to use the loo then breakfast will be ready in ten minutes,' said Spud.

Carruthers wandered over to the brick toilet and used the facilities. Whilst washing her face in the basin after brushing her teeth with her fingers, the outside door flung open and in walked a young girl. The girl was decked out in outdoor walking gear from head to foot with far too large spectacles balancing precariously on her nose. The girl was surprised by seeing Carruthers, who looked at her and weakly smiled. The girl abruptly turned around and fled.

'Mummy, Mummy, there's a witch in the toilet, I'm scared,' she shrieked.

A moment later, a small slim woman also bedecked in walking gear with a ridiculously multicoloured Peruvian bobble hat with tassels swinging from the ears of the hat poked her head into the toilet. She gazed at Carruthers, who was still standing in front of the basin applying cold water to her face, and said, 'Excuse me, how long will you be as my daughter wants to use the toilet?'

The vagabond replied with a surprisingly educated accent, 'I'm just finishing off and will out in a minute.'

'OK, thanks.'

Carruthers exited the toilet and noticed the young girl cowering in the back seat of the red Vauxhall Astra. She was now pointing at her, and her parents sitting in the front seats were also staring at her. Back at the camp, both tents had already been packed and the two instructors were sitting on the ground sheet eating porridge on plastic plates and slurping tea. Twiggy was sitting on the moorland next to the groundsheet.

Carruthers sat down where a plate full of porridge and a mug of tea were waiting for her, steaming away. The porridge had been doused in sugar and the tea was as before, milky and sweet.

After exchanging pleasantries, she consumed her food and drink in silence. Once finished, Spud picked up the plates, cutlery and general litter and headed off to the toilet. By now, the hill walking family had completed their ablutions and there were no cars at all in the car park. Puke Up packed away the stove and kicked out the fire and made three more mugs of tea, one of which he handed to Carruthers. Spud was back now and he sat on the ground sheet with his new cuppa.

'Let's go over the route for today,' Spud said, passing over the ordnance survey map and compass to Carruthers.

The circular route was around twelve miles, which took in Card Du peak at 873 metres, then onto Pen y Fan again and finally Cribyn peak at 795 metres before returning back and finishing at the car park. The circuit would take about eight hours, including regular breaks, to walk. This meant that the whole exercise would be completed in daylight. Carruthers studied the map and accepted it along with the compass which she hung around her neck. The map was handed over to her in a heavy plastic zipper bag. The mugs were emptied and dried using handfuls of grass, the groundsheet packed away and then they took up their standard positions. Puke Up waited to be instructed on how to carry Twiggy, and once Carruthers said that they would carry Twiggy again on their right shoulder and she'd take the front, he lifted Twiggy up.

Once they had set off, Spud retreated to the rear of the group and said, 'Right, Miss Brown, we will now follow your route.'

Carruthers was surprised by the sudden change of leadership but responded immediately. 'That's fine.'

Spud and Puke Up surreptitiously checked their watches and noted the time which was 07:57. Carruthers walked onwards and upwards. The sun had just broken through the cloud and there was still dew covering the heather and moorland. It was very tranquil in the early morning with an absence of humans and wildlife, save the odd bird of prey circling above using the thermals to good effect. Carruthers had consulted both the map and compass twice within two hours and had altered the route accordingly.

At 10:30, Puke Up said, 'Time for a natural break.'

Carruthers stopped and walked off the path where Twiggy was put down. She spent the time staring at the map, checking the landscape visually and applying her compass to the map whilst Puke Up relieved himself. She changed their direction and headed off into a valley with both instructors complying with her instructions. They carried on for a further two hours, changing directions on a further three occasions, which caused them to regularly go uphill and downhill. Twiggy was becoming not so much heavy but painful. Carrying it on her right shoulder over the two days had caused the skin to become raw and tender.

Carruthers said, 'Let's stop and take a break.'

The instructors complied and they walked away from the path where they stood awaiting Carruthers to share with them what she wanted.

She said, 'Let's take a fifteen-minute break and have a cuppa. I can read the map also.'

Twiggy was grounded and Spud pulled out the groundsheet and produced three mugs of tea and more digestive biscuits. Carruthers drank the tea, dunking her biscuits, and studied the map without consulting the compass. The fifteen-minute break passed quickly and then they were up in formation and off again. Spud and Puke Up both checked the time on their watches which said 12:51. Carruthers now instructed Puke Up that Twiggy would be carried on their left shoulder, and he complied. She continued to check her map, look at the surrounding landscape, check her compass against the map and occasionally change direction. Her thighs, which had recovered following a good night's sleep, were once again beginning to feel the strain. As there had been stretches of downhill walking today along with uphill stretches, her hamstrings were also beginning to tire. She set about her task with renewed determination and, despite not having great stamina, she pushed herself physically. After nearly two hours, Puke Up again requested a natural break. Once they moved off the path and rested Twiggy on the ground, Carruthers requested a tea break.

Spud set out the groundsheet, poured the tea and passed around the biscuits. Carruthers had her cuppa and then walked off out of their eye line where she relieved herself. Once back, she studied the map again, now muttering to herself. The temperature had been dropping steadily during the day and both instructors were well wrapped up.

Spud said, 'It's cold. Why don't you put your hat on.'

Carruthers fumbled in her sock and withdrew the plastic Lidl shopping bag. She shook it out and arranged it to form a makeshift hat and then fitted it on her head. The crumpled bag was immediately blown off by the strong breeze. Spud caught it and passed it back to her.

'You should cut off two pieces of string from your belt and tie one end to each of the handles. Then you can tie a bow under your chin,' said Spud, producing a small knife from his belt and passing it to her.

Carruthers cut two pieces off of her string belt and followed Spud's instructions. In a couple of minutes, she had an improvised hat on her head. She flattened the plastic bag on her head in order that it didn't flap about in the breeze. She picked up Twiggy and again placed it on her left shoulder which caused Puke Up to follow suit, and again they set off. Both men checked their watches and it was now 15:04. They headed uphill and turned onto a ridge. Heading towards them was a hill-walking family, clearly enjoying the day out by the laugher they jointly shared.

'Look, Mummy, it's the tramp from this morning,' squealed the little girl. 'And two soldiers are helping her carry a tree.'

The family edged passed Carruthers who was now wearing a plastic Lidl bag on her head as well as a hessian sack, fingerless gloves, long woolly socks and army boots. It had been a long day out in the wild countryside and Carruthers was also heavily speckled with mud and sand.

Carruthers looked at the family having heard the little girl's rather less than flattering comment and said bluntly, 'Good afternoon.'

The adults didn't know what to make of this well-spoken apparition but the girl chimed up, 'Is your broomstick not working?' looking at Twiggy.

The two instructions couldn't control themselves and burst out laughing. Carruthers wasn't in a jovial mood and ignored the comment. The little girl whose curiosity was spiked by the whole scenario was ushered away by her parents, but she periodically turned around to check on what the odd group were doing.

They carried on walking along the ridge and then Carruthers without consulting the map decided to descend into a valley. Both instructors exchanged glances as Carruthers' refusal to consult the map meant that she had effectively given up and was now going to wander around. Once they had descended into the valley, Carruthers called for another tea break. Spud said that they would set up camp, prepare dinner and now stay there overnight. He said matter of factly to Carruthers that after dinner, they would go through another map reading session.

Carruthers was both physically and mentally exhausted and was annoyed with herself, the army instructors, HR and MI5. This was a complete waste of time and pointless. She worked in an office, managed people, oversaw field operations and controlled budgets. So what if she couldn't map read or skin a squirrel, and what's the fucking point of carrying a branch around all day? She fumed whilst Spud and Puke Up set up camp and the two tents. She sat on the ground sheet with frantic action going on around her and then calm descended.

The two instructors and her sat on the ground sheet with mugs of tea and biscuits and again the cuppa ritual was observed. After a further twenty minutes, army ration dinner was served up and everyone wolfed down the food. By now, darkness had descended and there was a decent fire roaring away. The fire provided a fair amount of light, but both of the men had also put on head torches which were activated. After dinner, Puke Up disappeared for more than twenty minutes and returned with two armfuls of branches and twigs. Spud went through another session on map reading but Carruthers' ability to retain any of the information was zero. She was a spent force and needed to sleep.

He saw her eyes closing involuntarily and her head nod backwards and forwards a couple of times as she drifted off and finally said, 'Why don't you have a sleep? We'll be here, and when you wake up we'll have some more grub.'

Carruthers nodded and walked off towards her tent.

'Hey, don't forget Twiggy,' shouted out Spud.

She turned around, walked over to Twiggy, picked up one end and dragged it into the tent where she unceremoniously dropped it. She tried to kick off her boots but they wouldn't budge. She sat on her sleeping bag, undid the laces and then kicked off her boots. Exhausted, she got into the sleeping bag and zipped it up. Only then did she realise that not only was the tent flap open but she was still wearing everything. The only item that she dreamily removed was her hat and then she promptly fell asleep.

Spud withdrew his satellite phone with email and web access and created an email. Carruthers had not stopped every hour for a water break, she didn't stop for lunch, she didn't check her feet when they stopped, and she didn't check with them when map reading and ask for either help or confirmation of her action. She didn't ask Puke Up whether he wanted to change how Twiggy was being carried. She walked at a slow pace which betrayed her lack of stamina. She didn't communicate to the group what she was planning to do. In short, she wasn't a team player, she had poor communication skills and forgot all of the basics she had been told yesterday. He added to the email the route that they took, times walking, times of breaks and reason for breaks, food and drink consumed and position of final camp for overnight stop. He passed the draft over to Puke Up who reviewed it. The email was then sent.

Twenty-five minutes later, Spud heard a ping from his phone and checked his Inbox. He read the reply and passed it over to Puke Up who also read it, nodded and retuned the phone back to Spud. They decided that it was time for a fag and both sat there staring into the fire puffing away. They had a couple of cigarettes each and then put the butts into the plastic bag that they using to collect all of their litter.

At 21:30 Carruthers reappeared and Spud immediately set about putting on the stove another army rations meal for everyone. She looked even more exhausted than when she had retired earlier and sat on the groundsheet in a state of exhaustion. Spud looked at her whilst he was cooking and she got up, went back into her tent and dragged Twiggy back out. She dropped it by the edge of the groundsheet and flopped back down. Her boots were on but the laces weren't tied. The meal was eaten and everyone had a mug of tea. Carruthers began to brighten up and the food began reenergising her.

'Are we near a toilet?' she asked wearily.

'Afraid not,' said Spud matter of factly.

'Oh.'

'So, out here we use a latrine. We've dug a pit thirty metres over there which is downwind. You squat over it, use grass afterwards and throw that in the pit. Take this canteen as we all use this one for personal washing only, and wash your hands after. You can wash your face and elsewhere and brush your teeth also. In the morning, after breakfast we'll fill the latrine in. Clear?'

'Yes,' she replied, accepting the canteen.

'Best take the head torch also,' said Spud, taking off the head torch and putting it on her head and then adjusting the straps.

Carruthers slowly marched off into the inky dark and the two men took out another cigarette each and lit up. When she returned, Spud spent only ten minutes just going through the very basics of map reading with Carruthers. She looked vacant but at least had managed to clean off the mud and embedded sand encrusted on her. She accepted another mug of tea before retiring. Spud advised her that they would rise earlier tomorrow at 05:30 and again she would take the lead and that they would complete their mission. Ten minutes after she left, Puke Up got up, stretched and began to head out towards the latrine with the canteen of water.

'Here, don't forget this,' said Spud after rummaging in his rucksack and throwing over a roll of luxury toilet paper.

'Cheers, mate,' replied Puke Up as he caught the toilet roll.

05:30. The still was broken by the sound of two men rustling about in the cold dank mist. A fire was lit and then they prepared breakfast. Whilst efficiently going about their cooking tasks, they also set out a groundsheet and dismantled their tent. After ten minutes the food and drinks had been prepared and was ready to eat and drink.

Carruthers woke abruptly from a disturbing dream. In her dream, she had been chased by a pack of howling wolves through the streets of London. The pursuing pack were snarling and relentless in their chase. They were even the more terrifying because they were all the size of a human man with enlarged fangs dripping with angry saliva. No one came to her rescue and all ignored her pleas for help. This was a regular dream that she had and upon waking she always felt exhausted from the never-ending chase.

'Breakfast is up,' came the gruff call from Spud.

'I'll be straight out,' she replied whilst trying to remove the fog from her brain.

Slowly, she exited from her sleeping bag and felt the stiffness in her muscles. The exercise over the last two days was taking its toll and another day in the mountains would push her over the edge. Dressing was a non-event as she only needed to put on her boots and lace them up. She ran her fingers through her hair and rubbed the sleep out of her eyes before exiting the tent. She gingerly stretched outside of the tent and made no attempt to stifle a long, loud yawn.

A light bulb flickered in her head and she went back into the tent and retrieved Twiggy. Breakfast was a mute affair as the group focused on eating and drinking the hot fare. Once completed, Carruthers picked up the canteen and headed off to the latrine. By the time she returned, the tents and camp had been packed away save for the groundsheet. A final hot mug of sweet tea and biscuits was waiting for her which she gratefully accepted. Puke Up left with a fold up shovel and headed off to the latrine. Spud passed over a head torch and Carruthers fumbled with it as she positioned it over her head. Spud then explained again the basics of map reading including using a compass and went over their mission which was still expected to be completed. Carruthers didn't ask any questions but attempted to absorb the lesson in the darkness. Spud had no confidence that she had taken in enough information to affect their mission and continued to surreptitiously assess her performance.

'Latrine filled in,' said Puke Up, smiling as he returned and packed away the fold up shovel.

Both men then walked the camp area looking for anything that needed to be packed away or cleared up and then the groundsheet was placed in Spud's rucksack. The camp site now had been returned to its natural state and there was no evidence that anyone had been there. Both men then put on their rucksacks and stood motionless.

'I'll take the front of Twiggy. Right shoulder,' said Carruthers in a scratchy voice. 'And we'll head off along the path over there towards the ridge,' she continued, pointing towards her left.

Puke Up picked up his end of Twiggy, balancing it on his right shoulder, and Spud fell in behind both of them. Both men looked at their watches and noted that the time was 06:07. The start of the walk was very slow as Carruthers' leg muscles refused to release the stiffness. Fortunately the first thirty-five minutes were on a flat gravel path and that slowly eased the stiffness from Carruthers' protesting legs. They then began the ascent up the ridgeway path. Initially it was a slight incline up but then it became steeper and all of the while it was still dark. There was some artificial light provided by their three head torches but the beams only shone for a few metres ahead of where they were walking and only in long thin strips. The pathway was stony and this meant that their steps were occasionally unbalanced by the unevenness of it. There was no communication from Carruthers who was acting team leader to the other two men, and she again didn't consult with her map at any point in time.

They had walked another fifteen minutes on the uneventful climb when there was a commotion. Carruthers reacted to

Twiggy being violently projected away from her right shoulder by letting out a scream. She turned around and saw that Puke Up was lying face down on the path with his end of Twiggy nowhere near him. She was assimilating all of the information before her but wasn't actually doing or saying anything.

Puke Up was lying prone on the path emitting groans and making small movements with his arms and legs. Spud dropped his backpack and knelt down next to Puke Up.

'Puke Up, can you hear me?' said Spud. 'Can you get up?'

Puke Up continued to groan but started to move up into a dog-like position on all fours.

'Grab his arm,' said Spud, looking at Carruthers.

Carruthers moved to Puke Up's right side and threaded her arm under his armpit and lifted. Along with Spud on the other side and with Puke Up now gathering his senses, they both lifted him into a standing position. Spud continued to hold Puke Up firmly with his right hand and undid his rucksack with his left hand. Spud then threw off the rucksack which landed heavily in the sodden heathland. Spud inspected Puke Up's face and could see that blood was spouting down his face from a cut within his hairline that was under his hat.

'Are there any other injuries apart from your head wound?' inquired Spud.

Puke Up moved various body parts: arms, hands, fingers, elbows, neck, legs, knees, and stamped his feet.

'Everything good,' replied Puke Up shakily.

'What about your vision, hearing and any headache?' went on Spud.

'Strong headache but everything else is good,' came back the reply.

'Right. I'm going to check the head wound first,' said Spud, removing Puke Up's hat. 'No need to bend your head down. Lucky you're a midget.'

'Fuck off.'

Gently, Spud worked his fingers through Puke Up's scalp and found one small wound within his hair.

'Miss Brown, you keep a firm grip on him and I'll get out my first aid kit,' said Spud, looking at Carruthers.

'Yes, of course,' she replied.

Spud withdrew the first aid kit from his rucksack and then took out several items which he rested on the rucksack. He then took his canteen and applied a liberal dousing of water over the wound and over Puke Up's face.

'This may hurt,' said Spud as he applied an iodine pad directly to the wound.

Puke Up winced. Next, Spud pressed a sterile gauze pad directly over the wound and then wound a gauze bandage tightly around his head several times. Finally, tape was applied to the gauze bandage to ensure that it kept in place. Spud applied more water from his canteen onto Puke Up's face which washed away the remaining blood and then rinsed Puke Up's bloodied hat with more water.

'Take these,' Spud said, handing Puke Up two aspirin.

Puke Up put the two aspirin into his mouth and lifted the canteen to his mouth. He sucked out a small amount of water from the canteen and swallowed.

Spud looked into Puke Up's eyes, using his head torch to shine the light directly at his pupils, but couldn't see any pupil constriction. There was a strong possibility of concussion, especially as Puke Up had indicated that he had a headache.

'Right, this is what we are going to do,' said Spud. 'First I'm going to pitch up the two-man tent. Then I'm going to start a fire, brew up and set up some chow. I'll set Puke Up's hat to dry by the fire. After that I'm going to head off and get a medevac team here asap. Miss Brown, you need to go and gather all of the brushwood that you can find and bring it back here. You may need to make two or three journeys. Puke Up, you need to sit down here and stay awake.'

'Don't you have a phone?' appealed Carruthers.

'Nope. Anyway, there's no signal out here. Now, get a move on, this is an emergency.'

'OK, I'll be back soon.'

Spud started putting up the two-man tent and waited until Carruthers was out of sight.

'Oi, give us a hand,' shouted Spud.

'Sure. Thanks for tripping me up, mate. Appreciate the claret,' said Puke Up.

'Sorry about that. But it sure looked authentic what with all that claret. They wanted us to create an emergency and that was great.'

'Says he who wasn't headbutting rocks.'

'Yeah but at least the rocks weren't damaged.'

'Very funny.'

'Anyway, I'll call in the chopper and when she gets back, I'll head off. You know the rest of the plan, right?'

'Yeah.'

Spud extracted his satellite phone and phoned a preset number. He gave a code number, the extract co-ordinates and the extract time. He waited whilst the details were confirmed back to him and then he finished the call.

'OK, chopper will be here at 08:45. You know what to do.'

They finished off setting up the two-man tent with two sleeping bags, put out the groundsheet and cooking stove and filled it with water. Carruthers walked back with two armfuls of brush wood and they used that to create a fire. She then headed off and returned with another two armfuls. They all had a mug of sweet tea and some more biscuits. Some food was bubbling away on the stove.

'OK, I'm going to head off and arrange for a medevac team to come back. Time now is 07:14. I reckon they'll be here within one and a half hours. Remember to pick up everything and bring back all of our equipment,' Spud said, looking at Carruthers. 'And remember, Puke Up must stay awake at all times. Check on him occasionally. Ask him if he's feeling dizzy or has headaches or has hearing problems or has eyesight problems. Got that?'

'Yes. Should I give him any more aspirin?'

'No, he's had enough. Sweet tea is all he can have, and make a cuppa every half hour. I've left most of the water here. Both of you need regular hydration. I'll see you soon.'

And with that, Spud picked up the smaller rucksack and strode off down the ridgeway path with purpose. He made ground quickly and within ten minutes was out of sight. Around this time, daytime was replacing nighttime and there was natural light painting its way delicately over the Brecon Beacons. Despite this change, the wind was getting stronger and it was a bitterly cold November day. Carruthers started to shake with the cold and her teeth began to chatter. Puke Up realised that she wasn't going to survive out here dressed in a sack and that hypothermia was on her particular horizon.

'Why don't we get into the sleeping bags in the tent. It will be a lot warmer in there. We can come out and grab a cuppa at 07:45,' said Puke Up.

Carruthers looked at him suspiciously. He knew what she was thinking and decided to take positive action.

'Right. I'm getting into the sleeping bag. If you aren't in the tent behind me then I'm going to zip it up and keep warm.'

He then walked over to the tent and crawled into it. Right behind him was Carruthers. He took off his boots and got into his sleeping bag. Carruthers zipped up the tent and, after taking off her boots, got into the vacant sleeping bag. No mention of Twiggy.

'Is this the sleeping bag that I've been sleeping in?' asked Carruthers.

'No idea. I don't know if this is the one that I've been sleeping in.'

'Oh. Well, at least it's warm in here.'

'Toastie.'

'Toastie. Right,' replied a smiling Carruthers. 'I'll just check on you occasionally to make sure that you are awake.'

'Sure.'

Carruthers awoke with a start. Those bloody wolves were still chasing her all over London.

'Here, have a cuppa,' said the smiling Puke Up, thrusting a mug of tea into her hand.

'Oh, I must have dropped off. What time is it?'

'It's, um, not sure. I can't focus on my watch,' said Puke Up.

'What! Can't you see?' said the alarmed Carruthers.

'Not properly. Anyway, take a look at my watch.'

'08:15. Shit, I dropped off. Sorry, do you have any other symptoms, dizziness, hearing difficulties or a headache still?'

'Headache and blurry vision. No different than after a good night out.'

Carruthers laughed and took the mug from him. He got back into his sleeping bag and started drinking his own mug of tea. They both sighed and drank in silence.

Once finished, Carruthers took both mugs and threw the remnants out of the tent before zipping it back up and depositing the mugs next to her boots.

'So is your headache getting worse?' she asked.

'I guess it is. Perhaps a couple more aspirin will do the trick.'

'Sorry. Spud said no more aspirin. Maybe the cuppa will knock the edge off your headache.'

'I'll rest a bit. That should help with the headache.'

'OK.'

The wolves were closing in on her. The ground was vibrating and the noise was incredible. Whoomp, whoomp, whoomp. She awoke startled by the deafening sound, and it wasn't going away. She looked over to see an empty sleeping bag next to her. Puke Up was gone. This nightmare had taken an unusual and frightening turn. It was all too real. She got up, put on her boots, unzipped the tent and crawled outside. Puke Up was standing there talking into the ear of a crew member from a helicopter that was circling above but off from their actual location. The downdraft would have obliterated their camp if the helicopter was directly above. Both men turned to see her and started to walk over. This was not a dream.

Puke Up was now wearing the dried-out beanie hat which covered the bandaging. The helicopter crew man waited until they were almost touching each other and then shouted into Carruthers' ear.

'This man needs hospital attention asap. I'll winch him out. You need to stay here until your team member returns.'

'How long will that be?' asked a frightened Carruthers.

'My guess is one hour.' The crew man looked at his watch. 'So around 10:00.'

Puke Up nodded at Carruthers and she replied, 'I hope you are going to be OK.'

The two men walked away from the camp for some eighty metres. The helicopter stationed itself directly above at a height of sixty metres and lowered the winch. Both Puke Up and the crew man hooked on together. The crew man gave a thumbs up to the winch man and they began to ascend steadily. At the same time, the helicopter increased its power and began to fly away. The whoomp, whoomp emitted from the roster blades was deafening and Carruthers covered her ears in a vain attempt to lessen the roar. She watched as the helicopter left the area whilst winching in the two men. She couldn't make out what type of helicopter it was but it wasn't a military model and didn't have military livery. She concluded that the extraction was a civilian operation. The deep blue colour of the helicopter was rapidly disappearing into the distance. The helicopter was a Dauphin AS365 which was recently introduced as the favoured air transport of the SAS.

Carruthers added more brushwood to the fire, made herself a drink and looked at the food in the pot on the stove. The food had been there so long that it was burnt and stuck to the side in a hard, congealed mess. She was now angry and left the pot on the stove. Back in the snugness of her sleeping bag, she was annoyed that the rescue team didn't offer her a lift. She was also annoyed that she hadn't thought to ask for a lift. In fact, she thought that she should have pulled rank and demanded that she was airlifted out of here. As a mid-level manager in MI5, surely she was entitled to be on that helicopter. And as for this ridiculous exercise, well, Spud could do whatever he liked, but she wanted off of this mountain range asap. She sat in the tent unable to sleep and very frustrated for what seemed like an eternity. On a few occasions she poked her head out of the tent, but there was no sign of Spud or indeed any human life.

Eventually the combination of her anger and her frustration erupted. She had made a decision and she wasn't going to wait here any longer. She was going to travel light and make for a road. Once she met civilisation then she'd decide what her next step would be. First she took the canteen which was full of water. Next she rummaged through the rucksack to see whether there was anything in there worth taking. A packet of biscuits was selected and placed next to her canteen. Her eyes nearly popped out of her head when she saw what was nestling next in the rucksack.

'Fucking bastards,' she screamed.

In her hand was a luxury toilet roll. Without thinking, she threw it against the side of the tent and it unfurled like the toilet rolls that used to be thrown at football matches. The only other item that she took from the rucksack was a green beanie hat which she promptly put on her head, and she threw her makeshift hat on the ground. She stomped out of the tent and studied the map for several minutes. It looked to her that if she walked west in a straight line then she would meet up with a road. There was no point hanging around any longer, and off she set. The time was 09:50. In one hand she had a canteen and map and in her other hand she had a packet of digestive biscuits. Above her and secreted behind some rocks, her actions were being observed. Hidden behind an outcrop was Spud, who watched her walk off, and he realised that she wasn't going to return so he stood up, cleared up his camp and walked down into where Carruthers had been camped. He looked around and saw that the fire was still going, the stove was still on and that the tent and equipment were left untouched. Spud had left the camp earlier and circled around it until he had set up an observation hide.

He raised his walkie-talkie and spoke. 'Rabbit has run. Camp left intact and fire still burning. I'll pack everything away and clear the site. I'll tail Rabbit. Out.'

At the other end of the transmission, two men listened with interest. One of the men then typed out an encrypted email and sent it.

Carruthers walked for nearly two hours and then she finally met a road. The journey wasn't that unpleasant despite the cold wind, and she seemed to have gotten a new lease of life. During the walk, she focused on the actions of her two instructors. One idiot fell over and cut his head and then the other idiot just walked off. OK, he did arrange for an evacuation, but what a bloody clown. None of this would have happened if they weren't carrying Twiggy.

Twiggy, fucking Twiggy. I should have thrown that bastard on the fire, she repeatedly thought. *And to think, I thought that they were SAS. Weekend warriors at best. Probably not even Territorial Army being that they are totally incompetent. A pair of idiots who work in a shoe shop in Cheltenham giving themselves stupid nicknames; I bet they are called Barry and Nigel. Fucking financial cuts and then we're scrapping the bottom of the barrel for wannabes. Fuckers even brought their own loo roll. I'll write up my own report and raise a shit storm.*

Carruthers positioned herself by the side of the road and waited. Three cars slowed down to appraise her but didn't stop. The occupants all looked at the woman dressed in a sack, dirty, dishevelled, wearing cutoff gloves and a beanie hat, and decided that she wasn't someone that they wanted in their car. They all debated how someone could let themselves go so completely and all concluded that she had succumbed to drink, drugs or both. The fourth car had three occupants in it and it started to slow down some way up the road. Carruthers smiled and continued to motion her thumb in the fashion for requesting a lift. The red Vauxhall Astra drove past her with all occupants studying her intensely. In the back seat, a young girl had her face pressed up against the window which distorted it, and she was clearly shouting something. The car came to a stop several metres down the road. Carruthers picked up her pace and walked up to the car where the front passenger window had been half rolled down.

'Can I have a lift please?' Carruthers asked politely.

'Where are you going?' said the lady sitting in the front seat.

'Just to the nearest town please.'

The was a pause whilst the woman turned and looked at the man driving the car. He shrugged his shoulders.

'OK, get in.'

'Thanks.'

Carruthers opened the rear door and got into the car. Spud, who had been tracking her, raised his walkie-talkie and delivered a message into it which included details of the car including its number plate. The little girl, who had been watching Carruthers with fascination, broke the silence.

'Where's your broomstick?'

'Don't ask that,' said her mum.

'Where are the soldiers that were guarding you?'

'Don't ask that,' said her mum.

'Well, perhaps I can introduce myself. My name is Miss Brown and I'm studying how cold affects your body.'

'Is that why you are dressed like a tramp?' enquired the little girl.

'Don't ask that,' said her mum.

Carruthers laughed. 'Yes, we need to test in a difficult environment and perform tasks when cold and under duress.'

'Well, my name is Amy and this is Mummy and Daddy.'

'Pleased to meet you all, and thanks for stopping,' said a humbled Carruthers.

The two adults in the front seat remained silent and didn't engage in any conversation. Everything Carruthers had told them sounded like she was spinning them a line. Yes, she spoke with an educated accent, but she looked a right state, and stunk. The sooner that they unloaded her the better. In fact, they wouldn't have stopped at all except that Amy had spotted the witch and insisted that they stopped otherwise she would put a spell on them and then they would all die. Amy had a big imagination and stopping was preferable to having her talking about spells and curses for months.

They had been journeying for fifteen minutes when Daddy spoke. 'We are coming up to the car park where we first saw you yesterday morning.'

Carruthers became alert and looked into the car park. She saw two blue Ford Transit twelve-seater vans parked and standing outside were four men, two of which she recognised. One was Major Smith and the other one was the man who drove her down here.

'Stop the car,' Carruthers exclaimed as the car passed the car park.

Daddy obeyed and pulled up to a stop.

'Shall I reverse back into it?' asked Daddy.

'No, I'll get out here. Thanks for stopping and giving me a lift. You are a life saver.'

There was no reply from the front seat.

As Carruthers was getting out of the car, she heard Amy shout out, 'Don't put a spell on us. We don't want to die.'

'Don't say that,' said her mum.

Then the car pulled off.

Strange family, thought Carruthers.

Carruthers walked into the car park; the conversation stopped and four pairs of eyes focused on her.

'Good morning,' Carruthers said, looking directly at Major Smith.

'Good morning, Miss Brown. Are you OK?' replied Major Smith.

'I'm OK thanks.'

'So tell me what happened. Please start from the point of the medevac,' said Major Smith.

'Well, I waited around for a good while but then decided that I'd take the initiative and get off there. I walked to a road and then thumbed a lift from a family.'

'I see. And what were your actual instructions?'

'I think that I was supposed to wait until Spud returned.'

'So you disobeyed an order and left. You also left army equipment out there. What about the fire and the campsite? Did you clear it all up and put out the fire?'

'No.'

'But you have been taught that when out here, we observe the Countryside Code and leave everywhere as we found it.'

Carruthers didn't reply.

'What if the unattended fire caught light to the tent and started a countryside fire? Or what if an animal or a child wandered in and injured themselves in the camp?'

Again, Carruthers didn't reply.

'Quite frankly I'm disappointed with your behaviour and I'm perfectly entitled to throw you off the course. But I think that you need this course more than you realise. Your behaviour thus far is unacceptable and it will be reflected in your assessment. Furthermore you could have been injured out there on your own and we have our own man out there on his own. We never go on the Beacons alone as it's a harsh environment that can turn in a minute.'

Carruthers was realising that she hadn't thought through the potential dangers that could have materialised because of her actions.

'I think that seeing Puke Up airlifted out shook me up somewhat and I wasn't thinking clearly,' she said sheepishly. 'I owe Spud an apology.'

Major Smith had heard enough; his patience had been stretched to its limit.

'Right, your lift is here. You can get changed in the loo and you'll be dropped off.'

The man standing next to Major Smith beckoned Carruthers to follow him as he walked to one of the blue Ford transit vans and opened the door behind the front passenger door. Sitting on the seat were Carruthers' three Louis Vuitton cases. Carruthers leant inside the van and selected one of the cases. Without speaking, she headed into the sparse toilet. Ten minutes later, she re-emerged dressed in her designer clothes but the last couple of days had taken its toll. The pampering and haircut and highlighting were all but eroded and she looked haggard. In one hand she carried her case and in her other hand she had the hessian sack, a pair of boots with socks, gloves and a beanie hat stuck inside them along with some string. Spud was now standing beside Major Smith and he smiled weakly at her. He held out his hands and Carruthers passed over her gear.

She looked sheepishly at Spud.

'Sorry,' was all she managed before walking up to the van.

Carruthers got in the front seat and threw her case over and onto the rear seat. The driver started up the engine and Carruthers buckled up. As they left the car park, the driver leant forward and turned on the radio. Radio 2 started to envelope the van.

Major Smith looked at Spud. 'God help us if she represents the new breed of spooks.'

They had been driving fifteen minutes when Carruthers asked, 'What's the time?'

'It's 12:42.'

'So how long is the drive to Fort Monckton?'

'It's roughly four hours including one pit stop.'

The journey passed uneventfully and quietly as her driver didn't encourage any social intercourse. They arrived shortly before 17:00 and went through the security checks at the entrance with the civilian guards. Fort Monckton was surrounded by a razor wire security fence with CCTV in evidence everywhere. High intensity lighting augmented the security of the fort which had been heavily modified both in and around it. Here was where MI5, MI6, SAS and SBS underwent training.

Outside the admission building, a woman of nondescript appearance greeted Carruthers whilst the driver reversed his van and exited. It was evident that he had run this journey several times before. The woman led Carruthers into an adjacent building which was used as a dormitory and showed her to a room that housed a single bed, a wash basin and a wardrobe.

'The showers are at the end of the corridor. I daresay that you want to freshen up,' she said in a quiet voice. 'I'll be back at 18:00 and then you can grab some food before your first class.'

Carruthers nodded and unpacked some of her clothes before heading off to the shower unit with her wash bag and towel. There was no one else in there and whilst she had a steaming hot shower she sobbed. The experience on the Brecon Beacons has been overwhelming and she was out of her comfort zone. The sobbing soon passed and it had a cathartic effect. She decided that she would steel herself and recover from what was a poor start. If this course was a stepping stone to promotion, then she needed to shine from this point on.

10:00. Pope was sitting opposite Dr Hempel-Smith.

'I've got back the results of your eye test that you took yesterday.'

'That's quick.'

'Yes. Well, there's been a slight deterioration in your right eye. At this point I'd say that your current strength of glasses are fine. I assume that you don't suffer from headaches or blurred vision.'

'No, I feel OK. What do you reckon regarding the eye deterioration then? Will it speed up?'

'That's difficult to say. I think that regular eye tests are a must now and that way we can monitor any change.'

'Right. I'm an accredited marksman and I don't want anything to jeopardise that.'

'Yes, I see that on your records. There are correctional procedures that can help but for the moment I think that if we check every six months then we can check the situation and make the necessary call as and when. There's nothing to worry about. I assume that you wear your glasses when you are on the range or out in the field.'

'That's correct.'

'Well then, you're comfortable with your performance and that's good enough. Let's say another eye test in six months then.'

'OK.'

11:20. Pope, Chris Gould and Clare Hawkins had just completed a daily update on all operations under their control. The Luton operation remained high profile with a large number of interested parties requesting regular updates. Unfortunately there was nothing to report. The two undercover operatives at the Luton mosque had not found out anything suspicious, and for all intents and purposes the trail had gone cold. Pope remained stoic and felt that it was only a matter of time before something presented itself. His approach had a calming effect on everyone and in particular his team who felt reassured by his position. It also helped that Carruthers was out of the equation at the moment as she had a negative effect and had proven to be disruptive. The gossip mongers were working overtime speculating on why she had so suddenly and secretly disappeared.

'Are you going to watch the game tomorrow?' asked Chris.

Clare rolled her eyes. 'I'm off if you are going to talk about football.'

'Yes. I assume that it's live on terrestrial TV.'

'Yes, it is. I'm going to the game,' said Chris proudly.

'Really? How did you manage to get a ticket?'

'It was a birthday present from Melanie and she's coming along also. It will be her first ever football match.'

'Well, that's good. A World Cup qualifier at Wembley in front of a full house. Hard to top that.'

'You don't know her. She'll find something to moan about, she always does. Anyway, what do think the score will be?'

'Well we seem to be going OK so far. 4–0 against Bulgaria at home and 3–1 away to Switzerland so far. So I reckon 3–0 against Montenegro. What about you?'

'Dunno. We should win comfortably but our World Cup showing in the summer was so poor, there's a chance that we may implode,' lamented Chris.

'I really hope not. We can't keep living off of 1966.'

'You don't think that we are going to go to the Euros and win it, surely.'

'Well, first we need to get there. But once there and if everyone is fit then why not. We must have as good a chance as everyone else.'

'Perhaps, but Spain must be red hot favourites.'

'OK then, apart from Spain.'

12:00. The door bell rang. After a short wait it rang again.

'Hold your horses, I'm coming,' barked Ahmed as he walked lethargically to his front door.

He opened the door and was confronted by a young woman. She had long black shiny hair and a smallish round face. Her teeth were brilliant white and perfect. She was five feet three inches tall, slim build and was dressed casually in blue jeans, matching blue court shoes and a white T-shirt.

'Hi, is Dee in?' she said jauntily.

'Dee? Sorry, there's no Dee here,' Ahmed replied politely.

'Sure Dee does. You must be Ahmed. He's spoken about you often.'

Ahmed's grin was plastered all over his face as he puzzled over who the fuck was Dee. Then it dawned on him; Dee was Deepak.

'Oh, Dee, yeah, he's out at the moment. Can I be of assistance?' Ahmed said with as much charm as he could muster.

'Yes. I have the latest instalment of food from Mum. She reckons that both of you are consuming enough food to feed a small army. Dad thinks that he may need to get a second job to pay for all of the food that you guys are putting away,' laughed the small but perfectly formed goddess.

Ahmed laughed rather raucously considering that he didn't have a clue what she was talking about.

'I'm double parked outside, so we need to get the food in here quick,' said the goddess.

'OK, let's go.'

'Don't you want to put on some shoes first?' sang the goddess.

Ahmed was in uncharted waters now. 'Nah, I always go around in bare feet,' he bullshitted.

They ran down the metal stairs and out onto the street via a dirty alleyway. There below Ahmed's flat outside the chicken shop was a silver 2008 VW Golf GTI hatchback. The boot was opened by the Goddess and two holdalls removed. Ahmed showed his alpha male traits and carried both bags back up into the flat and then into the kitchen where he placed both of them on the small table.

'I need to take back the bags.'

'Sure,' he said, unzipping the bags and depositing the contents onto both the table and the draining board.

He passed over both empty holdalls and the goddess smiled.

'As Dad would say, "Lovely jubbly",' said the smiling goddess.

'Wasn't that...' blurted out Ahmed.

'Wasn't that what?'

'Oh, nothing.'

The goddess gracefully walked out of the flat. Ahmed was momentarily stunned. He then hobbled into the front room and peered out of the window from behind the grimy net curtains. He could just about make out her pert buttocks before she got into her chariot and floated away. Ahmed limped over to the settee and settled back down. He relived the last several minutes a number of times and chided himself for not asking her what her name was. He resolved to winkle out of Deepak as much information as he could about her and that would be his top priority. In the meantime, he concluded that there was no way that she was blood related to Deepak and that she must have been adopted. The more he thought about it though the more he thought that Deepak must be the one who was adopted. In fact, he decided that Deepak was probably found in a bin in Mumbai. That made more sense. He really needed to put all the food away rather than leave it lying around in the kitchen, but the soles of his feet felt like they had been cut to shreds. That was a price worth paying though as he demonstrated to the goddess that he was hardy. Anyway, 'Dee' could put it away when he got back.

Lying on the settee, Ahmed created a list of things that he needed to do. First he needed to get down the gym regularly and get buffed. Next he needed to buy a protein supplement. Then he needed to get a sharp haircut and finally he needed to upgrade his shabby wardrobe as he didn't really have a decent pair of jeans nor shoes nor T-shirt. He reflected that this job had pretty much turned him into a slob.

'Oh, and I better get some aftershave,' he concluded.

The front door of the flat opened at 15:20 and Deepak walked in.

'Hey, is everything alright?' Deepak shouted out.

'Yeah, just running a bit late,' came the reply from Ahmed, who was still lying on the settee.

Deepak was already in the front room and looking at Ahmed quizzically.

'So what time are you going then? I need to post the handover and I don't like covering for your habitual lateness.'

'Dee, you need to chill out.'

Deepak immediately became alert as Ahmed had never called him by that name before.

'Dee, I'm occasionally late but we all have our secrets, eh?'

Deepak continued to look at Ahmed suspiciously.

'Dee, I'll be off soon. That will allow you time on your own to cook some more food.'

'What's going on?' asked Deepak.

'Well now that you ask, I was resting on the settee earlier and there was a knock on the door. You'll never guess who it was,' went on Ahmed.

Deepak's head started to bobble but he offered no reply.

'Fucking Meals on Wheels, bro. Or to put it another way, your sister bringing up more of dear old Mummy's home cooking.'

'Oh,' muttered Deepak.

'Is that all you can say? Oh. All that shit about you cooking and it turns out that the whole of the Chopra family pop in and out of a safe house during an ongoing operation as if it's a fucking Indian take away. I don't know how many rules that you have broken but they would throw the book at you if this ever came out.'

'Yes, you are right. I'm sorry, I'll sort this out but please don't tell.'

'Don't tell? Bro, just get in the kitchen and put all of the grub away.'

'Right. Thanks.'

'And before you go, what is your sister's name?'

'Aisha.'

'Right. Tell her next time to park out the back and not in the High Street. No need to get a parking ticket. So anyway, what does she do for a job?'

Deepak was eager to appease Ahmed, 'She's a dentist in a practice in South London and she's twenty-three years old.'

That was easy, thought Ahmed. 'And one final question. Are you adopted?'

'What are you talking about?' replied Deepak.

'Nothing. Now, get on with putting the food away and then fill in your handover report that we did that at the mosque at 15:00. I'm going to get ready and go now,' said Ahmed.

And on the way I'll pop in and have a haircut, he thought, pleased with himself that he was going to tick off one item on his recently created to do list.

16:00. Seb Drake had entered Sir Dickie's office and was seated opposite him. Sir Dickie had a frown on his face and his thoughts were at a faraway place.

'I see that we've received an assessment from Sandra Carruthers' field trip,' said Seb.

Sir Dickie's reverie was broken. 'Yes, and she needs to pull her socks up on the rest of the course.'

'Well, the Brecon Beacons can be somewhat wet and windy at this time of year,' said Seb.

'I've played down there. Celtic Manor can be a tricky course with all that bloody wind and rain.'

'Yes. The SAS guys have really laid it on thick though. She won't listen and learn, isn't a team player, lacks fitness and is reckless,' said Seb, reading directly from the report that he had printed off.

'I've partnered a few like that and they always end up costing you the game and a bloody expensive round of drinks at the nineteenth hole,' said Sir Dickie crossly.

'The point about her being the worst person that they have ever encountered isn't good. It reflects on us also. We don't want our good name muddied by one pencil pusher.'

'Difficult to win any game carrying someone,' mused Sir Dickie.

'Quite,' said Seb. 'The report will be filed by HR and can be useful when we look at potential candidates for promotion.'

'Sitting in a comfy office moving parts about on paper is easy. Nothing beats getting out there to test one's mettle. I see the youngsters using golf simulators and spouting on about how they're improving. Utter balderdash. You need to be out there battling the elements and pitting your wits against a worthy opponent.'

'That reminds me, Sir Dickie. How did you fare with your golf match last Wednesday?'

'Last Wednesday? Ah, those bloody hedge fund managers. Damn braggarts. Dressed like pimps and they were clearly bandits. But they'll have to get up earlier in the morning to put one over me.'

'Well done, Sir Dickie,' trumped Seb, thinking that Sir Dickie could out cheat the Devil.

'Right then. We'll keep a close eye on the progress of our Miss Carruthers,' said Sir Dickie, dismissing Seb.

Seb Drake got in the lift and pressed the floor button for level -5. The lift descended a couple of floors and John Pope got in. He acknowledged Seb and pressed the ground floor button.

'Everything OK?' asked Seb.

'Good. Just a quick question though.'

'Sure, fire away.'

'Carruthers is out of the office and it's causing a bit of a stir with the troops,' said Pope, smiling.

'I would have thought that they would have been pleased,' replied Seb. 'Anyway, she's on a work experience placement courtesy of the Top Floor.'

'Isn't she a bit old for work experience?' quipped Pope.

'Obviously not,' retorted Seb.

Both men laughed.

'Seb, I can't put that out there. Can't you give me anything?'

'What I can say is that where she is currently, she's definitely making an impression, that's for sure.'

'So I can scotch the rumours that she is either having a face lift or a boob job.'

'Yes. But never say never.'

Again, both men laughed.

Pope looked at Seb as the doors opened on the ground floor.

'This is me,' Pope said as he exited.

Pope didn't know what to make of Seb's comments, but whatever was going on, Seb clearly thought that it was very amusing.

10:00. A fleet of stretch limos pulled up outside of the heavily guarded ExCel Centre in the heart of Docklands in London. They were accompanied by Metropolitan Police motorcycle outriders with their blue lights flashing. Behind barriers erected twenty metres away were vociferous demonstrators, and the sight of this cavalcade ignited their ire. Dormant placards were raised and shaken furiously accompanied by chants. The police on the other side of the barriers pushed back, hemming in the agitators. Unfazed by the commotion, a cordon of large men in dark suits, sunglasses and ear comms units emerged from the limos and spread out into a semi-circle. They resembled a bubble being blown up from a bubble wand. Once the bubble had expanded to its full size, the VIPs emerged from the limos. Most of them wore the traditional white thobes accompanied by the ghutra headwear. In amongst the group were three men dressed in military uniforms. They were whisked inside and away from both the prying eyes of the world's press and the noisy demonstrators.

The ExCel Centre was hosting the world's largest Arms Fair which was run by Defense and Security Equipment International (DSEI) jointly with the British government. This was a regular event and the very first one opened on 11th September 2001 when the 9/11 attacks took place in America. Over fifty countries from all around the world were invited to attend and see the wares presented by 1,500 exhibitors. The weaponry on display was the latest and greatest available.

Amongst the group that had just entered the ExCel Centre was General Faisal. Prior to arriving in the UK, his country had already gone through with a fine-tooth comb all of the weaponry that was going to be displayed here. Due diligence had been done on what would augment their existing arsenal. They had specific needs in that the weaponry needed to be robust and work in the harsh desert environment and in the surrounding seas. Money was not an inhibitor to an oil-rich country and only the best of breed would be purchased. They had seen ally countries operate in the deserts of the Arab countries and suffer mechanical and equipment failure during recent decades, and the manufactures had a bad habit of repeating the same mistakes over and over again. Sand whipped up by wind permeated everywhere, causing catastrophic failures. The group would spend two days going through the Arms Fair looking studiously at everything, but this was no more than a PR exercise. They were here in show, and it was important to friend and foe that they displayed strength and an eagerness to upgrade and improve their capabilities. However, the actual arms, equipment and said numbers had already been chosen, approved and budgeted for.

General Faisal projected a stern exterior and nodded whenever spoken to by one of the inner sanctum. He was bored by the whole pantomime and was looking forward to escaping from this place and these people. Tonight, following a plush meal he would head off to the casino, pick up one of the high-class hookers that frequented it and then head off to one of the many five-star hotels that adorned London. He had tried a number of the many lap dancing clubs that had sprung up in London in the previous decade and they ranged from elegant to downright dives, and there were willing girls there for the taking but he preferred the high-class hookers that hung around the casinos.

Tonight and tomorrow night were just reward for all of the work that he did not only on behalf of his country, but for the organisation that was planning to undermine the West through terrorist activities. London was a city that he always enjoyed, as at the right price it offered the finest of the finest and that was never truer than the hookers. As a senior general, he pretty much came and went as he pleased when on overseas duties. When asked why he was not attending functions, he simply said that he was undertaking missions of national security. That immediately silenced whoever was questioning his dedication. His entry into England was of note to a number of Arab countries, Western countries and Eastern European countries, and all of their security agencies were alerted. In some cases, the security agencies actively followed his movements.

13:00. In the secure comms room there were four senior Mossad agents sitting around the table. This inner sanctum was similar to every consular around the world. It allowed conversations of a sensitive nature to be conducted knowing that they were surrounded by hi-tech countermeasures that nullify all attempts at electronic eavesdropping. The Israeli embassy on the edge of Kensington Gardens maintained a high level of both physical and electronic security following several attacks over the previous decades.

The heavily set man in his early sixties with little hair and a pronounced stoop said, 'OK, let's go through it one more time.'

All eyes around the room remained focused on him.

'General Faisal will leave his hotel around 21:00. He will use public transport and go to a casino. He bets on the tables for a couple of hours and then heads off to the bar. He has a couple of drinks and will pick up a girl there. Then he leaves with the girl at around 01:00. If the girl has a flat or hotel suite, then he goes back there, otherwise he goes to another hotel and gets a room,' said the youngest man in the room who was over fifty years old and looked every day of it and more.

'And we are sure that he will do this?' quizzed the heavily set man.

'Yes. He follows the same routine when in London. In fact, it's the same routine whenever he's in Europe,' replied the youngest man.

'OK, carry on.'

'We'll pick him up outside the hotel and trail him. He doesn't do much dry cleaning. He'll get a cab then jump out at a station and get on the underground. Then he'll walk the last bit to the casino. We will follow initially in two cars. We'll send six people into the underground and when he emerges, we'll bring in four teams of two people who will swap over trailing him and we'll have a backup mobile unit tracking via the road systems. Once inside the casino, we'll lift something from him and then Agent J will take over. She'll drop the lifted item next to him and that will start the conversation. We have a hotel room and both rooms either side. Agent J will take him back and we have full visual and audio in that suite. There will be two teams, one in each room, and they will not only independently record everything but will also act as backup should the general get too boisterous.'

'The person who is going to lift. Is he one of ours?' asked the heavily set man gruffly.

'Yes. He's our best. His father was a famous pick pocket in Budapest. He was the scourge of the Red Army in the sixties. We used him a lot then and when it became too hot we relocated him to Tel Aviv as an instructor in the craft. The boy has been trained by the best.'

'Good. And Agent J?' he asked, although he already knew her and her family well.

'Recruited straight from the Army. In the field two years now and is a formidable and fearless agent.'

'Well then, let's see how General Faisal fares against us.'

He stood up and the other three men took that as a prompt that the meeting was over.

21:12. General Faisal walked swiftly through the hotel foyer and he went outside via the revolving door. It was raining and there were a glut of black London taxis waiting there eager to take anyone anywhere. He jumped into the back of the first taxi.

'Where to, guv?' said the driver in a heavy cockney accent.

'Oxford Circus.'

'Right you are, guv.'

The cab pulled out into the heavy evening traffic. As it did so, two cars that were parked on the main road also pulled out and headed off in the same direction. The black cab deftly took a number of back turns and arrived outside of Oxford Circus station in less than five minutes. The two cars had kept up the pursuit and stopped further back down the road. The rear doors opened and six men jumped out onto the pavements.

General Faisal pulled out of his brown leather wallet a crisp twenty-pound note and shoved it though the small Perspex window.

'Don't you want your change?' squawked the cockney sparrow.

General Faisal had already exited the cab and was heading down into Oxford Circus station.

'God bless,' shouted out the cabbie, and he turned on his For Hire neon yellow sign knowing that this was going to be his best tip tonight.

General Faisal darted down the grubby stairs and, using his London travel card, he passed through the barriers. He chose the escalators that were leading to the Central Line and joined the throng of people descending into the bowels of the station. Even at this time of the evening, Oxford Circus was busy. It was no wonder that Oxford Circus was the busiest underground station in London.

On the platform there was a fair crowd of people spread out over its full length. He moved along the platform to try and find more room and a train hurtled into the platform from the dark tunnel. The train doors swished open and passengers poured out. He, along with everyone else on the platform, anxiously pushed his way onto the train. The display board showed that the following train would only be three minutes away, but no one ever waited. He stood in the middle of the train, amongst fellow travellers.

In a carriage further down the train, two men managed to board the train just before it departed, leaving four colleagues in their wake. Both were blowing a bit as they had to sprint down the stairs, but they still had their quarry in their sights. The train had not journeyed more than two minutes when it pulled into Bond Street station. Again there was an exodus from the train and General Faisal was amongst the crowd. One of the men was hanging nonchalantly out of his carriage, staring to see whether the general had exited. He just caught the sight of the general's crown amongst the crowd moving towards the exit and he immediately jumped off. His colleague was caught in the rush of people getting on and the doors closed with him still inside. General Faisal exited Bond Street station and walked briskly down Davies Street. He raised the lapels on his overcoat to help ward off the rain. His pursuer had closed the gap by walking up the escalator rather than standing on the right-hand side and letting it carry him up.

Outside of the station, he spoke urgently into his phone before following the general from a distance and on the other side of the road. At Berkeley Square, the general turned left and then right into Berkeley Street. He continued to walk for a further three minutes before he headed off into an exclusive Mayfair casino. His tail casually walked past the casino and positioned himself some thirty metres away further down the road. He continued to talk urgently into his phone whilst remaining on guard in case the general exited from the casino.

A further ten minutes passed and two cars pulled up next to him. He exchanged hushed words into both cars and three people got out and went into the casino. Once inside, the two men headed off into the main gaming room and the other person headed off to the bar area. Despite having several teams available, it was down to one agent who managed to trail General Faisal to the casino. So far, the covert operation hadn't gone remotely to plan and they were following a man who used sloppy tradecraft.

After General Faisal had purchased £20,000 worth of chips, he took up a place at a busy roulette table. No one took much notice of the new punter wearing a navy two-piece suit, white shirt and blue tie. He was just another rich Arab in a sea of rich Arabs that frequented the gambling haunts in Mayfair. He ordered a twenty-five-year-old Chivas Regal whisky and once that arrived, relaxed into playing roulette. Crowds of people gathered around the tables as this was as much a spectator sport as that of a participating sport. The two men that arrived after the general were both dressed in black tuxedos and bow ties and were casually joining in amongst the watching crowd. The general was betting on every roll but wasn't having much luck, and the stash of chips soon dwindled to nothing. Unperturbed, the general replenished the chips stash with a further £30,000 worth and carried on betting. He had a number of decent wins and his stash increased to more than both of his stakes. He became more adventurous and placed larger bets on even numbers only. This tactic proved to be disastrous and he burned through his pile of chips. He showed no emotion having lost £50,000 in just over two hours when he got up and left without tipping the croupier.

He passed through the crowd and made his way to the gents' toilet. The two men who were standing in the crowd directly behind where he was seated watched him go into the toilet and walked with purpose into the bar. They sidled up to a young lady perched on a seat at the bar and, without speaking, passed over to her a gold lighter. The gold lighter was immediately placed into her purse. The activity took less than ten seconds and both men ordered a drink and moved to a table in the corner of the room. A text was sent and they settled into their surveillance roll.

The general walked into the bar and gazed all around. He noticed the groups of people chatting, couples and a number of single men and women dotted about. There was a vibrant hum about the place. Wealthy people who lost money gambling did not worry about it. There was always another day and another chance. In the meantime, there were drinks to be drunk, drugs to be taken and sex to be had. Life was all about living it in the fast lane, lots of laughter, mad moments and no regrets.

General Faisal's eyes lasered in on the young thin man who was twitching. He was standing with a group of similarly aged men but wasn't engaging in their loud, boorish behaviour. General Faisal nodded his head slightly and the twitching man gave a replying nod. General Faisal walked towards the men's toilet and the young man followed. No one in his crowd noticed him leaving them. Faisal was leaning against a hand basin when the young man walked in, having checked that there was no one else in the cubicles.

'Are you carrying?' enquired Faisal.

'It's been a while. How are you?' said the young toff with an educated accent.

'I want to score. How much?' said Faisal, ignoring the young man's attempt at pleasantries.

'I've got high grade Toot and top-quality Speedball.'

'What the fuck are you talking about? I want coke.'

'Toot is the street name for coke and Speedball is the street name for cocaine and heroin combined.'

Faisal grabbed the dealer by his throat and shook him with his big powerful hand.

'I don't want a lesson. Just give me £500 worth of coke.'

'Sure. Just let me go,' he replied timidly.

The harassed toff fumbled in his right-hand jacket pocket and produced several small plastic bags. They were all nestling in his now sweaty palm.

'Is that all I get for £500?'

'Yes. There's more than 500 quid's worth here but as you are a regular you can have the lot,' the junky dealer stammered.

Faisal swiped the bags from the toff's hand and put them in his own right-hand pocket. The toff's eyes were pleading with Faisal, fearing that he was going to take the drugs and not pay for them. Faisal looked at the pathetic sweating man and withdrew from his wallet ten fifty-pound notes. He then handed over the notes and went into one of the cubicles where he snorted the contents of one of the bags. When he came out of the cubicle, he checked his nose for any signs of powder and then went back into the bar. He hadn't noticed that the toff was no longer hanging around in the toilet. Faisal was beginning to feel the effects of the coke and gazed around the bar. He could have sworn that there were at least three very young blonde hookers dotted around earlier, but now they weren't anywhere to be seen. That was a shame, a real fucking shame, but it wasn't going to spoil his evening.

Shit, this coke gives a real buzz. I must take some more, he thought. *But first I'll have a drink and get a hooker.*

00:10. Faisal extended his arm and clicked his fingers loudly. A young woman dressed in a black jacket and matching black trousers with a white shirt and black bow tie scuttled over from the bar and took his order. He attracted a couple of looks from other patrons in the bar as his voice boomed when he ordered a whiskey. Once the whiskey arrives, his predatory instincts took over and he scanned the room. As a hunter, he was looking for prey that were on their own. They were easier to manipulate and control. Unlike the bars and clubs in the Middle East where he could nod at a girl and they came over knowing what to expect, in Europe the etiquette demanded that he first talked to them. Then he must buy them at least two drinks and all the while make small talk. This was an irritating practice especially as there weren't young girls available here.

Faisal got up and walked over to a young woman sitting on her own. He asked her if he could sit down and she said OK. He began the dance by asking her if she had had any luck at the tables. She shook her head and said that she had been playing poker but hadn't come away with any winnings. He offered to buy her a drink which she accepted and so the dance continued.

She was a lot older than he liked, although she had a charm about her which was made more seductive by her French accent. A burly man walked over, excused himself and told the female that her taxi was outside. She drained her drink, stood up, shook the general's hand and sauntered off. He sat there frustrated for several minutes and then went off into the toilet for another snort of coke. When he came back out, he decided to try his luck with the woman perched on a stool at the bar. He noticed that she had been sitting there all alone nursing a drink since he first walked into the bar. She was more likely to be a hooker than the previous female he'd approached, he thought. She was wearing a long strapless dress which was deep blue. She was slim with wide shoulders, developed by countless hours of swimming. Her hair was blonde and medium length but he knew that it was dyed by the darker roots that were evident. She had an oval face with dark brown eyes.

'Is this seat taken?' enquired the general in a rather loud voice.

'No,' she replied in a whispered voice.

The general shook the bar stool roughly and sat down on it.

'I never have any luck at this club,' he went on loudly.

'Really?'

'No. I swear that they fix the roulette tables by using magnets. It's an old trick and they can make the ball go into any pocket that they choose. It's rigged.'

'So why do you play here then?'

'Good question. I often ask myself that.'

She laughed.

'My name is Jenelle,' she proffered.

'That's an unusual name,' he shouted.

'It means Gift from God. I'm an only child and my parents had trouble conceiving.'

'My name is Majid and my parents had no trouble conceiving.'

Jenelle laughed again.

'What are you drinking?' he bellowed.

'A gin and tonic please.'

The general clicked his fingers loudly and the barman walked over.

'A gin and tonic for the lady, ice and slice, and I'll have another whiskey.'

Jenelle noticed that Majid's behaviour was not so much extrovert but more manic. This guy was wired.

'So do you go to any other casinos?' she asked.

'When I'm in London I go either here or to a couple of other clubs in Mayfair. What about you?'

'Oh, I only come here. It's a good place to meet people.'

'Don't you gamble?'

'No. I like to people watch, so I go into the main casino and watch people playing. There's an electricity around the table when someone is on a winning roll. The crowd spontaneously roar at every win and it's intoxicating.'

'What about when someone is losing?'

'Well that's also interesting but in a different way. The crowd watches silently as the player self-destructs. I think that they call it rubbernecking.'

'Never heard of that. Where do you come from? You have an unusual accent.'

'I was born in Austria but my family moved to Brooklyn when I was young.'

'A German Yank.'

'Not sure about the German bit but definitely a Yank.'

The general slung back his drink and beckoned over the barman.

'Two refills here,' he hollered.

The barman looked at him and then walked off to make the drinks. He could have heard the general's drinks order if he was standing outside in the street.

The general leant forward and placed his large hairy hand on Jenelle's knee. His rosy face was now inches from her own.

'What do you say we get out of here. I've got some great gear.'

Jenelle smiled and leaned back slightly, trying to avoid his foul breath.

'Yeah, sure. I have a hotel suite not far from here.'

'Good. Let's finish our drinks and we can get a cab. It's raining and there's no point in getting soaked.'

He was so loud now that almost everyone in the bar could hear their conversation. Well, his part of it anyway. He swung around to pick up his drink and knocked over both drinks. The glasses along with the bottle of tonic water flew off the bar and crashed onto the floor behind the bar. There was a loud noise as the glasses and bottle broke into pieces. The liquid spread all over the floor and the shards of glass began swimming in the alcoholic puddle. Everyone in the bar turned and looked towards the bar where the commotion had emanated from.

A hush had descended on the room until the barman smiled. 'No harm done. I'll clean this up.'

'Yes, and we'll have another couple of drinks then,' thundered the general.

Three large doormen appeared at the bar along with the floor manager.

'Sir, your taxi is waiting outside,' said the smiling floor manager.

'I haven't had my drink yet.'

'Sir, the taxi is waiting and your young lady wants to leave.'

'I need to get my coat.'

One of the doormen produced his overcoat and handed it to him. He also had Jenelle's coat and handed that over to her.

'OK, I need to settle up my bar bill.'

'Sir, that won't be necessary,' went on the floor manager.

Both the general and Jenelle dismounted their bar stools and, with their coats folded over their arms, followed the floor manager. The three doormen then followed behind both of them. They walked out into the opulent foyer with a magnificent chandelier as its centrepiece and headed towards the back of the casino. They walked through three rooms and then a door was opened to the rear of the casino. Outside on the street was a black taxicab parked with its engine running. The rain had become heavier than earlier and it was now teaming down. Both the general and Jenelle put their coats over their heads and made a dash to the cab.

The floor manager looked at the general as he passed by him. 'Sir, have a safe journey home and we'll see you soon.'

The floor manager held Jenelle by the arm for a moment as she passed by. 'Don't show your face in here again.'

Once in the cab, Jenelle gave the address of the hotel, and the cab headed off into the driving rain. The general leant over and forcibly pushed his tongue into her mouth. She was physically repulsed by this ogre but didn't reject his unwanted advance. The general suddenly disengaged and thrusted his head towards the partition that separated them from the driver.

'Change of plan. Take us to the Metropole,' he screamed.

'Right-oh, governor.'

A number of thoughts flooded Jenelle's mind but one thought overrode all of the others: *Keep calm*, she thought over and over.

'I thought that we were going back to my suite,' she said casually.

'I like the Metropole.'

The general walked up to the reception and demanded the key to his room. They ascended in the lift to his room in silence, although he continued to manhandle her breasts roughly. Once in the room, he poured a couple of drinks from the minibar. He plucked out the remaining plastic bags from his jacket pocket and put them on the table next to the drinks. He emptied the contents of three of the packets onto the table and spread the contents out into two lines. He leant over and snorted the thicker, bigger line through one of his nostrils whilst blocking the other nostril with his index finger. He received an immediate rush and slumped back into the plush sofa.

'Here, have this line,' he shouted, looking at Jenelle whilst pointing at the white talcum powder-like line on the table.

Jenelle leant forward and inhaled the line, mimicking his actions. She fell back into the sofa and was overcome by the rush that she was receiving.

'Wow, that's fucking great,' she shouted.

'Told you.'

01:40. Back at the casino, the twitching man felt his phone vibrating in his trouser pocket. He withdrew it and walked quickly into the toilet.

'Yeah, what's up?' he said in his posh accent.

'I've got some punters looking for Speedball. Do you still have the stash?'

'Yeah. I've unloaded all of the Toot though. So if anyone wants any then it won't be tonight.'

'Understood. That Speedball is high octane, right? So two bags shared between six should do. Right?'

'Yeah. It's the best we've ever had. A little goes a long way.'

'OK, I'll be outside in five minutes. Oh, and how much did you get for the Toot by the way?'

'Only £350, but he's a repeater,' he said, peeling off £150 from the roll and putting it in his shoe.

Under the branches of the trees at the edge of Berkeley, the two drug dealers conferred. The twitching man withdrew several plastic bags from his left-hand jacket pocket and passed them over. His confederate looked at them quizzically and then popped open one of the bags. He wet his little finger on his tongue and dabbed it gently in the bag. He then put his little finger into his mouth and rubbed it against his gums. All of the while the twitching man was looking at him perplexed.

'What the fuck is this?'

'What do you mean?' stammered the twitching man.

'This isn't Speedball, it's coke.'

'Oh fuck. That means I gave that Arab wanker Speedball. There's enough there to give the biggest, best and fatal fucking rush he'll ever have.'

'You're a real fucking twat. That was worth two grand at least and you gave it away for £350. And if he croaks then we'll have the old bill crawling all over us. You need to stop sampling the merchandise, it's fucking you up.'

'He hassled me and I got confused.'

The other man started to walk off after putting the several plastic bags into his coat pocket.

'Hey, where are you going?'

'To try and salvage your fuck up. I'll sell them this coke at a premium.'

'Thanks.'

'Fuck you.'

The general had finished his third drink and was rummaging through the minibar looking for more.

'I need to use the bathroom,' screeched Jenelle.

'Sure. I'll create another line that we can share,' he howled whilst sweating profusely.

Jenelle went into the bathroom and looked at herself in the mirror. Everything was going around at one hundred miles per hour. She wasn't in control and the plan had gone to shit. She had had coke before and this wasn't like anything that she had experienced. Maybe it was the drink along with the coke, she thought. But she'd only had a couple of drinks. It must be high-grade coke then, she thought. It wasn't only affecting her – that ogre was completely off his trolley and he was sweating like a pig. Hopefully he'd pass out before he wanted sex. She patted cold water onto her face and walked back out into the main room. The general was standing there facing her with a fixed look of anger on his face. The contents of her purse were strewn on the carpet and he had smashed everything under foot into smithereens.

'Is everything all right?' she shouted.

He strode up to her and punched her in the face with all of the force that he could muster. The blow knocked her backwards and she fell over. He immediately reigned down several kicks into her head and her body as she lay prone on the floor. He grabbed her by the hair and dragged her into the bathroom. Barely conscious, she was unable to defend herself. Once in the bathroom, he smashed her face into the basin several times. Her face was mush and there was blood everywhere in the bathroom. He threw the limp body into the bath. He looked in the bathroom mirror and saw that his face was splattered with blood and his suit and shirt were also covered. He looked down at his shoes and saw that they were covered in blood also. His heart rate was still racing. He was sweating but the red mist that had descended was lifting. He kicked off his shoes and stripped down to his underpants and then washed himself in the sink. He dried himself off and sat on the toilet. Beside it was a telephone and he dialled a number. The phone was answered after three rings.

'It's me. I'm at the Metropole, room 1309. There's been an accident and it needs cleaning. Bring me some clothes.'

'Twenty minutes.'

Faisal answered the knock on the door and the man carrying two suitcases swiftly walked into the room that bore the hallmarks of the aftermath of a violent crime scene. There was blood on the carpet and on the furniture. The table was upended and a vase with flowers was lying on the blood-soaked carpet. The man who was wearing gloves and a hat pulled down low to hide his face put the cases down, put on plastic covers over his shoes and walked into the bathroom. He surveyed the general's handiwork and returned to the main room.

'What the fuck happened here?'

'That bitch stole my lighter. I found it in her bag,' he shouted, holding up the gold lighter between his thumb and forefinger.

The man opened the first suitcase and withdrew a tracksuit, T-shirt, trainers and socks. He put all of the clothes on the bed which had not been contaminated with any blood or debris from the assault.

'OK, get changed and remain on the bed. I'm going to clean up this room first and then the bathroom.'

The general accepted the order and walked over to the bed, avoiding the blood on the carpet. The man walked around the room collecting all of the broken pieces of wood, glass, smashed contents from Agent J's bag and flowers strewn about the place and deposited everything into a couple of large plastic bags that he'd retrieved from one of the cases. He picked up from the table two small plastic bags containing powder and opened one of them. He then wet his little finger and dabbed the powder and rubbed his finger on his gums.

'How much of this stuff have you taken?'

'I don't know. Maybe four bags.'

The man withdrew his phone from his jacket pocket and speed-dialled a number.

'Bring up the medical bag right away.'

'What's the matter? What's going on?' wheezed the general.

Holding up the small plastic bag, the man said, 'This stuff is cocaine mixed with heroin and there's a lot of heroin.'

'Shit. I'll kill the dealer.'

'Let's not worry about him now. You need to remain calm and focus on taking deep breaths.'

The man then continued with cleaning up the room. He first threw onto the carpet an industrial-strength cleaning agent and then began vigorously cleaning away the blood and gunk. A knock on the door interrupted his endeavours and he walked over and opened the door. Another man, short and wearing a similar hat and gloves, nodded to him and walked into the room. The medical bag was put on the bedside table and the man withdrew a syringe and a small bottle. The syringe was filled with the contents of the bottle and the man looked at the general who was sat on the bed watching the events.

'Make a fist,' said the man.

'What's going on?' said the general, who was beginning to struggle for breath.

'You are experiencing a heroin overdose. That's why you can't breathe properly, it's slowing down your breathing. This is Naloxone and it will counteract the effects.'

The general made a fist and the man put the syringe's contents into a vein in the crook of his elbow. The man filled the syringe with the contents of another bottle and went into the bathroom. He returned and put the syringe and bottles into the medical bag.

He spoke to his partner. 'Go and get a cleaning cart and leave it outside the door.'

The small man picked up the medical bag and left without speaking. The man continued with cleaning the carpet and then retrieved from his case a small powerful vacuum cleaner and hoovered the carpet. He washed and cleaned the furniture and put everything back in its rightful place.

'I'm going to clean up the bathroom now. I'll be ten minutes,' he said, looking at the general.

'Is she dead?' said the still wheezing general.

'No but she needs medical attention.'

'Why not kill her and dump her?'

'Because it will be traced back to you. London has CCTV everywhere and you will have been captured on screen. Leave everything to me.'

The man went into the bathroom and ran the shower. He cleaned away blood from the still-limp body and cleaned up the rest of the bathroom. The general's bloodied clothes and shoes were strewn on the floor. He went through all of the general's pockets and retrieved all of his personal effects which he placed in a plastic bag. He then took the clothes and shoes and threw them into one of the big plastic bags in the main room. When he was satisfied that everything was respectable, he picked up Janelle and carried her out of the bathroom. He opened the front door and poked his head out. Satisfied that there was no one there, he quickly went out into the corridor where a cleaning cart was sitting and he dumped the body into the cart and covered it with some of the dirty linen. He went back into the room and slowly walked around, checking everywhere for anything that he may have missed. He did a similar inspection in the bathroom and ran the shower one final time. Back in the room, he refilled both suitcases. He looked at the general.

'We are leaving now. You can carry the two plastic sacks. And here's your personal stuff,' said the man, handing the general a plastic bag.

The general got up from the bed and stumbled towards the door.

The man held up his hand and said, 'Don't forget your lighter.'

The general stopped and went back and retrieved the gold lighter from the bedside table.

The man followed by the general pushed the cleaning cart which now also contained his two suitcases to the lift and pressed the button. A lift appeared almost instantaneously. They got in and descended into the basement car park. Once outside of the lift, a black Volvo estate car pulled up next to them and the smaller man darted out from it.

He looked all around, checking for any movements and, satisfied that that no one was around, he opened up the boot and then said, 'Quickly, get in.'

The other man threw his two suitcases into the boot and closed it. He then took the limp body from the laundry cart and put it safely into the rear passenger seat.

'Get in the front,' the man said to the general as he sat in the rear next to the body.

In less than two minutes, the car was pulling out of the underground car park into a quiet Edgware Road. The hotel garage CCTV had grabbed images of the black Volvo including its number plate.

'We are going to drop you off first. The hotel will charge you extra to cover the damages to your room but it's no worse than any party except that it's been cleaned up,' the man said in a tired voice.

'What about the girl?' asked the general, whose breathing was beginning to normalise.

'Don't worry about her.'

'I still think we should kill her. That's what I'd do in my country.'

'Well you aren't in your country now. And that doesn't work here.'

After ten minutes, the Volvo pulled up outside the general's hotel where he resided with his Arms Fair delegation. The general got out of the car, hesitated for a moment and then looked back into the car.

'Thanks.'

The was no reply, the front passenger door was closed and the Volvo pulled out into the quiet road. The car drove on for several minutes and stopped in a quiet side road. The man opened the rear passenger door and quickly pulled out the body and left it lying on the pavement. He got back into the car and it drove off. From his pocket he retrieved a burner phone.

He dialled 999. 'Hello, there's a badly injured woman in Glasgow Terrace.'

He closed the phone, not waiting for the operator to ask which service he required. He then leant over and put the burner phone into one of the plastic bags sitting in the boot of the estate car.

11:30. The delegation were sitting in a VIP room in the ExCel centre. They were taking a break from the tiring round of meetings and presentations that they had been attending since 08:30 this morning. They had had a long evening at their embassy the previous evening where a dinner party was thrown, and diplomats from many other nations along with politicians and a few celebrities had attended. The doors opened and through the security cordon emerged General Faisal wearing a freshly starched military uniform. He looked the picture of an important senior military man and walked briskly over to the group.

'Good morning,' he said with authority.

One of delegates looked at him and said sternly, 'Where have you been? We've been unable to contact you this morning. We came here without you and you were supposed to take the lead in a number of sessions.'

The general stood to his full height. 'I've been involved in matters of national security.'

'Even your own security detail didn't know where you were. We were all very worried. These are troubling times and we don't want our most high-profile general unaccounted for.'

'Yes, I agree. But the contacts that I have developed need to be protected. The information that they are providing is high grade and vital to our efforts. I cannot afford to jeopardise them.'

All of the men nodded in agreement. The general thought to himself that mentioning national security and meeting spies never failed to get him out of any situation no matter how tricky or embarrassing.

15:00. The group of four senior Mossad agents were again in the secure Inner Sanctum in the Israeli Embassy. With them was the operations manager who ran the covert operation mission to make contact with General Faisal. The object of the mission was to use a honeytrap to blackmail the general and obtain classified information. He had been selected because of his sexual proclivities and penchant for coupling that with drugs and gambling.

The heavily set man said, 'Start at the beginning and talk me through this clusterfuck.'

The air of confidence that suffused the meeting yesterday had been permanently punctured. No one looked at him and all were staring at the reports sitting on the desk in front of each of them.

The operations manager cleared his throat. 'The operation began at 21:15 and two cars followed Faisal who was in a taxi to Oxford Circus. He then descended into the underground and we followed him.'

'How many men were on his tail? Don't leave out anything,' growled the heavily set man.

'Sorry. Six men followed him into the station at 21:22 but four didn't get onto the platform because they couldn't get through the barriers. They needed to buy tickets and there were queues everywhere. Two followed him down and boarded the train at 21:28. The train stopped at Bond Street at 21:30 and one man followed him off the train. The other agent was caught on the train because of the surge of people getting on. Once

248

outside, our agent contacted the mobile team and began following Faisal whilst giving them a running commentary. At 21:45, Faisal entered the casino and the agent remained outside until the team arrived. The team went inside at 21:55. Agent J went and sat at the bar. The other two agents positioned themselves in the crowd watching the roulette table that Faisal was playing. He lost, according to our agents, a sum of £50,000 approximately and then left the table and went to the toilet. Whilst he was walking away from the table, a gold lighter was lifted from him. The lighter was then given to Agent J at 23:55 and the two agents then sat in the corner of the bar. Faisal went into the bar and left after several seconds and went back into the toilet. Whilst he was in there, the two agents walked up to three young blonde hookers who were on their own and asked them to go outside. They told them that they would make it worth their while.'

'Wait. This wasn't part of the plan that we discussed,' menaced the heavily set man.

'No, sir. They were using their initiative. They were aware that Faisal likes young girls and especially blondes and they wanted to remove all competition for Agent J,' said the operations manager without much conviction.

'Continue,' barked the heavily set man.

'At 00:08 our two agents and the three hookers left the casino. They went outside and walked around the corner. Once out of sight, they were offered £500 each to not go back inside the casino for the rest of the night. Initially it looked like they were going to accept the offer but then one of them asked for more money as she claimed that she would be losing money. The agents texted us and we agreed to treble the amount. She then said that she wanted £5,000 and that her "friends" also wanted £5,000. We agreed to that and then we had to get £15,000 over there. It was raining and the girls wouldn't stay outside, so we drove them to another hotel where they would wait for the money. They agreed only if the two agents accompanied them as they thought it was a scam. At 00:20 both the two agents and the three hookers were driven to a hotel where they waited for the money. The money arrived at 00:45 and the two agents rushed back to the casino. Whilst the two agents were away, there was a car sitting outside the front of the casino. The agents knew that Faisal hadn't left whilst they were away. They went straight into the bar at 00:52 but couldn't see either Faisal or Agent J. They checked all of the gaming rooms and all of the gents' toilets, but neither were in any of these places. They then asked the barman if he had seen their friend and described Agent J to him. He told them that Agent J left with a man answering Faisal's description after he had caused an incident. They spoke with the manager who declined to discuss any details regarding patrons and asked them to leave. One of them asked to use the toilet and in there he spoke to the attendant. The attendant told him that there was a back way out and that it was used to discreetly remove anyone behaving in an unacceptable manner. Apparently some patrons occasionally get upset after they suffer heavy losses and need to be removed as it upsets the general ambiance. That information cost another £200. They left the casino at 01:12. The agents at the honeytrap were contacted and told to report in as soon as Agent J arrived. In any event, they were told to report in every ten minutes anyway.'

'And was it escalated that an agent had gone missing?'

'No, sir. At this stage we thought that Faisal may have continued partying and gambling as he was only in the UK for a short visit.'

'Really? Continue.'

'We had the regular reports every ten minutes from the honeytrap. At 02:00 we sent a car back to Faisal's hotel. They checked at the reception if he had returned there but were told that he wasn't in his room. The car remained outside and at 02:55, he returned on his own in a black Volvo. We got the number plate and are running checks on the owner of the vehicle. What was strange was the general went out to the casino dressed up in an expensive suit and he returned in a tracksuit and trainers. General Faisal was picked up in an embassy car accompanied by another three cars at 11:00 and drove directly to the ExCel Centre, where he still is. At 02:05 we declared that Agent J was unaccounted for. We had been trying to contact her but her phone was switched off and we continued all day. We ran the usual checks i.e. hospitals, police, but didn't get a hit. At 11:45 we finally got a hit. A young woman had been admitted to St Thomas' Hospital on Westminster Bridge Road. An anonymous call was received at 02:43 and an ambulance despatched to Glasgow Terrace in Pimlico. She was found lying in the street unconscious and they took her straight into St Thomas'. She has multiple internal injuries which are consistent with being kicked many times by a heavy man. Her face has been smashed up and she has lost the sight in her right eye. The doctor said her injuries are far worse than someone being thrown head-first through the windscreen of a car doing sixty miles per hour that was in a head-on collision. She was in theatre for four hours and is out of danger but will need full facial reconstruction. We have a man and woman at her bedside and as part of her legend they are her mother and father. They will remain with her and get as much information as possible from her as soon as she is awake and able to communicate. The doctor said that she will need further facial reconstruction as his job is really just to put everything back in place. Because of the nature of her injuries and the fact that there was an anonymous call, the hospital has informed the police and they want to talk with her as soon as the doctors allow them to.'

'Is that everything?' said the incandescent heavily set man.

'Yes,' came back the timid reply.

'Are the two field agents who were supposed to be in the casino with Agent J outside?'

'Yes.'

'Please bring them in then.'

The two field agents who were looking and feeling haggard walked into the highly secure room and weren't invited to sit down. Beside them stood the operations manager.

'Gentleman, due to the seriousness of this incident and the complete lack of regard for protocol and the agreed plan, this is now a disciplinary hearing. Having heard the evidence as reported by the operations manager, the following measures will be implemented with immediate effect and there is no right of appeal. Both agents will be suspended for six months without pay. After the suspension has been completed, both of you will be sent back to training school where you will undergo all training starting from Phase One. Your records will be updated to reflect these measures but will not make any mention of the operation that caused these measures as that is classified. You will be on the next available flight back to Tel Aviv. Should you mention anything of this operation or your punishment to anyone, there will be the most severe consequence. Now get out.'

Both agents were visibly shaken by the wrath vented upon them and walked out of the secure room stunned.

'As operations manager, you endangered the life of an agent by your reckless behaviour. Your decision making and reaction to the unfolding events was exceptionally poor. You didn't escalate until it was far too late. You will be moved to liaison officer with the Army. You will become a border guard on the West Bank and remain there for one year. At the end of one year, your position within Mossad will be terminated. During your time as a border guard you will remain on Mossad pay. I do not need to remind you that there will be serious repercussions should you ever mention anything relating to this episode to anyone. Dismissed.'

There was quiet in the room for several minutes. The heavily set man had just driven a coach and horses through the whole wash up process and discipline procedures. Written manuals underpinned operational scenarios and they were used to define Mossad training. Where there were 'lessons learnt' out in the field, they were added to the ever-burgeoning manuals. Important lessons were incorporated in future training and if necessary, agents in the field would be either withdrawn for additional training or they would see the updates and acknowledge that they had absorbed the changes and would apply them forthwith.

One of the other men raised his head from looking at his recently handwritten notes and said, 'Perhaps we could talk through exactly what happened here.'

The heavily set man looked at him and smiled. 'Sure.'

'Surely we would want to wait for the written reports from the field agents and the operations manager to see whether there are lessons that need updating to our procedures. Once we have digested that, then we assess whether there was any further action to be taken and that would include promotion, citation or disciplinary action,' said Noah, who was sitting opposite the heavily set man who was called Jacob.

'There's no promotion or citation coming out of this fiasco,' said Jacob.

'That maybe so but we have an agreed process to follow,' replied Noah.

'An agent was left unprotected in the field by a bunch of incompetent fools and is now fighting for her life. That demands an instant response both internally and externally. We have dealt with the internal response and soon we will deal with the external response,' retorted Jacob.

'The reports from the—'

'Fuck the reports. We know what happened. And as you are so keen to see it in writing, take this down. Four agents who were on surveillance duty did not carry with them London Travel Oyster Cards. We knew the target would use the underground as part of his dry cleaning, but they didn't carry with them cards to get through the barriers. One agent remained on the train. He allowed a bunch of commuters and holiday makers to push him back onto the train. He should have barged them out of his way. The two agents who had specific orders to monitor Agent J deserted their posts. Without authorisation, they lured three prostitutes outside. Once there, they conducted some kind of negotiation and then with them and with another agent drove to a discreet hotel. A messenger was sent to a hotel to pay off the prostitutes and only then did the two agents return to the casino. There were two agents sitting outside the hotel and they didn't think to go inside and check that Agent J was OK. "Eyes on all times" is one of our pillars, is it not? And the operations manager didn't step in at any time and refocus the resources on supporting Agent J. He was embroiled in the negations with the three prostitutes and haggling with them. Once it was established that Agent J was no longer in the building, it should have been escalated. It wasn't escalated for nearly one hour,' said Noah as Jacob scribbled furiously on his note pad.

Noah looked grimly at his colleagues around the room. They in turn stared hard at their note pads.

'As for disciplinary procedures, the four morons who didn't bring their Oyster cards and subsequently were locked out of the underground, put them through disciplinary procedures. The idiot who got stuck on the train, arrange for a formal written warning. And the two goons who just sat outside the casino twiddling their thumbs, arrange for a month's pay to be docked. Find a replacement for the operations manager, arrange a five-day handover and then he's out of here. The two who drove off with the prostitutes will be sent back for more training. Right, that's covered everything, I believe. Oh, and get in replacements asap. We will meet here tomorrow 12:00. Before then, I want to know what exactly happened at the casino. Who picked up the general and Agent J and where they went. Who was driving the car that dropped off the general back at his hotel. If Agent J tells our agents anything at all, no matter how small, I want to hear it straight away,' said a still-furious Jacob as he got up and left the room.

No one spoke for a minute as they absorbed the edict.

Elijah spoke first. 'She is the daughter of one of Jacob's best friends. It's only natural that he's going to be upset.'

'Yes, but there are rules,' replied Daniel.

'Rules. They broke rules and left her in the hands of that animal,' said Elijah.

'Jacob won't back down and we won't challenge him. It's best if we get on with the tasks that he's set us,' said Daniel.

'Agreed. We don't want to fall foul of him and end up in his Kangaroo court,' lamented Elijah.

16:00. Pope and Chris Gould are sitting in the corner meeting room.

'So how did the match go yesterday evening?' inquired Pope.

'Frustrating really. The crowd were edgy and 0–0 against Montenegro didn't set the place alight. I think that there's still a hangover from that poor showing in the World Cup.'

'Yes. It didn't look great on TV. But we're still in a very strong position to qualify for the 2012 Euros though.'

'I just hope that when we get there we actually try and win it. There's no point qualifying and then not having a go.'

'Quite. Anyway, did Melanie enjoy her first game at Wembley?'

'She thinks that they are all overpaid and live in a bubble. Bankers and footballers are grossly overpaid and ignorant about austerity and the hardship of the working class. Christ, if I didn't know her, I'd think that she was a Commie.'

'But she didn't go on about that whilst the match was on, surely?'

'Don't you believe it. I thought she was going to start a chant for Arthur Scargill in the second half.'

'Come on.'

'Well, she did say that the hand dryer in the ladies' loo was fantastic.'

'Sounds like an interesting night.'

'Nope. It got worse. There was a queue to get into Wembley Park station that took forever. And once on the platforms, everyone squeezed onto the train. The whole process invaded her personal space. I guess that she won't be going to any more football matches.'

'OK, let's get back to work,' sighed Pope.

09:30. A strong rap on the door pierced the silence. Ahmed wearily dragged himself off the settee where he'd been fixated by the banal series of morning TV stories. Irritated by the interruption, he was determined to give a volley to whoever was behind the front door as he lived on a diet of TV programmes even though he didn't really enjoy most of what was on his menu. He pulled open the door with aggression complemented by an angry glare.

'Hi, Ahmed.'

The glare thawed instantly and the stiff body language melted. Ahmed's heart rate increased and his mouth opened and closes but no sound escaped from it. He was standing there gawping whilst catching flies.

'Here, take this bag,' she said, thrusting a large plastic bag into his hand as she demurely walked across the threshold.

Ahmed involuntarily stepped aside, accepting the bag as she shimmered into the front room. He regained his senses and dampened down his hair with his one free hand as he followed her into the front room. By this time, she had placed the other plastic bag on the bald table and was sat in the single chair.

'It's Dee's birthday today and I've brought up his presents,' said Aisha, pointing at the two large bags bursting with wrapped presents. 'Mum wanted him to open them on his birthday. I suppose that you will be going out for a drink to celebrate.'

Once again, Ahmed started catching flies.

'Yeah. We'll probably down a couple of pints.'

'Well, don't get him too drunk. He loses control of his legs and then it gets very messy,' Aisha said, laughing and displaying a perfect set of pearly teeth.

Ahmed immediately let out a raucous laugh.

'Put on the kettle then. I can't stay long but I'm dying for a cuppa.'

Ahmed scuttled out of the front room and set about completing the task with fervour. Meanwhile, Aisha scooped up the two plastic bags and followed him into the kitchen.

'Where are you going to hide them?'

'Hide what?'

'His presents. Obviously you want to surprise him and give him your card also.'

Ahmed took the two bags and disappeared into his bedroom. He threw the two bags onto his unmade bed and exited the foul-smelling cesspit, firmly shutting the door.

'I left my baby outside,' she sung whilst a choir of angels floated behind her.

'What? You have a baby?'

'Ahmed, don't be silly. My baby is a red VW New Beetle, 2007 model. Dee said that you told him to tell me to park it round the back. That way I'd avoid getting a parking ticket. Thanks for that.'

'No problem.'

'He said that you were limping. Did I do that when you helped me the other day?'

'What? No. I'm not limping, Dee got that wrong,' he replied, barely containing his rage.

'Good. Milk and two sugars. I'm going into the front room to watch a bit of daytime TV. I love it but don't ever get the chance to watch it. You are lucky to have a job with flexitime and can watch all of the best programmes.'

'Yeah. It's a perk,' he lied.

'Oh, and don't forget the bickies.'

Ahmed carried in two mugs of tea and half a packet of chocolate biscuits which he deposited on the table.

'You have had your hair cut.'

His reply was a curt nod.

'It looks nice. Mum was really pleased when she saw Dee's new haircut. She thinks that it makes him look grown-up. He's had the same floppy style since he was a boy and it makes him still look like a boy. Everyone in the family thinks that the new haircut suits him,' she said, glowing. 'Dee said that you told him to get it cut and recommended the new style. It's great, thanks.'

'Glad to be of help,' smiled Ahmed, thinking that Deepak looked like a football hooligan. *Well a wannabe anyway.*

'Mum is pleased that Dee has made a friend. I probably shouldn't say this but Dee didn't have many friends at school. He was quiet. But he talks about you a lot. He says that you are wise and always give him good advice. He says that you are loyal and a good friend as well as a work colleague.'

Ahmed smiled angelically whilst thinking, *Fucking hell. I'm on his case all of the time and I'm cruel to him and he thinks that the sun shines out of my arse. Perhaps I need to ease up on him. Nah, that's crazy, I'm going soft.*

'Can you speak to him? Mum has tried to call him every evening this week and he won't take the call. He works during the day and he claims he's working every evening as well. She's worried that he's overdoing it. He said not to come up for his birthday as he's working all weekend. That's why I brought up his presents. I had to take off half a day today so he got he presents to open on the day.'

Strange, thought Ahmed. *I didn't know that he was working every evening as I'm at the mosque. And he's definitely not there.*

'Perhaps he's got a bird,' laughed Ahmed.

'Not Dee.'

'Why not.'

'Because.'

'Because what?'

'Just because. Oh, and before I forget, take my number.'

Ahmed's heart raced as he fumbled for his phone and opened it up at the contacts icon.

'If there's an emergency you can call me and I'll pass it on.'

Ahmed was momentarily crushed but input her number. It saved him either illegally getting it via work databases or just bullying it out of Deepak.

'And give me your number.'

Aisha finished off her mug of tea, munching on her chocolate biscuit whilst talking to the TV. Ahmed finished off his mug of tea whilst watching Aisha talking to the TV. He could spend the rest of the day watching and listening to her talking to the TV. She got up and glided towards the front door.

'Bye, Ahmed. We'll catch up soon,' she said with a halo radiating liquid colours above her head and the same choir of angels singing softly in the background.

'Bye, Goddess,' he blurted out.

'What?'

'I said "My goodness". It's a saying that I got from my dad.'

'Strange,' she said, and with that the Goddess and her ensemble descended the stairs.

Ahmed slowly closed the front door.

'Fuck, fuck, fuck,' he muttered as he banged his head against the wall. He regained his composure as he heard the car sidle off. He even missed the opportunity to ogle her firm buttocks as she walked down the stairs to her baby. He was annoyed with himself and disappointed that he blurted out his thoughts despite making a heroic recovery. Calmness descended and he regained focus. He strode back into his health-hazard room, retrieved the two plastic bags and walked into the living room where he plonked both of them on the table.

'Right, what the fuck is that football hooligan up to,' he muttered to himself.

12:00. There was an air of expectancy in the Israeli secure room. The group had assembled and were waiting for Jacob to enter. He strode purposefully into the room with a small number of files under his arm and took up the seat at the head of the table.

He placed the files on the table and spoke softly. 'Gentlemen, please begin.'

'We had General Faisal under surveillance yesterday and he stayed with the entourage all day at the ExCel Centre. We had information that they were going back to the embassy and that there was going to be another embassy party that evening. However, they all left at 16:00 in a convoy with police outriders and went directly to Heathrow Airport. They were cleared through diplomatic channels and their private 747 took off at 17:30 heading for Zurich. Our agents confirmed that Faisal was in the convey and that he was seen at Heathrow Airport. We also know that he disembarked at Zurich and that the convoy went to their embassy. This morning the 747 left at 08:15 heading back to their capital and he was confirmed as being on board,' Daniel reported in a flat tone.

This drew no reaction from Jacob who was scribbling on a notepad.

'We spoke with the door security at the casino and they said that a gentleman and an escort girl were ejected from the casino the previous night. Apparently the gentleman was being very loud and drawing attention to himself which was disturbing other patrons. When he knocked over some drinks he was then discreetly removed. A black London taxi waiting out the front was asked to go around the back and pick up a member. They don't know the cabbie's name nor his licence number. There's over 20,000 black taxis in London and finding him won't be easy. We are going to ask every cabbie outside the casino between 22:00 and 03:00 whether they picked up Faisal and Agent J, and we have photos of both of them. We are going to say that Agent J was in an accident and we want to find out where she went prior to the accident. We'll do this every night and we'll stay on it for as long as it takes,' said Daniel.

Jacob continued to scribble in his notepad.

'The two agents sitting at Agent J's bedside have reported that Agent J remains unconscious. The doctors says that they don't believe that she's suffered any long-term brain damage but there is some swelling of the brain. They are monitoring her condition and remain hopeful that she will regain consciousness within a day or so. The doctor also said that blood tests revealed that she had taken both cocaine and heroin within twelve hours of her accident and also had alcohol in her bloodstream. Because of the heroin, they didn't give her the usual amounts of morphine and think that the heroin may have actually saved her as it reduced the pain that could have sent her into fatal shock,' said Elijah who had taken over the update before pausing.

The scribbling continued.

'We used our contact at the DVLA and got the name and address of the driver who dropped off Faisal at his hotel in a black Volvo at 02:55. We then used our police contact who told us that this man has a criminal record spread throughout his adult life. He's been involved in everything from burglary to driving getaway cars in bank robberies and anything in between,' continued Elijah.

Jacob stopped scribbling.

'I want him brought in and I'll question him. Take him to the safe house in Golders Green and when you are there let me know.'

'Jacob, we can't go around abducting people in another country. And we certainly can't torture them. It will cause a diplomatic storm,' Noah said.

'Just do it. He lost all rights when he assisted in the assault of Agent J. And no one is talking about torture; we're going to have a friendly fireside chat, that's all.'

Jacob scooped up his files and notepad, got up and left the secure room.

'He's taking this personally,' said Noah. 'And he's going to drag us all down with him. He's already dished out disciplinary actions without following due process and now he's going to lift a British citizen and question him.'

'That's only the half of it,' said Daniel. 'Yesterday he was openly talking about assassinating General Faisal. If he hadn't left on that 747, he'd have had a bullet with his name on it. The British authorities wouldn't have been happy with a dead Arab general on their streets and everything pointing at it being a Mossad hit. Not to mention what would happen back home. There would be a massive backlash from all of the Arab nations and who knows where that would lead. He's out of control.'

'Agent J may be a family friend but let's remember that she was involved in a honeytrap. We all know that those girls are glorified prostitutes,' said Noah.

'You have the same patronising attitude as the Russians. They use honey traps and treat their girls as meat. They are brave and are prepared to do anything and they risk their lives for their country. They are braver than you are and don't forget it,' raged Elijah.

'Agent J deserves a medal and don't let Jacob hear your views otherwise he might have a friendly fireside chat with you, Noah,' said Daniel.

'OK, before we end up tearing ourselves apart, let's go and pick up this character and see what information Jacob can elicit from him,' said Noah in a conciliatory voice.

262

10:30. A familiar ring tone repeated itself. Its familiarity nagged away until the owner woke with a start and fumbled for the mobile phone on the small table next to the bed. A cough cleared his throat as he pressed the digit to activate the phone.

'Hello,' he croaked.

'Ahmed, did I wake you?'

Ahmed sat bolt upright as an electric volt sped through his brain making it fully alert.

'No, how are you?'

'I'm well, thanks. Did Dee open his presents?' asked Aisha.

'Hang on.'

Ahmed sprung out of bed and walked into the front room. He fettled around the two plastic bags that were still on the old table. He then walked out and pushed open the bathroom door, then the second bedroom door and finally the kitchen door. Deepak was nowhere to be found.

'Aisha, he hasn't opened his presents yet and before you ask, he's not here.'

'Well, where is he? He didn't answer his phone yesterday evening and he's not answering it now.'

'Look, I don't know. I'll speak with him over the weekend and make sure that he phones home.'

'Thanks, Ahmed, Mum's upset. Did he come home last night?'

'I don't know. When I came home from work, I went straight to bed.'

'But didn't you see him at work yesterday evening? You work in the same place, right?'

'I didn't see him there. But he may have been in a different area.'

'Really? I'm confused. Dee said that you work in a small office.'

Ahmed screwed up his eyes.

'It is but I was in a small room going through a mountain of back files, so I wouldn't have seen him,' lied Ahmed, covering for Dee's earlier lie.

'OK. Thanks, Ahmed, and sorry to bother you.'

'No bother. Don't worry, he's just got a lot of work on his plate at the moment. That's all.'

'Bye then.'

'Bye.'

I need to nail that little bastard down and find out what is going on, thought Ahmed.

11:00. The silver BMW Series 5 model crunched on the stoney road that wended its way to the end of the industrial estate on the outskirts of Bedford. The car's suspension strained as it bounced over and through the potholes that permeated the badly preserved road. Muddy water splashed up against the shiny paintwork, leaving traces of stains. The further the car went, the more there was evidence of neglect to the buildings on this estate. The car stopped outside the last building at the end of the squirrelly road.

The four-storey commercial building was derelict and in a state of disrepair. It had been unused for several years and all exterior paintwork was peeling. Five people got out of the BMW and walked towards the front door, which had a large padlock and chain barring entry. The lead person retrieved a key from his pocket and unlocked the padlock. Everyone swiftly entered the building and the door was pushed shut from the inside. At least three pairs of eyes were watching them from concealed positions inside the building.

The noise of a car driving over the potholed and badly maintained road alerted the occupants in advance that someone was heading their way and they then took up positions to check who it was. Once inside, the pungent reek of marijuana filled everyone's nostrils. This was despite the fact that the building had been decked out with extractor fans. The fans were working at their absolute maximum but were overwhelmed by the number of plants that were being grown in this marijuana factory. There were heavy-duty plastic sheets on the walls, floors and even parts of the ceilings, and their function was to retain both heat and humidity. False ceilings had been fitted, and suspended from these low ceilings were batteries of 600-

watt hydroponic lamps. They were needed to feed the plants with eighteen hours of light every day. In addition, regular doses of water were required and this meant an adequate irrigation system was also in situ. Driving this was the stolen electricity power which was taken by bypassing the electric meter and thus keeping the clandestine business thriving. The plants were in pots and were regularly moved. Infant plants took up to twelve weeks to grow into mature plants when they could then be harvested. There could be three or four harvests per year. Each harvest yielded approximately 1,800 plants with a net worth of £600,000. All four floors were taken up with the growing of marijuana plants. The group walked through each of the floors inspecting the flourishing factory that was being cared for by five Chinese men who lived on the premises.

'Well, what do you think?' said the confident driver called Haroon.

'Impressive. In fact, I'm blown away,' replied Deepak.

'I told you, didn't I,' said Kareem.

'We control the manufacture and distribution from here,' boasted Younis.

'With this setup, I can see why you are riding around in a nice motor,' said Deepak, deliberately massaging their egos.

'Yeah, we are raking it in. But we need to be careful. We can't bank it otherwise it will trigger red flags and we can't spend too much otherwise people in our community will question where the money is coming from. Far too many nosey parkers,' Younis bragged again.

'So what do you do with money then?' enquired Deepak.

'Not now,' Siddiq said, firmly looking at Deepak with mistrust.

'You know why you've been recruited,' said Haroon sternly.

'Yup. I'm going to drop off the gear to the dealers around the Midlands and bring back their payments. Right?' Deepak answered confidently.

'That's right. The cash is collected by Siddiq outside of here and he looks after that end. Any dealer who is short or wants a tab then you just drive off and don't leave any gear with them. We'll look after that. If the word gets around that we're soft then everyone will try it on,' went on Haroon. 'Right, for this run, both me and Kareem will come with you. You have the list and the three burner phones?'

'Yes,' smiled Deepak as his head started to gently bobble.

'Let's do it then,' replied Haroon.

And with that, Deepak, Haroon and Kareem walked over to the dark blue 2007 Ford Fiesta that was parked by the side of building. The boot had already been filled with the packets of marijuana that had been packed and weighed by the Chinese workers. The car drove off and Siddiq stood impassively staring at the occupants. He had not fully bought into the new recruit Deepak. His antenna was tickled. There was something that wasn't quite right. Kareem had watched Deepak at the mosque for a while. He had quietly set about finding out about him and then had finally engaged him in conversation. Deepak was a mature student who had left his family in London and converted to Islam, and it was all too pat for Siddiq. Everyone else who was involved was a local Luton boy and everyone knew their families. But this guy has no background, and that spelt trouble.

15:30. The dark blue Ford Fiesta rested by the side of the dilapidated industrial building and the three occupants got out in unison. They circled the boot of the car and retrieved from it three sports holdalls. Then they smartly entered the padlocked front door, remembering to push it shut once inside. Their arrival had been tracked by the occupants who were busying themselves with their daily work but had halted. They recommenced their work once they had spied everyone had entered the building. The three men strode into a small room at the back of the ground floor. The door had peeled green paint exposing dry wood in badly need of treatment. The crispy paint flaked off in small pieces as they opened the door and went into the dank room. The three holdalls were thrown carelessly onto the table and the men grabbed rickety wooden chairs that were pushed against the cement walls and sat around the table.

'Deepak. This is your next lesson,' smiled Haroon. 'We now count all of the money again. Check it back against the entries that we made in the book. The money is then sorted by denomination and banded into bundles of £100. Got that?'

Deepak smiled and his head bobbled.

'OK, me and Haroon will leave you with Kareem and we'll be back in ten minutes,' said Younis, who was already seated in the small room expectantly.

And with that, Haroon and Younis got up and left the room, closing the door behind them.

Kareem unzipped the first holdall and turned it upside down. The spilled paper quickly built a small mountain as it flooded out of the bag. Kareem shook the holdall and turned it over, checking that all of its contents had been removed, and then tossed the empty bag onto the floor behind him. He repeated the exercise with the other two bags. The table now had a small mountain of cash, all in notes, on it.

'Right. I'll read out the names and the amounts of cash and you then collect that amount from the bundle and stack it in a pile. Each name I read out must have a pile,' said Kareem.

'OK.'

The exercise took twenty minutes and Kareem placed a tick in a column next to a name and amount in the small book that he took from inside his faded brown leather jacket. Neither Younis nor Haroon had returned by this time, but both Deepak and Kareem hadn't noticed as they were engrossed in their task.

Kareem then produced several handfuls of thick rubber bands from another pocket and threw them onto the table.

'Time to bundle up everything into £100 amounts,' Kareem said before adding, 'Always recount each bundle.'

They both set about the task with determination and the task was completed within fifteen minutes. Kareem pocketed the small book and the remainder of rubber bands before packing the cash bundles back into one of the holdalls and then deposited it, zipped up along with the other two holdalls onto the table. He took out his phone and jabbed out a small text.

'OK, we're done. Siddiq will come and pick us up,' said Kareem.

Right on queue, the door burst open and in walked Younis and Haroon, both smiling.

'Can we help?' laughed Younis, looking at the packed holdall and two deflated holdalls next to it.

'Nah, we managed without you,' eyed Kareem.

'Well, it was a good exercise for Deepak. He needs to learn the ropes,' continued Younis, still laughing.

'Anyway, time to have a smoke before Siddiq gets here,' laughed Haroon, producing two very large spliffs from his right hand which he had held behind his back.

'Looks like you have already had a smoke,' replied Kareem.

'We had to do something whilst Deepak was being schooled. 'Right?' laughed Younis.

Haroon lit the first spliff, inhaled deeply and passed the spliff to Deepak whilst exhaling the smoke into the room. The mustiness that pervaded the room was instantly overpowered by the pungent and recognisable smell of marijuana.

'Hey, Deepak, you do smoke, right?' quizzed Kareem.

'Of course,' lied Deepak, his head now furiously bobbling.

They all looked at Deepak as he inhaled. Their stares held until he exhaled the smoke through his nose and mouth and then coughed involuntarily several times.

'That's strong gear,' Deepak said whilst tears streamed from his eyes down his cheeks.

The other three howled with laughter and Deepak's draw was the initiation ceremony completed. He was part of their crew.

'Bro, that's skunk. It's the strongest and best there is. That's why we are taking control throughout the Midlands. Word is getting around about our product, and dealers want our gear rather than the weak shit,' said Haroon proudly.

Deepak passed the spliff onto Kareem, who took a long deep draw.

'Yeah, I can feel it already,' said Deepak, whose head was now bobbling a lot less.

The spliff went next to Younis, who was waiting patiently.

'Anyway, did you enjoy your first day?' enquired Kareem.

'Yeah. It was good. But the count routine seems a bit convoluted,' Deepak said.

'Don't let Siddiq hear you say that. It's his idea. We've tried to discuss it with him but he won't have it,' said Younis.

'Understood.'

'Let's just have a smoke. We've got another spliff to go and he'll be here in fifteen minutes,' said Kareem.

The room was filled with the smoke and the unmistakeable smell of skunk.

'The chinks always roll us a couple after we get back from a run. Can't understand a fucking word they say but they sure can grow the stuff and make a mean spliff. Good dudes,' said Younis.

Deepak had already made a mental note to get closer to Younis as he seemed to be the one who would spill information without too much cajoling.

'Younis, what makes skunk? Do the chinks need a lab?' asked Deepak, empowered by the heavy-duty blow.

'You really don't know shit, do you. Skunk is a plant that's been bred specifically. We get ours from Amsterdam but that's another story. The chinks are like gardeners. They plant it and grow it. Plus they give us a few rolled up. I guess they also smoke but we don't ask and they don't say,' said a relaxed Younis.

'Even if they told us, we wouldn't understand that gook shit,' said Kareem.

Everyone roared with laughter. The second spliff was smoked and the time was up. Siddiq had arrived in his silver BMW series 5 model and was sitting outside having just sent Haroon a text. They left with the three holdalls and re-padlocked the front door. The boot was open and the bags were thrown in it and a carpet placed over as a token. Once in the car, Kareem passed over the small book which Siddiq took and put in his jacket pocket.

'Everything go OK?'

'Like a dream. And everything is accounted for,' replied Kareem.

'You lot fucking stink,' said Siddiq as he put the car into gear and started to drive back out of the dead end.

Everyone smirked but didn't reply. Skunk got its name from the animal because it stank but it was the best. Upstairs several pairs of eyes watched the car depart before they returned to their gardening chores. Saddiq rolled down his window halfway even though it was a cold day.

Once they were halfway back to Luton on the A6, Saddiq looked in his rear mirror at Deepak.

'Where do you want dropping off?'

'I'm going back to the mosque, if that's OK.'

'Right, we'll drop you off first.'

The BMW pulled up outside the mosque and Deepak said goodbye to everyone and started to get out of the car.

'Hey, haven't you forgotten something?' Saddiq said, sharply turning around so that his head was facing Deepak.

Deepak froze.

Saddiq reached inside his jacket and produced a slightly bulging envelope.

'You did good today, bro. Kareem will be in touch,' smiled Saddiq.

The envelope was handed over and for the first time, Saddiq's tough exterior softened.

'Thanks.'

The BMW drove off and Deepak walked into the mosque with his head buzzing. He felt relaxed, awash with contentment but also with pangs of hunger. In the car, the talk was mainly about Deepak. The crew thought that he was a good guy, smart and would be an asset. Saddiq drank in their comments, kept his own counsel and hid his reservations.

One swallow does not make a summer, he thought.

Deepak walked aimlessly around the mosque for five minutes, waiting for the BMW to be well on its way to wherever it was going. He looked at his watch. It was now 17:10. He left the mosque and headed towards the flat. En route he stopped off at the chippie and bought two large cod and chips and two fish cakes. He was now feeling ravenous and couldn't wait to get home and devour this calorific, coronary heart attack mass.

He bumbled into the flat at 17:27, shouted out hello and put the wrapped fish and chips on the kitchen table. He placed one large cod, one fish cake and a heap of chips on a plate. They had already been salted and covered in vinegar by the chippie, so he only had to liberally add the tomato ketchup. Grabbing a knife and fork and after putting the kettle on, he wandered into the front room. Ahmed, sprawled out on the settee, carefully eyed him as Deepak sat in the armchair and began devouring the plate full of grub. Deepak chomped, chewed and swallowed the food in a frenzy. Tommie sauce splayed on both of his cheeks, lips and chin held firm when he let out a loud belch.

'Kettle's boiled, do you want a cuppa?' asked Deepak as he stood up.

Ahmed's eyes narrowed and his legs stretched over and beyond the end of tatty settee.

'Not for me.'

'What about some fish and chips then?' said the human tomato sauce man.

'No.'

'Good. I'm starving and wanted it anyway.'

Ahmed watched Deepak disappear into the kitchen. He puzzled over Deepak's odd behaviour but was interrupted when Deepak returned with an even bigger plate of food that was drowning in tomato sauce. Deepak went back out and returned with a mug of tea and an unopened packet of biscuits which he put on the table, brushing aside the two plastic bags full of his birthday presents. Deepak sat back down and loudly ate his way through the mountain of food on the plate. Without stopping, he swapped the sparse plate for the mug of tea and gulped down the mug's contents accompanied by four chocolate biscuits. His face was now covered in tomato sauce tinged with melted chocolate. He looked as if he had been in a fight and lost badly. He got up and let out an almighty belch. One that a lion would have been proud of following a feast of zebra, impala and wildebeest.

'Hungry then?' enquired Ahmed, still puzzled by Deepak's behaviour.

'Yeah, one more cuppa should do the trick,' said Deepak as he exited the room.

'Wash your face,' Ahmed shouted out after him.

Deepak returned with his face dripping with water and nonchalantly munched his way through another five chocolate biscuits whist disposing of another mug of tea. Deepak rested the mug on the table and melted back into the chair. Ahmed's blood was boiling nicely and he was ready to erupt.

'Bro, your sister turned up yesterday.'

Deepak smiled.

'Yeah, I'm not into getting in the middle of a domestic but neither do I want my ear bent.'

Deepak's smile endured.

'Bruv, you need to phone your mum.'

Deepak's smile emitted a sound. 'Chill.'

That was a red rag to a bull.

'Chill? Fucking chill? The fucking Chopra family were going to come up and blow out your birthday candles whilst we're in the fucking middle of a fucking under-fucking-cover operation. Don't fucking chill me, bro. You haven't even opened your presents that are sitting on the fucking table gathering fucking dust.'

Deepak stood up languidly.

'Where the fuck have you been? You say to your family that you are at the mosque, and I'm there so I know that you ain't. What the fuck is going on?'

'Chill out, man,' smiled Deepak, who was sated and relaxed.

Not a head bobble in sight. Ahmed's neck veins were pulsating manically and veins were appearing on his forehead. He was about to get up and physically confront Deepak. But two events happened simultaneously. First, Ahmed's phone started ringing and he gravitated towards it unthinkingly.

Second, Deepak walked out of the room, saying in his wake, 'I'm tired now and need a kip. Take a chill pill.'

Ahmed would have normally strangled Deepak and burned his body on a fire in woodland, but he noticed that the caller ID was Aisha aka the Goddess.

Fuck. I can't deal with her now, he thought.

And so the phone rang and rang and rang. Ahmed refusing to answer it, Aisha refusing to leave a message and Deepak lying on his bed, deep already in a dreamless slumber. There was no doubt that skunk was strong.

10:00. The lounge door tripped open and Ahmed ambled in. Full of sleep, he languidly stretched out dressed in a faded T-shirt and well-worn boxer shorts. Both under garments were in desperate need of cleaning following several days' worth of wear. His squinting eyes focused on everything in the room and then held a firm fix on Deepak, who was sitting on the settee – his settee.

'Good morning,' said an irritatingly perky Deepak.

'Is it?' croaked Ahmed, settling into Deepak's normal worn seat.

'I've opened all of my presents and cards,' said Deepak, pointing at the array of goods on the table surrounded by scrunched up wrapping paper with several birthday cards poking through.

'About time. I've been fielding questions from your family about your odd behaviour, bruv.'

'Thanks. I've spoken to everyone and made my peace,' Deepak said, waving ten ten-pound notes around that were inside his fist.

'Generous family you have, bruv, presents and money.'

Deepak quickly fumbled the money into his pocket just as his phone began to ring. He looked at the caller name that was being displayed and accepted the call.

'Yes. Right. See you there,' Deepak spat out and closed the phone.

Before Ahmed had a chance to begin his interrogation, Deepak sprung up from the settee and sped out of the lounge. Ahmed remained seated, awaiting his quarry's return. Ahmed sat there motionless for several minutes and heard Deepak leaving the bathroom. At that precise moment his phone rang and he saw the name of the caller. It was Aisha. He had no choice but to answer the call.

In the background he heard a muffled 'Bye' as the front door closed. His head spun around.

'Hello, hello, are you there, Ahmed?' Aisha said sweetly down the phone.

'Yeah,' he said in an annoyed tone, still staring daggers towards the front door.

'Have I called at a bad time? You sound stressed out.'

Gathering his composure, Ahmed said, 'No, everything is fine.'

'Well, that's good. I just wanted to say thanks. Dee phoned this morning and had a long chat with everyone and enjoyed all of the presents and cards. Mum is happy now but worried that he's working very long hours.'

'That's how it goes sometimes. Anyway, you are a very giving family what with giving him presents and all that money.'

'Ahmed, I don't know what you are talking about. We only ever give presents to each other. Giving money is lazy.'

'Right,' replied Ahmed, somewhat puzzled.

'So what are you up to now?'

'I'm off down the gym.'

'All right for some. Dee said that he has to go in today.'

'Did he? Well, I guess that he's still playing catch up then.'

'Well, you have a good time down at the gym. Bye.'

'Bye.'

Ahmed's mind was now moving into overdrive, *Where the fuck has that turd gone and where did he get that money from?* he thought. *I'm going to sort him out when he gets back. And he better not sit his arse on my settee either.*

10:45. Pope was dressed in a waterproof tracksuit and running shoes. Doodle was jumping up and yapping at him. Doodle's weekend runs had all but disappeared and whilst he got his regular daily walks, they were no compensation for the long weekend runs over Hampstead Heath.

'John, are you not going in today?' Jane said, standing squarely at the kitchen door.

'No, I need a day off. I'm going for a run, then down the pub and back for a family lunch at 16:00,' Pope said as he fixed Doodle's lead to his collar.

'It's going to be very muddy over there. It's tipping down.'

'Don't worry, I'll be OK.'

'It's not you I'm worried about. It's poor little Doodle.'

'Thanks.'

Daisy, dressed from head to foot in pink with a lurid pink bow on her head and a wand in her hand, danced awkwardly out of the front room and stood in front of Pope and Doodle, who was now straining at the lead.

Daisy looked sternly at Pope. 'Daddy, it's very wet out. Doodle will catch a cold, and don't forget that he has a sore bum.'

'Daisy, Doodle will be fine. Dogs like to be out in the rain,' said Pope sympathetically.

'Well, I don't know,' replied Daisy, standing her ground.

'Listen, we'll be back soon,' smiled Pope as he patted his mildly truculent daughter on her head.

Outside, Pope began to jog slowly up the road, warming up his muscles. Doodle continued to strain at the end of the lead. He had no interest in stopping at every tree and bush as was his want on a normal walk. He knew that they would soon be up on Hampstead Heath and then he would be free to run.

Pope's mind was quickly reprocessing events whilst he regulated his breathing in the driving rain that was hitting him at an angle and cutting into his eyes. He thought about all of the facets relating to the Luton operation before running through the facts and figures that made up his weekend project. Both were disturbing because there were no new leads and he really wanted to make some progress. The weekend work that Seb Drake had assigned to him personally were two high-profile cutting-edge UK scientific projects. The first related to a vaccine for Ebola and the second related to a filter for purifying water which was needed in Africa. Both had been infiltrated by French industrial espionage and as a result had irked senior captains of industry who had applied pressure to the prime minister.

As he ran over the Heath, slowly Pope's mind cleared and all that he focused on was his breathing. His muscles had settled into a rhythm and were working economically, compensating for both the uneven terrain and the muddiness under foot. He was vaguely aware that Doodle was changing colour before his eyes as the eager dog splashed over and through puddles in a near state of euphoria. They ploughed on in tandem and returned back home at 11:45. Both were a muddy spectacle and Pope removed his running shoes, leaving them outside in the rain.

Swiping up Doodle, he pressed the door bell and was greeted by Jane, who ran a critical eye over both of them before pronouncing, 'Both of you, straight upstairs and into the shower.'

Doodle eyed her dolefully and didn't move a muscle, secure in Pope's grasp as they headed upstairs and into the bathroom. He knew that there was a price to pay for returning home caked in mud and, despite not liking being put under the shower, accepted his fate. Pope spoke gently to him as he ran warm water over him, gently massaging doggie shampoo into his dull brown coat. In less than three minutes, Doodle's coat, legs and paws were now a dull white with all mud and leaves drained away. He stood there shivering whilst Pope roughly dried him with his towel. When Pope was satisfied that the job had been completed, he lifted Doodle out of the shower and placed him on the mat. Doodle shook himself vigorously several times, spraying beads of water all around the bathroom. Once he had completed that ritual, he sprinted out of the bathroom door and ran down the stairs where he ran in and out of every room. Without stopping, he sprinted back up the stairs and then ran in and out of every room upstairs save the bathroom. He completed another several laps and everyone watched, laughing as he kept up the pace. Finally he settled by Jane in the kitchen and lapped eagerly from his water bowl. With his fur still wet, he resembled a large rat rather than a Western Terrier.

Pope cleaned the shower out then dove under the piping hot water. It was instant relief following the long run in the driving cold wind and rain, and his brain was awash with endorphins. He dressed and headed down to the kitchen where a steaming mug of sweet tea was awaiting him. The mug of tea was despatched and Pope looked at Charlie, who was sitting silently opposite him at the table.

'Charlie, do me a favour. Pop your head outside and see whether Mr Khan is outside his house,' said Pope.

Charlie's scowl remained but she got up and walked out of the kitchen. Standing outside, she strained her neck around the porch and saw that Mr Khan was standing in the middle of his front garden. The rain had stopped and he was decked from head to foot in black. A black jacket over a black buttoned-down shirt with black trousers and black shoes. He was staring directly at her and she quickly moved back into cover in the porch. She retreated back into the kitchen.

'Yep. He's standing in the middle of his garden staring at our house. And he's dressed up. I guess he's going somewhere.'

Pope looked at Jane. 'Darling, can you give me a lift to the pub please?'

Jane eyed him curiously.

'Please. I need to take a day off. Listen, you get in the front and open the back door and I'll slip in from the back garden. He'll never notice.'

'John, really.'

Daisy, hearing the commotion, ambled in and stood in the middle of the floor, wand balanced in one hand.

'Right, Mum, I'm coming,' said Charlie mischievously.

'I'm coming also,' added Daisy, 'and so is Doodle.'

A smirk spread across Jane's face.

'OK. Looks like a family outing. John, anything to add?'

Pope was ambushed yet again by the Swans.

'Nope. I'll go out the back and come around the side. You lot just get in the car and be quiet.'

'Right, girls, get your coats, hats, gloves and wellies. We're off to sneak Daddy into the pub,' laughed Jane.

Both girls ran off to get their infiltration gear. Doodle was now up and running around in circles; clearly something was afoot, and he needed to be involved.

The girls returned bedecked and with Jane taking the lead they calmly walked out of the house, not looking up the road towards where Mr Khan was standing. The car was facing out of the drive and Jane got in the driver's seat. Charlie got in the front passenger seat and Daisy got in the seat behind Charlie. Doodle jumped onto Daisy's lap and Charlie reached back and closed Daisy's door. Jane deftly opened the passenger door behind her and started up the car engine. The rear passenger door mysteriously opened further and Pope crept in, remaining close to the floor. In one move, he turned and slowly and silently closed the door. Doodle instinctively joined in this wondrous game and leapt onto Pope's face, planting numerous licks on him. Daisy however was scowling as she couldn't fathom why her dad was lying on the floor of the backseat.

'Why is Daddy lying on the floor?' she screeched.

'He's playing a game of hide and seek with Mr Khan,' answered Jane calmly.

'Oh God. He walking down here,' shouted Charlie, looking directly at Mr Khan who was walking down the pavement towards them.

Jane was already in first gear, revving the engine, and upon hearing Charlie's shouts, dropped the clutch. The car wheel spun, creating a lot of noise, and skidded forward into the road. Fortune was with them as there were no other cars using the road and there was no chance of an accident. Jane yanked the steering wheel right and the car headed away from the very advancing Mr Khan. Everyone in the car started laughing and Doodle jumped around the car planting licks on everyone. The car quickly got to the end of the road and Jane took a left towards Hampstead Heath. Behind them, Mr Khan was standing with his hands on his hips, pondering the eccentric behaviour of Mrs Pope. He thought to himself that driving in that manner with children in the car was very irresponsible.

Once outside the pub that Pope used as his local, he got out of the car and popped his head back in. 'Thanks, girls. I'll be back later for Sunday lunch.'

The car pulled off in a more sedate fashion.

'Well, that's Dad's tradecraft in action,' quipped Charlie.

'I don't understand,' said a bemused Daisy.

'It's like witchcraft,' continued Charlie, teasing her younger sister.

'Daddy's not a witch,' said Daisy, who was getting visibly upset.

'That's enough now,' interjected Jane.

Doodle was still in full play mode and was jumping around the car licking everyone whilst wagging his tail.

'Now please calm Doodle down or he'll wee himself,' said Jane firmly.

15:12. It took a huge amount of effort over the last ten minutes but finally she had managed to prise open her eye. Her eyelids felt like they had been welded together and were not meant to be unsealed. Only full focus, concentration and what seemed like a Herculean amount of physical effort had achieved the goal of opening her eye. There was a film of liquid over her eyeball which was restricting her vision and her ability to re-close her eye. Around her eyeball and buried underneath her eyelids were small amounts of dried debris that felt like grains of sand and they were already irritating her. She wanted to rub her eye and clear away all of gunk but she knew something was seriously wrong.

It had taken several hours to get to this stage. She had travelled a long distance in that time. Starting from a state of deep unconsciousness, she had travelled through several unconsciousness layers and then finally she was on the positive journey as she traversed through several levels of consciousness until finally she reached a consciousness state where she was able to wake up. Travelling through all of the various levels created memories, and some were very fleeting whilst her brain tried to reboot. Primeval instincts worked, trying to restore the most important organ in the body back to its fully functioning state. The body had been desperately trying to reestablish a communication link with the brain and give it the millions of bytes of data per second that it always did. In return, the brain would return messages, and organs, muscles, ligaments, tendons and every cell in the body would act on those instructions. An unconscious brain reeked havoc to the most sophisticated animal on the planet. She knew that she felt disturbed and frightened during this journey but didn't have a recollection of what was happening within her brain. These were the dreams that someone had when they were having a nightmare and were suddenly woken up abruptly. These dreams, although she would never remember them fully, would haunt her for the rest of her life. Time and time again, she would relive this awaking process and wake up in a cold sweat fighting for breath. Her sleep would no longer be a peaceful experience but a battle. A battle with a faceless demon, her muted screams going unheard followed by a desperate struggle to wake up. Often after these regular night terrors, she would be mentally and physically exhausted for days. Seeking professional help would be out of the question as she would have to expose her fragile and tormented mind to a variety of 'mind doctors'. She would be certified unfit for the duties that she wanted to perform and she would be quietly pensioned off. She knew the outcome if her issues were exposed and preventing exposure meant that she would need to hide this vulnerability from everyone. This meant even sleeping with lovers. After the physical act of making love, she would never again experience the intertwining of bodies followed by sleep. Every aspect of her life needed guarding from now on from anyone who may choose to exploit, wittingly or otherwise, her weakness.

On two uncomfortable plastic chairs pushed against the wall of the sparse room sat two elderly people. The man, wearing a worn suit, with unbrushed shoes and a frayed collared shirt, was asleep at an uncomfortable angle. By his side, the elderly slim woman with brittle grey hair was studying the body opposite her in the hospital bed. The two seats were against the wall opposite the foot of the bed. The head which was swathed in bandages was propped up by several pillows whilst the rest of the body was lying under protective layers of blankets and sheets. A number of wires and tubes were attached to the body and head and were attached at the other end to three machines that were happily working away. The elderly woman had noticed that the body first was twitching and moving slightly. A few hours later, the head began to move, first side to side and then in an up and down motion. The girl was fighting. She was fighting for her life and fighting to recover her consciousness. The old lady moved her chair to be beside the bed and as near as possible to the bandaged head where she could see that a left eye was closed, protruding from fresh bandages. The right eye was packed and the bandages over it bulged out from the head.

That eye was damaged beyond repair and had already been removed.

Suddenly the left eyelids opened. First they were slits and then gradually they pushed back further. Behind them an eye started to move. It was surveying the room and moving about. The lady got up and briskly moved to the chair where the elderly man was sleeping fitfully.

'Wake up, Joseph,' she whispered. 'She's awake.'

Joseph's body shifted. The elderly lady dug her bony elbow into his exposed ribs and he sat bolt upright.

'What's going on?' he said, wiping the saliva away from the side of his mouth.

'Quick, she's awake.'

They scuttled back to the side of her bed and they both saw an eye peering at them out of the swathes of bandages. The elderly lady pulled back the bedclothes gently and exposed the arm and hand of the immobilised patient. Both arm and hand had tubes and monitoring wires attached to them. The elderly woman tenderly held the hand of the patient and looked into her eye and said in a calm mothering voice, 'If you can hear me, just squeeze my hand.'

The gunky eye looked at her somewhat alarmed and then moved around between the eyelids, trying to look elsewhere. She was desperately trying to make sense of what was going on.

'Please squeeze my hand. I'm here to help.'

Within the gnarly hand, the soft silky hand belonging to a young woman shook mildly and generated movement.

'That's good,' said the old lady. 'We don't have much time, so I'm going to ask you some questions. One squeeze for yes and two squeezes for no. OK?'

Another mild shake in the old woman's hand. Behind her, the old man had moved further back. He withdrew a phone from his pocket and hit a number in his contacts list.

He quietly mumbled a four-digit number and whispered, 'She's awake.'

The old lady smiled at the one eye.

'Do you know where you are?'

Two mild shakes within her grasp.

'Do you remember what happened to you?'

Another two mild shakes.

'Do you remember who you are?'

A mild shake in her hand.

'Good. You have done well. Now listen carefully. We have been sent here as part of your cover. I'm your mother and he is your dad. My name is Daliah, he's Joseph and you are Mia. Our family name is Berkovich. Don't worry if you forget any of that but don't say anything to anyone apart from us.'

The hand quivered again.

'Good. Everything will be OK. We're here with you now,' said the old lady, smiling at the bewildered and frightened eye.

Just then the door burst open and in strode a nurse. She moved past the old man and leant into the bandaged face, looking directly into the eye.

Her face was a mask of sternness, 'Good that you are awake. I'm going to get the doctor and he will come and examine you. OK?'

The eye looked at her and blinked.

'Once he's done then I'll clean up your eye. That will make you make comfortable,' said the nurse, now breaking into a smile.

The nurse moved towards the door and then addressed the two elderly people. 'Both of you will need to wait outside whilst the doctor examines your daughter Mia.'

'How long will that take?' asked Mrs Berkovich.

'Not that long but please come out with me now.'

The old lady leant into the bandaged head and regathered her left hand. 'We'll be outside whilst the doctor examines you. We'll come back in as soon as he has finished. We love you, Mia.'

There was a weak shake in her hand. The old lady knew that Agent J's strength was dwindling fast. The experience was overwhelming her but at least she had begun the very first baby step on a long, hard road towards her recovery.

Three men in long white coats with stethoscopes hanging from their necks marched past the elderly couple and into the single occupant room. There was a flurry of activity from the ward and a further three nurses scurried in after them. The blinds on the window and door to the room were closed. A nurse exited after five minutes and returned wheeling in a trolley laden with bandages and other materials. Another ten minutes passed slowly for the couple whilst they sat there in silence, anxiously staring at the door before the gaggle came out. The taller of the three men walked over to them and his two colleagues held back in deference. The nurses disappeared back into the side wards.

'My name is Mr Kent and I'm looking after your daughter's care.'

Both of them nodded and Mrs Berkovich smiled meekly.

'We've just examined Mia and are pleased with her. She's regained consciousness and that is very positive. We'll be monitoring her closely now for a few days to make sure that her brain activity remains stable. Her jaw is wired and she'll start on liquid feeds maybe tomorrow. Her cheek bones and skull have extensive damage but we've operated and everything there is as expected at this point. She has good skin which will heal but there are going to be multiple scars on her face. Her ribs are broken and there is damage to her internal organs including her kidneys and liver. We expect that, over time, these injuries will heal completely. One of her lungs has been punctured and a hollow needle has been inserted into her chest to remove air. It sounds worse than it is and she'll recover from that within a few weeks. Her right eye was damaged beyond repair and there were slivers of glass within it. We had no option but to remove her eye. We are managing her pain and I can assure you that she isn't really feeling any pain at the moment.'

Mr Kent paused to allow the information to be absorbed and Mrs Berkovich withdrew a crumpled handkerchief from her tatty handbag and blew her nose whilst shedding tears. She then dabbed her cheeks with the handkerchief where the tears were rolling down.

'Mia will remain under our care for at least two weeks until we are sure that all of her injuries are healing. We will get her out of bed tomorrow and start her physiotherapy. It's very important to her recovery that she gets up and moves around as soon as possible. I have to warn you though that her recovery will take a long time. In addition to her physical injuries there may be psychological injuries that will also need to be treated. A specialist in this area will come and see her in a few days and they will make an assessment and recommendation regarding her care.'

Mrs Berkovich continued to shed tears with her head bowed and Mr Berkovich placed his hand on her shoulder.

'The police are keen to speak to Mia as soon as possible due to the injuries that she suffered and I will need to inform them that she is awake.'

'But please, she's terribly injured and frightened. She needs to rest first,' Mrs Berkovich cried weakly.

'Yes. Whilst she's under my care, her health is the top priority. But you need to understand that any information she can give the police now will lead to the apprehension of whoever did this to Mia. They are anxious to speak to Mia as soon as possible.'

Mrs Berkovich nodded and continued to cry. She looked a shrivelled wreck and Mr Berkovich didn't look much better.

'I don't think that Mia will be ready for any conversation for at least forty-eight hours anyway. We need to keep her under strict observation,' said Mr Kent, hoping that that would lessen the distress that the couple were displaying.

'Now tell me, is Mia taking any medication or does she suffer from any long-term illnesses?'

'No. Mia is a healthy girl,' replied Mr Berkovich.

'That's good. But I do need to ask. Do you know if Mia takes drugs?'

'No, definitely not.'

'Thanks. I'll be back tomorrow and we can have a chat then. I know that you both have been here a long time. Why don't you see Mia and then go home and get some rest. We'll contact you if there's anything to report.'

'Thanks but we'd prefer to stay and be with Mia,' replied Mr Berkovich.

'Fine. I'll be back tomorrow and we can speak then. Mia doesn't know anything about her injuries and it's best not to mention anything to her yet. The shock could cause her to relapse, so please don't mention anything. I'll be speaking to her when the time is right.'

And with that, Mr Kent and his two colleagues walked off down the ward.

The nurse who was in the room shortly after Mia woke up walked over and said, 'Mia's cleaned up and has fresh bandages on, so you can go back in and see her.'

They both walked into the room and closed the door. Mia was propped up in the bed with brilliant white crisp bandages covering her head. Mrs Berkovich pulled up the chair and loosened the bed clothing enough to gently hold Mia's hand.

'Mia, you are doing really well. The doctors are pleased with your progress.'

The left eye looked at Mrs Berkovich. It was searching. There were so many questions. So, so many questions. The eyelids started closing slowly. Darkness was enveloping and there was nothing that Mia could do to stop it.

Mrs Berkovich sat there motionless, just looking at the closed eye, and finally she turned to her husband and whispered, 'She's asleep. Poor thing. Phone up control and tell them everything that the doctor just told us.'

Mr Berkovich nodded and walked to the window that faced out towards the River Thames and began a long whispered conversation.

19:20. Deepak walked into the front room and flopped into the chair. All of his presents, cards and wrapping paper were still on the table where he left them, although a space had been cleared by Ahmed so that he could park his mug and plate.

'Evening,' said Deepak, looking at Ahmed.

Ahmed remained sprawled out on the settee watching the TV.

'Have you been lying there all day?' went on Deepak.

'Nope. I've been very busy actually.'

'Really? What did you do then?'

'I went down the gym in the morning and then popped into the mosque after.'

'Oh. I haven't noticed any change in your physique. Perhaps you need to eat more protein or maybe increase the weights that you lift. I hear that...'

Ahmed's self-obsession with his physique was fuelled by the magazines and ads promoted by Adonis-type bodies that accompanied the articles and ads. He watched action films and all of the heroes had muscles bulging out of their muscles, and this further cemented in his mind that he needed to have a huge physique. This mindset had been further complicated because he had recently fallen head over heels in love and in his mind, his love would remain unrequited unless he had a powerful physique that would woo her and entrance her. He was desperate to win his prize and the idiot sitting opposite him was antagonising a very angry mind.

'Shut the fuck up. I don't need a stick insect giving me bodybuilding tips.'

'OK. You need to chillax.'

'Chillax, chillax. Who the fuck says that shit, and what the fuck does it mean anyway? I suppose it's another one of your dad's sayings,' raged Ahmed.

'Chillax is actually a combination of chill (out) and relax. It's rather cool actually, and no, it's not one of my dad's sayings. Aisha told it to me and she uses it all of the time.'

Ahmed's mouth started to open and close without making any sound at all. He was doing an excellent impression of a goldfish.

'Fuck this shit. I went to the mosque after training and you wasn't there. So?'

'Oh.'

'Yes, no fucking sign of you, bruv. Then I went out for a run in the afternoon and popped back into the mosque and no sign of you.'

'Oh.'

'Then I read all of your reports for the last two weeks and everything that Chris Gould and bossman Pope have written and I then went back to the mosque, and again, no sign of you.'

'Oh.'

'Yes, oh, bruv. Where the fuck have you been going? You tell your family that you are working and yet you ain't there.'

'I'm working, really.'

'Yeah. Not at the mosque where you are supposed to be, and there isn't one fucking word written about what you are up to. You ain't even having full fat meals in greasy spoons with fat fucking Chris. So what's fucking going on, bro?'

'Well, remember when you told me to integrate and get to know people in the mosque?'

'Yeah.'

'Well, that's exactly what I did.'

'Go on.'

'Well, there's a couple of young guys who go there and I started to talk to them. They asked me if I was interested in doing some work. It was cash in hand and they said that it was easy stuff and wouldn't interfere with my studying.'

Ahmed sat up and stared at Deepak intently.

'They were cagey and wouldn't say what the work was. But I told them my legend, that I've moved up here, converted and fell out with my family. They took it all in and I think that my new haircut really helped,' Deepak said, rubbing his crewcut haircut.

'Fuck your skinhead haircut.'

'I eventually met the others in their gang and they needed another person to help them. Apparently, one of their crew upped and left Luton.'

'So what exactly is your new tax avoiding fucking job then?'

'I deliver the product to outlet managers and collect payment for delivery of the goods. I'm a Midlands area manager.'

'Right, got all of that. So what exactly is the fucking product, bruv?'

'It has several names but it's commonly known as skunk.'

'Skunk,' exploded Ahmed, now standing up with both of his fists rolled up into two tight balls. 'What the fuck. You're a fucking drug dealer.'

'Well, that's one way of looking at it, I suppose.'

'Bruv, that's the ONLY fucking way of looking at it.'

'I'm infiltrating a gang. I'm going deep undercover and looking to see where this leads.'

'I'll fucking tell you where this leads, bruv. It leads straight to fucking prison.'

'I'm using my initiative.'

'Are you totally fucking nuts? No one has authorised this. You haven't reported anything at all. No one knows a fucking thing about what you are up to. For all intents and purposes you have gone rogue. You work for MI5 and have a specific, well-defined mission. Nowhere does it say anything about selling fucking skunk.'

'Well...'

'No fucking well. What if 5-0 gives you and your gang of fucking losers a tug? You are well and truly nicked – no get out of jail free card. Sacked from the job, no pension and no reference. Once you get out of the clink with no reference then what type of job do you think you'll get?'

'I guess you have a point.'

'Bruv, this is a fucking mess. It makes you and your family having tea parties where you sit around watching Bollywood movies at undercover sites look like fucking nothing. Seriously, are you a fucking retard?'

'We don't watch Bollywood movies.'

'Well that's a fucking relief, bro.'

'I'm only doing what you told me to do. You did tell me to integrate more.'

'Don't fucking drag me into this, bro. You fucked up and we need to sort this out.'

'OK. Thanks. What do we do?'

'First I've got to say that you stink, bruv. Same like yesterday.'

'Yeah, that's the skunk.'

'What, it gets into your clothes?'

'Not exactly.'

'What do you mean, not exactly?'

'I mean that I actually have a puff.'

'Bruv. You know that we have random drugs tests. You'll be fired straight away.'

'I had to do it to join in.'

'This gets fucking worse.'

'Would you like a puff? It's good gear.'

'No I fucking wouldn't. You need to ditch that shit, bruv, no fucking gear here, comprendez?'

'Cannabis is known for its medical healing properties and is legal in many countries and some states in America.'

'Bruv, you are selling skunk. That's illegal and it's fucking heavy gear that fucks people up. So stop talking bollocks. Now talk me through what going on. Who are the players and what is their operation?'

Deepak sighed and then recounted the names of the gang members and their history, and the desolated building in an industrial estate in Bedford where the skunk plants are grown. The Chinese men who tendered the plants and bagged up the skunk were next and then the distribution operation.

'Well, first, how much are you earning?' asked Ahmed.

'I've done two runs and I got two hundred pounds,' Deepak said, pulling out a wad of cash from his jeans pocket.

'Well, at least they are paying you well.'

'So what do we do?' asked Deepak, still quite relaxed from smoking a reefer earlier that evening back in Bedford after the drug distribution run.

'I need to think about this. You have dropped a fucking bombshell and I'm going to sleep on it. We can pick this up tomorrow.'

'OK, good,' said Deepak, getting up and heading out of the front room.

'Hang on. Is there anything else that you need to tell me before you fuck off, bruv?'

'No. I don't think so.'

'Good. That's fucking good.'

Deepak realised that his good intentions and motives were actually naive and he had crossed the line. He was now going to rely on Ahmed to dig him out of the very deep hole that he had dug himself into.

'By the way,' said a calmer Ahmed, 'I quite like chillax. In fact, I may use it myself.'

Deepak smiled and Ahmed began thinking about ways to increase his muscle mass.

05:00. The two stakeout teams had been monitoring the old brick house for nearly forty-eight hours continuously. It was a wet, cold dark winter morning and everyone was tired. They had little food and drink left and their vans stank. They could not leave the vans save to relieve themselves in trees and bushes in the surrounding streets. Whilst not knowing the background of their mission, they all knew that it was important and had been sanctioned at the highest level. They also knew that failure was not an option and would not be tolerated. That had been made clear to all of them by their section head prior to starting the mission. This had led to extra tension amongst the group whilst they patiently waited for their target to appear.

'It's freezing in here. Are we sure that he's inside?' said the grumpy agent.

'Yes. You know that he was tracked back to this address.'

'We should have another team come out and relieve us. That's standard operation procedures.'

'Stop whining. We were giving clear and unambiguous instructions. Wait here, follow him and pick him up and whoever he meets.'

Lights appeared in the house blinking on and off and ten minutes later a small man dressed in old clothes and trousers tucked into wellington boots appeared wearing a tattered deerstalker hat. He went to the rear of his black Volvo estate car and withdrew a basket and a long cylindrical tube. He closed the boot and walked out onto the street. There was a flurry of activity in the two vans. The several men were having multiple conversations via mobiles amongst each other without anyone taking the lead in the two vans and it was a cacophony of confusing noise. The little man carrying his load was already at the top of the street and turning right.

'OK, two follow him, and there will be two further teams behind. Don't get too close, and rotate regularly. We're exposed on this and he can easily spot us. So each split up on different sides of the road and get ahead of him occasionally. We'll drive the vans slowly behind, in case he's picked up somewhere.

Everyone keep in contact using the mobiles. Now, let's get to it,' said a strong voice taking command and tamping down on the chatter.

The little man had exited a house in Hackney and was heading eastwards. He wasn't doubling back, stopping and checking around. In fact, he was overtly displaying no tradecraft at all. This was helpful as the surveillance teams were exposed on the quiet streets of Hackney and would have been easy to flush out. It wasn't long before Hackney's urban dwellings gave way and the little man was on the footpath of the River Lea. He picked up his pace and headed northwards. Puddles were everywhere and he splashed through them, not noticing the inclement weather nor the colourful graffiti that was on the walls of tired buildings. On a fairly exposed path where there were no canal longboats moored, he slowed to a stop. He looked with intent at the flowing river. He noted the current and the position of various bushes that were leaning into the water and drinking from it. He looked up and down the river and seemed satisfied with what he saw in this particular swim. He didn't notice the group of men further back down the river who had also stopped and were fading back into the shadows. From his basket, he withdrew a small stool which he opened up and secured. He took out pieces of rod from the tube and snapped them into place. A reel was attached and worm bait from the box added to the hook. In less than two minutes he was seated on his stool with a rod on a stand next to him. A small smile spread across his face as he stretched his legs. He was hoping for perch but knew at this time of the year he'd more likely catch barbel. They were a challenge as they always fought hard once hooked. His keep net was lying flat next to the rod and he hoped to fill it up on this cold, wet morning.

His wandering thoughts were disturbed when a cyclist sped past close by, splashing him. The cyclist was heading towards the heart of London and cared not for pedestrians nor fishermen. These pathways were the domain of cyclists who rode far too fast and with zero consideration for any other users. Here they were kings and made sure everyone knew it. It was their terrain and unlike the dangerous streets of London where the motorist ruled, they exerted their power unforgivingly. He frowned as over the years he had grown to dislike intensely the aggressive behaviour of the cyclists.

Further back and out of his view, the group of men were in conference. They had made contact with their command centre and, after apprising them of the situation, had been given further orders. They waited there patiently until the two vans had positioned themselves in streets closest to where the man was fishing. The order was given to go and the newly constructed plan was put into action. One man set off from their concealed position and a minute passed before another man set off. Both walked casually, heads down in the driving rain. Both walked slow but not too slow that they would draw attention to themselves. The lone fisherman was aware of both men in his peripheral vision but paid no attention to either of them as they both casually walked past him and onwards up the towpath and around the next bend. Once they had got in position, they made contact confirming that they had secured the north exit. Three men then headed up the towpath. One man was leading by several feet and the other two were walking abreast. Like their colleagues before them, they all walked slowly in a manner as not to draw attention to themselves. The first man passed by the fisherman and slowed to a stop. At that precise moment, the second man had stopped directly behind the fisherman. The third and final man was now approaching the fisherman from his right-hand side. The fisherman hadn't noticed that he had been encircled and was staring at his float bobbing away in the water.

'How's the fishing going. Any luck?' inquired the man standing to his right-hand side.

The little man turned his head towards the man and smiled. 'No so far. But I've just—'

The man who was standing to his left and out of his vision had withdrawn a stun gun from his belt, activated it and then placed it against his neck. The fisherman involuntarily shook as 100,000 volts surged through his body. The stun gun remained hard against his neck for three seconds and then it was withdrawn. Three seconds of that amount of voltage applied to the human body incapacitated the recipient and rendered them unconscious. As soon as the stun gun was withdrawn, the fisherman slumped onto the ground. Looking around, they confirmed that no one had witnessed their attack.

'You two grab him and I'll follow with his gear. Head straight to the first van.'

The man speed-dialled a number and was surprised that it went to voicemail.

He said, 'Fish caught, head back immediately.'

He pocketed his mobile and hurriedly packed away the fishing rod seat and fish keep. His two colleagues were carrying the small man between them and were making good progress. From his position, it looked like two men carrying their friend home after a long alcoholic celebration. He caught up with them as they were quietly manhandling the limp body into the rear of the van. Slinging the fishing gear roughly into the back of the van, he said, 'Put the plasti-cuffs on him. Hands and feet and gag him.'

'Where are the other two?'

'No idea. We have to go but the other van will stay.'

The van drove off and headed west.

Back down the towpath, the two men were walking urgently from their designated place and were engaged in an argument.

'What the fuck was that about?' shouted one of them.

The second man had just listened to the voicemail. 'Shut up, we need to move it.'

A couple of minutes earlier, the two men were standing on the towpath side by side facing southwards. They were tense, ready to block and capture any attempted escape by the fisherman. Behind them, a cyclist who was cycling far too fast had come around a blind bend and skidded into one of them, uprooting him. The cyclist kept control of the bike but it had come to a stop with him in a crouched position, hanging onto his precious machine. The cyclist was momentarily shocked before he righted the bike and was about to cycle off. A burley arm clamped around the cyclist's throat. The fallen man had risen with speed, fuelled by anger and, despite being muddied, closed the gap and held the cyclist who began wriggling. An expletive was shouted and the angry man threw the cyclist into the River Lea. The Lycra-clad cyclist bobbed up, his florid yellow helmet shining brightly against the dark, dank water. He blew out air loudly three times, shocked by the coldness. Another cyclist who was also riding with fury had just come skidding around the corner in time to witness the cyclist fly unwillingly into the river.

'Oi, I saw that and I've captured everything on my helmet cam,' he shouted, tapping his helmet almost with pride.

The muddied man glared at him momentarily before commencing his attack. He focused on the cyclist's head and swiftly removed the helmet, leaving red marks on the rider's throat. The assault continued as the cyclist suffered a similar fate to his compadre. A loud splash followed as the flailing cyclist plummeted into the river. The angry man then threw the second cyclist's bike into the river, glaring at both of the cyclists who were now treading water. A third cyclist came around the bend but he was cycling with more control. He had a small stature and surveyed the scene in front of him, processing the surreal spectacle. In an instant, he had spun his bike around and frantically sped off in the direction from where he had just come.

The two men on the bank looked at each other and started to walk off quickly back from where they had come. The muddied man was still carrying the helmet camera in his hand.

When they reached the parked van, the driver nodded and they both got in the back. The van then reversed and headed off west.

'Where the fuck have you two been?'

'Long story,' replied the muddied man, unaware that he was still grasping the helmet camera in his closed fist.

07:30. The jaded bedroom door opened; the occupant in the bed stirred but didn't wake up. Lying on his side, he was aware that he still had at least five hours before he needed to wake up. His shoulders were shaken by the hands of the man who had entered his room.

'Wake up, wake up.'

'Uh, what's going on?' said the man, waking up with a start and confused.

The abrupt start had another effect on the sleeping man. He let out a volley of farts and it sounded like a series of cannons being fired.

'Fucking hell, bruv, you fucking stink and I ain't talking about that skunk shit either.'

Deepak's eyes were wide open as he sat up in bed yawning.

'What's the matter? Why all the fuss?' said Deepak, looking at Ahmed who was dressed and ready to go to the mosque for his shift.

'Right. I've got a plan. It's going to get you out of the shit.'

'Great.'

'Over the next couple of weeks, you are going to write up reports about your gang leading up to and including their criminal activities.'

Deepak didn't say anything but continued to stare at Ahmed.

'The first report will go out today. In it you will say that you have been speaking with a guy at the mosque for a couple of weeks. He's come up to you occasionally and chatted in general and you've told him your legend which he's accepted. Today he's mentioned that he's got some friends that he'd like you to meet.'

'What? That's it?'

'Yeah. We need to reel in HQ slowly and then you can get out of this without being fucking nicked. After a couple more reports on just him, you'll mention that you have a gut feeling that he may be radicalised and that you want to cultivate a relationship. Chris Gould will want to involve Team 4 and get background checks on all of your gang, their relatives and their associates.'

'I like the sound of your plan.'

'Good. Write the first report on the guy who made contact with you. I'll check it when you get home tonight and then you can send it off.'

'Kareem is his name.'

'Yeah, whatever.'

'So when do I mention about the grow house and the drug distribution then?'

'Bruv, are you mad? You ain't going to mention anything about being a drug dealer. In a few weeks the story will be out there and passed over to the old bill. Once Team 4 sniff around and see that it's a criminal gang without any radical ties then it will be of no interest.'

'OK. But what do I do when they want me to deliver skunk to the dealers?'

'For the moment, just keep going along. We have a few weeks to figure out how to get you away from the gang.'

Deepak's face displayed signs of anxiety. The plan was good but there was a lot that could go wrong.

Ahmed turned and walked out of the room.

'Chillax, bruv. And open a fucking window.'

08:00. The small man was sitting uncomfortably on a wooden chair. His hands were cuffed behind his back. His wellington boots had been removed and his ankles were also cuffed. The gag had remained in his mouth. He was sitting in the lounge of a detached house in Golders Green. It was a fairly large dwelling built post-war and the decoration was in need of freshening up. He looked around the room and saw that the curtains were still drawn and that the light in the room was coming from the central light fitting in the ceiling. There were three men in the room drinking coffee and staring at him. He'd been sitting in the seat for what seemed like eternity but in fact was only just over one hour. One of the men walked forward and removed the gag from his mouth.

'Do not shout or scream,' the man whispered into his ear.

'Please, please. I'll tell you everything. Please, just don't hurt me.'

The men looked at the small man, who had pissed himself and was smelling of it.

'Yes you will tell us everything,' said one of the men confidently.

'OK. It's about the 500 cloned credit cards and the card skimmer, right?'

The men looked at each other but said nothing.

'OK. It's about the carjacking to order. The Bimmers are nicked and driven straight onto the car ferry. Then they go straight to Eastern Europe. I'll tell you everything.'

The men looked at each other but still said nothing.

'It's about fencing all of the jewellery from the house robberies in Chelsea.'

The men cast glances at each other but remained silent.

'It's about—'

The gag was forced back into his mouth and silence reigned again.

The front door opened and three men entered. One of the men in the front room left and the other two men continued to drink coffee and stare at their prisoner. In the small kitchen, several men squeezed in, shuffling for space.

'Talk to me,' said the elderly man.

'We had him under surveillance and he left his premises at 05:10. We followed on foot and he went to the River Lea where he set up a place to fish. At around 05:30, we picked him up. We used a stun gun to zap him and then we took him back to the van. No one witnessed the operation and we came straight to the safe house.'

'Good. It's important that we remain under the radar with this operation. You guys have done a good job. Make sure everyone knows that.'

'Since he's been here, he's been restrained, gagged and is sitting on the wooden chair just as you asked. He's had no food or water nor has he been allowed to use the bathroom. He has pissed himself but that happened when he was zapped.'

'Right, it sounds like he's ready now for some old school interrogation. We'll take it from here.'

'Sure. I'll get the boys out of the front room then.'

The little man watched as the two men walked out of the room after another man came in and quietly talked in their ears. He was alone and fearful. It didn't last long because three middle-aged men walked into the room. The oldest of the men walked up to him and, without saying a word, he punched him in his right eye. The man throwing the punch was wearing a sovereign ring on his punching hand. The sovereign ring had the same effect as a knuckleduster but the jagged points on it caused more injury as it spiked into the soft eyeball. The little man was rocked back by the force of the punch and the wooden chair toppled over backwards in slow motion. The other two men stepped forward and righted the chair. They placed the bound man back on the chair. The little man's right eye was already beginning to swell and blood was oozing out from a couple of small cuts in his eyelid. He was squinting, trying to see out of his damaged eye, and began to wriggle about. The older man delivered a hefty blow direct to the little man's solar plexus, and the little man doubled up. The wind had been knocked out of him and he was breathing hard through his nose. Snot was running out of his nose as he tried to normalise his breathing.

The older man stood back and looked at the crumpled man. He was composing himself, taking in deep breaths. It had been a long while since he had interrogated a man in this manner and two vicious punches had already shown him that he was out of condition. That and not to mention that he was getting old. He gently pushed the little man back and into an upright sitting position. Blood was continuing to pour out of the eye cuts and run down onto his cheek, chin and clothes. The older man drew back his right fist and hit the little man with all the force that he could muster. The punch was again aimed at the right eye of the little man. The little man's body absorbed the force from the punch and his head involuntarily rolled back. His feet came off of the ground as once again he tipped backwards and onto the floor, still bound. The two men stepped forward once again and sat him back on the righted chair. The little man pissed himself and the air in the room was fetid. The little man's face was now a mask of excruciating pain with both of his eyes shut tight. The older man withdrew the gag from the little man's mouth and could see that he was experiencing deep distress. The other two men watched on but said nothing. The little man flopped forward onto the floor, letting out a number of short high-pitched screams. The other men gathered in groups throughout the house, heard the screams and knew that he was suffering. The man who had administered the beating knelt down and looked at the suffering man. He knew immediately that the little man was not playacting.

'Quickly, call our doctor. We need him here immediately,' said Jacob.

One of the men behind reacted immediately and dialled a number. The other man left the room and returned with a mug of cold water. He passed the mug to Jacob who tried to get the little man to drink from the mug. The little man's jaws were clamped shut and he was breathing in spurts through his teeth. The pain was such that the little man couldn't speak but continued to emit occasional screams. His eyes bulged and he gave out his final breath. His body convulsed and then it was over. Jacob looked at the other two men somewhat stunned and then stood up. The three men didn't speak. The stench was almost unbearable but they remained in the room. A further fifteen minutes passed before a portly middle-aged man carrying a medical case knocked on the front room door and entered. He surveyed the scene in front of him and then placed his bag next to the dead man. The doctor checked for a pulse, looked at his pupils and did a few other superficial checks before he stood up.

'He's dead. It looks to me like he suffered a fatal heart attack. Obviously a post-mortem would be needed to confirm the actual cause of death.'

No one spoke.

'Please have the decency to cut him loose,' went on the doctor.

Jacob bent over and cut the plasti-cuffs off of his ankles and his wrists.

'Did anyone check his medical records before he was interrogated? He may have a pre-existing heart condition, for example,' asked the doctor.

The three men stared at the floor.

The doctor then asked how long he had been here. The doctor was told that he was picked up about 05:30 and brought here. He was given no food nor water and had been knocked out by a stun gun. The doctor had already made a mental note of the eye injury that he had just suffered and said, 'You are all a fucking disgrace.'

Without waiting for a reply, the doctor packed his medical case and stormed out of the house. Jacob called into the front room the team leader of the surveillance team and gave him an explicit set of instructions. The body had to be disposed of along with his fishing gear. They had to take everything wrapped up to their contact at the Rainham landfill site and pay him £3,000 cash for disposal. Then the van that had been used to get him here and to the landfill site must be sold to a scrap dealer and the van crushed.

Jacob continued 'Change the van plates before you move the body. The other van because it isn't contaminated can still be used but the plates also need changing before it leaves here and goes back to base. This place needs deep cleaning and every trace of him must be removed.'

Jacob sat outside in the car with Noah and Daniel.

'I didn't expect him to be frail,' said a muted Jacob.

'No, nor did we,' replied Noah, trying to support Jacob.

'I wanted to teach him a lesson first. I wanted to blind his eye and inflict the same damage that was inflicted on Agent J. Then I was going to interrogate him and find out who he was working for.'

'He wasn't working for General Faisal then?' asked Noah.

'I don't think so. It will be difficult now to find out. But we need to follow up and see who he works for.'

'Jacob, we can't run around London pulling in anyone and interrogating them. You have made this personal and it's affected your judgement,' said Daniel.

There was a moment of quiet in the cold car.

'You are right. I'm going to step away from leading this investigation and Noah will take charge. I'll receive updates and that's all. Ultimately our goal is to find out exactly what happened and then bring the culprit to justice. I know that Faisal was involved but we need to do everything by the book from now on,' muttered a chastened Jacob.

'Agreed. Let's get back to base and put this on a proper footing,' said Noah.

09:15. Pope, Chris Gould and Clare Hawkins were sitting in their favoured corner meeting room drinking obnoxious coffee.

'Deepak's report is interesting,' started off Chris Gould.

'Well, it's a bit early to say where this lead is going,' piped up Clare.

'Perhaps. But this mosque seems to be a place where we stand our best chance of picking up a thread. It can't just be coincidence that we've had several unexplained characters turning up there and then disappearing,' replied Chris.

'I'm not saying that we are wasting our time there. I'm simply saying that the report is bare and we shouldn't necessarily get ahead of ourselves,' Clare said, trying to be pragmatic.

'I think the guys are doing well and we'll support them in any way that we can,' said Pope.

'Shall I pop up there and have a face to face with them?' said Chris Gould eagerly.

'Let's give them a bit of room. Deepak needs to have a degree of autonomy. It will be good for him,' Pope said.

'OK. I'll drop him a text and offer encouragement and say let us know if he needs anything,' replied Chris Gould.

'That's a good idea. I also think that we need to be cognisant that we don't really understand the cultural behaviour of the younger generation and in particular the Muslim guys that use the mosques. We need Deepak and Ahmed to do what they think is right. Ultimately they are the guys on the ground and they need to react in a natural way that won't draw any suspicion to themselves,' went on Pope.

'Anyway, where's Sandra Carruthers?' said Chris Gould mischievously.

'No idea. But I understand that she will be back next Monday,' replied Pope.

'Her PA is useless. I've spoken to her a couple of times in the ladies' and when Sandra's name is mentioned, she mumbles and then scurries off,' said Clare crossly.

'She's a real drip. I don't think I've ever heard her speak,' said Chris, trying to encourage a gossip session.

'She follows Carruthers about. When I see them, it always reminds me of that old record, 'Me and My Shadow'. I can't remember who sang that though as it was before my time and even my mum's,' Clare said.

'John will know,' Chris said.

'Thanks.'

'No, I didn't mean that you were THAT old. I know that you know your tunes, that's all.'

'OK, it was sung by many artists but probably Frank Sinatra and Sammy Davis Junior were best known for it.'

'Worth knowing,' Clare said as she rolled her eyes mockingly.

10:15. Carruthers was sitting in a car in the car park of Cascades shopping centre in the heart of Portsmouth. The missions for today had been explained after breakfast back at Fort Monckton. She had undergone two days of surveillance training in and around the fort's base and today she was going to undertake two exercises in the field. She was handed a description of the man that she was going to follow. She was told that he would be in Cascades shopping centre in the next ten minutes and that she needed to follow him and report back everything that he did. For this exercise she would not be miked up and would need to remember everything and then provide a verbal report. Carruthers nodded and left the car.

She travelled by lift up to the shopping floor and took up a position near the front entrance. She shifted about looking for her target and after twelve minutes, he walked into the centre. He was just over six feet tall, slim with short dark hair. He was dressed in grey trousers, brown shoes and a long brown overcoat closed tightly. In his right hand he carried a small black umbrella. He was talking on his mobile phone and didn't seem to notice any other shoppers. He walked into the large chemist shop and started walking up and down several aisles slowly. He was looking for something and finally stopped at the colds and remedies shelves. He studied many of the products and chose one of them.

Carruthers was in an adjacent aisle pretending to be studying the feminine hygiene products whilst keeping an eye on her target. He continued to walk around a few more aisles before he queued up and paid for the cold remedy product. He went out and then he walked into a card shop and once again walked up and down several aisles. Carruthers followed him into the shop and watched as he chose a birthday card and paid for it. He continued to go in and out of several other shops including a men's clothes shop where he spent time trying on three suits. He finally went into a coffee shop where he bought a large cappuccino and a blueberry muffin. He sat at a table in the corner and began to eat and drink. In between bites he wrote in the birthday card. Once he had finished writing, he placed the birthday card back inside the envelope and sealed it. He then vacated his seat and left his tray with the empty cup and rubbish on the table. It was busy in the coffee shop and as soon as he got up another man sat down in his place. Carruthers watched the man leave the coffee shop and then, without stopping anywhere, walk out of the shopping centre through the same entrance that he had arrived by. His exit signified the end of the exercise and Carruthers smiled smugly and headed back to the car park for her debrief.

In the car, Carruthers was sitting in the passenger seat. Her instructor was sitting in the driver's seat and in the rear seat was another instructor. Carruthers drew breath and then went through in detail everything that the man had done. She was confident that she had captured everything and when she finished her spiel she smiled confidently. The man sitting in the back seat then handed her instructor an envelope which he opened and withdrew from it a birthday card. Carruthers eyed the birthday card with suspicion. The instructor read the birthday card first to himself and then he read it out aloud to Carruthers. Her smile vanished as she heard the litany of errors that she had committed.

It started when she had stood very much in the open area near the entrance and her target had recognised her immediately. She should had been either in a shop or staring into a shop window checking everyone in the window's reflection. She followed him into every shop and was easily recognisable as she stood in adjacent aisles. She should have waited outside on occasion and varied her attire by perhaps taking off her coat or tying her hair differently or quite frankly doing anything. Finally, when he went into the coffee shop and wrote up his appraisal in the birthday card, she didn't notice that he left the birthday card and his umbrella on the table deliberately. The man who sat down was in fact the second instructor sitting behind her in the car. She was so engrossed with watching the target, she didn't even notice that a drop had taken place, and with someone she'd driven here with. The instructor was blunt with his assessment and told her that she wasn't taking any of this seriously and that her performance was substandard and that was how it would be reported. She was told that they were going to go ahead with the second exercise and that she needed to pull her socks up. The exercise would begin in an hour and she should go for a walk, clear her head and think about all of the surveillance techniques that she had been taught the previous couple of days.

12:45. Carruthers was sitting in the passenger seat and had been told the details of her surveillance mission. She was to follow an unwitting member of the public for more than one hour and report back all of the details. She wouldn't be miked and needed to retain every detail. She nodded again in acceptance. The instructor pointed to an elderly lady on the opposite side of the road. Carruthers got out of the car and crossed into Commercial Road. It was a pedestrianised road and one of the most popular shopping roads in Portsmouth. Carruthers thought about everything that she had been taught and all of the mistakes that she had made just a couple of hours earlier.

She kept her distance and pulled up the collar to her coat. It was bitterly cold and raining. Two men got out of a car parked ahead of Carruthers and started walking with speed ahead of both her and the old lady. Another man and woman got out of a van behind Carruthers and fell in behind her, keeping a discreet distance. The old lady walked slowly through the rain with her head down. She had a small umbrella up and was wearing a plastic hat to stave off the rain. She also had a small wicker wheelie basket that she was dragging behind her. Carruthers thought that following her would be an easy assignment but after this morning she realised that she needed to be vigilant. Carruthers even wondered if the old lady was an agent and if this was in some way a trap. She dismissed this idea and realised that she was becoming far too paranoid.

She crossed to the other side of the road and walked on the pavement, still keeping her distance. The old lady headed into Marks and Spencer and Carruthers decided that she would follow her. Once inside, the old lady headed painfully slowly to the food section where she collected a metal basket. Carruthers hung back in the women's clothing area and watched as the old lady started to make her way around. Carruthers decided that this probably would take some time and as part of her own cover that she would go around and grab some items. She decided that once the old lady was at the till then she'd ditch the basket and carry on with her surveillance.

The old lady stopped and studied a variety of food items. She was looking for price reductions which generally meant that the sell by date was either today or tomorrow. She would take the items home and then eat them within two weeks. This was the only way that she could manage on her meagre pension. She had a cat which also needed feeding and that was her only companion. It was a lonely life which she travelled through as if she was invisible. Being old meant that people didn't recognise you, they just passed by. Carruthers had picked up a microwave meal and was studying the calories and the horrific number of e additives. She was engrossed in the e's and trying to find out whether there was any real food in the meal when she was interrupted by a reedy voice.

'Hello, dear. Are you having trouble finding the sell by date on the meal? Here, let me show you.'

Carruthers looked down and there was a small face with the texture on a prune peering at her from under a plastic hat. A claw of a mottled hand took the microwave meal from her and began turning the plastic container over.

Fuck, thought Carruthers. *Where did she come from?*

'Look, dear. The sell by date is November, so you have plenty of time.'

The claw returned the microwave meal back into Carruthers' hands and the prune face expanded, displaying a gummy smile.

'Oh, thanks,' chocked out Carruthers.

'I'll tell you a secret,' whispered the prune face, looking around to check if anyone was eavesdropping. 'You can eat most everything weeks after the sell by date. They don't go off, you know.'

'That's good to know. Thanks for the advice.'

The old lady shuffled off. Carruthers stood there staring at the microwave meal whilst several pairs of eyes observed her from discreet placements. Carruthers abandoned her basket and went out into the women's clothes area, where she took up a position away from the food section exit. Carruthers looked at her watch. She had to follow the old lady for at least one hour and she had been going only twenty minutes. Worse than that, her target had contacted her. And as for eating food after the sell by date, Carruthers wrinkled her nose.

Jesus. Getting old sucks, she thought.

The old lady eventually came out of the food section, slowly dragging her wicker basket. She continued through the store, head down with no one paying any attention to her. Outside, she turned and headed back the way that she had just come from. It was raining even heavier now but she didn't put up her umbrella.

Carruthers came out of an entrance further down having walked along an aisle parallel to the old lady in the store. Carruthers darted to the other side of the pedestrian road and continued with her surveillance. The old lady stopped abruptly outside a well-known fast-food burger chain shop and then with great effort heaved the door open. Once inside, she queued alongside all of the noisy teenagers dressed in their school uniforms. After buying a small cup of coffee she grabbed ten sugar sachets and eight milks which were all slipped into her coat pockets. She then sat on a small table in the corner on her own. Carruthers saw her go inside the burger joint and realised that the old lady would be in there a long time, especially with the way that she moved. It was freezing and pissing down, so

Carruthers decided to go in, grab a coffee and warm up. Carruthers joined the back of the noisy queue and eventually bought a large coffee. The teenagers were mostly going upstairs and after she got a milk, she turned around and headed towards the front of the restaurant. There was a free table and she would have her back to the elderly lady but would still be able to observe her. Once seated, Carruthers removed the lid from the large cup and poured the milk into the steaming cup.

She was taking her third slurp and enjoying the infusion of caffeine when she was interrupted. 'Hello, dear,' said a reedy voice. 'Is that seat taken?'

Bollocks, thought Carruthers. 'No. Please sit down.'

The sodden wicker basket was banged up against the side of the plastic table, blocking the aisle between the tables, and then the old lady sat down opposite Carruthers. She was still wearing the plastic hat but it had slipped down and was covering her left eye. It had also steamed up and the left eye wasn't visible through the haze.

Not the most appealing of looks, thought Carruthers, smiling at the prune face.

'I thought it was you,' said the old lady. 'Where is your shopping though?'

This old buzzard would be fucking good at surveillance, thought Carruthers. *In fact, she'd be better than me.*

'Ah, you noticed,' said Carruthers in a patronising way. 'My husband picked up the bags. He's the lifter and shifter.'

There was a cackle, followed by four coughs as the old lady gasped for breath.

Before the old lady could say anything, two men in their thirties came up to the table carrying two trays full of burgers and asked if the other seats were free. The old lady sprang into life and said that they were welcome to sit down and join them. She could literally go weeks without talking to anyone and now today she was surrounded by companionship. The old lady without many teeth seemed to chew her coffee in an odd manner. Carruthers realised that the surveillance exercise was totally fucked up and decided that she might as well show some kindness.

'I'm going to get another coffee. Can I get you one?' she said, looking at the chewing prune.

'Oh yes, that would be nice.'

'Would you like a bigger cup?'

'Oh, that is so kind. And could I also have milk and sugar please.'

'Sure. Keep my seat and I'll be back in a minute.'

When Carruthers returned, the old lady was polishing off a portion of chips from a carton.

'Didn't fancy them,' said the young man, looking at Carruthers. 'And your friend said that she'd have them. I hope that's OK.'

'Yeah,' said Carruthers, placing a large coffee with milk and sugar cartons in front of the old lady. The mottled claw reached out, took all of the cartons and sachets and deposited them into her coat pocket.

Guess it's black coffee then, thought Carruthers.

Carruthers noticed that a youngish man and woman who were sitting on the table next to them were staring aimlessly around the place. This was surreal, thought Carruthers.

'Do you normally shop on a Tuesday?' rasped the old lady, looking at Carruthers.

'Not normally. My husband generally shops after work as I work long hours.'

'That's a shame. I thought that we could go for a coffee.'

'And chips,' chipped in the guy who had given her his chips.

The prune laughed raucously and then started coughing again. The plastic hat was slipping further down her face and was only stopped from completely covering it by the river of wrinkles that protruded from her forehead.

There was table conversation for nearly twenty minutes and the old lady explained that she was a widow with two children and five grandchildren who never visited her. She also explained that she had worked all of her life in a sweet shop. Everyone else contributed glimpses into their equally mundane lives and then it was time to disburse. The old lady was going to walk back to her house that was some fifteen minutes away and off she went. By now the haze over her left eye had cleared but she hadn't lifted her hat higher and no one had the heart to mention it to her. Carruthers left with her and peeled off at the top of Commercial Road. She stepped into the car and the instructor drove off.

Back at Monckton Fort, the instructor said that the debrief would be held in room one. Carruthers stopped off at the ladies' and then went into the room expecting another bollocking. She sat down and then the instructor walked in. He sat in silence and then three men and one woman walked in. Carruthers did a double take. The two men who had sat at her table chatting and feeding the old lady with chips looked at her. The couple who sat at the table next to her looking vacant also looked at her.

'Right, shall we begin?' said the instructor.

21:30. Pope and Doodle were walking in unison up the road. Pope was deep in thought, consumed with work. Doodle was straining on the lead. In his mind he was the lead husky pulling his master through the Canadian tundra. He swerved from lamppost to pavement wall, marking his territory as he went, panting from the exertion in the driving rain. No one was walking the streets, there were no cars driving and their only other companion was the constant pat, pat of the rain as it beat its drum on everything that it made contact with.

The sled team passed several houses and Pope had lowered his face, his hands in coat pockets trying to avoid being sandblasted from the rain. A man's voice pierced the silence. He was angry and even the walls of his house weren't sufficient to insulate the sound.

'You all are lazy bastards. I'm the only one who works. I put food on the table and clothes on your backs. Without me you all are nothing. Nothing. Remember that. I know that you all can hear me upstairs in bed. I'll be up soon and you better be asleep.'

A muffled voice said something. It only enraged the man even more.

'You're a lazy bitch as well. Keep your mouth shut. I should never have married you. You and your worthless family are beneath me.'

Pope's pace had slowed to a stop and he raised his head and stared at the house. The rain didn't notice the shouts emanating from the house and continued with its drum beat. Doodle stopped, stared at the house and then emitted a low rumbling growl. A high-pitched bark spat out of his mouth.

Pope's trance was broken and he looked down at the sodden dog, 'Good boy. Come on, let's enjoy our walk.'

Doodle's ears pricked up. He knew from the tone of the sled driver's voice that he had done good. He pulled and strained on the end of his lead. The sled started to move, first slowly and then with more pace. Time to head back over the tundra.

11:00. There was quiet in the room. The left eye looked out from behind her mask made of bandages and rolled her head from left to right. She counted three men in long white coats standing around the bed at different points and there were at least three female nurses dotted strategically around the room. The nurses had been busying themselves for the last ten minutes, making preparations for the grand entrance of the three men. Machines, monitoring wires and tubes had been checked. Charts clipped to the end of her bed had been updated.

'Mia, I want to talk to you about your injuries,' the tall man said in a sympathetic voice. 'You understand me, yes?'

The bandaged head nodded briefly and the left eye focused on him and him alone.

'Good. You were involved in an incident and as a result you have sustained a number of injuries.'

Her heartbeat quickened, her pulse rose and she gasped for breath. Her internal systems were triggering a fight or flight response and the monitor's readings instantaneously displayed the changes.

'Mia, try and relax. You are safe and well. My name is Mr Kent and I'm your doctor. If you prefer we can come back and talk to you later.'

The bandaged head shook from side to side slowly.

'OK, then I'll begin,' Mr Kent said in a calm and caring manner.

He described in a neutral tone the catalogue of injuries that she had suffered, the surgeries performed, the expected healing time for each of her injuries and then said that there would need to be further surgeries to rectify and restore her external features.

He paused for a moment and then told her that she had suffered one injury that they were unable to fix. He gently told her that her right eye had been damaged beyond repair and it had had to be removed. A tear filled her left eye and slowly rolled down into the corner where it then slipped out and beneath the bandages. It was followed by another tear and then another tear. Mr Kent told her that she was extremely fit and the physios were impressed with her strength and that she possessed good healing skin. These assets were signs that she would make a good recovery and he was very pleased with how everything had gone so far.

'Mia, I'll bring in your mum and dad now. They are waiting to see you. I'll be back to check on your progress tomorrow. Keep up the good work with the physios.'

The procession filed out of the room. The dam wall busted and tears flooded out of the left eye.

'Mr and Mrs Berkovich. I've spoken with Mia and explained everything to her. You both can now go in and see her,' said Mr Kent. 'By the way, is Mia known by any other name?'

Mrs Berkovich answered immediately. 'No. Why do you ask?'

'It's just that when staff call her, she doesn't always respond. When people don't know their name then there could be other issues. We'll monitor it and then decide if we need to run further tests.'

'Thank you, Mr Kent.'

The couple went into the room and saw a nurse bending over into Mia's face, talking in a soothing voice and dabbing her left eye with a tissue.

The nurse looked up at the elderly couple and said, 'I'll leave you all now.'

After the nurse left, Mrs Berkovich pulled up a chair next to where Mia was propped up and held her hand. She knew that the young lady was now not thinking about her broken body but was trying to make some sense out of what all of this meant. Her hopes and dreams were shattered, like a glass dropped from a great height. They were shattered into thousands of pieces and there was now no hope that they could ever be pieced back together. She'd grown up complimented on her beauty, and boys and men were always eager to be around her. This response bolstered her confidence and helped her in both her private and professional lives. Now there would be external scars forever permanent that would be matched and even dwarfed by her internal scars. And she now didn't have a right eye. Men always commented on her dark, sensual eyes. There would be no more comments, no more flattery, no more flirtatious behaviour. No more would heads turn when she walked into a room. Yes, there would be stares and sideways glances, but they wouldn't be admiring. Mrs Berkovich withdrew a hankie from her handbag and periodically dabbed the left eye gently. No words were spoken. There was nothing to say. Mr Berkovich was standing by the window and discreetly giving an update into his phone. The left eye closed eventually and darkness descended.

'Poor thing,' said the old lady to her husband.

After two hours the eye opened and the bandaged head swivelled around. The eye saw two elderly people slumped in two chairs. The old man was snoring loudly and that was probably what disturbed her slumber. Her movements had a different effect on the old lady who roused from her own sleep.

'Mia, are you OK?' whispered the old lady, gathering her hand again.

Mia squeezed her hand once. The old lady noticed that Mia's grip was getting stronger now. It was no longer feeble and this was a strong indicator that Mia was rapidly regaining her health.

'Mia, listen carefully. The doctor thinks that you may have suffered brain damage.'

The left eye began to flutter. Even more bad news. Does it never end?

'Don't worry, you are fine. It's because you don't respond when they call you Mia. You must respond now to that name. It's your name now until you leave. You understand? It's really important.'

The grip was strong.

'Good. That's very good, Mia.'

19:23. The door bell chimed.

'Now, who could that be? I'll get it,' shouted Jane, walking out of the kitchen towards the front door.

Jane opened the front door wide enough to look out. She didn't want the cold air to blast its way into the hall and replace the warm air that was circulating around the house. She saw the shape of a man standing in the porch. He had his back to the front door and was looking back out into the dark driveway. As the door opened he turned around, smile beaming, displaying a white set of teeth.

'Jane, good evening. How are you?' he said, flicking his jet-black locks.

'I'm fine, Mr Khan.'

'Zayhan, please. Is John in? I'd like a word.'

'Zayhan, please come in,' Jane said, opening the door a bit wider and stepping back into the hall.

Zayhan walked behind her into the hall, his eyes darting around. It was the first time that he had been in the Popes' home. He was immediately struck by how hot it was.

Their electricity bill must be huge, he thought.

His own house was never hot, not even warm. He kept a tight control over the thermostat and said that heat was a waste of money. If anyone was cold then put on a jumper or another vest, was his repetitive, stock response.

The noise had peaked Daisy's interest and she appeared out of the front room. She stood in the hall, dressed from head to foot in her garish pink dancing kit with a bright pink bow perched on her head and a pink wand in her right hand.

She looked directly at Zayhan Khan and shouted out, 'Daddy, Mr Khan is here. Are you going to hide now?'

Mr Khan's grin remained plastered on his face.

'Zayhan, come on into the front room and I'll get John,' said Jane, trying to skirt over Daisy's comment.

Mr Khan followed Jane past Daisy and into the front room. Doodle jumped down off of the settee and Mr Khan put his hand down to pat him. Doodle growled, baring his teeth, and made a motion to bite the adversary's hand. It was a mock charge and the bite was deliberately short. Nevertheless, Mr Khan withdrew his hand swiftly and stood up. The cheesy grin was still painted on his face.

'Doodle, behave,' said Jane sternly.

Daisy had followed Mr Khan into the room and was standing there looking at him.

'Doodle never bites anyone,' she said accusingly.

'Zayhan, please take a seat. Can I get you a drink?' Jane said, trying to de-escalate the situation.

Mr Khan sat down in the single seat still smiling.

'I'm fine thanks, Jane.'

'Daisy, why don't you go and get Daddy.'

Daisy was still staring at Mr Khan, a small bundle of pinkness.

'He's probably hiding,' Daisy replied with great earnest.

'Daisy, he's in the kitchen. Now go and get him please.'

Daisy complied and headed out of the room with Doodle in tow. She had a quarter of a biscuit in her left hand and Doodle always followed the food.

'Kids. She's obsessed with hide and seek and thinks that everyone is playing the game,' was the white lie that Jane's mouth ejected.

'Yes. I remember when my kids were young. It was games all of the time,' replied Mr Khan.

John Pope entered the front room followed by Daisy and Doodle. A smile broke over his face. He was at ease playing the genial host.

'Zayhan, how are you? Can I get you a drink?' Pope said, offering his right hand.

Zayhan stood up and shook hands.

'No thanks, John.'

Jane decided that a tactical retreat was in order before any more damage was done.

'Daisy, come on. We're going into the kitchen. And you, Doodle.'

Daisy stood there momentarily before following her mum out of the door. Her mind was whirring, mostly about why Daddy hadn't hidden. There were so many good places to hide in the house and that nasty Mr Khan would never be able to find him.

'Good to see you,' Pope said.

'Thanks. I haven't seen you for a while and I was wondering how things are,' said Zayhan.

'We're all good. How's your family?'

'Growing up fast.'

'Tell me about it.'

'I knocked on Sunday but there was no answer. I saw you return from a run and thought that you might want a drink.'

'Right.'

'Yeah. I then saw Jane go out in the car with the girls.'

Pope's suspicion that Khan was a nosey parker was being confirmed.

'I knocked several times, in fact,' said Khan, inviting an answer.

'I was working with my headphones on, so didn't hear a thing.'

'No problem. Jane was in a hurry. She charged out into the road, wheels spinning. She must have been in a hurry driving like that.'

Cheeky bastard, thought Pope but said blandly, 'Right.'

'Anyway, I was wondering if you fancied going for a drink again? It's been a while.'

'Oh. Yeah. Yeah, we should.'

'How about this Sunday? There's a good match on.'

'That's going to be difficult. There's a push on at work and I'm pulling weekenders at the moment.'

'The civil services pushes you hard. I thought that everyone was a strict nine to fiver, four weeks holiday and two weeks sick mandatory.'

'There's always an exception to every rule, you know,' smiled Pope.

'I guess so. I just didn't think that it would be in the pensions section though.'

'I'll let you into a secret. Civil services is all about pensions. Full salary pension, index linked, that's what motivates them. And if there's any problem, even the smallest, then retired or not they kick up a bloody storm.'

'OK. How about going out for a drink midweek then? Just a swift half one evening.'

Christ, this guy is relentless, thought Pope.

'Yeah, how about I call you in the next two weeks. Are there any nights during the week that aren't good for you?' said Pope.

A huge 500-watt grin spread across Mr Khan's face.

'John, any night is good.'

'You rich bankers have a lot of free time.'

'You know how it is.'

Khan got up and Pope walked him to the front door.

'Catch up soon then,' said Khan, mission accomplished.

'That we will,' Pope said, closing the front door.

Pope walked into the kitchen. Jane, Charlie, Daisy and Doodle all looked at him. No one spoke.

'What?' Pope said.

'Who's got a new friend then,' said Charlie through scrunched up eyes.

'Doodle doesn't like him,' added Daisy matter of factly.

'Cup of tea?' said Jane.

'Yeah, why not,' smiled Pope.

10:00. Carruthers was sitting in a car off of Commercial Road, Portsmouth with three other people. There were two other cars and a motorcycle rider that made up the surveillance unit. They had run a few drills in and around Monckton Fort the previous day in preparation for today's surveillance exercise. The instructors had set up and run the ops meeting earlier this morning, briefing the team on their objectives. There was a couple (man and wife) who they had to surveil. To make the exercise more realistic, the couple who worked for MI6 were also training on counter-surveillance before being deployed overseas and they were honing their skills. This bit of information had been withheld from Carruthers and her team.

'Right, everyone, we'll throw a net over these two and they won't know a thing,' said the eager young man in a Yorkshire accent sitting in the front passenger seat.

Carruthers, who was sitting directly behind the young man, had been smiling for the last several minutes. She was in a good mood. After breakfast there was enough time to have a long shower, dry and set her hair, put on her makeup and choose some designer clothes and matching handbag. This lifted her spirits, especially after the ghastly events during the previous two weeks.

'Off, off,' came the male voice in everyone's earpieces.

'Right, that's us,' boomed the Yorkshire accent as he opened his car door and exited the car.

'He's eager,' said Carruthers sarcastically, adjusting her hair.

'Let's just get this done,' said the young lady sharply as she exited the other back door, not looking directly at Carruthers.

Carruthers bit back the comment that was bubbling up in her throat.

These kids don't realise that once they pass then they'll be working for me. I'll beat some respect into them then, she thought spitefully.

Her real identity had been deliberately withheld from all of the current batch of students and from all but the most senior of instructors at Fort Monckton. In this batch of trainees, she was the oldest by some considerable distance. Recruitment was generally for the early to mid-twenties age range, but there were always exceptions and some 'oldies' were either on refresher training or training to be instructors.

'Where's Grandma?' said the Yorkshire accent loudly.

'Still putting her teeth in,' quipped the young lady.

The group had now swelled to eight people and all looked at Carruthers who was now out of the car and ambling towards them. The three drivers had remained in their cars and the motorcyclist had remained seated on his bike. Without speaking, the group split up into four teams of two and walked into Commercial Road, blending into the crowd of daily shoppers. It was a cold, wet day. But then again, when wasn't it cold, wet and bloody miserable?

They moved in formation, changing positions effortlessly and without communication. Sometimes in front, sometimes beside and sometimes behind their quarry. Hats changed, glasses worn and not worn, coats spun inside out to display another colour, the team were employing all the elements of tradecraft.

The couple went about their business in an effortless fashion and they seemed to have plenty of time to study the plentiful wares displayed in the shops and stores. They were a happy smiling couple at ease with each other. In reality they were running counter-surveillance techniques but very subtly. They didn't want to arouse any suspicion and alert anyone that they were checking for tails. Their own training had been about non-detection and that meant not being overt about checking for tails. Once they were deployed abroad, their very lives would depend on their skills to blend into their surroundings and go about their dangerous business without being detected. The opposition would always have the upper hand. They would be identified as soon as they arrived, followed, photographed and spied upon. It was a deadly game and one slip could have disastrous consequences not only for them but also for the indigenous agents that they would be running.

The couple had been shopping for nearly two hours and were now sitting down in a coffee shop. The surveillance team and the couple as the centrepiece had danced for a long while. The music was an extremely well-known piece; it was 'The Flight of the Bumblebee'. It evoked the seemingly chaotic and rapidly changing flying patterns of bumblebees, and they all had danced expertly.

The team had fanned out and the drivers were now on point. New faces to blend in the background and now there were new drivers in each car. The surveillance teams of two would now also be changed as part of the ongoing game. The couple enjoyed their medium cups of cappuccino with croissants, lazily surveilling the horizon. They smiled and chatted whilst checking their bounty. The shopping bags were opened up and the new clothes examined in full view. All the while they remained vigilant. They had picked up what appeared to be a tail but they were unable to flush it out and finally agreed that there wasn't anyone onto them. Carruthers was sitting at a table eating a sandwich when the Yorkshire voice boomed.

'I think we're working well as a team. They don't know that we're all over them like a rash.'

Carruthers nodded. She was more interested in eating her club sandwich. She knew that it was calorific but she'd been walking for nearly two hours and there was still maybe several more hours to go before the exercise finished and by then she'd burn off all of these calories. She then had a great idea: why not buy another club sandwich and she could eat that one later? Burning all of these calories literally demanded that she rewarded herself.

'We've got this in the bag.'

Carruthers was nudged out of her reverie by the incessant booming Yorkshire accent, whatever it was drivelling on about.

'I'm just going to grab another sandwich,' Carruthers said, finishing off the last mouthful of the current club sandwich.

'OK, hurry up though. They may be off soon,' boomed the Yorkshire accent to Carruthers' bespoke back.

The team had split up once the couple were parked in their coffee shop and Carruthers and her partner were in sandwich shop several shops down the road.

'Off, off,' came the voice in everyone's earpieces.

The bumblebees moved into formation, the music restarted and everyone danced to the tune. There was a tour of Cascades shopping centre for forty-five minutes and then the couple headed back to their car laden with bags. The car was parked in the same road as the surveillance wagon trail of three cars and the motorcycle. It was a delicate manoeuvre to allow the couple to return, collect their car and leave without exposing the surveillance team. The road was a choke point and the team was exposed. The four foot teams simply stayed away and waited until the car had left the area. The motorcycle had taken the lead and he was providing a running commentary. The cars followed his directions and closed ranks but at a safe distance.

For this exercise, the decision had been taken that the target vehicle would not be tagged. That meant that there was no electronic device planted on the couple's cars and that surveillance would be 'eyes on' only. In the field, there are many reasons why surveillance does not include using a tracking device. The lead car drove around the suburbs of Portsmouth whilst the three following cars and motorbike continued to dance around with it. The tune was the same but now the bumblebees were mechanical.

The lead car headed out onto the M27 motorway and the traffic was moderate with the rain splashing back up off the tarmac causing reduced visibility. The rain and the effects of it didn't deter all of the vehicles on the motorway from driving at speeds that were dangerous. Dangerous because of the reduced visibility and dangerous because the wet surface meant that the drivers didn't allow for sufficient braking distances between each other. The car turned onto the A32 and headed towards Gosport. As it neared the outskirts, the car pulled into the car park of an olde worlde pub. The couple got out and skipped quickly inside the pub. There was a hasty discussion over the mikes and it was agreed that one couple would go into the pub and keep 'eyes on' surveillance of the couple. Carruthers was listening into the conversation with some disinterest and her mind was wondering to what she'd eat for Sunday dinner once she was back home.

'OK, we'll do it,' boomed the Yorkshire accent.

Carruthers jumped in her seat. That meant she and the loud oaf were going to go into the pub.

'Remember to change your coat, remove your glasses and drop the hat,' shouted the Yorkshire accent.

'Yes. Yes. I know what I'm doing,' said an irritated Carruthers.

She moved around stiffly, re-arranging her garments in the back of the car.

The three cars and bike had pulled up in a turning after the pub. It was too exposed for them to park in the rather empty pub car park. As they entered the pub, the Yorkshire lump put his arm through the arm of Carruthers.

She instantly recoiled.

'Really,' she spat out, shooting him a look of daggers.

'Relax. Roleplay. We're just a mother and son out having a drink.'

'Fuck off,' she whispered, but she didn't remove his interlinked arm.

He laughed, emitting a sound of two drowning men screaming for help. A few stares bore down on this odd couple with the even odder laugh.

'Half of Best and a sweet sherry for Mum,' he boomed.

The barmaid nodded and went about pouring the drinks.

'Don't push it,' Carruthers said through gritted teeth whilst she slowly took in the pub's interior and punters.

It was typically dark inside with a low ceiling and her eyes were slowly adjusting to the permanent gloom. The lanky Yorkshire man was stooping to avoid scraping his head on the bowed ceiling. Drinks delivered and paid for, Carruthers walked deliberately to a rickety table away from the bar and sat down. She placed her two bags on the table. The couple that they were surveilling had taken a seat nearer to the front door and were engaged in a conversation, oblivious to everyone else in the pub. They had in front of them on their table two orange juices and two packets of crisps that they were munching away on. Carruthers and her 'bastard' son sat there sipping slowly on their drinks.

'So tell me, what type of music do you like?' said the Yorkshire voice in a fairly loud voice, which for him was near to a whisper.

Carruthers stared backed and then decided that she did need to roleplay.

'Classical.'

'That figures,' he replied.

'What does that mean?' she hissed.

'Nothing.'

There was then a standoff.

'Well, aren't you going to ask me what music I like?'

'Prey tell me, what music do you like?'

'Red Hot Chilli Peppers and the Stone Roses.'

'That figures,'

'I guess we both like our music for the same reasons. Both of my favourite bands were at their peak in 1990s when I was teenager and I suppose classical music was at its peak when you were a teenager in the eighteenth century.'

'Why are you so rude?'

'Not rude. Just Yorkshire humour.'

Just then the lady walked past them and carried on into the ladies' toilet.

'Are you going to follow her in there?'

'More Yorkshire humour?'

'What? No. What if she's making a drop or she's meeting someone?'

'You watch far too many films.'

'No. Check it out.'

Carruthers huffed slightly and then got up and headed into the toilet. It was cramped in there with the only stall occupied. Carruthers looked at the dingy sink, taps and mirror and wanted to escape but thought that that would look odd. No, she had to remain here and check the stall. The lady came out of the stall and smiled at Carruthers. Carruthers nodded and they moved around to let each other pass by in the cramped room. Carruthers sat quietly until she was happy that the lady had exited the toilet. She checked around the toilet looking for any signs of it being a drop box. She then stood on the toilet seat and checked in the cistern. The stall was clean; well, it wasn't a drop box at least. Carruthers went out and checked around the sink and hand dryer. Everything was in order and she washed her hands vigorously.

'Off, off,' she heard in her earpiece loudly.

It was the recognisable Yorkshire twat. She didn't finish drying her hands and hurried back to her table where the Yorkshireman was now standing with a stoop.

'Anything in the shithouse?' he said.

'No.'

'OK. We can hang back until they're out of the car park and on their way. The others will follow and we can pop around the corner and catch our lift.'

Carruthers nodded and nixed her schooner of sherry.

Actually that's not too bad, she thought to herself.

'Come on, they've gone.'

Carruthers picked up her two bags from the table and followed the lanky streak of piss out of the pub. Carruthers' car caught up with the group within three minutes and rejoined the dance. The car entered Gosport town centre and drove around sedately until it stopped at a popular chain hotel. The cars and motorbike pulled up in a side street and the team were about to set up surveillance in the hotel when they received a message from HQ advising that their mission had concluded and that they were to return for a full debrief. The surveillance had lasted just over four hours and the team were confident that it had been a success. They talked freely over the mikes and amongst themselves in each of the cars. There was a mood of victory and of a job well done.

Carruthers didn't join in the conversation. She didn't enjoy these exercises, this whole course and the constant roleplay. She remembered that she had a club sandwich and opened the bag containing it. On the way back to Fort Monckton she sat alone with her thoughts, grazing on the delicious sandwich. There was a constant babble going on in the background but boy, was this sandwich good.

A message was delivered to all three cars and to the motorcyclist that all material had to be handed back to the awaiting instructors and that the debrief would start sharply in fifteen minutes in meeting room 2. Carruthers digested the information and decided that there was enough time to go back to her room and change into another set of designer clothes. She spent the next three minutes whilst the convey sped back into the fort deciding what clothes would be best for an afternoon meeting. Arriving, she hastily made her way back to her room and, working efficiently, also managed to squeeze in a healthy dose of hairspray and a slight twist on her hairstyle before dashing off to room 2.

There was a buzz in room 2; the surveillance team were chatting about a job well done. Carruthers was contemplating whether there would be enough time on Sunday to have a pedicure or whether it made more sense to apply nail polish and get her PA to arrange a visit as early in the week as possible for a well-earned pedicure. Her thoughts were disturbed. The door opened and in walked three instructors, each weighed down with thick folders. They spread out behind the main desk and leant back against the wall holding indifferent poses. The surveillance group stared from their desks at the front of the classroom that was set out as any classroom up and down the country. The main instructor walked in and parked his backside on the edge of the teacher's desk facing the expectant students. The murmur ceased and the other instructors looked up and stared at his back.

'Everyone here?' said the head instructor, looking out at his audience.

Several heads nodded eagerly.

'Good. Let's get started then. All material returned?'

'Yes, Skip,' came a low growl from behind him.

The material had been numbered and every piece of paper had been counted back in. It was destined for the shredder and then would be bagged up, shipped out and incinerated by a company that was accredited with the destruction of classified material. The photos were the most prized of the material because they showed the faces of active British agents.

'First off. The couple that you followed work for 6. They are the best of the best regarding counter-surveillance and work in hostile environments.'

Smiles beamed back at him. Chests puffed out. The music now playing represented a victory and it was the '1812 Overture' and was moving swiftly to the climactic volley of cannon fire.

'We had five spotters out watching the whole operation and they were impressed with the team work and tradecraft displayed.'

The orchestra was building towards the famous crescendo and the team were enraptured.

'6 had their own team of spotters out monitoring primarily the performance of their agents and they reported back periodically that they were also impressed with your performance. That translates to that they weren't able to pick any of you out.'

Any second now and the climax would be reached with ringing chimes and brass fanfare accompanying the cannon volley. The group were bursting with pride.

'It was a bust,' the instructor said calmly.

'What?' they exclaimed in unison.

'A bust.'

'No way,' was the choir's reply.

Comments flew indiscriminately around the group. The orchestra had packed up their gear and were heading home. There was going to be no climax to the '1812 Overture'.

'Let's start at the beginning and walk through everything in detail.'

The stunned audience listened as they received the feedback. Very positive on all aspects of their tradecraft and teamwork tailing the couple around Commercial Road. The fanning out of the team when the couple settled down for a coffee break was praised. Again high praise about the tradecraft in Cascades shopping centre and the egress after when the target car left. That could have been a potential problem droned on the instructor but was managed seamlessly by teamwork and use of the motorcycle to take up the lead and guide the team back on and around the couple. More praise regarding the tradecraft used to hem the couple in when they stopped for a drink in a Gosport pub. There was a nod to the fact the weather was awful and that they coped well with the conditions. The group were numbed and the praise was falling on a set of collective deaf ears.

'It was in the pub when the tail was spotted,' the instructor said blandly.

The collective body language changed. They were all attentive now, coiled and ready to attack. The three instructors poised behind the lead instructor however continued to lounge against the wall, almost disinterested with the whole affair.

That noisy fucking Yorkshire twat, thought Carruthers. *Him and his stupid roleplay attracting attention. What a loud mouth.*

'The lady operative was going to the toilet when her attention was drawn to two items on a table where a couple were sitting.'

Fuck, thought Carruthers.

'There was a Hermes shoulder bag in bleu agate, I believe, and made of calfskin lying on the table. Very expensive, the agent noted. And next to the bag was a distinctive Pret a Manger bag. The agent thought how different they looked together and remembered seeing the same two bags in three different places in Cascades shopping centre. On the way back from the toilet, she took a look at the couple sitting at the table and remembered seeing them earlier. She noticed that on the earlier occasions they were wearing subtly different clothes, hats and even glasses. Her male partner glanced across and confirmed her awareness. When they left the pub as they drove back, they also remembered seeing both people sitting at the table earlier in the morning in Commercial Road but then they were with different partners.'

Snide glances were being shot at Carruthers from all comers. She remained silent, listening to the monologue, dressed impeccably and not one hair out of place.

'The agents communicated with their handlers who then contacted us. We had no choice at this stage but to halt the operation once they arrived at the hotel. You all would have swapped partners as per standard operating procedures and they would quickly have identified all of the surveillance team.'

Defeated, deflated and angry, the team sat there in silence, apportioning blame to Carruthers.

'Your opponents showed their undoubted skill. They were able to flush you all out by their powers of observation. Miss Brown is not to be blamed for this.'

A couple of mouths opened and in particular the big Yorkshire gob, but no one challenged the statement.

The instructor remained silent for a minute, letting that point sink in.

'You work as a team. You succeed as a team and you fail as a team. The stakes are high, your life, your colleagues' lives, agents' lives and members of the public as well as other services depend on your teamwork.'

Heads around the room nodded.

'Miss Brown took with her two bags into the pub. Why didn't someone in the car mention to her that she shouldn't take both bags, or even any bag?'

'You,' the instructor said, pointing at the big Yorkie, 'Why didn't you check your partner and make sure that she wasn't conspicuous? As a group, there was a lack of attention to detail.'

The look returned to the inspector from Yorkie was a sheepish one.

'Many of you will continue with your training here for some time and you all have learnt an invaluable lesson. You need to blend into the background, be unobtrusive. If you wear a distinctive wedding ring then take it off. If you wear ostentatious earrings, then remove them. Cover up tattoos. You can follow to the letter everything that we teach you about regularly changing clothes during surveillance but it is the little seemingly indistinctive things that our opponent will pick up on as you have found out today.'

They all now understood and agreed unreservedly with his sage comments.

'OK then. You will all be marked as failed for this exercise and the reason why will be included.'

The motorcycle rider could not disguise his thoughts. He was gutted!

All of the instructors headed towards the door in single file.

The head instructor turned and addressed the group, 'I hate losing to 6. They are smug bastards. Don't let it happen again.'

The group sat in silence, digesting the unwelcome but vital feedback.

'I hope that you enjoyed that fucking club sandwich,' boomed the big Yorkshireman.

22:00. Deepak sprung up as if he had received an electric shock. The wan smile on his face was one of *OK, you caught me in the act but don't start on me please.*

Ahmed's eyes roved from his settee to Deepak and back again. The fury was welling up inside and an explosion of volcanic proportions was moments away. Deepak retreated slowly towards his solitary single seat, still smiling and still holding Ahmed's stare. Ahmed was about to let rip when Deepak's left arm raised and in his hand was a TV remote control.

'Just finished tuning in the TV,' Deepak said meekly.

Ahmed's eyes darted around the room and then stopped at a TV.

'It's a forty-three inch flat screen.'

No response.

'LED.'

Still no response.

'Smart functionality inbuilt.'

Nope, nothing.

'Stand came with it.'

Still nothing.

Deepak pointed the remote control at the screen, hit a button, then another button. It came alive in a kaleidoscope of colours supported by rich sounds. Deepak adjusted the volume.

'Great sound.'

Ahmed sat back into his settee and started looking at the screen which was set up perfectly for watching from the ratty sofa. Not so from the frumpy single chair.

'Smart, you say?'

'Oh yes. WiFi enabled, web access too at your fingertips. And you can stream films and play games.'

'Where's the connection?'

'Wireless via N-Router.'

Ahmed nodded his head. The royal seal of approval. Deepak smiled again; the friendship remained intact. Hopefully the bonding had even improved. Watching sport was something that would definitely improve with this new shiny piece of techno-enriched kit. But where they both would co-join, support, dispute, argue, appreciate and follow fanatically were the talent shows and reality TV shows. They worked their Saturday around the talent shows, after show rap ups and then the Sunday sing offs. Judges were applauded and reviled, fallen contestants supported and booed. Emotions ran high, raised voices, perhaps one final cup of tea and then bed before another week kicked off.

'Pass the remote,' Ahmed said, stretching out on the settee.

Deepak got up and handed over the crown jewels. Ahmed started flicking through the channels. The natural order had been restored.

'I'll put the kettle on,' said Deepak happily.

A grunt was the reply as Teletext was imposed on the impressive forty-three-inch screen. To anyone walking into the room now it would feel like it was a cramped place, dominated by an ostentatious TV. A high-tech piece of kit out of place and out of time in a tired, old, scruffy small room. For the two guys who were the current inhabitants of the room, it was perfect.

Both were slurping their mugs of tea and devouring biscuits, hypnotised by the TV, even though they were watching the ads.

'So this was another birthday present,' Ahmed said, still in a trance.

'Not really.'

'Not really? What does that mean?'

'I bought it.'

'Really? How can you afford one of these on our wages?'

'Well, it wasn't paid for out of my wages.'

There was a silence. Ahmed sat up and the hair on the side of his head where he was lying down was flattened, giving his head an odd lopsided look. Another rage was welling up inside.

Deepak knew what was coming and stared intently at the ad on the TV.

'I used my drug money wages.'

'You fucking moron.'

'It made sense. I had all this cash and what was I supposed to do with it?'

'Nothing you do makes fucking sense. This is a government-owned property and you are filling it up with goods bought with drug money.'

'Technically the property is rented.'

'Don't get fucking smart. What if Fat Chris or the Boss comes up and sees all this swag? What the fuck are we going to tell them?'

'I won't buy anything else for the flat then.'

'Fucking right you won't.'

'Do you want me to get rid of it?'

'It's fucking here now. Just fucking leave it.'

'OK. Sorry.'

There was a sort of calm descending in the room.

'I hope that the young girl band doesn't get voted off Sunday,' Deepak said.

The ads were over.

05:30. Carruthers was wrapped up in a coat, hat, gloves, scarf, jeans and boots. The air was damp, a shower had just ceased and it was still dark in south London. She along with two others had just left the minivan and were heading up the garden path towards an old Victorian property. The lead person knocked gently on the back door. There were lights on in the kitchen. The wooden door creaked as it slowly opened outwards. A man's head popped out and he looked quickly from person to person before nodding. They all scurried inside, glad to get away from the biting cold wind.

'Go up,' he said flatly.

They walked in single file up three flights of stairs. The floorboards creaked under the threadbare carpet as they made their ascent. On the third floor there were three doors that led off the passageway and all were shut. The light was supplied by a single light bulb swinging gently on the thread suspended from the ceiling. It cast spooky shadows from all of them. There was an opening in the ceiling and an old wooden ladder had been placed against it. They made their way up into the cold loft that was just bearable due to a few small fan heaters chucking out modest amounts of warmth.

Once inside, the loft trapdoor was closed and their eyes worked frantically to adjust to the gloom. Carruthers was immediately struck by the stench. It was predominantly human body odour mingled with that musty odour that pervades all old lofts. She caught another smell; less pungent, but it was entwined nevertheless. The smell of urine was definitely there. Carruthers fiddled with her silk scarf and positioned it strategically over her nose and mouth. The loft was a very large space that, because of the dark, resembled a cavern. In the loft were three people. One was sitting in a small chair listening with headphones. Next to the chair was a recording device, the size of a small box. Another person was sitting in a battered old armchair. It had served its purpose in the house below and once it was no longer useable it had been shoved up into the loft. Now it was being used again. There was a box with a cloth on top of it and a laptop was sitting on top of the cloth. The laptop had a split screen displaying several small images on it. The images were in colour but the quality of each picture wasn't high quality. They were at best OK with blueish edges that were blurred. Headphones were also worn by that person. Further back in the recess of the loft was the final person. They were huddled over another laptop and were writing quickly using a standalone keyboard. A plastic bucket turned over so the flat base was their seat and a laptop was nestling on their knees. Headphones on that person also. Despite Carruthers' eyes having adjusted now, she wasn't able to make out the gender of the three inhabitants.

The person in front of her turned and whispered in her ear, 'Careful where you walk up here. It's easy to put your foot through the ceiling below. Keep to walking on the joists.'

Carruthers nodded and followed again as the three of them made their way carefully to the person watching the split screen.

The mid-twenties lady looked up from her screen at the group.

'May I introduce Miss Brown. She's on a training exercise and she's here to see how a live surveillance op is run,' said the lead person.

'Pleased to meet you,' said the young lady.

Carruthers nodded. The young lady recognised Carruthers immediately despite the fact that Carruthers resembled an eighteenth-century highwayman but said nothing.

She pointed to a dusty three-legged stool behind her and said, 'Grab that seat, make yourself comfy and I'll talk you through what's going on here.'

Carruthers dragged the stool over and sat down on it. There was nothing to be gained by cleaning the dust off it. It would only make the putrid air in here worse. The person in the recess who had been writing stopped and changed their screen to display a split screen and without being asked took over the monitoring role. The young lady explained that the house opposite contained two young Muslim men that were under surveillance. Cameras and audio equipment had been planted in several rooms in the house and the team here were watching and listening via a live feed. She talked through the roles that each of the team were performing currently and that the team were two hours into their twelve-hour shift. The surveillance operation was now into its third week and so far hadn't yielded anything significant. It was a cat and mouse game, said the girl. The guys were definitely acting suspicious and a number of characters had been observed coming and going and in that group were other 'people of interest'. An ever-expanding picture was being built and all of their behaviours, actions and habits no matter how small or how personal were being catalogued.

She looked at her watch and said, 'Target two will wake up in a few minutes or so and go and take a piss. He never washes his hands though.'

Charming, thought Carruthers.

Right on queue, there was a stir in one of the bedrooms. A head emerged from under a pillow followed by the bed clothes being thrown off. Like a drunk, he staggered into the bathroom and another hidden camera filmed his activities.

'Log that,' she said.

'Already done,' came the reply from the shadow in the recess.

'He's done now till 10:00 when he gets up,' she said to Carruthers.

The young lady went on to describe how they spent their day up here in the loft. Once she had completed that, Carruthers decided that she would ask her a number of questions. For the first time since Carruthers had been on the course, she was showing real interest. She was now seeing, smelling, hearing and tasting what it was really like to be on the frontline and involved in an ongoing op. Not a silly exercise or an even sillier roleplay.

'So tell me,' Carruthers said with earnest, 'what happens when you need to take a natural break?'

'Well, you see that old curtain hanging over there?'

'Yes.'

'Behind that is a bucket. There's an air freshener and hand wipes.'

That's the bloody smell, thought Carruthers. 'What about when you need to do a number two?'

'Most agents can survive without. That's one thing that happens automatically when you are on long surveillances. Your body adjusts as you need to be alert all the time. One trick that the newbies do though is that they take anti-diarrhoea products before they start their shift and constipation products when they leave.'

'Really?'

'Yeah. But if you are desperate then we have an arrangement with the owner that we can use the bathroom downstairs. To be honest, everyone on this gig has been around and that won't happen.'

Carruthers nodded.

'No one is stupid enough to go out for a curry before shift,' said the young lady.

The young lady then laughed and Carruthers laughed along with her.

'Oh, and as for the bucket. We just take it in turns when it's getting full. Pop downstairs and use the loo. It's no different than slopping out in prison really.'

'What about the people that live here? Aren't they curious or even put off by the slopping out routine?'

'No, they all just rent rooms here. The owner is a tough old bird who takes no nonsense. She's told them that it's none of their business what's going on in the loft.'

The young lady adjusted the screen in order that Carruthers could see the several different pictures that filled the screen simultaneously and handed her a set of headphones, gesturing to her to put them on. Carruthers did as she was asked and placed the headphones over her ears, making every effort not to dislodge her scarf that was acting as a filter to the fetid smell.

The young lady's mind had been racing the last several minutes and whilst she was able to present a calm exterior, internally she was in turmoil and reaching several conclusions. Her training had allowed her to remain calm but she was feeling the pressure. It had come as a shock when someone as senior as Carruthers had entered the hide. It was more alarming that she had used a false name and was trying to disguise herself by partially covering her face with a scarf. True, they had been pre-warned that there was going to be a visit from training school, but seeing Carruthers wasn't something that any of them could have expected.

Why was she here? What was her agenda? Why was she using an alias? Why was she trying to disguise herself by using a scarf? These were all the questions that were scurrying around inside the head of the young lady.

The conclusion was obvious and all roads led to the same endpoint. Carruthers was here to evaluate their performance. Maybe someone was being assessed for promotion. Maybe someone was being assessed for demotion or disciplinary action. Maybe there was assessment of their processes and controls. Whatever the reason, she needed to let the team know that they were being assessed and everyone needed to be both on their mettle and run everything by the book. Who spies on the spies? It was Carruthers, that's who, and she had a reputation for being a stickler. The young lady opened another laptop that was lying on the desk and created a message quickly. She then selected several names, marked the email as urgent and sent it. The email was sent from one of her private accounts and was sent over a commercial email network. This was to ensure that no trace nor audit trail would show up on MI5's private and secure network. As the message was sent over a network that employed low-grade encryption, it meant that there was a possibility that the message could be intercepted and read. That was an acceptable risk rather than leaving a footprint within MI5's network that would be retrievable forensic evidence. The message pinged on the personal laptops of the other two people working in the loft. It also pinged on several other personal laptops belonging to other members of the surveillance team. The message was read by everyone immediately as it was marked with 'High Priority'.

'Op under surveillance by HQ. Run everything by the book.'

There was no change in body language by the other two team members in the loft after they had read the message, and they carried on doing whatever they were doing. Carruthers was watching the split screen and listening to the audio feed, almost hypnotised by watching a live op, oblivious to the kerfuffle going on around her, caused by her.

Even though both targets were asleep in bed, Carruthers found the whole experience engrossing. So much so that she was gradually acclimatising to the awful smell in the loft.

Beside Carruthers, the young lady had already received several replies and in turn she had sent out replies. The pinging went on for several minutes until the young lady sent out an email to quiet it down otherwise Carruthers would become suspicious.

The other two people who had arrived with Carruthers were each sitting now with the other two operatives in the loft and both were receiving similar information regarding the current op that Carruthers had. Both of them were also similarly engrossed with seeing a live op. One of them was an instructor from Fort Monkton and the other one was a trainee. Both had noticed that there were emails being sent and received on a separate laptop but did not ask what was going on as they assumed that it related to something that was highly classified.

The young lady tapped Carruthers on the arm after several more minutes.

'Fancy a coffee?'

Hidden behind her scarf, Carruthers' face contorted. The thought of eating or drinking here went against her nature. However, she wanted to embrace everything that surveillance operatives did and muffled a reply.

'Sure.'

The girl withdrew a thermos flask from a bag by her side along with two mugs and poured out two cups. She also withdrew two chocolate bars.

'The coffee has already been sweetened and there's some milk in it but I like it strong. I hope that it's OK for you.'

'It's fine,' said Carruthers, accepting the steaming mug and chocolate bar.

Carruthers lowered her very expensive scarf and stared into the piping hot mug of coffee.

'We all bring in our own provisions and drinks. That way we don't leave our stations or get sidetracked. Even though we work as a team, we know that we must be vigilant at all times. And that means keeping our eyes and ears on the targets at all times.'

Carruthers blew into her mug and nodded. She was impressed by their dedication. The coffee had cooled sufficiently for Carruthers to take her first sip. She was overwhelmed by both how strong the coffee was and how sweet it was. In fact, it was unpleasant.

'Cor. That's one strong, sweet coffee,' smiled Carruthers.

'It helps keep me alert and provides energy.'

'I can see that.'

'The chocolate helps tone it down a bit and also boosts energy.'

Carruthers could feel an instant jolt as the coffee increased her alertness. Drinking the coffee and eating the chocolate bar worked as the young lady suggested and soon the coffee was drunk. Even though they were conversing, Carruthers noticed that the young lady focused exclusively on the screen. It was obvious that these were dedicated people who were not easily distracted.

'I generally have a coffee every two hours with some chocolate. I also have a couple of energy drinks, sweets, crisps and sandwiches.'

'That doesn't sound like a healthy diet.'

'It's all about staying alert. Everyone has their own way of dealing with twelve-hour shifts but I'd say most people use energy-boosting foods and drinks as their base. I know some who use health pills that are stimulants also but I've tried them and I'm not convinced that they are better than coffee and energy drinks.'

'What about when you go home? How can you sleep with all that coffee and sugar swimming around inside of you?'

'Most of us are exercise junkies. We head off to the gym or go for a run. It sweats out the crap, relaxes us and allows us to come down and sleep.'

'I don't think I could live like that.'

'You get used to it. The worst thing though is the location that we have to use for the surveillance.'

'Yes, I can see that,' said Carruthers, looking around the loft.

'Oh, this isn't too bad. It's worse when you are stuck inside some place that is freezing and you can't get warm even though you pile on the clothes, or in the summer when it's so hot that you feel dizzy with the heat. That really tests you both mentally and physically.'

'So talk me through a typical day.'

'We get here around 02:30 and go through a handover. We talk to each person individually and get all of their updates verbally. Then we run through all emails and read any reports. Usually they are off by 03:00 and we then pick up the reigns. Sometimes it takes longer to go through everything. So by the time we are due to start officially, everything is done and the handover is complete. In the afternoon, they will come in at 14:30 and we'll go through the handover in the same fashion. We all take two twenty-minute breaks and a one-hour lunch. We take them at separate times and that means that the others will cover. If there's any activity then we delay or skip the breaks and focus on the live op. Most people remain at their station and during their breaks read or watch films on their personal laptops. Obviously we don't use our work machines; and anyway, they have been hardened.

'As mentioned, we log everything that the targets do and say realtime. Anything suspicious is flagged up realtime. We liaise with the Walker teams and give them a heads up when the targets are getting ready to go out. Generally we know where they are going and what mode of transport they are going to take because they discuss it. We make sure that the Walker teams know all of this as it helps them prepare. Sometimes the targets talk about where they are going and how they plan to get there the night before. This is given straight to the Walker teams and they then plan routes and their own numbers required to follow them. It's mostly routine. Not at all like in the films when a target dashes out of the house and jumps on and off of buses and trains running dry cleaning routines. But everyone is looking for even the smallest change to their routine as that is when they will be up to something. The other thing that we check on is the surveillance equipment. We remotely check the signal strength and quality of feeds as we do get occasional equipment problems. Once the targets are out, then we go in and replace anything on the blink. We ship it back to HQ and another spare is sent over.'

'I didn't realise that our equipment was dodgy.'

'It isn't. There are many reasons why something isn't working. It ranges from interference to a loose connection, but we don't take any chances. We whip it out asap, replace it and keep up the electronic surveillance with minimal, if any, interruption.'

'So do you know where both targets are going to go today?'

'Yes. Target Two will get up at 10:00 and he'll go out just before 11:00 and go to the Department of Social Protection and sign on. Then he'll go to an address close by where someone will pick him up and he'll go to a flat. There he'll work as a labourer until 18:00 and will then get dropped back at the address that he was picked up from. He'll make his way back to the flat, maybe stopping off at the corner shop to pick up some groceries and be indoors by 18:30 where he'll remain.'

'Hang on. Are you saying that he's signing on today and then he's going to go to work?'

'Yes. He signs on once a month and he earns £35 per day cash in hand. He has a bank account but that is only used for receiving his weekly benefits. The cash in hand is spent mostly on gambling on the horses and some he transfers via Western Union back to his parents in Pakistan.'

'Cheeky little sod.'

'Yeah. But our role is to find out everything about him and intercept any terrorist activity that he may be involved in. If we tip off DSP that he's a benefit cheat then that may disrupt his plans and even spook him, so we don't interfere. Target One will get up and watch TV all day in the front room.'

Carruthers continued to be fascinated with being in the midst of a live op and had even forgotten to replace her scarf over her mouth and nose.

The young lady said that the plan was to rotate between all three operatives and that Miss Brown would go and sit with the person who was hugging the recess of the loft. Carruthers got up, leaving behind the headphones, and walked carefully into the darkened area of the loft. Once there, she was able to see that the person was a male and he was also in his twenties, although probably his late twenties. The person who was sitting with him stood up, nodded to Carruthers and retraced her steps. The vacant chair was a small plastic chair that was so grimy it was impossible to determine what colour it really was.

'Please take a seat. We don't have many visitors and there's not much here in the way of furniture,' he said in a pleasant tone.

'That's OK,' Carruthers said, sitting down in the uncomfortable chair.

'Nothing here will make it onto *Antiques Roadshow*,' he continued with an air of ease.

Carruthers laughed.

'I'll talk you through my day. There will be overlap with what you have already heard but I hope that you are OK with that.'

He went through his day. He was responsible for writing up realtime the daily report which was an activity log. He cross-referenced activities to times, camera and audios. He also monitored external cameras that were monitoring the outside of the house and back garden as well as the street. He was also the point of contact for both HQ and the Walker teams. The Walker teams had access to much of the feeds in a van based around the corner in a parallel street. Once the targets left then the Walker teams would use either cars or follow on foot and the van would remain there.

He heard a ping from his personal laptop and opened it nonchalantly whilst handing Carruthers a set of headphones in order that she could listen in to the live audio feed. He had his channel set up to communicate with the Walker team van.

'Asked a lot of questions. Be on your guard,' was the email text sent by the young lady to an eager group who desisted from firing back questions and comments.

The surveillance team were not only 'eyes on' the two targets but were now 'eyes on' Carruthers and her two cohorts. Carruthers put on the headphones, adjusted herself in the uncomfortable seat and sat there listening and watching the split screen intently. She remained engrossed at being in the heart of a live Op.

The young man studied Carruthers and decided to let her continue with her monitoring uninterrupted for the next twenty-five minutes.

Afterwards he tapped her on her arm and said, 'Fancy a coffee?'

Carruthers glanced at her watch and saw that the time was 08:30. The time was literally flying past and she remembered that the surveillance team stopped every two hours to ingest further quantities of caffeine and sugar. She had already gone past that point and felt in need of a stimulant.

'Yes please.'

The young man produced a flask and poured two mugs. Again, the coffee was steaming hot. He also gave her an energy bar. She let the coffee cool down a bit before daring to take a sip.

'This is sweet,' she said.

'Yeah. I reckon the sugar will rot my teeth within ten years.'

'Oh, that's not good.'

'No problem. I plan to skip fillings and go straight to implants. I'll have a real Hollywood smile.'

'Won't that be expensive?'

'Not really. There's already places in Eastern Europe that are offering cheap deals. In ten years' time, implants will be cheap as chips.'

'Sounds like you have thought this through.'

'Definitely.'

Carruthers sat in front of the screen watching and listening, totally absorbed. She watched as Target Two got up, readied himself and, as predicted, left before 11:00 and leisurely set off first to sign on and then get picked up and be driven to work. She heard the Walker team setting off ahead of him and plant someone at the Department of Social Protection and another person outside the flat that he'd then walk to. Other team members would either walk or drive as they followed his every step. It was an efficient net that they had thrown over him. There were two team members left in the van who would now relax somewhat and monitor Target One's predicted leisurely day.

At 11:30 the young man pointed to his colleague who was sitting in a small chair listening on headphones and said with charm, 'OK, Miss Brown, time to continue musical chairs. Go over and he'll explain his role.'

Carruthers exited from the gloom and her eyes adjusted to the extra light. There was another small chair next to the chair that was occupied by the young man. Upon inspection, he was a similar height, build and age as the chap that she had just spent a few hours with.

He handed her a set of headphones and told her not to put them on yet. He didn't remove his own headphones but continued to listen whilst he went through his role and daily activities. He explained that he was listening into any and all incoming and outgoing calls to the targets' address. Both of them had two mobile phones each. One was their personal phone and the other one was a burner phone. In addition there was a landline. The calls were all recorded within the box beside him and he could replay any of them at any time. Analysis of the calls was handled by Analysis Team 3 back at Thames House. In addition, the calls were sent to GCHQ who ran every call through voice recognition software that attempted to match up the voice on the call to a database of voices. New voices were added if the caller was new, thus expanding the list. Details such as their phone number and name were also appended. GCHQ would also identify the caller, all details attached to that phone number, and if it was a mobile phone it would also include the area from where the caller was making the call. This information would then be sent back to Analysis Team 3 to help build up an ever-expanding and detailed picture surrounding the two targets. The two burner phones were occasionally used but it appeared that they were being used when the targets had mislaid their personal phones. It meant that these guys were sloppy as burners were generally used no more than a few times and then disposed of.

'Would you like a coffee?' he asked politely.

'I would but first I need to use your rest room.'

'It's behind the curtain,' he replied.

Carruthers walked over and entered the partitioned area. She looked down at the bucket with some dismay as it was three quarters full. There was no time for decorum as she was busting.

'I think that we need to unload the bucket,' said the young lady sweetly from the other side of the curtain.

'Yes,' said Carruthers, swishing back the curtain.

The young lady said, 'We don't have many visitors and we should have already sorted this out. I'll pop downstairs and clear this out. It won't take a minute.'

'Why don't I do that? You have important work to do.'

'Are you sure?'

'Of course,' said Carruthers, picking up the bucket.

Carruthers made her way gingerly out of the loft. She did have an ulterior motive which was that by going downstairs, she'd be able to use a flush toilet and wash her hands thoroughly. The three operatives noted the gesture and even though Carruthers was there spying on them (in their opinion), she had just gone up a notch.

Back at her seat, Carruthers put on the headphones and started drinking the coffee that had now stewed for several hours. It was a very bitter taste and made her grimace but it powered up her senses immediately. Behind her there was a flurry of activity. The young lady was pointing at her screen and talking into her mic. The other operative in the recess was also doing the same.

'Target One is on the move. I repeat, Target One is on the move,' the voice said calmly through Carruthers' headphones.

'I'm out and on foot,' said a male voice Carruthers had never heard before.

'I'm going to trail in the van. We don't have enough bodies here to throw a net over him,' said another voice in the van.

'I'm going to assist. Tell the van driver to pull up outside the target address. I'll be right there,' said the Fort Monkton instructor, standing up in the loft.

'I'm going as well,' said Carruthers, standing up and dropping her headphones.

No one challenged Carruthers. The other person from Fort Monckton remained silent and he stayed put in the loft. The young lady relayed the message over the general communications channel.

Five minutes later, Carruthers was sitting in the back of the van slowly heading down the main road alongside her instructor. Both were already wearing throat mics and were listening into the stream of communications via earpieces. Target One had stopped at a bus stop and when the first bus arrived after five minutes, he boarded it and took a seat at the rear. The Walker had slipped onto the bus two people behind him and was standing in the centre of the bus looking out of the side window directly opposite the exit doors. He was strategically placed to follow the target should he decide to leave the bus at any point. The van was now following the bus at a discreet distance and, much to the ire of other drivers, continued to stop randomly, causing pockets of traffic jams. Whist all of this was going on, there was heavy traffic on the airwaves between the van, the stakeout team in the loft, the several people following Target Two and HQ. The decision from HQ was that four people in two vehicles deployed surveilling Target Two would peel off and join up with the van and the single Walker following Target One. The bus stopped outside Greenwich station and a throng of people got off.

12:20. Amongst the crowd was Target One and along with many of the passengers he headed up and into the station. The Walker kept his distance but followed him up the path whilst supplying a running commentary of the unfolding events. He had been asked several times whether Target One was carrying a rucksack or bag and replied on each occasion that he wasn't carrying anything. It was clear that people who were periodically joining in at HQ were concerned that the target may be about to carry out an attack. Target One bought a ticket from the automated ticket machine and the Walker was able to see that he had bought a return ticket to Charing Cross station.

The Walker relayed the information via his throat mic to everyone listening in, bought a similar ticket and smartly followed Target One over and onto platform two. The van pulled into the station forecourt and the two people in the rear jumped out and headed into the station, searching out directions to platform two whilst two tickets were purchased. Once on the platform, they positioned themselves a fair distance from where Target One was standing with his human shadow not too far away from him. The train that he was going to take was only five minutes away from arriving.

Meanwhile, one of the two cars assigned to Target Two had been reassigned and had hit a combination of traffic and roadworks, and their pursuit had ground to a halt. Hearing that Target One was heading to Charing Cross, they then made the decision to drive to Maze Hill station. It was on the same line and they were closer to that station. It would mean that they were unlikely to be on the same train but would be on the next train and would catch up in central London. They relayed their intentions via their comms link.

The train pulled into Greenwich and Target One boarded the train. He sat in a near empty carriage and was joined in that carriage by his shadow who sat further down next to another set of doors. In the next carriage sat Carruthers and the instructor. They deliberately faced forward without any direct eye contact on Target One who was also facing forward. The journey lasted only eight minutes and incorporated two stops before the train pulled into London Bridge station. The target got up lazily and stood at the exit doors behind an elderly couple as the train slowed. He stepped down onto the concrete platform and searched out an indicator board. He looked up at the board and there amongst the departures was a train scheduled to go to Charing Cross in thirteen minutes' time. This particular train would be departing from platform three. He smiled as he was standing on platform two and that meant that he didn't need to rush through the ever-present throng of humanity to another platform in the bewildering labyrinth that made up London Bridge station. He sat on one of the many uncomfortable metal seats and stared vacantly into space. So far, his behaviour was as predicted from the moment that he had purchased his return ticket. Many people in HQ had been studying the route from Greenwich and checking live timetables. They had fed back to all of the field operatives what they thought Target One's planned route would be. This information was useful as it gave the Walkers a 'heads up', although everyone knew that it was only a prediction.

The Charing Cross train pulled in and the target with his escort entered the train. This time though, Carruthers and the instructor had entered a carriage behind the carriage that he sat in. Once at Charing Cross station, there were several exits that he could choose and being ahead of him could be detrimental. They would tail him from a distance, following regular updates from his shadow.

Target One exited the station and headed up Villiers Street where he stood outside the burger bar. He had earphones on and was listening to music on his phone. It was another cold, wet grey day in London. The three operatives were both north and south of him on the grubby street looking in shop windows and blending into the crowd. An attractive white woman in her early twenties approached him and they kissed and embraced as friends do when they meet up. Words were exchanged and both smiled before entering the burger bar. They queued up, purchased a couple of burgers and chips that the young woman paid for with cash and then sat at one of the tables. His shadow joined in another queue and after buying his food, he sat near the entrance.

Carruthers and the instructor also purchased food and sat at a table in front of the couple. By discreetly leaning back, the instructor was able to pick up portions of their conversation. It was apparent that they had met at college and had kept in touch. A few names were mentioned and what they were now doing for a job since leaving college. The girl still lived at home with her parents in Chigwell in Essex and worked as a PA in an office not that far from here. She pressed her friend but he was evasive, saying that he was still looking for the right job. The eating took ten minutes and then they left. The instructor gave a rapid fire update into his throat mic as he was leaving the restaurant.

She placed her arm through his as they walked up to Charing Cross Road and crossed over together. His shadow followed and was several people behind him as they crossed the busy road at the pedestrian crossing. The target turned around and stared directly at his shadow. He held his gaze until the shadow couldn't help but look him in the eyes. There was no emotion, just a glare. The shadow turned directly left, stared at his watch and headed off with purpose towards Trafalgar Square. He knew that he had been made and once out of sight, he updated everyone via his comms. Carruthers and the instructor fell in behind the couple, keeping a cautious distance. The couple were slowly walking towards Covent Garden, stopping occasionally to look in the splendidly dressed shop windows.

The four operatives that had boarded the train at Maze Hill had caught up with Carruthers and her beau. They had run hard from Charing Cross station for several minutes. They immediately took over the surveillance and two of them followed from behind. One overtook and was ahead of them whilst the other person was on the other side of the road slightly behind them. The target was now boxed in and the woman with him had been photographed surreptitiously.

Over the channel another voice cut in. 'Target Two on the move. I repeat, Target Two on the move.'

At HQ, several pairs of eyes darted back and forth between each other, no one speaking. The group who were boxing in Target One didn't flinch but, like their colleagues at HQ, were now trying to make some sort of sense out of what was happening. Everyone was aware that Targets One and Two had set routines and today those routines had been torn up. The question was, was there something being planned, was something actually happening or was all of this just innocent?

'All units stay on the same channel until further notice. It's a combined operation,' said a voice from HQ.

Quickly, a decision had been made that everyone needed to share information. Breaking this into two separate operations may lead to errors being made. However, if it turned out that there were two separate attacks underway then that may lead to confusion if the communication channel was shared. The split would only happen if an attack started. As there was no indication so far that there was anything out of the ordinary happening, there was no escalation outside of MI5. It was being treated as purely surveillance of two targets.

Target Two walked down the road and headed towards the main road where he waited at a bus stop. He had already picked up a human shadow who was also waiting at the same bus stop. The other two people were sitting in a car parked off of the main road. Once again, the question was asked several times.

'Was he carrying a bag or wearing a rucksack?'

The answer came back that he was carrying a sports holdall. This triggered a flurry of communications over the comms link. HQ seemed concerned now that an attack was imminent.

One of the Walker team at Covent Garden cut in.

'Target Two carried a sports bag from his flat to DSP and then onto work. It's dark blue with a Slazenger motif. He carries his work gear in it and changes onsite. Loft surveillance can check the tapes and confirm.'

The young lady in the loft was already rerunning the surveillance tapes on her split screen and joined in the conversation.

'Confirmed. Target Two packed dark blue Slazenger holdall at 10:10 with work clothes, dark blue jeans, red T-shirt, brown crew neck jumper and brown boots.'

There were two clicks over the Comms. Target Two's shadow had confirmed that he was still wearing his work clothes and he had the same holdall with him.

Back at HQ, the anxiety levels had decreased but there was a possibility that there could be something in the sports bag. The shadow watched as Target Two picked up the holdall and knew that whatever was in there was very light, which suggested that he was carrying his other set of clothes. He sent a text and followed him onto the bus. After several minutes, Target Two got off the bus and walked to another bus stop. Another wait of ten minutes and Target Two then boarded another bus. He wasn't heading towards London. His shadow had been swapped over at the bus stop and the car was still following the bus.

Back at Covent Garden, Target One and his female companion had spent some time going in and out of a number of shops. The female had bought a jumper and a top in two different shops. It was possible that he was running a dry cleaning routine and the surveillance team were working hard to keep him boxed in without exposing themselves. In the meantime, the photo of the female had been run through several facial recognition databases and she had come back clean. That information had been broadcast over the comms link by HQ. The circuitous walk around Covent Garden had lasted just under one hour so far. The couple stopped outside an artisan coffee shop and then went inside. Further back down the road, the six Walkers conferred. The decision was to go into the coffee shop and the man and woman who had been following at a distance would enter and act as a couple. They were very aware that Target Two had already flushed out his original shadow and going in was a risk.

The couple were about to set off when Carruthers said, staring at the lady, 'Excuse me, but you can't go in wearing a designer shoulder bag and carrying that shopping bag.'

'Why ever not?'

'It's far too distinctive. He'll make you.'

'Don't be ridiculous. Anyway, you're a trainee.'

No one intervened. In fact, the other team members realised that Miss Brown had made a valid point.

'I'm not Miss Brown. I'm Sandra Carruthers and I assume that even though you don't recognise me you will have heard of me. Your boss will report to someone and that someone will then report to me. And for the record, I know of an op where someone was carrying a similar designer bag and also a sandwich bag and they were made just on those two items. So give me both bags and also let's swap coats and you can have my scarf.'

There was no dissent and the woman did as requested. The conversation was heard by everyone at HQ, in the loft stakeout and the other surveillance team. The instructor looked at the man who was a similar size and said that they should also swap jackets. It was an odd sight to see a group of adults swapping clothes in winter, in the middle of Covent Garden surrounded by tourists. No one paid any attention; the English are an odd nation with odd habits. The man put on a pair of spectacles and tousled his hair whilst the woman ran a comb through her hair, altering her current hairstyle. They then walked into the coffee house. The other two took up two separate positions, again north and south of the coffee shop whilst Carruthers and the instructor retreated some distance back down the road.

The instructor smiled at Carruthers and switched off his throat mic. 'I see that you learnt something on the course.'

There was no reply. After the coffee break, Target One hugged the female and headed off back to Charing Cross station. The female headed off up towards Seven Dials and she had now picked up a shadow. Where she worked will be logged and then Team 3 will get to work digging into her background.

Target Two had arrived back at the flat and changed into his casual gear. He put on the TV and lay down on the couch. Target One entered the flat sometime later and went into the lounge, drawn there by the sound of the TV. He remembered that he hadn't left it on when he went out.

'What's up?' he said, looking at the prostrate body lying on the couch with his arms covering his face.

'Not feeling well. I had to jack early. Anyway, where have you been?'

'Out. I went for a walk. Can't stay cooped up in here all of the time.'

'Yeah, I guess so.'

In the Walker van parked around the corner, the discussion on the split operation was well underway. They all agreed that Carruthers' intervention was 100% correct. The team leader said that it was a lesson that they needed to take onboard and as a team they had to sharpen up. Everyone nodded their heads. This was a deadly game and even the smallest mistake could be disastrous. He also wondered whether there would be any follow up or recriminations from Carruthers and whether that would reflect on his leadership skills, and more importantly his desire for promotion.

16:20. In the loft it was now crowded. The next shift had arrived at 14:15 but the incumbent shift had remained. The first shift were just completing writing up all of their reports and cross-referencing everything to both the audio and video tapes. Carruthers, the instructor and the trainee that was left in the loft earlier said their goodbyes and informed everyone that they would be back first thing tomorrow morning. The young lady sent out her final email for today to the group. In it she mentioned that Carruthers was supposed to be a desk jockey and aloof by reputation but she went out on a live op without hesitation, not knowing what dangers she may face, took charge when needed and made a valuable contribution. Perhaps her reputation was undeserved. She even slopped out! She went on to say she hoped that the Walkers hadn't blotted their copybook. They may be in trouble. First, they posted most of their resources around Target Two and then there was the incident in Covent Garden when they were picked up by not blending into the background and by not changing their appearances.

On the journey back to Fort Monckton the instructor asked Carruthers what she had learnt from today. Carruthers replied that the loft surveillance team were a dedicated bunch, working very long hours, used vast amounts of concentration and worked in difficult conditions. She went on that the Walker team responded to a dynamically changing situation effortlessly, communicated efficiently and effectively under pressure, and most of all everyone worked as a team and managed it well.

'A very long day. You must be tired,' said the instructor.

'No.'

'It must be all that coffee and sugar that you've had.'

'No. It's the adrenaline from being involved in a live op. That's both frightening and fulfilling at the same time. Quite a buzz.'

10:00. Mia was resting in her bed. She had already been up, had had a session with the ward physio and was now listening to the hospital radio. Her peace was disturbed when a group of nurses fluttered into the room. They were a welcome sea of smiles and they all cheerily said good morning whilst they fussed around her, straightening her sheets, plumping her pillows and fussing over her machines that were administering regular doses of medicine and monitoring her internal condition. The door opened again and in walked Mr Kent and his two associates. All displayed a chirpy bedside manner as they took up static positions around Mia's bed. The phalanx of nurses faded into the background and quiet descended.

'Mia, you continue to make very good progress,' started Mr Kent. 'With your permission, I'd like to take off your bandages.'

There was quiet. The bandaged head barely moved. The left eye looked at the surgeon quizzically.

'Exposing the wounds to air will accelerate the healing. This is important for the next phase of your treatment. Ointments will be applied regularly by the nursing team and the air will dry out the moisture and stop the weeping,' Mr Kent said gently. 'Also I'd like you to see for yourself how you look.'

The bandaged head slowly nodded.

'Mia, that's good,' said Mr Kent. 'Can we now clear the room please.'

All of the nurses save the ward sister filed out.

'Mia, the ward sister will remove your bandages and then you can have a look in the mirror. Before we start I must warn you that you will see a lot of bruises, cuts and puffiness. This is normal and over time most of this will clear up. There is a patch over your right eye and that will remain in place,' he said, just above a whisper. 'OK. Are you ready?'

There was another tentative nod from the bandaged head.

The ward sister leant in and slowly rolled off the bandages, carefully balling them up as she went. The bandages were all deposited in a bin beside the bed. Once the bandages had all been removed, Mr Kent said.

'Mia, ready?'

Another nod now.

Mr Kent held up a hand mirror and Mia looked into it. She was unable to recognise the reflection. Her brain didn't recognise the face. The face was broken. It was covered in cuts and discoloured. The skin displayed all the colours of the rainbow. Angry bruises sat around the cuts, some of which were now weeping. Her high cheekbones, slim face and small chin were all gone. Her face now was grotesque. Puffed out cheeks and what looked like multiple gum abscesses overwhelmed all of her previously defined, porcelain features. Tears flooded down her left cheek and her body shook uncontrollably. She put her left hand out and Mr Kent passed the mirror over to her. She moved the mirror around to several different positions and adjusted her head simultaneously. The different angles gave her different views of the face, neck and head that was unrecognisable but still staring back at her.

'Mia, I know that it's a shock but trust me. Over time you will recover. In fact, in the next two weeks, most of the swelling will go down. We can then better assess the next steps and then set out an action plan. You are a strong woman and have very good healing powers. These traits will help you. In the meantime, carry on with the physio, eat fruit and drink plenty of water.'

Mia was in shock and passed back the hand mirror face down to Mr Kent.

'Mia, I've already spoken with your mum and dad who are waiting outside and they know everything that I've just told you. I'll leave you with the nurses now and they will look after you. We'll be back tomorrow and check in on your progress.'

The three men in white coats left and were replaced in the room by a few nurses.

'Now Mia, why don't we wash your hair and style it. Then we'll apply cream to your face which will soothe it. Then you can see Mum and Dad,' said one of the nurses with a smile.

Mia nodded and became the centre of attention with everyone fussing around her in a positive and sympathetic fashion. During the act of washing Mia's hair, she had received several compliments on the loveliness of it. Once Mia's hair had been blow-dried, one of the nurses went to show Mia the style that had be applied using a hand-held mirror. As the mirror was being held up, Mia brushed it away and turned her head to one side. The nurses ignored Mia's rejection and then set about applying the ointments to her face and neck.

'There. All done,' said the ward sister. 'We'll leave you now and bring in your mum and dad.

Mia shook her head violently.

'Mia, they have been waiting outside for a very long time. Just let them say hello.'

Ignoring the further head shaking, the nurses left the room.

A couple of minutes later, the elderly couple shuffled into the room. The old lady sat by the bed and tried to clasp Mia's hand but was rejected. The old man took up a position standing directly behind his wife.

'Mia, I know that it must be a great shock. But I've spoken with Mr Kent and he believes that with reconstruction surgery, plastic surgery and then recuperation, you will recover. It will take time but you will get the best treatment that's available. Jacob has already assured me of that. He plans to visit you personally in the next few days. In the meantime he just wants you to focus on your recovery. I know that you won't but he said to remind you not to say anything to anyone about what happened,' said a croaky Mrs Berkovich.

Mia shook her head. How could they be so insensitive to remind her to keep her mouth shut when she had just seen the real extent of her life-changing injuries? Anyway, she couldn't remember a bloody thing.

'Mia, your hair really looks nice,' went on Mrs Berkovich.

Mia picked up her headphones and put them on. She turned up the music to a volume that was barely comfortable and closed her eye.

13:30. Mr Kent knocked on the door firmly three times and entered. Mia was sitting up erect in the bed with her headphones on and her eye closed. The distorted sound was bleeding out of the headphones but it wasn't of a quality that the song could be made out. Mrs Berkovich was sitting in a chair by the bed reading a tatty old book. Mr Berkovich was hanging off a chair propped against the wall opposite the foot of the bed, snoring.

'Mia, can I speak with you?' said Mr Kent.

There was no reply and Mrs Berkovich interrupted her reading to stare at him.

'Mia,' he said, gently nudging her elbow.

Her eye popped open and her body went rigid. She took off the headphones and looked at Mr Kent.

'Mia, the police are here and they want to talk with you. Do you feel strong enough to meet them?'

'She's had enough for one day, don't you think?' interjected Mrs Berkovich.

'If that is Mia's view then I can tell them that. But they do need to speak with her and I can't delay them for too much longer.'

Mia held up both her hands to get Mr Kent's attention. He turned away from looking at Mrs Berkovich and focused his gaze on Mia. She nodded her head in acceptance.

'Are you sure?' he quizzed.

Again, she nodded her head.

'OK, Mia, I will go and tell them that they can come in in say ten minutes.'

Another nod of the head.

'Fine. But I want to sit in with her during the interview,' rasped Mrs Berkovich.

'Of course. That makes perfect sense. I'll go and tell them now.'

Mr Kent spun around and left the room. Mia put her headphones back on. It was impossible to gather how she felt from reading her facial expressions, because her face was far too bashed up.

Two women walked into the room and introduced themselves at the foot of Mia's bed. She had removed her headphones and switched off the sound as soon as the door opened. Both of the women wore plain black trouser suits and flat shoes with overcoats thrown over their arms. They also had similar bob haircuts and wore minimal makeup, although one of them was wafting a pungent perfume. They were from the

Metropolitan Police Force's Criminal Investigation Department (CID) and were both of the Detective Constable (DC) rank. They explained that they wanted to introduce themselves as they had been assigned to investigate this particular case and that they had spoken with Mr Kent who had shared some information with them regarding Mia's injuries, treatment so far and her recovery to date. They assured Mia that they would do everything possible to find the perpetrator(s) and bring them to justice. They asked Mia if she understood and if she was willing to be interviewed and Mia nodded. They also knew that at the moment Mia wasn't able to speak but could nod for 'Yes' and shake her head for 'No.'

One of them then left the room and returned with a plastic chair. The other DC took the chair next to the snoring Mr Berkovich and both of them sat on the opposite side of the bed to the very suspicious Mrs Berkovich. Both of them retrieved note pads from their briefcases along with pens and started the interview.

The interview ran fifteen minutes and every question that was asked was met with a shake of Mia's head. The reality was that Mia had no recollection of the events leading up to and including those events that happened when she was brutally and savagely attacked. Also all events immediately following the attack were not available in Mia's memory. Her memory held events of the day before the attack and then started again when she woke up in hospital.

The two DCs attempted to befriend Mia and were sympathetic to her non-responses. They even mentioned that Mr Kent had warned them that Mia may not be able to remember much if anything at the moment but over time fragments would return. They went on to explain that they wanted to speak with Mia because if she did have any information then they would follow up whilst the trail was still fairly hot. They then mentioned that they were also following up other leads, so Mia shouldn't worry too much. Mrs Berkovich was showing less strain now as Mia had performed well and it looked like the interview was coming to a conclusion. The women without conferring asked almost innocuously whether Mia was either a regular or infrequent drug taker. Mia for the first time didn't shake her head. This question confused her and she just stared at both of them. Mrs Berkovich opened her mouth to say something when one of the DCs said that both heroin and cocaine were found in Mia's blood sample and in large quantities. Mia was shocked by this announcement and didn't move a muscle. The DC went on and said that the blood results indicated that a cocktail of both heroin and cocaine known as Speedball was what she had taken. They then asked her if she had ever taken Speedball. Mia shook her head vigorously.

Mrs Berkovich finally spoke up. 'I think that that is enough for today.'

Both DCs nodded, thanked Mia for seeing them and said that they would come back in a few days and check on her progress. One of the DCs handed Mrs Berkovich a card and said that they wanted to be contacted immediately if Mia remembered anything.

After they left the room, the apparently snoring Mr Berkovich sprung to life, whispered in his wife's ear, smiled at Mia and stood at the widow urgently typing out an email. Mrs Berkovich said to Mia that she had done a great job. Mia put her headphones back on and turned up the volume. This was the worst day of her life. Her beauty had been crushed along with her confidence and dreams. Then she found out that she had taken Speedball.

14:00. Carruthers was home and had been busy. She had just finished unpacking and putting away the clothes and shoes that weren't worn on her two-week training course. She had put the rest of her clothes into various piles. There was a pile of whites and another pile of colours destined for the washing machine. There were a further two piles for dry cleaning. They had been sorted by how badly they were stained. The worst pile were the clothes that she had worn whilst out on the live op. The loft was a musty, dirty place and it had already affected her breathing as she dry-coughed again. Finally, there was a bag containing two pairs of shoes and one shoulder bag. She had great confidence that her dry cleaner would take care of the cleaning and the cost which would be exorbitant was acceptable in her mind. She mildly mulled over whether she would put in the cleaning cost as expenses but decided against it. Since being home earlier that morning, she had already taken two showers and she had already decided that she would take another shower as she still felt grimy. She had also spent time going through all of her emails and attachments. Even though she had read most of them whilst on the course and dealt with them, she wanted to go through them all again and make sure that she hadn't made any errors due to being on the mind-numbing course. Also it was a way of refreshing herself ahead of returning back to work tomorrow. She calculated that another couple of hours would complete the task of catching up and then she'd hit the ground running tomorrow. She fired off an email to her PA requesting that an appointment for a pedicure and hairdo was arranged asap and carried on with catching up. Ten minutes later a ping alerted Carruthers that an email had arrived in her inbox. In was a reply from her PA.

'Appointment with Carrie booked for 16:20 tomorrow and pedicure after.'

She smiled; at least her PA was efficient.

She daydreamed and thought that the Saturday spent in the loft had passed relatively uneventfully. The two targets had followed their predicted routines to a tee. The twelve-hour shift that she spent with the three-person team in the loft passed quickly and she found that she actually enjoyed the experience. In some way, studying screens intently for long periods, listening into the audio feeds and writing up activity reports realtime mirrored her days in finance which she remembered with fondness.

When both targets went out, they were trailed by the Walkers and the communication with the loft was comprehensive as were the reports that were completed in near realtime along with accompanying photos. Back at Fort Monckton that evening, she had had her end-of-course appraisal with three instructors. In this meeting they went over all of the course modules and how they had rated her performance in general terms. Their comments were an odd combination of blunt and circumspect, as if every word had been carefully chosen. At the end of the appraisal, they never gave her an overall performance rating. They qualified this by saying that it wasn't required because she wasn't a trainee. This was an obvious and blatant cop out.

When Fort Monckton were told that a senior line manager from Thames House was going on a bespoke course that was sanctioned by the director general, alarm bells rang and they were highly suspicious of the underlying motives. This broke all protocol and standard working practices, especially as the course had to be cobbled together at short notice and both personnel and schedules needed jigging around to accommodate it. Was the fort being assessed? With all of the cuts and budget scrutiny going on, was the fort now in the spotlight? There was a directive from HQ detailing everything that 'Miss Brown' required training on e.g. basic field training, target practice with live ammo, tradecraft, sit in on a live op, high speed car manoeuvring as well as regular PT classes. It also stipulated that she wasn't to undergo any personal interrogation classes nor any survival technique classes. This was very much a personalised training course. Upon receiving the initial request from Thames House HR department, the fort's senior management team met to discuss this highly unusual request and after much debate, some of it heated, some dubious second-guessing and some off-the-wall brainstorming, the consensus was to play everything by the book and follow the script as decreed by HQ. They would follow everything to the letter and send back interim and final reports as written by the instructors without any review or interference. No sugar coating, no bias; the reports would go out unvarnished. Intra-course reporting was unheard of but this request would be accommodated. The only thing that was added by the senior management team was that a copy of every report would be sent immediately to them. They in turn met and poured over the contents of every report. Once again they analysed, argued and second-guessed what the real motive was for sending Miss Brown on this customised course. The sessions were unhealthy because everything was based on speculation. Worse than that was that they obsessed and became sidetracked, arguing furiously over the words, sentences and, in their opinion, ambiguous paragraphs within the reports. In fact, the only action points coming out of their meetings were that a few instructors should be sent on report writing courses.

The three instructors were summoned to a meeting with the senior management on the Sunday morning. In that meeting they had to go through the appraisal meeting with Miss Brown in minute detail. It felt for like a court of inquiry rather than a normal meeting. What was clear was that the senior management team wanted to know everything Miss Brown had said and especially what she'd said at the end when she was asked to give her verbal feedback on the course, the actual training, course material, the competence of her instructors, any comment on any of the other trainees, what she learnt from the course, anything in particular that she would implement into her daily work, and finally, any proposed improvements that could be made to any module or the course in general. Her response was minimal, almost to the point of disinterest, although she did comment that she enjoyed the two days' observation of a live op spent mostly in the loft. The self-assessment form was sent electronically to her inbox from the fort's admin section and she agreed to complete and return it within five days. The senior management team would meet as soon as the completed form was returned and they would pour over her every word, again wondering whether the fate of the fort hung on the words of Miss Brown. They knew that a copy of her self-assessment was to be sent immediately to both the director general and Seb Drake at HQ and that meant that this whole exercise had high profile and potentially dire consequences.

Carruthers liked everything orderly and done on time and to agreed deadlines and she was musing over filling in the self-assessment form. She poured herself another glass of red wine and sank back into the sofa, listening to Vivaldi's 'Four Seasons' pounding out of her sound system. She decided that in light of the exertions of the last two weeks, she'd first polish off the bottle of red and then have another shower. After that, she planned to then sit down and complete the self-assessment form and that would be another item ticked off as complete from her to do list.

17:00. Carruthers was sitting uncomfortably on her sofa with her left leg perched on the coffee table supported by a pillow. On her lap was her laptop and she was grimacing and breathing heavily. She had already taken a dose of strong painkillers and was now supping large slugs out of a glass full of whiskey. The pain was beginning to dull in her ankle and she could see that it was visibly swelling minute on minute. She was wearing her pjs and was still wet from recently taking a shower. When stepping out of the shower, she'd slipped and her right leg had shot out and away from her. Her left ankle wrenched as it took the full force of her twisting, falling body. She screamed several times from the searing pain as she lay on the floor. Her bathroom floor surface often became slippery when water from the bath spilled onto it and she had on several occasions slipped but always managed to correct herself and avoid falling over. She had cursed on each occasion and vowed to change the floor surface to something that wasn't slippery when doused with water but never got around to it.

She sat up and looked at her ankle. Nothing but pain filled her mind. Sitting there wasn't an option, so with the help of the side of the bath she rose to her full height but didn't put any weight on her left leg. She awkwardly towelled herself down in the bathroom that now was steaming up whilst the shower continued to pump out hot water. She leant in, turned off the taps and left the wet towel on the floor soaking up some of the water and then hopped out of the bathroom. She used her arms to assist with balancing her as she unsteadily made her way into her bedroom, grunting loudly as she went. She took out her pjs and carefully put them on before flopping onto the bed. She closed her eyes, put a pillow under her left ankle, shut her eyes and lay there. The effort required from getting to the bedroom from the bathroom had depleted most of her energy.

After several minutes, she decided that she needed to get up and take some painkillers. Then she would go into the lounge, put on the TV and have a stiff drink. She'd rest a bit and then carry on with her work. She didn't think that anything was broken, most probably a bad sprain; certainly not worth sitting in A&E for five hours. Anyway, she'd get it looked at by their own quack when she went into work. Now that she had a plan, she set about following it albeit very slowly and very painfully. Painkillers administered first. Next she took out the bottle of whiskey and rather than as her plan just pour a large glass, she took the bottle over to the sofa and sat it on the floor next to her. She quickly hammered back a full glass of whiskey and, without thinking, filled up another glass full of whiskey.

Into her second large glass of whiskey, she decided that she would now continue with her work. She'd become increasingly angry and irrational and now all of thoughts were of blame. Her injury now was the fault of being on the two-week course, the fault of the instructors, the fault of Seb Drake and by far the fault of that fucking old dinosaur Sir Dickie Crampton and his muse Sheila Beavers. Unable to dampen the flames of anger, she logged on and accessed the self-assessment form in her inbox.

'Right, they want feedback? I'll fucking give them feedback.'

Carruthers went to town. She gave herself top marks in every box on the form and supported each mark with a hugely bias opinion of her performance. In the 'Any Other Comments' field she slaughtered both Puke-Up and Spud, accusing them of being weekend warriors who were wannabes. She supported that opening remark by recounting the staged accident (although she didn't know that that's what it was) as an example of their incompetence. She went on to say that she'd had no option but to get off of the mountain under her own steam when Puke-Up left evac'd by chopper and Spud just plodded off. With ever-changing weather conditions that could be life-threatening, it was a decision that she hadn't taken lightly. She'd made her way back to the car park and rendezvoused with Major Smith. She added that she had twisted her ankle badly on the exercise and that prompted her to focus on her safety and getting off of the mountain. The ankle was still extremely painful now and she intended seeking medical attention in the next couple of days to assess the damage. She questioned the selfish action of Spud leaving her alone to fend for herself when she was injured.

Now in full swing, she recounted the group surveillance training exercise that she went on in Portsmouth. The object was to follow a couple, report back and not get spotted by them. She said that she and her partner went into a pub as part of the operation, and he'd behaved in a brash, loud manner which drew attention to both of them. She felt strongly that his uncouth behaviour alerted the couple initially who then exposed them. She went on that, in her opinion after working alongside him, he needed a lot more training if he ever was to pass out. Furthermore, currently he was a danger to himself, his colleagues and to the Service. She had stuck the knife in deep, intending to inflict a mortal wound. Following on, she described in detail the live op when she joined in and, in her opinion, stopped what could have been a catastrophe. One Walker had already been spotted by Target One and a Walker couple were going into a cafe without changing their appearance. Only her intervention probably saved not only the day but potentially the whole op. She was on full throttle now and was about to launch an attack on the driving instructors when she gathered some composure and decided that if she attacked everything about the course then that would potentially lead to questions about her credibility.

Anyway, the combination of the painkillers and the booze had kicked in and the pain was lessening. Writing up her version of events had had a cathartic effect and the raging anger within her was ebbing out. She saved a copy of the self-assessment form to her personal folder and then sent it back to the fort attached to an encrypted email. She logged out and lay back on the sofa, carefully positioning the pillow under her left ankle. Her eyelids were heavy now and deep sleep invaded her.

19:00. Ahmed was sprawled out on the settee enjoying watching the HD TV. Deepak wandered in with his customary plate full of food courtesy of the chicken shop below. He sat in his seat and began tucking in viciously. The mountain of food was soon despatched and Deepak took out the plate having used his fingers to eat the food. He returned and sunk into his chair. He had been working both Saturday and Sunday on his 'other' job. He moaned that Kareem was supposed to work with him yesterday but he was a no show. Today Haroon was supposed to work with him and again he was also a no show. He had texted both but didn't get a reply from either of them. He was run off of his feet doing all of the deliveries, collecting the cash and then reconciling everything and updating the book accordingly. Siddiq turned up at the skunk warehouse, picked up all of the cash and book, gave him £160 for two days' work, didn't say anything, didn't ask where the other two were and then drove off. His wages were £40 light. He had to use his own car and that meant he paid for the petrol out of his own pocket.

He lamented, 'No wonder the other bloke left. That's no way to run a business. They are very unprofessional.'

Ahmed was seething. 'Stop fucking moaning. What do you expect? They are a fucking drug running gang.'

'I'm exhausted working seven days a week. It's too much.'

'Here's an idea. Why don't you start by stop smoking skunk. Maybe that's why you feel fucking tired.'

'It's the only thing that helps me. I'm stressed out with their behaviour. The chinks not only roll a stonking spliff but they are really good blokes.'

'Oh, so now you're a fucking expert on rolling joints? And the chinks don't even speak English, so how do you know what they are like?'

'That's just detail. Anyway, I can pack smoking in whenever I want.'

'Good. Because when you walk into your next blood test at HQ with that shit in you it will be curtains.'

'When do you think that I can quit this job then?'

'Realistically it going to be a few weeks. Chris Gould is using Team 4 to run background checks and we need to let that run its course. They'll establish that there's no terrorist link and then it will be passed over to the old bill. That will be the time to walk away with HQ's blessing.'

'So what did you do today?'

'I went out for a run this morning. Read the papers and lazed around. Then I went down to the gym for a session this afternoon.'

Deepak looked at him and blurted out, 'Is this gym thing really working?'

'Why?' snapped back Ahmed.

'It's just that I can't see any change.'

'What the fuck do you know?'

'Nothing. Just saying, that's all.'

'Worry about yourself. Especially with all of the shit that you are in. Fucking self-inflicted, by the way.'

'OK, no need to be so sensitive.'

The conversation was over and both combatants sat there watching the TV in silence.

19:50. 'I'll put the kettle on. Fancy a cuppa?' asked Deepak.

'Yeah,' grunted Ahmed.

The kettle was boiled, two mugs of tea made and another packet of chocolate biscuits opened. Both men were slurping from their mugs of tea and munching away on chocolate biscuits when the clock struck 20:00. The reality TV show flared up on the humongous TV.

'God. I hope that the young girl band doesn't get voted off.'

'Sssshhh.'

08:00. Carruthers was sitting at her desk looking out from her glass office over the open floor office. There were a number of people busily working away. It was 24/7 working hours and always staffed up. She winced and put her left foot up on a chair that she had wheeled around to be her side of the desk.

'Good morning, can I get you a tea or coffee?' said her PA, poking her head into Carruthers' office.

'A strong tea would be nice.'

Carruthers went through the log on protocol that would take a few minutes. By the time she was logged on with access to all of the systems that she wanted, the PA was back with her tea.

'Oh dear, what happened to you?'

'I twisted my ankle several days ago whilst I was on a course.'

'That must be painful. Have you seen a doctor?'

'No.'

'Would you like me to make an appointment?'

'Not at the moment. Let's see how it feels first.'

'OK.'

Carruthers had had a tortuous journey into work, barely able to put any weight on her left ankle and in the end had flagged down a passing taxi. A thought flashed through her head and she quickly accessed her email and she then selected her outbox. She next selected the last email that she sent and was about to delete it when she saw that it already had been delivered.

Shit, she thought. That was a bit strong. Still, they deserved it.

Carruthers then opened up the attachment and read what she had written in the self-assessment form. Sober now but with a mild hangover, she reread it a few times. Each time it read worse and she decided that she should stop rereading it. Her comments weren't completely true and were in some cases inflammatory and outright lies. Putting it in writing could come back to bite her and documenting anything untruthful was a mistake. Nothing to do but brazen it out. Another email arrived in her inbox and she opened it. HR had advised her that she had an appointment with Dr Hempel-Smith at 09:00. No doubt the comments in her self-assessment were already having ramifications. She finished her tea and removed her card from the card reader next to her PC. This action instantly locked it. She took several deep breaths and then began her slow journey down to see the quack. Limping heavily through the office, several sets of eyes darted her way but no one said anything apart from, 'Good morning.'

Carruthers was lying back on the couch, only the rustle of the paper over the couch making any noise. Dr Hempel-Smith had finished washing and drying his hands and walked over to her.

'Now, tell me what happened here?' he said with sympathy.

'Well, I was out walking on the hills several days ago and I stood on a rock. My ankle took all of my weight when I fell over. It was an accident.'

'I see,' he said, gently running both of his hands over the swollen ankle.

'Can you move your toes for me.'

A couple of Carruthers' toes moved fractionally.

'Good. Can you move your ankle?'

The swollen ankle moved slightly.

'Good. Now, you say that this happened several days ago,' he said, still looking at the swollen ankle that was beginning to discolour.

'That's correct.'

'Hhmm. Well, the good news is that it's not broken. It's badly sprained though and you should stay off of it for a few days until it settles down. I'll sign you off for four days.'

'No chance. I've been away for two weeks and there's no way that I'm taking more time off. Give me some tablets and I'll be on my way.'

'Rest is the quickest way to recover and heal this type of injury.'

'There's too much going on. Just give my something to control the pain.'

'OK, but you still need to do a number of other things. First, your foot must be elevated at all times. Put it on a chair and put a pillow under it. Apply cold to it every four hours for no more than twenty minutes. I'll arrange for an icepack to be prepared and someone can pick it up. I'll give you something strong for the pain and something to reduce the swelling. I'll see you in seven days.'

'Great.'

'Oh and don't drink any alcohol whilst you are taking these pills.'

The doctor went over to a cabinet and took out two pill boxes. He then went out and returned with a pair of crutches and a pillow.

'Take two pills every six hours from both boxes. Now, do you know how to use crutches?'

'Yes. I used them a couple of times when I was at school. Horse riding accidents. Good leg first when going up and damaged leg first when going down stairs, right?'

Dr Hempel-Smith nodded and opened the surgery door. The small PA was seated timidly outside.

'Come in please. Can you take the pillow for Miss Carruthers and her icepack and also her meds please. She needs to get a fresh icepack every four hours, so you need to pick one up from the nurses' station next door and the ankle should be iced for no more than twenty minutes at a time. Pills to be taken every six hours and foot elevated with a pillow under it at all times. Is that all clear?'

'Yes, and what about an icepack at home?' the PA whispered.

'Buy a large pack of peas and keep it in the deep freezer. Then apply every four hours as normal. And diarise that I want to see Miss Carruthers again in seven days at the same time for a follow up appointment.'

Carruthers was now standing with both arms inside the crutches applying pressure onto the handles with her left leg bent up behind her.

'Any problems then contact me,' he said as the pair of women slowly left his room.

Dr Hempel-Smith completed a form with his diagnosis, treatment and next follow up appointment. He then sent a bland email to HR stating that Carruthers had a badly sprained ankle but was fit for work. He then composed a lengthy, detailed email that he sent to Seb Drake and in the email he said that he'd seen many sprains in the field and that in his opinion this sprain whilst bad was less than one day old. The discolouring had only just begun and the swelling would still continue. Whatever caused the injury wasn't done several days ago.

09:30. The senior management team at Fort Monckton were in session. Carruthers' self-assessment was anything but complimentary and there were a number of controversial points. They had just finished talking with Major Smith and he had refuted the allegation that she had suffered an injury and was then left to fend for herself on the mountainside. He said that when she turned up, he remembered her being unimpeded by any injury. He was tasked with speaking to both of the two SAS instructors and to check whether either or both of them had witnessed Carruthers injuring herself or limping as a result of an injury and then write a report. He had to have all of their statements rolled up in the report and sent back to the fort within twenty-four hours. The senior instructor was tasked with conducting interviews with everyone who took part in the surveillance exercise, and he needed to talk to MI6 and find out from their two agents whether they were alerted by the male's behaviour in the pub or whether it was as originally documented: that it was Carruthers carrying two distinct bags that had alerted them. The instructor that went out on the live op with Carruthers and witnessed the surveillance in Covent Garden needed to be pulled off of his teaching course today. He needed to be in front of them at 10:00 explaining in detail everything that had happened. Afterwards, he would need to write it up.

Finally, everyone who had any contact with Carruthers since she went on the Brecon Beacons exercise would need to be contacted and asked whether they were aware that she was carrying an injury and if she actually mentioned to any of them that she had injured her left ankle. Fort Monckton was used to training MI6 officers as that was their raison d'être, but there was also training given to MI5, and the senior management team agreed that they needed the ongoing work to make the fort financially viable. If this was an attempt to take work away from the fort then they were going to fight it tooth and nail.

10:15. Seb Drake was seated in Sir Dickie Crampton's office. Sir Dickie was pacing about slightly agitated. He had spent the weekend on the east coast of Scotland playing on a links course. The wind had played havoc with his long drives and despite his best efforts to drive the ball lower, the ball never stayed on the fairway. Losing to a couple of Scottish national politicians was not his idea of fun. He was happy to listen to their devolution rhetoric and stories about how better off Scotland would be post-independence, although they still needed to use English currency and have access to the national health system and subsidies from England and the protection of the British Army etc., etc., but losing stuck in his craw.

'Carruthers' self-assessment is pretty scathing,' said Seb dryly.

'Yes. It will ruffle a few feathers down at the fort,' replied Sir Dickie, picking up his belly putter.

'Without putting a too-fine point on it though, she's been somewhat economical with the truth,' Seb went on.

'Really?'

'Yes. Our doctor has examined her and he's convinced that her ankle sprain isn't even one day old.'

'She manages to stir up the pot even when she's not here. Well, no point working ourselves up into a lather. Let's wait and see what the fort does.'

'OK.'

'They can overreact. Always worried about their damn budget. Played a round not that long ago with them down by the coast and they feel it's only a matter of time before the Whitehall Mandarins squeeze their funding. Anyway, beat the buggers so it was a good day out.'

10:30. A sharp bang on the door and it was immediately opened.

'Sorry to interrupt but we have four 6 chaps downstairs in reception waiting to start their course. They've been here since 08:15 and they are getting a wee bit antsy,' said the middle-aged lady from the admin department over the top of her horn-rimmed glasses.

The man sitting at the head of the table tapped his pen on the table a few times.

'Really? Can't have them antsy, no, definitely not antsy.'

He looked at the instructor who was standing in front of him and had been grilled for half an hour so far about the live op in Covent Garden.

'Is the psycho still here?'

'Which one?' asked the instructor.

'There's only one psycho. That bloody Yank CIA interrogator.'

'Oh, Captain...'

'Yes, him,' interrupted the senior man.

'Yes, sir, he is.'

'Right then. Get them billeted sharpish and then straight down to the House. Two sessions in the rooms with whizz bangs and smoke grenades. Then straight in the chamber for tear gas induction. Follow that up with a couple of hours' interrogation. Make sure that it's hoods on, white noise, cuffed hands and feet and body in stress positions. Then onto waterboarding with Captain Psycho. A spot of late lunch then out on the beach for a few sprints followed by a session of treading water should do the trick.'

The instructor and admin lady stood perfectly still.

'Anything else?'

'What about the stuff we were just discussing?'

'We'll take a fifteen-minute break for coffee. That'll give you time to rustle up someone to get the ball rolling and we'll reconvene then.'

'Sir,' acknowledged the instructor as he turned to leave the room along with the admin lady who was looking somewhat flustered.

There were a few smirks on the faces of the senior management team. It looked like the current crop of 6 agents in for a refresher course were going to have a hard day. The usual classroom modules as a light intro were off the menu. And it was blowing a gale outside. This morning was chaotic in the fort. Instructors had been pulled off of their courses and duties.

They were scrambling around, checking existing reporting to refute the allegations made in Carruthers' self-assessment. Trainees were sitting around in groups waiting for some direction. The small admin team were busy compiling a new report and appending supporting statements.

16:00. Carruthers had shut down her PC and was getting gingerly to her feet aided by her crutches. Her ankle was throbbing and sitting at her desk for several hours proved to be uncomfortable, particularly with her left leg up and with her body in an unnatural position. Her PA had just cancelled her haircut and pedicure and when she asked when the appointment should be rescheduled, she was told by Carruthers that it was far too early to think about that. The PA had arranged for an in-house driver to take Carruthers home. On the way down to the basement car park, the PA carried Carruthers' bags and put them on the rear seat of the car whilst Carruthers positioned herself in the front passenger seat that had already been pushed back as far as it could go.

'There's two large bags of peas also for icing your ankle. They need to go straight into your deep freezer when you get home,' said the PA.

'You are a sweetie,' replied Carruthers, smiling weakly.

17:30. Seb Drake walked into Sir Dickie's room having received a request from Sheila Beavers to 'pop in for a moment'.

'I've read the instructor's final appraisal with Carruthers, reread all of the interim appraisals and Carruthers' version of events in her self-assessment,' Seb said before taking a seat.

'Right. And your conclusion?'

'She didn't really try at all throughout the course.'

'Quite,' said Sir Dickie, studying the base of his belly putter intently.

'Apart from, that is, when she went out on the live op,' went on Seb. 'Although she even distorted some of the details there in her favour.'

'Go on.'

'She was at fault when she went out on the group surveillance training exercise but other team members weren't exactly blameless. At least one of them should have noticed and told her to change her appearance when entering the pub and especially the "two bags issue". That was a real rookie's gaff.'

'Hhmm.'

'As I mentioned this morning, she never injured her ankle on the mountain exercise. Our doc checked her out first thing and he's of the opinion that her ankle sprain isn't even twenty-four hours old. Worst of all, she's attempted to throw two experienced SAS guys and a trainee under the bus. That's wholly unacceptable.'

Sir Dickie Crampton's bushy eyebrows creased and he sucked his teeth.

'We can't do nothing. That's tantamount to condoning her behaviour. Worse still, it will get on all of their records.'

'Agreed.'

'What do you suggest then, sir?'

'Well, the fort will be compiling a report the size of *War and Peace* as we speak and we'll be getting that delivered in a bloody artic lorry tomorrow. Or maybe they'll just send it over the secure net, slow down the whole system and fill up all of the disc memory.'

Seb let out a small laugh.

'We'll have to sit on the mountain of paper for a couple of days. That way they'll think that we've actually read through everything. I dare say that it will be similar in size to the R&A's Rules of Golf and probably just as confusing.'

'OK.'

'Then we'll get HR to reply. Nice and bland, something along the lines of "Thanks for providing a detailed report on the recent bespoke course. Everyone at the fort, SAS instructors, and trainees have performed to the highest standards. This has been an extremely useful joint exercise," blah, blah, blah. Then we bury it.'

'Good,' replied Seb.

'No, it's not good. Carruthers is divisive. She'd start a row in a phone box. Look at the amount of time, money and manpower wasted because of her and she only went on a damn course! I'll have to mend some broken bridges. Probably will invite them up for a round at my club. Dammed if I'll lose the game though. A nice lunch and a few at the nineteenth hole should smooth it over.'

'I know that we haven't spoken about it. But what about the other report that they sent? The one where they refer to her recurring nightmares. CCTV records the trainees even when they are asleep and her sleep pattern was flagged up. Their sleep consultant said that she displayed some very disturbing behaviour that may need treatment. They recommended that she was referred to a clinical psychologist as they believe that she has a sleeping disorder. She wakes up following her dreams in a real state apparently and her behaviour could be a weakness that could be exploited by a foreign power. Friend or foe could target her and manipulate her.'

'Quite frankly I'd like to lock her up in a padded cell. But that isn't going to happen. It's fluffy nonsense, so it gets buried along with everything else.'

'Of course.'

'Oh, and Seb. Can I leave it with you to coordinate with HR and get the reply out a couple of days after we receive the fort's handiwork?'

'Of course.'

18:00. The mobile phone sang aloud. Carruthers picked it up and stared at the number. It wasn't one that she'd plugged into her phone, nor was it a number that she recognised. The display informed her 'Unknown Caller'. She bridled as she knew it was an unknown caller.

'Hello.'

'Hello, is that Miss Carruthers?'

'Yes. Who's calling?'

'It's Catherine.'

'Who?'

'Catherine Egerton.'

There was silence on the phone.

'Catherine, your PA.'

'Oh yes. Right.'

'I was calling to remind you that it's time to put the icepack on your ankle for twenty minutes.'

'Thank you. I wish everyone was as diligent as you.'

'Thanks.'

Click. Carruthers eased herself off the couch and hopped into the kitchen via the bathroom where she picked up a towel. She returned to the couch hopping and put the towel over the pillow and then gently rested her ankle on it before applying the large pack of peas. She was immediately hit by a burning sensation from her ankle and flinched. She looked at the wall clock, gritted her teeth and counted down twenty slow, very slow, minutes.

20:00. Another shrill burst from Carruthers' phone. She didn't recognise the number once again.

'Hello.'

'Hello, is that Miss Carruthers?'

'Yes.'

'Hello, it's Catherine, your PA.'

There was a long pause.

'I was phoning up to remind you to take the two sets of tablets.'

'Thanks.'

'I've arranged for a car to pick you up at 07:20 tomorrow morning. I assume that you still plan to come into the office.'

'Of course.'

'Also, would you like me to pick up some groceries for you?'

'Oh, that would be wonderful.'

'If you send me a list, then I'll pick it up and have it ready for when you go home tomorrow. I think that the driver will be able to carry up your shopping for you.'

'I'll create a list and pop it in an email.'

'OK.'

'You are a real treasure.'

'Goodnight.'

Click. Carruthers hopped into the kitchen and took her pills before returning back to her couch. The surround system was majestically playing Handel's 'Zadok the Priest' which always made the hairs on the back of Carruthers' neck stand up. This was her favourite Handel's arrangement. She was relaxed now due to the combination of pills and the inspiring music, and the throbbing in her ankle was ebbing away at last. Her thoughts turned as always to her work; it was all consuming. She momentarily thought of her tiny PA and that she was turning out to be a real asset. In times like this, she was someone that she could actually rely on. A dark cloud started to descend, not like that fucking dinosaur Crampton and his sidekick, that prick Drake. She deliberately inhaled deep breaths several times and cleared her mind. Focusing on the music pushed the negative thoughts out of her mind. It would be good to just lie there, relax and be in state of tranquillity for a few hours. Especially if she was going to have another night punctuated with those awful, recurring nightmares.

09:45. The old lady slowly stooped, riddled with arthritis. She blew out her cheeks with the effort and scooped up the two pieces of mail that had just been delivered through the rusty letterbox. The letterbox squealed and drummed loudly whenever it yawned open, which wasn't that often. Mail shot was the normal fare, local takeaways and mini cabs trying to grab any business that they could, and it all went straight into the bin. But from behind her hazy glasses she saw that one of the letters bore a familiar stamp. It was from Kabul. The handwriting however wasn't one that she instantly recognised. The other letter looked like something official and that would be dealt with later.

She walked slowly back into the kitchen and laid the Afghanistan letter on the table in front of her husband. He squinted and picked up the letter, turning it over in his mottled hand. There were no other markings of any kind on the reverse of the envelope. His other hand patted the front of his shirt, tapped the top of his head and ran over the kitchen surface. Admitting defeat, he put out his hand, palm faced upwards. The old lady removed the dirty glasses that were perched on her nose and placed them into the waiting palm. He put the glasses onto his bulbous nose and then slowly tore open the envelope. He reached inside and retrieved the folded paper and opened it. Now he moved the glasses further down his nose in a vain attempt to get a clear focus on the contents. He squinted, pulled the note closer to him and that was the best vision that he was going to achieve. All the while the old lady stood silently opposite him, rasping with her own poor breathing and ignoring his short gasps for breath through a phlegm-riddled chest. He read the short message written in his mother tongue, turned over the paper and rechecked inside the empty envelope. He then slid the note across the table. It was now the old lady's turn to hold out her hand and he responded by returning the glasses to her. She replaced the glasses into the grooves on the side of her nose and picked up the note. She read it and put it on the table, looking at her husband angrily. She didn't like it when he didn't shave as he looked unkempt with the mass of silver stubble covering his face and neck. Shaving was another task that he doesn't do regularly as he was now struggling with doing even the mundane tasks. Both of their sets of clothes were threadbare and in need of a wash; a further indication that they were no longer able to cope or care for each other. They had reluctantly accepted that their time was nearly up but tried as best they could to have some sort of daily routine.

He painfully got up and turned around, placing both of his hands on the sides of the dirty kitchen sink. Leaning over, he coughed deliberately three times and spat the mouthful of phlegm into the sink before he turned on the cold tap and swished the phlegm down the plug hole. He then put his head under the tap and sucked in some water before he turned around and looked impassively at his wife whilst wiping his mouth. The small terraced house in southwest Luton that they'd lived in for twenty-one years was a reflection of the couple. It was decaying inside and there was nothing that they could do about it. How she hated him spitting in the sink, how she hated him getting old, how she hated herself getting old and how she hated the news that they had just received.

The spidery handwringing in Pashto was short and succinct.
Uncle will be arriving soon and he's looking forward to seeing both of you.
They spoke in whispers, not because they were trying to be secretive but because that was how they spoke. They would clean and tidy up the house in the coming days. The goods that were left here by those young men a couple of months ago had remained exactly in the same place as they were instructed to leave them. They would burn today's grim news and destroy the evidence. But first they would sit down and remember together what the items were that they'd originally stored and where they were stored. It was a puzzle but they worked hard trying to remember the items, talking simultaneously and answering their own questions if the answer pinged in their head.

'Wasn't there two alarm clocks?'

'Yes.'

'But where did we put them?'

'One is in our bedroom on top of the big chest of drawers and the other one in the dining room on the sideboard.'

'Next was three rucksacks?'

'Right. We wrapped them up as if they were going to be presents and put them under our bed.'

'That's right. Oh, I think we had three alarms clocks. One for each rucksack. Now, where did we put the other one then?'

'In the chest of drawers. Better take it out and put it next to the bed in the back room. What next?'

'Lots of bags of nails and washers. Carrying that lot out to the shed was tiring.'

'Finally there were all of those bottles of cleaning fluid. Yes, they are under the sink.'

Their faces displayed smiles through the mass of wrinkles. The old lady walked over to the sink and opened the cabinet doors. There were the bottles of cleaning fluids. She was showing her husband proof of their joint memory recollection skills. She closed the battered cabinet doors and went out into the garden. He shuffled over to the window and watched as she managed with some effort to access the shed.

Several minutes passed before she returned to the kitchen and then said, 'There's several boxes of electrical items and boxes of batteries in the shed that we forgot.'

'Right. Let's write everything down and we'll test each other every day.'

'OK. We do need to remember otherwise "Uncle" will be angry.'

17:10. Pope walked into the small pub in Pimlico and was discreetly checking all of the customers as he walked up to the bar. He had instantly recognised Dr Hempel-Smith nursing a pint in the corner and reading a copy of the *London Evening Standard*. Several thoughts raced through Pope's mind whilst the friendly Polish barmaid hand-pulled a pint of Best bitter. He paid for the pint and took a decent swig from the malty-flavoured beer and made a decision. If Hempel-Smith was on his case then he'd flush him out. His thoughts were borderline paranoia. He turned and walked over to the table where Dr Hempel-Smith was sitting studiously studying the sports pages.

'Can I join you, Doc?' Pope enquired.

Hempel-Smith looked up from the newspaper, flicked his green flecked eyes over the top of his half-moon glasses and smiled.

'Please take a seat,' he murmured as he folded the newspaper.

'I haven't seen you in here before,' said Pope, planting his pint glass on the burnished wooden table.

'No, I thought I'd give it a go. Far too many tourists and civil servants near our place. Difficult to get a seat and it can take the devil of a time to get served.'

'Quite.'

'And I read that this is a CAMRA real ale pub.'

'That's why I pop in, Doc.'

'Simon, please.'

'OK. Anything interesting in the paper, Simon?'

'No. Just the usual paper chat on who Capello should pick for the match tomorrow.'

'I don't understand how he survived after the 2010 World Cup.'

'Really. I don't understand how he got the job in the first place.'

Both laughed.

'Yeah. The first English manager who couldn't even speak English,' went on Hempel-Smith. 'High altitude training in

Austria ahead of the WC after a full English season. It's no wonder they lacked spark. Bloody knackered, they were.'

'Is that your medical opinion?'

'Nope. That's a frustrated football fan's opinion. Can't imagine anyone in any job performing well if they are dead on their feet, and then they have to listen to a bloke who doesn't speak the lingo doling out tactics and trying to motivate everyone.'

'It didn't help though when your keeper let in a howler. At least he's out of the equation now.'

'Yes, 1–1 with USA wasn't acceptable. I still don't understand though how Capello got through the interview process. Surely one of the old farts must have realised that he didn't speak English.'

'Ready for another?' said Pope, draining his pint and standing up.

'Yeah, why not. Pint of Best,' replied Hempel-Smith, taking a couple of urgent gulps.

Pope went to the bar and ordered a round. He was warming to this genial medical man who clearly had a passion for football and in particular England's international team. Hempel-Smith had noticed Pope when he first entered the pub and, driven part by paranoia, had thought that he had been followed by him but now was revising that opinion. Pope deposited both frothing glasses on the table and eased back into the old threadbare seat.

'If you don't mind, Simon, where were you before joining us?'

'I was a military psychiatrist and served in both Iraq and Afghanistan.'

'Really? That must have been interesting.'

'It had its moment but quite frankly it left a bad taste in my mouth, John.'

'Oh. Is it OK to discuss?'

'It's not covered by the Official Secrets Act, if that's what you mean. And even if it was, I wouldn't care.'

Pope admired this man's frankness.

'I dealt with soldiers suffering from combat stress reaction, or COS, which is not to be confused with PTSD.'

'What's the difference?'

'COS is short-term reaction whereas PTSD is the long-term reaction. Both are serious but require different treatments.'

Both men took swigs from their respective pints.

'It's complicated but I was then seconded to be an observer at interrogations and that was when I realised that we had lost the plot. Our American cousins were driven by results and they ignored the Geneva Convention. Our political masters didn't stand up to them and the unethical, inhumane methods used yielded garbage. Yes, there was some useful information gained, but if you torture someone then they will tell you whatever you want to hear. We raised it at the time but were told to butt out. Only now is the truth beginning to surface.'

'So do your psychiatric qualifications allow you to treat us?'

'No. I was a geek. First I trained as a medical doctor and then I trained as a psychiatrist. All paid for by the Army.'

'Really? You must have spent a long time studying.'

'Many hours spent in college bars chasing college students.'

'So it wasn't all work and no play then.'

'No, and the drinks are cheap in those college bars as I remember. My round I think, John.'

Pope raised his near-empty glass and smiled. Hempel-Smith returned with another two pints of bitter.

'So, without giving away any secrets, what's happening on your side of the fence?' asked Hempel-Smith, who was now slightly slurring his words. The years spent in those college bars whilst hunting down his qualifications had taken their toll.

'Well, we're still trying to adjust to the ever-changing landscape. We still have far left activists organising rallies in the City and using that as cover to vandalise property and just run amok. Far right still fuel racial hatred in inner cities and whilst both sets of extremists were high on our radar pre 9/11, they have slipped down our list of priorities. MI5 and MI6 have over time refocused our combined efforts on extreme terror groups purporting to represent Muslims. It's very messy and the battle lines are blurred. We still have the stigma hanging over us courtesy of Burgess, Maclean, Philby and others and that drives the paranoia about Communist spies and traitors. But even this has reduced since the fall of the Berlin Wall, the breakup of the

USSR, and the rise of the oligarchs and their influence in Russia, Europe and globally. They are seen as shining examples of a shift in Russia's core ideology. They've even taken over football in the Premiership, for God's sake. That being said, Putin is a formidable opponent in the game of global politics. He's like a chess grandmaster and is always thinking several plays ahead. He needs to be treated with respect and wariness in equal measures. Germany buddied up to him and were hit along with many other European countries last year when gas supplies were shutdown. He wanted to show that Russia remains a super power and he wanted in particular to reel in Ukraine who wants to join the EEC. The Cold War isn't over, and I say that with caution. Maybe it's beginning to thaw. China is growing rapidly and they want to acquire technology any way that they can and are becoming a cyber espionage threat that is a real problem. We don't have the manpower or the budget to have coverage on everything that I've mentioned. Far right and far left activist groups and individuals have been handed off mostly to the police forces around the UK, with Special Branch providing first-line support and then we assist as and when. Will Russia and China become a real threat? Only time will tell, but for now our political masters aren't so sure. So we focus on the Muslim fanatics who are hellbent on wreaking destruction and death anywhere and everywhere.'

'Wow. I should have stuck to asking about football.'

'Simon, you are part of our team. We need everyone in our team to be on their game because we don't know when it's coming but we do know that it's coming. We just need to be able to read the tea leaves and intercept anything ahead of time.'

Simon blew out his cheeks and stood up.

'I'm going to head off, John, but it was good to catch up outside of the office. Maybe we could do it again sometime.'

'Why not. The beer here is good. And we can discuss how the Euro campaign is going for England.'

Pope watched Hempel-Smith shuffle out of the door leaving an empty glass on the table and recognised that he was a decent man and a work colleague who he could discuss pretty much any topic with albeit not the spook stuff. Ten minutes later, Seb Drake walked in.

'I see that you have been interviewing,' he said.

'He's a good bloke.'

'I did pop in earlier but when I saw you with him I left.'

'Did you? I didn't see you.'

'No, but he did.'

'Anyway, what can I get you before we get down to the nitty gritty.'

22:15. In the background, Pope could hear the ever-angry male voice berating his wife in the bedroom. The small top window was slightly ajar and let out the sounds, distinct and clear into the cold wet November sky.

'They will never amount to anything. They are all lazy. I'm the only one who makes any money and don't ever forget that,' the   voice   raged.

Man and dog were one house before where the regular bullying emanated from. Pope bent down, patted the slightly sodden Doodle and unclipped his lead. Doodle scampered ahead and into the driveway of the noisy house. He ran into the middle of the sloshy lawn and defecated. His ears remained pinned back, eyes scanning the house. He was on full alert as he was now in the enemy's camp. Pope had pulled up the lapels of his long black gabardine overcoat, pulled down the tweed peak cap and slightly increased his pace without glancing sideways. He glided past the house unnoticed and passed a further three houses before the small wet dog lightly nudged his leg. Pope slowed and in one motion retrieved the leash from his coat pocket and hooked it onto the collar of the expectant Doodle. Doodle, familiar with the snap sound of the lead hooking onto his dog collar, started to strain on the lead.

'Good boy,' whispered Pope.

Doodle gave the merest of nods and then bucked hard on the lead. He was once more the lead dog pulling the sled with all his might. Behind them sitting in the middle of the fussed over lawn was a steaming turd. Doodle accepted his multifunctional role in his family with grace and equanimity. He would run hard, fast and far at the weekend with the man. He walked with him daily, mostly in the late evenings, and would sit out in the garden when the man was having a crafty fag. He was tolerant when on the evening walks the man talked through his day in minute detail and shared with him dark forbidden secrets. Moreover, the man would use the peace and quiet to replay problems and they would then work on a solution. They were a team; he was a confidante and a key player. On a number of occasions the man would repeat at the end of a particularly revealing dialogue the same spiel but always with a jaunty tone.

'Doodle, if you ever repeat anything that I've just told you to anyone then I'd have no choice but to kill you. All legal, old chap, covered under the Official Secrets Act.'

Doodle's kind eyes would look up at the man and think, *What a silly man, He must know that I'm the main man.*

18:00. Pope was sitting at the kitchen table eating his evening meal. Unusually, both girls were not around, nor Doodle, and Jane was quieter than usual, facing the kitchen sink busying herself with making sandwiches. Pope paid no attention to the stillness, although he had deliberately come home earlier in order that he could sit down and eat with his family. Daisy walked urgently into the kitchen, a mass of screaming pink, carrying a pink wand in one hand and her somewhat beaten up teddy bear in her other hand. The distressed teddy bear was an ominous sign; it always appeared when Daisy was stressed out about something. And if Daisy was stressed out then everyone would end up stressed out by the time she had calmed down. Ignoring the fact that Pope had arrived home, Daisy stood in the middle of the kitchen staring earnestly at Jane's back.

'Mummy, is Charlie going to have her foot cut off?' Daisy quivered.

'No, darling.'

'She told me she is,' went on Daisy, still grizzly.

'No, darling, she's fine.'

'But it's in a bandage and she's crying,' implored Daisy, her voice now rising and tears flowing freely down her cheeks.

Jane wasn't able to satisfy Daisy's inquisitiveness with her bland answers.

'Mummy, if Charlie has her foot chopped off then she will only need one shoe. That will save a lot of money. Could I have some more pocket money then?'

'No one is getting their foot chopped off and there's no more pocket money,' replied Jane.

Pope downed his knife and fork mid-mouthful.

'Jane, what's going on?' he said, also talking to Jane's back.

'I'll tell you after dinner.'

'No, tell me now,' said Pope, standing up and moving away from the table, still talking to Jane's back.

'Mummy...' started off Daisy.

Pope interrupted her.

'Go and check Doodle's bum.'

'Why?'

'Because it may be sore,' replied Pope.

Daisy's face was a picture of confusion with tears staining her small cheeks. She thought about Charlie and then skated out of the room, heading off to find an unsuspecting Doodle. Jane finally turned around, wiping her hands on a cloth, and looked sheepishly at Pope. He was waiting for an explanation. And it had better be good.

'Well, you know what teenage girls are like,' started off a not so confident Jane.

'No, I don't.'

'Well, she's been talking about it for a while, you know.'

'What?'

'Teenage girls talk about a lot of things really and mostly it's just talk.'

'What EXACTLY has happened?'

'She's had a tattoo.'

'Fucking Christ, she not even sixteen. You know that it's illegal to have a tattoo under the age of eighteen.'

'Yes.'

'Where did she get it?'

'A friend at school, her brother is a budding artist and a number of girls have already had tattoos from him.'

'Fuck. What did she have done?'

'She had a rose flower on her instep.'

'Right, I'm going up.'

'Don't you want to finish your dinner first?' said Jane, hoping to buy some time in order that Pope would calm down.

No reply. Pope exited the kitchen and bounded up the stairs with Jane following in his wake. He thrust open Charlie's bedroom door without knocking and waiting for the customary 'Come' when Charlie was ready. To enter Charlie's room without knocking and then being invited in would normally result in a massive, hysterical argument. Not this time. Charlie was propped up in her bed with three pillows behind her head and a further two pillows under her left foot. Her eyes screwed up and it didn't help that the mascara that she had liberally applied was now spread across her face due to the ongoing floods of tears.

If Pope had been in a calmer mood he would have registered her face and thought, *Now, what's the name of the actor who plays the main character in Beetlejuice?*

But there was no time for frivolity. He walked to the foot of Charlie's bed and drew back the duvet cover. Charlie started crying again. Her foot was exposed below her pj bottoms and was swollen under the fresh bandage. Pope stared angrily at the bandaged foot.

'Daddy,' came the Bambi-like noise from his daughter.

'Well,' stepped in Jane. 'The doctor says that it's just a reaction to the ink. There's no infection. She must stay off her feet for three to four days and the swelling will go down along with the pain.'

'What's his name?' said Pope, still fixated with the bandaged foot.

'Who?' sobbed Charlie.

'The tattooist. The twat brother of your school friend.'

'No, Daddy. Please.'

'Where does he live?'

'No, Daddy, don't.'

'You are underage and it's illegal to tattoo anyone under the age of eighteen.'

'John, you are right. I'll speak to the boy's mum. Let's go downstairs,' interrupted Jane.

'Best you do. Otherwise I'll speak to the budding artist and he won't be tattooing anyone for a very long time, if ever.'

John continued to stare at the bandaged foot.

'How much?'

'It was £20, Daddy.'

'Jane, get the money back.'

'Yes, John.'

'She's supposed to be studying for her GCSEs. This is a very important year for her.'

'Charlie can study at home for a few days. It won't affect her grades. Come on, John. Let's go downstairs,' said Jane calmly.

Daisy burst into the room, full of energy and squealed gleefully, 'Doodle's bum is OK.'

Pope turned around without speaking, nor re-covering Charlie's foot with the duvet, and walked out of the room.

Daisy's smile was warm and affectionate but he didn't notice her. Charlie was scowling and looking straight ahead, also ignoring her little sister, who was bursting with good news. Jane placed her hand on Daisy's head and gently turned it towards the door.

'Come on,' Jane said, gently marching the smiling face out of the room.

The bedroom door was gently closed by Jane, and Charlie burst out crying.

10:30. Showered and with the house locked up securely, Pope entered the bedroom. Jane was sitting up in bed reading her romance novel. She didn't speak as Pope plugged in his mobile phone and got under the covers. He lay on his back for several minutes, staring absently at the ceiling. In his mind he wondered whether he could actually have delayed his shower and had it in the morning. This was his preferred time to have a shower and it was something that he had done pretty much all of his career. Starting the day with a shower was invigorating. He was still angry. Angry that he had to take a shower at night. Angry that if he left it until tomorrow then Charlie would probably be in there anyway. Angry that Charlie had a tattoo and it would now be with her for the rest of her life. Angry that Jane knew that Charlie was thinking about having a tattoo but never mentioned it. Angry that he didn't have a clue what went through Charlie's mind. His job was to protect her until she was able to make independent decisions and in his mind this was a sign of rebellion. Rebellion to what though? He thought that he was a liberal type of guy and that all of his family had a lot of freedom within reason. Tattoos now, what next? Move into a squat, become a fucking goth? Are goths still around? His mind was spinning. Jane put her book down on the bedside table and snuggled up to Pope. Her hand moved down between his legs and grabbed his flaccid member. There was a stirring.

She whispered in his ear, 'Everything alright?'

Pope rolled onto his side facing towards the window and Jane's hand was left grasping fresh air. Jane rolled onto her side and was now facing the bedroom door. No sex tonight.

Click. The light went off and all that was left in the bedroom was the frosty atmosphere.

09:30. Pope was in level -five in Thames House and had entered the secure area which had automatically locked behind him. Jenkins was seated at his customary desk filling in documents which were stored inside a large plastic binder.

'Good morning, sir,' said Jenkins in his best cockney accent.

'Good morning, Jenkins. It's been a while; perhaps I could try out my gun on the range today with dummy ammo. I'll also take a Browning High-Power with dummy ammo for two magazines also.'

'Right you are, sir,' replied Jenkins, checking that the stock was showing up on his computer screen, although he knew exactly what was in stock, out in the field, on order or out being repaired.

The paperwork was completed and Jenkins updated his screen with Pope's details and what he was going to use on the range today.

Pope went into the range and retrieved glasses, ear defenders and five targets. He could hear that a number of lanes were being used and there was a cacophony of noise within the soundproofed range. He then went on down to lane nine and put up his first target which he then sent down range. He had already made up his mind that he'd unload the Browning High-Power ammo first on four targets. This was his regular practice exercise and he wanted to do that first before he savoured handling his favourite hand weapon. As a sniper he would also favour sniper rifles over any other weapon. The accuracy over unbelievable distances and ability to deliver lethal force always outweighed all other guns and rifles in his opinion. Yes, other weapons delivered more rounds, weighed considerably less, made no sound and were great in urban or general warfare, but they simply didn't match a sniper rifle.

He set the four targets at distances from fifteen metres first, then incremented five metres until the final distance was thirty metres. Today he fired from a standing position, retrieving the gun from either his inside jacket pocket or his outside jacket pocket using his right hand. He scrutinised briefly each target post firing several rounds into it and made notes on the target. Today's date, gun, ammo, range and where the gun was drawn from. This information would be dissected later and added into his shooting diary. The targets would be kept and filed along with all of the other targets. Pope was a true marksman and all weapons firing had a purpose and therefore the results were important. He knew from briefly looking at the mauled targets that the results were of a standard that he would be OK with. A sniper was a perfectionist and always strived for improvement. There was always room for improvement even if minuscule. After checking that there wasn't a round in the chamber then setting the safety, the Browning High Power, along with the targets and emptied ammo boxes, was on a side table within the booth.

Pope now picked up his 'personal' firearm that had been liberated in a black op early 2002 in Afghanistan. The handgun was taken from a Russian observer who was with the Taliban unit targeted and ultimately perished in the firefight. The weapon or trophy was stashed by a member of the SAS unit as they went through the Taliban unit looking for intel. The gun and a quantity of ammo found its way back into the UK and passed through several hands before it was offered to Pope. Pope was interested in the gun because it had a range far and away superior to handguns and pistols available anywhere. He wanted to see the weapon in action before he made any decision about purchasing it and a test was arranged in the harsh Hereford countryside in mid-December. The gun performed as advertised. Most handguns had a killing range up to fifty metres. This gun had a reported range up to 1,500 metres and so to a sniper that was rifle range. The weapon had been customised at some point and that improved its overall performance. The ammo had also been tweaked and whoever made the modifications was a world-class expert in guns. Pope had seen with his own eyes and by firing the weapon that it would be a useful acquisition and it would excel in certain operational scenarios if used by someone with his skill set. He went back to Thames House and spoke with Seb Drake about the possibility of purchasing this weapon which did have a murky background. Seb listened intently to Pope making his case and then said that he would need to think about it and check internally whether it was possible. Seb met Sir Dickie who was director general designate for dinner at a private club. He had spent hours choosing the words and phrases that would portray the need for procuring the weapon.

Sir Dickie's eyebrows knitted after a couple of minutes of Seb's monologue and he cut in. 'No point having a bloody sniper onboard if he hasn't got the tools, eh. I wouldn't take a shot from the tee with a putter.'

That was settled then; only time for some of the finest Napoleon brandy. Seb came back several days later and said that the gun would need to be inspected first and only then would MI5 consider purchasing it. The gun was delivered and checked out. It appeared that this particular gun was traced back to having being originally sold to the Georgian army. The high-tech modifications which included an adjustable sight for either wind or elevation set at 1,000 yards were definitely the handiwork of Russian craftsmanship. The standard adjustable sight was set at 100 yards. Pope was given the green light to purchase the gun and cash was exchanged for the weapon and all of its customised ammo. There were unwritten rules regarding the purchase that Pope was told were non-negotiable. Pope had to purchase the weapon himself. The seller was not to know the sale would be direct to MI5. There was to be no paper trail of the purchase. The weapon would be held in Thames House Armoury. It would not be registered on any computer and there would be no paper trail either. The Armoury would only be allowed to hand out the gun to Pope either for use on the range or for an op. Pope was extremely happy with Seb's purchase and ongoing arrangements for handling the gun.

Pope picked up the FN Five-seven semi-automatic weapon. The gun was built by Fabrique Nationale d'Arms de Guerre-Herstal, a Belgium small arms manufacturer who'd first sold the weapon in 2000. It weighed 1.6 lbs loaded. It was 8.2 inches long, barrel length 4.8 inches originally with a height of 5.4 inches and a width of 1.4 inches. It could fire eleven, twenty-one or thirty-one rounds depending on the magazine type used. The cartridges were 5.7 by 28mm in size and the diameter of each cartridge was also smaller than the 9 by 19mm cartridges which it was specifically designed to compete against. These changes meant that more bullets could be put in each magazine for less weight. There was 30% less recoil than 9 by 19mm cartridges which improved the controllability. There was a loud report (noise when the gun fired) and it produced considerable muzzle flash. In Pope's hand the gun felt familiar; it had the same grip angle as a Browning High-Power. The Russian gunsmith master had extended the barrel from 4.8 inches to 6.2 inches and this gave the weapon extended range and accuracy when firing the rounds. The rounds had also been customised to account for the longer barrel and they subtly flew in a flatter trajectory to the target with more lethal force up to 1,400 metres before they started to reduce their final lethal force.

He inserted the magazine that had already been loaded with five dummy bullets. He felt the gun and almost caressed it before putting it back down on the table. He then put up the final target and sent it down range to a distance of sixty-five metres which was the furthest that the targets could be set at. Rather than go through his standard protocol of drawing and firing as if simulating a real-life situation, he drew up the firearm, steadied his breathing, took aim and then fired. He then pulled back the target using the automated mechanism and checked the position of the hit on the target. He then sent back down range the target marking the hit with the number of that particular shot. He made adjustments after every shot as he would when using a rifle. He savoured firing this unique weapon as a foodie would savour each morsel of a gourmet meal. It was lighter than the Browning High-Power and that needed the adjustment that he made with his eye–hand coordination and muscle power applied. Once he had finished firing the five rounds he packed up everything, returning the goggles and ear defenders back into the used box where they would be thoroughly cleaned by Jenkins before anyone else used then.

'Everything OK, sir?' enquired Jenkins when Pope returned the two weapons and empty ammo boxes.

'Yes, thanks,' replied Pope.

'I'll pop a bit of oil into your special and give it a thorough wipe down,' said Jenkins with relish.

'That would be much appreciated,' Pope replied.

'Well, we don't often get the opportunity to have something like that in here,' went on Jenkins as if talking about a priceless painting that was painted by one of the Masters. 'We need to make sure that it's given all the care that it deserves.'

'Thanks, Jenkins. I'll see you soon.'

'Yes, sir.'

Jenkins updated the computer with the relevant details and returned the weapons to their respective places having gone through his routine of checking that they were clear of any rounds and the safeties had been applied. The computer wasn't aware that there was an FN Five-Seven semi-automatic in stock. Nor was it aware that it had be customised. Jenkins was aware and he was in a very small group of people who knew about this weapon.

11:20. A broad smile painted Hamiza's face as he strode towards the table where his two familiar friends were sitting.

'Here he is,' said Usam, looking at Hamiza as he approached the table already laden with plates of food, mugs of coffee, a couple of daily newspapers screaming salacious gossip out from most of the pages and the usual array of bottles and other condiments that adorned cafes.

'What are you going to have?' asked Zeehan with mock sincerity.

Before Hamiza answered, Usam butted in.

'Bacon sarnie, bro, what else.'

Usam and Zeehan both roared with laughter. Usam slapped the palm of his right hand on the table before they both raised their hands and engaged in an enthusiastic high-five. Others in the cafe stopped and looked at the unruly behaviour coming from one of the tables.

'Oi, keep the bloody noise down over there,' shouted the owner-cum-chef from behind the counter as he slaved over a hot greasy frying pan.

He was a loud, friendly man who actually relished banter with all of his customers. He was passionate about football and was an armchair supporter of Luton Town. Every week, young men in their droves headed off into London to watch their chosen teams playing in the Premiership. If only they would follow his beloved Luton Town, then that would generate the money to buy better players and then they could also play in the Premiership. This was a well-told story and many just put up with his rants, claiming that the fumes from all that grease had rotted his brain.

Hamiza sank into the chair.

'Listen, bro, don't be going saying that.'

He was only adding fuel to the fire.

He whispered, 'Keep it down in fucking public. You don't know who could be listening.'

More laughter and slaps on the table.

'I just told you lot. Hey, Hamiza, if you ain't buying anything then clear off,' bellowed the owner/chef.

'Sorry, boss. Can I have two eggs, chips and beans with a mug of tea?' shouted out Hamiza.

'Coming up.'

'So what's happening?' enquired Usam.

'Not much,' replied Hamiza.

'Yeah, quiet all round,' said Usam.

'I still haven't spoken to Rahan. Have you?' said Zeehan just above a whisper.

Hamiza shook his head and the three conspirators' moods changed instantly as they then sat in silence. Hamiza's mug of tea was placed on the tabletop by the young girl and she walked away without speaking.

'I just don't get it. Rahan loved his phone. Texts, emails, WhatsApp; he just didn't stop. In fact, he was the only guy who followed up everything with a phone call. And now nada,' said Usam.

'It's fucking weird, bruv. He's sent to Bradford by the Ayatollah on some secret squirrel mission and we don't hear a thing. He occasionally sends out some shit text just to say that he's OK but that just ain't his style,' added Hamiza.

'I agree, but if he's really doing some dangerous mission then I suppose it does make sense. Anyway, I do know that his family are really worried but he got into this with his eyes open, just like the rest of us,' said Zeehan gravely.

Hamiza's plate full of greasy food arrived and the girl disappeared after planting it on the table.

'Anyway, no word from the Ayatollah of Doom and Fucking Gloom,' whispered Usam.

'No but I reckon that it can't be long now,' Zeehan said in a lowered voice, eyes darting around the cafe.

'Why do you say that?' spat out Hamiza, rather too defensively.

'Well, I see those three guys occasionally around Luton. They are never together but always in and out of internet cafes. They look like bulldogs chewing a wasp. Whatever is going to happen will involve them and they look like they are ready to fucking explode, I'm telling you, bro,' continued Zeehan.

'Anyway, why the concern? We are ready, right?' he added, not too convincingly.

Usam nodded without any real conviction.

'Dad has being talking about it for years, yeah,' said Hamiza shakily.

'Talking about what?' said Usam whilst his expression changed from concern to aggression.

'It's something that he's always wanted to do and he said that when he does it he'll take the old man,' meandered Hamiza.

There was no reply from the other two, just the background noise of a cafe half full of diners chomping away on their food.

'Anyway, I was surprised when he said that he was going to do it now. And I was even more surprised when he asked if I'd like to go with them. What could I say really?'

'Fucking spit it out. Where are you lot going?' said Usam with venom.

'Er. Well, we're going to the Hajj,' said Hamiza with his eyes looking down at the table.

'Great. You leave us with the Ayatollah AND we're already one man down because Rahan ain't around,' Usam said.

'Rahan isn't here because the Ayatollah sent him away, so that isn't down to me. Anyway, we don't know when we'll be needed, so it might not happen until I get back. There's no way I was going to say no. Everyone has to go to the Hajj at least once in their life, if they are able. You know that. Once my dad asked, I couldn't refuse.'

'OK, so when do you go on the pilgrimage to Mecca?' said Usam, calming down a bit.

'We leave on 13th. This year it's from 14th November to 19th November. We will leave Saudi Arabia and fly onto Islamabad and stay with family for three weeks. Dad wants the old man to do the pilgrimage and see the family before the end. You know he's getting frail now and this will be his last chance.'

Both Usam and Zeehan nodded somewhat begrudgingly.

'Look, I'll be back on 10th December and then we'll do whatever is needed.'

'Four weeks without a bacon sarnie. How are you and your dad going to survive?' Zeehan said.

Again there was an explosion of laughter and high-fives.

'Oi, I told you lot to keep the noise down,' came a growl from behind the counter.

'So what do we tell him if he turns up whilst you are away?' smiled Zeehan.

'Tell him the truth. I went on Hajj with my family and then went to visit family in Islamabad. He's an Imam, he'll understand,' replied Hamiza.

The other two shook their heads. There was one thing that was 100% sure; he definitely wouldn't understand.

'Bruv. Remember that he's already sent away four guys. He'll probably bring them back to sort you out,' said Usam.

'Maybe he'll bring Rahan back as well,' Hamiza retorted.

Rahan Iqbal would not be coming back. His throat cut by the Imam, he was already buried in a shallow grave in a park up in Bedfordshire. With their food consumed, the three of them then settled their individual bills and walked out of the cafe.

'Why don't you lot do something useful and get yourselves along to the next home game? Luton could do with the support. Even if it is bloody rabble,' came the stinging words as they exited the cafe.

09:35. Pope, Clare Hawkins and Chris Gould were sitting in their favoured seats in the corner meeting room. Files and laptops were already opened and ready. They had all taken a sip from their ersatz coffee and it wasn't mood enhancing.

'Christ, this stuff is getting worse,' said Chris after taking another sip.

'I don't think that we should give it to any visitors,' added Clare sagely.

'Well it's lucky then 'cause we don't get any visitors,' replied Chris sarcastically.

'OK, let's go through the agenda,' said Pope. 'Clare, will you minute and add new actions and update existing action points?'

Clare nodded, fingers hovering over her keyboard. Chris was able to type after a fashion. He used his index finger on his right hand and could move fairly rapidly but generally wrote notes on paper copies and typed it up later. Clare typed like a seasoned pro with both hands and many fingers, much like a pianist playing their keyboard, other than her music wasn't melodious. Pope was a painfully slow typist, similar to Chris in style but much, much slower. He ran the meeting and therefore he delegated the minutes to Chris and Clare alternatively. They ran through the items with efficiency as there were few meaningful updates and no new action points. The meeting was wrapped up in under ten minutes and they started to pack away their stuff.

'I hear that Sandra Carruthers is planning to close down the Luton op and return it to how it was before,' said Chris in an even tone, looking at Pope.

'Can't say that I've heard that,' replied Pope.

'Yes. It's been doing the rounds in the last couple of days,' added Clare.

'Rumours. This place is a gossip shop,' said Pope balefully.

'That's what you get when you fill a place up with spies,' Chris said, smiling.

'It will need to go up to the Top Floor and she hasn't done that. That was where this mission was sanctioned and they will need to approve any changes to the mission parameters,' Pope said, making it sound very official.

'Anyway, she's still limping and no one knows exactly how she managed to injure herself. I don't suppose you have any idea, John?' asked Chris, throwing out his line, seeing whether he'd get a bite.

Pope was already up and heading towards the door.

'Just a rumour,' Pope muttered.

Chris sat bolt upright, mouth hanging open, tongue lolling out, anticipating a tasty morsel.

'I heard that she tripped over her ego,' Pope continued slyly.

Pope was now out of the room. Clare sniggered and Chris hastily gathered up his stuff and shuffled out.

16:00. Pope and Boris were sitting in a corner seat in a hotel off Mayfair. Boris was a senior officer in SVR which was Russia's Foreign Intelligence Agency, working in foreign countries. The coffee had just been served. Three tables away, Boris's two assistants sat, periodically scanning the opulent room and everyone in it. They were conspicuous because of their size. A couple of gorillas squeezed into ill-fitting brown suits topped off with elephantine heads.

'John. How's the coffee?'

'Better than we get at the office.'

'Good. Very good,' said Boris, not really listening to John's obtuse answer.

'John, I have a problem,' Boris went on.

John placed the cup on the table and stared at Boris.

'I gave all of the information to our people back home and they aren't doing anything with it. I can't just let this go. If you are right then the whole supply route from Afghanistan right up to and including delivery in Moscow can be eradicated. Heroin is destroying many, many lives in Russia and it needs to be stopped,' said Boris with steel.

'What can I do?' said Pope earnestly.

'I'd like to hear the whole story from the guy who was on the op. There may be something in there, a small morsel maybe that I can then go back with and get those imbeciles in FSS to do their fucking job,' said Boris angrily.

A few people heard the baritone profanities and looked towards where Pope and Boris were sitting. The two gorillas stared hard at those individuals, and once they had locked eyes, the individuals promptly stopped looking towards Pope's table for the remainder of their time in the room.

'That's a big ask.'

'I know but I wouldn't ask if it wasn't important. John, I promise you that if you are able to grant me this favour then I'll be indebted to you. A debt that I will repay,' said Boris, leaning forward until he was invading Pope's personal space.

'Remember what we spoke about before, Victor,' said Pope now, trying to leverage what he perceived as an advantage.

'What, John?'

'I don't want any trouble on our streets. Not in London, not anywhere in the UK. No feuds, no assassinations, no nothing.'

'John, we spoke about this. There's nothing to worry about. The Cold War is over, yes? Russia is a friend. We want what you want. Peace and prosperity. We have elections now. You know that, right? Elected leaders, elected by the people. The future is bright.'

'Was that a party political broadcast?' said Pope dryly.

'Why pick on the Russians? Always, the blame goes to Russia. Britain is paranoid about all embassy workers in all Eastern European embassies who lawfully go about their business. What about Mossad?' rebutted Boris.

'What about Mossad?' said Pope, trying to disguise his peaked interest.

'It's OK for them to murder a British citizen but if a Russian drops a bit of litter then that's a diplomatic incident which leads to the expulsion of fifty diplomats and their families,' ranted Boris.

'Victor, what are you talking about? Do you know something? What's this about Mossad murdering a British citizen?'

Boris faltered. He was processing the information and running through the implications of telling Pope that Mossad had recently picked up a low-level criminal and, during interrogation, he'd died of a heart attack. Technically it wasn't murder but it was kidnap and there was torture, by a foreign agency on British sovereign soil. Many laws had been broken, not to mention a man lost his life. But if he shared this information then Mossad would realise that there was a mole in their ranks and they would be relentless in their pursuit. No, protecting the mole was far too important. Having a mole in Mossad was far, far too invaluable. In fact, it was priceless.

'Nothing, John. I was angry, that's all,' said Boris. 'I'm sorry.'

'OK.'

'Anyway, I really need your help with this heroin supply line.'

'Victor, leave it with me. I'll see what I can do. And for the record, it is illegal to drop litter.'

Pope's attempt at British humour went over Boris's head.

Pope drained his coffee, stood up, shook the huge paw that was offered by Boris, turned and left, ignoring the two gorillas who looked over towards him.

10:12. Ahmed was walking through The Mall shopping centre dressed in old jeans and tattered trainers, topped off with an Arsenal football shirt. He was distracted and deep in thought. Deepak's naive behaviour, the fact that he unilaterally entered into an unauthorised undercover operation, was testament to his lack of maturity and went against everything that every agent had been taught. Add to that that he was now regularly smoking skunk, and it was further proof that Deepak had a seriously flawed character. He could fail a routine drug test and be summarily dismissed. Finally, he had been taking cash payments for supplying cannabis to the drug dealers in the Midlands. Ahmed was annoyed and getting very vexed.

'Hey, watch where you're going,' shouted the tall, slim, young man dressed in the latest fashion with a smart haircut.

Ahmed had accidentally bumped into the young man, caused by his focus being fully on Deepak's self-inflicted drama.

'Fuck off,' spat back Ahmed, venting his anger.

The young man raised his arms and shouted out something that Ahmed didn't quite catch because of the din, the piped music and the anger swirling around inside his head. Five young men appeared around the young man that Ahmed had bumped into. They were are all well-dressed with smart haircuts. Ahmed could see fingers being pointed at him and then the group started to spread out in an arc formation and march menacingly towards him. Ahmed read the signs, turned on his heels and started to run. The pack followed, shouting and howling. Morning shoppers either fled out of the way or stood frozen to the spot as Ahmed deftly swerved through the throng. The following pack weren't as graceful and pushed aside anyone in their way.

Ahmed was past the large entrance to The Mall and off down the road. He decided to turn right onto John Street with the pack still in pursuit but split. There was one of them that was clearly a decent sprinter and he was at the arrow head of their formation and closing. At the back was the person who Ahmed had confronted. He was on his mobile phone and having an earnest conversation whilst still trying to keep up. Ahmed didn't let up and sprinted left onto Church Street. He was darting in and out of the road, looking for gaps and trying to maintain his top end speed. A car horn tooted twice. Ahmed looked across and saw the smiling face of Deepak who was waving at him.

'Want a lift?' shouted Deepak through the open passenger door.

'Yeah.'

The car indicated and pulled into a gap. Ahmed dashed into the car, put on his seat belt and locked the door.

'Right, move it,' shouted Ahmed right in Deepak's smiling visage.

A hand was now banging on the roof of the car and it was making an awful din inside the vehicle.

'Fucking move it!' screamed Ahmed, still only inches away from the broad smiley face.

Deepak's reactions took over and the car jumped out into the traffic. There were several cars' horns sounding all together. A number of cars had to brake sharply to let out the intruder. Inside the cars, drivers and passengers speculated. Another weekend driver, some old sod who should have his licence taken away, someone in a hurry probably late for a wedding. No one speculated that it was two MI5 undercover agents exfiltrating whilst being chased by Luton Town football hooligans. They were part of the notorious MIGs (Men in Gear) gang that followed Luton Town. They were always dressed in smart casual gear as fashion was as much part of the cult as following their beloved team.

Ahmed looked over his shoulder anxiously a couple of times. Deepak also checked his mirror but he was more concerned about the gaggle of angry motorists that he had just cut up.

'Fuck,' said Ahmed. 'Fuck.'

The guy who had been sprinting after Ahmed and had nearly grabbed him, had chased him down the road after their car had stopped. He gave up the chase when Deepak started to really accelerate and now was jumping into a car that had swerved in and out of the traffic and was part of the pursuit. Worse still, there appeared to be another two cars in that caravan.

'What's going on?' enquired a concerned Deepak.

Ahmed said that they had picked up a tail and there were at least three cars chasing them. Deepak was now at the junction with the A6. He looked in his mirror, deliberated and then turned left onto the A6. He increased his speed, checking his mirror periodically, and noticed that indeed there were three cars that were following them. He was driving the dark blue Ford Fiesta that was used by the gang to deliver drugs and collect cash. It wasn't a high-performance car, so outrunning the chasing vehicles probably wasn't going to be an option. Deepak accessed his phone and spoke briefly. The person on the other end had given him clear and concise instructions.

'OK, so what's this all about?' said Deepak calmly.

'I was in The Mall earlier minding my own business when some bloke came up and pushed me. Next thing I know, there were several of them surrounding me and I just legged it,' said Ahmed, truncating and modifying the events to fit.

'Why would someone just push into you?'

'Well, that's obvious, bruv. I'm wearing my Gooner shirt and they are MIGs.'

'What's a MIG?'

'Not what, who. They're the hooligan firm that follows Luton Town.'

'So this is all about football then?'

'Yeah, of course. What else could it be about?'

'Well, it could have been connected to work.'

'How the fuck could that be connected to work?'

'What about a racially motivated attack?'

'Look, I just explained what happened and why. I was fucking there.'

'Hhmm.'

Deepak picked up his mobile phone and gave some further information in a hushed voice. Once again he was told that the arrangements discussed still remained.

'Anyway, what are we going to do?' said Ahmed, turning around and seeing that the three cars were still in pursuit but not gaining significantly. Clearly they were cars with similar poke to the Ford Fiesta.

Deepak explained the plan and Ahmed nodded very begrudgingly. The chase continued for nearly forty minutes and Deepak drove fast but with care. Finally, Deepak bounced the car over the potholed road until it reached the final building in the industrial estate at the end of the road. A silver BMW Series 5 was parked outside of the dilapidated building and Deepak skidded the car to a halt next to it, splashing water everywhere in a dramatic fashion. The front door of the building creaked open and out came the crew that Deepak knew. Haroon, Kareem, Younis and Siddiq, who was the leader of the drug gang. They were all carrying either a baseball bat or a length of pipe. Deepak got out of the car and so did Ahmed reluctantly.

It was now raining, that fine spray that often covered Bedfordshire. Siddiq greeted both Ahmed and Deepak with a nod. The noise of three cars had been increasing, and then before the small group appeared, the cars were bouncing up and down as the suspensions on them struggled with the uneven surface. The cars stopped still in single file and then eight very well-dressed young men appeared and formed a line in front of the cars. They were not carrying any weapons but had numerical superiority. They also did this on a regular basis and were well versed in their particular warfare. There was no sound, adrenaline coursing through their veins. This was a familiar ritual before any ruck. It was normal to be scared but that was crushed when it all kicked off. The buzz from the row was euphoric. It was hypnotic and addictive. Only a hooli understood that. The MIGs walked forward in unison. A pride of lions stalking their prey, before they would explode and attack. The group of impalas stood their ground, tails swishing in the air almost nonchalantly. The gap was closing and still the impalas stood their ground. Sometimes a prey is frozen with fear and accepts the inevitable without either fighting back or deploying evasion tactics. But there was something different going on here.

'Geoff, hold on,' said a guy to the right of the leader.

Geoff stopped and everyone's eyes scanned 360'. Behind them standing in a line were five small Chinese men of indeterminable age. Each was armed with either a meat cleaver or a long knife. Hardly gardening tools for growing skunk. The impalas had buddied up with hippos and nobody, not even a pride of lions, would square up to these mean bastards. OK, the hippos were considerably smaller than their jungle buddies, but this wasn't the time nor the place to go head to head. Geoff deliberated and his pals waited for the nod. Geoff looked directly at Ahmed and pointed.

'Gooner. You've got away with it today. But if I catch you again in Luton then you're in for a right kicking.'

Geoff and his group turned around slowly and walked back to their cars. The group of Chinese men waited until the cars had reversed back down the road before they melted into the fine rain.

'So Deepak said that you are going to work with him. I know that he's been out on his own recently and an extra pair of hands is welcome,' Saddiq said, smiling and looking at Ahmed.

Ahmed's mouth opened and closed but no sound came out. He was catching flies again. Deepak's head started to bobble.

'Sure. We're going out today and I'll teach him the ropes,' said Deepak, deliberately avoiding any eye contact with Ahmed.

'Listen, I have to dash but I'll see you all later. Oh, and don't worry about them. They won't be back,' said Saddiq confidently as he got into his BMW.

Haroon, Younis and Kareem stayed put and they all went inside to get away from the incessant rain.

'Why is Saddiq so sure that they won't come back?' asked Deepak.

'He'll have a word. That crowd buy skunk that we supply, so it isn't in their interest to cause aggro. And besides, they like a row with other firms and we ain't into that. For us it's a living but fuck with us and we have serious backup. This is big money we are talking about here,' replied Younis.

Just then, three Chinese appeared with two massive joints and proffered them. This group who were about to go out on a delivery run looked at the joints and took them, smiling.

Ahmed took his first ever puff. He was simply reacting, almost in a state of shock, to the events that were unfolding around him which were spinning out of control.

What a fucking morning, Ahmed thought. *These boys and the chinks saved me. They aren't that bad after all. Mind you, Deepak has excelled himself. I'm now part of the drug gang and it's his fault that I bumped into that bloody football nutter in the first place. He's a walking fucking disaster. Still, at least he got me away from them.*

He took another drag. 'Yeah, this gear ain't that bad. No not that bad at all.'

Ahmed was mellowing albeit pharmaceutically induced.

10:30. A meeting had just finished in the lavish conference room on the Top Floor. Senior Management had left along with a couple of the aides and PAs who had security clearance to attend these meetings. Seb was slowly gathering his papers having seen Sir Dickie give him a slight nod during the meeting, which meant hang back at the end. Sir Dickie's PA was the last to leave the room and gently closed the door, leaving both of them together.

'Carruthers is like a dog with a bone. She won't leave the damn thing alone,' growled Sir Dickie.

'It's certainly curious behaviour. The amount of time that she's spent on trying to shut down Luton when there's far more important things on her plate. It doesn't make much sense,' replied Seb.

'Oh it makes bloody sense alright,' said Sir Dickie.

'How so?'

'She's making this personal and she's on a crusade,' went on Sir Dickie.

Seb raised his eyebrows as his head dropped into his hands that were supported by his elbows leaning on the highly polished oak table. It was unusual to speak with Sir Dickie without him waving a golf club around, Seb thought.

'She's challenging my authority. I don't doubt for a minute that this is her way of extracting some revenge for being sent on that course recently.'

'The one where she sprained her ankle...allegedly,' smiled Seb.

'She's made it very clear not through her direct management line that the op is highly unusual and not run according to procedure. Having to listen to that crap in the meeting just now by three people who should know better is bloody irritating. Yet again Mizzz Carruthers bypasses processes and gets other people to do her dirty work. And yet she claims to be an advocate of procedures,' fumed Sir Dickie.

'We agree that Pope was playing the "long game". He was using his years of experience and working on a gut feeling; call it intuition or a hunch. But there was far too much going on there in that one mosque to ignore it. If Carruthers had any experience then she would have boosted that op by pulling in agents from other areas. We had to intervene and do that originally.'

'Her bloody experience is with spreadsheets,' howled Sir Dickie.

'Yes. I hear she's a wizzo at writing macros.'

Sir Dickie furrowed his eyebrows having no idea what Seb was on about.

'Well, we are backed into a corner now. There's no point digging in over this one. Enough of our group support her on this, so it's done. Tell Pope that the Luton op reverts at the end of the month and the extra support and surveillance stops then also. He can make the necessary changes on the shop floor. And make sure that the guys up in Luton know that we really appreciate their efforts.'

'Sure. Lose the battle but win the war.'

'Exactly. Seb, she's dangerous. I've heard several whispers through the club's grapevines that she's been building powerful alliances for some considerable time. She's been on a smooching offensive but at the same time she's out of her depth and she's really playing with fire. We'll keep our powder dry for the time being.'

'OK. We are quietly building our own evidence. The interim reports from her course was way below acceptable. She was unbelievably poor on the field exercise and didn't bother to learn map reading. On the range, her marksmanship was very low. In the two surveillance exercises she was identified. In the first one, she was spotted by an old lady who then joined her for a Big Mac along with the trainers. No leadership qualities displayed...'

Sir Dickie butted in.

'Yes, I get the picture. I've seen this before. A decent player who is picked to play for the first team but thinks that they should be a fixture there then gets picked to play for the seconds. They go to the match but don't play well. It's obvious that they haven't prepared well and aren't 100% committed on the day. They let the second team down, they let the club down and they let everyone who has ever represented the club down. No matter what team you play for, you always play your best. Shabby attitude leads to poor performance. Players like that are prima donnas and generally don't get picked for the first team again.'

'Right.'

'Seb. Get her to put in writing why the op should be closed. Just usual paperwork, if she asks. If she's wrong about Luton, then that's critical evidence that will be used against her. Her days are numbered, mark my words.'

09:30. Jacob was sitting at the bedside of Agent J. Outside of the room sitting in the corridor were the pair of agents that had been assigned to her. The elderly couple were using the legends of Joseph and Dalia Berkovich and were the 'parents' of Mia. Mia had been the victim of a crime and had suffered many horrific injuries sustained by person or persons unknown. She had lost the sight of her right eye and would need facial reconstruction, followed by several rounds of plastic surgery before she would be fixed. Well, fixed as far as modern medicine could make her. The Metropolitan Police were investigating the case but were making zero headway with their investigation.

Mossad were conducting their own inquiry and had through over-zealous behaviour caused the death of their only lead. They knew that General Faisal was involved in Agent J's near fatal atrocity but their own agents had left Agent J unprotected at the critical time of the covert operation. She had been transferred from St Thomas' Hospital on Westminster Bridge Road where she was first treated to Clementine Churchill Hospital which sat in large grounds at the base of Harrow on the Hill. Here in this private hospital, Agent J would begin the lengthy reconstruction and rehabilitation process.

'Mia. I'm sorry but I have to call you by this name whilst you remain in the field. I'm sure that you understand. We are all praying for you. This operation is the first step towards getting you back to where you were before the incident. The surgeon is a brilliant man. One of the top men in oral and maxillofacial surgery. He will be able to do everything: teeth, jawbone, skull and facial muscles. He's confident that two, maybe three surgeries, and then everything will be done. Once that's over then there will be plastic surgery to follow but we can talk about that phase later,' said Jacob softly, looking at the battered face of Agent J/Mia.

Mia, who was wearing a hospital gown, spoke awkwardly through her wired teeth.

'Thanks.'

'There's nothing to be worried about. I'll be here when you wake up as will Joseph and Dalia. They will be with you now all of the time. They love you and want you to be happy. I know that you miss your parents but until you are better and we understand what exactly happened to you then it is in everyone's interest that we manage your recovery. You won't come to any harm again, I can promise you that,' went on Jacob as if reading a script.

Mia thought, *It's a bit late, protecting me now. Why wasn't I protected before? This should never have happened.*

'Mia, do you remember anything from the night of the incident?'

'No. The days leading up to the incident are also a blank.'

'The nurses will be here shortly. You have a private room with dedicated nurses 24/7 and access to the beautiful grounds, so you can get out and about should you desire. Although it's not great in winter, I must say. The food served will be excellent but if you need anything then Joseph and Dalia will arrange for it to be brought in. We're sending over a trainer so you can work out. They have physios here but I imagine that you will want to start training. If there's anything, anything at all that you want, then tell Joseph.'

Mia nodded.

'After you have finished with the plastic surgery, you will recover in Jaffa. It will be good to be back home. You will stay there as long as you want. There's a place waiting for you with us. It will be ready whenever you feel ready to return. You have served your country and now your country will serve you,' said Jacob with pride.

'Jacob, what will my role be?'

'Mia, we can discuss that at the right time. Let's just focus on getting you better first, eh.'

The door opened and in walked two nurses and two orderlies with a gurney. It was time.

19:45. Pope was approaching on foot the small Syrian restaurant off of the Edgware Road. He turned to the tough, wiry man walking beside him.

'Give him the details but no names, no units or departments involved.'

'Fine,' came the curt reply.

The SAS signals officer from D Squadron had been told to get up to London asap, as the spooks wanted him for some mission. He wasn't given any other details and was pulled out of the training exercise on Dartmoor, put on a train and told to report to Thames House. Pope met him at the entrance and took him through the security barriers after signing him in and getting a temporary pass for him. They then went up to the first floor and into a small enclosed meeting room, and Pope explained what he wanted the SAS warrior to do. The SAS guy was given time to gather his thoughts and reconstruct the story that he had previously told Seb Drake. He sat in the room collecting his thoughts whilst drinking the worst cup of coffee that he'd ever tasted.

Pope walked into the restaurant, past the two gorillas without any acknowledgement and met Victor Sokolov aka Boris at his customary table. This time it was tense; there was just a nod and then another nod to the man behind Pope.

Once seated, Boris said, 'Can I get you anything? A drink?'

'No, we're fine,' replied Pope. 'Let's get started. I'll hand straight over to my man.'

The SAS man breathed in and then went through the op that he was on. The SAS were contacted and asked to escort someone up to Badghis province, near the border with Turkmenistan. They helicoptered from their base in Helmand province to the jumping-off point in Badghis and then walked for three days to the target.

'Can I ask what the target was?' enquired Boris.

Pope nodded.

'We had gold intel that there was a Somalian terrorist training camp there and there were high-value targets also there at that time. Anyway, we scouted the whole area and there was no evidence of any camp. A convoy of lorries arrived late evening. We counted eight of them and they parked outside the village, stopping overnight. The drivers all went into the village, leaving their lorries unguarded. Probably because this was such a remote area, they figured that it would be OK. We went down and looked into all of the lorries along with our guest. In each lorry were three or three barrels of oil and Afghan rugs. Our friend popped up into one of the lorries and planted a tracker on one of the barrels. It wasn't one of ours. He then said that we should evac, so we called for a chopper. We escorted him to the pick-up point. He left and we were ordered to stay with new mission orders. We lay low for five days and another convoy arrived. We then went back and dismantled one of the barrels. There was a false bottom. In there, sealed in a compartment, was heroin. We put the barrel back together and then put one of our own trackers in it. So we plotted the whole route of the convoy. It crossed the border into Turkmenistan and then went to the port of Turkmenbashi. There's a ferry that crosses the Caspian Sea and goes to Olya in Russia. From Olya the convoy went to Astrakhan. This is the where the Caspian Highway starts. It's known as the M6 and travels some 860 miles approximately up to Moscow. The convey stopped at an industrial estate in the east of Moscow. The district is called Basmanny and there are many abandoned warehouses, although I guess that you know this.'

Boris nodded.

'The warehouse is owned by a company that sells Afghan rugs and carpets throughout the whole of Russia. This was the final destination. We lost our tracker at this point and we suspect that the oil drum was discarded.'

Boris nodded.

'Thank you. That was very comprehensive. I do still have a couple of questions though.'

Pope nodded.

'Going into Badghis province was a risk, no? That's under US control with US Rangers running around. Weren't you concerned about friendly fire? The US have been upping their Strike First policy and even if it isn't their ground forces then they send in Predators.'

'It was a black op but our friend said that we wouldn't be targeted.'

'I see. And your friend said that this was a Somali camp with high-value targets also?'

'Yes.'

'And he only planted a tracker?'

Pope's eyes flickered. Boris looked at him and they both knew.

'Right, I think that we are done,' Pope said, getting up.

'Thanks, John, and to you also,' said Boris.

Pope left with the man following in his wake.

Outside, the SAS warrior said, 'Everything alright?'

'Yes. Why shouldn't it be?'

'No reason. One minute we are sharing classified info then we're out of there as if the place is on fire.'

'Listen, can you make your own way back?' said Pope, offering his hand.

'Sure.'

'Thanks for everything,' said Pope as he hustled off on his own.

Pope had his hands in his pockets, trying to keep warm as he walked down Park Lane. He realised that he had been played. Boris wasn't interested in the route; he had previously been given that information. FSS wanted more and weren't doing anything was a ruse. Boris wanted to know about one thing and one thing only. Pope had been sucker-punched and it didn't feel good. He'd have to tell Seb. This was way above his pay grade. It was weird; there were a lot of pieces just floating about and then all of a sudden, they all fell into place. A perfect fit. Boris was trying to find out how CIA manage to get their hi-tech spy equipment into Moscow. The equipment that the CIA agents and Russian traitors use to gather information and then send to waiting spy satellites via encrypted fast-burst frequency transmissions. Diplomatic baggage was supposed to be immune from any type of examination. But everyone knew that they were X-rayed and subjected to other types of scanning between unloading from the plane and being picked up in baggage reclaim. Diplomats walked through the 'Nothing to Declare' area and were walking through highly sensitive scanners and anything and everything on them was identified, even their shiny new fake teeth. The CIA were always looking for a secure route to transport their James Bond equipment into Russia. What better way than to conceal it in a heroin consignment. The route was as secure as it could get. Customs officers, border guards, army, police and mafias would all have had their palms greased. Large amounts of cash would be paid to allow safe passage of heroin into Moscow and through several checkpoints en route. There'd always been a market for 100% pure heroin and the rich and famous will pay a fortune. Further down the food chain, poor, raddled addicts and the desperate will pay for 2% heroin cut with any old shit. Moscow was a great market. No one would dare look inside the lorries and at their content. At a push, someone could be concealed in one of the trucks also, if they ever needed to get someone in under the radar. The CIA would only need to payoff the Afghan warlords and get access to the lorries where they could hide their wares. No wonder the lorry drivers went into town overnight and left their lorries packed with heroin unguarded. They were under instructions from the warlords. It was a brilliant plan. It was a brilliant plan and Pope had royally fucked it up.

The CIA route was about to be closed permanently and Pope needed to let Seb know. Pope felt really bad about how easily Boris had deceived him and that would stick in his craw for a very long time. It didn't lessen Pope's feelings of guilt but at the end of the day, Seb was the one who'd instructed him to share the information and Seb should shoulder most of the blame if there was any fallout. It was Seb's decision whether he told MI6 or whether he contacted the CIA direct or whether he said nothing. It certainly explained clearly why MI6 had done nothing when they'd heard about the heroin route originally. They probably knew all along that it was a heroin route. The SAS guest that was on the original mission was probably an MI6 operative. The Russians had two choices: one was to leave

the route open and intercept the CIA gear and get a handle of
the latest kit that they were using, or just blow the shit out
everything and close the route down. Pope knew that despite it
going to cause an absolute shit storm, Seb would have to tell the
CIA. The route was compromised and they wouldn't want any
of their kit to end up in Ivan's hands. And neither would they
want any operatives caught when they turned up to collect the
kit. Pope opened his phone and dialled Seb.

20:00. Pope was sitting at the table in the kitchen having finished his dinner. Daisy had already gone upstairs and was in bed. Doodle was sitting expectantly under the kitchen table. Jane was preparing sandwiches for both herself and the girls for tomorrow. Charlie was sitting opposite Pope with a small scowl plastered on her face.

'Daddy, look at my foot. It's healing well now and it will be fully healed on Wednesday the 17th, which is not far away now.'

Pope's expression changed and the muscles in his jaw started to ripple. He looked hard into the half-full mug of tea. Charlie flashed up her left foot, nearly under Pope's nose. She had deliberately removed the elasticated stocking bandage before sitting down at the table. She was proud of her tattoo and wanted her stubborn father to at least like it. So far, he was ignoring it but it would be a permanent fixture and Charlie was going to apply pressure on him. Like any daughter, Charlie was able to wrap her dad around her little finger. He would come round, of that she was confident. It would only be a question of when. Start with a softly, softly approach and if that didn't work then up the ante. There was always the nuclear option, screaming tantrums, hysterical behaviour combined with the silent treatment, but best to exhaust other avenues first. Charlie wiggled her foot. The tattoo on her instep was angry and demanded attention.

'Look Daddy. It's a red rose with a stem. Isn't it beautiful?'

Pope's jaw muscles were flexing as he involuntarily ground his teeth. It was impossible not to look at Charlie's dainty foot, twirling before him.

'Do you know what a red rose and stem symbolises?'

Doodle's ears pricked up. He could hear Pope's teeth grinding away and that wasn't a good sign.

'No? Well, a red rose symbolises hope, love, promise and new beginnings. Isn't it wonderful?'

'Darling, take your foot out of Daddy's face. He's trying to have his dinner,' said Jane, preparing to act as referee.

'You are now scarred for life,' blurted out Pope.

The waggling foot started to retreat.

'You're underage and getting a tattoo is illegal.'

'John,' said the referee.

'She had better not get another tattoo until she's eighteen,' said John, staring at the referee.

He then turned his glare back to Charlie. 'When you are eighteen then you can do what you want. But I tell you now, it won't be under my roof. Understand!'

'Calm down John,' said the referee, realising that she was rapidly losing control of the match.

'Calm down. Calm down. I'll sort that little scrote out. When I'm finished with him, he won't be able to write his name, never mind tattoo anyone.'

Charlie dashed out of the kitchen and slammed the door behind her as she stomped up the stairs and into her bedroom.

'Satisfied?' said Jane.

'Not yet. Did you get the money back from that little gobshite?'

'John, why don't you take Doodle out for a walk. He needs to lift his leg.'

Doodle, upon hearing his name, poked his snow-white head out from under the table. Ears cocked, two jet-black eyes pleading and an even blacker little wet nose looked intensely at Pope. Pope got up and said, 'I'll get my coat boy and we'll be off.'

Doodle yapped and launched himself several times at Pope's thighs. Out on their medium route, Pope started to calm down. He wasn't just going to let Charlie off that easily no matter what Jane said.

A tattoo now, what next? Drinking, drugs, more tattoos, face piercing, nipple piercing? And then boyfriends. Pope shuddered.

His thoughts were interrupted. Doodle had stopped walking and was now refusing to move. Pope looked around and saw that they were adjacent to The House. He quietly unhooked Doodle and walked on briskly. Doodle scampered into the middle of the front garden and left a steaming package before catching up with Pope.

22:30. Pope was lying on his back in bed having just had his shower.

Jane put down her book. 'I had a chat with Nadia today.'

Nadia was the wife of Zayhan Khan who had been trying desperately to befriend Pope, and they along with their children lived further up the road. Khan worked in the back office of a bank in the City.

'Oh yeah.'

'Yes. Nadia mentioned that there's dog poo in the middle of her garden. It's been happening on a regular basis for some time. She's upset because she thinks that it's deliberate.'

'Oh yeah.'

'Nadia is a lovely lady. The kids are great. She has to go out and clear it up. She doesn't want the kids getting covered in it.'

'Oh yeah.'

'It can't be easy for her or her kids. You know. Living with someone like that.'

'There are urban foxes around here. They have moved off of living on the Heath and are getting bolder,' said Pope unconvincingly.

'Bold foxes, really? Well, it's time now that they stop.'

Pope didn't reply but made a mental note not to let Doodle off the lead any more on their regular walks. There was silence for a while and Pope remained lying on his back with his eyes staring blankly at the ceiling.

'John. Don't be too hard on Charlie. It's just a flower.'

Pope's views were a lot stronger than his wife and the tattoo had for some reason touched a nerve.

'Anyway, it's just a phase that she's going through,' continued Jane matter of factly.

Pope rolled onto his side, now facing the window. No sex tonight.

It's just a phase I'm going through, thought Pope.

Click. The bedroom light went out.

11:24. Ahmed Hussain was back at his family home in east London. He'd been chatting with his mum for over an hour. She had been filling him in on all of the family gossip and updating him on what had been going on in the local neighbourhood. Ahmed liked listening to his mum. She had a special skill of saying mundane things and making them sound very interesting. As usual, she avoided two topics. The first was asking anything about his work. And the second was mentioning anything about Ahmed's dad. Ahmed and his father had been at loggerheads for as long as she could remember. Ahmed's father was brought up under strict conditions and he did the same with his children. Ahmed, who was strong-willed, rebelled and this led to many arguments. Ahmed wanted to be Muslim but he also wanted to be British and do many of the things that others at school and university did, and took for granted. He defied his father and sought out his own path and career. They had, even now, a strained relationship.

Mr Hussain arrived home unexpectedly from his clerical job at the local council. 'Ahmed, how are you?'

'I'm well thanks, Dad. How are you?'

'Good, all is well. To what do we owe the pleasure?'

'No reason. Just dropping in.'

'It's good because I wanted to speak with you.'

Ahmed's mum sat down. She wasn't feeling well and knew that this wasn't going to make her feel any better.

'OK.'

'Ahmed, you are twenty-eight years old and still not married. Soon you will be an old man. Life is passing you by. You need to marry, have children. That will make your mother happy.'

'Really?'

'Have you not met any nice Muslim girls?'

'I'm focusing on work. It's my career where I spend my time.'

'Yes, yes. Work is admirable but you need a work–life balance.'

'When the time is right.'

'I had an arranged marriage. You know that. Your mum and me both came to England from Pakistan and our parents arranged our marriage. I am a prominent person in our community and I can arrange your marriage. I consider it my duty to ensure that my first-born son is married to a suitable partner. It's common Islamic practice.'

'Dad, I'll choose my own bride and in my own good time.'

His dad banged his fist down on the table in anger. The same anger that Ahmed had inherited.

'In my house...'

Ahmed interrupted him.

'I don't live in your house. In fact, I'll tell you now, I probably won't marry a Muslim. And there's one thing that's a dead cert, I'll choose my wife and for the reasons that I want.'

Ahmed was close to revealing that he had already identified his future wife. Deepak's sister, Aisha, had stolen his heart. OK, she didn't know that, and no, they hadn't even been on a date. In fact, he had barely spoken to her. Mostly because he was tongue-tied whenever he was around her. But once he put on some more muscle, he was sure that with his newfound (muscle) confidence and personality he would win her over.

'This is how you treat your mum. You should be ashamed of yourself,' ranted his dad.

'I'm off. I can't take this shit. See you soon, Mum,' shouted Ahmed as he got up and bolted for the front door.

There was a loud noise as the door slammed shut. Ahmed was already close to his car and readying himself for the drive back to Luton.

'Swearing is disrespectful. He's ungrateful as well. There are many who wish that their parents would arrange their marriages for them.'

Both parents sat in silence, divided by space and tolerance.

'Is it me or is Ahmed losing weight?' said his mum, breaking the stony silence.

20:45. The car pulled up quietly to a stop at the edge of the large car park. Neither man was speaking and the windows were open. It was a cold night but the passenger insisted that the windows were partially opened as soon as they disembarked the P&O ferry at Harwich. The driver was someone who unfortunately suffered from sea sickness. On this particular journey from the Hook of Holland, the North Sea waters weren't particularly choppy but it still affected the young man. He had pretty much occupied one of the toilets on the ferry for the whole of the crossing, much to the annoyance of other passengers who were also in need.

The Hook ferry was popular for groups travelling to and from the continent who were celebrating. The ferry was carrying back the now quieter groups. Boozed out, fagged out and partied out. Everyone was looking to get back home and readying themselves for next week when it would be back to work. The car was on the ferry before 14:15 CET when it always left promptly and sailed its regular route, arriving at Harwich at 19:45 GMT. The car left the parked ferry and headed out of Harwich, picking up the A12. It cruised along at 50mph until it reached the sign for Chelmsford Service station. It indicated and left the busy main road and accessed the service station via a junction.

The passenger was dressed as an Imam with very little of his face visible. He was angry. Angry that once again the driver who was masquerading as his nephew had drawn unnecessary attention to himself on the ferry. Eyes were drawn to him as he staggered in and out of the toilet. Some were sympathetic, recognising that he was not well. Others drew nudges and sniggers; they recognised someone suffering from overindulgence. The Imam was offended by the smell that was in the air and in every crevice in the car. The smell of sick. His own journey had started out in the Middle East where he had flown to Zurich. He had stayed there for three days before flying on to Schiphol airport under an assumed name. It was here that he was picked up by his nephew in a new car and also here where both of them assumed new identities that he carried with him.

A car slowly circled the car park and then reversed into a space next to their car. In the darkened corner, they were the only cars occupying any space. The driver of the other car looked over at the nephew and nodded. The nephew got out of the car and walked to rear of his car where he opened the boot. Inside the boot was a medium-sized black travel case and a sports bag. The driver of the other car got out and retrieved a tradesman tool bag from his own boot. He hefted the bag out of his boot. It was fully laden with plumbers' tools and he shifted it awkwardly over to the nephew's car and dropped it in the boot. It made a fairly loud noise as it thudded on the base of the boot.

'Is everything in there?' asked the nephew in a low voice.

The man took two paces back, the awful breath nearly knocking him off of his feet.

'Yes. In fact, it's got everything you could ever need to do a job.' he said confidently.

'Not traceable?'

'Nope.'

'Good. We'll leave now. Have a coffee and something to eat and stay here for an hour. You can then go back but don't use the same route that you came here by.'

'Understood.'

The man closed his boot, locked the car using his key fob and walked towards the well-lit restaurant.

The nephew got back into the car and started the ignition.

'Everything go OK?' asked the Imam.

'Yes. He brought everything that you could possibly want and confirmed that its untraceable.'

'Good,' replied the Iman, almost throwing up after getting a waft of spew.

The man entered the restaurant and looked at the queue. It would take fifteen minutes to get served and he hated queuing. He turned around and slowly walked back to where his car was parked. He got in and started the ignition. He went back onto the A12 and headed back along the exact route that he'd come by, only a few minutes behind the Imam's car.

'Sod dog's breath,' he muttered as he drove.

22:55. The car pulled up outside the mid-terrace house in the southwest of Luton. The Imam put on a pair of latex gloves, got out and went to the boot which was already open. He retrieved both the medium-sized black travel case and the tradesman tool bag, placed them both on the pavement and closed the boot. The car drove off and the driver quickly closed the windows; he was freezing. The Imam picked up both of the bags and staggered towards the front door, straining under the weight of the tool bag. The door opened before he had reached it and he walked inside. The little old lady quietly shut the door and he dropped both bags to the floor in the cramped, musty hallway.

She nodded at the Imam.

'I'll take the bags upstairs. Perhaps I could have a meal in half an hour,' he said in Pashto.

She nodded and walked stiffly back into the kitchen. The Imam grabbed the tool bag with two hands and struggled upstairs with it. He came back down straight away and took the travel bag up to his room. In the room, he sat on the bed for a couple of minutes breathing heavily. Once he had regathered his breath, he withdrew from his case a burner phone. He inserted the SIM card and logged on. He took out a piece of paper from his thobe and created a message. It was a string of numbers.

1011160400

He then sent the string of numbers as a text message to three telephone numbers. He then created another message, again as a string of numbers.

1011160430

He then sent that text message to another three telephone numbers also as text messages. He refolded the piece of paper containing a list of numbers that were telephone numbers, other than they were written back to front, and put it back in his pocket. He took the SIM card out of the phone and used brute strength to fold the SIM card. Next he used his Janbiya (dagger) and he cut it up. He then crushed the burner phone. The SIM pieces were flushed down the toilet and the burner phone pieces placed in a plastic bag which went back inside his case.

The first text displayed on Usam's, Zeehan's and Hamiza's phones. The instruction was clear. The message was simple.

1011160400 meant that they were to pick him up at 04:00 on 16th November 2010.

To read the text, you just read from right to left as MM:HH DD MM YY.

The second text displayed on the burner phones of the three martyrs was exactly the same; simple encryption.

1011160430 meant that they were to be at the Luton mosque at 04:30 on 16th November 2010.

Both groups had their instructions. The plan was being activated.

The Imam locked his case and went downstairs and into the kitchen. The old lady ladled a broth into a bowl and put it on the table. There was a loaf of bread already on the table. He sat at the seat and she shakily put the brimming bowl in front of him. She nodded and left him alone in the kitchen. He ate heartily; it had been some time since he had last eaten. Wiping his mouth with the back of his gloved hand, he walked over to the cupboard set on the wall and opened it. He was studying it intensely and didn't notice that both the old woman and old man had entered the kitchen and were standing directly behind him.
'Would you like a cup of tea?' the old lady asked.
The Imam spun around, leaving the cupboard door open. 'Yes.'

The old lady walked past him and closed the cupboard door. Inside the cupboard were both the electricity and gas meters. She went over to the kettle and put it on. The Imam sat back down and no words were exchanged. The tea was made and he was given a cup heavily dosed with sugar. It was an Afghan tradition to have the first cup of tea heavily sweetened and the next cup with no sugar at all. The Imam caught the old lady staring at his hands that were still wearing black latex gloves.

'I have a rare skin affliction on my hands. It is highly contagious, so I'm wearing gloves,' he said.

She nodded.

'Anyway. First thing tomorrow, I'd like all of the equipment that was delivered here sent up to my room.'

'Yes. First thing,' she replied.

Both her and her husband left the kitchen and went back into the front room. They continued listening to the radio and heard the Imam's footfall on the stairs. They waited and then heard the creaking sound of the bedroom door closing.

'I wonder what he was doing looking in the cupboard,' she whispered.

'No idea. We should go to bed now. We have an early start tomorrow,' replied her husband, huffing as he grappled with getting out of his seat.

18:00. The little Afghanistan lady was sitting in the front room on the ratty chair. She looked over to her husband who was half lying on the settee. The general aches and pains that they both suffered along with never-ending pains from their arthritic joints had magnified several fold. Today they had been very busy. Up early to prepare food for the day. Then they had the job of ferrying the items up to the Imam's room. They had been given instructions to leave the items outside the bedroom after each journey, knock on the door and then begin the next run. By the time they had returned with the next set of items, the previous set had been scooped up by the Imam and the space left bare.

By mid-morning, the old man could no longer make the journey up the stairs. His frail body's capacity for climbing the stairs had been fully exhausted. He then concentrated on ferrying the goods from their hiding place to the bottom of the stairs. His wife would then struggle up and down the stairs, huffing and puffing all of the time. They started off by emptying the garden shed of the items. It was a cold, wet morning and this added to their discomfort. Early on they jointly decided that each load should be fairly light otherwise they wouldn't get everything upstairs. They stopped for a couple of breaks and refuelled with hot sweet tea and sandwiches, which temporarily revived both of them. The Imam didn't leave his room but accepted the tea and sandwiches which, after consuming, he then left the empty plate and mug outside the door for removing. Lunch was a lamb stew made Afghani style. They ate it in the kitchen whilst the Imam remained in his room, eating alone. By late afternoon they had placed all of the goods secreted all over their property outside of the bedroom. Before placing the last set of items outside of the bedroom door, the elderly couple had sat down in the kitchen and checked not once but three times that they had delivered all of the items. They had been counting the items and checking them off of a scrappy list that they'd prepared the night they received a letter telling them in code that the Imam would be joining them. They smiled at each other; they were confident that they had completed their task. It was both a mentally and physically demanding task that pushed both of them to their limits, but it was completed.

After the last item was delivered, the old lady knocked on the door and said proudly, 'That's everything. There's no more to deliver.'

Later on, the frail woman went upstairs and knocked on the bedroom door, 'We are going to have our dinner now. Would you like to join us or shall I bring it up?'

'Serve. I'll be down in ten minutes.'

The old lady turned around and painfully went down the stairs.

'He's having dinner with us,' she said, looking at her decrepit husband.

He moved himself up into a sitting position, grimacing and gasping for air.

'He stayed in the room all day. He could have helped and carried some of the stuff up himself,' she said with contempt.

'It's done. Let's enjoy dinner and then maybe an early night,' replied her husband, trying to placate her.

Up in the bedroom, the Imam had been making preparations all day. Along with items stashed at this property, he also had a number of critical components that he had in his black travel case. These items had been purchased in Belgium and Germany and then delivered to his 'nephew's' address, who then packed them in the case that he'd been instructed to buy. He was pleased with the progress that he'd made. First, everything was there. There were no missing parts. Second, there was a strict order to building the destructive weapons that would be concealed in the rucksacks. It was crucial to build the weapon(s) in such a way that there was no chance of it accidentally going off before the planned time. He had spent a lot of time first in Libya, then in Syria and finally in Afghanistan perfecting his bomb-making trade. Along the way, he had witnessed a number of trainee bomb makers blow themselves to smithereens and sometimes other people foolish enough to stand within the bomb blast area. He had lasted this long because he was meticulous in his preparation. For this build he was going to use a unique priming device. Very simple but ideal for the target. He had tested it himself and had gone through a few dry runs with a dummy weapon using future martyrs. He knew that the devices would work. The reason that he was implementing a new priming method was that there was a chance that the weapon could accidentally go off before it was at the target. Tomorrow he would start constructing the weapons in earnest. Wearing latex gloves all of the time was becoming irritating but he knew that it was essential. Tonight he'd dine and then sleep well.

22:30. The huge TV was blearing out the commentator's animated protestations. Three different angles, all in slow motion, and the forward was fractionally offside. How did the assistant referee miss that one? Easy with technology and several different camera angles, but still, the assistant referee needed castigating and in another time and era probably publicly flogging also.
'Who would be a Lino?' said Deepak.
'Must be mad,' replied the horizontal Ahmed.
'Are you coming out tomorrow?' probed Deepak.
'Nope.'
'Oh, I thought that you were going to help?'
'Are you fucking crazy? They are a drug gang.'
'But they helped you out.'
'Yeah, and I'm grateful but I ain't getting involved.'
'So what about the money that you got paid last week then?' asked Deepak.
'What about it? I worked and I got paid. Simple.'
'Well perhaps you could give it to my mum.'
'Why would I do that?'
'I know that I bought the TV with some of the money but the rest I give to my mum.'
'Why the fuck would you give your mum drug money, bruv? She's now an accessory after the fact.'
'Strictly speaking, she isn't, actually. To be an accessory she would need to know that an offence had been committed and she doesn't.'

'Now you're a fucking expert in law? You'll be fucking handy when she's nicked and needs a defence lawyer,' said Ahmed, getting more annoyed. 'Anyway, answer the question.'

'Sorry, what was the question?'

'Why the fuck should I give the money to your mum?'

'Because she sends up mountains of food every week. She cooks the food, packs it up and then it's transported up here. She then washes all of the pots, pans, our plates and cutlery and returns it with the next batch. It's costing her a fortune to feed us, not to mention the petrol and someone driving up here.'

Ahmed sat there, looking at Deepak. He hadn't really thought that much about how much the cost and effort was to feed them before.

'We do eat a lot of food every week,' went on Deepak. 'Or to be precise, you eat a lot of food. I'm not a big eater.'

'No, except after you've been on the puff.'

'True, but then I eat mostly from the chicken shop. That's when I love their food the most.'

Ahmed continued to stare menacingly at Deepak.

'You know that's true. How often have you said that eating all of this freshly cooked food is good for your training? Maybe it is but I think that you need to change your training routine.'

Ahmed's hand thrust into his jeans pocket and he withdrew a bundle of twenty pound notes and threw them at Deepak.

'Here, have the lot.'

'Thanks.'

'Now shut the fuck up, I'm missing the footie.'

Deepak's head started to bobble as Ahmed sunk back into his horizontal position.

10:30. Usam and Zeehan were standing in the car park of The Mall shopping centre. Even at this time of day, there were quite a few cars parked there. Zeehan was leaning against his car, a T Porter SE130, five-door black people carrier with tinted windows.

'Hamiza flew out yesterday to the Hajj. Did he mention anything regarding the text?'

'Not to me. What about you?' replied Usam.

'No.'

'I guess then we'll just have to explain everything to the Ayatollah.'

'Yeah. I don't fancy doing that. He'll explode,' said Zeehan.

'I'll do it. You drive us around, that's enough to focus on. And you are also part of the security team since Rahan went up to Bradford.'

'Should we try and get someone else to be part of the security team as now there's only us two?' asked Zeehan.

'No, it's too risky. Anyway, the Ayatollah's a control freak. He'll want to do his security checks first. Whatever they are,' replied Usam.

'Usam, the more I think about this, the more I don't like it,' said Zeehan in a faltering voice.

'I know what you mean. A few years ago we all went down to Finsbury Park and listened to the speeches. It was intoxicating. Suddenly we had a purpose. We wanted to be involved. There were recruiters in the crowds and we jumped in, feet first. We had our own private meetings. A proper little spy group out on an adventure,' said Usam.

Zeehan laughed, 'Yeah, we were committed but naive. Where did it all go wrong?'

'We grew up. The trouble was once the romance washed away, we were left in a nightmare.'

'But what do we do now?' implored Zeehan.

Usam shrugged his shoulders. He stared at the cold facade of The Mall.

'We're in too deep, you know that,' said Usam.

'Yes.'

'We can't back out. I think that we go along with the plan. After this is over then we lie low here in Luton for a while. We get the gang back together. You, me, Hamiza and Rahan and we get out. Start afresh, we go somewhere where the Ayatollah can't find us.'

'Bristol,' Zeehan blurted out.

'Could be.'

'And we start a business together.'

'Why not.'

'I'm in,' replied Zeehan.

'First though we have to stick together. If we make a mistake, we'll get caught. Imagine the effect on our families. It will be devastating for them.'

'I do think about that all of the time. Also, we don't really know what the plan is. We just ferry the Imam to and from the mosque and make sure no one interrupts him in the basement. We're really pawns and no more,' went on Zeehan, knowing that that was a lame excuse.

'We are pawns. But if we were to disappear now, think about it. The Imam knows where we live and our families also. The retribution on our families would be unthinkable,' said Usam sternly.

'We made a big mistake getting involved,' groaned Zeehan.

'Yes, we did.'

11:30. The meeting of regional heads in the Cage was wrapping up. Everyone had given their update. Salient points from last week. Key objectives for this week. The last item on the agenda – AOB (Any Other Business). A few minor HR issues were banded about but no one was really interested in either listening to or voicing an opinion. HR staff issues were a poison chalice. It led into worker rights, health & safety and any number of European laws being flung about. In this business, with the need for absolute secrecy, people needed to walk away if they didn't have the stomach for the work. That wasn't to say that MI5 shouldn't work within the parameters set out for them alongside full accountability. But it wasn't an office nine to five environment.

Carruthers looked up but not directly at Pope who, like his colleagues, was waiting now for the meeting to end so that they could get on with their work.

'I have made contact with senior management and advised them that in my opinion the Luton operation that is currently being run in a non-standard way should be stopped and the resources resume they previously agreed modus operandi.'

Some papers were rustled but no one looked either at Pope or at Carruthers. This was an awkward moment.

'The senior management team has endorsed my proposal and the change will be implemented soonest,' she blathered on in typical management speak.

'I see. What about the support given by Team 4?' asked Pope.

'That will also cease.'

'It's only light touch though,' said Pope.

'It's manpower resources that could be better utilised.'

'Really? This still represents one of our best leads but we need to utilise our resources better. There was significant activity there with what appears to be external support from someone purporting to be an Imam. And there were several young guys sighted there at the same time,' went on Pope.

'Yes, we know that. But there's been no activity there for a while. The trail has gone dead. We need to move on,' Carruthers said confidently, now looking directly at Pope.

'In my opinion, the original activity represented the planning phase. The actual operation will be run from the same place. They don't know that we have two very capable guys inserted in there. We are in a strong position to catch them before they strike.'

'That is one opinion. But there are many other mosques in Luton and this potential attack that you are describing could as easily be launched from one of the other mosques,' she said smugly.

'Well, I guess that is it.'

'Good.'

'I'll need to let the team know when everything is going to be rearranged, so what is the date?'

'Yes of course. The last day is 30th November.'

'OK. And that goes for the support from Team 4 and the CCTV coverage from the street camera outside the mosque?'

Carruthers' eyes flickered, 'As I said, the operation in its current guise ceases on 30th November.'

Carruthers looked around the room.

'Anymore AOB? No? Then same time next week,' she said, getting up.

Her PA busied herself gathering up Carruthers' papers and scuttled out of the room after her. Several people got up and followed Carruthers out. Pope remained seated, staring into space. Tony Crook, James Davison, Frank Selly, Callum Drake and Steve McLeish all remained in their seats.

'Bad luck,' said Tony Crook. 'She's on a power trip.'

'Yeah, mate. She's making sure that she's able to get senior management to back her. It's not personal,' added Frank Selly.

'It's not about that. My concern is that there really is something going on AND that mosque is at the heart of it. I know it. I just know it,' replied Pope.

'She's still limping about,' added Callum Drake. 'Hopefully it really hurts.'

'Now, now.' said Tony Crook, laughing.

Team 4 had received in their inbox authorisation from Carruthers that they were no longer supporting directly anything coming from the Luton mosque operation. In addition, the CCTV camera was to be deactivated and removed. Both were effective immediately.

03:55. The black T Porter, five-seater people carrier stopped outside the terraced house in the south west of Luton. The front door creaked open and the stooping figure strode out into the drizzling rain and then on towards the car. He was carrying in his right hand a black medium-sized travel case. The rear passenger door opened and out stepped Usam. The Imam swept past him and onto the bench seat, keeping the case firmly on his lap. Usam got back in and the door automatically closed. As the car slowly pulled away along the quiet street, the Imam scanned the interior of the people carrier.

'Where is he?' he said with venom.

Zeehan focused on the empty street, driving well within the speed limit.

'Hamiza?' squeaked Usam.

'Who else would I be talking about?' countered the Imam.

'He's gone to the Hajj,' replied Usam.

The Imam glared at him, not saying a word but demanding through the silence more details.

'He went with his dad and his grandfather. They left on Saturday and after they plan to go on to Islamabad and visit family there.'

'He knew this but didn't tell anyone?' said the Imam with annoyance.

'No, we didn't know. He told us just before he left,' replied Usam.

'He has jeopardised everything.'

'His grandfather is old and this is probably his last chance to make it to the Hajj.. And then see his family back home.'

'That I understand. But the fool knew that this trip was planned. I don't doubt that it's taken years to plan and get the money saved for it.'

Usam nodded. Zeehan continued to be focused fully on driving, although he also nodded slyly.

'He could have mentioned this last month, last year or even last decade,' went on the Imam.

Usam again nodded, although he thought that Hamiza and all of the Ali family planning anything for over a decade was pushing it. Not that he was going to raise this point with the Imam.

'Well, we will have to carry on without him. I hope to speak with him in the future and share with him my disappointment. I expect both of you to station yourselves at the bottom of the stairs and bar entrance to anyone. The three martyrs will be arriving at 04:30 so we need to hurry up.'

Zeehan pressed his foot down on the accelerator and the car sped towards the mosque.

The previous evening in three bathrooms in Luton, three young men underwent the ritual. They spent time shaving off all of their body hair. Upon entering paradise a martyr would receive seventy-two virgins and this thought occupied their minds during shaving. All three had been preparing their own personal message. The Imam had left them with the task of writing their own unique message and he explained to them that their message was important. They had to speak confidently and with authority when the time came. These would be their last words that would be shared with the world. Future generations would be able to see their speeches and it would inspire them to follow in their footsteps. After the cleansing ritual had been completed, all three of them alone would go through their speeches in their bedrooms again several times.

The Imam and his two bodyguards entered the quiet mosque and headed down to the basement without encountering anyone. They made their way to the furthest room and Usam unlocked the room. He switched on the light and breathed in the damp, dusty air.

The Imam placed his case on the table, took the key and said, 'I'll lock the door. You know the knock routine. Bring down each of them when they arrive but make sure one of you always remains at the bottom of the stairs.'

Usam and Zeehan, who remained at the door, both nodded. The door was closed and they both heard the door being locked. They turned around and walked back to the bottom of the stairs, taking up their sentry duties. Usam glanced at his watch. The luminous dial told him that it was 04:24. He held up the watch face to Zeehan.

'Not bad. We made it on time.'

'Yes. But he's really annoyed with Hamiza,' whispered Zeehan.

'You don't say,' replied Usam dryly.

'What was that all about when he said that he was going to speak with him and share his disappointment with him?' muttered Zeehan.

'No idea. But he's right. The Ali family didn't do this on the spur of the moment. Hamiza knew about this for a long time. He's a crafty little sod.'

'I wonder what the Ayatollah would have done if we'd told him that the Ali family were into bacon sarnies,' sniggered Zeehan.

'Leave off.'

'Hey. I've got a new nickname for Hamiza. We should call him Hamy. Get it? Ham-y. Ham...'

'Yeah, I get it,' interrupted Usam.

The upstairs door opened and there were loud footsteps as the person trod their way down. Zeehan swung the door open and there before him was one of the martyrs. They all looked at each other, recognising one another from before.

'Follow me,' said Usam to the young man.

Another set of loud footfalls echoed down the stairs. Zeehan waited until the person got to the bottom and swung open the door. The young man was mildly startled and then stared at Zeehan. He started to walk past him. Zeehan's hand flashed up and pressed against the young man's chest.

'Wait,' said Zeehan with an air of authority.

The young man stared at him saying nothing but did as he was told. He stopped pressing forward, releasing pressure from Zeehan's hand that was firmly imprinted against his chest. They stood there, both staring at each other, neither one speaking. Usam had been aware that someone else had turned up and he hurried back down the corridor. He saw both of them standing close together, just staring at each other.

He put his hand on Zeehan's shoulder, looked at the young man and said, 'Follow me.'

Zeehan stepped aside and the young man obeyed Usam's command. Again there were loud footfalls on the stairs and Zeehan followed the same routine. Swing the door open, block his entrance, wait for Usam, let him pass. It worked like clockwork. Usam and him were a good team. Usam came back after delivering the third and final martyr and looked at his watch again. He smiled and swung the watch face up and into Zeehan's face. The dial shone out in deep red 04:30.

'Perfect,' said Zeehan.

The Imam had spread out the large black flag on the table. It was hanging over the sides of the table menacingly. The three martyrs had taken all of the chairs and stacked them in a corner, making more space in the small room. The Imam was rummaging around inside the travel case which he had placed on top of the flag and was busily taking out several items that he then also placed on top of the flag. Once he was satisfied that he had retrieved all of the items that he needed, he then put the case on top of the stacked chairs. He then asked the martyrs to pass over to him their handwritten messages. The martyr's suicide message was a personal message that they had written. It was a propaganda tool and a very powerful one at that. It served two distinct purposes. The first was that it was regarded as an 'external' message. This was meant to demoralise and humiliate the opposition and their forces. The second purpose was that it was regarded as an 'internal' message. This was primarily used as a recruitment tool.

He read with difficulty the scrawly almost illegible notes and then said that they should use the term 'martyrdom operations' in their speech when referring to the suicide atrocity that they were going to commit. He said to the nearest young man that he would be filmed first. He passed over two black balaclavas to the other two and told them to put them on. He then passed over a well-worn, tatty, brown, wool Pakol to the young man who was going to be filmed first. The young man immediately put on the ill-fitting cap. A Pakol was a round cap made popular by the Afghani mujahideen fighters who fought the Soviets in the 1980s.

The Iman next picked up the small handheld video camera and checked that it was ready to work. This was a new camcorder that his 'nephew' had bought in Belgium for cash. It was the exact same camcorder that he had back home to film his family. He was very familiar and comfortable with this make of camcorder. He then passed the black Islamic flag over to the now hooded two men. They were all nearly ready to film the first message. The two men stepped back to the far wall and spread apart until the flag was taut. The young man then stood in front of the flag in the middle, as directed by the Imam. The Imam looked through the viewfinder and was happy with the setting. The flag was horizontal, the two hooded holders of the flag added threatening drama, the young man in the centre dressed as a freedom fighter and the added effect of the small dank room. He was a director, excited just like when he filmed his family swimming or eating a meal to celebrate an event. He then gave a thumbs up and the young English-born man started to recite his message.

The extremist views held by the very small group who advocate suicide bombing are not supported or considered religiously justified by the global population of Muslim people.

The Iman had taken out of the case a fairly heavy rucksack and put it on the table. The items that he had previously taken out of the case had been packed away and the case was now back sitting on top of the chairs. He had already taken four chairs off the stack and placed then in the centre of the room. Three of the chairs were facing the other chair.

'Sit please,' he said, pointing to the three chairs.

The three young men did as they were asked without speaking.

'It is time to go through the plan. You will be remembered forever. You are warriors and martyrs and your reward will be given to all of you in paradise,' he went on solemnly.

'The target is the football match tomorrow at Wembley. England play France but when you are finished there won't be a match. France are a supporter of oppression and this is the perfect time to strike the infidels. Wembley is a place that is known all around the world. English and French supporters will be mingling together heading towards the match. It is here where the martyrdom operation will take place.'

The young men waited in anticipation. Now the details of their mission would be given to them. They had been waiting for this moment for a long time. Even before they travelled to be trained in camps hidden away on the Afghanistan/Pakistan border.

'You will all travel to Wembley Stadium. You have all travelled there several times. Yes?'

They all nodded. One of the tasks given by the Imam when they last met was to travel to Wembley Stadium. First they would travel during the quiet daytime and then at the time of early evening which was when their mission would take place. Always on the train and underground system and always alone.

'When you all get to Wembley Park station, you will walk to the right side of the station after you go through the ticket barriers. Here is where the steep stairs take you down under the road and on towards Wembley Stadium along Wembley Way. This is pedestrian only and the main route to the stadium. On your journey to the stadium, do not acknowledge each other, sit in separate carriages and arrive at the same time. If any of you arrive there alone and idly stand around, you may draw attention to yourselves. Security at Wembley will be tight with a lot of police milling about. If one of you are late then send a text to the others and reschedule the meeting time. That way the others can move off down the road towards Wembley Park shops and mingle with the crowd until it is time to meet. This is very important. Do you understand?'

'Yes,' they mumbled in unison.

'Good. Once everyone is together, the bombs will be activated. Up until then the bombs will not be primed. I'll talk you through the process in a minute but first we must finish going through the plan. After you meet up in the corner, where you'll all prime the weapons, you will then split up.'

Pointing to the young man facing him on his right-hand side, the Imam said, 'You are number one.'

Pointing at the young man sitting in the middle of the group, he said, 'You are number two.'

Pointing at the young man facing him on his left-hand side, he said, 'You are number three.'

'The weapons will be primed to go off in eight minutes. Number one, you must walk briskly down the stairs and along Wembley Way. You will walk all of the way and stop on the walkway near the statue outside Wembley Stadium. You can't miss it. It's twenty feet high and will be right in front of you as you approach on your right-hand side.'

'Yes, Imam, I know the statue. It's of a famous footballer called Bobby Moore.'

The Imam looked at him with disdain. 'Quite.'

The Iman paused again.

'Number two, you will also walk down the stairs and along Wembley Way but you will walk slower and stop where Wembley Way crosses over Fulton Road. This is the first road that you meet on Wembley Way and it is only a couple of minutes to get there, so walk slowly. Once there, stay in the middle of Wembley Way.'

Number two nodded.

'Number three, you will position yourself in the middle set of steps at the top of the stairs leading down and onto Wembley Way. You will need to wait seven minutes at the side and you need to keep out of the way and read a newspaper. That way you won't draw any attention to yourself.'

'Yes. I'll get the free newspaper. It's called the *London Evening Standard*,' he said, trying to show his knowledge of London.

The Imam's patience was being tried. 'Good.'

The Imam paused. 'The time that you should all be at Wembley Park station is 18:25. This will be the busiest time when there will be the most amount of French and English infidels walking towards Wembley Stadium. The effect and impact that you cause will be immense. It will not only strike at the heart of both infidel countries but it will reverberate around the world. Your names will be revered for generations and there will be songs created to remember your bravery and deeds.'

The young men allowed themselves a sneaky look at each other and a shared smile. Even the Imam was smiling with his hands and arms spread out wide.

'Do you all understand what it is you need to do tomorrow?'

Once again they all nodded. The plan was fairly simple. Get to Wembley. prime the weapons and get to their designated locations within eight minutes.

'Now, let's go over the route for tomorrow. You will leave from Luton station on the 17:28 London-bound train and get off at West Hampstead at 17:54. Then you leave the station, turn right and walk up to West Hampstead underground station. This should take eight minutes and then there will be a slight wait on the platform before the train leaves for Wembley Park station. You should arrive there at around 18:21. Then you will walk up from the platform and meet at the rendezvous point at 18:25. Once you are all there then you will prime the weapons immediately and get on with the mission. The whole journey will be uncomfortable. Not only are you travelling in rush hour but there will be all of the people travelling to watch the game, cramming into the trains and blocking the pavements. It will be better to stand all of the way on both trains. Keep your rucksacks with you but on the trains, take them off and plant them between your feet. That way they won't draw any attention towards you.'

The Imam got up and went back to the table where the rucksack was placed.

'Please return all of the stairs,' he said, pointing to the stack of chairs in the corner.

The chairs were re-stacked and the young men stayed in the corner, hesitant.

'Gather round. It's perfectly safe.'

The trio clumsily formed a semicircle behind the Imam.

'First, I want you all to try on the rucksack, walk around the room and get the feel of it. Number one, you are first.'

All of the martyrs picked up the rucksack with some foreboding, put it on their back using the shoulder straps and walked around the room, initially looking at their feet.

'No. No. You must walk normal. Stand up straight and look straight ahead,' instructed the Imam.

They all tried to rectify their stoop but continued to walk gingerly. The Imam unlocked the door and walked out into the narrow corridor. He ignored the two silhouetted faces that were anxiously looking at him.

'Number three. Out here, please.'

The young man still wearing the rucksack tiptoed out into the corridor.

'Now walk up to the end, turn around and walk back.'

The young man did the exercise several times before the Imam said that he now looked like a person going about his business. The Imam made the other two do the same repetitive exercise until he was satisfied that they also were walking normally.

They went back inside the room and the Imam said, 'Good. It's important that tomorrow you blend in.'

'Yes. The rucksack is quite heavy and it's that maybe that we were conscious of,' said number one.

'Tomorrow when you put on your own rucksack, adjust the shoulder straps to make it comfortable. You can also use the waist and chest clips to add stability. But I'd prefer that you don't. OK. There will be some more weight added when we fill up the pockets but I've chosen this rucksack specifically for the task. Some rucksacks are far too large and extend above your head. This one can fit in everything and isn't cumbersome.'

Again, they all nodded. The Imam helped take the rucksack off number three and put it on the table.

'Now we'll go through arming the weapon. It's a very simple task.'

The Imam unclipped the rucksack's top and lifted it up. Inside was a small alarm clock with two wires attached to it. The rest of the two wires disappeared into the belly of the pack. He turned the alarm clock and was now facing the back of it. He opened the area that contained the one battery, took it out, turned it around and put it back it. He then flicked up the switch on the top. The second hand on the face was already moving clockwise around the face. He rested the alarm clock back in its place, pulled down the top and reset the clip.

'Done,' he said, looking at the three inquisitive faces.

'That's all that you have to do. The alarm timer will be set before I hand over the rucksack. It is set for eight minutes. The battery is inside but it's facing the wrong way. You just turn it around and replace it, then the clock will start. Flick up the little button on the top of the alarm and that activates the alarm function on the clock. The weapon is now activated. Now, I want each of you to do it five times whilst the rucksack it sitting on the table.'

The Imam undid the rucksack and reset the alarm clock back to its original inert state and then shut the rucksack.

'Number one, you go first.'

The trio rapidly went through the exercise with ease.

'OK, now we'll go through the exercise again. This time it will be done exactly how it must be done tomorrow. Rather than taking the rucksacks off and each of you arming your own weapon, you will arm each other's. It's vital that you don't draw any attention, and by doing it the way that I'll explain, no one will take any notice.'

The trio waited for the final piece of information quietly.

'Number one will stand at the top of the stairs facing towards Wembley Stadium. Number three will stand behind him and open the rucksack, set the alarm and close the rucksack. As soon as the rucksack is closed, number one will head off immediately to the statue outside Wembley Stadium. Number two will then arm the weapon in number three's rucksack. And finally number three will arm number two's weapon. Once completed, number two will go off to the designated point at the intersection with Fulton Road. Now, we'll run through the drill a few times.'

The trio were slow and clumsy, partly due to the difference in height which meant that number two had to almost squat to allow number three comfortable access to his rucksack. The drill was also unwieldy because they had to stop after each go, reset the alarm and pass the rucksack onto the next person. They ran through the drill several times without the Imam speaking. He watched on and let them make mistakes, talk to each other, correct the mistakes. It was important that they worked as a team. Finally, they went through a near-perfect run. The Imam didn't say anything. The group was working as a unit. They repeated the drill now another several times smoothly and with ease. The Imam was confident that they could go through this well-rehearsed routine in the full glare of the multitude of football fans and security forces without anyone becoming suspicious of their activities.

'Good. You can stop now. That's very good.'

Finally, the trio were getting praise. The Imam was a stern hard taskmaster. He packed away the rucksack in the travel case and then said, 'Gather the chairs and we'll talk.'

The chairs were again placed in almost the same places as before and everyone took their original seat.

'Tomorrow you will all wear the jackets and trousers that I asked you all to buy,' he said.

They all nodded. They had bought the specific clothes that he'd ordered them to purchase. They had used the cash that he'd previously given them and they had travelled down to London, where they'd bought the items.

'Remember to bring your burner phones tomorrow and only have each other's numbers in the phones. Also don't forget to wear your watches. Finally, check your rooms tonight, don't leave anything there that could be incriminating. No notes, nothing. They will be checking everything and everywhere after the attack and we don't want to leave anything around.'

They all nodded again. There was a lot of information and drills that they had gone through this morning. They were now cramming in the information, and it was beginning to show. It was now time to stop.

'I'll see all of you tomorrow, here. Please arrive at 15:30. And don't eat or drink anything after 12:30. Once you get here, there can't be any breaks. You understand? Once the mission starts nothing, and I mean nothing, can interrupt it. You must remain vigilant at all times.'

Again, no reply.

'Number one, you can go now.'

The Imam got up and unlocked the door. The young man walked through it and the Imam locked it again. The young man walked up to the end of the corridor and Zeehan opened the door. No words were spoken.

'Good. I'm busting for a leak. Can't be long now,' Zeehan whispered.

Usam nodded. It was 07:55 according to his watch. Another young man followed after two minutes and then another young man after a further two minutes and finally the Imam arrived carrying his case. Usam led the way having taken back the door key, followed by the Imam and then Zeehan. They walked in single file, briskly out of the back entrance and towards Zeehan's people carrier that was parked in the corner on its own. A pair of eyes had tracked them leaving the basement. He was concealed in the shadows, and no one ever paid any attention to him anyway.

15:30. Pope let himself through his front door. Doodle bounced down the stairs and greeted him. A bundle of fur and a wet tongue leaped up at him as he took off his coat and then his jacket. Pope patted the wildly excited little dog and walked into the kitchen. Doodle however bounced back upstairs.

'You're home early,' said Jane, turning around from the kitchen side.

'Yes. I needed some quiet time to think over a problem, so I left the madhouse.'

'Good idea. The kettle's on, I'll make a cuppa.'

'Great. I'm going to go for a run after.'

'Not over the Heath. It's really wet now and in the dark you could easily slip over.'

'No, I'm going to go for a road run instead.'

'Good. That means Doodle will stay at home.'

'Yes.'

'Daisy's convinced that there's something wrong with his bum and she's in the middle of a thorough examination.'

'I wondered what you lot got up to before I got home,' Pope quipped.

'It's not that funny. I'm thinking of having a quiet word with her. This has gone on far too long.'

Pope's brow was already furrowed. He was only half listening. Carruthers' behaviour had irked him. Seb hadn't stepped in as he'd expected and put her in her place. The mission was important and Pope felt that even though Carruthers was his boss, she lacked experience. Worse though was she didn't accept nor seek advice from people like him. People who had years of field experience. She was a loose cannon in his opinion, and she was going to make a monumental mistake. One that would cost lives, he just knew it. He was also as irked with Chris and Clare who kept on probing. Their main tactic was to lob the latest office gossip at him and see what reaction that produced. He was beginning to get fed up with their puerile behaviour and maybe it was time to bring the axe down on it.

'John. Have you even heard a word that I've said?'

'Yes, of course. Daisy is being a pain in the arse. Well, Doodle's arse, actually.'

'Very funny.'

'I'm going to go and get changed into my running gear. Pour the tea and I'll be straight down.'

Pope finished the dregs of his tea and the last mouthful of a biscuit.

'Right, I'm off then,'

Charlie burst into the kitchen and sat on the wooden stool next to Pope. In one movement her bare foot was up and almost under Pope's nose.

'Daddy, look. The rose and stem are now healed. Isn't it beautiful?'

Pope's face flushed with anger. He saw the slender foot wiggling and noticed that Charlie's toenails were painted a garish blood red. He barely registered the fresh tattoo.

'Charlie, don't push your luck,' he growled.

Pope got up and stormed out of the kitchen. Charlie's face reconfigured back into its now natural scowl.

'Charlie. Not now, Daddy's busy,' said Jane calmly.

'He's always busy,' snapped Charlie.

In the hallway Pope dug in his pocket to gather his keys and phone. He was about to put both into his waterproof running jacket when he glanced at his phone and saw eight missed calls.

Christ, he thought, logging onto the phone.

It exploded into life. Missed call from Ahmed x 2. Missed call from Chris x 3. Missed call from Clare x 1. Missed call from Control Centre x 2. A few were when he was travelling on the underground back home. The rest since then. He turned the phone over and realised that he must have accidentally set the phone to mute. He pressed redial against the last number. It was picked up instantly and he knew that he was on speaker phone at the other end.

'John. We have a crisis. I'm currently taking lead. Sandra Carruthers is on her way and she'll take over lead. The Top Floor are aware and linked into the situation. Seb Drake will also be joining us here in control,' boomed Tony Crook in a tinny voice.

'Go on.'

'Ahmed has called in from Luton mosque. A guy there has reported activity. He's seen men going into the basement. He's not sure but maybe four of them. They were carrying rucksacks and one of them is the dead spit of our friend the Hawk.'

'Jesus Christ.'

'Look, they're in there now and have been in there for we think twenty minutes.'

'Where's Deepak?'

'He's been contacted and will be back there within thirty.'

'This guy reckons that they were in there yesterday also but early in the morning. No rucksacks but the Hawk was carrying a suitcase.'

'OK. So we have good intel.'

'Ahmed thinks so.'

Pope walked into the dining room and went over to the cabinet. Charlie screwed up her face and stared at him. He should have knocked first, was her initial thought. Pope was pulling out books and folders from the cabinet and throwing them onto the dining room table. This was winding Charlie up; she was only moments away now from exploding. Pope, with the phone cradled between his ear and his shoulder, removed the large dogeared A to Z Road Atlas and put it on the dining room table. He was spinning the pages over until he found the right one. He squinted hard and tried to see the details on the large map clearly. His index finger was drawing a line from Finchley up via a blue line to a turning and then off to Luton. Charlie was leaning over and watching her dad with interest.

'Tony, I'm at home in Finchley. I'm going to leave now and head up to Luton. I'll be there in an hour.'

'Are you carrying?'

'No. I don't have a weapon on me.'

Jane had entered the room and upon hearing that comment, she folded her arms. Charlie shot her mum a worrying glance.

'We're pulling in everyone here into the control room. We've alerted the Met and they are now speaking with Beds police. Luton Fire Brigade and Luton and Dunstable hospital have been alerted and both ambulance and fire engine crews are being despatched to Luton and will rendezvous behind Luton station. We've also notified the Army and they are sending up a bomb disposal team.'

'What's the Army's ETA?'

'17:15.'

Pope put his hand over the phone. 'Where's my pair of glasses?'

Jane and Charlie looked at each other.

'I think Daisy has them,' replied Charlie meekly.

Pope dashed through the door and upstairs. He found Daisy and Doodle both standing in the bath. Daisy had the pair of spectacles in her hand. Pope snatched them and ran back downstairs. He clumsily put them on and both Charlie and Jane stood there in front of him agog. There were flecks of dog shit on his face. Also there was a small piece dangling from the end of his glasses just behind his right ear.

'Right. I'm going to Luton. I need you to read me the directions as soon as I get off of the motorway,' Pope said to Jane, pointing at the A-Z.

'Yes, John,' she replied.

'Daddy, I can google the route and check for traffic reports?' added Charlie eagerly.

'Yes,' said Pope, turning around and rushing into the kitchen.

Pope opened the kitchen drawer and scrambled around, finally pulling out a large, shiny carving knife. He turned around and in the kitchen was confronted by Jane, Charlie and Daisy. They were all staring at him with a mixture of emotions.

'Call me on my mobile before I leave, so I know that we have comms,' said Pope to Jane.

Jane dashed over to the kitchen table and picked up her phone, dialling via speed dial.

Pope, who wasn't proficient with technology, fumbled to connect to Jane's call as he was already on a call to control. Charlie leapt into action and pressed a couple of buttons on his phone.

'Hello,' said Jane.

'Good,' said Pope, hearing her both on the phone and direct as she was only two feet in front of him.

Pope dashed out of the house in his running kit, picking up his case on the way, leaving Daisy, Charlie and Jane in the kitchen.

'Does he know?' said Charlie, looking at Jane with a smirk.

'Please, Charlie,' said an exasperated Jane.

Daisy said, 'What's wrong with Daddy?'

'He's going to save the world,' chirped in Charlie.

Daisy's face was a picture of confusion and misery.

'Yes, and Doodle's poo is his camouflage,' laughed Charlie.

Daisy was about to burst into tears and Jane tried to diffuse the situation.

'It's good luck.'

Daisy smiled and then went back upstairs.

It was 16:02.

'Mummy, Mummy, quickly,' screamed Daisy.

Pope was just joining the start of the M1 near Brent Cross shopping centre. The traffic, as usual, was crawling and the journey from Finchley was excruciatingly slow. There was a GPS system in the car but he had never got to grips with it. Jane loved it and Charlie was forever fiddling with it but he was a technophobe and it was no more than an ornament. Pope relied on his memory, maps and road signs to get around. Today though, he needed assistance as he wasn't familiar with Luton nor getting there and he wished that he had learnt how to use the GPS. Now he was involving his family and that made him feel uncomfortable.

The phone, still on speaker, was sitting in its cradle.

'I'm on the M1 now.'

'OK, Daddy. Your exit is 10.'

'Exit 10. Thanks, Charlie. Where's Mum?'

'She's upstairs with Daisy. She'll be back soon.'

Pope could see that there was an incoming call and fiddled with the phone.

'John, are you there? John?' shouted Tony Crook.

'Here, Tony. What's up?'

'Just to let you know. There are three Met Trojan units on their way. They are probably forty minutes behind you but once they are on the M1 we expect them to make up time.'

The Metropolitan Police have a full-time armed response unit that are known as Trojan units. One of their duties is to provide firearm support against all terrorist activities including terrorist attacks.

'OK.'

'There's been a couple of non-related incidents in London which the Trojans have been dealing with and there's traffic jams everywhere. They've just been released and are heading up now from east London.'

'Thanks,' said Pope, and he fiddled with a couple of buttons.

'Charlie, is Mum there?'

'No. Why, is there a problem?'

'No, I was just checking. Listen, I'll be back in a minute, I just need to have a quick chat with the office. OK?'

Pope fiddled again with a couple of buttons and was back on the conference call with Tony Crook.

'Tony.'

'Yes, John.'

'Listen, have we got the CCTV pictures from outside the mosque? There must be good intel there. We should be able to ID all vehicles, their registration numbers and get facial recognition on anyone entering the front door,' said Pope.

'John, there's been a problem.'

'What type of problem?'

'The CCTV has been switched off.'

'OK, so switch it back on.'

'Unfortunately we can't. The CCTV camera was removed yesterday afternoon.'

'What!' bristled Pope. 'That camera was supposed to be there until the end of the month.'

'That's our understanding also. But it's not there now and we can't divert resources to look into that at the moment.'

'What about Team 4?'

'They were also stood down. But we are now in a crisis, so everyone is on this.'

There was a pause on the line.

'John. Sandra Carruthers has just walked in. I'm going on mute and will bring her up to speed then she'll be running the show.'

'OK.'

Pope stayed on the line.

How the hell did the CCTV get pulled? he thought to himself.

It couldn't have been a mistake. He then thought that only one person could have authorised that.

'John, are you there?' said Sandra Carruthers.

'Yes, Sandra.'

'I understand that you're going up there and you don't have any weapon, is that correct?'

Pope looked at the large, sharp carving knife lying on the passenger seat.

'That's correct, Sandra.'

'Beds police are going to have two armed officers who'll work with you.'

'OK. Can they supply me with a weapon?'

'Sorry, John.'

'What weapons will they be carrying?'

'I'll check.'

Carruthers flicked the mute button. Someone in the control room behind her was already asking that question to a senior officer in Beds police force. She received the answer in thirty seconds.

'John. Both will be carrying sidearms. They both have Glock 17 semis. They also each have Tasers and CS spray with several sets of PlastiCuffs.'

'No chance of them getting a rifle?'

'John. We go with what we've been told. Don't forget that the Trojans will be carrying a lot of firepower. The local officers are moving into a position as we speak near the mosque and will rendezvous with you when you get there. We're working on the plan at the moment. But we'll look to get everyone out of the mosque and then use the Trojans. You'll be there first and if they make any move, then you along with the two officers will contain them. We'll need our two undercover agents to be our eyes and ears on the inside.'

'Understood. Deepak isn't there yet but he's on his way.'

'OK, John. If there's any changes to the plan then we'll let you know.'

'Thanks.'

Pope continued to fiddle with the buttons on his phone without really knowing what he was actually doing. But he was able to straddle between two calls in an unwieldy fashion.

'Charlie. I've gone past Junction 9. Next up is Junction 10. Make sure that you are ready to instruct me into Luton and then up towards the mosque.'

'Yes Daddy. I've got it up on Google Maps also. It's straight forward really. You should be there in fifteen minutes, once you leave the motorway. When you get off the motorway, Luton is on your right-hand side. So you need to follow the junction around and over to the other side of the motorway. Then it's relatively straight forward.'

'Thanks.'

The sign for Junction 10 was blazoned before Pope. He glanced at his watch. It was 16:52.

'Charlie, I'm turning off now at Junction 10.'

'OK, Daddy, follow the signs to Luton. As we discussed, follow around the large roundabout over the M1. When you are on the other side, take the first left which is the A1081. It's also called New Airport Way.'

'OK, Charlie, that's clear. I'm now on the New Airport Way.'

'Daddy, you need to stay on that road for a few minutes. It's going to lead up to Luton Airport but it splits into two. The left-hand side will go up and over the top of you and onto Luton Airport. You need to get into the right-hand lane when it splits and go under it and onto a roundabout.'

'Charlie, is this the quickest way into Luton?'

'Yes. You will avoid all of the traffic. If you don't want my help then I can stop now.'

'Charlie, please.'

Pope could see that control was calling.

'Charlie, hang on. The office is calling, I'll be right back.'

Pope once again clumsily managed to reconnect with the conference call.

'John?'

'Yes, Sandra. Go ahead.'

'Listen. A target has just left the mosque. He's on foot and wearing a rucksack. He's wearing a black jacket and dark trousers that plumbers wear. The ones with many pockets. It looks like the rucksack is fairly heavy and it's bulging.'

'Right.'

'Agent Ahmed Hussain is following him and he's constantly updating us on another line. The target left about two minutes ago and he's heading towards Luton town centre.'

Pope looked at his watch. It was 16:55.

'Is Deepak Chopra at the mosque?' asked Pope.

'Yes, John. He arrived at 16:48,' answered Carruthers.

Where the hell has Deepak been? thought John. *He should have been there twenty minutes ago.*

'John. Target is still heading into town. We are running assessment now,' said Carruthers calmly. 'Can you change course and head now to the town centre? The police unit have been alerted and they are heading into the town centre where they'll meet up with you. We've also alerted the Trojan units and the Army bomb disposal team who are making great time and may beat you there.'

'I'll just drop off for a minute,' said Pope, who was again pressing buttons with more fury now.

'Charlie. Listen up. I need to go straight into the town centre now and not to the mosque. Does that change my route?'

'No, Daddy. I'm a genius. The route that you are going on will take you straight into the town centre,' Charlie said smugly.

'I'll be right back,' said Pope, reconnecting with the conference call.

'John. The target is still heading into the town centre. The consensus is that he's going to go into London. There's no high-value target in Luton this evening. We think that he's going to go into London and set off his bomb either on the underground, bus or maybe even in Theatreland.'

'No,' said Pope emphatically. 'He going to Wembley. He's targeting the football match this evening.'

Carruthers stood up from leaning over the speaker phone. And with dramatic effect, she rolled her eyes up. Everyone in the room was watching her.

'John, we've run an assessment and it's highly likely that this is another copycat of the 7/7 attack.'

The 7/7 attack, as it was known, was an orchestrated attack on London's public transport on 7th July 2005.

'But he's on his own and an attack at the football match would make more sense,' railed Pope.

Carruthers was leaning forward towards the speaker phone, ready to make another pronouncement when she felt a slight squeeze of her elbow. Seb Drake was now standing at her side.

'John, Seb Drake here. Thanks for raising that with us. We need to also include Wembley as a potential target. We'll start on that right now and come back.'

Carruthers shot Drake a look but he ignored her and said loudly, 'Factor in an attack at Wembley, everyone, and let's get an updated plan out pronto. John, head to Luton town station, we'll tell your police guys to meet you outside the main ticket office and we'll advise the bomb disposal team to head there.'

Pope left the call.

'Charlie, I'm in the right-hand lane and going towards the roundabout.'

'OK. At the roundabout, turn left onto Kimpton Road. Then you go straight ahead. You will come to a roundabout. Just carry on straight. You are still on the Kimpton Road.'

'Thanks, Charlie. You are doing a fantastic job. I need to go direct to Luton station now. Can you check and let me know the route?'

Charlie was pleased to be praised. It was exciting being involved in a real-life drama. Much better than the dramas that she and many of her friends at school were embellishing daily. Charlie set the phone onto camera mode and then took a close-up photo of her tattoo. She looked at the tattoo, bristling with love and admiration for it. She then sent a copy of the photo to her dad's phone. Pope heard the ping notifying him that he had just received a new email. He wasn't that sure how he'd access the email and keep on the line with the two calls. He had no choice but to check the email. It could be critical to the mission. He again fiddled with a few buttons and accessed his email account. He then clicked on the email and saw a colour picture. His blood literally boiled.

'What the fuck?' Pope shouted, thumping the steering wheel with his fist.

In front of Pope was a 1990 white Transit Cargo van trundling along. It was sitting low at the back straining under the weight that the owner/driver was carrying. He closed the gap quickly and stuck his nose out to overtake. There were cars coming in the opposite direction and there was little room to make a move. Pope saw that in front of the slow-moving transit van was a yawning gap. The driver touched his break several times and then slowed down. Pope tried to swerve out but was met by honking horns from cars driving on the opposite side of the road. He took a gamble and accelerated out. Unfamiliar with the road, he didn't recognise how close he was to the roundabout that Charlie had mentioned and had no choice but to break and remain behind the van. He saw the van driver angrily gesticulating in his wing mirror.

Pope quickly pressed a few buttons and said, 'Charlie, I've just gone over the roundabout. What's up next?'

'OK, at the end of this road, turn right onto Windmill Road and head onto the next roundabout.'

Pope tried to overtake again but the van moved out also and cut off any opportunity to overtake. Pope pounded on his horn. The van driver pounded back and slowed even more whilst hitting the breaks several times, which lit up the break lights. With the steady stream of traffic coming on the other side of the road, Pope had no opportunity to overtake this road hog. The road was finishing. It was a T junction and the Transit van slowed gently to a stop. The little man in a flat cap and bottle-top glasses leant out of the window and screamed a volley of obscenities at Pope.

Pope wound down the passenger window and shouted out, 'Oi, who are you calling a cunt? You fucking cunt!'

Pope accelerated forward and was level with the Transit van. The old man who was still hanging out of the driver window angrily banged his fist on the roof of Pope's car. Pope saw the gap and skidded away, leaving the van driver sitting there.

'Daddy, you owe a lot of money to the swear box,' said Charlie with mock indignation.

'Charlie, not now please.'

Pope was hurtling towards the next roundabout. He checked his mirror and the Transit van had turned left at the T junction and was becoming a speck as it drove slowly away from Pope.

'Approaching the roundabout now. Which exit, Charlie?'

'Take the second cunting left,' replied Charlie. 'It's called St Mary's Road. Go straight ahead. It becomes Church Street and you take the third cunting turning on your left.'

Jane had just walked into the dining room.

'What did you just say?' shouted Jane.

Charlie's head swivelled and she was surprised to see her mum almost behind her.

'Nothing.'

'I've told you that you never use the C word,' Jane said crossly. 'John?' she went on, looking for support.

'Not now please. Anyway, is everything OK?' Pope said, driving with focus as he increased his speed.

'Just great. Doodle had massive diarrhoea and Daisy slipped over in it. Luckily they were both in the bath. I've cleaned up the mess. Daisy needed a scrub down and she's now in bed in a state of shock. Doodle needed a doggie shampoo and he's in his bed in the kitchen. Daisy's clothes are all in the washing machine now but I needed to hand wash them first. Just great.'

'Not good,' Pope said, trying to show sympathy for Jane's trials and tribulations.

'Right, Charlie, I'm approaching third left. Where now?'

'Turn. Go straight ahead. Directly on your right is Luton station.'

'Thanks, Charlie.'

'Daddy, did you like the photo I sent you? I think that the rose will look better when I take a photo of it in natural sunlight.'

BZZZZ.

'Hello? Daddy, are you there?'

Charlie looked at her mum, annoyed.

'Well, how rude. I direct him to Luton and he cuts me off.'

'Charlie, he's really busy, you understand that. Anyway, I haven't forgotten about your language and we'll have a chat later,' Jane said, picking up her phone and walking out of the dining room.

Pope's hands were gripping the steering wheel tightly and he released his grip slightly.

'John, the Trojans are probably twenty-five minutes away now. Your two police contacts are standing at the ticket window. The Army guys are there and setting up in a room that you can use,' said Carruthers. 'There's now a large police presence at St Pancreas station and they are already looking for anyone wearing a rucksack who fits the MO. All trains are still running normally, we don't want to alert them. There could be someone monitoring the news.'

Pope was now on the road leading up to the station. He looked at his watch. It was now 17:02. He pulled up just past the station and mounted the pavement.

'I'm here now. Patch me through to Deepak,' he said, picking up the phone and also the large carving knife that was lying motionless on the passenger seat on top of his case.

The Imam had completed the bombs building process. Everything had been triple checked and the three rucksacks were packed tight. He had the bags of nuts, bolts, nails and washers sitting on the bed. His travel case was packed and also sitting on the bed along side the tradesman tool bag. The large wrench was out and on the bed along with a few other tools.

The Imam walked downstairs and into the kitchen. The old man was sitting at the table eating a broth. The Imam walked up behind him and in one swift movement, drew his janbiya and slit his throat. The old man coughed and his hands went to his throat. There was no chance of stemming the flow of blood. His head lolled forward and his life ebbed away. The old woman, who was standing at the kitchen sink, turned around and witnessed her husband take his last breath. She stood her ground, eyes burning with hatred, and the Imam walked over to her, took out the front door key that she kept in her right trouser pocket and calmly slit her throat. She fell to the ground immediately, a crumpled mess swimming slowly in her own blood. The Imam ran the knife under the tap and left the kitchen. He returned with a number of tools and went to the cupboard that contained the gas meter. The gas joint was loosened sufficiently, thus causing a leak. He checked and was happy that it was a small leak only. He then left the kitchen, making sure that he avoided the dark red pools of blood that were covering parts of the kitchen floor. He repacked all of the plumbing tools and carried the heavy bag downstairs. He went up and brought down the travel case that was now very light along with the bags of nuts, bolts, nails and washers. He then went up and carried down each of the fairly heavy rucksacks. Everything was now stored by the door. He went back upstairs and checked the bathroom and then the bedroom for anything that could be evidence of his stay there. Once satisfied, he walked back down and stood in the front room, looking out at the street.

14:35. The black people carrier pulled up outside the mid-terrace house and Usam got out and walked up to the door. The Imam opened the door and passed him the tradesman tool bag. They quickly ferried all of the items from in the hallway into the people carrier and then left. When they arrived at the mosque, Zeehan parked in the same spot. As ordered by the Imam, they each carried a rucksack and bags of nuts, bolts, nails and washers and went into the mosque in single file via the back door. Once inside, they made their way to the door that led down to the basement. Usam was taking the lead and out from a side corridor, a small elderly man appeared. Usam didn't have time to alter his course and pushed the elderly man aside. The elderly man who was small and frail was caught out and fell backwards onto the floor.

'Out of the way, old man,' said Usam with disdain.

The old man grimaced. Falling over was painful for someone who was riddled with arthritis and he sat there, struggling to get his breath regulated. The three-man team walked on without stopping to check whether the old man had injured himself. He watched them from his sitting position as they headed off. When they had got into their room in the basement and the three rucksacks were sitting on the table, the Imam tuned to Usam.

'Who was that old man?'

'He's nobody. He hangs around here and he cleans the rooms. They give him drinks and some sandwiches for his work. Don't worry, no one ever talks to him.'

'OK. Take your posts, the martyrs will be here soon.'

Usam and Zeehan went back down to the door where they generally stood guard and the Imam locked the door from the inside once again.

15:35. All three of the young men were seated in their places in the room with the Imam seated opposite them. He had checked that they all had their burner phones and only the contact numbers of each other in the phones. They all were wearing their watches and the times on each of the watches was synchronised. And he could see that they were all wearing the jackets and trousers that they needed for the mission.

'First I want all of you to see your final messages. They are great messages, this is a great moment and you all are great people.'

They all smiled. He was a master of manipulation.

'Gather round and we can watch each of them. I'll use the playback function on the camcorder.'

The three young men stood behind the Imam, looked into the small viewfinder and watched and listened to their messages. It had a powerful, galvanising effect on the group.

Ahmed was walking through the mosque when he saw the little cleaner limping.

'Hey, how's it going? Are you OK?' said Ahmed with concern.

No one bothered talking to the old man. He had been working at the mosque for several years now without much recognition from anyone. He studied Ahmed for a minute with suspicion.

'I'm OK.'

'You are limping though. I've seen you around and you walk normally. Have you had an accident?' asked a concerned Ahmed.

'It wasn't an accident. I was attacked,' said the little old man.

'Attacked? What happened?'

'I was walking out the back. Just going to get a broom and then three of them bumped into me and knocked me over. Same group that was here yesterday morning in the basement.'

'Really? Can you describe them?'

'Two young guys who come here regularly with their families. One's a cab driver and his car is outside. The other one is an Imam. Not a regular. I saw him here a few months ago and he disappeared. They were all carrying a rucksack.'

'Where are they now?'

'In the basement. You won't get in there. They stand at the bottom of the stairs and guard it. The only ones allowed in are the others.'

'What others? Who are they?'

'Don't know. Young guys, not from around here. I don't know, there could be two or even five of them.'

'Listen. You take care. I just remembered that I need to make a call. See you later,' said Ahmed as he headed off towards the rear of the mosque.

He went out into the car park and recognised Zeehan's people carrier. This was the one that the Hawk used last time he was here. Ahmed dialled Pope's number but it wasn't connected. He dialled Chris Gould and explained what he had just heard. Chris asked whether Ahmed had spoken with Pope yet. Ahmed said no, he wasn't getting a connection. Chris tried Pope also but wasn't getting connected. Chris spoke with Clare in whispered tones and they jointly agreed that this was a potential crisis. Chris sent out the relevant message and headed into the control room. People were moving swiftly into the control room and Tony Crook as senior person there took the lead. Ahmed was on speaker phone and repeated everything that the cleaner had told him. He was told to go back inside, monitor the basement and send regular updates. Control would set up and they'd advise him of the plan.

Ahmed walked back into the mosque and moved around to a position where he could discreetly surveil the basement entrance. He dialled Deepak who picked up the phone after several rings.

'Dee, I need you at the mosque now,' whispered Ahmed.

'Oh. I'm in Cambridge,' replied Deepak cheerfully.

'Please don't tell me you are doing your other job,' growled Ahmed.

'Yes. Someone was ill and they—'

Ahmed interrupted Deepak. 'Get the fuck back here now. We have a major situation. The Hawk is here and there's guys running around with rucksacks.'

'Shit. I'm on my way.'

Ahmed cut the call and dialled Chris Gould.

'Chris, Deepak is on his way. He'll be here in forty minutes.'

'I'll pass it on. Also I'll dial back from the crisis number and then you're hooked in.'

Ahmed cut the call. Deepak needed to put his foot down and if he did then forty minutes was doable. Ahmed looked at his watch. It was 15:45.

16:10. The group in the basement were all sitting back in their usual chairs. The Imam had put the camcorder back on the table. He was calm and not exuding his normal menace. The three martyrs fed off of his more relaxed posture and they in turn were not tense. He wanted them to be focused and not feeling too much pressure. Feeling pressure was when people made mistakes and he wanted this group to react and behave as they had trained.

'I want each of you to talk me through what you will be doing from the moment that you leave the mosque. Number one, why don't you start?' the Imam said, smiling.

The group sat there and listened to each of them repeat the plan, timings and their own particular tasks. All of the while the Imam nodded, smiled and occasionally said the word 'Good'. Everything was going well. They all knew to the minute what time they were to leave the basement, right through to their final position and the time that the world would change for ever.

16:30. The Imam got up and smiled at all of them. 'I will leave now. It's part of the mission.'

He then hugged each of them and again told them that they'd made great messages, were on a great mission and were great people.

He picked up the camcorder and before walking to the locked door, said to them, 'Now, fill up all of your pockets in your jackets and trousers with the plastic bags of nuts, bolts, nails and washers.'

'Shall we remove them from their bags?' asked number two.

'No need. It's better to leave them in the bags. Easier to transport. I'll leave the door unlocked now and the guards will also come with me for our part of this great mission.'

They all nodded; the Imam was also going on a dangerous, secret mission. With that, he swept out the door.

Mr Butt was flustered and deeply upset.

'Ahmed, I have the most terrible news,' he said, planting both hands on Ahmed's shoulders and turning him around to face him.

Mr Butt started to walk slowly but Ahmed's feet weren't moving in time with him. Ahmed had reluctantly turned around from facing the basement door but he wasn't going to desert his post. They both slowly walked a few steps into a side room and Ahmed deliberately left the door open. He did not have direct sight of the door leading to the basement and wanted this impromptu meeting over asap. If Mr Butt entered into one of his monologues, then he had no choice but to leave him in the room as there was something afoot and he needed to be on his A game.

'Ahmed, it's awful. Have you heard?' said Mr Butt tearfully.

'No, I haven't. What's happened?' replied Ahmed, trying to sound interested.

'It's the Ali family. There's been a terrible accident.'

'Which one, Mr Butt? There's quite a few Ali families in the community.'

'A terrible, terrible accident,' rambled on Mr Butt, not really hearing Ahmed's question.

'We don't have all the details but the Saudis have confirmed it's them. It was an accident.'

'Right. What happened?' said Ahmed, frustrated that Mr Butt was not being articulate.

'It happened at the Hajj on Monday. They were in a van and it lost control and hit an oncoming lorry. Everyone in the van was killed instantly. The old man, Mr Ali, and the son, Hamiza.'

'What! I know Hamiza. That's horrific.'

'That's what I've been saying. This trip had been planned for a number of years. They were all so much looking forward to it.'

'Well, thanks for letting me know. I will pray for them and their families.'

'Yes. Ahmed, you are a good boy. I'll speak with you later when I get more details.'

Ahmed turned around and resumed his place opposite the basement entrance.

Outside in the car park, the three shadowy characters got quickly into the people carrier and left the car park. They started the journey back to the Afghanis' house.

'Shouldn't we have remained with them and guard them? What if something happens?' Usam queried.

'Nothing will happen,' spat the Imam.

The journey back was conducted in stony silence. The people carrier pulled up outside the mid-terrace abode of the Afghanis.

'Usam, can you come inside?' asked the Imam firmly.

'Oh. OK,' Usam replied.

They walked quickly to the front door and the Imam produced a door key from inside his thobe. He unlocked the front door and Usam followed him inside. Usam stood in the hallway awaiting his next instruction.

'They are in the kitchen. Please, after you,' said the Imam calmly, standing aside to let Usam pass.

Usam walked unsuspectingly into the kitchen. Once inside he was greeted by carnage. The pools of blood were dark now and there was a metallic smell in the air. He was about to gag when a sharp blade cut deep across his neck. It came from behind and cut both carotid arteries on both sides of his neck as well as slicing deep into his throat. His hands instinctively came up and felt the gushing blood flow out. He was in a state of shock and there was a shove from behind. He fell forward and thrashed about on the floor. It was to no avail; the wound was deep, deliberate and mortal. His assassin stood back, watching the helpless fish thrash about. It was over quickly and the Imam was able to find a bloodless path to the kitchen sink and clean the janbiya. He re-sheathed his killing knife and carefully left the kitchen. He relocked the front door and sat in the seat behind Zeehan.

'Where's Usam?' asked Zeehan suspiciously.

'He's staying with the old couple and helping them. After you drop me off, go back and pick him up. He'll be finished by then.'

The Imam then told Zeehan an address to drive to. Zeehan knew the road and drove off.

16:48. Deepak entered the mosque and saw Ahmed prowling the edge of a small square with a phone pressed to his right ear.

'Deepak's onsite,' whispered Ahmed, nodding to Deepak.

'Roger that,' replied Carruthers. 'Get him to join the call.'

Ahmed muted his phone and showed Deepak the number displayed and said, 'Dial this number. You need to get onto the call.'

Deepak dialled in.

'Are you up to speed?' asked Carruthers.

'Yes. Ahmed has been updating me whilst I was getting here.'

'Good. Then you know the plan,' said Carruthers, who was clearly enjoying being the centre of attention.

16:52. The door to the basement opened and out walked a young man wearing a black ski jacket. It had four pockets on the front of it and one pocket on each of the sleeves. The grey pants had external pockets. The wearer of the clothes was hooded and looked like a Michelin Man with all the pockets burgeoning. He was slightly straining from carrying the rucksack but stood up erect and walked towards the front door.

'Target on the move,' said Ahmed into the phone as he turned sideways to avoid eye contact with him.

There was a stir in control as everyone waited for the next order. Seb Drake stood up and looked at Carruthers.

'Follow target and report. Do not engage,' said Carruthers. 'Chopra, remain on station.'

'Copy that,' said Ahmed as he headed briskly towards the front door.

'Copy that,' said Deepak as he slunk back into the corner.

Ahmed poked his head outside and saw the young man heading off towards the town centre. He held back and waited until the young man had turned the corner at the end of the road and then set off. He had already given an accurate description of the clothes, rucksack, height and approximate weight of his quarry. The information was spinning out into ether. Control, MI5 analyst teams, Beds police, the Met police, GCHQ, Army bomb disposal unit and John Pope were all getting verbal and electronic updates. The CCTV in Luton was all being invaded by GCHQ who were now looking to hunt the terrorist remotely. They would share the images but wanted to get a photo and then search all face recognition databases and put a name to the person. Once identified, MI5 teams would search for relatives, contacts and known associates. There would be knocks on doors when he had been neutralised.

16:54. The door to the basement opened and another young man exited from it. He was dressed in similar garb to his confederate and he was also carrying a rucksack. He looked around the small square and reset the rucksack on his back before heading off towards the front door. There was only a couple of people milling around and a young guy who was on his phone with his back to him. He didn't feel threatened by what he saw and thought only about getting to the train station on time.

'Target Two on the move,' whispered Deepak.

'Say again,' replied a strained Carruthers.

'Target Two on the move. He's going out the front door. Dressed the same as Target One and carrying a rucksack.'

Carruthers looked at Seb Drake who remained impassive.

'Seb, there could be more in the basement. Also we haven't seen the Hawk leave yet,' she said.

Seb waited, thinking through the options.

'I recommend that Chopra stays put. The Hawk is a high-value target,' she went on.

'I concur. It could be that the two that are out in the field are the two that arrived with the Hawk and he's next. Unlikely though because the planners don't sacrifice themselves.'

Carruthers nodded. 'Chopra. Stay on station.'

Carruthers didn't hear Deepak reply, 'Copy that.'

She told Command Comms to tell GCHQ that there was now another target and that they needed to track him on CCTV.

'Just stuck my head out. Target Two is heading towards town,' piped up Deepak.

16:56. Deepak spied another young man leaving the basement. He walked away as he talked into his mobile phone.

The young man, wearing a rucksack and dressed similar to the other two guys, headed towards the front door, paying no attention to anyone in the mosque.

The news that there was now a third person carrying a rucksack reverberated around control. Whatever was being planned was big and it was going to happen soon. Once again, Carruthers directed Deepak to stay put. He needed to keep an eye on what the bombers HQ was and report back any further developments including if there were any more bombers leaving there. GCHQ were tracking Target One and could see Ahmed in pursuit. As yet they hadn't picked up Target Two and now they had a third target to find and follow. Deepak was able to confirm that Target Three, like the two others, was heading towards the town centre.

17:15. The people carrier drew up outside the self-store garage. It was the final one at the end of a long row of self-store garages. Like all of the other garages, it had a moss-green rollover door.

'OK, this is it,' said Zeehan.

The Imam was sitting directly behind him and leant over. The janbiya was pressed against Zeehan's throat. A man emerged from the shadows next to the last garage and opened Zeehan's driver door. He produced a cloth from his coat pocket and pressed it hard over Zeehan's mouth and nose. Zeehan's eyes widened, confirming that he was in a state of panic. The knife pressing firmly to his throat meant that Zeehan complied. It took a couple of minutes for halothane to have its desired effect. His pupils rolled, then his eyelids shut and he fell unconscious. The nephew pushed Zeehan's limp body over and sat in the driver's seat. The Imam picked up his light travel case and the heavy tradesman tool bag and got out of the people carrier. He placed both bags next to the garage door. The door had already been unlocked by his nephew who had made the necessary preparations in the garage. The Imam bent down and rolled up the door. The car slowly rolled in and the garage door was closed. The nephew stopped the car and went around to the back of it. He had a long hose and clip that he took off a hook on the wall. He busied himself attaching the hose to the hot exhaust pipe.

Once he was satisfied that the hose was secure, he took the other end of it and went to the driver's window which he slightly opened and fed it into the car. He then fetched an old 45lb barbell plate that was lying on the floor and went back to the driver's side. He started up the car, checking that it was in neutral, placed the barbell on the accelerator and closed the door. The engine roared and the deadly gas spewed into the car. He checked through the window that everything was working as he expected and then checked that the exhaust pipe and hose was secure. He gave a thumbs up to the Imam and they both exited the garage which was then locked. The two bags were picked up and they both casually walked up the road and around the corner. Once inside the car, the Imam looked at his watch.

'17:28. Good. Let's go to Harwich. We can have something to eat there. Our ferry is not until 23:00 so we'll have time to stretch our legs also. We can dump the tool bag somewhere on the way.'

The nephew nodded and started the car. He wasn't looking forward to another sea crossing. The sea sickness tablets that he took coming over were useless.

Pope jogged up to the station entrance. The crowds were already beginning to backlog to the end of the road and there was a jam as people tried to get through the four meagre ticket barriers. The two burly police officers were standing inside the station entrance shying away from the fine rain that was spraying down on this cold winter's evening. Their breath was forming clouds as they peered out. Pope stopped in front of them on the pavement which made them look even taller. Both were wearing hi-viz jackets.

'Mr Brown, MI5,' Pope said, thrusting out his ID card.

'PC Jones and PC Wilmot,' said PC Jones. 'We have a room and the Army boys are setting up in there. Follow me.'

Pope followed the two PCs into the station door beside the main counter and then down a corridor. The third door on the right was ajar and they went inside. Pope quickly looked around the smallish room and saw that in addition to the four military men there were also four people dressed in Thameslink rail uniforms.

He said to the Army group, 'Who's in charge?'

'I am. Sergeant Richards, and we are setting up in the corner. One chap is putting on the bomb suit as you can see. The other two are helping him get into it. One of them will drive the bomb disposal robot if it's needed and the other one is backup. We have brought a spare bomb suit and three shields. We're five minutes away from being ready to go.'

'Good. I'm Mr Brown from MI5 and I'm the lead person here. PC Jones and PC Wilmot will support me.'

There were nods all round.

Pope then looked at the four railway people and said, 'This could become a lethal zone if we bring in someone carrying a bomb. I suggest that you all make yourselves scarce.'

'It's my station and I'm bleeding staying,' said the portly, balding man.

Pope shrugged his shoulders as the other three left the room sprightly.

Pope put his phone to his ear and said, 'Ahmed. John here. Can you see what Target One has in his hands.'

'John, I've been close up and now I'm back in the crowd. I can confirm that he isn't wearing gloves and that he has nothing in his hands.'

'Good. That means it's not a suicide vest. What about his jacket? Is it extra thick?'

'It's a ski jacket and bulky but I can't confirm that he's got any extra protection under it.'

'Ahmed, thanks. I'll be back shortly.'

Pope beckoned the two PCs over and they stood in a tight group.

'OK, the target is wearing a thick ski jacket and trousers both with external pockets. I want us to be outside near the end of this road. I'll be nearest the railway side. PC Jones will be on the far side. We all walk up behind him. PC Wilmot will overtake him and turn around and say to me, "Hi, Bob, are you going to the match?" Then you Taser him in his left thigh. We'll grab his arms and keep them away from his body. Ahmed will be right behind and he'll cover the rucksack. We'll march him into this room then cuff his hands in front of him and his ankles and his knees. PC Jones will do the cuffing. If he moves then PC Wilmot will Taser him again. Once he's incapacitated the Army guys will remove the rucksack. I'll then cut off his clothes as he could be booby trapped. We need to be quick as there are another two targets coming and we need go back out and take them down as they come in.'

'What? There's three bombers?' yelped PC Wilmot.

'Yes, so far,' replied Pope.

'We haven't been getting much intel from our HQ,' bemoaned PC Jones.

'Listen, it is what it is. Often in a crisis information doesn't all get through to the front line. But we have everything and we have a plan, agreed?'

'Yes, agreed.' They nodded.

Pope looked at the Army crew who were working feverishly.

'Guys. We going to bring them in one at a time. We'll cuff them then you take off their rucksacks and work on them. I'll check them out for any other surprises. So far we expect three of them but the situation is fluid.'

'Right. We'll get another suit on then,' shouted Sergeant Richards.

Pope went on the phone and explained to Ahmed exactly what he wanted from him and what everyone else was going to do who was involved in executing the plan. Pope knew that control was on the phone and that they could demand a change to the plan. There was no objection raised.

'Get rid of your viz jackets, guys. This isn't the time to let everyone know you are about,' smiled Pope, who was wearing his tatty old running gear.

17:17. The crowds were moving slowly towards the station along the road. Ahmed raised his hand and Pope and the two PCs moved out from the side and moved into their positions behind Target One. PC Wilmot then moved forward and in front of Target One before turning around.

'Hi, Bob, are you going to the match?' said PC Wilmot, looking at Pope.

Whilst the words were spilling out, PC Wilmot's Taser swung up from his side and fired from almost point-blank range into the left thigh of Target One. He counted to four in his head as he held the trigger. That was enough for anyone to lose muscle control and fall over. Pope and PC Jones had Target One in arm locks and Ahmed was holding the rucksack. The group quickened their pace and dragged the limp terrorist between them into the station and then into their seconded room.

The immobilised and disorientated terrorist was sat on the floor and the PlastiCuffs quickly bound to his wrists, ankles and knees. The Taser prongs were left in his thigh and PC Wilmot was ready to administer another long dose if the bomber put up any form of struggle. Sergeant Richards swooped over the inert figure and looked all around the straps of the bomb, delicately pulling here and there. Once satisfied that the rucksack wasn't boobytrapped, he unclipped it slowly and then gently removed it. He carried it over to the corner where one of the guys was wearing a bomb suit and put it on the wooden table. The three shields were placed around the bomb disposal expert as extra protection for everyone else in room. In such an enclosed space, this actually offered little protection if the bomb were to detonate.

Pope was kneeling over the bomber who was slowly coming to. The two PCs were stationed beside him. Pope started to check over the jacket, looking for any trip wires, but it was clean. He unzipped it slowly, cautiously looking inside the jacket as he did so but again there was no evidence of trip wires. The jacket was undone. Pope checked under each sleeve for any trip wires. He then went behind the bomber and lifted the jacket up above his head and examined his back. Pope stood up and withdrew a large carving knife from inside his running jacket. Both PCs gave quizzical looks but said nothing. Pope felt gently around the bomber's chest and abdomen and then sliced through his T shirt, exposing his front. He checked under his armpits and then went behind him before performing the same exercise again.

Ahmed was listening in on the phone for any external developments and was giving a running commentary of everything happening in the room.

'John. First Trojan unit has just pulled up outside and they are coming in,' said Ahmed with an air of authority.

'I'll go out and bring them in here,' said the portly station manager as he waddled off.

The bomber's eyes were open and he was taking in his surroundings. Pope looked at him, their faces only inches apart.

'Stay still,' Pope said menacingly.

The bomber wriggled slightly but realised that he was bound tight. Pope slowly removed both of his trainers and checked inside them before placing them to the side and away from the bomber. Sergeant Richards was conferring with the soldier in the bomb suit and turned around.

'Mr Brown, can we have a word?' Richards barked with typical army authority.

Pope jumped up and walked over to their corner.

'We've unpacked this baby. It wasn't primed. They were going to have to set the detonator manually by putting the battery into the clock. It was set for eight minutes before it would go off. It would definitely be lethal up to a fifteen-yard radius. We haven't seen anything like this before.'

Pope picked up his phone and repeated everything that Sergeant Richards had told him for control's benefit. He went back to the bomber and pulled off first his right sock before checking his foot and the sock. He then pulled off his left sock and stared intently. His got up and kicked the bomber in the chest and then grabbed him by the collar before delivering a right cross onto the chin of the defenceless man. The two PCs and Ahmed grabbed Pope and pulled him away.

'Calm down,' said PC Wilmot.

Pope was distracted as the office door was opened by the station manager and in walked two Trojans carrying Heckler & Koch MP5SF 9mm carbines slung across their chests.

Pope looked at them, recognising that they worked as a three-man team which meant that the driver had remained in the car.

'Where are the other two Trojan units?' Pope said, regaining his composure.

'We got separated due to the volume of people making their way to the station. They are two minutes behind us.'

Ahmed was leaning down and talking quietly to the manacled man who was now bleeding from a cut in his mouth.

'Bruv, your boss smells of dog shit.'

Ahmed nodded.

Outside in the road, the two Trojan units pulled in amidst the mass of people heading towards the station. They had been made aware via their comms that Target Two and Target Three were now together and heading along the last eighty-five metres to the station. GHHQ had managed to pick them both up on CCTV and were relaying the route to both the Met Police and control. The Trojans jumped out of their cars and ran towards the two unsuspecting terrorists. Pope realised that the bombs in the rucksacks would have had to have been made by the same bomb maker and therefore they would need to have been manually activated. He sprinted out of the room and then out into the main throng. He was trying to push his way against a sea of humanity that was pressing onward towards the trains that would take them into the suburbs of London and then onto Wembley.

He was desperately pushing his way through the crowd, and he bellowed, 'The bombs are inactive. The bombs are inactive.'

The Trojans had formed a semi-circle line and had both bombers caught in their crosshairs. People were screaming and panicking as they pushed, ran and fell over each other to get away from the kill zone. There was fear everywhere and a huge gap opened up around the two would-be bombers. The bombers stopped and turned to face their assailants.

The Trojans were screaming at them but in the melee no one could hear anything. One of the bombers started to move behind the other one. The Trojans were still screaming but he continued on his journey.

Both of the bombers were now shouting, 'Allahu Akbar.' God is Great.

The Trojans unleashed their Heckler & Koch MP5SF weapons. The sound was deafening. It filled the ink sky and drowned out the screams from the terrified innocents who were only guilty of being in the wrong place at the wrong time. The innocents were scattering everywhere and fleeing the killing zone. The two bombers fell to the ground, blood pouring out of multiple wounds, and their short lives were spent.

Pope rushed up to the scene screaming now, 'Stop. Stop. We need them alive.'

The Trojans had ceased their rage of gunfire after seven seconds. It was over that quickly. They turned towards Pope with their weapons still smoking.

'They have valuable information. We wanted them captured alive. Their bombs weren't armed,' shouted Pope.

'I have the safety of the public to consider. I also have the safety of my men to consider. I don't want to call a spouse and say that their husband won't be coming home tonight,' said the inspector who was in charge of the three-car team.

Pope looked at him and then at the lifeless bodies and realised that the inspector was right. The Trojans had acted based on the information that they had and they had acted in the correct manner. It was the only course of action that they could have taken.

'Yes, you are right,' Pope said with sincerity.

There was loud gun report and everyone turned back towards the station. Pope and the Trojans instantaneously broke into a sprint. There was no one in their path as everyone had already fled. They all rushed into the room with Pope taking the lead with the exception of two Trojans who remained standing over the two dead would-be terrorists. The bomber was lying on the floor near the corner where the Army bomb disposal team had dismantled and analysed the first rucksack.

'What happened?' panted Pope.

'Bloody fool just upped and made a lunge towards the rucksack. The armed officer saw him making the move and fired,' said Sergeant Richards.

Pope looked at Ahmed who just nodded. Pope realised that any chance of getting valuable intel was rapidly disappearing, but he also knew that the Trojan had acted correctly. The Trojan had just arrived and wasn't to know that the bomb had been rendered inoperable.

The body of the manacled bomber lay partially clothed in a heap on the floor. His left foot was facing upwards and on his instep was a skull and crossbones in vivid colours.

Pope talked into his phone.

'Three bombers down. They have been neutralised. We need to get back to the mosque and round up whoever is there. Deepak, are you there?'

'Yes, John.'

'Any movement from the basement?'

'No, John.'

'OK, we're coming over,' said Pope. 'Right, let's get over to the mosque. I'll jump in one of your cars.'

Pope paused and then said, 'PC Wilmot and PC Jones, great job. Can you stay here and liaise with the locals? The forensics will need to document both scenes and then the bodies will need to be picked up. We need to keep the public from tramping all over the area. We'll want prints and anything else we can get off of the bodies asap. You Army guys need to go out and check that those rucksacks are not primed and that the two bombers aren't boobytrapped.'

'John. You need to go,' said Carruthers. 'We'll sort this end out with Beds police and other services.'

'Right,' said Pope, picking up his carving knife and putting it back in his jacket. 'Ahmed, you're with me.'

Pope and Ahmed were sitting in the back of the second BMW fast pursuit car.

'Ahmed, we need you to remain undercover. We'll drop you off at the end of the road and you can make your own way to the mosque.'

'OK, John.'

'Do we have permission to enter the mosque?' asked John over the phone.

'Confirmed by Legal. Under the Prevention of Terrorism Act, no warrant is necessary. Try not to be too heavy-handed with the local community, but rounding up the others is your priority,' said Carruthers.

Pope removed his phone and told the driver and other Trojans in the car what he had been told and that they would be dropping Ahmed off, who would still be operating as an undercover agent. The Trojan who was on comms relayed the message to the other two cars as they sped through Luton. John then told the driver to also relay to the team that there was another undercover agent onsite and described him in detail. Pope wanted to make sure that Deepak was neither identified as being an undercover agent nor shot by the Trojans.

Ahmed jumped out of the car at the end of the road and started walking briskly towards the mosque. It looked tranquil on this quiet street but that was all about to change. The first Trojan car went into the car park and stopped outside the rear entrance. The other two cars pulled up outside the front entrance. The Trojans with Pope taking the lead headed to the front door. At the same time, two Trojans entered the back door. Once inside, Pope walked towards where Deepak was stationed. He was listening to Deepak on his phone guiding him there. Men, women and children panicked when they saw several heavily armed police officers dressed as Storm Troopers and a bloke in tatty running gear walking through the mosque. The Trojans took up defensive positions in the small square with their firepower aimed at the basement door. Pope spoke to Deepak and got confirmation that no one had exited the basement since the third and last bomber at 16:56. Pope spoke to the inspector and agreed that the Trojans would go into the basement straight away. The two Trojans who had entered by the rear door had appeared and now their number swelled to seven. There was one Trojan outside the rear door and another Trojan outside the front door covering the only two access points into and out of the mosque. Local police units were now in position at the end of each entrance to the road and the road was blocked off. An ambulance and two fire appliances were also minutes away.

Beds police had been sending all available units to Luton since the ballon went up. The phalanx of police vehicles was congregated mainly around Luton station and the officers who were not dealing with preserving the scenes where three terrorists were shot dead were dealing with crowd control. There was near pandemonium caused by it being rush hour and the extra volume of people who were planning on going to the football match. The football crowd who were close to the incident had dispersed and panicked, but there were others who hadn't witnessed the events and were now arriving. Some were demanding access to get their train, but the police cordon was up and no one was getting into the station. Trains now were no longer stopping at Luton. The trains at the station were sitting at red lights and the passengers on the trains were getting no information, nor were the doors being opened.

Along the rail tracks, trains were slowing down and backlogs were beginning. The local news companies had received calls, as had local radio stations, and their reporters were dashing towards the station. This was their five minutes of fame. Their reporting would make national TV, radio and newspapers and would then disperse around the globe. Another task for Beds police to juggle with. Real-time reporting was a recent phenomena and police sources needed to be made available for the avarice press.

The Trojans were shielded from the hubris surrounding Luton station. They had focus and strict mission parameters. The inspector was just about to give the order to enter the basement when several males of senior age walked into the square.

'Who is in charge?' enquired a tall, willowy figure with a long grey beard.

The inspector looked at Pope and raised his eyebrows.

'I am,' said Pope.

'What is your name and why have you entered this holy place?' demanded the same man, who was clearly the leader of this group.

'There's been a serious terrorist incident at Luton station and we believe that there are co-conspirators in your basement.'

'Impossible. Where is your warrant?'

'I don't need a warrant under the Prevention of Terrorism Act. Sir, you need to move away now as this is a—'

'Imam. Please, there were three bombers at Luton station. They were going to London to blow people up. We need to help now and prevent any further chance of people being blown up,' said Ahmed in a calming tone.

The Imam looked at Ahmed, who he recognised as a member of the community, and thought silently for a moment. The news that Ahmed had just imparted was earth shaking. The Muslim faithful were peace-loving and didn't support wanton killing, but if this mosque was somehow involved then that would heighten tensions further with the non-Muslim communities.

'Yes. How can we help?' said the man looking at Ahmed.

'Well. We should tell everyone to stay where they are. And then we should go into the cafe and wait for the police to do whatever it is they need to do,' replied Ahmed.

The Imam nodded and the group left the square accompanied by Ahmed. Pope watched Ahmed leave, leading the group, and recognised that Ahmed had averted a situation.

The inspector nodded and the Trojan group stealthily headed into the basement. They returned five minutes later empty-handed. Deepak was puzzled; there was no other way out of the basement.

Ahmed, who was listening in on his phone, left the Imam and his group and dashed towards the rear door, saying into the phone, 'Tell the Trojan covering the rear door that undercover agent Ahmed Hussain is coming out. I don't want to get shot.'

Ahmed opened the door and, before showing himself, shouted out his name and that he worked for MI5. The Trojan shouted back that he could come out with his hands up. Ahmed walked out with his hands up. He looked past the Trojan to where Zeehan had parked his people carrier earlier on. The space was empty. Ahmed looked around the rest of the half-full car park but the car was nowhere to be seen. Ahmed shouted out that he was going back inside and the Trojan nodded.

Once inside, Ahmed said into his phone, 'John. Zeehan's car isn't here. I don't know how they did it but they've gone.'

Pope acknowledged Ahmed's message and made a decision.

'Inspector, the people that we are after probably have gone. Their car is no longer here. Can you sweep this place? Room by room just to make sure. Then the locals can take over.'

The inspector split his team into three teams and they all took a floor each, looking for anyone carrying a rucksack and anyone matching the description of the Hawk.

Pope went back on his phone, 'You heard Ahmed's comment. We need an APW (All Ports Warning) on Zeehan Begum who's driving a black T Porter people carrier. We have his details in the system. We need to put out the mugshot for the Hawk as they will be travelling together.'

'John. We have our people on that now,' replied Carruthers.

'There's one other with them. I think it's Usam Mia. I didn't get a full description from the cleaner but he's known to us also,' added Ahmed.

'OK, Ahmed, we'll add him into the APW,' replied Carruthers.

Pope waited as Ahmed walked into the square.

'What happened?' said Pope to Deepak and Ahmed, covering his phone with his hand.

Ahmed and Deepak muted their phones.

'They never left whilst I was watching,' blurted out Deepak.

'Same for me,' added Ahmed.

Ahmed shot Deepak a murderous glance.

'OK. You guys need to stay here. Mingle and see what the gossip is. The Trojans are sweeping the place but our guys are long gone,' said Pope.

'You don't think that they may come back?' asked Deepak.

'No chance. The local bill will be all over this place now for the next twenty-four hours. They will get all the names of everyone here and will start collecting statements,' replied Pope.

'The cleaner is the guy with the intel,' said Ahmed dryly.

'Yes. Speak to him. Get his details and we'll do a full debrief tomorrow. Chris Gould will pick him up. As soon as the Trojans are done then I'll get a lift back to the station. Both of you have been brilliant today. We have stopped a major terrorist attack. Stay sharp though. It will be a big day tomorrow. Both of you will need to be back in here and you will also need to submit your reports on today's events. I'll check in later with both of you.'

Pope put his phone to his ear and listened. COBRA (Cabinet Office Briefing Rooms) was sitting. The prime minster was chairing the meeting which included several senior ministers, senior Met officers, director general of MI5, chief of MI6, director of GCHQ and a couple of Whitehall mandarins. One of the suicide bombers had on them a piece of paper which had a timetable of trains. Luton 17:28 to West Hampstead 17:54. West Hampstead 18:04 to Wembley Park 18:16. The decision based on information known so far was that the match at Wembley would go ahead, but it was the target. Extra police were being drafted into all three Wembley train stations. The ever-evolving plan was to stop anyone carrying a rucksack and search them. Two Army bomb disposal Units were on their way and would supplement the one unit that was already in situ. A statement had been prepared and reviewed by COBRA which a local Beds police officer would read out to the news teams that were congregating around Luton station. It would be bland and say that an attempted terrorist attack had been foiled by a joint operation and that further details would be released later. They could confirm that there had been no civilian casualties. Various platforms were already publishing eye witness accounts that claimed anything from several terrorists shot dead to unarmed civilians caught in crossfire with multiple casualties. There was no public mention of APW; the suspects were not going to be given any information that may help them evade capture. GCHQ were now working at maximum capacity. They were hunting for the black T Porter people carrier. The number plate would get recognised on the standard surveillance cameras but they were trying to extend the search area and look at areas that it could have travelled to in three hours. They were also looking at cameras at West Hampstead, Luton and Wembley, searching for likely suspects carrying a rucksack and going back through earlier footage. Pope knew that the wider operation was now in place.

The inspector walked up to Pope.

'We've searched everywhere. It's clean.'

Pope updated control and said that he was now going to go back to the station. First he walked into the cafe followed by the inspector and stood in front of the group of men who had earlier confronted him.

'Thank you for your cooperation. We have searched everywhere and the people that we are looking for aren't here.'

'Who are you looking for?' demanded the leader.

'I'm not at liberty to say,' replied Pope. He didn't want anyone here tipping them off.

The Imam was irate.

'We will leave now but the Bedfordshire police will be coming in and they will want to speak to everyone,' went on Pope.

'Thank you. I'm sure everyone wants to help out. Especially as there could have been loss of life,' interceded Ahmed.

The Imam looked at the young man but said nothing.

'We'll be off. But thanks once again,' said Pope diplomatically, appreciating Ahmed's second interruption.

'You never told us your name,' said the Imam to Pope's back.

There was no reply. Pope spoke into his phone and said that Beds local police could now enter and start gathering statements. Pope looked at his watch. It was 18:32. The three

Trojan cars drove back to the train station at a more sedate speed. There was no chatter in the cars. It had been an intense few hours. All the training had paid off and they had done their job. Pope sent a discreet text to Jane.

'Job done. Just paperwork to do. Don't wait up.'

The Beds police liaison officer stood in front of the mics, cameras and lights and read the statement. Once he had finished, several reporters started shouting at the same time. Their questions melded into an unintelligible noise and he said that there would be a further briefing soon.

The three Trojan cars were parked outside the station. Three armed Trojan officers walked towards the end of the road where they took up prominent positions. Everyone else including Pope walked back inside the station and into the room where the would-be suicide bomber's body was being placed inside a body bag. The body was removed and placed inside a windowless van. The deceased had had his fingerprints taken along with facial photos and body shots including his distinctive foot tattoo. The information had been transferred into multiple databases trying to find a match. The other two accomplices were already packed in the van and their details were also in the Big Machine. The van would be driven straight to an undisclosed hospital in London where preparations had already been made to carry out three autopsies. All of their clothes, bags of bolts, nails and washers, phones and rucksacks had been tagged and bagged. These items were on their way back to Thames House in a commandeered police car. Outside the station, barriers had been erected and a tent put up around the killing zone. The crowd were no longer fizzing with energy, looking forward to watching an international football match with France. The mood was sombre and they marched slowly without complaint in single file towards the eerie platforms. Trains were just beginning to run again from Luton to London. The backlog of trains, many half empty, would soon be bursting with too many passengers after they had stopped at Luton. The trains that were coming up from London however were not stopping at Luton. Passengers were being advised to get off before Luton at Luton Airport Parkway or get off after Luton at Leagrave.

The prime minister finished a call in COBRA with the prime minister of France. They had jointly agreed that the match should go ahead. They didn't want to bow to terrorism or show any sign of weakness. They had discussed the information that was available and the measures that the English PM would put in place not only for the security of all of the spectators but also for the French football team. The English PM was confident that the incident had been contained. He did share in the strictest of confidence that a manhunt was now underway for the bomb planner and two others. The French team that were being delayed at their hotel were told that the French PM wanted the match to go ahead and that they would be very well looked after by their hosts. With reluctance, they boarded the team bus and noticed that there were several hard, wiry men sitting in it. Behind the bus were two Land Rovers with another one sitting directly in front of it. Each Land Rover contained four hard, wiry men. The English PM was as good as his word. The famed SAS would be acting as bodyguards until the French team were safely away from the UK. The motorcycle outriders led the cavalcade which also included three police cars. All of the police lights were blazing in a show of force. After the match, the team bus would be escorted straight away to Heathrow airport where a plane was waiting to fly the squad back to Paris. The match had been rescheduled for a 20:15 start. News was now interrupting TV programmes and radio programmes alike and would continue to do so for the rest of the night.

19:10. The Hawk and his nephew had finished eating their meal in a rustic pub restaurant in Harwich town centre. They walked back out to the car in the side car park.

'I want to get rid of the tool bag now. Stop near one of those big bins behind the restaurants and I'll throw it in there,' said the Hawk.

The nephew drove slowly around the road in front of the pier looking for an alleyway with several large bins. It wasn't hard to find something in this area. The Hawk got out, retrieved the tradesman tool bag and travel case and disappeared down the alleyway. The nephew kept a keen watch on the traffic and the pavements, looking for anything untoward. The passenger door opened and in stepped a man with thick light brown hair, glasses and wearing a black suit with a pale shirt.

'Oi, mate, what are you doing?' said the nephew, pushing out his left arm towards the intruder.

'Relax, it's me,' said the Hawk.

'You scared me,' replied the nephew.

'I've changed my appearance. They might be looking for an Imam.'

'You certainly have. I didn't recognise you. Do you have a new passport?'

The Hawk flashed his new Belgium passport with another identity.

'I'm a friend of yours and you are giving me a lift back after a holiday, if anyone asks. I've been staying with family in Chelmsford,' said the Hawk.

'OK,' acknowledged the nephew, unnerved by the Hawk's wig and Western appearance.

'Let us listen to the radio. We should hear that the martyrs have struck a blow to the infidels,' said the Hawk.

The nephew turned on the car radio and started channel hopping.

Pope was talking to Sergeant Richards and getting all of the details regarding the rucksack bombs. They were all made exactly the same and they all had the same time set on their alarm clocks. Once armed, they would all go off after eight minutes. Sergeant Richards speculated that the three bombers would have armed their bombs in a group and then set off to different points. They would have caused many fatalities not least because the bags of nails, washers and bolts that they had all added into their many pockets would become deadly shrapnel and increase the potency of the weapons several fold. The Army bomb disposal team had packed away some of their gear. They were getting ready to stand down but that order hadn't been delivered yet. Pope knew that there was almost no likelihood of any further would-be bombers out there, but it wasn't right to stand down just yet. There were still people going to Wembley and they couldn't drop their guard just yet.

The Army team were sharing a flask of tea and sandwiches that they had brought with them and they were listening to a radio which was repeating over and over bare details of the terrorist incident at Luton station along with details of the rescheduled match at Wembley. Pope had drained all of the information that he could from Sergeant Richards and went back to listening to everything that was being communicated at control. He learnt all about the match details including the SAS and the hot flight back to Paris after the match for the French squad. The rest of the Trojan team were also in the small room and were fidgeting. The stout station manager bounced in and all eyes turned towards him.

'I've arranged for tea and coffee. It'll be here any minute and there's chocolates, biscuits and a few sandwiches,' he said cheerily.

'Thanks,' said the Trojans.

'Don't thank me. The lady who runs the tea kiosk on platform three has rustled it all up.'

'What do we owe her?' said the inspector.

'Have it on me,' said the station manager. 'You've earned it.'

'Cheers, mate.'

19:20. Pope retrieved his case with his laptop from his car. He then chatted with the Trojan inspector and they went through everything that the Trojans had done since they'd arrived at Luton. The inspector recounted everything in a chronological order and Pope made mental notes.

As the inspector finished, he said, 'Just one more thing. When the two bombers were facing us off and one of them was trying to get behind the other one, they were both screaming "Allahu Akbar", but it was in a northern accent.'

'Do you know where?'

'Can't be sure but Bob reckons it sounded Bradford.'

Pope nearly jumped as if he had been delivered an electric shock. He just remembered that Ahmed had spoken with the first bomber.

He put his phone to his ear. 'Ahmed, are you there?'

'Yes, John.'

'Listen. You spoke to the first bomber. Do you remember what accent he spoke with?'

Ahmed paused and thought about what the guy said and then replied, 'John, he had a Bradford accent.'

'Are you sure?'

'Yes. I've got family up there.'

'Sandra. We have confirmation that all three had northern accents and that they are probably from Bradford. Can you feed that into the checks that's currently being run?'

'John. Thanks. That's very useful information and it's being done as we speak,' said Carruthers.

19:30. The TV news cameras camped outside 10 Downing Street were handed a note saying that the prime minister would address the nation live tomorrow morning at 08:30. In the meantime there would be regular updates as and when there was any information to deliver. The information was broadcast live on all UK TV stations and fired off immediately around the world. Studio commentators speculated and guest 'experts' gave their opinions, filling airtime with hyperbole and even more speculation. Three Trojans had refuelled then swapped over with the three Trojans who had taken up positions at the end of the road earlier. Pope took the opportunity to logon and start creating his report of events. He was going to include all of the information that he had gleaned from both Sergeant Richards and the Trojan inspector even though it was second-hand. It would be useful to cross check the reports from the Trojans and the Army bomb disposal unit and make sure that there were no inaccuracies or inconsistencies. The backlog of people going to Wembley from Luton had decreased now to a dribble. That translated into massive queues on the road at West Hampstead between the line from Luton and the underground station along with a dangerously overfull platform at the underground station and overcrowding on all trains that stopped there heading towards Wembley.

20:20. The friendly match at Wembley kicked off.

Four young men carrying rucksacks had been hustled off and detained inside Wembley Park station. Their rucksacks were searched by Army disposal unit soldiers and nothing deadly was found. All complained but were given short thrift. They all ended up late for the kick off and three of them lamented loudly that they would be making complaints to their MPs, the Police Complaints Authority, national newspapers and Uncle Tom

Cobley. The forth one was in possession of fourteen thumbed pornographic magazines, a well-worn butt plug and a rather weathered deflated plastic blow-up doll. He was less vociferous, vowing silently that he would never again transport his wanking paraphernalia to another public event.

There was a longer than usual queuing time to enter the Harwich International terminal. Every car was being searched and there were sniffer dogs out. The Hawk checked his watch and it was 20:30. Boarding was open and they just needed to check in. They had been listening to the radio for a while and the news was repetitive but unequivocal. The mission had failed and the martyrs had been caught at Luton station. Still no details about the fate of the martyrs had been broadcast. Had they been captured, had they been shot and wounded or had they been shot and killed? The Hawk was anxious to get onto the ferry as it may offer them concealment until the ferry sailed at 23:00.

The car edged forward slowly until they were at the front of the queue and able to see the amassed group of customs officers and dogs. The Hawk passed over the ferry tickets to his nephew. The nephew exhibited some fear and studied the tickets. He slightly relaxed when he saw that the Hawk's ticket was in the name of his latest alias. The customs officers looked at both of them and checked the two photos and identikit photo of the Hawk. Neither resembled the people on the APW and after a quick check in the boot they were allowed to drive into the bowels of the ferry. The Hawk was still wearing latex gloves which meant that he had not left any fingerprint DNA anywhere since he'd arrived in the UK. He relished the moment when he'd got dropped off at Schiphol airport and could rid himself of these awful accessories. He wouldn't relax though until he was on his flight and heading back to the Middle East. The failure of the mission would need to be examined and he would be accountable for that, but first he needed to get away before the net tightened around him. And he was now stuck with this oaf who would spend the journey chucking his guts up.

Pope went onto his phone. 'Ahmed, what's happening at the mosque?'

'John. It's subdued here. The local police have taken everyone's names and details and will be arranging interviews starting tomorrow. We've been caught up in that and I guess we need to cooperate and keep our cover.'

'That's a definite, Ahmed.'

'Everyone here has heard that there's been a tragic accident at the Hajj. The Ali family were all killed in a road accident on Monday. That was Hamiza, his dad and his grandfather. No one is really focusing on what has happened at Luton station, nor that the bombers were here first. The community is in shock.'

'OK, Ahmed, stick with it,' said Pope.

Carruthers announced over the phone that Pope had permanently stuck to his ear that West Yorkshire police had assembled several teams and they were awaiting instructions. There were teams to speak to the families of the deceased and other teams that were search and capture teams. They were all primed and ready to go and were housed in Trafalgar House police station in the heart of Bradford.

21:00. Carruthers announced that the Army bomb disposal team in Luton would be stood down. Pope walked outside to where their two vans were parked and shook the hand of every one of them and thanked them all for everything that they had done this evening. In another ten minutes they would be packed up and on their way back to their base.

21:15. Carruthers was a bit animated with the latest news. GCHQ had found the IDs of all three dead bombers. Facial recognition software had identified them. They were faces in the crowd of a gathering outside a mosque where an extremist Imam was preaching four years ago in Bradford. They had all then flown to Syria where they stayed for three months. Syria was notorious for hosting terrorist training camps. After they returned, they were all interviewed but claimed that they were visiting relatives. All were flagged as potentials but had not surfaced until now. The Bradford units were given the green light to start the operations. MI5, police and other agencies were now looking heavily into their backgrounds, families in the UK and abroad and any contacts. Phone numbers, email accounts and other online platform accounts were being intercepted and data gathered along with reading and listening to any new information that appeared. The names, personal details and photos were being uploaded and would soon be broadcast to a waiting world. The PM agreed with other members of COBRA that it was time to release further information and a statement was drafted and reviewed before it was sent to Bedford police. The Bedford police liaison office stood in front of the increasing press corp and read out the statement that confirmed that three terror suspects who were all carrying bombs in their rucksacks had been shot dead by police and that there were no police or civilian casualties. The press corp erupted with multiple questions but the shouts all melded into one indistinguishable noise. The police liaison officer walked off to a barrage of noise, saying that further details would be released as and when there was something to share. Newspapers in London were all holding back printing their papers. Editors were experiencing blood pressure readings close to heart attack levels. The editors wanted more information and greater sensational headlines that would capture the public tomorrow and boost their sales.

22:10. The friendly match at Wembley had finished and France had won 2–1. Peter Crouch had scored for England in a lacklustre game where all of the players did their best but were aware that there had been a major incident in Luton. The crowd were also flat and they were subdued by the news that was being drip-fed from Luton.

The three Trojan teams were advised that they were going to be relieved by two new Trojan teams and that they should be there in fifteen minutes. They were to return directly to New Scotland Yard and hand in all of their weapons and ammunition. The weapons and ammunition would be held and form part of the evidence and enquiry that was going to follow.

22:30. Pope got on the phone and told Ahmed and Deepak that unless they had a reason then they should now head off home and that they needed to be back in the mosque no later than 08:00 tomorrow. He told them that they both had done an excellent job today, which they both appreciated, especially as the great and the good were also on the call. Seb Drake came on the line next and told John that he should also wrap it up and head off home. He told Pope that he should aim to get in the office tomorrow around 10ish.

Underground trains, overground trains and buses in London going out to all points on the compass were swelled with the crowd now going home late from Wembley. The Met police and other police forces were stretched and Beds police were straining to the point that officers from surrounding counties were being drafted in to assist in policing Luton. The train station staff who were always the unsung heroes knew that it was going to be a late finish as the service had been seriously disrupted and was still being pieced back together.

22:40. The three Trojan teams had done their handover with the incoming two teams and were readying themselves for the journey back down to London. Pope finished having a chat and thanking the portly station manager for his assistance, who was in turn talking passionately about the difficulty of managing a station as large as Luton.

Pope disengaged with the station manager who was beginning to get on his soap box after thanking him once again and his team for their support and professionalism. Pope then jogged over to the Trojan inspector.

'Your team were excellent this evening. Great job,' Pope said earnestly.

'Thanks. We appreciate it,' replied the inspector. 'We're going back into London now. If you want, we can stick you in the middle and we'll get you home quick. We're going "Blues and Twos".'

'Yeah, I'll take you up on that offer,' Pope said with a smile.

'Where are you heading to in the Smoke?'

'I'm off the Finchley Road.'

'Well, we can take you there. We go straight past there and onto St Johns Wood where we go via Lords cricket ground, Marble Arch then Park Lane and past Buck House, along Birdcage Walk then along Victoria Embankment. From you it should be forty-two minutes back to base but we'll do that in eighteen minutes.'

'What a nerd,' said one of the Trojans.

They all laughed.

'Anyway, is your motor some tricked out, souped up beast? James Bond-like?' asked a Trojan.

'No, it's my wife's pride and joy. If I prang it, she'll have my guts for garters,' laughed Pope.

The Trojans roared heartily.

'So that stonking knife you carry under your dippy running disguise, that's your wife's also?'

''Fraid so.'

The Trojans roared again.

'Let's get going. We need to get back, debriefed and square everything away,' said the inspector. 'OK, you'll be car three in our convey.'

Pope nodded and headed back to his car with the phone still stuck to his ear.

23:00. The ferry rumbled to life and left its berth at Harwich. The Hawk was mildly relieved. They had managed to leave the port without any further mishaps or questions. Despite the mission failing, he smiled to himself. There was still one more surprise in store that would throw the UK services into chaos and strike terror into the general population.

Deepak and Ahmed were sitting in the front room sipping tea and watching the TV. A new bulletin was being broadcast. Again the Beds police liaison officer faced the cameras and microphones. This time he read out the names and ages of the dead bombers. He added that they all hailed from Bradford. Photos of the three were circulated. This was the information

that the daily newspapers were hoping for. It would be splashed
all over the front pages with salacious headlines. The police
liaison officer added that there wouldn't be any more press
briefings until tomorrow morning. Hardly anyone was listening
to him though as they all poured the information back to either
their editors or out to the TV audiences.

'Where the fuck were you?' said Ahmed.

'You know that I was in Cambridge,'

'You should have been there by 16:30.'

'Well it wasn't that easy to just up and leave. They wanted
to finish the drop but I told them that I had to get back as my
dad was having a heart attack.'

'I was having a fucking heart attack. Listen, if you were in
the flat where you should have been then you could have been
at the mosque by 16:00.'

'I'm sorry.'

'You fucking resign tomorrow. No one month notice shit.
You tell them that you ain't going in anymore. Finito. Oh, and
before you start. Cancel Mum's takeaway, I don't want it and I
don't want to hear no more shit about how much it costs to feed
us. We'll eat local.'

'Fine.'

'And no more fucking skunk.'

'OK.'

'Good.'

'I do have one question though,' said Deepak timidly.

'Go on,' growled Ahmed.

'How did the Hawk and the other two get out? I know that
they didn't leave when I was there.'

Ahmed paused momentarily.

'No idea. They never left when I was there either,' said
Ahmed.

'Strange.'

'Listen. Just write up your report and I'll write up mine. And
you had better have a good reason for being up in Cambridge
also.'

Deepak shrugged. Ahmed knew that Mr Butt had dragged
him into the room to explain that the Ali family had been killed
in an accident at the Hajj. It must have been at that moment

when they'd come out of the basement. That was not going to go into his report though.

Pope was flooring it and the car was shuddering at 85 mph. He was cocooned in between the Trojan convoy with their blaring lights and screaming sirens clearing a path in the outside lane of the southbound M1 motorway. It was still raining but it was now turning into a downpour. The traffic in both directions was heavy and moving far too fast considering the conditions. That being said, all of the motorists bowed before the Trojan convoy and vacated the fast lane early. A couple of cars that dozed in the fast lane awoke abruptly when the lead car breathed heavily on their rear bumper with increased lights and louder sirens, and they quickly scooted out of their way. It was obvious to Pope that the convoy would have been moving even faster if he wasn't sitting squarely in their midst. He daydreamed momentarily, thinking that it would be very efficient if he travelled all around London in this convoy. It would significantly reduce the time that it took to get from A to B.

'John, are you there?' enquired Tony Crook.

'Yes, Tony, go ahead.'

'Great job tonight. Just to let you know, you kept us on an open line all day. Right.'

There was a pause before Tony Crook continued. 'Two points. Is Doodle OK now, and do you want us to redirect your Trojan convoy after that pikey van driver who deliberately blocked you overtaking him and sort him out?'

'Ha, ha, very funny.'

'Yeah, we waited until Carruthers had left control before we contacted you. And don't worry, she didn't even notice when you took the third cunting left. Even we were surprised when she missed that,' chuckled Tony Crook.

Pope didn't reply and heard muffled laughter coming from the group in control. In any tense, life-threatening situation, there was always a time for laughter, as it released tension for a small period of time.

The convoy left the M1 Motorway and headed up to Finchley. There was still heavy traffic in and around the North

Circular Road with people still heading home from the match at Wembley, and the Trojans cut through the gridlock like a hot knife through butter. The convey was nearing Finchley Road underground station when Pope flashed his lights. In unison, the cars smoothly pulled over and into the inside lane where they stopped. Pope jumped out of his car and jogged up to the lead car and poked his head in. He took the time to shake hands with all three of the occupants and thanked them for their bravery and professionalism today. He repeated the same actions with the occupants of both cars two and three. The fast cars pushed back out into the traffic, closed ranks and sped back towards London, lights and sirens on full pelt. They still had paperwork to do and also had to hand in their weapons and ammo. Their night wasn't over yet. Without his escort, Pope indicated and turned sedately left up the hilly road.

11:18. Pope strode into the bedroom. Jane looked up from the romance novel that she was reading and saw that Pope was aroused and ready to pounce. Brief thoughts flitted across her mind around the lack of action in the bedroom in recent months. She looked at Pope and got a mild waft of Doodle's poo from the flecks that were still on his face.

'John, why don't you have a quick shower first,' she said sweetly.

'Right,' said Pope, and he bumbled off.

When Pope returned five minutes later, his state of excitement had not diminished. He entered the bed and asserted himself. Jane was compliant, willing and excited. Her long neck stretched out high. They synchronised their actions and glanced continually at each other. Jane was enraptured and gently fluttered her wings. Once they had finished, Pope rolled off, sated. It was a very physical, intense lovemaking session. No words were spoken as they lay there recovering. Minutes later, Pope rolled over and their lovemaking began again. It was as intense and physical as the first time. There would be one further lovemaking act during the night and whispered conversations between Pope and Jane about the violent day that had unfolded. It was a cathartic moment because they then spoke about their own hopes and dreams and that they were now spending most of their time ferrying the kids around and supporting their every whim. They decided that they would insert a measure of change and spend more time together. They needed an occasional spark and romance to rekindle their own relationship.

At one point during their whispered conversation, Jane remarked, 'We can't wait for you to thwart a terrorist attack to get horny.'

'Quite,' replied Pope, smiling as his member began to engorge again...

08:00. Pope walked into the kitchen and his brood were already gathered there.

'Good morning,' he said breezily.

'Good morning,' cooed Jane.

Charlie smiled.

'Charlie, thanks for your help yesterday,' said Pope, patting her on her head.

'That's all right, Daddy,' beamed Charlie, eager for praise.

Daisy, who was sitting there eating a small bowl of cornflakes, looked at Pope earnestly. 'Daddy, did you save the world then?'

Pope looked at his youngest, precious cygnet, trying to figure out what she was going on about.

Charlie piped up. 'Of course he did.'

Daisy's face broke out into a wide, beaming smile and all of the females were looking at each other with identical smiles.

Daisy broke away from her unfinished breakfast, saying, 'I'll tell Doodle that he was a good luck charm.'

She skipped energetically out of the kitchen. Pope's look of confusion continued as a mug of tea was placed in front of him.

08:30. The young British prime minister addressed the world's press from a hastily erected podium outside 10 Downing Street. The broadcast was live on all UK TV channels and many others throughout the world. It was raining and he was shrouded beneath umbrellas as he delivered the anodyne statement. He started off by saying that a terrorist attempt yesterday was thwarted by UK services and thanked all of the men and women involved in the operation. The target was the friendly football match at Wembley between England and France. He said that the French PM was consulted and it was jointly agreed that the match would go ahead. He thanked both teams for playing the match and that both France and England were determined not to bow to terrorists. He commended the bravery of the police who dealt with the situation and the ongoing dedication by the services that made our country safe and secure. There was no direct mention of MI5 or GCHQ, just implication. He confirmed the names of the now dead terrorists and that their next of kin had been informed. He restated that the swift actions of the police had ensured that there was neither injury nor loss of life to the general public. He concluded that it was still an ongoing operation and that the police along with other services were still hunting for three other suspects, but no details were available. David Cameron had been PM for barely six months.

10:15. Pope walked in the main door to his office. He'd had the luxury of a shower in the morning and ablutions before he left home and was feeling perky. People in the office stared at him as he made his way towards his desk. He smiled and said 'Good morning' as he passed on his way to his desk. One middle-aged man seated at a desk near the window stood up and applauded. Then another stood up and applauded. Before he reached his desk, the whole of the office was standing and applauding. Pope felt the heat rising in his cheeks. He didn't seek the limelight and was uncomfortable. The applause was polite, respectful and a joint show of admiration. In their world, success was but a fleeting moment that should be savoured because the next potential attack was always just around the corner.

Pope smiled to the adoring audience, sat down and that was the end. He logged onto all of his systems and waited until they all fired up. Carruthers was looking on from her ivory tower, hands on hips and fuming. Pope attended the 11:00 meeting chaired by Carruthers. The group jointly praised Pope for his performance and management yesterday before the business got under way. There were reports regarding the dead terrorists and the surveillance already in place on their relatives, friends and associates. There were further reports regarding the hunt for the Hawk and the two local men who'd left the mosque with him, but so far that was drawing a blank. Carruthers said that CCTV surveillance was being reinstalled outside the mosque and that extra resources would be available for surveillance not only at that mosque but for other mosques in Luton, and that Team 4 were now fully engaged and back online. She didn't mention how and why the CCTV and Team 4 support had been prematurely withdrawn and it wasn't either the time or the place for that particular discussion. There had been feedback that mosque elders and community leaders were pushing back and baulking at the blanket requests for interviews. They were suggesting that there was no evidence of any involvement from the mosque community and were raising the spectre of discrimination and victimisation. MI5 were going to sit this one out and it was between the police liaison and community leaders to resolve it in a way that satisfied all parties. Pope briefed everyone that Chris Gould was already up in Luton and he was interviewing the mosque cleaner who had alerted Ahmed to the fact that the Hawk was there and that there were others with him carrying rucksacks. Pope planned to go up to Luton after the meeting with Clare Hawkins and meet up with the Luton team for a debrief and action plan. Carruthers was curt throughout the meeting and left, followed by her little shadow. Her limp had returned.

Once she had left the room, the usual group stayed behind. There was much animated discussion about the measures that Carruthers had hastily put in place, and all eyes fell on Pope. He said that it was all too late now. The horse has bolted; or was that the Hawk had flown away? The mosque as a front for any terrorist operation had been blown. The only thing now was to get the details of who was involved, what their involvement was and how they'd originally got involved. Pope was going to focus all resources on answering those questions and most importantly find out anything and everything about the Hawk, as he was behind everything.

Pope left the meeting and headed up to the Top Floor where he was ushered straight in by Sheila Beavers. The door closed and Seb Drake turned and smiled at Pope. Sir Dickie Crampton, director general of MI5, was putting with his belly putter.

'John, I know that you are in the middle of the op. But I wanted to offer my thanks to both you and your boys up in Luton. A sterling job yesterday.'

'Thanks, Sir Dickie.'

'I know that you will, but please pass that message onto both of them.'

'I'm going up there now and it will be done.'

'I was just saying to Seb before you arrived. We need to have a recruiting drive for more ethnic minorities. The chaps proved that. They were invaluable.'

'Absolutely agreed,' said Seb Drake.

'I know that the Whitehall Mandarins want to slash our budget and push more to GCHQ but this has proved that we are just as important. Worst of all, they think that Mother Russia is now a bloody big cuddly bear. Mark my words, once they have finished updating their Cold War technology, they'll be twice as vicious as before. We'll be fighting on two fronts then. Mr Putin and extremist Muslim terrorists,' went on Sir Dickie.

'We need to adapt now,' chimed up Seb Drake.

'Anyway, we won't keep you, John,' said Sir Dickie, taking a practice swing with his dreaded belly putter.

Pope and Clare Hawkins drove up to Luton and arrived there at 13:35. Chris Gould was already in the coffee shop in The Mall shopping centre wearing a frappe coffee moustache and a croissant-covered shirt. Once another round of coffees was bought, Chris gave them both a whispered update. He had interviewed the cleaner earlier that morning and the cleaner had recounted his story in broken English. The cleaner was adamant that he had seen a few months earlier three local men and the Hawk enter the basement early one morning. After that, he had counted seven young men also go in to the basement. Pope asked Chris if he'd rechecked the numbers with the cleaner and Chris said that he had and that the cleaner was resolute. The cleaner then said that he saw two local young men and the Hawk go into the basement twice in the two previous days and that they were followed in there by another three young men. Chris pressed him as to whether he could identify the three young men as part of the original group of seven, but the cleaner couldn't. The cleaner was able to identify all of the local young men from photos that Chris had shown him. In fact, there were four locals in total as Rahan Iqbal was identified as being in the earlier group but not the recent group, and Zeehan Begum was only in the recent group.

The cleaner had a remarkable ability to recall faces. The cleaner had told Chris Gould that he was scared and Chris had reassured him that everything was going to be OK and that he was safe. Chris gave him a telephone number that he could call anytime and that he would get help. Chris also said that if he ever felt any imminent personal danger then he should also call the police. Pope stated the obvious. If there were seven originally and three had been neutralised, then where were the other four. It was possible that they were sleepers and would surface when the next terrorist attack went live. The other possibility was that the current attack had not finished and that the threat was both credible and imminent. Pope then got on the phone and relayed the information back to Thames House. Added to the mix was that the manhunt for the Hawk and the other two as yet hadn't turned up anything. It was as if he along with Usam, Zeehan and his car had disappeared off the face of the Earth.

14:10. An enormous explosion shattered the nervous quiet in south east Luton. The violence demolished the elderly mid-terraced house. What was once the exterior walls and slate roof were now piles of bricks and broken slate strewn everywhere. Timber roof structures were broken and thrown like javelins in every direction. The glass in the windows had been shattered and spat out as part of the violence. A fire had started and was trying to burn the evidence that this place was once a dwelling. Pouring rain was stopping the flames from spreading. The houses on either side of the explosion had also suffered damage but were largely still intact albeit without many windows and a number of holes in their roofs. Fortunately, no one was standing outside the dwelling when it exploded, otherwise they would have perished. Occupants in both adjacent houses were injured but not fatally. Other people in the street, whilst not physically injured, were in a state of shock. The noise coming from the explosion could be heard all over Luton. The emergency switchboard went into meltdown as they were inundated with calls. The switchboard operators who were trained to deal with emergencies directed the emergency services to the location where the explosion had occurred. In light of what had happened the previous day, the news of an explosion was passed up the escalation tree and within ten minutes MI5 were setting up in control, GCHQ were watching and listening to electronic traffic in Luton, COBRA was being convened, several Trojan teams were heading towards Luton, two bomb disposal units were dispatched from Didcot and John Pope along with Clare and Chris Gould were speeding towards the epicentre.

The police had put a cordon up around the street and were ferrying the residents out. They were cautiously going door to door and moving out all of the occupants. Some were trying to resist and were gently manhandled away. At the end of the street in both directions, ambulances, police vehicles and fire appliances idled with their lights flashing. A mobile control centre had arrived and information was flowing to their respective Bedfordshire headquarters and down into London. The first priority was to affect an orderly evacuation and this was completed at 14:35. Whilst this was going on, the perimeter was established. Apart from the house that had exploded, there were no fatalities reported and the injured were transported to the Dunstable hospital in a small fleet of ambulances. The decision was taken that no one would enter the site until the bomb disposal unit had checked it out. MI5 were hypothesising that the property could be a bomb-making factory. The rucksack bombs that were seized yesterday had had to have been built somewhere and it just may be that they were built there. Also, there still could be further bombs and potential boobytraps hidden within the debris. Following MI5's recommendation, COBRA had instructed the local services that they were not to enter the site until the bomb disposal unit had conducted their search and determined that the area was safe.

Once again Luton had become the centre of world news reporting. The local news reporters were converging on the site with speed. The police liaison officer was onsite and preparing the first statement that was going to flash around the globe. The statement was read back to COBRA who insisted on wordsmithing it. At 15:10 the first statement was read out and it said that there had been an explosion at an address in south east Luton and that the emergency services were attending. Several local people were now being treated in hospital for minor injuries and shock. Once again speculation was rife amongst the reporting and most of it inferred that there had been a terrorist attack.

15:50. The Army bomb disposal unit had arrived and quickly unpacked their gear away from the prying eyes of the press. Two men put on their bomb suits and walked out into the desolate street. Slowly, they walked up to the remains of the house and studied the destruction ahead of them, paying particular attention to the houses on either side. Both still looked sturdy, which was a plus. They then retreated and, along with the other members of their unit, agreed that they should send in the bomb disposal robot. It would do a quick recce and then a thorough investigation of the site which they could all monitor realtime via the cameras that the robot carried with it.

The bomb disposal robot crawled up, over and under the site for twenty-five minutes. The cameras didn't detect anything that resembled either bombs or bomb-making materials during its search, but it displayed pictures of human body parts. Before doing the human search, the Army bomb disposal team spoke with the fire brigade and requested that both the gas and the electricity to the street were switched off. The fire brigade did as they were asked and the two-man team then went in.

They had helmet and body cameras and their investigation was watched not only by their comrades onsite but also by other agencies who were plugged into the feed. Once onsite, their gas leak detectors picked up that there was an excessive amount of gas there. The men painstakingly picked their way through the remains of the property and were satisfied that it was not a bomb factory, nor were there any boobytraps there. They saw body parts strewn within the building wreckage and concluded that there were at least three people who had lost their lives. They also noted that the centre of the explosion was in what would have been the kitchen and that it was highly likely that the explosion was caused by a gas leak. They next checked the back garden and the remains of the garden shed. The men then retreated back to their group and conferred. Everyone watching via the monitors agreed with the conclusion of the two men. Their verdict was then passed onto the fire brigade and also to the various emergency groups that had been hastily convened. The fire brigade were told to secure the property and retrieve all of the human remains. The scene was going to be examined in minute detail by forensic experts and it needed to be preserved.

Whilst it may have been an unfortunate gas leak that caused the explosion, experts would crawl all over it and the back garden, including the remains of a rickety shed, looking for any clues and any scrap of evidence that there could have been terrorist activities carried out there. Pope had been speaking with the Army bomb disposal team regularly since they had arrived and once they had concluded that it was a gas leak that caused the explosion, he ran several scenarios through his mind. COBRA created a statement that would be communicated to the press via the police liaison officer. Public anxiety was high as a result of yesterday's thwarted terrorist attack. People needed to be reassured that the country was safe and that the government was in control, and nowhere more than Luton. The statement would say that there had been a gas leak that caused an explosion and that the services were now making the area safe. People who lived in the street would be given accommodation for a few days. Unfortunately there had been loss of life in one property and their next of kin would be informed in due course. TV stations around the globe were running this story live.

In a hotel in the Middle East, the Hawk smiled to himself as he sipped a large single malt whiskey whilst watching the latest news flash. He had left no loose ends. There was no one in the UK left alive who could identify him or provide even morsels of information to the pursuing security agencies.

18:20. Pope was once again back in the coffee shop in the Mall. Deepak and Ahmed had joined Pope along with Clare Hawkins and Chris Gould. Pope was running through all of the information that had been gathered in the last twenty-four hours or so. The investigation and manhunt were both proceeding with speed and a huge amount of data had been gathered and analysed in that relatively short period of time. The bombers who'd hailed originally from Bradford were having their backgrounds scrutinised and it was unearthing potentially useful information. Pope went on that MI5 were now going to up the level of resources in the Luton area along with reinstalling the CCTV cameras and assistance from Team 4. He said that the new team members would need to be brought up to speed and suggested that Chris set up a team meeting asap. He also suggested that Deepak and Ahmed would take the lead and update everyone on the events and key players. He added that MI5 had contacted Mabaheth (Saudi Arabia's internal security agency) and they had confirmed that the death of the three male members of the Ali family at the Hajj was as a result of an unfortunate car accident and that there was nothing suspicious about the incident. Ahmed then said that the community were reeling from that loss and still did not want to admit that their mosque could in some way be connected with the thwarted terrorist attack yesterday. The community were convinced that both Usam Mia and Zeehan Begum who were still unaccounted for were in no way involved. In fact, the rumours were that they may have been forced against their will to assist in the escape of the mysterious Imam.

Pope said that the cleaner needed support and that they all had to keep an eye on him for the next several weeks. He told Chris that he needed to arrange for him to be brought into Thames House asap for a more detailed interview and that they should arrange for an interpreter to assist and conduct the interview in his own language. Pope once again thanked everyone for their professionalism yesterday and then asked if they had any questions or thoughts.

Ahmed waited briefly and then said that in his opinion the mosque was no longer a place where there would be any further terrorist planning or meetings, nor would the Hawk appear there again. He went on and said that it now was about gathering anything and everything that related to yesterday's events.

Pope paused and then said that Ahmed had raised valid points but they needed to proceed with caution until they were absolutely sure. He also said that with the extra resources and support that they could put more coverage in all of the other Luton mosques and see what that threw up. He mentioned glibly that in other mosques they may uncover local criminal elements but apart from reporting it, it wasn't their business. Ahmed and Deepak nodded a little too enthusiastically, but that wasn't picked up by the others.

A news alert containing photos and brief details filled TV screens. The newscasters read the prepared statement that contained the names, ages and occupations of the three Bradford-born would-be bombers. These details would make the front pages of tomorrow's newspapers not only in the UK but all about the world. The details relating to the gas explosion in Luton was relegated to a small item on the scheduled TV news and it mentioned that two elderly people who'd lived in the house had been killed and that there was also another body of a young man who as yet hadn't been identified.

Clare was driving Pope and Chris back down the M1 in a pool car when all of their phones rang, pinged and lit up. They all answered immediately and heard that Luton police had searched a storage garage where they had found Zeehan Begum's T Porter, five-door black people carrier. Inside the car they had discovered Zeehan dead. They were treating the death as suicide because the car had a pipe leading from the exhaust into the driver's window and his body showed no signs of a struggle. The forensic team had been requested to examine the scene which was cordoned off and their results would be shared. The police had spoken with the company who rented out the garage and they had confirmed that the unit had been rented out for six months in Zeehan's name and that it had been paid for with cash a couple of months ago. The records seemed in order and the young lady who had filled in the paperwork had since left the company. The Hawk's 'nephew' had acquired the garage using false documentation and the former employee would not remember any details of the event when questioned. Pope decided that nothing would be gained by turning around and heading back up to Luton, and the nondescript car plodded along with the rest of the early evening traffic back towards the capital.

11:00. Ahmed was sitting in the cafeteria area engrossed in his online studying. He'd been in the mosque since 08:00 this morning partially studying and also keeping an eye on the latest MI5 undercover agent who had recently qualified in the role. Ahmed had been mentoring two newbies for just over two weeks and he would shortly be moving onto another undercover role at two other mosques in Luton. It'd been three weeks since the attempted suicide attack and the community had settled back in to their normal routine. Life went on and everyone quickly got over the initial shock. The only people who never recovered are those who had family and friends either connected to the terrorists or anyone injured or killed by the terrorist act.

The community and families within it were coming to grips with a spate of tragedies, although there would be permanent scars caused by several deaths that were apparently unrelated to the terrorist event. Mr Butt bustled in and sat in the seat opposite Ahmed.

'Good morning, Ahmed, how are you today?'

'I'm well, and how are you?' said Ahmed, logging off from the university course, knowing that Mr Butt could waffle on for ages.

'I take it day by day. There's been far too much death recently,' he said with sadness. 'I've visited the Ali family this morning. I doubt that they will ever recover. To lose three males in one family is tragic. But to lose them at the Hajj is awful. It's the one event that we all aspire to attend at least one time in our lives and to be killed in an automobile accident is terrible.'

'Yes, the family must be in pain. But there are deaths every year at the Hajj. It seems that if you gather that amount of people in a smallish area then there's always going to be tragic accidents. I know that doesn't make it right,' said Ahmed sympathetically.

'No, it's terrible. Then we have Zeehan's family. I went and saw them yesterday. They are grieving. They can't understand why he'd take his life. He was such a good boy, respectful. He also worked very hard as a cab driver.'

'I didn't know him well but everyone says he was a great guy. It's strange. Some people just struggle with life and before you know it, they are gone,' said Ahmed, thinking that Zeehan was a main player in this whole crazy thing and was the last known person to see and be with the Hawk.

'It's as if we are being punished,' explained Mr Butt.

'How so?'

'Usam Mia; a very clever young man. He was blown up in that horrible gas explosion. No one knows why he was at that house. It's a mystery. The house was decrepit and unsafe by all accounts. The two elderly Afghanis who lived there weren't involved in the community from what I hear. They didn't worship but were believers. A tragic accident.'

'He was in the wrong place at the wrong time. It happens,' replied Ahmed.

'That may be so but what about young Rahan Iqbal? He goes missing for a few months and then he's found dead. Murdered in Malden Woods. With his throat cut,' said a clearly agitated Mr Butt.

'Yes, that was nasty.'

'Nasty! It was murder. There's a maniac on the loose and what are the police doing about it? Nothing. I tell you Ahmed, no one is safe. He was such a good boy.'

'I agree in part. If that dog walker hadn't discovered him, he would have lain there in that woodland forever.'

'What I don't understand is that he was sending texts saying that he was in Bradford. How could that be the case? He was murdered and left in a shallow grave,' went on Mr Butt.

'Mr Butt, the forensic examination and autopsy couldn't determine the exact date of his death. The body was far too decomposed. He could have been up in Bradford and then came back when he was then murdered. We need to be careful here. There's no point spreading rumours, it will only distress the family.'

'Ahmed, mark my words, there's something very fishy about young Rahan's death.'

'We need to be guided by the evidence. And let's not forget that the police are conducting a murder investigation. It's only been ten days since his body was found. It takes time.'

'The police won't capture Rahan's killer, everyone knows that. We are cursed,' shouted an almost hysterical Mr Butt.

People in the cafeteria turned and looked towards where Ahmed and Mr Butt were sitting. Mr Butt had already got up and was waddling towards the door. Ahmed stared after him. MI5 weren't connecting everything up regarding the recent spate of deaths. The Hawk was a very clever, cunning opponent. It was ironic because if Hamiza Ali hadn't have been killed in the car accident at the Hajj, then he would have died by the hand of the Hawk.

19:40. Pope and Jane had waited patiently for twenty minutes. Their time had come and they were now going to see Miss Stephens, who was Daisy's teacher. They stepped forward and sat at the two chairs on the opposite side of her desk. The walls of the classroom were festooned with all manner of pictures that were painted by the children. It was a bright, vivid collage that brightened up the drab interior.

'Good evening,' said the young teacher.

'Good evening, Miss Stephens,' replied Jane.

Pope just smiled at the teacher.

Miss Stephens rattled through Daisy's academic performance which was in the top quartile. She mentioned that Daisy was popular with all of the other children and had an infectious smile. The report was pleasing and Jane squeezed Pope's hand.

'There is one thing though,' said Miss Stephens at the conclusion of the meeting.

Pope and Jane sat there expectantly.

'Daisy has a very active mind but maybe a bit too much imagination.'

Jane bristled. 'What exactly do you mean?'

'Well, recently all of the children were asked to talk a little bit about their family and Daisy stood up and told the class that, and I quote, "My daddy had just saved the world and it was a big secret." She then said that her dog was also involved. I think that she said he was called Dibble.'

Pope squeezed Jane's hand, hoping that she wasn't going to react.

Miss Stephens went on forcefully. 'Obviously we encourage all of the children to express themselves and have a vivid imagination. But, and I must emphasis this, we do want them to respect each other and be truthful when conversing.'

Pope was still squeezing Jane's hand but tighter now.

'She's five years old,' growled Jane.

Pope butted in. 'Thanks very much for your time.'

He half manhandled Jane as he got up and they left abruptly. Miss Stephens sat there with her mouth open as they marched off, Pope still squeezing Jane's hand.

In the car on the short journey home, Jane broke the stoney silence.

'All of this political correctness is now even affecting our kids. It's utter madness.'

'I agree. Anyway, what was all of that stuff about Doodle?'

'Shut up, John.'

The rest of the short journey was completed in silence.

12:00. The temperature was twenty-two degrees and sunny in the Kingdom of Bahrain. It was a typical warm, dusty day in the Al Markh village. The small village still made canvas and sails using the traditional methods that had been around for a thousand plus years. All of the people that were gathered in the villa on the edge of the village had spent a long morning driving around Bahrain. They either arrived at Bahrain International Airport or had crossed from Saudi Arabia via the sixteen-mile-long King Fahd Causeway. Once in Bahrain they had been picked up individually and had swapped cars three times. The purpose of so many car changes was to check for and lose any tails. Once the security team were confident that there were no tails, the people were delivered to the villa. A journey from Bahrain International Airport to Al Markh would normally take thirty-one minutes along Shaikh Khalifa Bin Highway, but today they had all been driven around the main island in the archipelago that made up Bahrain for over three hours. There was visible security both inside the villa and within its grounds as well as several SUVs parked at strategic points close to the villa. No one would be able to get close to the villa without being spotted and intercepted. Bahrain's Nation Security Agency were maintaining the security perimeter and they ensured that there was no breach. The location was also chosen because it was in a place where foreign drones were not over flying, intent on spying. The West had increased the use of drones for both spying and kill missions in a number of Middle East countries as well as Afghanistan but hadn't extended their reach into the skies above a number of countries that were allies... as yet.

In the whitewashed stonewalled room dominated by three ceiling fans spinning furiously sat the seven men. This was their first meeting since the failed attack in London three weeks ago and since they had met in Dubai. Mr Manzur checked that everyone was seated with a traditional cup of coffee in front of them before welcoming everyone. They sat listening intensely to him as he explained that for security reasons they had now chosen an out-of-the-way place and that in future all meetings would be held in similar venues rather than in the brash, gaudy hotels in places like Dubai. The group solemnly nodded at the wise decision.

General Faisal, who was dressed in a dark blue suit, matching tie, white shirt and black polished shoes, boomed, 'No more fornicating for you now. If you want to fuck then there's a goat outside.'

He laughed thunderously at his uncouth behaviour but it only drew uncomfortable smiles from the rest of the men in the room. He was not liked by any of them but they all realised that in his position as general in one of the most powerful armies in the Middle East, he was indispensable. Mr Manzur's mind flashed back to the last meeting in the middle of August. Post the meeting, everyone was supposed to leave the hotel immediately, but the general had stayed and picked up a prostitute in a bar. He then took her back to a room that he had booked where he beat her viciously, resulting in her having to receive hospital treatment. Not only that but the general had the arrogance/ignorance to book the room in his own name. It was up to Mr Manzur and Mr Salhi, who acted as security, to sort out the mess and make sure that the CCTV cameras were also wiped clean. In fact, the only reason that they were here in this backwater was because of General Faisal's grotesque behaviour.

'I would now like to hand over to the Imam who will brief us on the outcome of the last mission,' said Mr Manzur, trying to keep his composure.

The Imam was still wearing his traditional clothes. He cleared his throat and spoke about the recruitment of seven British-born martyrs and said that three had been killed when going on their suicide mission. He explained that as yet he hadn't discovered how the mission had been compromised but he would continue to investigate. He said that he himself had not been compromised and that he had taken measures to ensure that anyone involved with the mission in England had been eliminated.

The general butted in. 'Well then, we can conclude that the mission was a failure.'

The Imam faced towards the general, his black eyes blazing with fury, and he was about to reply when Mr Manzur spoke calmly.

'I think that we will all agree that the mission was a success.'

No one said a word; they were waiting for the reasons why Mr Manzur had made that statement.

'First, we are up against a country that has a highly sophisticated and mature security system. We caused maximum panic within their country and stretched their resources. The publicity from the attack was global news and many countries were taking live feeds. Then the next day, the gas explosion caused a similar reaction.'

'I thought that the gas explosion was an accident,' interrupted the general.

'No, General. The Imam had deliberately caused that and delayed the timing in order to cause maximum confusion and terror,' replied Mr Manzur.

The Imam bowed his head slightly, acknowledging the praise heaped on him by Mr Manzur. The others in the group rose to their feet and applauded the Imam. He in turn raised his right hand as acceptance.

'The campaign will be fought not only by us but by our children and by our children's children. We will prevail but it will take time,' went on Mr Manzur. 'We will defeat the infidels as we have Allah on our side.'

The Imam then went on to explain that he along with his network and cells would be conducting a campaign focusing on mainland Europe in 2011. He predicted that they would enjoy many successes, not least because there were lax security measures in place, and the freedom of people movement across country borders meant that both terrorists and their weapons could move more freely.

Mr Tariq asked whether any further attacks were being planned in the UK. The Imam said that they would be in due course but certainly for 2011 the focus was on mainland Europe only. If anyone was listening to this meeting, they would have thought that the group were a senior executive group of a company discussing their strategy for rolling out their product and increasing their sales. Not a despot group planning the murder of innocent civilians.

Mr Manzur next explained that a further 10 million in funds had been made available as per the Imam's request. The denominations and their amounts were 4 million in euros, 4 million in US dollars and 2 million in GB pounds. The funds in cash were currently being fitted into the Imam's three purpose-built suitcases during this meeting within concealed compartments. As his cases travelled under diplomatic immunity, there would be little chance of discovery of the terrorist funds. In addition, 3 million US dollars had been wired into the various personal accounts that the Imam had specified for payment for the next phase of the plan for Europe. Mr Manzur thanked both Mr Ebeid and Mr Karim, who were responsible for managing the complex financial arrangements. They both acknowledged his kind words.

Next, Mr Manzur asked for an update on recruitment, training and deployment into Europe of martyrs and their support cells from Mr Tariq. Mr Tariq said that al-Qaeda training camps in Pakistan were fertile recruiting grounds in particular. These were camps that were originally based in Afghanistan but had been relocated due to the increased and persistent military actions against them by US-lead coalition forces. There were still camps within Afghanistan but they were increasingly difficult to access. Iraq had training camps but their fighters were fighting against the Western forces that had invaded Iraq. He said that there was a breakaway group who planned to move into Syria next year and create their own group and they would be called ISIS, he believed. He hoped that he would then be able to recruit from that new group in time. Whilst he didn't have exact numbers, he said that he was confident that he would be able to resource all requests from the Imam in the coming year. He said that cells were already in place in several European countries and were just awaiting activation. He thanked Mr Salhi for his ongoing support in the recruitment, training and placement drive. Mr Manzur wrapped up the meeting and thanked everyone for their professionalism, dedication and ongoing support before asking if there was AOB (any other business).

General Faisal wrapped his knuckles on the table, 'We released 6 million in euros, GB pounds and US dollars only four months ago and paid the venerable Imam 2 million US dollars and now we are releasing another 13 million in various currencies. We never see any expenses or any evidence of how the funds are being spent. Surely we should receive some information on budget forecasts and expenditure?'

Mr Manzur was barely able to contain himself but replied quietly, 'The less anyone knows about the details, the better our security is, General. We deliberately share nothing but bare details. What if someone here was captured? How long do you think it will be before the Americans will squeeze the information out of them?'

'I wouldn't give them any information,' bellowed the general.

'Maybe not, General. But what about the rest of us? We are professional people without any military or counter-terrorism experience.'

'Well, we seem to be giving the Imam an open chequebook and he's being extremely well paid also.'

'Please don't worry about the funding. I can assure you that it's just a drop in the ocean. We have unlimited funds and as for the Imam, he's the one taking all of the risks. He's the one who is doing the detailed planning and executing the plans in the heart of the infidels. We will never question his dedication to the cause nor his meagre rewards.'

The general realised that in trying to make his point, he was only antagonising the group and said through gritted teeth, 'Thank you for that explanation, Mr Manzur.'

The meeting adjourned and everyone filed out expect the Imam and Mr Manzur.

'Imam, I do apologise for General Faisal's behaviour,' said Mr Manzur.

'Please don't worry on my account. I thought that you handled the situation well.'

'Thank you. I have many years' experience of dealing with buffoons. He needs to focus on what he's here for and try to not get involved in matters that he doesn't even understand.'

'Yes. A typical military man.'

'Unfortunately they get used to giving orders and think that they can order everyone around. Anyway, leave him to me. You continue to deliver against our plan in 2011. That's all we ask of you.'

'Thanks,' said the Imam.

He was already thinking about how much out of the 10 million in cash he'd steal and deposit into one of his personal Swiss bank accounts.

Outside, a few of the cars had already left the villa and the occupants were beginning the multiple car changes and several hours' criss-cross journey through Bahrain before they left. Mr Ebeid and Mr Karim had chosen a secluded and shaded corner in the garden to engage in a private conversation. Their drivers were sitting patiently in their new Mercedes cars and several members of the security detail were hovering around them at a discreet distance. Mr Karim had requested that they had a chat and Mr Ebeid had said that they should do it face to face here. Mr Ebeid, who had been siphoning off funds for years, wanted this opportunity to allay Mr Karim's concerns. Mr Karim had noticed that there were several discrepancies in the funds transferred and the associated accounting and had raised that with Mr Ebeid in August.

'Mr Karim, your work in identifying that there's funds missing has not gone unnoticed and the leaders of this great movement are grateful to you.'

'What! You speak to people above Mr Manzur?' cried Mr Karim.

Mr Ebeid looked around conspiratorially and said, 'I speak to the bosses of Mr Manzur's boss.'

'I, I didn't know,' stuttered Mr Karim.

'Well, now you do and I know that you will treat that information as confidential.'

Mr Karim nodded enthusiastically.

'Not only has your work been noticed but I've been told to tell you that you will be handsomely rewarded. I have been authorised to tell you that we are aware that millions have been siphoned off and that we will capture the perpetrator and any accomplices. They will not go unpunished. But you need to be aware that what is most important and in fact is the only important thing is the success of this mission. You mustn't say anything to anyone about either your suspicions or this conversation as you could be talking to the thief and that could jeopardise not only this mission but future missions and even the organisation itself. The message from on high to you is, and I quote, "Don't worry about the missing money. It can easily be replaced."'

Mr Karim smiled. Finally he had been recognised and it felt good. All of the years running around without so much as a thank you from everyone senior to him and at last praise.

'Thank you, Mr Ebeid, for bringing me into your confidence. Please let them know that I won't let them down.'

'I will,' said Mr Ebeid. 'Now come, our cars are waiting for us.'

Mr Karim spent his journey back home bolstered by the praise heaped on him. Mr Ebeid spent his journey back home thinking about ways to kill Mr Karim after he had planted enough false evidence to connect him to stealing multi-millions from the organisation. In the end, he thought that he didn't have it in him to kill the mild Mr Karim, but he knew that General Faisal had no compunction or compassion and he'd do it willingly. It now was a question of planting the trail of false evidence at his leisure.

16:00. Within MI5, the legend of John Pope was expanding and growing daily. Tales of his daring deeds had been embellished and had risen to preposterous heights. He had entered into MI5 folklore. John Pope was the alpha male in a pack of dangerous wolves. He wandered the streets, hunting terrorists with his pack of snarling, rabid Trojans. He led the faithful pack, jogging everywhere in his rank, sweaty jogging gear armed with a carving knife. The pack delivered at his behest instant sentencing and terminal justice. Black humour was part of life in this environment and it allowed people who worked 24/7 without public recognition to unwind a bit. Pope, who had previously been a soldier, was thick-skinned enough to realise that banter was part and parcel of belonging and took no notice. In fact, he thought that it was funny. Clare Hawkins, who was strung a little too tight, thought that the comments were inappropriate and berated a couple of colleagues who engaged in building Pope's mythology. MI5 legends were being created daily relating to Pope's feats and exploits, most of which were imaginary.

18:00. The meeting had been arranged and quite a few people who had involvement in the MI5 operation had turned up in the quiet pub off of Victoria situated on the corner of Great Peter Street. Team 4 turned up en mass as they were always looking for a decent night out apart from the unlucky couple who were on duty. A number of people who had been in the control centre on 17th November were also there including Tony Crook, Steve McLeish and Frank Selly. Pope, Clare Hawkins and Chris Gould were in there along with Deepak and Ahmed who had made their way down from Luton to attend. Word had got out about this soirée and a few Walkers had turned up. As a job, they followed people aka targets, and scrounging a few drinkers was something that they did routinely. A tab was opened up behind the bar and Seb Drake promised to pick it up. Although he had made it clear that he wasn't staying there all evening. The cliques formed quickly and everyone began to relax as the drinks flowed. This pub didn't offer a big screen, music or fruit machines and was a favourite for a get together.

The groups interchanged and mingled and the noise levels grew from muted to just below raucous. MI5 employees were the main group in the pub and there was a splattering of MPs dotted about who used the place to avoid the barflies in Westminster's inner hostelries. How it started was irrelevant, but there was a rumour circulating that John Pope had lost it with the first terrorist that had been caught. Apparently Pope was meticulously cutting off the guy's clothes looking for any sign of a bobby trap when he removed his shoes and socks. The rumour went on that Pope looked at the tattoo on the guy's foot and really lost it. He reigned in blows and kicks, causing the guy to end up with blood pouring out of several facial cuts. The guy was cuffed tight, bound hand, foot and even knee, but Pope battered him until he was dragged off. The word was that Pope hated tattoos. Team 4, ever eager to get involved in any gossip, checked on their phones and confirmed 'unofficially' that the tattoo on the guy's left foot was a brightly coloured skull and crossbones. They checked the pathologist reports and squashed all rumours that Pope had slashed the guy's face to pieces with his carving knife and that Pope had stamped on his face several times thereby shattering his jaw and nose.

The evening was progressing nicely and even though Seb Drake withdrew graciously at 20:30 along within his credit card, the beers kept flowing. The smokers in the party had periodically spilled out onto the street for a crafty fag. Ahmed was out there along with a few others including three Walkers when one of Walkers said, 'I see Rodney has come down from Luton.'

His mate replied, 'What a plonker.'

The Walkers laughed and Ahmed smiled.

He then thought, *Who the fuck are they talking about?* before he squared up to one of them and said, 'Are you talking about Deepak?'

'Might be,' came back the reply.

Ahmed pushed the Walker forcefully in the chest and he staggered backwards. The Walker regained his balance and then pushed Ahmed straight back.

One of the other Walkers stepped in between them shouting, 'Dave, calm down, mate. Please calm down.'

'Why did that fucker just push me?' came the reply.

Several people had heard the commotion inside the boozer and they had all piled outside. Deepak was in the group and shouted at Ahmed, 'Ahmed, what's going on?'

'Nothing, bruv.'

'I'll tell you. We were just saying that you had come down from Luton, Rodney, when he started pushing me.'

'Ahmed, mate. I've known those guys for years. We even trained together before we joined "5" and they always call me Rodney. It's a nickname that I've had for years,' said Deepak.

'Oh, I thought that they were taking the piss,' Ahmed said.

'Look, mate, I'm sorry,' he said, looking at the Walker who he'd just manhandled.

'No problem. We're going back inside anyway, brass monkeys out here,' the Walker replied, and everyone apart from Ahmed and Deepak went back inside.

'Everything good?' asked Deepak.

'Yeah, but they're still white institutionalised racist bastards,' replied Ahmed.

Deepak shook his head. Inside the pub, the manager had pulled Pope over to one corner and said that any more of that behaviour and everyone would be barred. Pope nodded and accepted the guvnor's decision.

'What time are you guys going back tonight?' asked Pope when Deepak and Ahmed reappeared.

'Probably catch the 23:00 train.'

The Walkers had regrouped in the corner near the toilets and were laughing. That flare up had just offered them an opportunity to slap on a new nickname. Not only was there Rodney but he was now joined by Uncle Albert.

Ahmed wasn't going to be happy when he heard that he had acquired a new nickname that would stick with him for the rest of his career.

09:00. Pope was sitting at his desk. Despite it being the weekend, Thames House was a hive of activity. He was about to start on work pertaining to the side project that Seb Drake had given him when he thought that he'd take a look at recent MI6 reports on activity from Russia. Since 9/11 there was more cooperation and sharing of information between departments, organisations and services that historically were reluctant to share. 9/11 highlighted to the world that even the USA was vulnerable, and that vulnerability was in no small part due to services refusing to share critical intel. The UK was significantly smaller in every respect to the USA and sharing information was vital, especially in the war on terror. There had been changes and improvements but there was still a long way to go before all information was shared with the relevant people in other services.

Pope scrolled through the reports that were Moscow related and within a heavily redacted report, he saw that there had been a huge fire in the Basmanny district. He clicked on the various links and also searched on news reports via the web. He pieced together the story of a fire in a huge warehouse that destroyed it and all of its contents. The warehouse was the main supplier of Afghan rugs and carpets to not only Moscow but to the whole of Russia. The fire investigation report concluded that the fire was started in the rear office section at night and was triggered by faulty electrical wiring. The faulty electrical wiring had been highlighted to the owners in two previous independent inspections, one by their own insurance company and the other by the local fire brigade. The owners were being prosecuted for not addressing the shortcomings and three of the main shareholders were currently in prison awaiting trial. The fire raged for nearly twenty-four hours before the fire brigade were able to bring it under control. There was substantial damage to three other warehouses and their goods as well as several derelict warehouses which were used by homeless people. It wasn't clear exactly how many people had perished in the fire but there were six known fatalities and thirty-five people treated in hospital for either burns or smoke inhalation issues. The local press said that eyewitnesses reported plumes of white powder being ejected from the burning building and clouds of it floating over the local neighbourhood. People in the area reported feeling euphoria then drowsiness and extreme itching followed by nausea. The police said that the effects experienced by some local people were caused by hemp in the carpets that mixed with quantities of stored talcum powder.

Pope then trawled through any stories relating to Olya village and read that several workers on the ferry route to Turkmenbashi in Turkmenistan were killed in a mysterious boating accident. A further four senior politicians died when their private plane crashed. And three customs officers along with two policemen were killed in an ambush which had been blamed on Chechen rebels. All of these events had happened in the last three weeks. Pope then checked accidents and deaths for the same period of time for Astrakhan city and found a string of similar events. He then checked for any articles relating to the Caspian highway that runs from Moscow to Astrakhan and read that there had been several dismissals, resignations and retirements of police officers that manned the various checkpoints along the 860-mile route in the last three weeks. He had gathered enough evidence to know that Boris had given the information that they along with the SAS signals officer had discussed regarding the Afghan heroin supply route to Moscow to the FSS (Federal Secret Service) and that they had eliminated anyone and everyone connected with the supply and distribution chain within Russia. Pope tried to find any information regarding the Turkmenistan leg of the supply chain but MI6 didn't operate there and there was precious little information as it was a closed country, although there was a small British consulate operating from an office based in a hotel. He was not successful in finding any information relating to that leg of the journey.

Pope drew all of the relevant strands together and created a document that he then sent onto Seb Drake. He knew that he'd be bringing this up with Boris in the next meeting and expected that there would be a few vodkas drunk as they toasted the demise of a major heroin supply route and all of the profiteers.

Pope's office phone rang two minutes after he sent the report to Seb Drake and he saw on his phone Seb's name displayed.

'Seb. Good morning.'

'And good morning to you, John. Thanks for sending over that report. I'll take a look at it later. Do you have a minute?'

'Sure.'

'I was wondering how you were getting along with that side project that I sent you. I know that it's been manic since the Luton episode but Sir Dickie is getting pressure from the PM.'

'I have to be honest, Seb, I've had little time recently to give any attention to looking into it.'

'I see.'

'I came in today to try and pick it up but I thought that I'd first off take a look and see whether there had been any developments with the heroin route, and as you can see the FSS have moped it up in their place.'

'Yes. That is credit in the bank and thanks for that. But where are you and what do I tell Sir Dickie?'

'I'm a one-man team with this one and it's taking time. I agree that there's a leak and that there's definitely been French industrial espionage, but it's going to take time to track down who's involved. There's no connection that immediately stands out between the two British companies. One is creating a vaccine for Ebola using genetic DNA engineering that will tackle and treat the disease even when it mutates. The other is producing clean water by taking dirty water and passing it through a nanofiltration process. I'm still shifting through the CVs and security checks of all of each company's employees. Then I need to go through their subcontractors and their employees and all of the contractors and agency employees. Then I need to look at their finances and see if any of them are spending above their means or receiving unusually large funds into their accounts. If this is urgent then I need to bring in more resources and ramp it up. I think that if I had four dedicated resources alongside myself then I'd have an answer for you in six months.'

'John. I made it clear that you and you alone would be working on this.'

'OK, and at the moment that is exactly what is happening. I was just explaining what was needed if you wanted quicker results. On my own – and remember that I may have to drop it if there's another incident like Luton – then I'd say you are looking at two years. Obviously, if I get a break then it will be cracked quicker, but that's the bottom line.'

'John, I appreciate your candour. I'll tell Sir Dickie and he'll spin it to the PM. I think that we'll go with "It's a complex situation and the spies have received inside information and have covered their tracks extremely well." The PM will be annoyed as the captains of industry are pressing him hard for a result but they don't understand what's involved smoking out the spies.'

'I'm sorry that I can't give you anything more positive.'

'John. Just stick with it. You have both Sir Dickie's and my support on this.'

Pope put the phone back down. Once again he was puzzled as to why Sir Dickie and or Seb Drake hadn't authorised more resources to tackle this blatant industrial espionage by the French. They had their reasons but they weren't prepared to share them with Pope.

Pope then read the latest police report. It said that officers had interviewed the young woman who had rented the garage to Zeehan Begum. She had worked in the rental office for several months but resigned on 24th November and was now working part-time in the office of a mini cab company owned by her uncle. She couldn't confirm whether the photos shown to her were Zeehan or not. She did confirm that she had rented the garage on the 15th November and he had paid cash when they showed her the actual paperwork with her signatures sprawled all over it. Pope decided to forward everything to Team 4 and run a check on her. He didn't expect that it would throw up anything but he was determined to follow every and any lead. The suicide of Zeehan was a mystery not only because there was no suicide note left, but also because everyone interviewed had said that Zeehan was a bubbly character who had much to live for and had never displayed any signs of depression or displayed suicidal tendencies. Team 4 were already checking with his doctor and running a profile on Zeehan, looking for drug/alcohol abuse, debts, gambling vice or any other number of issues that may have caused him to commit suicide. But young men did without any apparent reason or forewarning occasionally commit suicide and this looked like one of those cases.

The Hawk's 'nephew' who had rented the garage using fake documentation had not been identified by the young lady and another possible lead had now been lost.

12:30. Charlie was sitting in front of her PC in the dining room. She'd been studying for two and a half hours so far. Her sixteenth birthday was only two months away and her thoughts had turned towards that date. It was a significant milestone with all teenagers and she wanted more freedom. Freedom to go out at the weekend without having to be back home by 21:00 and freedom not to explain every minute detail about where she was going and who she was going with when she went out. She wasn't that interested in drinking alcohol but seriously thought about smoking as that was what most girls of her age did at school. She knew that she was going to end up having serious rows with her mum but she wanted more freedom. Her hormones were on fire and what she wanted most of all was a boyfriend.

She had recently started joining internet chatrooms that had been recommended to her by girls at school. These chatrooms were allegedly filled with boys a year or so older than herself. The boys in her year at school were OK but they seemed so young. She wanted a boyfriend a year or so older. That would be really cool and would make her friends super jealous. Even though some of the girls had been using the chatrooms for several months, none of them had been on a date. It was as if the boys were great at chatting online but were reluctant to meet up face to face. There was much debate at school regarding who was the hottest man and who they would date. Most of the girls fancied professional footballers mainly because they had the best legs and were rich and famous. Some were still following Justin Bieber but he was mainly popular with the younger girls. She had a crush on Jonny Wilkinson, the rugby player, but her friends didn't get how anyone could fancy a man who wasn't super rich. She would settle for Cliff in the year above her but despite her best smile whenever they passed in the school corridors he never paid her any attention. She knew that he didn't have a girlfriend so planned to persevere with smiling at him until he spoke to her. Meanwhile, she'd chat to the cool young guys in the chatrooms and maybe even meet up with one of them.

13:45. Ahmed was sitting at his customary table in the cafeteria looking at his laptop. He was working on his Open University course whilst waiting for someone to show up. He had cleared it with John Pope first and he was going to try and recruit a local person. The only way that any operation had a chance of being long term was by local, indigenous resources being recruited. He had chosen the ideal candidate. Someone who made it their business to find out what was going on and who was quite happy to spread and share all gossip.

'Ahmed, good afternoon, and how are you this fine day?' said a vibrant Mr Butt as he planted his ample backside in the seat opposite Ahmed.

'I'm very well, and how are you?'

'I'm holding up, just.'

'Yes, it's a difficult time.'

'Ahmed, that's an understatement. We are all suffering. The whole of the community is rocked. Rocked to the very foundations, I tell you.'

'I do understand. Perhaps there's something that you could do to help the community,' said Ahmed, treading carefully.

'I would help in any way that I can. What are you suggesting?'

'Well, you know everyone and you know everything that goes on here. Perhaps you could share some of that information on an ongoing basis.'

'Share information? Share it with who?' questioned Mr Butt, whose eyes narrowed.

'Share information with people whose job it is to protect everyone.'

'What? The police? They need to do more to protect us. There are far too many right-wing rallies and marches in Luton. People are frightened. We need better protection and all of the rallies and intimidation needs to be stopped.'

'I wasn't thinking of the police exactly,' went on Ahmed.

'Well, who are you thinking of?'

'The security forces that protect our country.'

'I don't understand.'

'Well. Put it another way. Recently we had in our mosque an Imam that no one knew about and then we had a failed terrorist bomb attack.'

'Ahmed. We've had several deaths in our community in the last few weeks. It's been a very bad time for everyone what with all of these accidents. We need to support all of the grieving families. They are all hard-working people who are pillars of our community. As for this Imam character. It's been blown out of all proportion. The elders aren't aware of him or his presence and no one else has even seen him.'

Ahmed was about to say that he had caught a glimpse of the Imam and also that the cleaner had identified him, but he didn't want to give this gossip any information that may be detrimental to either the ongoing enquiry or to the cleaner.

'Mr Butt, I suppose you are right,' said Ahmed, trying to appease Mr Butt.

'Yes, I am,' said Mr Butt as he got up and toddled off.

Ahmed sat there for a few minutes contemplating. His first attempt at recruiting someone inside the mosque had failed. Mr Butt was blinded by loyalty. Loyalty for the local community usurped loyalty for The Greater Good.

09:30. Pope and family were sitting at the kitchen table finishing off their breakfasts. Doodle was moving around the table deftly, propping his front paws on everyone's knees. His eyes implored them and his tail wagged a friendly signal towards them. Only Daisy dropped soggy breakfast cereals that his grateful tongue scooped up from the tiled floor. Pope was steeling himself for a long, mundane day in the office working through the details of his 'special' project that Seb Drake had assigned him.

Nestling a mug of steaming tea in her hands, Jane spoke. 'Girls, Daddy and I have something to tell you.'

The girls broke away from eating and stared at their mum. Pope did likewise as he wasn't aware that there was any new news. Certainly he and Jane hadn't discussed any details regarding the next family holiday.

'Starting in the New Year, Daddy and myself are going to be going out regularly together.'

Charlie's eyes began to scrunch together. Daisy was now beaming a huge infectious smile, although she didn't really understand what was being said to her. She patted Doodle's head a little too firmly whilst listening to her mum.

'What do you mean?' snarled Charlie.

'We will go and see a film, maybe go for a meal or even go and see an exhibition.'

'So what do we do?' butted in Charlie.

'Well, you are old enough now to spend an evening at home without us.'

'I'm not babysitting.'

'No one is asking you to. Daisy will go to bed at her normal time.'

'So, can I bring a friend around?'

'No. You can carry on with your homework.'

'We can study together.'

'No. I don't want anyone else here whilst we are out.'

'What you are saying is that you don't trust me,' argued Charlie.

'Charlie, stop please,' said Jane.

'Anyway, why are you going out?' went on Charlie.

'It's a date night,' replied Jane.

'How gross.'

'Why?'

'At your age.'

'What do you mean? Do you think that we shouldn't have our own lives? Just wash, clean, feed and run you around?' said Jane testily.

'Jane,' interrupted Pope.

There was quiet for a moment.

'Doodle and me will come with you. We want to go on a date night,' squealed Daisy.

'Darling, Doodle isn't allowed in cinemas or restaurants, and besides, you need to be in bed and get your sleep otherwise you will be tired the next day for school. And you don't want to miss school, do you?' said Jane with empathy.

Daisy reluctantly nodded her head in agreement, looking tearful.

'Right then. I'm off to work. I'll see you all this evening. Have a good day,' said Pope, getting up and heading towards the hall.

He gathered his coat, case, phone and car keys and was opening the front door when he heard, 'Isn't date night an American thing?'

'Charlie. Just stop now!'

13:00. The group who regularly met for a drink every Sunday had gathered and were standing in a group of twenty. They were all dressed smartly and had put fifteen pounds each into the whip. It would allow them to drink all afternoon whilst both Premiership football games were shown on Sky TV. They were Luton Town football hooligans, MIGs (Men In Gear) and were in their favourite watering hole in the outskirts of Luton and in a place where they were known to the landlord and their boisterous behaviour was accepted. That along with the regular custom that they brought in a time when money was tight and pubs up and down the country were closing on a daily basis.

'Here, Geoff, you'll never guess who I bumped into in the gym this morning.'

'Go on. It wasn't one of our players, was it?'

'Nope. Remember that Gooner we chased up to Bedford and he was then backed up by that drug crew and some chinks?'

'Yeah, I remember that twat.'

'Well, he was in there pumping iron.'

'What's he like?'

'Lifts light and he's skinny. He'll never be anything. Not without taking gear.'

'No juice, no gain,' said Geoff.

Everyone laughed.

'He'll need to take a lot of juice, that little fucker.'

'At least we know where he's at. Keep an eye on that skinny little prick.'

'Yeah, no problem.'

'Fucking Gooner,' said Geoff. 'Right, who's getting them in then?'

16:00. The drive up to the industrial estate in Bedford had been carried out in virtual silence. Unlike the last time when Deepak was driving fast and trying to outrun the MIG's convey who were in hot pursuit of Ahmed. Ahmed had come up with today's plan and Deepak had reluctantly agreed to it.

Deepak had been out on a drugs run in Cambridge when Ahmed had called him and said that he needed him at the mosque straight away as the Hawk was there along with other guys carrying rucksacks. Deepak took longer than expected to get back and in the confusion, the Hawk had escaped. Ahmed said that that was the final straw and there was to be no more involvement with the drug gang and today they both would leave their employment. Deepak agreed to leave all of the talking to Ahmed. In reality they would both be staying in Luton for the foreseeable future but would move onto other mosques and start cultivating new contacts there. They would be training up the latest set of undercover agents that were going to be assigned to Luton and mentor them but their work at that particular mosque was now coming to a close. When they arrived at the four-storey derelict building, Siddiq's silver BMW series 5 model was already parked outside next to the dark blue Ford Fiesta that was used by the gang to deliver the drugs to all of their dealers and to collect the cash payments for delivery. Kareem, who had recruited Deepak at the mosque, was waiting for them at the front door. Deepak and Ahmed hot-footed it into the dank building to escape from the cold, drab rainy day. Kareem smiled at them both warmly and they all went into the small office at the back where Haroon, Younis and Siddiq, who was the leader of the gang, were waiting for them. Everyone nodded and said hello.

'You asked for this meet, so what's up?' said Siddiq, who was sitting behind a weathered metal desk painted in bright green.

'We have both decided that we're going to go back down to London,' started Ahmed slightly hesitantly.

'Right,' said Siddiq.

'We both want to continue with our Online University degrees but we don't want to stay in Luton anymore,' said Ahmed, and then added, 'Too much has happened here not only in the mosque but also in the local community. Quite frankly, Luton is cursed and we want away.'

Everyone nodded in agreement. They all privately thought that the place was cursed with so many horrendous fatal accidents happening in such a short space of time and right in the middle of it all, a failed terrorist attack which resulted in a further three deaths.

'We'll be going our separate ways in London as we both have different sets of contacts but we wanted to come up and say good bye,' added Ahmed smoothly, now getting into his stride.

'Well, thanks for letting us know. If you ever want to get some work in London then let me know. I have several contacts down there,' said Siddiq.

'Thanks. We have your number and we'll definitely consider it,' said Ahmed.

Ahmed and Deepak then turned around and were about to leave.

'Wait,' shouted Siddiq.

Ahmed and Deepak froze. Both feared that things were about to take a turn for the worse. Siddiq opened the top drawer of the desk. As it opened, it squealed painfully as the contorted metal resisted. Siddiq put his hand slowly in the desk and retrieved a huge spliff.

Smiling, Siddiq said, 'Fancy sharing one last joint? Best skunk there is.'

Deepak's face lit up and his head bobbled.

Ahmed knew that he was cornered and replied, 'Love to.'

When Ahmed and Deepak finally left the skunk factory after a couple more shared spliffs, several pairs of Chinese eyes watched them from windows dotted about the building.

08:10. There was almost a crush in the lift. This was the time of the morning when there was peak flow of people into Thames House. The doors began to slowly close for the third time and then two more bodies squeezed in. The doors slid back to their starting positions quickly and the loud ping noise sounded, proudly telling everyone that the doors were now open...again. People shuffled and readjusted, partly to accommodate the extra two bodies but more out of frustration.

Why couldn't they have waited for the next lift? thought the group in unison.

But each one of them had performed the very same annoying act on many occasions. The two women were oblivious to the reaction around them and leant over to check that their floor had already been requested on the panel.

'Anyway, there was a commotion and then literally everyone ran outside,' said the first lady in a hushed tone.

'No way, what caused it?' asked her companion.

'Dave was having a smoke with a couple of the Walker team when one of the undercover guys from Luton started on him.'

'What did Dave do?'

The doors had groaned but were finally shut and the lift was about to start its slow ascent, stopping off at every floor.

'I spoke to him and he said that he never did a thing. He was just chatting when the guy pushed him.'

'So what happened next?'

'Handbags. A bit of pushing and then the other undercover bloke from Luton stepped in.'

'Probably good to get outside for a couple of minutes and get some fresh air anyway.'

'Would be if they weren't outside smoking like beagles.'

Both women sniggered. The lift was easing past the second floor and despite people getting out, it was still rammed.

'Anyway, I heard the strangest story.'

'Go on.'

'Well, you know John Pope?' she whispered, having lowered her voice even more.

'Yes.'

'Apparently when he was searching the first terrorist in the station, he lost it completely.'

'Really? He always comes across as super calm.'

'True. But not on this occasion.'

The lift was still slowly going up and people were still drifting out of it at every stop.

'The story goes that Pope was stripping the guy, looking for any hidden boobytraps, and the bomb disposal guys were working on disarming the bomb in the rucksack when he went berserk.'

The crowd in the lift were able to breathe and spread out a bit.

'Anyway, the terrorist was restrained, bound hand and foot, and Pope had his shoes and socks off when he started kicking the crap out of him. The local old bill and a couple of others pulled Pope off him.'

'Why did he do that?'

'This is the really bizarre bit. The story goes that Pope saw a tattoo on the guy's foot and then launched into him.'

'That is bizarre. What was the tattoo of?'

A loud ping sounded and the lift doors slowly opened.

'Here's our floor,' said the first lady easing out.

The doors closed. In the corner behind where the two ladies were standing, another lady raised her head and stood up to her full height. Sandra Carruthers waited until the lift stopped at the next floor and then got off. She stood in the corridor and pressed the down button, as she had travelled a few floors past where she worked.

Carruthers logged onto all of her systems and retrieved all of the accounts written by everyone in the small room in Luton station from that fateful evening. She read through all of the individual reports including the one written by the acting assistant station manager (strange job title, she thought) but couldn't find any mention of Pope laying into the guy. She read that in a couple of the reports Pope was praised for both his calm leadership skills and courage. She checked the post-mortem report and there was mention of blood on the terrorist's face caused by a cut in his mouth but nothing else suspicious. Carruthers then called up the photos of the body and she saw that he had a skull and cross bones tattoo on his left foot. She sat there for several minutes, deciding her next course of action. Finally she leant forward and created a new email. Carruthers' wasplike fingers stung the keyboard, every finger stroke delivering deadly venom into her email. She quickly reread the email and then fired it out to the HR dept.

10:15. Chris Gould knocked on the door rather than using the wonky door knocker. The door was opened almost immediately and a pretty young Indian girl smiled at him.

'Oh. Is Deepak or Ahmed in?' Chris said, surprised to see a female in this address.

'Dee is at work but Ahmed is in. Who are you?'

'Chris from work.'

'I'll just call him,' she replied, smiling as she slightly closed the door.

Ahmed appeared at the door in short time and was clearly flustered.

'Chris. How's it going?' Ahmed stuttered. 'Please come in.'

Ahmed led Chris Gould into the front room. Chris could not help but notice the gigantic TV that dwarfed the small room and was booming out a daytime house renovation programme.

'Take a seat, Chris,' said Ahmed, pointing at his favourite settee that was placed opposite the TV.

Ahmed picked up the TV remote control and lowered the volume to a few decibels less than a commercial aircraft taking off.

'I thought that I'd pop up and see how things are going. I know that I didn't give you any advanced notice. I hope that that's OK,' said Chris, easing his ample body down and onto the now straining settee.

Ahmed was standing, moving from foot to foot almost dance-like. He was nervous and it was being displayed by his edgy behaviour and the fact that he didn't know where Aisha was or what she was doing.

'No. Yeah. Good to see you. Dee's at work. Do you want me to call him?' Ahmed blathered.

'No need. We can catch up and you can update him later,' replied Chris, whose eyes were drawn to and fixed on the huge TV. 'Also, you can update the rest of the team at your leisure.'

'Yeah. Right. Update Dee and update the rest of the team,' said Ahmed, parrot fashion, still hopping from foot to foot.

The lounge door burst open and Aisha walked in carrying a tray with three mugs, a sugar bowl, milk and a plate full of biscuits.

'I've made some tea for us. And there's biscuits,' Aisha said, sweetly putting the fully laden tray down on the aged table.

Chris looked at Ahmed, whose mouth was now opening and closing. It was a look that fish gave when they were out of water and struggling to survive in an unnatural habitat.

'I'm sorry, we haven't been introduced,' said Chris, half standing and extending his hand towards Aisha.

This position was extremely precarious for Chris. His trousers, jacket and shirt were all stretched to their extreme. A further several seconds in that position and he would begin to resemble the trigger point when Dr Bruce Banner turns into the Hulk and all his clothes shred. Fortunately for him, Aisha put her delicate hand in his sweaty mitt.

'Aisha,' she said, smiling her perfect set of teeth at him.

'Chris,' he replied before flopping back into his seat. 'I work with Ahmed and Deepak.'

'Do you now?' Aisha went on, passing him a mug of tea. 'Milk and sugar?'

'Yes please. Three sugars and a dash.'

'That's not good for your teeth,' Aisha said as she scooped three sugars into his mug, followed by a slop of milk from the carton.

Chris Gould smiled at the gentle, smiling female.

'I'm a dentist and far too many people have problems caused by excessive sugar.'

Chris was salivating. Despite having just demolished a builder's breakfast in a cafe, he was eyeing the plate full of biscuits. He wasn't feeling guilty as he had read online a new training routine that he was going to start at the weekend and that along with the latest batch of supplements that he had ordered online would turn him into a lean, mean fighting machine just like the guy in the ad. And it only took six weeks. This new routine and supplements, unlike the last one and the one before that, would transform him in next to no time. Ahmed was still standing there; the fish gasping, not knowing how long he could survive in this hostile environment.

'Ahmed, why don't you sit in the chair and I'll sit next to Chris,' said Aisha, taking control of the dying fish.

'Aisha, if you don't mind, why are you here?' said Chris, beginning his interrogation.

'Oh, don't you know?' said Aisha, smiling back at Chris. 'I'm Ahmed's girlfriend.'

Chris smiled and nodded his head as he grabbed a couple of biscuits. He planted one into his mouth whole and the crumbs spread across his face and also dropped like raindrops onto his shirt. He munched the dry biscuit and then swallowed more tea to change the biscuit's texture. He looked at Ahmed and raised his eyebrows as if surprised. Ahmed's face had already froze with a rictus smile but at least it was a better look than the dying fish that he had been mimicking for the last few minutes.

'Oh yes. I pop up occasionally and see him,' went on Aisha cheerily. 'It can be difficult. What with work demands and that I live in London. But we make it work.'

Chris nodded as he devoured the second biscuit, still looking with curiosity at Ahmed. The crumbs on Chris's shirt and jacket now looked like a serious case of brownish dandruff. Ahmed somehow managed to pick up the mug and put it shakily to his semi-smiling lips and then took a sip. So far he hadn't blinked but at least he was still breathing.

'How's your tea, Chris? Are you ready for another?' said Aisha in a song-like voice.

Chris looked into his mug and gulped it down. He knew that there were still several biscuits on the plate that had his name on them and that they would taste better if accompanied by a mug of tea.

'Yes. You make a great cup,' said Chris, looking at Aisha through a field of crumbs.

'Right, boys, I'll be back in a moment.'

Aisha looked at Ahmed who hadn't drunk more than a thimble full of tea, and didn't bother asking him if he wanted another mug.

After she had left the room, Chris leant forward and whispered, 'Ahmed, this is all highly irregular. You know that. You shouldn't have anyone onsite during an op. Also, have you declared Aisha as a partner? Background checks, mate, you know the rules.'

Ahmed was sitting there. Some form of life was bubbling under the surface as Ahmed was blinking in time to all of Chris's statements.

'And what's with the TV? You know that we don't jazz up any of our sites. That's top of the bloody range,' said Chris, pointing at the oversized screen.

Aisha had just entered the room with two fresh mugs of tea.

'Oh, you like the TV, Chris? It's mine. I just leant it to Ahmed for a while. Funny, I really miss it,' said Aisha, plonking Chris's mug back on the table.

'Isn't that right, Ahmed?' Aisha said, looking at Ahmed.

Ahmed started to catch flies as his mouth opened and closed but nothing came out.

'It's highly irregular to upgrade government property without completing the necessary paperwork and then receiving authorisation,' said Chris in an officious tone.

'Civil servants. All wrapped up in red tape. It's no wonder nothing ever gets done!' quipped Aisha.

Chris shot Ahmed a glare of disapproval but Ahmed was still catching flies and his mug of tea was getting colder by the minute. There was some further small talk which Ahmed managed to join in with. Chris managed to munch through a further three biscuits before he decided that it was time to leave. There was no point trying to have a work discussion here. He'd drop Ahmed an email on the way back to London and he'd propose a time when they could catch up later today via a secure telephone line. Chris stood up and crumbs flew everywhere.

'Nice to meet you, Aisha, and thanks for the tea,' said Chris, pouring crumbs over everywhere as he leant over and shook her hand.

'Oh, going already? Shame. There's a great programme coming up. It follows sheriffs going around the country repossessing properties, seizing goods or getting payments,' said Aisha.

'No, I do need to get going. Ahmed, walk me out,' said Chris, laying a trail of crumbles behind him as he left the room.

Chris walked outside of the flat and pulled the front door to after Ahmed had followed him.

'There's some paperwork to catch up on. A vetting form and a gifts form,' said Chris.

Ahmed frowned. Chris replayed in his head all of the great work that Ahmed and Deepak had recently done which had averted a national disaster and then followed up.

'If you are still with your girlfriend in January then think about submitting a vetting form, eh? Plus, bringing civilians into our properties isn't on. You need to sort that out pronto. Either meet in London or get a room somewhere.'

With that, Chris headed off down the stairs.

Ahmed walked back into the front room and Aisha was standing there smiling her heart-melting smile at him.

'I bet you're now glad that I came up today with food from Mum. She worries about both of you and she and Dad don't understand why Dee cancelled the food run. She's insulted, she thinks that you don't like her food.'

Without much pause, she said, 'My quick thinking got you out of trouble then'.

Ahmed started to catch flies again. His mouth just opened and closed repeatedly.

'Chris thinks that I'm your girlfriend,' Aisha went on, still smiling.

No reply.

Aisha closed the gap between them and pressed her seductive lips against his quivering lips. She forcefully pushed her tongue into his compliant mouth. After several seconds, she withdrew and looked into his eyes, which were flickering.

'Well, I guess that I am your girlfriend now,' she whispered.

The front room was ridiculously overcrowded. The huge TV swallowed up a significant portion of the tardy room. The choir of angels appeared singing divinely whilst playing harps supported by cherubs playing lyres, horns and violins, and all were floating delicately above and slightly behind Aisha. Ahmed could smell the soft musk smell of her perfume as his arms embraced her around her waist. Aisha's arms moved around his neck and they embraced him gently.

'What are you thinking? What will your dad say now that you are consorting with the enemy?' Aisha said, laughing loudly.

'What do you mean?' replied Ahmed, eager to keep her in his grip.

'You know. There's no love lost between Pakistan and India when they play cricket.'

Ahmed laughed loudly.

Ahmed thought about his dad and his intransigent position. 'I don't think cricket will be an issue.'

'No. What will then?'

'Religion. My dad wants me to marry a Muslim. He even wants to arrange my marriage, and any kids have to be brought up as Muslims.'

'Wow. I want to bring up my children to respect everyone, don't break the law and just work hard,' Aisha replied.

'I have a similar view but with one add on.'

'What's that?'

'They will all be Gooners. No way will they be allowed to support Spurs.'

They both laughed.

'Seems reasonable,' replied Aisha, and she added cheekily, 'Now we need to set a date.'

They kissed again and the choir and ensemble raised their wonderful, rapturous volume.

15:20. Pope was sitting at his desk. He gently tapped his pen on the edge of the desk and alternated between looking out of the window at the view over the River Thames and looking at his PC. It was already dark outside and there were lights twinkling everywhere. Cars, boats and streetlights were painted onto London's majestic canvas. Some were like stars in the sky, moving slowly as they orbited. Others were static; they illuminated their small patch of the canvas. He occasionally dragged up some information onto his screen and studied it. He was looking at the ongoing developments relating to the Luton incident. Like a big puzzle, small pieces kept getting added but the picture was still far from complete.

The three dead terrorists' accommodation in Luton didn't harvest any results. Neither did the backgrounds of the people who owned or sublet the rooms. The internet cafes where they watched the propaganda and terrorists supporting websites drew a blank, although there were now several lines of inquiries being followed by Bedfordshire police force, most relating to illegal pornographic material. Even their mobile phones were lacking any information that could initiate a material lead. There were six deaths, one of which was murder, of people who were connected to the Hawk, but none of them yielded a clue. Rahan Iqbal had had his throat slit and he was buried in a shallow grave in parkland. Three members of the Ali family were killed in a road accident at the Hajj in Saudi Arabia. Zeehan Begum had committed suicide when he fed an exhaust pipe into his car in a garage. And Usam Mia was killed along with two elderly Afghanistanis when there was a gas explosion at their property. There were plenty of peculiar and bizarre aspects to their individual and combined deaths but there was no evidence linking them. Even when the forensic team went over the remains of the Afghani house with a fine tooth comb, they couldn't find any evidence relating to the Luton incident. The bodies were shredded by the force of the explosion and one medical examiner said that the bodies may have had their throats cut before the explosion. Other medical examiners vigorously disagreed with his view, stating that there was no evidence to support such a position. Pope logged the contrasting position but knew that unless there was any further evidence, it wasn't useful espousing that position as it only fuelled conspiracy theories, and that just clouded everything. What was clear though was that there were another four would-be bombers out there and they needed to be hunted and captured before they committed their heinous and deadly act. As important as finding them was finding and capturing the Hawk.

He was the key to stopping everything and he was a cunning, determined, heartless foe.

Pope tapped his pen on the edge of his desk again when he heard the ping of a new email. He logged into his inbox and read the email. He then shut down his PC, put on his jacket and walked out of the office. Several minutes later, Pope was in one of the lower levels of Thames House. He knocked on the door.

'Come in,' came the voice from the other side of the door.

Pope entered and walked towards the desk.

'John, thanks for coming,' said Doctor Hempel-Smith, smiling. 'Please take a seat.'

Pope sat down and smiled at Dr Hempel-Smith. He wondered if this was a follow up regarding his rising blood pressure, or perhaps a checkup on his slightly worsening eyesight. Hempel-Smith had a pro-forma on the desk in front of him.

'John, as part of our ongoing support and evaluation of all officers involved in a major incident, I'd like to conduct an interview with you. There's a number of questions that I'd like to ask. Are you OK with that?' asked the genial doctor.

'Sure,' said Pope indifferently.

'Good, let's begin then. Since the incident, how are you sleeping?'

'Good, thanks.'

'No nightmares?'

'None.'

'Are you eating OK?'

'Yes.'

'Are you taking regular exercise?'

'When I can.'

'Anything troubling you?'

'No.'

'Any anxiety or depression?'

'No.'

'Any suicidal thoughts?'

'Never.'

'Feeling angry?'

'No.'

'What's your feelings about religion?'

Pope just shrugged his shoulders.

'How do you feel about Christian views?'

'I'm fine with them.'

'What about Jewish views?'

'The same.'

'And what about Muslim views?'

'No different.'

Without looking up from the notes that he was studiously writing on the pro-forma, Dr Hempel-Smith asked, 'And what's your views on body art?'

Pope didn't answer; he just glared at the top of Dr Hempel-Smith's thinning pate as he hunched over his paperwork, pen poised in his right hand.

'In particular, what do you think about tattoos?'

There was complete silence. Dr Hempel-Smith sat back upright and looked at Pope.

Both men sat there, eyes unblinking, locked in contact.

- THE END -